# Blood Feud

## Draegonstorm: The Elders Saga

### Book One

NOVELS IN THE DRAEGONSTORM: ELDERS SAGA


BLOOD FEUD

NIGHTFALL

THE DRAGON LORD

SONS OF THE DRAGON

THE ORDER OF THE DRAGON

# Blood Feud
## Draegonstorm: The Elders Saga
### Book One
#### K.R. Fraser

Dragonrock
Press

DRAGONROCK PRESS

BLOOD FEUD
DRAEGONSTORM: THE ELDERS SAGA

Published by Dragonrock Press, a division of Dragonrock Enterprises Inc.
Copyright © 2019 by K.R. Fraser
Foreword copyright © by K.R. Fraser

Dragonrock Press, Dragonrock, and the Dragonrock logo are all trademarks of the
Dragonrock Enterprises Inc. group of companies.
Dragonrock ® is a registered trademark of Dragonrock Enterprises Inc.

Cover art by Leah Keeler

A Dragonrock Book
Published by Dragonrock Press, LLC
P.O. Box 752
980 Wheeler Way
Langhorne, PA. 19047

ISBN 978-1-7333787-2-7
Printed in the United States of America

*For Ian, who always loved the magic of my world.*
*For Laura, who never stopped believing and for being my*
*cheering section.*
*For Stephen, who discovered that magic is real and found*
*himself in the process.*
*For Aimee, who still believes in chasing dreams.*
*For Crystal, who thought they were Christmas lights the*
*first time she saw them.*
*For Erin, who is still wandering the wild.*
*For Tony, who helped me find myself again.*
*For Josh, who fell in love with Dragons.*
*For my chosen family, who walked this journey with me*
*through the years.*
*For my mom - I wish you were here...*
*For my dad and Jane for all the love and support.*
*For my friends, who kept me going through everything*
*and never let me give up.*
*For all the fans who have ridden the long journey with me.*
*Most importantly, for my best friend, John, who has*
*always been there for me and helped me over too many*
*hurdles to count, and my designated partner in crime, my*
*best friend, Jim, who spent way too many nights sitting*
*with me on the phone and living the adventure of a*
*lifetime in Draegonstorm.*

*~ Te Iubesc ~*


DEDICATED TO SETH E. GAINER
YOU LEFT US TOO SOON AND YOU ARE FOREVER MISSED.
10/14/1991 – 07/03/2018

# Table of Contents

# Foreword

When I first sat down and began to create the world of Draegonstorm, I never imagined it would grow so much. It began as stories for my children, who grew up with Tolkien, Salvatore, Brooks and a myriad of other incredibly creative storytellers. Bedtimes became journeys into magical realms full of fantastical creatures who ignited their imaginations.

In those first few years, the characters were still young and not overly developed. But as time went by, they evolved and came very much to life. Friends who would visit occasionally at night often listened in as I told these tales and loved them as much as my children did. Before long, the world of Draegonstorm began to emerge and take shape. I began to write down details so I would not forget them. I think this is where the true birth of these novels began.

It wasn't long before I found myself writing down the adventures and piecing together how they developed, and before long, I had my first story. Then the day came when I printed off the first pages from my printer, only to see my children racing to the living room to see who could get to them first. It was one of the most inspiring moments I've ever experienced, and the joy I saw in their eyes stayed with me. That was when I decided that I wanted to make this series something more. I wanted to share that excitement with the whole world.

That was all so many years ago. In the years that followed, I got a complete college education in media and communications, business management and marketing. I had begun to work in the field, primarily writing and editing for magazines and newspapers. I wrote and published poetry and finally, short stories. I edited some more, attended dozens of writer's conferences and learned about and worked with the publishing industry. Throughout those years, I slowly developed what would come to be my baby: Draegonstorm.

When I began to mentor my first student, he had a moment when he wanted to quit writing because friends had told him it was weird. As an answer, I told him this world we live in is often dark. Many people lose sight of their goals and with them, their happiness. The artists, composers, musicians, authors, film makers, entertainers... we are the light bringers. We take those who dive into our work on a guided tour through the realm of the imagination, where the impossible becomes possible, and where life is not as hard as it is in the real world. When they sit down to read, watch television, listen to music, or even delve into looking at pictures, for the time they can forget their troubles. They are there in that place we've created, living that story. It is there that they finally remember to dream.

Those dreams are what keep people going each day. It gives them a reason to smile, to laugh, to share fun with their friends, to believe there is always something better, and it gives them the courage to dare to dream. Every dream has merit, even when others think it impossible.

Gene Roddenberry once imagined this thing called a communicator. People thought it simple science fiction and an impossibility when it first appeared in his stories. Then the first cell phone was invented. Edison, Tesla and even Benjamin Franklin believed electricity could be harnessed to benefit humanity, and they were at one point, each called insane. Now, it's common in every home and business around the globe.

The future is always built on new dreams when they become real. When we dream, we have to believe in that dream, for it is only then that we can discover just how far that dream will take us. Dare to dream and believe...

K.R. Fraser

# Blood Feud

## Draegonstorm: The Elders Saga

### Book One

# BLOOD FEUD

## Chapter One
## Betrayal

A single figure glided silently through the shadows of the night, hugging the tree line to avoid the moon's rays that broke through the clouds to bathe the landscape in pale light. Hooded and cloaked, Ceros Valfort slipped across a clearing to disappear once more among the trees. Finally, he paused and scanned the forest behind him. When he was satisfied that he had not been followed, he let out a soft whistle. The cold September air chilled him, as he waited for a response. He drew his cloak tighter around himself with a shiver.

"I was beginning to think you had second thoughts about meeting me." A silhouette stepped from the shadows behind him and slowly approached.

Valfort turned around. "You know better than that, based on my reputation alone. Do you really think I would take such a risk if I had no intention of following it through?"

His companion shrugged. "You know once you do this, there is no going back?"

"I understood the consequences long before I requested this meeting," Valfort stated dryly.

The man lowered his voice. "You must take the rite tonight. Are you ready?"

Valfort shook his head. "I have one more thing to do. Can you wait for me?"

His companion shifted slightly and glanced around in obvious discomfort. "I can, but not for long. I have no intention of being here long enough for their scouts to find me."

Valfort growled and glared at him. "I won't be long! Climb a tree and stay out of sight!"

Clearly displeased, the man disappeared into the canopy above. "You have one hour."

Valfort ignored him and headed back the way he had come, staying alert as he hurried through the woods. Then he spotted the sentries on the outskirts of the Alliance encampment and dropped out of sight. He moved forward cautiously, knowing if caught, it would be his undoing.

A few feet away, a sentry stopped and turned, as if sensing someone was there. He peered into the trees, searching the shadows for any sign of movement.

Valfort froze and waited for the guard to move on. Then he hustled over the crossing.

The camp was just beginning to come alive. Reveille sounded, and a scurry of activity ensued, allowing him to slip in unnoticed. With grim purpose, he entered the cluster of ramshackle shelters and made his way to the hill's summit where the officer's quarters stood, their silhouettes outlined in the moonlight.

* * * * *

*The Alliance... never before have I heard so grossly a misused name for a fellowship of disorganized chaos. Our world is in turmoil, burning from the fires of war, and still the Council bickers endlessly, as each seeks to dominate control of the territories. Here on the fighting field we die by the thousands for their war. Loyalty is demanded of us as their children and their power is absolute. It is said that a hierarchy in which everyone knows their place brings order from chaos, but in truth does it not also bring slavery, where no man is free to speak his own mind for fear of retribution? When serving the Council, one must always remember his loyalty is to his tribe first and balance out his decisions, weighing the consequences of every action. Step wrong and death will find you. Serve and fight. Fight and kill. This is the legacy of the dark.*
    *Lord Reivn Draegon*

* * * * *

Reivn stepped out onto the porch of his temporary quarters shortly after sunset. The breeze blew his black hair around his shoulders, but he paid no attention. Though his tall, muscular frame cut an imposing figure, fatigue darkened his handsome and youthful face. He leaned on the railing and stared at the horizon. Then a cloud of dust on the road caught his attention, as a rider approached.

His scout had returned.

Reivn stepped down to meet him. "Report, Corporal!"

The soldier saluted. "They are just over the ridge, sir! I counted six divisions headed this way! Two corps, sir! What are your orders?"

Weariness lined Reivn's face as he studied the surrounding hills. Then his jaw tightened, and his eyes narrowed. "Tell the men to prepare for battle. We move in an hour's time!"

"Yes, sir!" The Corporal saluted again. Then he turned his horse and galloped down the hill toward the encampment.

Reivn headed for the officer's quarters. They had already assembled, so he joined them at the table. "There are two full corps headed this way," he began. "We will engage them within the hour. We have barely three divisions and those have been hammered hard these last few nights. I sent for reinforcements, but I do not know when they will arrive." He glanced at the man across from him. "Commander... take your cavalry and cover the left flank. I will lead my men to the right. You will have to spread thin, but the flanks must not fall. If they get past us, they will not stop until they take London."

Lunitar studied the map, and his long white hair spilled over his shoulder. A pale reflection of his father, he was nearly as tall as Reivn, his muscles and tanned, scarred complexion the result of years on the battlefield. "I will not fail, my lord. We will hold to the last man," he promised.

Reivn stared at his men, noting their discouraged and weary expressions. "Let us hope it does not come to that," he growled. Then he gazed at the map, assessing the terrain. "Captain, you will launch the frontal assault. Take your regiment up the center here."

Gideon studied the map carefully. He was handsome with boyish charm, and his dark hair was almost as black as Reivn's. "It shall be done," he replied.

"Your command must divide both left and right. While you draw their attention, our cavalry will close in from the flanks and destroy them." Reivn moved the markers on the map. "We execute a pincer movement. Their numbers will be a disadvantage when they are forced together. They will have nowhere to run, and we can cut them down."

Lunitar frowned. "My lord, this is a risky tactic with our few numbers. If even one aspect of this fails, we will lose the battle."

"It is indeed risky, but it is the only chance we have to hold this ground," Reivn answered, eyeing his men. "Remember what we fight for. We are all that stands between the Principatus and the destruction of the Alliance. We must be an unmovable wall... unyielding to the last."

The men shifted uneasily, gazing at one another in silence. Finally, Lunitar spoke up. "My lord. We will of course fight to the last if need be, but what of our reinforcements? Should we even expect any or are we on our own again?"

Reivn noted the tension in the air. "I do not know. I have not had any news from the other Warlords for several nights now. Now unless there are any more questions, you are dismissed."

Each man considered the weight of his words. Then one by one, they saluted and left.

Lunitar waited until he and Reivn were alone. "Permission to speak, my lord?" he asked.

"Speak your mind," Reivn replied, as he stared at the map.

"We don't have enough warriors among the whole lot to win this," Lunitar stated. "I know every soldier under your command would lay down their life for you, but would it not be wiser to fall back to a better location and regroup?"

At that, Reivn looked up. "Fall back?" he repeated and frowned. "There is nowhere left to fall back to. No… the battle will be here, and we shall either prevail or die tonight." His eyes carried the full weight of those words and he looked away.

"I see. Then I shall go prepare." Lunitar knelt on his right knee and crossed his right fist over his chest in salute. Then he got up and turned to leave.

"Lunitar…" Reivn said quietly.

"Yes, my lord?" Lunitar paused and turned around.

Reivn stared at his son intently before answering. "Watch your back out there tonight."

Lunitar nodded. "You as well, father." He walked out, leaving the Warlord to his thoughts.

When Reivn finally left headquarters, he headed toward the stables. One glance at the encampment told him his soldiers were already falling into ranks.

"Lord Reivn!" a voice hailed him from behind.

Reivn turned around, and then raised an eyebrow in annoyance.

Valfort was walking up the road from camp, headed toward him.

Reivn dropped his hands behind his back and slowed his pace. "What do you want, Ceros?" he asked in irritation.

Valfort joined him, and they descended the hill together.

Reivn glanced at him and frowned. "Our warriors are preparing for battle and yet you are here. Did you deliver my request to Polusporta?"

"I know how to do my job. I am leaving after we speak," Valfort answered coldly.

Reivn shot him an angry look. "You were supposed to deliver my request last night! Time is of the essence! In a short while, a large Principatus contingent is marching on Rowton Heath and we have less than half enough warriors to meet them! I need those reinforcements now!"

Valfort stopped and stared at him. "Have you ever wondered why?"

"Why what?" Reivn asked in annoyance.

Valfort's tone changed. "Have you ever questioned the reason for this war? Or why the Council has made puppets of us all?"

"Those are dangerous words," Reivn growled, chastising him. "Our allegiance is to the Council and obedience our sacred duty. If we fail them, mortal men pay the price. You know this better than anyone as Mastric's firstborn."

Valfort's eyes grew cold. "I am fully aware of the Council's mandates, but like most men, I still dream. Do you not remember your life before Mastric claimed you? Or what it was to be human?" Bitterness seeped into his voice. "You cannot tell me you have never desired the freedom the Council holds from us… what our own father denies us!"

Reivn briskly walked the remaining distance to the stables, where his aide was already brushing down their horses. "Girard, saddle Zaitan. We leave as soon as possible!" Then he turned to Valfort, his anger readily apparent. "I remember who and what I once was, and how you destroyed that! None of that is who we are now! Hubris will not win this war, nor will treasonous words! That was why you were demoted in the first place! Perhaps you should remember that when you question father's judgment! Now excuse me, I have to see to my men!"

Valfort watched Reivn walk away, his dark eyes unreadable. "You are a fool," he whispered. "Farewell then. We will meet again soon. I hope your loyalty and honor find you better fortune than did mine…" His decision made, he retrieved his horse and headed out of camp and onto the road still muddy from the day's rain.

In the hours that followed, Reivn's forces fought continuous waves of Principatus, desperately struggling to hold their ground. Their soldiers were well-seasoned, but their numbers were dwindling, and reinforcements had still not arrived. The Renegades had vastly outnumbered them from the onset and pounded on them throughout the night. Brief respites gave Reivn just enough time to regroup his remaining troops before they had to push forward again. Corpses of the fallen burned with intense heat that scorched the once green and fertile earth, the acrid smoke rising from their charred remains to blend into the dark haze above. Cracks of lightning lit the sky with brilliant hues of blue and white, tearing momentary holes in the deep shadows of the night. Thunder echoed off the surrounding hills and shook the ground with its intensity, heralding the approaching storm, as nature's fury added to the sounds of war.

Desperate to regain lost ground, their tattered brigades of mounted cavalry joined devastated remnants of foot soldier battalions near the town's outskirts.

Reivn rode hard down the front of the battle line, the hooves of his Friesian thundering beneath him. His black wool cloak and tunic rippled in the wind, and the twin sanguine dragons adorning his chest caught the moonlight, giving him an eerie appearance as he galloped past his soldiers. He shouted to his officers, rallying them to prepare for another attack. "They're trying to cut us off! Girard, ride to Lunitar! Tell him to gather what cavalry remains and reinforce the left flank! Marcus, tell your people to tighten their ranks and shore up that hole on the right! We must hold our ground! If either side gives, we won't survive the night!" He made for the end of the column and assessed the battle. When he saw how few were still standing, he frowned. *Where is Valfort?* he wondered. *He should have returned by now.* Spotting Gideon, he urged his mount forward. "Gideon, has Valfort reported in?"

"There's been no word, my lord!" Gideon answered, reining his horse in to keep pace with Reivn's. "Another wave is preparing to attack, sire! We cannot hold them this time! There aren't enough of us left!" They stopped and surveyed the battlefield.

Soldiers scrambled in every direction, many bleeding from wounds they did not have time to close. Clerics dotted the landscape with flashes of light as they summoned the spirals, using their magic to heal the more seriously injured. Others collected the dead to the waiting wagons.

Reivn growled. "Pull four squads to the center and prevent them from breaking through! If our cavalry can defend the outer flanks, we may yet hold!"

"Yes, sir!" Gideon saluted and then rejoined his troops.

Reivn reined in his horse, his eyes narrowing as he gazed across the field.

This battle, like every other, lay hidden beneath the conflicts of humanity. The English civil war had been raging for several years, as the unrest in Europe escalated. The Renegades were determined to get a foothold in Europe. So while Cromwell battled for power and the throne, they were using the conflict as a front for their own assaults. Now the Alliance struggled to defend their territories from the numbers that opposed them.

Reivn's eyes grew dark as he spotted movement in the distance. *They are going to hit us again, God help us. We must hold, no matter what the cost. If we fail, we risk losing England.*

As if in answer to prayer Lucian, the Thylacinian Warlord, pushed through the lines and rode to Reivn's side. "Sorry I'm late," he apologized. His dark animalistic appearance and rugged complexion echoed the features of his father, Thylacinos.

"You are a welcome sight, Lucian, but I hope you brought troops with you," Reivn replied. "We are badly outnumbered."

Lucian turned around and pointed. "Fifteen thousand. Look behind you."

Reivn turned and saw three full Brigades filling the gaps in his ragged lines. Soldiers and mounted Cavalry from every tribe were joining their ranks. "How did you get so many?"

Lucian smiled and pointed further down the line.

Following his gaze, Reivn saw two of his other Warlords riding along the line, shouting out orders as fresh troops strengthened their position.

Several field defense teams of Mastrics were also with them. The magic-users immediately spread out and summoned the Spirals, casting a force shield in front of their forces. They were led by his sister, Elena.

She was one of the few kin Reivn felt any connection to, and her appearance on the battlefield was so uncharacteristic to her gentle nature that he frowned, her presence unsettling him. *Elena…* he telepathied. *You should not be here.*

Elena smiled affectionately and glanced in his direction. *Do not worry, little brother. I will be careful. I will see you when the battle is over.*

Then Reivn growled and turned to Lucian. "Why is she here? She is a healer, not a warrior! Why did the Council send her? Did Valfort not explain just how bad our situation is?"

"Valfort? What are you talking about?" Lucian asked in confusion. "None of us have even seen him since he was reassigned to your detail. The Council sent us because they had not heard from you. They assumed you would need us. Was he supposed to report in?"

Reivn's eyes filled with fury. "You never received my messages?"

Lucian's answer was lost, as a voice yelled, "Here they come!"

"Hold the line! Let them come closer!" Reivn shouted. He drew his sword, his attention returning to the battle. His stallion danced nervously under him, sensing the tension in the air.

The Renegades surged across the field, bearing down on them in vast numbers.

Reivn shouted to his men. "Bugler, sound the charge! Defend this ground! Forward!"

At his side, Lucian grinned and leaned into the wind, the pending fight filling him with anticipation. He drew his scimitar and let out a howling battle cry to his nearby tribesmen, smiling when every voice took up the call.

Elena's Mastrics waited until the Alliance forces reached the barrier before they dissolved it. Then they bombarded the Renegades with lightning and fire. When the Alliance's forces moved past them, they continued their assault from behind the line, their devastating magic effectively damaging the approaching enemy ranks.

The two armies collided with savage brutality, and Reivn's fresh troops cut into their enemy with fierce resolve. Both sides fought with desperate zeal, ripping into each other in a frenzy of steel and blood. Explosions of magic lit the field in brilliant hues of blue and red, casting an eerie glow on the furious conflict. The cavalry routed and charged, countering the Renegades that assaulted the flanks, and foot soldiers pressed forward in the center, attacking with renewed determination. Battle cries filled the air as officers rallied their troops, as the ground ran red with the blood of the fallen.

A mounted Renegade charged Reivn, brandishing a wickedly barbed spear.

Reivn was brutally efficient and drove his blade through the man's heart. The sound of a pistol erupted near him and his side exploded in agonizing pain, as the bullet tore through him. He touched his ribs and checked the wound, and then through sheer willpower pushed away the pain. He turned and swung wide, cleaving the shooter's arm off.

The injured Renegade howled in pain and tried to defend himself from the furious Warlord.

But enraged, Reivn only fought harder, forcing the frightened Renegade back until he overpowered the man and sliced through his abdomen with deadly precision.

The soldier toppled from his horse, futilely grabbing at the wound.

Reivn turned his attention on three Principatus who blocked his path. Two wielded swords, the third a heavy chain.

They sneered and circled him. Then one attacked, swinging his sword wildly.

Reivn caught the Renegade's arm mid-swing. Then he pulled the man closer, decapitated him, and kicked his body from his saddle.

The second Renegade yelled and charged him, swinging the chain over his head.

"Seliaprinde!" Reivn shouted. A fireball formed in his hand and he threw it at his attacker. Then he dodged as the chain flew mere inches from his head. The fireball hit the Renegade's chest and enveloped him.

The man screamed and tried to drop the heavy chain, but the intense heat had fused the now molten metal to his flesh. Horrified, he struggled with the remnants in his hands. The horse bolted in terror, dragging his screaming, burning body with it.

The remaining Renegade snarled with rage and attacked, swinging his blade like a madman.

Reivn forced the man's weapon aside.

His attacker brought his saber up to block him, but when their swords collided, the hilts locked, and it turned into a test of strength as each tried to disarm the other.

Reivn's eyes narrowed. He formed another fireball and launched it.

The Renegade lost his momentum and fell from his saddle as the flames swallowed him.

Without a second glance at the dying man, Reivn plunged back into battle.

Lucian attacked the Renegades with the ferocity of his tribe, leaving a bloody trail of bodies behind him. Enemy soldiers saw him and charged, intent on taking him down, but he was ready for them. He drove his sword into the first man's skull, and then grabbed a spear from a corpse and hurled it at the second Renegade.

The impact sent the soldier flying from his saddle as the spear ripped through his chest to protrude from his spinal cord.

"That is what happens to all those who turn on their Elders, boy!" Lucian snarled. Then he spotted Reivn.

Several Renegades had surrounded the Mastric Warlord. They attempted to drag him from his saddle, but he fought them off. "Entae Seliaprinde!" he shouted. Fireball after fireball formed in his hand, and he threw them at his attackers.

The Renegades' bodies were devoured by the blaze. Their screams died with them.

Reivn's stallion reared in terror and shied away from the flames. Calming the beast, he scanned the battlefield, searching for his sister. His sharp eyes quickly found her.

Elena was outnumbered and struggling to keep from being dragged to the ground.

Reivn's sudden need to get to her drove him back into action. He rejoined the fight, attacking his enemies with desperate fury and laying waste to those in his path.

Lucian realized Reivn was pushing left and tried to follow, but an enemy Captain plowed his horse into the Thylacinian, unsaddling them both. He hit the ground and rolled, recovering his footing quickly. Then he spun around and roared. "Come on, then!"

The Renegade rose to meet him and growled "Alliance scum! You will beg for mercy before I am finished with you!"

Lucian wiped the blood from his torn lip and grinned. "Then you'd best get to it."

Attempting to overpower the Warlord, his attacker barreled into him.

Lucian slid back a step, letting the Renegade's sword slice a thin line across his neck.

The man saw the blood on his blade and let out a howl of delight, pushing harder.

Without warning, Lucian dropped back and side-stepped his attacker. Then he lunged.

Surprised, the Captain's own inertia propelled him forward and he fell. His eyes registered shock as Lucian's sword buried itself in his chest.

The Thylacinian kicked him off and pulled his weapon free. Then he threw his head back, howled a cry of victory, and turned back to the fight.

Near the center of the field, the Principatus began to break through their defenses. Reivn saw the breach, fell back, and grabbed a courier. "They are pushing through! Find Lord Gideon! Tell him to pull three more squads to the front! Tell him he must hold the line!"

The courier rode hard to where Gideon's command fought to maintain their position.

Reivn spurred his mount forward again, his sharp eyes searching for Elena until he found her once more. Well past Gideon's position, she still struggled to stay in her saddle. He quickly analyzed the situation. In the distance, he could see Lunitar's division. It was being pounded by enemy ranks, but strengthened by their reinforcements, they were slowly pushing ahead. Gideon's men had reformed and closed the gap in the center. Now they were pressing forward. The Alliance was gradually regaining ground on every front.

Then another enemy wave charged across the field, catching Reivn's attention. He stared.

Valfort was leading the enemy in their charge.

Reivn was stunned. Then he followed Valfort's gaze and fear gripped his heart.

The traitor was heading directly for Elena.

"Elena, watch out!" Reivn yelled. He kicked his stallion into motion. Telepathy was impossible in the chaos. He fought his way over the corpses that littered the ground, but the new attack slowed his progress. "Elena!" he shouted again. Fury driving him, he deflected a blow from another attacker and cut him in two.

Elena heard his warning too late.

Valfort jumped onto her horse and dragged her to the ground.

"Let me go!" Elena screamed, struggling to free herself. "Ceros, let go of me!" Then her voice filled with terror. "Reivn, help me!"

Ignoring her cries, Valfort grabbed her hair and forced her to her feet. Then he viciously drove his blade through her back, cutting a path to her heart.

"No!" Reivn shouted, desperation filling him as he fought to reach them.

Valfort ripped out her heart and held it up in triumph. With a grin, he crushed it.

Elena slid to the ground, shock frozen on her face.

Reivn broke free of the chaos and charged at him.

"Give my condolences to father, little brother!" Valfort's laughter filled the air.

"I will kill you for this! Seliaprinde!" Reivn roared, unleashing a massive fireball.

Flames exploded in every direction, but when the smoke cleared, the traitor had vanished.

Reivn jumped from his horse and ran to Elena. He dropped to his knees beside her and pulled her into his arms, brushing her hair from her face. The ashen pallor of death had already claimed her. "I failed you. Forgive me," he whispered. He got up, carrying her lifeless body with him. Then he screamed, his anguish filling the air.

Valfort had betrayed the Alliance. In slaughtering his sister, he had declared war on the Council and his own brethren.

Reivn's grief merged with fury over his brother's betrayal and he looked around, seeking vengeance. There would be none that night.

Strengthened by their reinforcements, the Alliance had driven back the Principatus on every front. The enemy's line had collapsed, and they were running. Then the cavalry closed in and cut them down until only a scattered few remained. The field was slowly falling quiet.

Several Mastrics approached Reivn and he turned. "Take her to Draegonstorm," he ordered, his expression unreadable. "Then inform Lord Mastric that Valfort has betrayed us. Convey my request that he send a Warlord to replace me. I want blood for blood."

Bowing to him, they carefully took her body, saluted him and headed back to camp and a portal that would take them to his fortress.

Reivn turned his attention to the battlefield and stared at the devastation in silence.

A Cleric saw him and approached. "My lord, let me attend you."

Reivn did not answer. *The fighting is over for now and we held, but at what cost?* He grimly stared across the field at the remnants of the fighting, watching as Lucian finished his last kill.

Lucian was covered in blood, some from his own deep wounds. Satisfied with the night's victory, he lifted his head and howled. As other

26

voices raised in response, he turned and headed toward the hill's summit where the remaining forces were gathering.

Hundreds of warriors limped from the field. The more serious injured were being evacuated by Clerics, and flashes of light dotted the landscape like fireflies, as they healed any too critical to move. The scent of blood and death hung heavy in the air from the sea of corpses covering the ground. Those who could were searching for survivors and burning the bodies of the dead, moving slowly across the battlefield with grim purpose.

"My lord Reivn," the healer ventured again. "My lord, you are wounded. Let me attend you."

Jolted back from his thoughts by her voice, Reivn turned and nodded. Then he sat down so the Cleric could see to his injuries.

The girl skillfully withdrew the bullet and closed the hole, knitting flesh and bone back together with her magic. Then she worked closed his other wounds one by one.

"Thank you. Now leave me. I must see to our troops, and there are others who need you," Reivn stated. He watched in silence as she bowed and walked away.

A bugle sounded recall in the distance and Reivn turned his attention to the field once more. Searching for his own banners, relief filled him when he spotted them across the field. Lunitar was leading the cavalry back to camp. Then his eyes fell on the dark-haired man who rode at his side. Gideon had joined his brother as they headed for much-needed rest.

Reivn looked away. His mind on his sons, he walked over to his horse and climbed into the saddle. Then mulling over recent events, he rode back to camp to debrief his officers. "Luck was with us... this time," he mused in frustration. "Our reinforcements secured this territory for now, but the Renegades will return. Elena's death will ignite Mastric's rage, and he will declare a hunt on Valfort like no other. We won the battle tonight, but this war has only just begun..."

# BLOOD FEUD

## Chapter Two
## Innocence Lost

*There are many forces in this world the average person cannot explain.
Often have I watched as the world has burned in one war after another,
always with the lie each one tells himself that what he does is right. Are all
so blind to themselves then? Do we not defeat the very reason we exist
when we declare ourselves so perfect as to not need each other in the end?
For myself, I need those around me. My existence would be empty without
the companionship and love I share with my kin. Do they feel the same, I
wonder?*

*The betrayal of so many leads me to grieve for those lost. It weighs
heavy on my heart and lays like an iron yoke upon my shoulders. All light
and laughter has fled, yielding to the gloom of loneliness. Did all my joy
flee with the passing of the sunlight, or was it at the turning of so many
ages? My sister knew of my heart and would often counsel me to find
renewed strength in the hope that springs from our Jihad. She used to tell
me that defending the innocent has long been a worthy charge, but to this I
say were not the ones I now hunt once each an innocent?*

*I am weary of hunting the young, so foolishly misled by their own
newly found power. They possess not the wisdom to govern themselves,
nor do they take heed of the shadows that would cover all the world in
darkness if we gave in to our bestial desires. I obey the laws of our sires
and bring to justice those who would bring chaos to order, but I take no
pleasure in the killing of a child I may once have called friend. And yet... I
still hear the cries of the dead, those condemned by their own greed,
judged by the Ancients, hunted and executed often by my own hand. It is
true indeed that a race divided is a race doomed from the moment the
fighting begins.*

*Lord Reivn Draegon*

\* \* \* \* \*

August 1670. Vienna, Austria

The Inn was lit by a fire that crackled in the large stone hearth and bathed
the interior in its soft glow. Planked wood walls rose to meet huge
crossbeams that ran the full length of the ceiling. Two rough-hewn support
columns of aged oak stood side by side like sentinels, dominating the
center of the room. For a roadside Inn, it was unusually quiet. The few

mismatched worn tables and chairs remained empty, as a serving girl busily tidied up from the last occupants to have dined. An old man shuffled back and forth by the bar, cleaning needlessly, for it had barely been touched that night. His eyes shifted back to a chair facing the fire, where his master sat staring at the flames in silent contemplation. The old man's gaze lingered for a moment. Then he disappeared down the hall at the back of the Inn.

Valfort did not look up. He waited while the girl finished her work, listening for the latch to click on the back door as she headed home. He stared at the fire, revisiting memories of the past, but the silence told him it was time to leave and his body demanded sustenance.

"Time to go," he groaned and got up. In an almost agitated state, he grabbed a cloak hanging next to the door and walked out into the night. Minutes later, he exited the Inn's stables and urged his horse to a full gallop, disappearing in a cloud of dust on the road.

After an hour's hard ride, he reined in the lathered animal in front of a well-lit estate. Music drifted from its open doorways. Neo-classic arches curved gracefully over the stone staircase leading to the Villa's front entry. Marble sculptures adorned the walls around windows and door-side panels of elegant stained glass. The soft yellow stucco walls glowed in the light of the streetlamps that dotted the property, their pale radiance extending down the front drive and grand stairway. Guests arrived in carriages, attired in an array of brilliant colors, and lined the steps as they waited to be announced. Ladies turned to stare as he dismounted, their excited chatter filling the air. He handed the reins to a groom, dusted himself off and climbed the steps.

A servant greeted him at the door. "Whom shall I announce, my lord?"

"Lord Ceros Valfort," he answered and handed the man his cloak with a smile, as a few curious eyes glanced his way. He waited patiently while his name was announced. Then he stepped through the doors and his senses came alive. He closed his eyes and let the rush of emotion in the room flow through him in a wave of intense pleasure. His irrepressible hunger demanded sustenance and he looked slowly around the room.

The ballroom was well lit by chandeliers that illuminated the 16th-century architecture in golden hues. Rich velvet drapes of deep blue and gold framed the French doors and windows, where marble statues of Greek heroes stood guarding their openings. The assembled guests moved about, filling the air with conversation.

Valfort stood in the shadows and leaned nonchalantly against the wall, his dark eyes alert as he searched the crowd. Finally, he spotted a young blonde talking with two men and smiled. *This is going to be a good night,* he thought. He casually approached his prey and reached out with his senses. Then he slipped into her mind and began to whisper, seducing her. However, when he drew closer to his target, he caught the odor of spirits and curled his nose in disgust. *She has been drinking. God, I hate the acerbic taste it leaves in my mouth. Not her then...* He released her mind and turned to search for an acceptable substitute.

Across the room, another young woman sat viewing the festivities with only mild interest. Angelique watched the dancing from her corner in boredom and covered her mouth to hide a yawn. She leaned back, her copper curls glistening in the light as she moved. Her thoughts wandered and the guest's laughter faded into the background. Then a sudden icy chill washed over her, causing her to shiver. She looked around in mild discomfort, but nothing appeared to be out of place. Still, she could not shake the sensation that something was different, so she got up and began searching for the source of her uneasiness.

Valfort scanned the room, his annoyance causing indifference over the selection before him. Then he felt it... the uncertainty flowing from someone nearby. *Interesting...* he thought with a smile. He was a centuries-old creature to whom legends had given the name Vampyre. He came from the second oldest tribe of a society of ordered hierarchy known as the Alliance. Now he was a Renegade and a traitor to his own kind. This did not deter him though, for he reveled in his newfound freedom. These were his hunting grounds, and this society was his prey. His senses were far keener than any human's. He could hear every whisper, heartbeat, and breath of those nearby. He could even feel the steady throb of emotions in those around him. As he circled the room, a different emotion began to fill his mind... one of mild alarm. It did not take him long to find the source. He smiled again when his eyes settled on red curls and green eyes. His selection made, he approached her.

Angelique felt his gaze before she even saw him. She turned and found herself staring at the most surreal man she had ever met.

His face was almost white in contrast to the black strands of hair that fell to his shoulders, despite the ribbon restraining them. His dark eyes bore into the very fabric of her soul. They tore at her, compelling her to his side. Then his thoughts filled her mind.

*Beautiful child, come to me...*

Spellbound, she obeyed.

"Come... dance with me." He took her arm and led her out among the moving crowd. Then he gently folded his arms around her and began waltzing to the music. The notes became a pulse, blending them together in one fluid motion.

Angelique could not tear her gaze from him. His chiseled features and dark hair hovered on the outskirts of eyes that consumed her soul. She barely noticed when the room disappeared from her awareness. His voice filled her senses, all else fading as it echoed in her mind.

Valfort brushed against her ear with his lips and whispered. "Do you like magic, little one?"

His voice mesmerized her. She tried to answer, but speech failed her.

He smiled again, whirling her around even faster.

All sound vanished from her awareness and only he remained, as he led her out through the ballroom doors into the garden beyond. Her instincts told her to be afraid and run, but she found herself immobile, lost in the fathomless depth of those eyes.

With inhuman speed, he took her farther into the garden until they disappeared from view. Climbing roses arched over the pathway like gentle guardians, blotting out the moon's rays and shrouding them in shadow. "Then I shall give you a gift you will never forget." He pulled her closer and swept her hair from her neck.

She could feel his lips against her cheek and an unnamable fear crept into her heart.

His thoughts filled her mind. *You belong to me.*

*I don't understand*, she began, but the words never reached her mouth. Her eyes went wide with fear as his fangs opened her flesh. Then he began to drink, and her awareness faded. Finally, she slipped into unconsciousness.

He held her close as she went limp, sinking his fangs even deeper. Her heartbeat faded to a whisper and her breathing grew shallow. Finally he withdrew, gasping with ecstasy. The blood on the edges of his mouth vanished and his skin took on a healthier glow. He groaned as her innocence filled his senses with desire... and something else he could not name. He lowered her to the ground, and then stood gazing at her in silence. *A mere child...* he observed. He knelt at her side, deep in thought. Something had drawn him to her. He searched her mind until he found the thread still clinging to life. *Angelique?* he mused. W*hat are you? A resistor? An angel?*

He knew taking her was dangerous, but instinct told him letting her go would be even more so. He had not been hunting for her, but she had crossed his path. She had sensed his presence when others could not, and that meant he was exposed in his own hunting grounds. He usually took only what he needed to survive so he could hide his whereabouts, making sure his victims remembered nothing. The need to protect himself had driven him to risk everything. He had drained her and meant for her to die.

Valfort's thoughts turned back to her. He watched her until her life had all but faded. He was toying with ideas for her fate, weighing the odds of awakening her. Then just as her skin grayed with death's kiss, he opened a vein in his neck. "You will be special. I will make you the strongest of my young. Drink and live." He lifted her up and put her lips to his wound. The surge of blood that poured into her mouth became a living thing as it ran down her throat. When she could take no more, he pulled away and willed his wound closed. He smiled at the rare creature he had created. Then taking her with him, he disappeared into the night.

Angelique's final moments of life exploded in a symphony of visions. As the curse wound itself around her soul, she drifted into a place beyond oblivion. Her happiest memories appeared and vanished with vivid clarity, swallowed by the void that was forming in her mind. In desperation, she clung to one name... *Blake.* She was betrothed to the only son of the Duke of Kent. Now, as her soul was cursed to the night, his face became an anchor while she fought to cling to her mortality. Somewhere in the dark, she heard him call her name. Then when the last vestiges of her life extinguished, his voice silenced, and the images gradually faded to black.

When she finally awoke, it was to strange surroundings. *Where am I?* she wondered. Then she remembered the garden. Fear coursed through her and she touched her neck, but found nothing. She looked around in confusion.

The old wooden walls of the room did little to keep out the night air. A single candle on a bedside table flickered in the draft, its flame dimly lighting the chamber. The room's interior was sparsely furnished. A chair sat in the corner by the door, and a wardrobe leaned against the far wall. These and the bed were the only furniture present.

Disoriented, she got up and went to the door. It was locked. Anxious, she called out. "Can anyone hear me? Hello?"

Keys rattled, and the lock clicked.

A wave of relief flooded through her. "Oh, thank God! I could not get the door open," she exclaimed when it swung wide. Light poured in and she winced from the sudden glare. Then her eyes adjusted, and fear gripped her heart.

An old man with pale skin and sunken eyes stood in the threshold. His hair resembled an old tuft of raw cotton left in the sun too long.

"Who are you?" Though terrified, she managed to keep a calm outward appearance.

"You're awake at last," the old man rasped with a smile. "I am Maratoli. My master bid me teach you everything you need to survive. Now then, let's have a look at you," he stated, observing her with a critical eye.

At that, Angelique backed away, staring at him in confusion. "What are you talking about?"

"All your questions will be answered, but first you must feed," he calmly explained. "You are weak. Strength is important if you are to live. There are many who will try to take your life, so you must be prepared. Come now." He took out a knife and opened his wrist.

Horrified, she cried "What are you doing?"

In response, he held his wrist closer, letting her smell the blood.

Without warning, her stomach twisted into excruciating knots of pain and her senses exploded. She staggered back in agony. The savage desire to take what he offered overwhelmed her. "No!" she screamed. She stumbled and fell as she attempted to move away. Then she tried to crawl, but she was weak with painful need and could barely move.

He pushed his wrist toward her again. "Feed or you'll die."

"Let me die then," she choked out. "I don't want this!" Wracked with pain, she curled into a ball. "What did he do to me?"

He knelt and cradled her in his arms. Then he gently put his wrist to her lips.

She could taste the blood. Her remaining strength gone, her fangs extended on their own. She grabbed his wrist. The hot, sweet fluid excited her on a powerful level and she sucked it down until he began to pull away. Desires drove her that she could not control, and she clung to him.

He firmly freed his arm and gazed down at her. "Lick the wound," he ordered. His voice unmistakably carried urgency.

She stared at him in shock, realizing what she had just done. She was shaking uncontrollably, and new sensations flooded her senses.

"Lick the wound," he commanded again. "...and it will close. If you don't, I'll die."

Revulsion and sickness overwhelmed her, and she closed her eyes. Then she leaned forward and ran her tongue across the leathery surface of his skin. Her senses were reeling. She collapsed on the cold stone floor, trying to shut out the euphoria flooding her body. When she could finally open her eyes again, Maratoli was moving about the room as though nothing had happened. "Please," she begged. "Tell me what has happened to me?"

Maratoli stopped and turned around. "You have been reborn. You are here until you can care for yourself," he explained, staring at her briefly before resuming his work. "You are a night creature... an Immortal, what humans call Vampyre. Daylight is your enemy. You can only travel freely after dark. You must forget your old life. My master is your maker and you, his child. I will teach you to feed and use your power. When you are ready, he will come for you."

Angelique listened in stunned silence.

"That is enough for now. You have much to learn, but tonight has been a great shock. You must rest. Tomorrow I will tell you more." He helped her up walked her over to the bed.

She let him care for her without protest. There were sensations pulsing through her she could not understand. When he went to leave, she stopped him. "What will happen to me now?"

He turned around, his eyes settling on her troubled face. Finally, he responded. "You are a creature of power and magic. To live, you must feed on blood. You must never reveal yourself to humans. They would kill you. You will grow stronger, but you will never grow old." Then he left, locking the door behind him and leaving her to absorb all she had learned that night.

Tears clouded her vision. She wiped them away and was shocked to see blood on her hand. "God help me," she whispered.

Countless days and nights passed, until Angelique could no longer tell what date it was. While she adjusted to her new life, Maratoli taught her about her newfound abilities. She learned to hear, see and sense everything around her. He was a kind and patient teacher, but he never spoke of the man who had stripped her innocence from her. He never spoke of Valfort.

## Chapter Three
## Blood Hunt

*Fate has a strange way of twisting things, always bringing forth something one does not expect. In pursuit of the traitor, Valfort, I have come to know self-loathing. The young that defend his lairs are so much weaker than those of us that pursue them that killing them seems pointless and cruel. They pose little threat. Many have not learned the full measure of their new abilities. Drunk on bloodlust and hungry for more power, most do not even understand what they have truly become. Promises of wealth and conquest lure the young, for they have not had time to turn away from worldly things.*

*So foolish, the child that willingly runs into my blade, giving their immortality for a cause they cannot hope to truly grasp meaning from. God take their souls, for their innocence is fleeting and wasted in the darkness of our world. Like lambs led to slaughter by wolves, they are created and given over that a coward may flee to live another night.*

*We have followed Valfort's trail for many years. I had hoped this would be over long before now, but he continues to avoid us. Now the hunt has led us to Vienna. If he is here, so too will there be more killing of children. It is his way. Is the taking of so many young on his soul or mine? Do I damn myself by freeing those whose lives he has already stolen? Some would argue that a life... any life... is better than the death that awaits at the end of my sword. When I encounter the next lair he has made and take countless more lives, am I the murderer? Or am I merely the hand of God striking vengeance in the realm of the forgotten? Whose soul do I then pray for... those I send to meet their doom, or my own at the battle's end?*

*Lord Reivn Draegon*

\* \* \* \* \*

It was well past midnight when the ship bearing Reivn and his son finally reached the coast of France. The night was crisp and clear, an early winter chill having settled in the air. The moon broke through clouds and painted the dock in shades of blue. Calais was bustling with commotion. Ships filled the harbor, some loading cargo in preparation to depart. Others were securing their lines, having only just arrived. Ramshackle wooden storehouses stood bunched together on either side of the wharves, their great doors a flurry of activity. The roads leading into the harbor were hard-packed earth and cobblestone, with ruts worn into them from the wagons traveling their lengths night and day.

From the deck, Reivn slowly surveyed the shore. His hair danced around his face in the breeze, but he paid no attention. His eyes swept across the dock as he searched for their contact.

Gideon stood patiently beside him awaiting orders and studying the shoreline. He knew the Council had sent people to meet them.

*There*, Reivn telepathied his son. He nodded toward two men seated on horseback, each holding a riderless horse by the reins and watching the ship.

Gideon followed his gaze, then shouldered their packs and followed him down the gangplank.

They approached the riders cautiously and called out a greeting. The waiting men responded by handing over the spare horses. Reivn and Gideon fastened down their packs and mounted up without a word. Then the four men rode off into the night.

Hours later, the group arrived at a small roadside tavern. After seeing to the horses, they stomped the mud from their boots and went inside. Then they found an empty table in a corner of the main room and sat down.

"We can talk here in private," Reivn stated, glancing around at the Inn's occupants.

Gideon settled into the chair closest to the room's center to keep watch.

Reivn leaned over the table and spoke in hushed tones. "Tell me who you are and everything you know thus far."

The man across from him lowered his hood. "I am Jack Dunn. My companion is Grimel."

Grimel bowed his head in silent greeting.

"Well, I assume you already know who I am," Reivn replied, shaking Jack's hand. "This is my son, Gideon."

Gideon looked around at the mention of his name and nodded quietly.

"We were sent by the Council to aid in hunting the Renegade," Jack continued in hushed tones. We tracked Valfort here and then to Vienna, where we lost him. He has to be there somewhere. I'd bank on him having at least one hidden stronghold near there."

Reivn agreed. "Valfort is no fool. He probably has more than one. He knows he is being hunted and will not make it easy for us."

Jack shifted in his seat and moved closer to Reivn. "We at least have an idea where he's been feeding," he answered quietly. "We may be able to track his whereabouts from there. We still have at least four hours until daybreak. If we leave now, we can get a good start. We have more than eight hundred miles to cover over the next few weeks."

"The horses are spent and need rest," Reivn pointed out, disagreeing with the Epochian. "Valfort is arrogant. He has been toying with us. If he has set up a stronghold, he is not going to leave it willingly. Our departure can wait until tomorrow. I suggest we find adequate shelter to retreat from the day."

"I suppose so," Jack finally agreed grudgingly. "I read your reports. He's almost certainly sired more children by now. If he has, there'll be more than one to deal with."

Reivn nodded grimly. "We rest today and ride out after sunset tomorrow."

The whispered conversation lasted a few more minutes. Then they got up in one fluid motion and exited out into the night. They quickly retrieved their horses and mounted up, preparing for the hard ride ahead.

Jack's mare danced nervously, sensing her rider's urgency. "There's a deserted farm not far from here," he stated, calming the animal. "The house is ruined, but the barns are still intact. We can rest there."

The group headed down the road, pushing their tired mounts to a gallop, and within the hour, they arrived at an old abandoned farm. The night creatures fell silent when they approached.

Reivn ignored the house, which was burnt and partially collapsed, and rode on to the larger of the two barns. When he dismounted, a sound from within caused him to draw his sword.

Jack jumped down beside him and quickly pulled his own blade. Then he nodded to Reivn and disappeared behind the building, moving at inhuman speed.

Gideon and Grimel drew their weapons and joined Reivn as he approached the barn.

"*Now!*" Reivn telepathied. Then he threw open the doors.

Jack jumped through the loft window and landed on the floor at the back of the barn. A scream rang out and he spun around just in time to see a ragged form darting into one of the stalls. He dove after it and hauled an old man, shabby and dirty, from his hiding place.

"Please," the man stuttered in fright, as he sat trembling before him. "I won't tell anyone. I saw nothin', I swear!"

Motioning for the others to secure the barn, Reivn approached Jack and his prisoner.

The old farmer cowered in terror.

"What is it you think you saw, old man?" Reivn calmly asked.

"He... he flew to that window," the old man whimpered and pointed first to Jack, then the window. "He's a Daemon! He ain't natural!"

The man shuddered when Reivn pulled him to his feet. "You will remember nothing of this." Reivn's voice changed, echoing with power.

The old man's face went blank as his mind was overthrown, and his trembling stopped.

"Today, you will sleep in a bed," Reivn continued. "Tomorrow you begin rebuilding this farm. You have one thousand pounds in an account. The papers are in your satchel. Now sleep."

The farmer slumped forward and Reivn caught him effortlessly. "Drink only what you need. He will be well paid." He pulled a piece of paper from his pouch and stuffed it into the farmer's waist-side bag. Then he handed the old man back to Jack.

The Epochian passed him on to Grimel. "I prefer to drink from my own stores. However," he added and pulled a small bag from inside his cloak. "You can stick this in his satchel too. Gold on hand will aid him with his appearance. You don't drink?"

Reivn shook his head. "I will feed later."

When Gideon and Grimel were finished feeding, Jack pulled Grimel aside and spoke with him in hushed tones. Minutes later the Thylacinian departed, taking the aged farmer back to town to stay in the Inn. After they left, Jack turned to Reivn. "He will watch over our friend while he recovers and rendezvous with us tomorrow after sunset."

Not bothering to answer, Reivn inspected the stalls, searching for a clean place to rest. After finding what he wanted, he fetched hay from the loft and spread it on the floor, wrinkling his nose at its musty smell. With a yawn, he pulled a blanket from his pack and spread it across the makeshift bed. Then he laid down and pulled his cloak around him.

Gideon saw to the horses and then settled into the stall near his father.

Jack set himself up in another stall nearby and the barn fell silent.

The following night, Grimel returned as they were saddling their horses. "Our friend is making his arrangements," he reported. "This farm will thrive again."

Jack looked at Reivn in satisfaction. "You're a good man. Not many of our kind pay the mortals for what we take," he observed in admiration. "But I must ask, why give him so much? The bank note?"

Reivn shook his head. "I keep accounts set up for contingencies such as this. Just because we do not kill them does not mean we do not harm them when we take from them. I merely give back what I acquire."

Jack snickered and climbed into his saddle. "Let's go," he replied, ignoring Reivn's frown. The others urged their horses forward and followed him out of the yard.

Reivn's expression unfathomable, he caught up to Jack. "Why do you doubt my sincerity? It is sound reasoning. Balance is what our world exists on."

Jack chuckled at Reivn's serious expression. "Reivn old boy, you can deny it all you wish and even convince yourself, but I know a soft heart when I see one." At Reivn's irritated expression, he rode on, his laughter filling the night air.

After two weeks of hunting by night and stopping at wayside locations at dawn each day, they finally arrived in Vienna. The streets were empty except for occasional passers-by.

Reivn joined Jack. "It will be dawn soon. We should head for the Eagle's Rest Inn in the southern quarter. I have contacts there who will give us rooms, no questions asked. We can start our search tomorrow." They turned and headed for the southern end of the city.

The Inn was a two-story worn-down building, its roof still the thatching of older years. A single lantern lit the door, casting reflections on its worn wood frame. When their group approached and dismounted, a stable boy appeared and led their horses away. Then they stepped inside and looked around.

The interior was simple, but clean, its tables and chairs polished to a smooth surface from repeated scrubbings. Crossbeams ran the length of the ceiling, intercepting the worn wood pillars that supported the central structure. A fire burned in the great stone hearth on the far wall and candles flickered in heavy iron sconces, leaving hardened mounds of wax on the hardwood floor.

Reivn received a warm smile from the girl behind the counter. He approached her and whispered in her ear. In response, she giggled and motioned for him and his companions to follow as she headed for a set of stairs.

Jack shook his head in resignation and followed the Warlord to the second floor.

Grimel shouldered his bag and joined them. Keeping his own counsel had long been a habit that allowed him to observe, often unnoticed, while others went about their business.

Gideon glanced around the room, carefully noting its occupants, and then followed them.

Jack and Grimel disappeared into a room the girl pointed out. Then Reivn picked her up and carried her into the adjoining room.

Gideon entered behind his father. He stood and watched Reivn tease her for a moment, their laughter filling the room. Then he silently took out his bedroll and threw it on a cot in the corner. He quickly unrolled it and laid down, facing the wall and covering himself with his blanket. He tried to shut out the sounds of his father's coupling as he fed on the girl. Though he knew she was willing, it still disturbed him. His thoughts drifting into the past, he slipped into slumber.

Reivn ignored his son and lounged in the large bed, holding the now unconscious woman in his arms. Her scent pleased him, but she had slipped into unconsciousness too soon. Listening to the quiet sounds of her breathing, he glanced over at Gideon, and saw sleep had already claimed him. His thoughts on his son, the troubled Warlord finally closed his eyes.

Jack was annoyed. He disapproved of Reivn's actions. *She may be a regular donor, but I don't like it,* he telepathied Grimel. *Humans who know too much about us are dangerous.*

Grimel merely shrugged, keeping his opinion to himself. The room fell silent as they secured their position and settled into their cots.

The following night they began the hunt again. Reivn waited atop his stallion on a street at the edge of town while Jack and Grimel searched nearby and Gideon made local inquiries.

When Gideon returned, his expression told Reivn there were still no leads.

Reivn cursed silently. "Report!" he growled.

"He's covered his tracks well, my lord. No one remembers such a man," Gideon said, and then paused, noting his father's furious countenance. "The peasants' minds were wiped clean."

Reivn stared at the dark street ahead. "Valfort has not remained hidden this long by being a fool. Of all the Elders to have gone Renegade, he is the most dangerous. Mastric only charged me with finding him because I know him so well." Reivn paused, his eyes still focused on the road as he watched for their companions.

Gideon stared at his father, questions filling his mind. But any response was silenced as their companions rode up.

Jack reined in beside them and saluted. "We have a lead," he told them. "A woman in the western quarter remembers seeing a man fitting Valfort's description. She works at one of the estates outside the city. A few weeks ago, they held a masque' ball. She remembers the ball because the daughter of an aristocrat went missing that night and has yet to be found. The whole estate is in an uproar. Sound familiar?"

"Let us hope she is not enduring a new life," Reivn growled. "I dislike killing young girls." He turned his stallion toward city limits. "It seems the estate is a good place to start."

Jack kept pace with Reivn. "What's your plan?"

His eyes unreadable, Reivn replied, "He is going to lead us right to him."

"You really think it will be that easy?" Jack asked with a frown. "I'm not so certain of that."

Reivn chuckled at Jack's expression. "This time, he was foolish. He took a member of the aristocracy, Jack. That will give us an unmistakable trail. If he killed her and left her for dead, we will not be able to track him. However, an arrogant newborn will not be difficult to find."

The small company rode on in silence, their senses alert to the shadows around them. Their horse's hooves gave off an eerie sound, as night creatures fell silent at their passing.

Jack's thoughts were dark. *I know the trail will be difficult to find, because it is weeks old. Still, there are ways to see things mortals cannot.*

The hunting party finally arrived at the gates of the sumptuous manor. The Neo-classic estate boasted a row of marble statues on either side of a staircase that rose to its entrance, and stain-glassed windows shone with candle-lit brilliance against the night sky.

Reivn signaled for the group to halt by the gate. Then he dismounted and handed his reins to Gideon. "Wait here. I will not be long," he ordered. Then he stepped back and summoned the Spirals. "Liatulnae Arovite!" he uttered and began to transform. His body shifted and grew smaller, as his arms sprouted feathers and gracefully curved into fine wings. In moments, a black raven hovered where he had been standing.

*Good luck*, Jack telepathied.

Reivn flew over the gates and slowly circled around the property, his wings riding the air as he descended. He searched for something humans could not find. As he neared lavish gardens beyond the grand ballroom, he caught a scent. He dropped down closer and tested the air with his senses. The faint odor of old blood still lingered. He settled on a bush and looked around until his sharp eyes found its source. A single drop stained a leaf of the climbing roses covering the walk. It carried a telltale aroma. Plucking the leaf from its stem, he flew back to the waiting group. He landed on Jack's outstretched hand.

Jack took the leaf from Reivn and examined it. "Only our kind could have found this," he remarked and handed it back to Reivn, who had jumped down and shifted forms again.

"Valfort! It has to be!" Reivn stated, inspecting the leaf. "This is potent blood." He turned the leaf over, carefully inhaling the scent. "I do not think he killed her though."

Jack's expression was solemn. "No, I don't think he did." He turned to the others. "He is making children again!"

Reivn swung himself into his saddle, and then looked at Jack. "We search in a circular pattern, checking every house, home, abandoned building, cave, anything!" he ordered. "Leave nothing to chance! We must find him before yet another child reaches maturity! He may already have others who are fully developed! Let us be sure he cannot add any more to their ranks!"

"We should split up. We can cover more ground. I'll head east, Grimel south." Jack's mount danced nervously as he spoke, sensing his rider's urgency. "Send Gideon west and you head north. We meet at the Eagle's Rest in two night's time. If Valfort is found, no one engages him until after we rendezvous!" Without waiting for an answer, he disappeared down the east road.

Reivn watched him ride out of sight, and then nodded to Gideon. "See you in two days!" He kicked his heels into his stallion's sides. The beast reared, dancing for a second before galloping north. Gideon and Grimel separated and rode off. All four men were determined to cover as much ground as possible, hoping to be at the end of their hunt.

For two nights Reivn searched every place he came across, but found no clues. *It is as though he vanished into the mist*, he thought in frustration. Finally, he headed back to the Eagle's Rest Inn. A soft rain began to fall, so he pulled his cloak around him and donned its hood. Then he rode silently on through the dark.

When he arrived at the Inn, Gideon had not yet returned, but Jack and Grimel were waiting for him. Jack raised a hand in greeting. "Any news?" he asked.

Reivn's face darkened, realizing they had also returned empty-handed. "Let us hope my son had better luck than the rest of us."

The sound of hooves pounding furiously up the road caused them to turn, weapons drawn.

Gideon rode hard toward them, the wind tearing at his hair and clothes. "I found him!" he shouted when he was in range. "He has an Inn not far from Liesing! We've got him!"

Reivn nodded and turned to Jack, ignoring anything further from Gideon.

Jack looked from father to son, noting the tension. Then he smiled. "Well done Gideon," he stated. "Your father must be proud."

Reivn frowned, his countenance darkening. "My son does not require praise for performing his duties. The important matter here is catching our quarry! Now... let's move out!"

Jack stared at Reivn's back as they rode down the street, but kept quiet. He was disturbed at the Warlord's reaction and apparent indifference to his son.

Gideon followed in silence, his expression brooding.

The hunting party rode all night, stopping only when necessary. Shortly before dawn, they arrived in Liesing. They avoided the town and rode on, wanting to reach the Inn before daybreak. Finally, it came into sight.

Set just off the road, the small building was protected on two sides by trees. Smoke rose from the chimney, but the yard remained empty. The stars were veiled, and the moon had slipped behind the clouds, hiding the landscape in deep shadows. Their horses were exhausted from the two-hour run, so the group tied their mounts in a secluded spot among the trees. From there they went on foot, moving with deathly silence. They drew their weapons and prepared to enter, unaware that a pair of eyes watched them from a hidden vantage point.

Valfort sent a silent warning to the old man inside.

Maratoli's eyes went wide and he shouted the alarm. Then he ran for the back hall. Angelique had just finished bathing and dressing when he burst into the room. "Milady, quickly! Come with me! They've found us!" he cried as he hastily gathered a few of her belongings and stuffed them into a sack. "You must leave at once! Anything you need will be brought to you when my brother can safely deliver it!"

In the hall, Angelique could hear screams, shouts, and the sounds of fighting. She stared at the door in terror, frozen to the spot.

Maratoli grabbed her arm, pushed a money purse into her hands, and dragged her out before she could grasp what he was saying. He spoke rapidly as he hurried her along the dark hall and down the back stairs. "Don't forget, Milady! Sleep protected by day, and feed or you'll die!" he reminded her. "Live and be strong!" A carriage waited behind the Inn, and he looked sad when he shoved her into its dark interior. "Go, Jarvis!" he shouted, and they raced into the night. It was the last time she ever saw her strange friend.

Angelique stared back in fright at the building she had lived in since her abduction. It was a narrow escape. Now, as the carriage sped toward some unknown destination, this new turn of events terrified her. *Who found us?* she wondered fearfully. Gazing in silence at the countryside that flew by, she could only pray she was not pursued by the unknown assailant.

The Inn was filled with terrifying sounds as Reivn and his companions charged into the main room of the building, cutting down anything that moved. Several young, but trained Vampyres flew at them, only to be ripped apart by the Elders attacking them.

Reivn's blade was soaked in blood from those who lay beheaded on the floor. He had briefly seen a flash of copper curls in the back hall behind the bar. But before he could follow it, one of the initiates charged him, weapon raised to strike. He met his attacker and cut through the Renegade's chest in one massive stroke.

His momentum cut short, the young Vampyre fell to his knees and looked at his wound. Then he looked up, fear in his eyes.

Without hesitation, Reivn cut his head from his shoulders, letting it fall to the floor.

A snarl from the door drew the attention of those in the room.

Reivn spun around, his eyes blazing with fury. He saw Valfort and they locked eyes.

Jack finished off another fledgling and turned, leaving the girl where she fell. "Valfort! Defend yourself!" he shouted.

Valfort faced the Epochian, his expression cold as ice. "Arrogant fool!" he growled and dropped his voice to a chant.

Jack crumpled to the floor as Valfort's mind assaulted him.

"Seliacaliea!" Reivn roared, summoning a lightning bolt. He threw it at Valfort. It was enough to break the Renegade's hold on the Epochian.

Valfort snarled in rage and turned on his brother. "We meet again, Reivn! Have you come to my house to play?"

Gideon looked up from killing another of Valfort's children. "Father, behind you!" he yelled.

Reivn heard Gideon and spun around, just as an old man emerged from the hall. He immediately cast a fireball at the approaching attacker.

Maratoli fell, writhing and screaming in agony as the flames devoured him.

Reivn turned his attention back to Valfort.

Valfort stared at him, hatred burning in his eyes. "This is far from over, brother." His words faded, and he disappeared.

"Coward!" Reivn snarled and leapt across the room, but his hand closed on empty air. Valfort was gone. He cursed as he turned and surveyed the room. Blood covered the floor and walls, eleven more of Valfort's children lay incapacitated or dead, ...*and someone escaped through the back*. "Burn them!" he ordered. Then grabbing a cloth from the nearest table, he wiped the blood from his sword and stalked out into the night. A soft breeze greeted him, cooling the fever in his blood. He fell to his knees, thinking of the young he had just destroyed, and unseen by his companions, drove his sword into the ground, crossed himself and prayed.

It was apparent to Angelique that dawn was fast approaching, but their pace had not slowed. *What happens if we have not sought shelter by daybreak?*

As if in answer to her question, they pulled to a stop in front of a small house hidden in the woods. The driver opened the door and held out his hand to help her down. "Here we are, milady. You'll be safe here."

Angelique stepped down and followed him into the house.

He chattered on, unaware of her discomfort. "My name's Jarvis, milady. Follow me. It's this way." He led her into one of the rooms and threw back a small rug, revealing a trap door in the floor. Then he waved her toward it and lifted the latch.

"You want me to go down there?" she asked uneasily.

"Well, yes," he replied, "unless you wish to brave the daylight."

Frightened now, she descended the steps into the darkness.

Jarvis followed her and began to light candles in its dark interior.

As light removed the shadows, she saw it was beautifully furnished. *At least it is clean and comfortable*, she thought in relief.

"I must go, Milady. I will be back with your things as soon as it's safe," he stated, and began to ascend the steps. "The house is at your disposal. The trap door opens easily, and if you crack it like this…" He lifted the latch, showing her the mechanism to unlock it. "…you can see if daylight has come or gone without harm."

She nodded. *What am I supposed to do now that I'm on my own?*

"Good luck, milady," he smiled and shut the trap door, leaving her alone.

In exhaustion, she retired to the bed to sleep, and as slumber began to overtake her, one thought filled her mind. *What will happen to me now?*

Night had fallen again when Angelique awoke suddenly, sensing she was not alone. She sat up and looked around. Immediately, she saw Valfort sitting in a chair across from her.

He was watching her with interest.

"You!" she cried, instinctively backing up.

"You're awake," he smiled. "Good." He got up and approached.

She screamed and scrambled across the bed. "Stay away!"

"Child, be still! I will not harm you," he admonished impatiently. "You're already mine to command. You need to feed. I came to be sure you do." He stared at her, his eyes reflecting the light from their black depths.

She backed into the corner of the room, poised to run at the first opportunity. "Why did you do this to me?" she wailed.

He smiled cruelly, mocking her. "I gave you a gift."

"I never asked for this!" she sobbed.

His smile vanished, and his voice went cold. "You knew me. You sought me out in my own hunting grounds. No, you did not ask for life. You asked for death. I was merciful."

"Merciful?" she screamed. "How can you call this merciful? Look what you've done to me!"

"What I have done?" he laughed, sending a chill through her. "I made you Immortal. Come, I will show you." He caught her arm and pulled her to him.

"No…" she whimpered. Her strength failed her. She wanted to fight him, but something powerful held her back.

Valfort brushed her hair from her neck. "You need to accept your new life. Denial will not save you." Then he bit into her and drank until she felt weak.

Angelique could feel her life's fluid coursing through him, and their shared blood opened her senses to everything he felt. When he finished, he pushed her head toward his throat, slicing himself open with a razor-sharp fingernail. "It is time for you to grow up, daughter. You are destined to take your place at my side."

The smell of blood rose to her senses and that intense need to feed took over, driving her into a familiar, irrepressible oblivion. Droplets of red covered her in a fine sheen of sweat as she fought to maintain self-control. She struggled to free herself, desperate to retain what humanity she had left, but he was relentless. Finally, she could not fight it anymore and drank, the fierceness of her hunger tearing at her soul. The warm liquid pulsated through her like fire, the heat rising to sear the core of her being. An irresistible power welled up in her while she fed from him and it confused her. *I did not feel this when I fed at the inn. Why is this so different?*

"It is the power of an Elder's blood coursing through you," he answered with a smile.

She backed away again, unnerved by his statement and asked, "How did you know what I was thinking?"

His hand shot out and caught her again with no effort. "I can read your thoughts," he explained. "Now after today, you'll have to hunt and feed for yourself. Here is a brief list of safe places you can stay. Do not contact your family or friends. They cannot help you, nor would they understand. When you are ready, I will find you."

His warning ringing in her ears, he vanished as the paper slowly drifted to the floor. "Wait!" her voice trailed off when she realized he was already gone. *I do not even know your name.*

Angelique paced the room for hours after he left. Twice he had come to her and both times, he had changed her. She knew only one thing for sure. She never wanted to see him again.

When Jarvis returned with the carriage two nights later, Angelique approached him cautiously. "Would you be kind enough to give me the carriage? I wish to leave tonight." She figured she still had to be somewhere near Vienna and decided to travel west until she was able to get her bearings. She knew in her heart she could not go home and fought the fear she would be alone forever.

Jarvis stared at her in shock. "Milady, the sun is rising! It's suicide for you to leave! Wait until tonight. I'll stay to help you."

She was surprised by his answer. "If you don't mind, then yes, tomorrow will be fine. Good day," she answered. Returning to the secret room, she descended again into darkness.

The next night as promised, he hitched up the horses When he finished, he approached her. "I was not able to save your belongings. They burned in the fire. So, I brought you these. It will help you when you get where you're going." He handed her a bank note and a small bag of gold. She was astonished that he did not question where she was going. She climbed into the driver's seat and drove off, feeling the first ray of hope in weeks, as one thought crossed her mind. *I will be free again.*

## Chapter Four
## A Deadly Game

*England...home of the child princess. Vicious beyond imagining, she is nonetheless effective in controlling her territory. She is not one I look forward to meeting face to face. I have grown so weary of this game. The power my brother wields destroys lesser men and few could stop him. This is why I am still on the hunt. Mastric wants him above all others and will stop at nothing to get him. Perhaps Jack is right about the young Valfort throws in our way, then again, perhaps not. Who can say for certain, when none have tried to cool the fever in their blood?*

*Lord, you have made me your instrument and the justice I mete out, I do in your name, but we are all slaves to one master or another here. I am no exception. There are none among the Council who will ever let me leave my appointed position or the duties therein. Perhaps this is part of the exhaustion I feel in my heart. I see the world change with each new passing of a century, but hope has long since ceased to renew itself. Man continues to rise, and we continue our retreat into the shadows, where beasts wait to feast upon our flesh.*

*The nights of pursuit give me little time to dwell on my thoughts, but this is most likely to my advantage. Many of those thoughts could be considered disloyal were they to find their way back to the halls of our great Council, but that is not my intent.*

*My only thought is for the rigid way in which we continue to view the world. It changes all around us, but we do not yield ourselves to its rhythm. If we are truly part of this world, then why do we keep ourselves so far from its ever-changing cycle of motion?*

*Lord Reivn Draegon*

\* \* \* \* \*

For many nights after the battle at the Inn, Reivn and his companions searched the surrounding areas for any sign of Valfort. Their horses were worn, their nerves on edge, and Reivn's brooding visage kept the others at a respectful distance.

Jack had long since grown discouraged and his thoughts were grim. *Valfort has covered his tracks well. He is long gone by now.*

Reivn pulled up beside him. "This is pointless. It will be weeks before we pick up his trail again. He has also hidden his child well, or we would have found some trace of it by now. We need to break for a night or so to refresh our mounts and gather more supplies."

Jack glanced at Grimel and Gideon and then agreed. He turned to Reivn with a sigh. "I could use a little rest. I'm tired of choking down road dust. We passed a town about an hour ago. Shall we ride back and find some rooms?"

Turning his horse around, Reivn answered by heading back up the road. His temper did nothing to improve their moods, and frustration followed them as they rode for the town.

Once they were settled into chairs at the tavern, they talked quietly while Gideon kept watch. Reivn's irritation was apparent. "I think it is time to return to Polusporta. Valfort has run again instead of facing me, so he has no doubt fled the country as he did the last two times we found him. This game of cat and mouse is pointless. I am tired of killing the young he hides behind." He leaned back and closed his eyes wearily. "There is no honor in it," he whispered.

Jack almost did not hear Reivn's last remark. He leaned forward and looked hard at Reivn. "No there isn't, my friend," he responded quietly. "However, what we are doing is right. Valfort's children would only end up joining the rebellion. You know this makes them dangerous. Better to eliminate them while they are weak than to wait until they grow in strength and power." He heaved a sigh. "Valfort is determined to evade us. You have been on his trail longer than I, and considering what I am thinking, it must be worse for you."

Reivn's gaze was intense. "Do you want the bitter truth, Jack? I do not believe we will find him until he wants to be found. He is too clever for that." Then he added, "...and he knows me well."

Gideon glanced sharply at his father. "Are you giving up the hunt then?" he asked. The look of annoyance from across the table would have shaken most men, but Gideon was undaunted.

"I am not giving up the hunt, but I believe we are better served on the front at present. Valfort will still be around when this war is over," Reivn stated with a scowl.

Jack cleared his throat to ease the tension and got up. "I think we need to get some sleep. We have been on the road for too many nights with little time to gather any real strength. If we are going to return to Polusporta, then it will not hurt to tarry awhile to get some much-needed rest."

Reivn placed a hand on his arm. "There is one thing we must consider, Jack, and that is exactly what we will report to the Council. They are not the most forgiving, as you well know."

Reivn's statement reminded Jack they were returning with news of their failure, and he sat back down, his mind racing ahead. "They will want to know details."

"The fact Valfort is still running loose after killing Elena does not sit well with me, and my father felt her loss far more than I," Reivn advised quietly, the edge in his voice cutting into them. "Even if the Council accepts this news stoically, he will not."

Jack frowned. Reivn's words worried him. They all knew Mastric's reputation.

After minutes of contemplative silence, Reivn finally sighed and shook his head. "Well, it is not something we can resolve tonight. We will have time on the road to think about it." He stood up and stretched. "You are right, Jack. This has worn on all of us and we need rest. It will be dawn soon, so we should get situated. We leave for the Sahara tomorrow night."

Jack stared at Reivn, his usual disposition silenced. Then he got up.

Gideon quickly joined them, knowing Reivn expected him to see to his duties.

Grimel continued to stare silently at the fire, thinking of his own father and the rivalry he bore with Mastric. *Thylacinos will consider this a failure and use it to further his objections to Reivn's leadership with the Warlords. This is not going to end well.* Heaving a sigh, he frowned and rose to join his companions.

The usual camaraderie dampened, they divided as they had many times in the past few months and went to their separate rooms. Long after the others had settled, Reivn lay awake, fighting the unstoppable lethargy that was slowly creeping over him. His thoughts were chaotic as he dwelt on the coming confrontation with his father. *Mastric will not be pleased, no question, but I wonder if he really understands the nature of the man he created in my brother.* He glanced across the room at Gideon, who was already asleep. He briefly considered his relationship with his own son and a resigned sigh escaped his lips. Troubled, he turned away and let his thoughts return to the hunt until sleep finally claimed him.

Dusk had barely shrouded the sky the following night when Reivn heard his master's voice.

"Rise, Reivn. We must speak." Mastric's summons broke through the haze that held his son.

Reivn sat up immediately, jolted awake by the call.

Mastric stood before him, his face hidden by his dark cowled hood. The glyph on his forehead glowed beneath it, its brilliant blue casting an eerie shadow on eyes that pierced the Warlord's soul.

Instantly scrambling from his bed, Reivn dropped to his right knee and raised his right fist over his chest in salute. "How can I serve you, my lord?"

"You are not to return to Polusporta. I know your plans and they bear no fruit," Mastric stated coldly. "Valfort fled to England and has re-established himself there. You and your team must travel to London. I have already paid a visit to the child Prince and she will aid you."

Reivn glanced up at the mention of England's Prince and frowned. "Portia? Dealing with her could prove as dangerous as dealing with Valfort."

Mastric's laugh dissolved the silence like shattering glass. "It is not she you need fear. Valfort is long overdue being brought to bay. His very existence vexes me. I have matters I must attend to, or I would hunt and kill him myself. Thus, you will continue to hunt him. I will accept nothing less. Remember your duties, Warlord…" His voice faded as he disappeared.

*I did not realize he was following my activities so closely,* Reivn thought, scowling profusely when he saw Gideon was still asleep. *You would think the boy would wake with an Ancient in the room.* He pulled on his boots and left without a backward glance.

As soon as the door closed, Gideon sat up. He sighed in relief that both Mastric and his father were finally gone. His thoughts were in turmoil. *Mastric is displeased. If father does not watch his step, he will end up in grandfather's laboratory, just as so many others have.* He quickly made his way downstairs.

Reivn looked up from his conversation with Jack when Gideon entered the great room. "It is about time you saw fit to join us. We were just discussing our plans to resume the hunt for Valfort. Perhaps you should sit down and try to keep up."

Gideon's jaw tightened. "I could serve better seeing to the supplies and preparing for our departure," he replied. Then he bowed and headed for the door.

Reivn growled, his response stopping Gideon in his tracks. "Mind your tongue! You do not yet know our plans!" he reprimanded coldly.

"I have a fair idea. We're going to England," Gideon answered and walked out.

Jack's gaze followed him. "I don't know what the issue is between you two, but you have a far more loyal child in that one than you give credit for. He tries to please you and yet cannot."

"Loyalty alone cannot erase the past," Reivn interrupted, his voice uncharacteristically bitter.

Ignoring Grimel's warning look, Jack leaned back and crossed his arms, undaunted. "You must have loved him enough once, because you awakened him. What could he possibly have done to have incurred such anger in you? He..."

Reivn bristled and cut him off. "He is not your concern!"

"...does not deserve this," Jack finished, annoyed.

Reivn ignored him and returned to discussing their plans. "As I was saying, we are heading to London. We can start at the wharves to see if he went by ship. The English Channel is a bit unfriendly this time of year, but I will book us passage when we arrive in Calais."

Jack's resigned sigh echoed his weary thoughts and he dropped the subject, turning once more to their plans. "We have some hard riding ahead of us... again. Dear God, I wish there was a way to hunt him by portal. It would be far less taxing."

Grimel growled in frustration. "Does this mean Mastric intends to keep us on the hunt until we locate Valfort and take him down?"

"Most probably," Reivn answered gruffly. "He wants Valfort worse than we do. He is not likely to allow us to return empty-handed."

"Then let's not keep him waiting," Jack replied, getting up. "It's a long ride to Calais, and it will be longer still before we see our own homes again!" He strode to the doors and stormed out.

Grimel rose quietly and followed Jack out the door.

Reivn turned to stare at the fire, mulling over his father's final words. It had been a clear threat, and one he dared not ignore. He was still sitting there when Gideon returned.

"Father, a moment if you please?" Gideon asked, facing his father.

Reivn answered him harshly, his irritation apparent. "What is it, Gideon?"

Gideon met his father's eyes with a steady gaze. "I know you think little of me and I know it is not my place, but you should be more careful with Mastric. You are angering him too often."

"You are right! You should not meddle in my affairs! If you recall, it is what cost you my favor to begin with!" Abruptly, Reivn kicked his chair back and stood up. He strode to the door, then stopped and looked back. "Stick to your duties and leave my affairs to me!" Without another word, he disappeared into the night.

Gideon stared after him. "Aye, my duties," he bitterly reminded himself. "Now as it was then, watching over you. Had I not been there that night…" His voice tinged with sadness, he whispered, "God, it is folly to trust to hope where there is none." With a sigh, he exited out into the night, caught his reins from Grimel and quickly mounted his horse.

Reivn ignored him. "Move out!" he commanded and spurred his stallion forward. The others followed him, anxious to be on their way. Within moments, they had disappeared in a cloud of dust, galloping down the road toward Calais and England.

London was cold and wet when Reivn and his companions disembarked. The rain fell in a torrential downpour, stinging their eyes and half-blinding them. Thunder shook the ground beneath them and lightning streaked across the sky. The wind whipped around them with deafening strength as the storm raged overhead. Few people were about the dock other than the sailors who struggled to unload their cargo.

All four men were soaked by the time their horses were brought down the gangplank.

Reivn pulled his hood further over his head and hunched forward to avoid the drops of rain that pelted the weary group while they saddled their horses. The roads were bogged down with water and mud, so they walked their animals into the city. Finally, he pointed at an Inn ahead and yelled to his companions. "We will stop there tonight! It will be dawn in a few hours!"

Jack signaled the others and followed as they headed toward the structure.

The group trudged wearily into the yard on the side of the Inn. When no one appeared to take the animals, Reivn tossed his reins to Gideon and slogged through the mud toward the door.

Grimel took charge of his and Jack's horses when they dismounted, and then led them to the stables at the back of the property.

Gideon stared after his father until he disappeared, his thoughts unreadable. Then he turned and followed his companion, leading their mounts behind him.

Jack entered the building and stomped off the mud. Then he slammed the door behind him and strode over to where Reivn was settling into a chair near the fire. "What exactly is your problem with Gideon? You need to tell me here and now!" he demanded. "This could spill over into our mission and endanger us all!"

Reivn sat back and scowled at him. "Stay out of it, Jack. Do not meddle in Mastrics' affairs. Just sit down and have a drink."

Jack dropped into a chair opposite him. "This isn't Mastrics' business and you know it," he shot back. "This is personal. Why are you punishing him? What has he done?"

"Why must you pry into my affairs?" Reivn growled. "There are things better left alone."

Flashing him a dark look, Jack frowned. "And some things are better when dealt with instead of ignoring them!" he retorted, shaking his head. "I'll leave it alone for now, but I don't like it."

Reivn closed his eyes and leaned back. "This is not something we can discuss. Gideon knows his place and will continue to serve me loyally. Of that, I have no doubt."

Annoyed, Jack sat back and stared at the fire. "If it interferes with our assignment, we will all pay the price. I hope you will remember that. I like my head where it is, not hanging as a trophy on a wall in the Council's chambers."

Grimel and Gideon came in, shaking off the rain and mud, abruptly ending the conversation as they joined the two men and sat down.

Gideon cleared his throat. "The horses are stabled and cared for, my lord."

Reivn nodded and the group slipped into an awkward silence.

Finally, Jack stood up. "It's been a long night and tomorrow will be even more so," he stated. "Dawn will come soon enough. I am securing our rooms and turning in."

Grimel hastily rose to join him, nodding to Reivn and Gideon.

Reivn scowled, but he got up and walked over to the desk with them. Still seated, Gideon stared after them, his mind preoccupied.

Jack paid for their accommodations and turned to Reivn. "Here," he offered, handing him a key. "You have the room next to us."

Reivn took it without a word. Then motioning for Gideon to accompany him, he headed for the stairs and what he hoped was a decent bed.

Gideon moved to follow, but Jack grabbed his arm. "Hold on, Gideon. I want to talk to you," he insisted, and directed him toward the table.

The two men sat down again, and Jack leaned forward, his expression serious. "I want to know what happened between you and your father."

Gideon opened his mouth to respond, but Jack held up his hand. "Wait," he cautioned. "Before you say anything, understand this. I've already asked your father, and he refused to speak of it. I'd like to help solve this if I can."

"You don't know him, obviously," Gideon answered, the bitterness creeping into his voice. "His pride will never let him forgive me."

Jack disagreed and shook his head. "I don't think that's true. Behind that wall of anger, there is something else… something he doesn't want you to see. Now tell me what happened."

"I stepped wrong, plain and simple. I made a mistake," Gideon responded in disgust. "He was already angry with me when I was awakened. It was more of an eternal sentence than a gift. Then his wife, Alora, tried to murder him while he lay unconscious. I managed to fight her off and drive her from the Keep. He believes I killed her and it's best that way. He would look for her if he knew the truth, and some things are better left forgotten."

Jack frowned. "But this is not best left forgotten. Son, you need to speak with him about it. You can't just let it alone."

"If I push the issue with him, it could end far worse," Gideon argued. "He has never released me, so I am his to do with as he pleases."

Leaning back, Jack closed his eyes and groaned. "He still holds you in thrall? No wonder you're so obedient. As long as you have no rights, you really have no choice either. It would seem I'm going to have to try to speak with him again."

Gideon shook his head. "Just leave it alone. You will only anger him. He has not been himself since that night. Sometimes I think… ah, never mind. It does not matter."

Jack gazed at him intently. "Doesn't it?"

"Look, Jack. My father is a good man. Do not think otherwise based on his treatment of me. I am the exception to the rule." Gideon's eyes demanded understanding. "I have accepted it and now, so must you. He is far too valuable to the cause to worry about a problem as small as this."

Jack was silent for a moment before replying. "Are you sure this is what you want?"

Gideon nodded. "It is," he answered and stood up. "My father is waiting for me and I must attend to my duties. Good day." Without another word, he stalked off.

Jack sat deep in thought long after Gideon had gone, mulling over the conversation until dawn. Troubled by the distance between his friends and disturbed by Gideon's revelation, he made up his mind to do a little investigating on his own.

When they rose that night, the weather was clear once more, with only a slight mist covering the ground to remind them of the previous night's storm.

As they prepared for the ride to London, Jack pulled Grimel away from Reivn and Gideon, and then handed him a letter. "Take this to Galatia and await her orders," he instructed. "We'll go on to Portia's court. Say nothing of this to anyone other than her. It is strictly confidential."

Grimel took it and tucked it into his coat. "Will you need me to rendezvous with you later?"

Jack shook his head. "No, we'll be fine. This is far more important. I need to know a few things and the matter cannot wait. Do not use the Mastric's portals until you are clear of England. Travel only by conventional means. The damned wizards are too adept at finding out things we do not need them to know right now. Now go. I'll deal with the others."

Grimel nodded and slipped away, walking his horse quietly out the side gate. Once on the road, he mounted and galloped away, his destination the distant Sahara and Polusporta fortress.

Jack rejoined the others and began saddling his horse.

Reivn looked up from loading his saddlebags. "Where is Grimel?" he asked.

"He had other business to attend to. We don't really need him here and this could not be delayed," Jack informed him.

Reivn frowned. "We cannot wait for him. We are already overdue presenting ourselves in Portia's court. We have to be there tonight."

Jack nodded nonchalantly. "I realized this and told him as much," he replied. "He has a long way to go anyway, so we will be down a man." He busied himself with his own saddlebags. "I'll be ready to ride in five."

A short while later the three men rode out of the yard. Moving at a rapid pace, they made good time through the outskirts of London until they reached the city's central hub. They slowed their mounts and headed down the cobblestone lanes. Extravagant mansions lined the street and reached upward into the night, their fronts lit by lanterns that cast an eerie glow on the riders as they passed. Many sported huge iron gates and great wooden doors, with grand entryways that boasted of money, position, and power. This was the heart of England's aristocracy… all of whom vied to remain close to the royal court and its sovereignty.

The group rode up to a sumptuous manor, the gates of which were barred shut and guarded.

Reivn approached the guard and introduced himself, requesting entrance.

The soldier's eyes went wide at the mention of his name. He rushed to open the gates for them and then bowed as they passed.

They rode up the winding drive in silence, stopping when they reached front of the great structure. Grooms appeared to take their horses, and a well-dressed servant waited for them when they approached the front steps. Bowing silently, he led them up to the grand entryway. "Her royal majesty is expecting you, my lords," he informed them. "She will see you immediately."

Jack scratched his head in frustration. Portia was well known for her ruthlessness, and displeasure at their late arrival had no doubt put her in a foul mood. "Shouldn't we clean up a bit first?" he asked politely.

The servant shook his head. "No, sir. I was instructed to show you in as soon as you arrived."

*Of course,* Jack thought wryly as they walked along. He glanced at Reivn.

The Warlord appeared composed, following the servant in solemn silence.

The child prince was seated on a large mahogany throne encrusted with blood-red rubies and cushioned with embroidered silk pillows. Portia, who would forever resemble a twelve-year-old child, gazed at them expectantly when they entered. Her hair was tucked under a pearl and diamond caplet crown that sparkled radiantly in the light of the multitude of candles burning throughout the hall. Dressed in a purple velvet gown trimmed with black satin ribbons, she held her scepter, the symbol of her high office, with delicate little hands.

Twilight-blue drapes hung over the windows, held open by gold-tasseled tiebacks. The walls were intricately crafted in rich mahogany, giving the room a warmth that belied the cold creature whose eyes now settled on them. "You are late, Warlord! I expected you last night!" Portia's icy stare sent a chill through the room.

Reivn and his companions bowed low. Then he stepped forward. "I apologize for the delay. We encountered severe weather and our ship was slow putting into port. We disembarked just before Dawn. So we came here directly after rising this evening."

Portia pouted, as though wanting a different response. "I am quite aware of when you arrived, my lord. My scouts reported the moment your ship docked. I am disappointed," she chided. "It seems your reputation is not as well placed as I heard."

His face darkening, Reivn stiffened at the insult. "I was likewise aware of your scouts. I did not imagine I would have to justify myself in a city so well-protected by her Prince."

"Princess," Portia corrected impatiently. Then she smiled, her eyes cold. "You are here because you need my help in finding your renegade brother!"

Reivn bristled, reaching the edge of his control. "I should remind you, Portia, that I am a Council Warlord, higher in rank than you, and youngest son to the master of the spirals! I do not answer to you except as a courtesy!"

Without even flinching, Portia responded, "and might I remind you, Lord Reivn, that I am Victus' oldest and most cherished child! Perhaps I should speak to him of your rudeness?"

"Speak to whomever you will, Portia," Reivn challenged coldly. "I have no time for games. I must continue the chase while his trail is still fresh. I am sure Lord Victus will understand why you are hindering the hunt for a dangerous fugitive. Now are you going to be of assistance in this matter, or shall I contact the Council for aid from other means?"

The child prince sat back, fury flaring in her eyes. "You have made your point, Warlord! I will help you, but I will not forget this insult!" she countered hotly.

"I certainly hope not," Reivn growled, his eyes taking on a dangerous look.

Sighing to indicate her irritation, Portia shrugged and ignored his comment, moving instead to the subject at hand. "My scouts have been searching for Valfort in anticipation of your arrival, and I know where he was headed. Wendell will show you the way."

Reivn raised his eyebrow and cast a quick glance at Jack.

Jack's expression told him the idea of having her servant ride along was not at all appealing.

Suppressing a chuckle, Reivn turned back to meet Portia's gaze. "I appreciate your offer, but in truth, we need only the knowledge he will provide, not his services as a guide."

"I see," she answered slowly, a sardonic smile on her lips. "Then glean from him what information you will and be gone from my court. But be warned, all of England is mine!"

Reivn ignored her and joined the others as they exited the throne room.

Wendell was waiting for them. He bowed his head slightly in recognition of the furious Warlord when they approached. "My lord, I was told you wanted information on the whereabouts of Ceros Valfort?"

Waving the others toward the doors, Reivn turned and began walking with the mousy man. Their voices faded around the corner and they disappeared.

Jack and Gideon emerged once more into the night. Their horses were waiting, and they mounted up, eager to put distance between themselves and the vengeful child on the throne.

Moments later Reivn appeared, moving briskly down the steps to join them. "We have many long months ahead of us," he told them, climbing into his saddle. "I'll explain on the way."

## Chapter Five
## One Good Turn

*I have always believed that those around us pay for our darkness... the curse that holds us bound to eternal shadows. The humans that fall into our paths suffer whether we mean for them to or not. I made a promise to myself that I shall not bring that destruction upon them unless I am left with no other choice. They see enough when we let out the beast that lies within us.*

*This incessant hunt... I believe now that it will not end until I have brought my brother to bay. I begin to wonder just what makes him so important as to warrant this continued folly, when it has become abundantly clear that I will not find him until he is ready for the confrontation I know is coming. He is preparing for something, but what is still a complete mystery to me. His bitterness at our father's harsh treatment turned him to this, but just where it has taken him, I know not. Hatred can twist you into something so foul... so dark, there is no way back from it once you begin down that path. I believe this is the road he has traveled.*

*Gideon has been at my side since this hunt began, but I have still not found a resolution to the problem with him. He seems so genuine in his devotion, and yet what he did... the past cannot be so easily erased. He is my blood, but I am still looking for the similarity he holds to me. He is weak. Perhaps I should never have taken him with me. Had I left him where I found him, he would have grown old and died believing in what he did. Had I killed him, it would have been merciful, but he would never have learned the truth, and I owed her that. My greatest failure, the two of them... they will forever be the ghosts that haunt me...*

*Lord Reivn Draegon*

\* \* \* \* \*

Jack watched the surrounding countryside for a place they could retreat from the coming daylight. Finally, he spotted a farmhouse set back off the road. Cattle grazed in the field just beyond the building, and horses roamed the paddock beside a large barn near the home. He shouted to Reivn and they turned up the dirt road leading to the house.

A teenaged girl walked out the door, tying on an apron, as they approached. "What do you want?" she asked cautiously, eyeing them with mistrust.

"We need a place to sleep. We've been riding all night and are exhausted from our travels," Jack answered, smiling at her.

The girl backed away. "There are no rooms here," she exclaimed with fear in her eyes.

Reivn dismounted and strode over to her. "What is your name child?" he asked gently.

"Keira, sir," she stuttered. Her eyes were wide with fright.

The door to the house opened and a child of five or six years came out. "What is it, Keira? Who are they?" she asked.

Keira turned slightly, refusing to take her eyes off Reivn, who stood mere inches from her. "Go back inside, Casey! And lock the door!"

Speaking softly, Reivn looked at the little girl standing as if rooted in stone on the front stoop. "It is all right, child. I will not harm either you or your sister," he assured her calmly. "We are lost and looking for shelter. Do you know where we can rest for the day?"

Casey ran over and grabbed his hand. "Oh, yes! I know where! Follow me!" She pulled him in the direction of the barn. "Come on, Keira!"

Keira looked on in horror, as Reivn followed Casey and his companions began to dismount. "Casey, no! We don't know them or what they'll do!"

Ignoring her sister, Casey tugged on the big barn door. "Ugh! It's too big, mister!"

With a chuckle, Reivn lifted her onto his shoulder and pulled the door open with ease. "There we go. Now Casey, where is the darkest corner of the barn? I wouldn't want to have our nap spoiled by sunlight."

Still perched on his shoulder, she pointed to the back of the barn in excitement. "Over there, mister! That's where Charlie sometimes sleeps."

"Charlie?" Reivn asked cautiously and looked up at her. "Is he your friend?"

She squealed with laughter. "No, mister! He's my cat!" Then she squirmed and patted his shoulder to be set down.

Keira entered the barn breathless, followed by Jack and Gideon. Red in the face, she glared at them. "Mister, we don't have nothing here you'd want. Please just go. I don't want no trouble."

"I brought her along, so she wouldn't run off to get help," Jack explained with a grin.

Reivn shook his head. "Let her alone. You're frightening her."

Jack lifted his hands in resignation and left Reivn to negotiate their accommodations.

Turning to the frightened girl, Reivn sighed. "I am sorry about that. My friend meant well. I told you we mean no harm. We are willing to pay for the use of your barn. We were riding all night and need to sleep for a few hours. Then we will go, and I doubt you will ever see us again." To prove his point, he pulled out his pouch filled with gold coin and handed it to her. "If you will let us rest here undisturbed for the day, then this is yours."

Her eyes grew wide at so large a sum of money and she stared. "All of it?" she asked shyly.

"All of it. You can have it right now. I'll even add to it if we can bring in the horses and give them feed and water." Reivn smiled warmly at her, knowing he had already won.

Contemplating the money in her hand, Keira nodded slowly at first, and then beamed radiantly at him. "Alright, you can stay… your horses too."

Casey ran to Reivn and hugged him. He smiled and tousled her hair, but when he looked up, the pain in Gideon's eyes caused him to look away, guilt gnawing at him.

Gideon abruptly pushed the doors open and walked out to collect the horses.

Jack investigated the back of the barn and found several bales of clean hay. He promptly set to work preparing their beds, knowing the sun was rising.

Reivn shooed the girls out, leaving the gold with Keira, who gave him a dazzling smile. Casey grumbled as they headed back toward the farmhouse, and he teased them both. "We need to sleep now. You can visit with us after we wake."

Gideon had returned with the horses and was settling them into nearby stalls. Then one by one, they spread out their bedding and prepared to turn in.

Jack finished with his own bags and dropped onto the nearest bed, pulling off his boots. With no further thought to his companions, he leaned back and closed his eyes.

Reivn closed the doors just as the first rays of light touched the barn. Then he settled in, pulled his cloak around him and quickly slipped into slumber.

Gideon sat staring at his father until he could no longer fight that familiar tugging at the edge of his mind. Finally, he lay down and closed his eyes, letting sleep claim him.

Reivn was jolted awake by terrified screams. He sat up, the usual lethargy gone. He instantly recognized Keira and Casey's voices. They were struggling with unknown assailants. As silent and swift as death, he leaned over and woke Gideon from slumber. "Shhh," he whispered, putting a finger to his lips. "There's trouble. Wake Jack."

Gideon quickly roused the Epochian and warned him not to make a sound.

Jack nodded and quickly pulled on his boots.

Within seconds, the three men were armed and at the doors to the barn. Reivn cautiously cracked one open and looked outside. The last rays of day met his eyes. The girls were nowhere in sight and the door to the house was ajar. He turned back to the others. "It is not yet sunset," he whispered. "You can stay here or follow me, but it is going to be a painful trip."

"What are we waiting for?" Jack grinned, waving his sword in the dim light.

Gideon readied himself as Reivn cracked the doors open once more.

They silently slipped out into the last rays of light and ran for the house. A familiar burning sensation greeted them, and soft wisps of smoke rose from their bodies in reaction to the forbidden daystar. They ignored the pain, focusing instead on the sounds coming from within. Three horses stood tethered to a tree near the house, but there were no riders in sight.

Reivn growled and kicked in the door. Then he burst into the little home, Jack and Gideon behind him.

A ragged and dirty soldier spun around at the intrusion, Reivn's coin pouch in his hands. He stared at the newcomers in confusion.

From his vantage point, Reivn could see Keira on her bed in the back of the house. She was pinned by one of the men, her clothes torn and bloodied. Her tear-streaked face was contorted with fear and pain as she struggled to get free. "Help me!" she begged.

From a corner of the room, Casey squirmed in another captor's arms. "Oh, let go!" Seeing Reivn, she cried out. "Help mister, they're hurting Keira!"

The soldier restraining Casey covered her mouth, and she bit down. "Ow! Little beast!" he yelled and cuffed her in the head.

Reivn snarled and charged the soldier restraining Casey, while Jack leapt at the man holding the coin purse.

Casey hit the floor, as the man let her go and ran for the door, where he collided with Gideon.

After Reivn secured Casey's safety, he turned his attention to the soldier that had Keira.

The man was simultaneously struggling to pull up his breeches and grab for his weapon.

In one swing, Reivn cut him in two, killing him instantly.

Jack had little trouble dispatching the man with the coin pouch, and Gideon detained the one that had hit Casey. The man begged for his life, falling to his knees.

Reivn ignored him. "Keira?" he ventured softly, approaching her.

Keira did not answer. She had rolled over and buried her face in a pillow. Now she was weeping uncontrollably.

Reivn sat down next to her, noting her near-naked state and the blood on the sheets. He carefully pulled her into his arms. "You and your sister are safe now," he whispered as he held her. Then looking up at Jack, his eyes grew dark with fury. "Take that filth outside and dispose of them. Bury the bodies where they will never be found."

Gideon collected the two bodies, swiftly wrapped them in one of the bloodied blankets and dragged them outside.

Jack grabbed the remaining deserter, who still cowered on the floor. "Move!"

The man yelped, pointlessly struggling to free himself as he was forcefully taken outside.

"Casey, go with my friends," Reivn told her quietly. He waited until she was gone, and then turned to Keira, examining her injuries. "Just lay still. I am going to take care of you."

Keira stared at the ceiling, her expression blank. She had gone into shock.

Reivn carefully brushed his hand across her eyes, closing them and sending her into a deep sleep. Then he summoned the spirals, and his hands began to glow with the power that poured forth, encompassing them both.

Keira gasped as the warmth covered her in a blanket of comfort.

Casey had slipped back in unnoticed and stood silently watching as Keira's wounds disappeared and her pallor returned to a healthier shade.

Within moments, Keira was resting comfortably, but Reivn was not finished. Placing his hand gently on her forehead, he reached into her mind where the nightmares had already begun. With careful consideration, he sifted through her memories until he found what he was looking for and erased them.

Keira sighed as all traces of the night's brutality disappeared, slipping into content dreams of happier days.

Reivn brushed her damp hair from her forehead. "Sleep well," he whispered gently and covered her with a blanket.

When he stepped away from the bed, he realized Casey was there, staring wide-eyed at him. "Do not be afraid. I made your sister feel better," he soothed, picking her up. He retrieved his pouch from the floor and handed it to her. "This belongs to you and Keira."

Casey curled up to him as he walked to the front room, bearing her in his arms. "Why'd they hurt Keira?" she asked furtively.

Startled by her question, he stared down at her for a moment before answering. "They were bad men, Casey, but do not worry," he replied and gently placed his hand on her forehead. "You will not remember it."

Casey pushed his hand away. "Yes, I will!" she exclaimed adamantly.

He touched her forehead again and reached into her mind. He found a certain familiarity staring back at him. "Forget tonight, Casey," he murmured into her thoughts.

Casey wiggled out of his grip and put her hands on his face, mimicking him. "Why?" she asked, her bright eyes full of curiosity.

He gazed at her intently. *She is a resistor...* he realized in surprise. "Well," he began slowly, searching for an answer, "...because I am going to take care of you and Keira from now on."

Her eyes wide, Casey squealed with delight. "You mean you're going to be my daddy?"

Reivn hesitated, contemplating this notion in silence. Then he smiled. "Yes... yes, I am."

A few nights later, Reivn, Jack and Gideon rode out of the farmyard, waving their goodbyes.

Keira stood holding Casey's hand, while the child danced in excitement. Behind them were four newly hired farmhands ready to make the farm flourish again.

Jack chuckled as they headed out onto the open road.

Reivn glared at him. "None of your jokes, Jack! Those girls needed help, and after they had given us shelter, I was not going to repay that by abandoning them to their fates!"

Laughing, Jack spurred his horse forward. "Anything you say... daddy!"

Reivn and his companions returned to the hunt and for the next three years, they searched England with little success. When Grimel finished at Polusporta, he returned, joining them once more in their search for the traitor, but Valfort had vanished without a trace. With each new lair they found came the inevitable battle, and the slaughter of young ones. Finally, their search took them back to the coast of England.

The four men rode into Portsmouth just hours after sunset. The town was busy despite the late hour. Carts travelled up from the docks, horse-drawn carriages and riders traveled the streets, and the faint sound of merriment drifted from nearby taverns.

Looking around, Reivn frowned. "We need to split up. We know a lair is here. Our reports have given us that much, so let's locate it, flush it out and be done with it!"

"The sooner, the better!" Jack agreed.

"I will meet you back here one hour before dawn!" Turning his mount, Reivn headed further into the city, leaving his companions to choose their own paths.

Grimel smiled and rode down the road leading to the north end of the city.

Gideon briefly stared after his father and then headed back the way they had come.

Jack watched Gideon's retreating figure for a moment, then growled and dismounted. "Those two really need to sort out their differences!" Walking his horse behind him, he approached the nearest tavern. Stopping long enough to tether the animal to a post, he slipped in the door and looked around.

Wooden beams ran the length of the ceiling, connecting with walls made of solid stone. The fireplace was small for a tavern, leaving much of the chill about the room, but its occupants were too busy to notice. Sailors and travelers filled almost every table, while serving girls bustled back and forth with drinks and food. At length, Jack spied an empty spot near a rather loud group. He moved casually across the room, settled into a chair, and waved to a barmaid.

The girl hurried over, a bright smile on her face. Soft brown hair peeked out from her cap, and her chest bulged from her tight bustier when she leaned over, moving so they jiggled under his nose. "What'll you have, mister?"

Sitting back to put a little distance between them, Jack sighed. "Ale..."

Obviously disappointed, she left him to retrieve his drink.

Jack began to survey the room, listening to nearby conversations. Talk of trade and crops assaulted his ears, so he shifted to another group, only to hear shipboard tales. A shrill laugh told him he would not get his drink anytime soon. The barmaid was frolicking with a drunk sailor. Irritated, he got up and prepared to leave, when a conversation caught his attention.

"I tell you, Jerry, them people's not right... movin' about at night, and not a one of 'em out durin' the day! Comings and goings of all sorts of strange folk!" Two old men sitting near the fire were engrossed in conversation.

"Ah, yer daft! They just keep to themselves. Maybe even thieves... I might bite my tongue were I you afore they cut it out fer ya!" Jerry argued, shaking his head.

Jack shifted positions, so he could hear them better.

"No Jerry! Those people's witches or somethin', mark me on it! I seen things... one of 'em picked a horse right up off the ground, he did! And have you seen 'em buy anything at market? I ain't... so how do they eat?" The old fellow looked around nervously.

Jack smiled to himself. They had found their mark. Getting up slowly, he staggered slightly to appear drunk and moved toward the two old men. "...I know what you're talkin' about... I seen things too. Is it the same place I've been seein'?"

The talkative fellow squinted up at him. "The dock-house down by the pier?"

"Shhh, Tom! I am not knowin' this fellow!" Jerry cautioned.

"Ah, it's not a problem mate, I'll go, but be warned! I say they're witches! Should stay away from there..." Jack swaggered to the door and out into the street, where he straightened up and walked back to his mount. "Come on girl, we need to find Lord Reivn."

Reivn was just exiting the third Inn he had searched when Jack came up the street at a hurried clip. "What did you find?" he asked, as Jack reined his horse in and leapt down.

"I found out where the bastard's lair is!" Jack responded eagerly. "We can finish here within the hour and be on our way!"

Closing his eyes, Reivn telepathied Gideon and Grimel. *It has been found. Return at once.*

Within minutes, Grimel came trotting up the road toward them, his own eagerness to finally catch their quarry evident in his expression. He jumped down and walked over to Jack.

Jack quickly filled him in, keeping his volume low in case there were any passersby.

Reivn paced back and forth, stopping every few moments to stare up the road before resuming his vigil.

Finally, Gideon came galloping up the road, pulling to a halt in front of them.

Giving his son a dark look, Reivn mounted up and growled, "Move out!"

The four men kicked their horses into motion and rode toward the piers.

When they reached the docks twenty minutes later, they dismounted and tied their horses well away from the small warehouse. Then they moved silently toward the building.

Reivn motioned for Jack and Grimel to go around behind the structure, while he and Gideon used the front entrance. Then drawing his sword, he kicked in the door.

The main room was almost empty, with only a few piles of scattered crates around the room.

Jack entered from the back with Grimel and they searched the rear of the building. Then they joined Reivn and Gideon. "There's no one back there. It's empty."

"No... they are here. I can sense their presence." Reivn cast a meaningful glance at the floor.

Jack's eyes narrowed. "Gophers?"

They began moving the crates. Then Grimel uncovered a trap door. "Over here!" he called.

Reivn motioned for Gideon to lift the trap door. Then summoning the spirals, he hurled a fireball into the hole. The fire quickly spread and screams for mercy broke out below. He closed his eyes and silently committed their souls to God. Then he turned to Jack. "Burn it all to cover the remains. Valfort is not here… only these pathetic young he left to hide like animals. Give them peace." Turning his back, he walked out into the night once more.

Jack, Grimel and Gideon went to work, setting the building ablaze. Valfort's brood were trapped beneath the floorboards in the raging inferno they left in their wake. When they exited the building, the screams of young unfortunates could still be heard from within.

Reivn stood watching the warehouse burn. Finally the cries stopped, and a deadly silence filled the air. Only the sound of crackling, burning timber remained. He closed his eyes for a moment, wondering how many more had just died at his hands.

Jack and Grimel walked back to the horses with Gideon.

"Jack…" Reivn almost whispered as the Epochian passed him.

Turning around, Jack looked at the weary Warlord. "Yes?"

Reivn shifted his gaze from the fire and stared at his companion. "We are returning to the Sahara. It is time I spoke with my father."

Jack nodded. "I figured we would have to sooner or later. It might as well be now. I won't mind the rest, although I'm not sure how pleased Mastric will be to see us return empty-handed."

"It matters not! We're heading back!" Reivn growled.

Gideon glanced up at his father's bitter tone in surprise, and then looked away, his own thoughts bordering on relief.

As he mounted up, Jack took one final glance at the structure that had succumbed to the flames and sighed. *There will be others… there always is. One thing we can count on is Valfort's cruelty. He revels in it.*

Reivn swung himself back into the saddle. Then without a backward glance, he turned his stallion around and headed back down Portsmouth's now almost deserted streets. His companions followed him in silence as they headed out onto the open road once more, beginning the long, slow journey to the Sahara and Polusporta fortress.

## Chapter Six
## Bloodlines

*Child of the night, are you afraid? You have barely taken your first steps and already someone marches against you, ready to snuff out your life. I begin to understand the true nature of the curse that forever binds us to darkness. It is not the lack of the daystar, or even our own thirst. It is the measured killing... always the killing, for among beasts there is no true rest. Instinct drives us, governed only by our knowledge... the only quality that raises us above lesser animals. We follow the Council to the end, but to the end of what? A lesson in rhetoric, I think.*

*There will never truly be an end to hatred. It is the insanity that ignites armies to slaughter the innocent and causes father and son to turn on one another. What breeds such contempt among brothers? Greed? Malcontent? Jealousy? If these are the only legacies given to those we love, then why do so many still hold true? With the penchant to fall into the shadows that consume the night, it is necessary to govern ourselves with an iron hand. Those that choose to turn from sound judgment and moral conscience sentence themselves to fall into madness and a bloodlust beyond what any know how to truly control.*

*Still, with so many forced into the world in which we dwell, I must wonder if there is a way to reconcile these youths to the right path again. Those who do not know of the struggle between either side have not yet chosen their allegiance. Why destroy them merely because of the blood that flows in their veins? Should we not judge each on their own merit? If even one child proved to have loyalty and potential, what would it mean for the future of our kind? If we continue our present course, I fear it will ultimately be ourselves we destroy.*

*Lord Reivn Draegon*

\* \* \* \* \*

Deep in the Sahara, other events were unfolding. In the vast expanse of the desert, there was no sleep. The Ancients were gathering at the seat of Alliance sovereignty… Polusporta fortress. The archaic citadel lay hidden from mortal sight by the power of the Ancients themselves.

Originally built near Mysia and later moved to its present location, its primordial walls were of massive hewn stones and mimicked a Roman stronghold. Massive studded iron outer doors loomed in the darkness of the desert night. Closed and bolted from the inside, they were the solitary entrance into the foreboding fortress. The small courtyard held stables stocked with Arabian horses, bred for life in this unfriendly terrain. An armory filled with armor and weapons of every age stood to the left of the stable, and a granary to the right. The moon cast eerie shadows on a courtyard that laid bereft of any other light. By day the sun filled the open square with intense light and heat, warming deep underground chambers that had been added after the upper fortress was relocated from its original foundations following the fall of Troy. Across from the main gate were the massive inner doors of aged oak, bound with great iron hinges. Adorned with carvings of Angels and Daemons locked in eternal warfare, bearing elaborate details of an empire defying description, they guarded the entrance to its immense interior.

Once past the vast entryway, the great Council hall dominated much of the first floor. The walls were of finely sculpted and polished basalt and the floors of refined obsidian. Torches burned in archaic sconces, lighting the halls as they had for countless centuries. On the far side of the room's great expanse, there were nine thrones in a half-circle upon a dais one foot off the floor. Banners, faded from time hung behind every throne, each bearing the crest of one of the nine tribes whose founders resided here. Gargoyles crafted by magic into living stone kept silent sentry duty from the chamber's vast walls, their black eyes blending eerily into the shadows. Deep within the protected interior where human eyes never venture, there was no peace. The oldest among the Ancients stood up and began pacing, as the others listened in silence.

"He is not the first of the Elders to elude our grasp, Galatia! You know this! He is merely more dangerous because of his abilities!" Victus turned and gazed at her. The raw power pouring from his resonant voice filled the room with his presence. First-born among them, he was their chosen sovereign. His dark hair was tinged with silver streaks and his black robes moved with a life of their own, adding to the potency of his aura.

Galatia stirred in her seat. Her gold diaphanous Grecian gown hugged her perfect figure. Her platinum hair was interwoven with strands of gold chain and arranged atop her head, and tiny wisps of curls hung softly about her flawless face. Her pale skin glowed in the torchlight like an alabaster statue carved in the image of a Goddess. Mother of the Galatian tribe and mistress of wisdom and beauty, she was once worshiped by mortals as both Athena and Aphrodite. Her tribe was behind both the greatest heroes and the greatest wars, for their passion was uncontainable and of unparalleled magnificence. Seductive eyes as blue as the morning sky gazed slowly around the room before coming to rest on Victus' face. "There is no denying the danger Valfort presents to us, but his creations strengthen the dark ones' cause. Even those he abandons are eventually brought into their service." She paused, contemplating this thought. "Our laws have long called for the destruction of all Renegades and their children. By allowing any one of them to escape, we are merely giving them the chance to build an even stronger force against us."

A low rumble from the corner interrupted her. The shadows moved and a figure more wolf than man stepped into the light, his body moving with the fluid paces of a predator. Thylacinos growled, sounding much like the animal whose features he resembled so clearly. He and his children embraced their bestial nature, much more animal than the rest of the Ancients. However, he was as shrewd and intelligent as he was feral. "You should have assigned more of my children to the party you sent to track him. They are harder to fool. The Mastric Warlord only holds my son back." As he spoke, Thylacinos sauntered across to the thrones. Sniffing casually, he comfortably sprawled out in front of one on the floor.

"That may or may not be true, Thylacinos. They are not tracking a novice, but one of the oldest among their generation. He is not easy prey," Victus paused, knowing there was contention as to which of the tribes had the most skilled hunters. "That is why we sent his brother to find him. They did spend considerable time together before Valfort betrayed us."

Thylacinos growled in disagreement. "I do not believe one brother should hunt the other. There are conflicts of a much different nature to consider. We cannot afford to lose any more of our firstborn to such dangerous ideas."

Silvanus had been lounging on his throne quietly listening, but now he spoke up. "I have to agree with Thylacinos. Trusting this to the Mastric Warlord was folly. Their tribe has a problematic history with keeping Warlords that none ours shares. I believe it was a mistake to send Reivn. He's too unpredictable." Of all the tribes, Silvanus' was the most nomadic. Most of his children came from the Rrom of Europe, whom he prized above all else. He had long since adopted their mode of dress, sporting an open-front shirt, sash, breeches, and boots. His Dracanas were known for their ability to communicate with Dragons, and their tribe held to the ways of the wagon, making it hard for outsiders to learn their secrets. "What if that traitor convinces Reivn to join him? Valfort did train him, after all. Does anyone know how strong their bond actually was? If they were close enough, Valfort could turn the Warlord to the twisted doctrines he now follows."

"I can see I'm not the only one concerned with that possibility," Thylacinos snickered. "It has been my problem with this whole venture to begin with. This Council has maintained the balance by counterweights and measures. Every rank has an opposing force within our numbers to keep them in check. Yet somehow the Mastrics seem to have been beyond these thrice now."

Victus looked from one to the other, obviously irritated with them both. "Mastric rules his children with a harsher hand than most of us. Reivn has given us no cause to doubt his loyalty thus far, and Mastric will not willingly allow you to remove him without good reason." He paused, thinking of the wrath Mastric would visit on them all if this continued. "You know as well as I that offering insult to the Lord of the Spirals is dangerous. It was a sound decision to assign Reivn to this, because it does test his loyalty. We have Jack there as our eyes and ears. He will not allow Reivn to go astray without putting a bullet in his back if need be."

Thylacinos would not back down. He growled again. "I have yielded to your judgement on the matter thus far, but I still do so with great objection. Testing his loyalty is just as easily done on the battlefield, or in new explorations where his strength and mettle are pushed beyond endurance. If he still maintains our laws under such circumstances, then and only then would I consider recognizing him myself." He stretched out, a slow rumble sounding in his throat.

The woman seated next to him looked down at him in disgust. Her dark eyes glistened, reflecting the torchlight in their black depths. "Thylacinos, why do you persist in lying on the floor like a beast? It's beneath you!" Annoyed, Armenia played with a stray lock of her hair. Her burgundy Roman gown was ornately trimmed in gold thread, and bejeweled cobra armbands, the eyes of which looked alive, glowing red as the gems caught the light, adorned her arms. Her children were the guardians of all the history and knowledge of their race. Under her leadership, the Armenians had developed an extensive network of communication, rivaled only by The Caelum Invictus Imperium, a secret society known only to the Ancients or its own members.

Thylacinos grinned, his white fangs brilliant against the fur around his face. "I sit here because I find it comfortable."

Victus cleared his throat, interrupting their dispute. "If you two are finished…"

Armenia closed her mouth and bowed her head respectfully in Victus' direction, but continued to glare at Thylacinos.

Thylacinos grinned and stretched out further, watching Armenia with an amused expression.

"I have summoned the rest of the Council. When the others arrive, we must discuss our next move. The Renegades grow stronger every day," Victus paced the room. "If they are not stopped, they will eventually try to attack us here."

Silvanus chuckled, interrupting Victus. "They may be growing in number, but they will never penetrate our defenses here. None other than Martu or Semerkhet is strong enough, and they are only two. We are many. I cannot see even Martu as being that foolish."

"I am not so confident in our invincibility. Martu's attacks on the Mastrics strongholds have increased." Victus gazed at his younger brother intently. "He grows bolder by the day and as more young ones join them, he will become increasingly more so."

Silvanus laughed. "I think you worry too much. It is true our brother's numbers grow. I see it every night. But he has never directly challenged even the weakest among us. He always attacks the younger generations." Silvanus spent most of his time among his Rrom, preferring their company to that of the Council's. Now boredom turned his thoughts back to them. "Are we going to just sit here until our brethren join us? I have other plans."

Victus held up his hand. "Patience, Silvanus. Our brothers had matters of their own to attend to before they could join us. They will not be long."

As if in response, the center of the hall began to fill with thick, black mist. It moved like a living entity as it grew, its tendrils stretching in every direction. In the heart of the spinning vortex, a silhouette appeared… an eerie blue glow radiating from the denseness of the cloud. The other Council members looked up as the figure emerged. Hooded and cloaked in a black robe, Mastric's only visible aspects were the two steel-flecked eyes that gazed intently from its dark expanse and the glowing blue glyph emblazoned on his forehead.

Victus stood and greeted him respectfully. "Mastric... welcome back. We have been anticipating your arrival."

The Master of magic glided across the floor and took his seat. "I have just come from my Council. Much of my tribe is in an uproar. There have been unusual disturbances in the Spirals."

Victus stood silent for a moment, contemplating the possibilities. He knew there was little Mastric did not know of the Mystic Spirals. Of all the firstborns, he was the only one to command their full power. Finally, he spoke. "Well, we know the Renegades have been calling Daemons up from Gehenna in larger numbers of late. Perhaps that is the source of these disturbances. I too, have felt those stirrings, but then my skills are but a shadow to yours."

Mastric bowed his head in acknowledgement of the compliment. He knew his brethren did not trust him, and in fact feared him. The respect with which Victus spoke was due merely to his discomfort, and that of the rest of the Council's from his presence.

The Mastrics were the most adept of the tribes in arcane arts and the most feared among the Alliance. Their ability to manipulate the Spiral's magic was almost limitless. But as respected as his tribe was, their footsteps were shadowed with mistrust. It was well known that Mastric had the power to take control of the entire race if he chose. It was fear of this fact that drove the others to both recognize and acquiesce to the importance of his place among the nine tribes. Mastric usually kept his own counsel and spoke only when he felt it pertinent to do so. The underground lair in London was the base for his own tribe's Council and his personal sanctuary. The other Ancients had approached him there to move the fortress they now sat in from Mysia to its present location when fear of discovery drove them into hiding from mortal kind. Only his magic was powerful enough to accomplish the task of moving such an immense structure... and move it he did... he and his eldest son.

Mastric eyed Victus expectantly. "Is there any word on Valfort or my youngest son? Reivn has not yet reported to me."

Victus tried to hide his surprise. "A few days ago, they destroyed another of Valfort's lairs. This time it was a dock-house in Portsmouth." He returned to his own throne. "There were several children also, with total fatalities. However, at least one escaped during a previous raid, maybe more. He and his party are still tracking Valfort, but there has been no further word."

Scratching his head, Thylacinos stretched and got up. "I told you I should have sent more of my scouts. Their tracking abilities are far superior even to the Mastric's magic. If you had let Grimel lead the party, they would have found your traitor son by now." His barb was directed at Mastric, but his eyes wandered around the chamber. He ambled across the room and sniffed the air before turning back to his companions. "Sharrukin has arrived."

At that moment the great doors opened, and a tall figure strode into the room. Attired in the desert garb of the Arabs, his turban, tunic, and abaya were brilliant white, but as Sharrukin moved and the fabric fluttered open, the black fathomless depth of the astrophysical world could be seen in the folds of his robe. His skin was dark and weathered, though no daylight had ever touched his face. Once the first king of Akkadia, he was father of the Sargonian tribe, and his power was awe-inspiring even by Council standards. As lord of the astral plain, Sharrukin knew how to manipulate the lost souls within its infinite space. This ability was what made it possible to keep watch on the Renegades' activities. He dwelt deep in the desert among the Bedouin, only returning when urgent matters called. Now he approached the thrones and bowed, touching his forehead and heart in greeting. "Assalamu alaikum," he stated calmly and moved to his throne.

"And with you, my brother," Victus answered with a nod. He looked around, then motioned to Thylacinos, bidding him to join them.

Wandering back to his throne, Thylacinos dropped at its base once more and smiled at Armenia's scowl.

Victus briefly glanced at Galatia and their eyes locked. He averted his gaze, staring instead at the empty throne next to him. *The Time Lord is not yet come*, he observed silently.

Chronos was the father of the Epochians and the master of time. Some said he could wander in and out of the time stream at will, though none had ever seen it. His determination to protect the forces that moved the time streams dominated his tribe, and he rarely if ever used his power openly. His fortress was hidden deep in the Carpathian Mountains.

The throne next to his, belonging to Mithras, was also empty. Mithras spent a great deal of time with Chronos, who often acted as an advisor to Mithranian tribal disputes, so it was not surprising they were both late. Masters of weaponry and war, the Mithranians were warriors unrivaled. Their abilities let them move within the domain of shadows freely, making them very hard to kill. However, this same strength also made them temperamental by nature.

Victus stared at the empty thrones, deep in thought. His own power rivaled that of his brethren. His birthright gave his tribe the reigning ranks most often among the territories, with only a handful of the ruling class rising from other tribes. He had emerged from the desert and their exile with his father to seek out the other Ancients in the beginning and had served as his father's right hand until war had driven them apart. Now he sat contemplating its beginning. *The war... it destroyed the world once, when those of us that dwell in the pits of flame and torment tried to retake the gates of infinite light, guarded by the holy veil. Men's souls became the prize for a battle neither side has ever won, and that prize is still unclaimed, waiting for the final war that will end all things. Now we come to it at last...*

The soft murmur of voices filled the room as the other Ancients talked among themselves.

Victus stared at them, lost in thought. *We formed this Council to stop the senseless destruction. Our faith has carried us since we joined forces against the fires of Gehenna, giving us holy power even in our own dark curse.* It was the war that had brought them together. Now they awaited the arrival of the last of their brethren, contemplating what the discovery of yet another growing segment of the Renegades meant for the future.

"Victus, your mind betrays you. You dwell too much on the past," Sharrukin observed quietly. He spoke much like a wizened father, though seventh born and still only a youth when Victus had reached his age of immortality. "What troubles you?"

Reaching inside his robes, Victus retrieved the reports he had received. "I called this gathering before these arrived, but they add new urgency to our plans. Our enemy has more recent activity than we suspected. They are building their numbers to dangerous levels."

Silvanus snorted in contempt. "Please, Victus! They have been trying to build their army for centuries. They are no match for us. You worry too much about something that is insignificant at best. We will do as we always have. We will hunt and destroy them. Problem solved."

"Not if we cannot easily find them," a voice interrupted from across the room.

Victus looked up as Mithras and Chronos walked in. It was Mithras who had spoken.

The Mithranian Ancient was wearing chainmail, and a black tunic and cloak that flowed behind him. His long silver hair hung loose and in disarray, giving the appearance of having just returned from battle. His booted feet made no sound as he strode toward them.

At his side, Chronos contrasted greatly by comparison, wearing archaic Grecian robes, his black hair restrained by a thin leather cord. His dark eyes could pierce a soul in one glance. It was apparent he had once more been at Mithras' halls.

The solemn pair took their seats, while Victus waited for the explanation rather impatiently.

Finally, Mithras continued. "I have had my people out searching for any new Renegade strongholds recently emerged in every hotbed across the globe. Only a scattered few could be located. They are hiding too well. I believe they struck some kind of new deal with the creatures from the pit. We must be more cautious if we are to maintain a hold on our territories."

Silvanus sighed in resignation. "I knew this was going to be a long night..."

Turning to look at Silvanus, Chronos raised an eyebrow. "Wanted to run back to those wagons of yours, Silvanus? Keep in mind those humans are often hunted, just as the Renegades hunt us. How will you defend their Kumpanias when the hunt begins again? You are in the middle of a war that sits on your doorstep, and it concerns you as much as the rest of us. Take heed, for the grief born in your camp will be great in the nights to come."

"Peace, peace..." Victus stood and strode to the center of the room. "I did not call you here to quarrel. We must plan a strategy for the future of all our tribes if we are to survive. The Principatus is growing rapidly despite our attempts to crush them. We must resolve this now."

Armenia interrupted him. "That is part of the curse, is it not? To quote the verse... the battle shall then be yours to fight... Remember?"

"That's only part of it," Galatia interjected. "...you know that."

Exasperated, Victus held up his hand. "Sceptrum Ellibre!" His staff appeared instantly and flew to him. "Enough!" he demanded, slamming its base into the floor. A crack of thunder reverberated through the room as he stood glaring at those around him. The pure power of his presence filled the chamber and caused all but Mastric to cringe inwardly. His birthright's potency was not lost on them. "There is no time! Even as we speak, the territories defend themselves from repeated attacks on every front! If the

Renegades are using the dark powers to hide themselves, then our people are in danger! We must decide on a new strategy... tonight!"

Mithras got up and went to stand at Victus side. "If you will allow me, brother..."

Victus gazed at him in silence, and then nodded. He released the room from thrall and sat down with a sigh of relief.

Turning so he addressed them all, Mithras explained. "In recent nights, it was brought to my attention that the Principatus has expanded to the new world. Allowing them to establish themselves unchecked there could prove a fatal mistake. I have long heard the opposing views you each have concerning the present state of affairs, and I think I have a plan..."

## Chapter Seven
## A Change of Plans

*I have returned to the Council's halls weary of the hunt. Valfort will not be found so easily as I first imagined. I have long thought if I returned to the battlefield, I would have more success. His past involvement in the war has shown his desire for blood and leaves no lack of potential targets to satisfy his lust for destruction. Still, Mastric's anger is far greater than his acceptance of failure. He wants Valfort at all costs. He will not be pleased at my return, but I see no other recourse. It would be folly to continue chasing Valfort and killing the young he so obviously creates to bait me. He knows I suffer with each one I kill, and he revels in it. His blood lust cannot be satiated. He is too much like the Renegades whose doctrines he has embraced.*

*In my recent travels, I heard of the new world and the Renegades that have begun to migrate there. Soon they will have their own continent to rule. Will they still wish to wage war against us here, or will they become as the Shokou Azuma in the East, ruling their own Empires in conflict with each other and leaving Europe to finally have peace among the Alliance territories? What will the Alliance do with these territories once the war has ended?*

*Seeing the sometimes-petty disagreements that pass between many of my kind, I cannot but question the wisdom in attempting to be of a social nature at all. I think we would do well to fall into that state in which we withdraw from all life and from each other, staying instead in the confines of our own lairs. I cannot say it would displease me to return to Draegonstorm to squander my nights with my family in peace and the pursuit of knowledge. In my mind, such would be a far more noble charge than the killing of the innocent...*

*Lord Reivn Draegon*

\* \* \* \* \*

Reivn strode into Polusporta's throne room, Jack at his side. Seeing only empty thrones, he called out, "My Lord Mastric! I must speak with you!"

Torches flared, and a soft voice rose from the shadows. "You dare to raise your voice in this chamber? Have you no respect for your forefathers, child?"

Jack immediately dropped to one knee, grabbing Reivn's arm to pull him down beside him. He knew the Warlord's fury would get him killed if he did not recognize their sovereignty.

Galatia stepped into the light. "You are obviously troubled, Reivn. Open your mind to me."

"Galatia! He is not yours to command! Leave him!" Victus materialized on his throne. "Stand and approach, Reivn. You can give me your report. Your father has retired to his chambers and does not wish to be disturbed."

Galatia retreated to her throne to stare with sultry eyes at the two men kneeling before them.

Reivn rose from bended knee, his eyes flashing like fire. "Valfort has eluded us yet again! He makes young to be slaughtered so he can evade us, and I am weary of killing children! I believe my skills are far more useful to this Council if I return to the front lines!"

"Weary of killing?" Laughter filled the hall, as Thylacinos emerged from the shadows. "Killing is what you were chosen for. You serve us as a Warlord, and you live to serve. Are you saying you will no longer obey? Dangerous words, boy!" In a flash, the Ancient was at his side, staring at him through fathomless black pools, as his long claws extended from his hand.

Reivn bowed and averted his gaze. "I do not disobey, my lord. I merely state my grievances at my brother's actions. I serve as I always have… loyally."

Victus noted his lack of fear. "You have courage, Reivn. Be careful it is not mistaken for rebellion. I understand your distaste, but Valfort is dangerous, and few are strong enough to face him. His children would strengthen the renegades if not destroyed. You do what must be done."

Jack looked up. "Permission to speak, my lord?"

Victus waved him forward.

Jack got up and bowed respectfully, before approaching the nine thrones. "My lord, what Lord Reivn is saying is that there are more detrimental issues arising for the Alliance than an Elder going Renegade. The number of children Valfort makes is an annoyance beside a greater problem. This hunt revealed that the Renegades have changed tactics. They have not only grown in number. They have a new purpose." He paused and glanced at Reivn.

Reivn remained silent, his dark eyes unreadable as he listened to Jack's report. He stared at the floor in front of him, knowing if he looked up, Victus would see the fury in his expression. He knew the Council did not trust him, any more than they trusted his father. In truth, he hoped Jack would be able to sway their decision in favor of their abandoning the hunt until the war was over. It was a dangerous gamble.

Jack continued. "Since the discovery of the New World, many have gone there to establish new territories. I believe they seek to build a nation from which they can launch large-scale assaults on the Alliance. We need to send an expedition to the Americas to disrupt their efforts. Forgive me. I do not mean to speak out of turn. I merely seek to offer a solution to what has become a dangerously growing threat."

Galatia held her hand up, motioning for silence. "We are aware of the problem. We believe they were responsible for the disappearance of the Roanoke colony, as well as the troubles at Jamestown. As we speak, Mastric discusses the matter with his own Council. We plan to expand into the new world, but must do so under the guise of humanity until we have a strong position from which to defend ourselves. Perhaps…" Her voice trailed into silence and she glanced at Victus. *This could be a good time to execute the plan Mithras has and rid ourselves of the Mastric Warlord at the same time.*

*Careful, Galatia,* Victus telepathied. *Reivn would indeed be useful in the New World because he is strong, and many follow him loyally. But if we do this, then we must do it for that reason alone. We cannot afford to lost either he or his father right now. We need him.*

Reivn and Jack knew the Ancients had exchanged thoughts, but their content would remain unknown. They quietly waited for Victus to speak again.

Victus got up and walked over to Reivn. "Rise and stand before me."

Reivn did as ordered and got to his feet. But when he lifted his eyes to meet Victus' gaze, there was no fear in them.

"You do not wish to hunt your brother anymore," Victus began, his eyes narrowing when he saw Reivn's jaw tighten. "So, what if we send you to establish a stronghold in the new world? You would be the first Warlord ever assigned to the Americas. You could even take your sons with you. What say you? Forget Valfort. I will assign another to hunt him."

Reivn stared at Victus in silence. He calculated the possibilities of being so far from the Councils' reach and home. *Is this opportunity or exile?* he wondered.

*Consider it opportunity,* Victus answered as easily as if Reivn had spoken. "You forget, I can read your thoughts. Now, will you serve in the new world?"

Reivn dropped on his right knee and placed his fist over his chest in salute. He knew there was no point in arguing. It was either serve or be destroyed. "Yes, my lord."

Galatia smiled from her seat. *I will assign someone to watch him,* she telepathied Victus.

Victus gave no indication she had sent him anything. "Good. I will contact your father and inform him you will lead the mission to the colonies." He nodded in satisfaction. "You must guide our people in building an enduring presence. The young ones will benefit from your knowledge and experience."

Jack stepped forward. "Am I to go as well, my lord?"

Victus shook his head. "You will continue the hunt for Valfort. This time Thylacinos will send more of his own with you." Victus turned to his younger brother. "Does that please you?"

"You should have done that in the first place," Thylacinos growled. "Then that traitor would be dead by now."

Jack bowed. "I will be ready to leave within the hour, my lord."

Victus nodded and dismissed them both.

Reivn turned and walked out with Jack. "I am sorry, Jack. I am being sent into exile and you to hunt Valfort possibly to your own death. I go because I believe in our cause. God be with you. We may not meet again."

"I'm not that easy to get rid of, my friend." Jack smiled. "You are an honorable man. I hope you will count me among your friends. You will see me again. Take care of Gideon. He's a good lad. Farewell and Godspeed." The two shook hands and parted.

A short while later, Reivn watched from a balcony as Jack rode into the desert night, the sands churning into a cloud of dust under his horse's hooves. Grimel and seven other riders had joined him, and in minutes, they vanished on the horizon.

For the next three weeks, apprehension filled the air as Reivn prepared for his mission. He sent for Lunitar, and had Gideon gather supplies, while he assembled the list of names of those who would go with him. He spent hours poring over books in Polusporta's library, gathering knowledge that would aid them in the months or years to come. He realized then that he did not know when or even if he or his sons would ever see home again.

The night of their departure, Reivn and his company traveled by portal to docks off the coast of Africa. There he and his companions, Gideon, Lunitar and Thylacinos' own son, Morgan Wolfe among them, boarded ships bound for the Americas.

As they stood on deck watching their home fade from view, a young Mastric woman assigned to the team approached Reivn. "I am Serena De Fontaine, my lord. I sensed your pain when we boarded. I am a cleric. If you will allow me, perhaps I can be of assistance..."

Reivn glanced down at her. "Why? I do not need healing."

"We all have our place in this world, my lord. Mine is to heal those in need. I see terrible pain in you." Serena met his powerful gaze with an equally intense one of her own.

Lunitar stood nearby, observing in silence. He was concerned by his father's behavior.

From the bow of the ship, Gideon also watched the pair. He grew hopeful when he saw his father and the woman together, but it quickly faded when Reivn turned his back and abruptly walked away, leaving the girl alone in the chill night air. He made his way down to her. "Hello," he called politely. "May I join you?"

Turning around, Serena smiled. "Please do."

Gideon joined her. "I'm sorry. My father isn't always like that."

"Isn't he? He is in a great deal of pain. I can feel it. I offered to help, but he refused me." Serena stared at the dark horizon. "Tell me, what causes his pain?"

Gideon looked around to make sure they were alone. "His wife betrayed him. She would have murdered him while he was unconscious had I not been there. I fought her off that night, but her betrayal changed him somehow."

Her eyes unreadable, she gazed at him in pity. "So, you are loyal in spite of his anger. Do you watch over him to pay a debt? Does he know the nature of her betrayal?"

"He knows, but it matters not. I should not have interfered. That is the law. But he was in a helpless state, and she would have succeeded had I not stopped her. I could not stand by and let her murder him." He frowned, remembering that night.

"What is your name?" Serena's voice brought him back to the present.

"Gideon Aurelius Draegon. And you are..."

She smiled. "Serena. It's a pleasure to meet you."

From across the deck, a familiar voice interrupted. "Gideon!"

Gideon turned to see Reivn striding toward them. "Yes, father?"

Reivn scowled at Serena. "We have work to do. Plans will not make themselves. If you would excuse us, lady..." Without another word, he turned and stormed off.

"Goodnight, Serena." Gideon hesitated, as if to say more, then changed his mind and followed Reivn. He turned and smiled at her once more before disappearing below deck.

Watching him go, Serena shook her head and sighed. *Galatia is right. Gaining his trust will not be easy. If not for his importance to our cause, it would not be worth the effort. Still, I have my assignment...*

Lunitar closed his eyes, digesting what he had just seen. Then after careful consideration, he descended from the upper deck and walked over to where Serena stood staring out at the dark ocean water. He cleared his throat politely to get her attention, then said simply, "Be mindful where you tread, my lady. Lord Reivn is not pleased with Gideon. Keeping him from his duties is unwise. And can cause you both a great deal of grief."

Serena turned around, her sharp eyes carefully observing every inch of the man in front of her. "I do not believe we have met."

"Who I am is not as important as what dangerous waters you tread. His lordship is presently not himself. I believe the concerns of this mission have put him in foul graces," Lunitar stated calmly. He studied her intently, suspecting there was more to her than met the eye.

Serena smiled at him, "I am only trying to do my job, sir. I was assigned to this mission as a cleric. As such, I try to put my skills to use where they are needed."

"Fair enough. Just remember what I have said, or you may regret not having done so. Now I will bid you a good night." Lunitar bowed and walked away, heading below to join his father.

Serena watched him go in silence, then turned and headed to her own cabin. The deck fell silent except for the crew that moved about tending the ship as they moved swiftly through the night, destined for a new land...

## Chapter Eight
## The Journey Home

*I have wondered often about those I hunt. What kind of existence do they carve out for themselves here in the vast night? What muse have I silenced with one stroke? Those Valfort took from their mortal lives were from every station... the very poorest to the aristocracy. That girl... she escaped her fate that night, but in how many more encounters will she find herself that lucky? Her very existence tempts fate to strike at her from the shadows. Where will she go, I wonder, to hide from the will of the Council? How much does she know of this war, and will she join in its insanity? There are too many questions left unanswered that I must know.*

*For years, Valfort has run and abandoned many... too many, to death. The young are untrained and unruly. If he did this with all of them, then his purpose is clear. Their creations were merely to distract us from his true intentions, and we have done naught but waste ourselves for his amusement. While they are all so new to our world and ways, I could take them and attempt to turn them to our cause. It is not the blood that makes them hate so, but rather the doctrines of rebellion. Can we not teach them instead to have faith in what is right and good? Has God so completely abandoned us to the abyss?*

*This girl... born to a pampered world of privilege, and sheltered from the brutality the world offers up... How can she possibly be anything other than cannon fodder so my brother can keep barriers between himself and his hunters? Moreover, if he has abandoned her, how does she survive? Does she even know the truth of her own existence, or does she live in the shadow of his lies? Find her remaining mortal connection, and I shall find her as well...*

*Lord Reivn Draegon*

\* \* \* \* \*

For three years after her escape, Angelique wandered in delusional madness. She drifted from place to place, tormented by nightmares and existing in her own hell. She fought the urge to feed until she was so wracked with pain, she could no longer control it. Then she would feed only enough to stop the agony. Days turned to weeks, weeks to months, and months to years. She had all but succumbed to insanity when a fading memory called to her. She stood on an unknown street in a nameless town.

*Blake...* She turned around, her eyes searching.

*Remember Blake...* She knew that name, but from where?

*Find Blake...* The memory echoed from the darkness. With only a fragment of her crumbling sanity, she remembered, and clinging to that hope, she began the journey back to England. On the coast of France, she boarded the ship '*The Sea Hawke*' bound for England.

Angelique would not set foot on English soil for ten years. While her ship sailed the channel, an event took place that would forever change her life, and she would not remember it for three hundred and twenty-six years.

When she arrived in England, it was aboard '*Le Dupre*' ten years later. She awoke to the sound of Frenchmen calling out as they docked. She was shocked when she learned the date and year. *What happened?* She could not recall even the slightest detail of where she had been. Assuming her insanity had taken over, she wondered if her mysterious creator had helped her. *No! I will not believe that!* She shoved the thought aside.

After disembarking, Angelique traveled for three nights across England to Blake's home, stopping only to pass the days in safety. She arrived in the town one mile outside his estates shortly before dawn and rented rooms at the local inn. She withdrew from the daylight, closing the shutters. Then she looked around and nodded in satisfaction. It was small, but clean. The bed against the far wall was worn, but comfortable. An old chest rested by the door, a washbasin placed neatly atop it. There was a nightstand with a half-burnt candle next to the bed, and one chair. The remainder of the room was bare. Her trunk sat in a corner, unloaded by the coachman when she had arrived. With a sigh, she sat down and removed her shoes, frowning at their mud-stained toes. Then after bathing and dressing, she crawled into bed.

When Angelique awoke the following night, her thoughts returned to Blake. It occurred to her he might have a new life, perhaps even a wife and children. *It would be better if I levitated and went in unseen by the balcony door*, she decided, and then frowned. *When did I learn to do that?* Troubled with her apparent changes, she set out for the estate.

As she drew near the mansion, her apprehension grew. Blake's ancestral home loomed ahead, its twin towers barely visible in the dark. A few lights flickered in windows, as servants tended their affairs. The great fountain in front of the entryway flowed with gentle rhythm.

She stared down at the water. *How do I explain my absence… or my disappearance itself?* She looked up at the balcony she had known since her youth. Then she whispered archaic words she did not understand, and to her surprise, she rose into the air. Moments later, she landed on the cold stone balcony and slipped quietly in.

The room was decorated in masculine tones, with heavy velvet drapes hanging over the windows and door to the balcony, and soft wispy curtains encircled the bed. The old wardrobe was still in the corner, its mahogany hues catching the light from the single candle, and a gilded mirror hung on the wall.

A sigh rose from the bed, so Angelique crept forward and peeked in. Blake was alone.

As she silently watched him, sadness filled her. "My dearest friend, how you have changed."

Even in slumber, his face held grief and revealed how much he had aged.

When he rolled over, she realized how much she had missed him. She sat down, gently brushed his hair from his brow and whispered, "My love, wake."

He moaned and opened his eyes. He gasped when he saw her. "Oh, my God! Angelique, have you finally come to haunt me?" His voice broke, and he reached out to touch the ghost that haunted his dreams. He tenderly stroked her cheek as a tear trailed down his face to land on her hand. "Are you real? Or have I finally died, and you are an angel come to bring me home?" His words were heavy with anguish.

Sorrow filled her and she finally understood Maratoli's warning. Blake's pain had been far greater than her own. "This is but a dream, my love," she whispered.

He sat up and pulled her into his embrace, afraid she would disappear again.

She could feel his heart racing and resisted the urge to taste him. She caught his scent and her desire for him grew. Minutes passed in silence, until finally, her hunger took over. She bit into him, drinking deeply. His blood was warm and tantalizing, setting her senses on fire, her hunger only serving to make it sweeter.

When she finally regained control, she had drained him nearly to the point of death. "What have I done? You can't… you mustn't die! Blake!"

she cried, laying him down. Then she bit her wrist and held it to his lips. "Drink!" she urged. "Drink and live!"

Barely conscious, Blake opened his mouth and accepted her offer. When his strength began to return, he grabbed her wrist with a frantic desire to cling to life and her. Finally, she pulled away, as he lost consciousness and the curse consumed him. She willed her wound closed and lay down beside him. In her mind, she was screaming at what she had done, but she knew her survival depended on it.

It was almost dawn when Blake awoke. When he saw she was indeed really there, he was full of questions.

Angelique knew they needed to get to the safety of the Inn. "My love," she put her fingers to his lips. "We cannot stay here. It isn't safe! I promise I will answer your questions when we get to the Inn."

"I don't understand, but I'll take you wherever you want to go." He would agree to anything rather than lose her again. He dressed quickly. and then took her hand. But when he headed for the door, she stopped. "What's wrong?" he asked.

"I didn't come that way and no one knows I am here but you. It would be really difficult to explain how I got here," she replied, and then paused at his confused look. "I'll explain later. I should leave the way I came. We can meet near the front gate, and from there, ride to the Inn."

Reluctantly, Blake agreed.

Angelique glanced at his pale face, worried about his ability to travel so soon after the turning. "Are you well enough to ride?"

"I'll be fine. Just make sure you do not disappear again," he replied.

As she descended from the balcony, she looked back, afraid he would see her, but the room was already empty.

Blake arrived at the gates half-believing it had all been a dream. He looked anxiously around until he spotted Angelique and rode to her side. Then he pulled her up behind him, and they raced away into the night.

They rode into the Inn's yard just as the sun was rising. Blake tossed the reins to a stable boy. "Take care of him!" he called over his shoulder, as they ran for the door. Then they raced up the stairs to her room.

Blake slammed the door behind them, and they collapsed on the floor laughing, just as they had when they were children. Then he immediately sobered. "You're not a dream! You're real and you're here! God, I have missed you!" He pulled her into his arms and hugged her tight. "What happened? Where have you been?"

"We must rest," she answered, pulling away. She took his hand and led him to the bed. "When we wake, I'll tell you everything."

Blake reluctantly closed his eyes and wrapped his arms around her, as though to shield her from the world.

*I wonder if he'll be this way when he knows the truth*, Angelique thought sadly.

They awoke still intertwined. Blake was full of questions about her disappearance. When she told him how she had been changed and where she had ended up, his eyes registered both understanding and confusion. He held her close and stroked her hair gently. "Whatever you've been through and whatever your reasons, you sought me out. I have never stopped loving you. Armand and I tried for years to find you." Angelique opened her mouth to speak, but he silenced her. "I never thought I would see you again, and I'm not going to lose you now. I am here for as long as you'll have me. I have nothing waiting for me in the world except a cold home of wood and stone." He gently kissed her cheek. "I would give up anything to be with you for eternity, even my humanity. But I will not believe you're a monster. You have never seemed more vulnerable to me than you do right now."

She realized in that moment that this was what she had yearned for most... the companionship of someone, who like her, would live eternally by night.

They talked for most of the night, and Angelique learned of all that had transpired since her disappearance. She was broken-hearted at the news of her parent's deaths. Her estates had been left in Blake's care in the hope she was found. "What of Armand?" she asked.

Blake's eyes took on a distant look. "Armand all but gave up his shipping business to find you, but after twelve years of searching, he returned to the sea. He rarely puts to shore these days," he explained quietly.

Her thoughts on the man she called brother, his face stared back at her from the dark. The three of them had been inseparable. She smiled to herself, only half-listening as Blake talked.

That night they decided to return to St. Etienne.

They spent the next two weeks making travel plans. Angelique also wanted to find Armand, but Blake was very much against the idea. "He has already mourned for you. Let him remember you as you were. I'm not sure he could accept the change in either of us."

She disagreed. "He needs to know I'm alive! We shouldn't leave him believing I'm dead!"

He frowned. "He won't understand, Angelique. Remember the legends among the locals about creatures like us. You can't let your feelings get in the way of reason."

"He's always been your closest friend! How can you think he would be that way?" She grew angry. "He's always trusted you! I will not believe he would betray us!"

Blake paced back and forth, struggling to contain his anger. "It's not that simple, and you know it! You were gone for thirteen years before you came looking for me. You had to have known this wasn't something you just randomly tell someone, no matter how close they are!"

She shook her head and caught his arm. "I would explain it to him just as I have you. When he realizes I had no choice, he will…?"

"Will what?" Blake interrupted angrily. "…say it is all right, here is my blood, now I'll go home and forget? For Heaven's sake, Angelique! He's as superstitious as the rest of the world!"

At his outburst, Angelique fell silent.

"He rarely even comes to our shores anymore," he continued, softening his tone. "Even rarer is his appearance at my home." He did not tell her he had not seen Armand since his own return a year ago. He was thankful when she finally dropped the discussion.

Angelique had started teaching Blake to use his abilities, and the last nights at the Inn, he took it upon himself to hunt for them both, bringing someone back for her to feed on. It had not escaped his notice that she despised the idea of drinking blood to survive. She had always been delicate, but something in her had changed. With shock, he realized it was her innocence.

When they arrived at St. Etienne, Angelique was leaning out the carriage window, trying to catch a glimpse of the old chateau. *Has it changed? Is it as I remember?*

Blake looked across the carriage and smiled. "Don't worry, love," he teased, laughing at her expression. "It has been well cared for. It will be as you remember it."

The chateau loomed in the dark, lights in the windows welcoming them as they approached. When the carriage pulled to a stop, she could barely contain her excitement.

Then the great oak doors opened, and an elderly couple came down the steps.

She scrambled out of the carriage, totally forgetting she had been gone for thirteen years. She knew these people and wanted nothing more than to see them again.

She was about to run up the steps when he gently took her arm and restrained her.

In surprise, she looked up, a question in her eyes.

"Remember," he reminded her.

Understanding crossed her features and she slowed her pace, tucking her arm in his.

The old woman wiped her eyes. "We had given up hope, Milady. We thought you dead."

Angelique glanced at Blake, who stood calmly at her side.

He took her hand and squeezed it affectionately, his eyes offering comfort. "Let's go inside, shall we?" he suggested, wrapping his arm around her. "The Comtesse has had a long journey." He escorted her up the stairs and into the great hall of St. Etienne.

When they stepped inside, Angelique keenly felt her parent's absence and was filled with grief at the emptiness of the hall. Memories flooded her senses and she clung to Blake, momentarily forgetting the old couple standing just behind them.

He squeezed her arm reassuringly and helped her over to the great staircase. "The Comtesse is exhausted from travelling. I'm going to insist she not be disturbed tomorrow. She needs to rest," he ordered, taking command without hesitation.

She leaned on his arm heavily as they climbed the stairs.

The housekeeper was more than willing to follow Blake's orders. Lighting a lantern, she climbed the steps behind them. "I'll put her in her old room," she offered immediately.

Blake shook his head. "No. A room where morning light will not so easily wake her would be better. I also want to be near her, in case she wakes during the day and becomes frightened. I think the old west wing is more suitable."

The housekeeper gasped and turned to look at him incredulously. "Monsieur Blake, that wing hasn't been used since her parents..." her voice trailed off when she saw his steely-eyed expression. "Yes, monsieur, as you wish."

Half-carrying Angelique, Blake followed the old woman, his own thoughts wandering to what lay ahead for them. *Once she has rested, we will have to make careful plans if we are to avoid the servants discovering the truth.*

When they were settled, Blake sat watch while Angelique slept through the first part of the day. He was troubled. *I know how much she needed to see home, but we will be in grave danger if we remain here too long. We are going to have to leave again... soon.* He sat mulling over their situation until he could no longer fight the urge to sleep. Then he went to the adjoining room and slipped quietly into bed.

They remained undisturbed as requested and woke just after nightfall to a cool breeze blowing in through the windows. The velvet drapes had done their job well, preventing sunlight from penetrating the dark chambers.

At dusk when Angelique awoke, she briefly forgot where she was. "Blake?"

"I'm here," Blake answered from the next room. He had awakened only seconds before her and was changing to put in an appearance downstairs.

She remembered then where they were and relief filled her, and she quickly did the same.

They went downstairs arm in arm...neither sure of what waited below.

There was no one around when they entered the dining room, but there were sounds coming from the kitchen. The table was set, and wine was poured. They could hear the excited chatter as the servants prepared the evening meal. They stared at each other in dismay.

Angelique telepathied him. *How are we going to get through dinner without revealing we are not eating anything?*

A bark from outside the door gave them an unexpected answer as the butler entered, three beautiful Great Danes behind him. "Good evening my Lady...my Lord. I beg but a moment of your time, if I may?"

Angelique nodded, more alert then she had been the previous night. "But of course, monsieur. Please..." She motioned for him to approach.

"These dogs, Mademoiselle, they are not the ones you remember from your childhood," the butler paused. "But these are their pups. I thought you might like to have them here. Your mother liked them to be near the family on evenings such as these."

Angelique and Blake smiled at each other. "Yes!" they answered simultaneously.

The butler bowed respectfully and left, closing the doors and leaving the dogs to wander the room under Blake's watchful eyes.

An hour later, all three dogs lay fast asleep near the hearth, having dined well on a myriad of delicious foods. The fire sizzled as the last of the wine burned in its flames.

Blake took Angelique's hand and led her from the table. "There is no music to dance to and for that I am sorry. It has been a great many years since last we shared a waltz." He pulled her into his arms and swung her around. His playfulness made her laugh, and her voice echoed in the vastness of the dining hall.

He smiled warmly. "God, I missed you. I am blessed with good fortune to have you back." Then his tone changed. "You know we cannot stay here."

She pulled away from him. "I know," she whispered. "The only way we can keep St. Etienne is to adopt children and bring them here as our own. But if we do that too soon, people will get suspicious."

"There are many orphans in both England and France who would be grateful to be rid of the beggar's life. The problem will be finding a brother and sister that carry characteristics of both our families." Blake frowned as he spoke, thinking of the possibilities.

Angelique turned to stare at the fire. "The time we spend searching will give us the appearance of having married and had children." Her voice betrayed her sadness.

Blake rested his hand on her shoulder, trying to comfort her. He remembered how they had once planned to fill the halls of their two great houses with the laughter of their children.

Just then, the dogs leapt up and bounded to the door, sniffing the air excitedly. Booted feet sounded on the wood flooring outside, and they both turned as the door opened.

"You could have told me she was home!" Ruben came striding into the room. A loyal servant of sorts, he had lived in the province since birth. Angelique, Blake, and Armand had often played with him and others in the village as children. The six-foot tall man had grown considerably since Angelique had last seen him.

She looked at Blake, a question on her face. "I took the liberty of placing him in charge as Overseer of the Chateau shortly after its care fell into my hands," he explained.

Angelique turned back to the man she had known as a boy. "Life has been good to you, Ruben," she observed, smiling. "I hadn't thought to see anyone I knew so long ago. I'm happy to know there are at least some good folk still at St. Etienne."

Ruben knelt beside her. "Welcome back Angelique... Comtesse!" Taking her hand, he kissed it. "It brings me great joy to see you safely returned to St. Etienne."

Blake stared at her over Ruben's shoulder, and then telepathied her.

Angelique glanced up in surprise. Not all so young were telepathic, but Blake appeared to have mastered it. *What is it, my love?* she asked.

*Make him yours by shared blood,* he told her.

Looking back at Ruben, she agreed. *Watch the doors.*

As she circled around him, Ruben bowed his head respectfully.

She began to weave a web across his mind, enslaving it. She hesitated for a moment, contemplating what she was about to do. Ruben seemed so fragile. *So alive,* she mused. Finally, she swept his hair back and bit into his neck. The sweet taste of his blood awakened her senses. She almost forgot her intent. Then she caught herself and withdrew before taking too much. She desired him to retain life.

Ruben had gasped at the sudden pain, but he remained motionless even when Angelique pulled away.

Angelique opened a vein in her wrist and dropped liquid fire down his throat. She had not taken enough to turn him, but he still belonged to her. By not taking all his blood, while still sharing her own, she had made him a blood servant. Then she gave him back his own thoughts and waited for the questions that would come.

Ruben slowly turned around, his eyes registering clarity. He faced her with a complete absence of fear. "My Lady? I don't understand," he stated in confusion. "Why did you not just ask for my loyalty? I know of your kind. Is this why you were gone so long?"

She stared at him in surprise. "How is it so many fear the legends, yet you do not?"

He smiled. "There was another like you many years ago. I was an orphan and she took me in. She had her servants adopt me as their son. They were the ones you knew. When I was old enough to fend for myself, they went with her. She told me to remember her kindness. She said she had seen the future and knew there would be others like her who would need my help. I never saw her again, but I never forgot."

Listening in amazement, she glanced at Blake, at a loss for words.

Blake cleared his throat uncomfortably. "Her ladyship didn't tell you her intentions because she's been hunted before. She couldn't take the risk of it reoccurring."

"I understand," Ruben smiled, bowing before them.

Angelique walked to the fire and stared into the flames, deep in thought. Moments passed in silence until finally, she turned around. "I need you to travel with us to keep up appearances. We can't stay, or those here at the Chateau will find out the truth."

Ruben shifted uncomfortably. "My Lady, I am recently wed. My wife, Genevieve, is my life. What of her?"

She thought for a moment. "She would come also. It would give you her company during the day, and I do need a lady's maid. I have been without one since I left."

Ruben obediently bowed. "Then I will gladly serve you, as will my own."

The three convened to a private study and spoke long into the night. Angelique told Ruben everything, and what she and Blake had decided.

Ruben listened in astonishment. He realized she had taken countless chances with her safety. He kissed her ring. "I swore to serve you and his lordship. To that vow I hold."

The decision to leave now settled, the trio carefully made their plans. It was agreed all Chateau affairs would be handled through courier, as would all business for Blake's estates. They would contract a ship and sail for the Orient, settling somewhere remote to make discovery of their true nature less likely.

Three nights later, Angelique had a new lady's maid and found herself once more on a ship bound for foreign shores.

*Finally,* she thought as she looked out over the dark water. *I will have peace.*

# BLOOD FEUD

## Chapter Nine
## The New World

*Standing for countless nights and watching the black water of a sunless ocean swirl past, I have had much time to contemplate not only my position, but the fates of my sons and the others with me. We cross the oceans to an unknown destination to establish a presence in the New World, leaving behind our homes and the people we know and love. What awaits us there? I smile and promise those with me that we will succeed in our mission, but I have no real guarantee. Though I would fight until death took me to defend them, will it be enough against the tide of Principatus that are reported as already present?*

*If I cannot get them safely established, then what becomes of us if not ruin and death? I feel this burden is mine alone to bear, for if we are indeed to survive, I must push to the very edge of my endurance to see them through. They look to me to secure their positions in territories I have never laid eyes on and I will see it done not for my own sake, but for the many that followed me to this desolate place.*

*I heard nothing from Jack prior to my leaving Europe other than the fact there has been no further sign of Valfort's activity, nor of the child we tried to find. By now, it has learned how to use the Spirals in as twisted a way as its sire. I do not envy Jack when he finds it, for killing it will not be as easy as it may once have been. So many things Valfort could have done, and instead he creates nightmares for the innocent, leaving them abandoned and bereft of their previous lives. Killing that child would be merciful I think, and yet one must wonder...*

*Lord Reivn Draegon*

\* \* \* \* \*

From the moment their ship docked, Reivn knew survival would be a struggle. America was a wilderness. Amboyle was still populated primarily by natives, with only a scattered few buildings existing as a town near the port to give evidence that Europe had come at all. "Opportunity indeed," he scowled as he studied the landscape from the deck.

The fleet had anchored hours earlier, but he and his company had waited for sunset before emerging from their cabins. Now they stared in silence at what would be their new home for many years to come.

Gideon hovered near his father, but his eyes traveled over the assembly until he found a familiar face. He smiled as Serena's eyes met his own. Reivn had barely given him any peace since that first night on deck, keeping him occupied with the planning of the structures that would have to be built upon their arrival. For reasons undisclosed, Reivn's mood had been inexplicably foul since meeting her.

Not far from them, Lunitar stood gazing stoically at their new home. He frowned, knowing Reivn would be more driven than ever to see to their security. This also meant his mood would disintegrate further. He glanced over and caught Gideon's smile. When he saw the source, hope filled him. *Perhaps he will finally find some happiness.*

Reivn caught Gideon's expression and followed his son's gaze. He scowled when he saw Serena. "It's time to go!" he growled and walked down the gangplank.

Serena shook her head and followed silently as the party began to disembark.

Lunitar waited until the rest of their group had descended the gangplank before heading down himself, instead carefully observing the woman who disturbed his father so much.

Reivn stepped off the docks into the mud. His boots sank into the soft, wet earth, and he looked around in disgust. Finally, he spotted a man harnessing a horse and cart nearby. "Wait here," he told his team. Then he motioned for Lunitar and Gideon to join him.

The man looked up as they approached, suspicion crossing his features. "What do you want?" he asked. His speech was slurred with too much ale.

Reivn stepped closer and then wrinkled his nose in revulsion as the smell of sweat and urine assaulted his senses.

Gideon recoiled when he inhaled the foul stench that hung in the air.

From his position behind Gideon, Lunitar frowned, dismissing the man as a mere drunkard. Then he studied their surroundings, watching for trouble.

Reivn pulled a few gold coins from the pouch at his side. "Take us to an Inn or farm where my traveling companions and I can stay for a few days."

"There's only one Inn, and it won't hold all of you. Some of em' will have to stay here til you can make other arrangements." The man eyed the English coins in annoyance, and then smirked when he saw Reivn's hesitation. "Ships don't usually leave for three days. Take it or leave it. Them coins aren't much use 'round here no how, and I'm headin' home."

Reivn turned to Lunitar, his irritation apparent. "Travel with us long enough to see where we are staying. Then return to the ships. Make sure at least half the women go with you." Leaning closer, he telepathied, *Take control of the fleet. Make sure they do not leave until we are safely installed in the new guild. We cannot afford any losses.*

Lunitar walked back to those waiting behind them and ordered one of the Mastrics to take the majority back on board. Then he rejoined his father and climbed into the waiting wagon.

Minutes later, Reivn and those who went with him were headed into the settlement, unsure of what awaited them. The cart came to a stop in front of a crude building, the town's only Inn. The party alighted from their uncomfortable seats and stood in silence in front of its ramshackle entryway, as the cart disappeared up the road.

Reivn stared at the dilapidated structure. "Tomorrow we combine all our skills to build a guild here. For now, we share quarters to ensure our safety," he ordered. "All humans here must be dominated so they guard us during the day." He turned to find Serena on Gideon's arm and scowled. Then he headed into the building.

Within the hour, they had control of the settlement. They wasted no time preparing a perimeter. Then settling into their assigned rooms, most of the group retired to a nervous sleep.

Gideon walked Serena to her room, fully aware of his father's disapproval. He gently kissed her hand before leaving her to join his father.

Reivn frowned as he watched the interchange. *Why does she irritate me so?* He waited until Gideon had joined him before he returned to the great room.

Gideon drew a deep breath and caught up to him. "Father, may I speak to you?"

Reivn ignored him and pulled out plans for the Guild. "Lunitar," he called.

"Yes, my lord?" Lunitar answered from the door, as he walked in. He could feel the tension in the air.

Reivn lowered his voice. "This place is not secure enough to defend from an attack. See to the security of those ships to buy us time, then return tomorrow night. I need your skills here. We have much work to do and no time to waste."

Lunitar bowed. "It will be done, my lord."

"Father, I would speak with you now!" Gideon's tone became insistent. Finally, he grabbed Reivn's arm. "Father!"

His eyes cold as steel, Reivn spun around and grabbed Gideon by the throat. "You dare?" He forced his son to his knees and snarled. "You forget your place!"

Lunitar took a step back and lowered his eyes. He knew better than to intervene. To challenge his father, even in his brother's defense, would be a fool's errand.

Gideon gasped at the pain and fought his father's grasp. "Forgive me!" he choked out. "I only wanted to talk with you. She's not your enemy!"

Reivn let him go. "It is no concern of yours how I view my subordinates! She is a cleric! Why trouble myself with her?"

"Because she wants to help you! You are ill, father! You have been for some time!" Gideon cried. His neck was painfully bruised. "I only ask that you listen to what she has to say! Please!"

Reivn growled at his son, his irritation apparent.

Gideon struggled to his knees, the pain he felt evident in his expression.

A thread of guilt passed through Reivn, but he shoved it aside. "I promise nothing! Now leave me! We have work to do come the morrow!" Without a second glance, he turned back to Lunitar. "Where were we?"

"I was asking if there were any other supplies I need to bring with me," Lunitar stated.

Reivn shook his head. "No. We will use the spirals to construct the Guild. Between the three of us and the other skilled Mastrics, we have all the knowledge and abilities we need.

Lunitar bowed. "Then with your permission, I will take my leave and attend to my duties," he replied. As he passed Gideon, Lunitar telepathied him. *Don't… not right now.*

Reivn left Gideon to tend himself and retired, shutting out the grief he felt at his son's pain.

The next night at sunset, he began banging on doors and ordering his people to assemble.

Gideon followed him, quiet and withdrawn.

Before his people had even gathered, Lunitar arrived, bringing the most skilled Mastrics from the ship with him. They quickly joined the gathering group.

Just then, Serena exited her room and ran right into Reivn as he passed her door. She quickly backed up to avoid him, tripping on her dress and losing her footing.

Reivn caught her and pulled her to her feet. Then he held her wrist, staring at her in silence.

The rest of the group fell quiet. His animosity toward her was no secret.

Lunitar shook his head in resignation.

Serena met Reivn's gaze and their eyes locked. Instinctively, she reached out with her mind, trying to connect with his. She found only a wall.

"You did not honestly think it would be that easy, did you?" Reivn growled. "You are not a Renegade, so who sent you?" He tightened his grip on her wrist.

Unflinching, Serena ignited her palm and a brilliant ball of energy engulfed both of their hands in intense heat.

Reivn's flesh began to burn, but he refused to let go. Instead, he tightened his hold until an audible snap was heard in the silence.

Most of the assembled group backed off, shocked by her act of defiance and the battle of wills that had begun. But Lunitar slowly stepped forward, reluctantly prepared to intervene. His father was uncharacteristically angry, and it troubled him.

The pain in Serena's wrist was so intense she almost faltered. "I will not yield!" she cried defiantly, fine beads of blood appearing on her forehead from the strain.

"You will find I can withstand a great deal of pain, Miss DeFontaine! You will tell me what I want to know, or I will break you!" Reivn also showed signs of strain, as a telltale trickle of blood wound its way down the side of his face.

Gideon stared in horror at the conflict. He feared for Serena, but worry for his father was greater still. "Father," he whispered.

Lunitar put his hand on Gideon's arm and shook his head. *This is not your fight*.

Reivn heard Gideon and looked up, suddenly remembering they were not alone. His people stood there watching in mute silence. Their shock only served to further his rage. He shoved Serena backward into the room and slammed the door. "Now it's just you and me!" he growled.

She backed away when he let go. Her wrist was crushed and turning angry shades of purple. "I am not going to let you intimidate me as you do your son, Lord Reivn."

"My son is not your concern!" he snarled, his eyes filled with fury. "You openly attacked me! Now, I will have an answer to my query. I know someone sent you and I want to know who! Make no mistake, I will do whatever is necessary to extract that information." In his anger, Reivn failed to notice that Lunitar had entered the room.

Serena realized she was cornered. "No, I can't!" Her words were cut off as Reivn grabbed her by the throat. She gasped in pain.

He pulled her close. "I punished my son for his rebellion last night," he growled, and squeezed, choking off any reply she would have given. "Now you will learn your place! I am a Warlord and your superior! You will submit!"

Lunitar quickly crossed the room and interrupted him. "Father, if you want to interrogate her, then just take it from her blood."

Reivn looked up, his eyes pitch black. "What did you say?" he snapped.

"None here are foolish enough to challenge you," Lunitar replied calmly. "I was merely saying if it is information you want, then take it from her blood and mind."

Reivn gazed intently at his son for a moment, then back at the woman in his hand.

Serena struggled to free herself, pulling at the hand around her neck.

He lifted her off the floor and dangled her in the air.

"Father," Lunitar ventured. "Search her mind and be done with it. Our work cannot wait."

Shaking himself, Reivn regained his senses and pulled her into his arms. Then he roughly bent her head back to expose her neck, and savagely began to drink.

Serena's scream filled the hall and Gideon shuddered. He knew how ruthless his father's interrogations could be. He closed his eyes, trying to shut out the painful sounds coming from the room, but his mind offered no illusions about what was happening beyond that door. He turned away, heading for the stairs and anywhere.

When Reivn finished, Serena lay staring into empty space, drained and pale, her strength gone. He sat down beside her and entered her consciousness. Once the doorways of her mind opened, he found what he sought. *So... Galatia sent you, fearful I would betray the Council and join the Renegades. Let us see what other surprises you hold.* He explored further into her inner being. Then he found the edges of her soul and saw the truth of her existence. Shame filled him. "My God!" he cried, recoiling in shock.

"Did you find what you were looking for?" Lunitar asked quietly.

Not answering, Reivn withdrew quickly from her mind. He bent his head and licked her wound closed. Then he sat back and tore his wrist open, shoving it into her mouth.

Serena gasped and sucked down his blood, the need for sustenance driving her.

Once satisfied she was out of danger, he pulled away. "I am... sorry."

She slowly sat up. She was shaking badly. His probing had found far more than she had ever told anyone, and it frightened her.

"What would you report of me then?" he asked quietly.

Lunitar listened in silence, disturbed by his father's words.

Serena said nothing. She gazed up at Reivn, her eyes troubled.

Reivn stared at her. "Please understand my position. I could not risk harm to this group. If there was any chance you were here to sabotage it, I could not allow it. Forgive me, please."

"Did what you see answer your questions, my lord?" she asked quietly.

He closed his eyes for a second before answering. Finally, he said, "That and more. Look, Miss DeFontaine, I am no threat to the Alliance. I am loyal to the Council, even here in exile."

Touching her hand to his forehead, she reached out with her mind again, this time allowing him to see what he had not. The radiating light from her inner core was so brilliant it engulfed his mind, as the revelation of her true being filled his thoughts.

Concerned now, Lunitar stepped close enough to defend Reivn should she try to harm him.

After a moment, Serena pulled away. "So, you see," she explained, "you did not learn as much as you thought." She was not sure Reivn's remorse was genuine, but when he looked up, she could see his agony. "All right," she finally answered. "I was sent because your behavior has come to the Council's attention. Will you allow me?" Her question rang in the silence.

Reivn glanced up at his son.

Lunitar nodded. "We can spare the time if you need it, father. I will stay while she works."

Reivn sighed and finally agreed. "Very well."

Serena gently pushed him back on her bed. Then she knelt at his side. She raised her hands to his chest and summoned her own power, searching for the source of the problem.

Lunitar sat down near them and watched in silence.

Reivn closed his eyes, forcing himself to ignore her invasive probing. His discomfort was shadowed by the guilt he felt at his abuse of her.

Her eyes grew wide when she found the cause. Centered in his heart was a black mass. When she looked deeper, she realized it was a Daemon seed, the tendrils of which had begun to embed themselves in his heart's outer walls. This was the cause of the changes so poignantly noticed in him, and if not removed soon, it would eventually take over completely. "It is not what I imagined, but it is bad. It will take months to completely heal you. However, I can start tonight." She focused on the seed and summoned her power. "All right, then. Let's see what we can do."

The silence in the room was her only answer.

## Chapter Ten
## Unexpected Reunions

*I am exiled in Hell. This is a foul and unknown place. The land is hostile and rejects every attempt we make to strengthen our defenses here. I am struggling just to keep those with me protected by day from both sunlight and the wilderness we have come to.*

*If the Council sought to punish me for my desire to cease the hunt for Valfort, they could not have found a more perfect penance. I have spent more time in recent months crawling through the mud to build the foundations of our strongholds than any other task collectively at hand. God help us all if we cannot get the humans to strengthen their own presence here. We cannot survive without them, and those that flock to the Americas are the outcasts among their people or the religious zealots who can find no peace in their own lands.*

*Some are rugged, but many are unschooled and poor, and come with dreams of freedom or wealth. The land here is merciless, and I have doubts as to the permanence of even our own presence. Many of my people were fearful and disheartened when we disembarked, including my own sons, I believe, and it is only worse now that we have seen what awaits us.*

*God give me the strength to defend my people and lead them on the right course to our survival or be merciful and strike them down by day while they sleep, but do not let them suffer. I will gladly accept that burden to spare any one of them the agony of suffering or death. I have seen how the fever takes them when they are injured beyond what our healing can repair... when the madness pulls them into death. I would not see any succumb to that horrific end.*

*Lord Reivn Draegon*

* * * * *

Angelique stood on the bow of the ship bound for Mediterranean waters. She stared at the vast dark ocean, as she had for the past two nights, until raised voices drew her attention. Curious as to the cause, she turned and headed across the deck.

A fight had broken out between two shipmates, and one of them had drawn a dagger. Another crewman ran for the captain's quarters, banging on the door frantically.

When they had first boarded, Angelique had heard the ship's captain was a recluse. Curious over both the commotion and the mysterious captain, she made her way closer.

"Careful, miss!" one of the crew called out. "A bit rough back there right now! Not at all a place for a Lady such as yourself!"

Angelique stepped over to the railing, where she could watch safely.

The two men rolled around with their knives drawn, locked in combat. The crew's shouts carried across the deck when one drew first blood. Then the Captain stormed from his cabin, interrupting what would have been a bloodbath. "Not on my ship! Break it up!" he shouted.

Angelique stared at his back. There was something familiar in the way he moved.

He had both men restrained by shipmates while he spoke with them. It was obvious he commanded a great deal of respect from his crew.

She watched the tense moments that followed, until the men were released and shook hands.

Satisfied that his men were settled, the captain turned to head back to his cabin. He froze when he saw her. There was a sharp intake of breath and he snatched his hat from his head, his dark hair blowing in the wind. "My God!"

Angelique stared at him in disbelief.

He quickly crossed the deck to join her. Then he took her hand and helped her down to stand next to him. "Angelique?" his question was painful. "Is it really you?"

Silently, she touched his cheek on impulse.

"You are frozen to the bone," he exclaimed, not wanting to believe she was real. "You should not be standing on the deck in this cold." He motioned toward the men he had just left. "The crew can be rough this time of night. Come, I'll take you below." He turned to lead her toward the captain's quarters.

"Armand, wait!" Angelique cried, breaking her silence. "Blake's here too. Perhaps you should send for him, then we can all talk together."

Armand turned and looked at her sharply. "So... it is you. And Blake is traveling with you? Perhaps you should get him first then." He stared at her, his dark eyes unreadable. "The two of you can join me in my quarters when you are ready." As he walked away, she heard him whisper, "Why did Blake not tell me he found her?"

Angelique stared in stunned silence at the retreating figure. *How are we supposed to explain this?* she wondered. *He knows us too well to lie to him.* She frowned, trying to think of some way to rationalize their presence.

Blake's voice interrupted her thoughts. "Angelique?" He was standing somewhat disarrayed behind her. "I sensed your pain. What happened?" Seeing her expression, he hurried to her side. "What's wrong?"

Angelique quietly explained.

As Blake listened, his face creased with worry. "Armand? This is one of his ships?"

Neither of them noticed when Armand emerged from his cabin again and approached. "What is wrong, Blake? Surely you are not distressed at seeing your oldest friend? For the love of God! You never even told me you found her." He glared at Blake.

Blake stared at the man he called brother. *How can I possibly explain our new life?*

"Well, Blake? Have you nothing to say? I aided you for twelve years. Do you not think I should have been told she was finally found?" Armand looked both angry and sad.

Angelique could bear it no longer. "Stop it, Armand! You are still our brother and dearest friend. It is just that..." Blake shot her a warning look and she fell silent.

Armand did not miss his expression and turned on him, anger seething in his eyes. "Let her finish! You owe me that much!"

Blake held up his hand. "Hold on! I can explain."

Furious now, Armand swung at him.

Angelique cried out, "Look out!"

Blake caught his fist mid-air with ease.

Armand winced as his arm was forced back, and he gasped in pain.

Distraught, Angelique pushed between them. "Blake! Armand! Stop it!" She turned to Armand. "I will tell you why he is so guarded, Armand! We are being hunted! We are going somewhere safe!"

Armand stared at Blake angrily, searching his face for answers as the two of them continued their test of strength and wills.

"It's true!" she cried. Then she turned to Blake in desperation. "Blake! Tell him!"

Ashamed now, Blake let go of Armand's arm. "It's true," he confirmed.

Armand glared at the two of them. "Well, that's just beautiful! Why didn't you tell me? I would have helped you! I still can!"

"We didn't want to put you at risk." Angelique put her hand on his shoulder. "Those hunting us are dangerous and powerful. Blake didn't want to ruin your life here."

"After all these years, do you know me so little? If you are not a part of my life, then it is ruined!" Armand shook his head in disbelief, his tone rising as his anger exploded. "I spent twelve years searching for you! Twelve years! Does that say nothing? You, Blake," he growled. "Haven't I always called you brother?"

A voice from the deck interrupted his tirade. "Mon Capitaine, is something wrong?"

Suddenly aware that several pairs of eyes were watching them, Armand waved his crewmen away. Then he lowered his voice. "We should continue this in my quarters. After you..." He stepped aside and waited.

Blake and Angelique glanced at each other, and then went inside.

The cabin was comfortably furnished. A small table stood in the center of the room, annexed by two chairs. The bunk, still in disarray, stretched along one wall next to a washstand with a hand-hammered steel pitcher and basin. Charts and a mess of other papers lay scattered across a bench seat beneath the window at the back of the cabin, and a chest filled one corner.

Armand closed the door, and then faced them, crossing his arms. "Now," he began, his tone edged with anger. "Start from the beginning. Where have you been for the last thirteen years?" He directed the question at Angelique, but his eyes were locked with Blake's.

Blake stood in front of her protectively.

She sighed and started pacing. "You are right. We were wrong to doubt you."

Armand turned to look at her, and the pain in his eyes tore at her soul.

"I promise I will explain, so please…" Her eyes pleaded for understanding.

Armand stared at her for a moment, then finally nodded and dropped into a chair.

Angelique telepathied Blake. *He deserves the truth*. Without waiting for an answer, she began to tell Armand her story, including everything she could remember from the escape at the Inn to Blake's change and her own.

Armand listened in stunned silence. He knew there could be no journey back for them. He had loved Angelique from the moment they met, but because of his friendship with Blake, had never spoken of it, choosing instead to protect her even to his own death. Now his heart sank.

"Have you been listening?" Angelique was staring at him.

He realized his thoughts had been wandering. "Yes, but I am also thinking of the possibilities. I want to help."

Blake had been silently brooding while Angelique talked. Now he shook his head and sat down in the chair across from his friend. "I was afraid you would say that. It is why I did not involve you. There is nothing you can do for us other than getting us to the orient."

Deep in thought, Armand frowned.

"There is no reason why we cannot stay in touch. You obviously do not fear us." Angelique looked from one to the other.

Armand met her gaze, a strange expression in his eyes. "Take me with you. Make me one of you. Then we will all be together again."

Blake slammed his fist on the table. "No!" he snapped, his rage building. "Don't you understand what we have become? We exist off the blood of others, stalking people like an animal… predators who hunt by night preying on innocent victims to survive!" He pushed away from the table, choosing to ignore Angelique, who winced at his words. *I know this is hard on her, but this has gone too far.* "Is this the kind of existence you would choose?" he snarled. Without warning, he grabbed Angelique and savagely tore into her throat.

"Stop!" Angelique gasped. She could feel his rage. "Please, Blake…stop!" she cried again, trying to break his hold on her.

With a growl, he licked her wound and closed it. Then he stared at Armand, who sat tight-lipped, white and as still as a marble statue. "Is this what you wish to be… old friend?" he asked.

Shaking uncontrollably, Angelique grabbed the table for support, fighting to keep her own hunger at bay. She was unwilling to show her thirst in front of Armand.

Armand slowly got to his feet. His desire to be close to them again far outweighed his revulsion to what he had witnessed, but he was unsure how to voice what he felt.

In disgust, Blake stormed from the cabin without waiting for an answer.

"Do the people you feed from remember?" Armand finally asked quietly. "Or do you kill them?" He turned and stared out the window at the churning waves flowing past the ship's stern, waiting for her answer.

"We don't kill anyone," she whispered. "If we did, it would be too easy for humans to discover what we are." Reeling from blood loss, she began to shake. "We make them forget when we feed from them. It is safer that way."

He nodded, unable to meet her eyes. "Then I will send someone to you." Abruptly, he turned and walked out, leaving her alone in the cabin.

She sank into a chair. *What have we done?* she wondered, shaken by the encounter. Her heart ached for the pain she knew Armand felt, and she began to cry, her crimson tears staining the wood planks beneath her.

After a few minutes, she got up and poured water into the washbasin. She quickly washed her face, finishing as a knock at the door told her Armand had kept his word. "Come in." she answered softly.

A young crewman came in and looked around. Seeing her, he shyly approached. "Mon Capitaine said you needed my help, mademoiselle?" He shifted uncomfortably, and she realized how out of the ordinary this must be.

"Oui, I do. Please... sit." Angelique motioned to a chair near him.

He sat down, his eyes vacant as she dominated his senses.

She circled around behind him, gently whispering in his ear and slipping into his mind. His head finally nodded forward, and he fell into a deep trance. She caught him and bit into his neck, drinking her fill. Her strength returned quickly. When she was finished, she licked the wound closed, leaving no trace behind. Then she sifted through the youth's thoughts.

Deep in his consciousness was the memory of what she had done, his fear of death molding it into horror. She wiped away all traces of it and returned him to the chair. Then she revived him.

He opened his eyes groggily. "Mademoiselle? I'm sorry. I didn't mean to..." he looked embarrassed.

She stopped him mid-sentence. "It is all right. You already brought me what I needed. Don't you remember?" she asked, guiding his thoughts and pointing to a paper and quill on the table. "You brought me those. I only told you to sit because you looked tired. Perhaps you should get some rest? It seems you have been working too hard."

The confused youth got up and bowed, and then scurried away.

Angelique realized with a start that Armand was by the door, watching her in silence. "How long have you been standing there?" she asked quietly.

He leaned against the wall playing with something in his hands. "Long enough..."

She looked shocked. "How could you just...I mean, you saw?"

He nodded, his face emotionless. He could not look at her.

With a start, Angelique realized he was holding a small dagger. "Armand, you're not going to..." Her voice trailed into silence and she backed away fearfully.

"Be serious!" he objected, sounding hurt. "I thought you knew me better than that. I only use this to carve wood." Crossing the room to the chest, he knelt beside it, set the dagger on the floor and opened the top. "See?" he answered and held up an exquisitely hand-carved ship.

She walked over and took it from him. "It's beautiful," she whispered. "Is this what you do when you're alone?"

He leaned back against the wall and looked down. "I have a great deal of time on my hands. I can do my duties either by day or night, but there's never been much point to being on deck for both. I have ship's officers that deal with those duties most of the time."

Angelique handed him the carving and turned away. "I am sorry we caused you so much pain. I would never have..." she stopped, choking on her words as she tried not to cry again.

Putting the figure away, Armand picked up his dagger and got up. Then he caught her arm and turned her around. "You did not do this, Angelique! The one who made you did... when he stole your innocence thirteen years ago!" Armand's tone softened. "You cannot blame yourself."

Angelique could not meet his gaze.

"I never gave up hope that we would find you," Armand continued. "I could not forgive myself for not..." he stopped himself before he said too much.

"You could not have changed anything, Armand," she murmured, "You would, in fact, be dead had you tried to deny him his prey."

The cabin door flew open, interrupting them, and they turned at the sudden intrusion.

Blake stood in the doorway, rage twisting his features. He glanced from Angelique to Armand, who still had a grip on her arm, and then at the dagger in his hand.

Armand followed his gaze and realized too late what the situation looked like.

"You bastard! I knew something was wrong!" Roaring with anger, Blake charged him.

"Blake… no!" Angelique screamed, but he already had Armand by the neck.

Blake curled his fingers around Armand's throat and squeezed, sinking his claws into the delicate flesh and tearing it open. It was over in seconds. He threw Armand across the room and stood between he and Angelique.

She grabbed Blake's arm, restraining him. "He wasn't trying to hurt me! He uses that dagger to carve wood!" she shouted. "He was trying to comfort me! Stop it or you'll kill him!"

Blake looked down at her and with sudden shock, realized he had made a terrible mistake. Turning back to Armand, he stared at the unconscious man on the floor.

Armand lay in a heap where he had landed. Blood poured from his throat, running in small rivulets across the floor.

She ran over and rolled him on his back. Then she looked up with a horrified expression. "He's dying!"

Blake was stunned. He realized he had just condemned his best friend to their existence. "You must change him," he whispered. "It's the only way you can save him now."

Angelique did not hesitate. She drained him the rest of the way, and then bit her wrist and fed him her blood. Then she closed both their wounds and sank to the floor to wait.

Blake listened to her weep for a moment, and then turned to leave. "For what it's worth… I'm sorry," he whispered as he walked out.

Angelique sat for hours waiting for Armand to awaken. She blamed herself, seeing the fury in Blake's eyes. She had destroyed their lives and cursed them to live her nightmare. Finally, a groan from Armand brought her back to the present. She stroked his hair and he opened his eyes. "You're awake," she whispered. "How do you feel?"

Armand stared at her, trying to clear the fog from his mind. "My skin feels like it's on fire. What happened? The last thing I remember is Blake charging at me." Trying to sit up, he noticed his blood-soaked shirt. "What the…" He started to check himself for injury.

Angelique caught his hand. "You were hurt, Armand… badly." She averted her eyes. "I did the only thing I could. I'm sorry." Falling silent, she waited for his condemnation.

He reached up and turned her to meet his gaze. "Are you saying I have joined the family?"

Unable to voice her shame, she pulled away as a sob escaped her.

"It's all right," he assured her. "I wanted this. Now perhaps the rift can mend." Then he noticed his friend's absence. "Where's Blake?"

She glanced at the door. "He went to our quarters. He is quite upset."

"Then perhaps it's time we renew old bonds." Still shaky from his transformation, he got up. "I have a great deal I need to learn. Come," he held out his hand. "Let's go find my brother." He helped her up and almost lost his balance. She put her arm around him, but he shook her off. "No, I need to do this on my own."

Armand staggered over to the chest, pulled out a clean shirt and put it on. Then he took her hand and led her up to the deck.

Angelique avoided looking at the men who stared at them as they made their way toward the passenger cabins.

He was used to his crew's curiosity and ignored them. He concentrated instead on the new sensations pulsing through his body. All his senses had come alive. Focusing on an object on the far side of the ship, he could see it with complete clarity. He could hear the chatter of the crew. He could even taste the salt in the air. Glancing at her, he finally understood how unhappy she had been. New clarity filled him when he felt her presence through the connection of blood they now shared. He understood how Blake had made the mistake he did. *He could feel her fear,* he realized. *That's why he was so angry. He thought her in danger.*

They reached the steps to the lower cabins and Armand helped her down them. Blake's door was open, so they went in.

Blake was sitting on his bunk, head in hands. "I suppose you're here to demand an explanation then?" he asked without looking up.

Armand walked over and sat down beside him. "I am neither here to ask for an explanation nor to condemn you. You have been and always shall be my brother. Now we share the same blood and truly are a family.

Please, no more harsh words between us." He held up his arms to embrace his life-long friend, but Blake pushed him away.

"You have no idea what you are condemned to…or what I have done! You will not be able to stay on your ships! All the years you put into building your fleet… it means nothing now!" Blake ran his hands through his hair in frustration, the strain showing on his face.

Armand opened his mouth to speak, but Ruben, who had heard Blake's outburst, stopped him. "There is no need for us to leave this or any ship in his fleet," he turned to Angelique. "Milady, as you know, you are able to make your prey forget they have been fed from, yes?"

Angelique nodded, curious now.

He looked at Armand. "Monsieur, is it not true your crews change out at different ports when the men take time away from the sea?"

Now it was Armand's turn for curiosity. "Usually."

"Well then, it should not be difficult to make sure the same crewmen never get on the ship twice outside of a certain number of years. Each lifetime is measured to hide our secret." Ruben smiled at them. "If the crew doesn't know you, then they won't notice you don't age."

Blake stared at him. "What of the Orient?"

Ruben turned to face him. "We can go there if it is what you wish, but it is not a necessity. We would be just as safe here as we would in the wilds, perhaps safer."

Angelique stared at Blake, praying he would forgive himself for what he considered his crime. She shared his pain, but Armand's happiness had somewhat eased her mind.

Seeing her expression, Blake could not deny what she asked. His love for her, and for Armand, was too strong. He stood defeated and gazed at them through eyes filled with pain.

Angelique took both their hands and pulled them to their feet. Then the three stood together in silence, the bonds of friendship and love that held them together renewed.

Ruben nodded in satisfaction. Then he slipped out quietly, leaving them to talk. *They have a great deal to catch up on,* he decided. *I'll return before sunrise, so they can feed.* Ascending the steps into the night air on deck, he positioned himself near the entrance to keep watch.

Those below talked for hours, close bonds and memories sparking to life once more. Little did they know their journey had not yet truly begun.

## Chapter Eleven
## Revenge

*I finally received a communiqué from Jack. Valfort's trail went cold
again... no lairs, no children, nothing. He vanished without a trace. Jack
has returned to the Sahara, after continued weeks of hunting left him
without even the smallest of clues. After killing Valfort's Principatus
liaison, the only lead Jack was able to track down, he was reassigned
elsewhere. He will no doubt suffer a similar fate to mine. Had I been
there... ah, but that is my own folly. I asked to cease hunting him and have
none to blame save myself. I was tired of killing young ones, and so
despised him for his success in evading me that I let it drive me to
disgrace. I am still not certain if it was his cleverness or my own temper
that defeated me, and I do not think I care to know the truth of that answer.*

*I wrote Jack and asked about his reassignment, but it will be days
before I hear anything. I would ask for his company here, but he will be
well en route to his new duties by the time he gets my letter. I am going to
begin inquiries of my own as to Valfort's whereabouts and with any due
luck, I'll at least find out his general location. Without my previous status,
I cannot do much. However, the information may at least serve to help
others find him and take him down before he can cause further harm.*

*How he must hate me for hunting him as I did. After having to evade
the Council's grip once more, he must be so bitter. His betrayal was
equally so, however, and just as he gave no mercy to Elena, so too, shall
he have none. Let him keep running. The day will come when I will find
and end him.*

*Lord Reivn Draegon*

\* \* \* \* \*

"I want her found, Winston! No more mistakes!" Valfort paced back and
forth in irritation.

His servant stood nearby, blood dripping from a fresh wound on his
lip. The skin around the injury was turning purple from the blow he had
received. "Yes, my lord."

Valfort stopped to look at him. "Ah, Winston," he cooed. "I do not
wish to punish you, but you left me no choice. There is too much at stake
for you to be so careless. You let her slip through your fingers twice. I will
not allow it a third time. You are far easier replaced than she."

Winston cringed at his words, knowing they were true. In Valfort's eyes, he was expendable. "I will not fail you again, my lord," he answered quietly.

"I know. You must understand she is one of only a handful to have survived this long, and has no doubt created at least one of her own. Reivn spent so many years destroying my children that only a few managed to reach maturity. She has, and this means strength to my cause," Valfort growled. He began pacing again. "Angelique will be a great asset to the fight. She knows nothing yet of the Alliance or our rebellion."

"My lord, how do you know she will join us?" Winston asked.

Valfort laughed. "You speak as though she has a choice. I created her, I and will destroy her if she does not obey me. Now, I have work to do. Leave me." Waving his hand, he dismissed Winston and turned his attention to other matters.

The secrets that the Mastrics harbored in their libraries were of great interest to Valfort, and he sought a way to gain access to them. He was meeting with Principatus leaders soon, and any plans they had to steal those secrets had to be carefully laid out if they were to be successful.

He rubbed his neck, reminding himself of the reason for his hatred of Mastric. The angry scar across his throat was evidence of a failure and ultimately, punishment. He had refused to suffer through it again and had turned on the Alliance. As he sat down and dug through the extensive material he had collected, his thoughts drifted to the girl he had awakened, and his annoyance grew. *I should not have left her that night. This search is taking far longer than I expected.*

Frustrated, Valfort focused on his plans. He knew the layout of the London Guild, but attacking it would not be easy. It was Mastric's main seat of power. He remembered the years he spent with the others Mastric had created, and how he had once had a place among them. His own position had long since been filled by his aspiring brother, Reivn. *Now he crawls before Mastric as I once did. I look forward to finding him alone.*

He drew a blueprint of the guild, noting exits and rooms to avoid, and marking clear lines to the library, which was where their secreted knowledge was kept. Mulling over the possibilities, he lost track of time. When a knock on the door heralded the arrival of his guests, he quickly put away his work.

Two heavily cloaked figures entered.

"Welcome. You know who I am. Whom do I have the pleasure of hosting?" Valfort asked. He walked over to the table and sat down expectantly.

The taller of the two stepped forward, but did not remove his hood. "Our identities are of no consequence. All that matters are what plans we accomplish." They joined him and sat down, their faces hidden behind the cowls they wore.

From his hiding place in the hall, Winston waited until the door closed and their voices were shielded from prying ears. When he was sure those within were well engaged in conversation, he made for the back of the building and slipped out into the night. He knew where the girl had last been seen and planned to start searching again from there. He took a horse from the stable and headed north.

Valfort listened impatiently to the man in front of him.

"We are not ready for such a bold move yet. We have few strong enough to take on that many of your tribe, especially those of their age and power," the tall man stated. "We need to gain more victories to rally our soldiers first. It will give us the edge we need to bring the Alliance to its knees."

Hatred burned in Valfort's eyes. "If we act now, we can harness that magic to use in our campaign," he argued. "Leave the Elders to me. I am not afraid of my own brethren."

The man sighed again and glanced at his companion, who sat silent and disapproving. Then he turned to Valfort. "We understand your frustration," he answered. "The hatred you bear for the Alliance is of no small consequence. We have been lucky in the numbers that have joined us, but there are few among your rank and age turning to our cause." The man paused. "What we need right now is for you to go to the Americas and protect our interests there. News has reached us that Lord Reivn Draegon, your enemy, has set up a base there and is building their strength. You are strong enough to defeat him and have your own agendas where he is concerned. This other matter will keep for now. Will you go? For the cause?"

"If I do, it's with the understanding that I am in command of any troops you send. My servants will be hunting for my lost children in my absence. When they are found, I reserve the right to leave the situation there to retrieve them," Valfort demanded. He knew their ways, but he also knew they needed his power.

His second guest interrupted. "Have you performed the bond-breaking rite?" she asked.

Valfort nodded. "Many years ago. My father would have already forcefully summoned me back had I not. He cannot trace me, so I am free to go where I will without discovery."

"I would have thought one in your previous position would have been reluctant to give up such a seat of privilege. Your abandonment was most unexpected, but advantageous to our cause. With you in the Americas, we will gain a firmer foothold on territories that may yet win the revolution against the Alliance." She stood up, indicating the meeting was at an end.

Valfort got up. "How soon do you want me to depart?"

They turned to leave. "Tomorrow night," the man answered over his shoulder. "Make what plans you must tonight. There is no time to waste. Every night the Alliance settlement grows stronger. If we are to maintain our presence there, we must move now. Once you are established, we will send others to rule the territories, leaving you free to continue your own pursuits. We are counting on you..." His words dissipated as he and his companion disappeared into the shadows.

"I will be successful. Have no fear of that... and if my brother gets in my way, I'll crush him. We will have our victory," Valfort growled, not moving until the door shut once more. Then he went to the desk and began digging through old papers. Looking up names he remembered, he started putting together a list of those he could recruit for the assignment. His irritation at having to put off the attack on Mastric's lair was only eased by the idea of finally having the opportunity to destroy Reivn once and for all.

Semerkhet followed Martu in silence. Once they were out of earshot, she lowered her hood and stared at her brother. "Do you think he suspected anything?"

"Of course, he did," Martu replied. "He is Mastric's firstborn and has seen much of this war. It is fortunate he holds no love for that pompous fool. His betrayal gave us the opportunity we have been waiting for. Mastric always destroyed any of his children that went Renegade, but Valfort is far stronger than the others. His power can turn the tide in our favor. He is also arrogant, and that gives us the advantage we need. He did not realize who he was talking to, and that was why we could so easily manipulate him."

She smiled at the thought. "Then let us send our best with him and hope he destroys Lord Reivn. He is the only other of Mastric's children that remains a threat to us. The rest are by far weaker than he, and are no match for our strength. Then destroying the Guilds and all that remains of their defenses would be a simple task."

Martu chuckled, as they slipped into an underground entrance to the tunnels below. "We shall see. We shall indeed see…"

By sunrise Valfort had notified those to be traveling with him, gathered the necessary designs for underground structures, and acquired the funding. When he laid down to sleep, he smiled and thought of the battles to come. The idea of his greatest enemy falling at his hands filled him with pleasure as he drifted into slumber.

When Valfort reached the Pennsylvania colony months later, his mood quickly soured. He stared in distaste at the muddied shoreline and sparse docks. *This place is little more than wilderness. Gods… what did I let them talk me into? I doubt there is an aristocrat within a thousand miles of here. Finding someone that doesn't taste of swill will be impossible!* he thought in disgust.

The dock was devoid of activity when he and his associates disembarked, and he frowned profusely. Spotting scattered lights not too far up the street, he hoped to at least acquire a safe location to stay in until they were established.

As he moved down the gangplank, a boy of thirteen ran up to greet him. "Mister… I'll carry your bag for a coin. Hire me and I can show you the town too!"

Valfort looked to see if any humans were around and smiled when he saw no one in sight. He grabbed the youth and sank his fangs in. But he only took a little. Then he tore open his wrist and forced the boy to drink. "I don't need to pay you!" he laughed. "You belong to me! Carry the bags and take me to the best accommodations this putrid place can offer. Then find accommodations for my men." He cuffed the boy in the ear and sent him sprawling into the mud.

The youngster yelped in pain and held his ear, which was quickly turning shades of blue. "Yes… yes, sir!" he cried, scrambling to his feet. He quickly gathered Valfort's bags.

"That's master, boy. Master! Don't forget that!" Valfort growled. Then he stretched and started walking again. *I will send for the horses tomorrow night.* The youth would see to it, he knew. Fear was a wonderful tool. *Boy... hmmm.* He glanced at the kid who now followed him obediently, his eyes wide with fear. "Boy!"

The lad immediately responded. "Yes, master?"

Valfort grinned. "What is your name?"

The boy trembled, remembering the bite. "It's Tommy, my lord," he answered quietly.

Valfort nodded in satisfaction and continued down the street toward what he hoped was a hot bath and a decently clean maid for company.

Tommy struggled behind him, carrying his bags and trying to keep up. He was under no illusions about his new owner, nor did he question the sudden loss of his freedom. He was just happy his life had been spared by the creature he now followed into town.

Two hours later, Valfort was ensconced in the town's best Inn and soaking in a wood tub of hot water. He had run Tommy ferociously, beating the boy frequently as he scrambled to fulfill his duties. Now he leaned back and closed his eyes, enjoying the warmth from the bath.

Tommy lay curled in a ball on the floor, half his face swollen in mottled shades of black and blue. His lip was split open and bleeding from the blows. Too afraid to even whimper, he closed his eyes and tried to will away the pain. To his surprise, it eased a bit and his wounds healed slightly. He glanced up, wondering if his master had shown him some mercy at last. But Valfort ignored his suffering. He sighed and put his head back down, waiting for his next command, which would not be long in coming.

Valfort stirred in his bath, his hunger awakened. "Tommy, go downstairs and find a maid," he ordered. "Make sure she is relatively clean, pretty and well-shaped. I want company."

"Yes, master." Tommy ran to the door, ignoring the painful reminders of his earlier beatings. He knew if he was to survive, he had to be quick and invaluable to Valfort, and that meant finding anything he needed. He hurried downstairs. Then he scanned the crowd until he spotted a pretty blond serving drinks. He slowed his pace and walked over to her. Pulling on her sleeve, he forced a smile despite his pain. "Excuse me miss. My lord would like your company. He'll pay you a fortune in gold for your time."

The girl looked down at him. "Lord's mercy, boy. Did he do this to you?" she asked.

Tommy feigned shock and shook his head. "No, miss! My lord is kind and generous. I was jumped in the market. Will you come?"

She smiled at him then. "Lead the way. I haven't made much serving this drunken lot."

Tommy took her hand and led her up the stairs to the back of the Inn where Valfort waited. When he opened the door and ushered her in, he looked around to see if anyone had seen them.

The room was pitch black. Moving into the gloom, the girl called out. "Hello? Where are you? May I light a lantern? Ugh…"

Her voice ended with a strangled gurgle when Valfort viciously tore into her throat. He savagely raped her while draining her, suddenly and brutally ending her life. Then he looked up and his eyes leveled on Tommy, who stood frozen with horror. "Dump the body in the alley among the refuse. When found, people will assume she was killed by some vagrant." He pulled out a dagger and slit her throat, covering her jagged wounds. Then he shoved her body toward the boy.

Tommy shook with terror, as he pulled her corpse toward the window and opened it. He looked down into the alley, making sure no one would see the figure that seconds later fell to the ground below. It was almost sunrise and the streets were silent. He stared down at the girl's still form for long moments, and then slowly closed the window.

Valfort settled into his bed after casting a lock spell on the door. It would open for no one until he removed it. He closed his eyes. "Sleep lightly," he warned. Then he let sleep claim him, leaving Tommy to sit alone in the silence until exhaustion claimed him.

Sometime later, a scream jolted Tommy awake again. Voices filled the air with the discovery below. He glanced up at Valfort, and realized black eyes were staring back at him. "Mm… master?" he stuttered. The low rumble of laughter from across the room caused a shudder to ripple through him. He turned over, trying to shut out the sounds below, as the body of the girl was taken away.

The following night, Valfort roused Tommy from slumber and had him prepare to leave.

"Where are we going, master?" the boy asked hesitantly.

Valfort smiled at him. "We are going deep into the Pennsylvania colonies to our brothers. There we shall find shelter and protection from discovery. They control this area, and it grows more with each passing year. Come, we have much to do."

# BLOOD FEUD

## Chapter Twelve
## Tribe of the East

*Sister or enemy, who are you? In thinking back to the night you fled your fate, one must wonder if you would not have rather it ended there. You would be wise to fear that which is to come. Following the path your father has set before you can only lead to certain death at the hands of those who hunt you. If you have not already embraced the twisted and corrupt doctrines of your father's, then do not, or I pray there is no hope for your redemption when the long night has run its course.*

*The truth is that our immortality is a charade, for none are truly immortal. We merely die far more violently than our human counterparts. There is no mercy for those who live outside the pulse of life. You must bend your head to the ferocity that lies in the winds of our war, or it will snatch you up in its fiery breath and consume you in its core.*

*Child, who are you? When I do find you, and I will eventually find you, will you bow your head and submit to the Council, or will you be set ablaze to burn in your own corruption? Valfort has such a foul habit of leaving his young to fend for themselves that I fear he has stolen your life merely to let you die from sheer lack of anything that even resembles useful knowledge.*

*God teach the weak to be steadfast, and the strong to be merciful, lest compassion be made to fade into the bitterness of our hardened hearts. How I long to see the sun in all its radiant glory, but to do so would spell my fate. So too, does the child who embraces the corrupt and twisted teachings of the Renegades succumb to the death that awaits them when justice reaches out her mighty hand to slay them at last.*

*Lord Reivn Draegon*

\* \* \* \* \*

For three centuries, Angelique and her companions traveled the world, hiding from civilization. The great sailing ships eventually disappeared, replaced by the steel freighters of a new age. Over time, Armand sold most of his fleet and focused on learning his new skills. When they finally settled, it was in the Caribbean islands, where the natives readily accepted their presence. From there, Armand could keep his remaining ship in operation with a new Captain while retiring from operation himself.

Generations of children had lived and died since the first orphans adopted and taken to both their ancestral homes, and their descendants kept the secrets handed down to them. Both estates continued to yield a fortune, a portion of which was always allotted to their true owners. With such peace surrounding their lives, Angelique, Blake, and Armand forgot they had ever been hunted or in any danger. But all that changed when they decided to travel to America.

They sailed into a harbor near Atlantic City in August of 1995. When they disembarked, Blake and Ruben took Genevieve with them and went to secure a place for them to stay, while Armand arranged for the ship to stay in dock for repairs.

Angelique had stayed with Armand, only half-listening as he spoke with the harbor supervisor. While she waited, she noticed a man closely watching them and pulled on Armand's sleeve. "Armand," she whispered. "I think you should finish your business, so we can leave." Then she telepathied both he and Blake. *We are being watched. I think he's another Vampyre.*

Blake responded immediately. *We're almost there. Try to be as inconspicuous as possible.*

Armand quickly finished the paperwork. Then holding her arm, he turned to leave. "Come on," he whispered, keenly aware when the man followed them from the office.

They were still waiting for Blake when the man approached. "Excuse me," he called out.

Armand stepped protectively in front of Angelique. "Can I help you?"

"No, but perhaps I can help you," the stranger stated, walking up to them. "Good evening, my lady." He bowed to her. "I am Lord Kuromoto. I noticed you came in on that ship. I think perhaps you need a guide here."

Armand looked at him suspiciously. He was obviously of Oriental background and looked as out of place as they did. "What are you talking about?"

Kuromoto bowed again. "You know very well. You are Immortal, as are your companions. I too, have that honor."

Angelique stared him. *Surely, I know him from somewhere.*

Just then, a car pulled up and Blake jumped out.

Kuromoto bowed to him, introducing himself again. "So... now you are all here." He turned to Angelique. "You are their creator, no? You have come to an Alliance city. If you are to stay alive, you must be introduced to their Prince. Their tenets require it."

Blake exchanged glances with Armand. "Tenets?"

Kuromoto nodded. "Their laws," he explained. "There are many of them."

Angelique frowned. "How do we know we can trust you?"

"Do you really have a choice?" Kuromoto smiled.

She glanced at her companions. Neither one liked the idea, but they agreed.

Blake spoke first. "What exactly are we supposed to do?"

Kuromoto gazed at him. "You have done the first part. You found a place to stay, yes?"

Though Blake nodded in affirmation, he did not volunteer any information.

"Then you wait until they gather again, and you introduce yourself to the Immortals of the city." Kuromoto smiled. "This is the custom of our kind." He turned to leave, then stopped and looked at them. "Do not worry, I will find you when the time comes. If you meet others like us, tell them you are of my tribe, the Eastern Lords."

Kuromoto walked away.

Speechless, Angelique stared after him. They had never heard of anything even close to what Kuromoto had told them. They had never stayed in too many largely populated areas and had rarely met any other Vampyres over the centuries. Those they had seen were usually just as interested in staying anonymous as Angelique and her family were.

Armand broke the silence. "Alliance? Vampyre Lord? Tribes of Vampyres? What is he talking about?"

"Please Blake, let's go. He said something about staying alive." Angelique shuddered at the thought. "I don't like the sound of that. What if others are watching us too?"

Blake frowned. "I think we need to talk about this and decide what our next move will be. Come on. We can talk when we get to our rooms. I rented some at a hotel." He helped Angelique into the car. Then he and Armand climbed in and Ruben started the car.

Angelique's voice rose from the back seat. "Where's Genevieve?"

Propping his arm over the seat, Blake turned to look at her. "She's fine. I left her at the hotel to prep the rooms. This car is a little on the small side and it would have been crowded. I plan to get a larger one tomorrow. We rented this one."

She nodded and fell silent, staring out the windows at the new world they had come to, wondering what laid in wait for them. Though none voiced it, there was tension in the air.

Once they had settled in their rooms, they decided Ruben would keep watch by day, ignoring his usual duties until nightfall.

Angelique stared at Blake, afraid to close her eyes.

He pulled her into his arms. "Don't worry. I'm not going to let anything happen to you. Armand and I can handle anything. Rest now. I'll see you at sunset." He gently stroked her hair.

When he turned to walk away, she grabbed his hand. "I don't want to be alone. I'm afraid. Please...hold me."

He looked down at her and his eyes softened. His love for her had never diminished.

Armand's voice broke the moment. "I think we need to stay together. It will be easier for Ruben to keep watch and more difficult for anyone to catch us by surprise."

Blake agreed. "I'll have Genevieve set up an extra bed on the floor."

When Genevieve returned from the other rooms, Ruben quickly explained their plans, and she hurried away to gather the extra bedding.

Blake watched over Angelique until she fell asleep. Then he sat down with Armand and Ruben and quietly formed a plan in case they were attacked during the day. The sun had already risen by the time they settled down to sleep.

Ruben cleaned his guns and sat by the door, listening to the day's activities outside and watching over his sleeping friends.

The day passed uneventfully and when the sun set, one by one, the Immortals awakened.

Angelique was relieved and smiled at Blake.

Armand sat up, complaining. "Damned floor!" he groaned. "Remind me to buy a mattress if we must do this again."

She looked over at him and giggled. "Getting old, Armand?"

He growled. "Very funny! You try sleeping on a hard floor when the day claims you and see if you're not sore!"

Blake had just returned from dressing for the day. He grinned and threw a towel at Armand. "The only one that sleeps in a bed next to me is the Lady. You don't qualify!"

Armand ignored him and headed to his own room. Then he leaned against his door and closed his eyes. *Why do I do this to myself? I know they're happy.* He was lost in his thoughts until he heard his name.

Blake knocked again. "Armand! Are you in there?"

"Yeah, I'm here," Armand replied and opened the door.

Blake raised an eyebrow. "I've been knocking for the last five minutes. Are you all right?"

Armand looked embarrassed, so he did not pry further. "Why don't you shower and meet us downstairs?" he suggested. Then he left and went down to meet Angelique.

A short while later Armand headed downstairs to join them.

Blake hailed him as he approached. "We need to learn our way around the city, so we have some knowledge of the streets and nightlife."

Angelique touched his arm. "We should do some shopping too. The clothing here is different from what we wore in the islands."

"Ruben and I can shop for a car while you take her to the stores," Armand stated. "I trust you to find something suitable for me."

Blake nodded. "It's true we'll cover more territory if we split up, but it will also be easier for someone to attack us, so watch your backs!"

"Agreed!" Armand answered. Then he and Ruben left.

Genevieve was about to return to her duties when Angelique stopped her. "I want you with us too. You are not safe here by yourself."

Genevieve smiled. "As you wish, milady. I was going to clean up a bit, but it will keep."

Blake escorted them out to a waiting taxi. "Driver, take us to the most upscale stores your city offers. You will be generously paid for your time."

"Yes, sir! Right away!" The driver quickly called his dispatch to inform them his fare would be keeping him the rest of the night, smiling at the thought of the money he would make. Music blared over the radio as the trio took careful note of the roads they traveled on, all the while wondering what secrets this city would soon reveal.

Several weeks passed and Angelique began to believe Kuromoto was just an eccentric trying to scare them. Blake disagreed and continued to take precautions to safeguard them all. He and Armand took turns keeping watch at night, while Ruben guarded them by day.

One night Armand spotted something unusual in one of the upstairs windows of the building across the street. The glint of a reflection from a small lens and a shadowed outline were easily visible to his keen senses. They were being watched. He quickly telepathied Blake. *There... that window on the third floor... fourth from the left.*

*Say nothing to Angelique,* Blake answered silently. *There is no point in frightening her. Just keep watching for now. We'll tell her if something changes.*

Armand agreed, and silently watched the street. In his opinion, Angelique had become far too wise in the ways of the world, and less like the refined lady she had once been. She still carried herself with grace, but Armand feared this too would disappear, changing his gentle friend forever. *As long as I live this life, whatever it is, I won't let that happen.* Then movement below caught his attention.

Two figures were coming silently up the street, keeping to the shadows.

Armand signaled Blake, then looked back out the window just in time to see the figures disappear, as they entered the lobby downstairs.

Blake wasted no time in rousing Ruben, and telepathing Angelique, who was in the next room with Genevieve. When he got no answer, he grabbed Armand, and the two of them raced down the hall.

They burst through the door, and Blake froze when he saw the figures standing in the room. They were hooded and cloaked, so he could not see their faces, but he saw Angelique's and felt her fear. "Get away from her!" he snarled.

One of the strangers pushed back their hood and both men drew to a halt, staring at the dark eyes that met theirs without fear. Tall and thin, long raven-black hair streaming down her back, she was unearthly beautiful. Of obvious Eastern origin, her ethereal appearance un-nerved Armand.

Blake stared at her with suspicion.

She bowed to them. "I am Lady Takara. My companion and I have come to bring you to our Lord's dwelling. We mean you no harm, this I swear to you."

Blake pushed past them to stand by Angelique. "How do we know we can trust you?" He studied her face carefully, awaiting her response.

Takara waved her hand, and her companion removed her hood as well.

Blake looked from one to the other in astonishment.

Angelique stared in surprise at their guests.

"This is Lady Akihana," Takara said, motioning toward her companion. "She is also of our people, the Shokou Azuma."

Lady Akihana was shorter than her tall eastern companion, but just as beautiful. Her dark eyes were observant, and she smiled at them. Then her gaze shifted to Angelique.

Angelique looked away, feeling as though she had met this woman before.

The room fell silent.

Takara looked from one to the other. "Will you come? My Lord is trying to help you. There are others watching you who are not so friendly. He will explain all when you meet with him."

Angelique spoke first. "We will come, but not unprotected. My companions and I are ready to defend ourselves." Blake nodded when she cast a meaningful glance his way.

Their strange guests said nothing more. They just stepped into the hall to wait for them.

Blake threw Angelique's cloak over her shoulders. Then they followed their new companions out to a waiting car.

The ride was quiet. Blake took careful note of the roads they traveled. He had no idea how many of these people there were going to be, or how powerful. Glancing over at Angelique, who sat silently between their hosts, he grew worried. *She is not sitting where I can easily help her.* She looked up then, and he saw the uncertainty in her eyes. *Don't worry, we'll be fine,* he telepathied. He was not at all certain what he would do, but she did not need to know that.

Before long, they pulled up in front of an abandoned building with boarded up windows and doors, and Blake and Armand exchanged worried glances, not trusting the location.

Their mysterious hosts, however, calmly led them to one of the side entrances. Then Takara stepped forward and waved her hand, uttering words they did not understand. The door in front of them disappeared and she entered, motioning for them to follow.

After cautioning them with a look, Blake walked in first, in case they were attacked.

Armand put his arm around Angelique protectively, and they followed.

Once in the entryway, they stared in shock. The interior resembled an oriental palace.

"Your Lord has a palace in the heart of Atlantic City?" Blake asked incredulously.

Akihana smiled at his question. "It is only the house of a Lord, not an Emperor. There are many such hidden lairs in our world. Have you not had elegant homes of your own?" She looked at Angelique as she spoke.

Angelique again had the nagging feeling they had met before. She never had the chance to answer though, because a voice interrupted the conversation.

"Welcome to my home. I am pleased you have come at last. You are my honored guests."

Takara and Akihana disappeared through a door across from the entryway.

Angelique nodded to Blake, and then followed their hosts.

When they entered the room, they came face to face with the man they had met on the docks. But Kuromoto was not dressed in the modern attire he had worn in their previous meeting. Instead, he now wore the traditional garb of Japanese Lords. Angelique curtsied, casting a sideways glance at Blake. Grudgingly, he and Armand followed suit with a bow.

Takara and Akihana stood behind Kuromoto. The robes they had worn to conceal themselves were gone, revealing that they too were beautifully garbed.

Kuromoto chuckled at their formality. "Please, no more. We are all brothers. There is much to speak of. Come." He turned and walked over to a sliding wood door. Then he opened it and stepped aside for them to enter.

A young girl was seated on a cushion inside. Other cushions had been carefully placed around the room.

Armand entered first, removed his shoes, and then sat as he had learned in the Orient during his travels. The others quickly followed his example, not wanting to insult their host.

Kuromoto joined them, smiling broadly. "Ah, you know our ways."

Armand nodded, still unsure about trusting him.

"This pleases me. It is good when one does not insult one's guest, but it is also a wise man who does not insult his host." Kuromoto glanced at the girl and she got up immediately.

She moved silently around, pouring cups of a dark liquid and handing them to each in turn.

Kuromoto continued to talk, ignoring her presence completely. "You shall enjoy all my humble abode has to offer. I have waited a long time for this moment."

Blake sniffed the cup in his hand. "This is Sake! We can't…"

With a laugh, Kuromoto downed his own drink. "Yes, Sake… laced with blood and completely safe. Honor me and drink. It sits well." The girl refilled his cup and mutely retreated again to her seat.

Blake stared at her. "Doesn't she talk?" he asked. His gaze returned to Kuromoto, his eyes demanding an answer.

"It pleases me for her to be silent. She has been a loyal servant for some five hundred years now," Kuromoto answered, his dark eyes veiled. He gazed intently at Blake.

Angelique interrupted, returning to the purpose of their visit. "Why did you wish to see us, my Lord?" She spoke with the utmost respect. Her curiosity aroused, she was both fascinated and repulsed by him.

Armand sat deep in thought, but he looked up at her question.

"I do not wish disrespect you or your hospitality, my Lord," Angelique continued softly, "but I must confess, I do not know what possible interest you could have in us. We have kept to ourselves for many years now."

Armand downed his drink and laughed in surprise. "Amazing! Hey, Blake, you have to try this!" Then realizing how rude his outburst had been, he looked sheepishly at his host. "Sorry."

Blake glared at him, knowing the potential offense his behavior could give. Then turning to their host, he raised his cup in salute and downed its contents.

Kuromoto nodded in recognition of the apology. Then he began to speak, looking past them as if recounting a distant memory. "I have been alive for uncounted centuries, and have served my noble lord a with honor." He paused. "Three centuries ago I was told of a girl who was brought into our tribe. But before she could be taught our ways, she disappeared. I was dispatched to find her. Find her I did, aboard a ship bound for England. She had succumbed to madness, so I took her with me and healed her. I taught her how to use her power and how to hunt. Then I was ordered to let her prove her ability to survive, as is our custom. I let her go, after erasing all memory of me." Kuromoto stopped and gazed intently at Angelique.

She stared at him in shock. "I put her on another ship and let her continue her journey, but I watched over her for years. I have waited a long time, Angelique. You have done well."

She sat gaping at him. "...And yet I have no memory of you. Why?"

Kuromoto rubbed the scruff on his chin. "Because I took those memories from your mind to protect you. I did not wish for you to come to any harm."

She frowned. "Then you know the man who made me?"

"He is one of us," Kuromoto answered with a smile.

Blake had been quiet up to this point, but now he grew angry. "Am I supposed to believe you let her survive all this time without your help because some higher power ordered you to? How do we know you are telling the truth?"

"Ever the protective and faithful child," Kuromoto answered in amusement. "Did you forget? She is older and stronger than you. She is your master and your maker. You speak as though she were yours to protect."

Blake's eyes flashed dangerously. "I love her and will not let her come to harm! I know she is strong. I also know how much she despises what she has become!"

Angelique held up her hand, stopping him. "I do despise having to feed, but I have grown accustomed to the night and its ways. It has been my well-placed faith in you and Armand that has been behind my complacency."

Kuromoto motioned for them to be silent. "Friends please, I do not wish you to be angry with each other. If you would but give me time, I will share all I know with you. I offer you to come to live here. If you agree, I will send someone to fetch your servants and your belongings this very night. What say you?"

Angelique sat back and thought quietly for a minute. Finally, she looked up. "I would ask that you give us the freedom of knowing how to enter and leave, and that we are roomed near our friends. They are not just our servants." Blake started to speak but she silenced him with a look. Then she her attention back to the man in front of her. "I want to know more about the other Vampyres you spoke of. If my family and I," she waved her hand toward Blake and Armand, "are going to survive, then we need to know more about their society and the laws you spoke of."

Kuromoto smiled broadly. "Already demanding terms. I can see you have grown much since we last met. We will get along well, I think. Come, let us make our plans." He motioned to his servant and without a word, she refilled their cups again.

Blake watched her in silence, disturbed by both her acquiescence and Kuromoto's earlier statement that bordered on tyranny, but he said nothing.

Kuromoto raised his cup and offered a toast. "Here is to a profitable future."

They joined him and raised their cups in unison, each keeping to their own thoughts as they toasted their newfound friend. "To the future!"

Nights passed quickly as they learned of the world they had avoided for so long. Angelique was full of questions, and spent hours talking with Kuromoto or Akihana. They did not see much of Takara, but they hardly noticed.

Blake spent as much time as possible honing his skills and power, determined to gain more strength and ability. He did not trust Kuromoto. Something about the man bothered him, and there were things he found questionable. One night, he mentioned his concerns to Armand.

Armand laughed at him. "You're just jealous of the time Angelique spends with her new tutor." While his companions were learning of Vampyre society, he had been spending his own time studying the laws and learning about their trade industries. He desired to increase his own business again. A servant girl could frequently be found standing silently by to refill his cup with sake. He found this to be a pleasant substitute to feeding, and when mixed with other liquors, the sake still held the ability to intoxicate. His secret pain became easier to manage and gave him a reason to be alone. However, he and Blake did frequently practice swordplay, learning the Eastern techniques from Akihana, who proved quite adept with a blade. Their goals were different though, and they spent weeks merely seeing each other in passing.

Angelique spent little time with Blake at night. She did not reveal the reasons for her thirst of information about the past or present. Her lack of memory disturbed her, and she hoped to regain some small part of them.

Akihana took interest in both Angelique and Genevieve. She spent hours teaching them the ancient herbal medicines of the Orient and their healing power. They learned the art of infusing their work with magic to make it more potent. She whispered secrets of the old ones into their ears, teaching them powerful medicine far more advanced than anything they had ever imagined.

Angelique learned everything she could, rapidly growing in knowledge and strength, and the nights passed in relative peace learning about their new life from Kuromoto and his house. For a while, they forgot the dangers the world outside held for them, but it would not be long before time would find them again.

One night when Angelique, Blake and Armand awakened, they were instructed by Kuromoto to dress for formal court. When they were done, he met them in the front hall. "I am honored. I am also sorry for such short notice, but here they are not as organized as perhaps more civilized parts of the world. Tonight you will meet the Prince and be made known to those who live here. It is the law of their Council. We must go, or we will be late."

As they drove to the court, Angelique stared out the window in silence. *I hope they are willing to accept us. I haven't been in the presence of royalty since I was with my father in Paris.*

They arrived at an immaculately kept manor on the outskirts of the suburbs. The antique estate was surrounded by high stone walls. The only entrance was through large wrought iron gates. Other cars waited in a line to gain admittance while security men at the entrance checked each vehicle. Then they drove up the winding drive to the house and servants opened their doors. The parking was left to the attendants, and they ascended the steps.

When they walked through the grand entryway, Angelique stared at the sight before them. People were everywhere they looked, presumably all Immortals. She whispered to Kuromoto, "They couldn't all possibly be Vampyres...could they?"

He took her arm and guided her toward the main ballroom, while the others followed. "Yes, my dear. They are. Welcome to our society."

The doors were open, and an incredible sight met their eyes. The grand ballroom, lit by candelabras and chandeliers dimmed to a soft glow, was bustling with activity. At the far end, an empty throne sat flanked by two smaller thrones. Above those, a live orchestra played on a balcony that overlooked the room. Couples waltzed on the dance floor, and guests sat at tables, quietly conversing and sharing wine. There were ladies in ball gowns of almost every era. The men were clad in everything from Knight's tunics to modern dress suits, and they were from nearly every corner of the globe.

Angelique sighed in relief. *I had feared I would be out of place in this gown, but that is obviously not the case.*

As they walked through the room, several guests curtsied or bowed, and voiced greetings to Kuromoto. Then Takara and Akihana waved them to a table. As they sat down, the sound of trumpets heralded the arrival of the territory's sovereign.

Two doors opened on the far side of the room and the Prince entered with an entourage of people behind him. Tall and thin, with dark hair and a tan complexion, he reminded her of the gypsies she had seen roaming in the hills near her home in France. The man next to him had long, light brown hair and pale skin, and was slightly taller and better built. Although these two were dressed much like the old aristocracy of Europe, the men with them were all dressed in modern black suits. They took positions around the throne, making it apparent that they were his personal guard. The room buzzed with conversation

Angelique observed the room's occupants, only half listening while Blake and Armand conversed with Takara. She quietly explained what was expected of them when they met the Prince.

Kuromoto smiled at Angelique, patted her hand reassuringly, and then turned his attention to the man on the throne.

# BLOOD FEUD

## Chapter Thirteen
## Building an Empire

*This new World is such a difficult place to survive, yet I find myself drawn to it like a moth to flame. Much of what has happened since our arrival has put my greatest skills to the test, and still I find myself looking for more. The world I left behind seems a dream now. I do not miss it. This place has made me stronger, faster and more resilient than I have ever been. I have seen similar changes in many of those with me. The difficulties we have faced here have pushed them all to their limits, and they have responded with an incredible amount of determination.*

*We have just begun to establish ourselves here in this wilderness and already I am looking to our borders. I know the Renegades are not far, and if they have discovered our presence, then we can expect an attack at some point. The only advantage we have is the fact so many Mastrics came here with me. That at least gives us the advantage of the Spirals to use against them. What I would not give for a few more Mithranians among our numbers though. They are more skilled in battle than most of the Mastrics here and could defend us with far less difficulty.*

*I put Gideon in charge of organizing our defenses while I finish getting the necessary buildings erected underground. Much of what our human counterparts have built could not withstand a skirmish with our enemies, so it is necessary to dig deep in order to have adequate protection should the need arise. The Guild is done, but there are so many other structures to finish. God help us all if I cannot get this area secured. It would be my own people that would go missing. This would have been easier if I were still in command of my army instead of an expedition of wizards and young ones that sought adventure...*

*Lord Reivn Draegon*

\* \* \* \* \*

The new world held many challenges for Reivn and his people, the foremost of which was to establish themselves securely. The first few years after their arrival were spent constructing more than a hundred structures beneath the surface, giving the Alliance a firm grip on the territory. The Guild was the first completed, and with it, a portal that allowed for more efficient travel than ships. With each structure's completion, their numbers grew. Then they built buildings above ground.

Through influence and manipulation, they were able to engineer the growth of not only Amboyle, but other nearby regions as well. Once they had a good foothold on the upper east coast, Reivn sent word to the Council requesting further instructions. Their answer came with the arrival of a new monarch.

Hidden beneath the crowns of the human world, all Vampyre territories had their own sovereignty, and each had its own Lord. Domains were vast, encompassing cities and sometimes entire countries. The Lords that governed them were ruthless and unforgiving, chosen for their power and prestige. The Prince that arrived was no exception.

Lord Sorin Mandrulano was Victulian, and his birthright gave him the power to dominate his brethren. The second moment he arrived, his presence filled their minds... all but Reivn's.

Reivn stood a short distance from the group waiting to greet the new ruler of the territory. He watched in silence, as each of the people he had worked with for years now, bowed before their new sovereign. As he waited for the meeting he knew would come, he wondered what the Council had planned for him, and what the arrival of Lord Sorin would mean to his own future.

Then the greetings ended and Lord Sorin stood in front of him, offering him a scroll. "This is for you," he explained. "New orders, my Lord."

Without a word, Reivn accepted and read it. When he finished, he lowered it to face the man before him. "I am to retain my station here?" he stated, surprised by the letter's contents.

Lord Sorin smiled and shook his hand. "You have taken control of a rather large portion of land, my Lord. It is the Council's wish that you continue to oversee its growth as the first Warlord ever assigned here. You were a Warlord in Europe and have been both Commander and Warlord here. Now you will continue as judge, jury, and executioner to those who would break our tenets." He turned to look at the gathered group. Then he raised his voice. "Lord Reivn has been given the honor of being the first Warlord ever assigned to the New World."

Reivn gazed at his sons, who stood nearby. Their eyes met, and Gideon bowed. Then one by one, those assembled began kissing his ring and congratulating him.

Lunitar approached last, bowed, and kissed his father's hand in silence. He was concerned now that the Council had no intention of letting them return home.

Over the centuries that followed, through the wars that ravaged the colonies and later the newly formed nation, Reivn led campaigns to defend their territories from the Renegades. Using the Revolutionary War and later the Civil War as a front, the Principatus tried repeatedly to take control of the east coast. But the Council regularly sent more troops, building the numbers loyal to them to impressive levels. Amboyle became Perth Amboy and it flourished.

During those years, permission had been openly granted for the creation of children, until they grew too numerous and the Council began having difficulties controlling the population. Then it became law that each new child was to be brought before the Council for approval. It enabled a careful counting of heads that prevented further betrayal within the massive populace of their own people. As the ages passed, newly awakened brought with them new technologies. However, not all awakened wanted the life the Alliance offered and left to join the Principatus. Over time, as their list of names grew, the Book of the Dead was born.

Reivn's primary assignment became that of an executioner. He destroyed countless young ones, and his name was spoken in whispers. When Lord Sorin moved his seat of power to Atlantic City, Reivn was the iron hand that backed him as he brought the population under control. Serena stayed at his side, continuing her slow healing to withdraw the Daemon seed. Her healing was thorough, but he grew cold, as the continuous killing of those who had once been loyal slowly corroded him. Between hunts, he travelled home to Draegonstorm, deep in Australia's mountains, or visited his father at the main guild in London.

One night, while visiting home, an urgent summons arrived from Lord Sorin.

*My Lord Reivn,*

*Several unknowns were recently discovered here. Knowing the Council has listed every child created in the Alliance in the last hundred years or so, the presence of three is too much of an*

*anomaly to ignore. I believe they may be Renegade spies. Your*
*immediate assistance is needed in this matter.*
    *My thanks old friend, SM*

Reivn immediately sent for Lunitar and Gideon.

They entered together and bowed respectfully.

Lunitar look up. "You sent for us, father?"

Reivn motioned for them to sit down. "We're heading back to Atlantic City tomorrow night. There is a matter that needs my immediate attention. Gideon, contact the enforcers and have them rendezvous with us there. Then join me. Lunitar, you are coming with me. Three unknowns have been discovered and have not yet presented themselves. If you consider our enemy's activities of late, they could be spies. Sorin has requested my presence to deal with the matter. Inform Moventius he will be in charge of the Keep. We leave at dusk." With that, he waved a hand in dismissal.

Lunitar bowed again. "I'll let him know. I'll meet you in the portal chamber at the appointed hour, father." Then he turned and left.

After Lunitar closed the door, Gideon cleared his throat. "Father?" he ventured.

Reivn growled. "Yes?"

"I would like to remain here. I feel Gabriel bears watching. He speaks out against you and…" Gideon's words trailed into silence at his father's icy stare.

"Must I remind you that Gabriel is your brother? He is well-tended and does not need you to watch him! We leave at dusk as planned! Now leave me!"

Gideon bowed and swiftly left the room. He went to his quarters, quickly packed, and then dropped onto his bed. He stared at the ceiling. *Father is a fool. He refuses to see the truth. Gabriel will kill him if he gets the chance. That much is certain.* His thoughts troubled, he drifted into sleep.

Reivn finished his plans and headed to the lower levels of his stronghold to see his eldest son.

Gabriel sat reading by candlelight against the far wall of his chamber. His dark hair was tousled and partially covered his face, but piercing eyes, devoid of irises their black depths, missed nothing. He looked up, flexing immense black-feathered wings when Reivn entered, his face showing no emotion. "Father?"

Reivn sat down across from his son. "I must leave again tomorrow night. I am sorry. I had hoped to have a little more time with you."

Gabriel laughed bitterly. "It won't be the first time you've left me alone." He held up a chain attached to the wall. The other end was securely fastened to a collar around his neck. Both chain and collar emanated immense magic. "Take these off me. I am no dog."

"No, my son. I know how many years it has been, but you still have not learned to control yourself," Reivn answered. "Your blood surges through you with far greater ferocity than those of us from human origin. Do not worry. The servants will see to it you have everything you need."

"Take these off and set me free!" Gabriel snapped the chain taught. The collar glowed blue and a spark shot out, encircling his neck. He gasped at the sudden pain.

"You know this is for your own good. Should harm befall you, I could not forgive myself. You must continue to be patient." Reivn moved to Gabriel's side and gently stroked his hair for a moment. "This shall pass." Then he got up and walked to the door. "Until I return, farewell."

Gabriel stared after him, hatred burning in his eyes. *Keep your promises for yourself, you pompous Peacock. The day will come when I will have my vengeance.*

Reivn arrived in Atlantic City the week before Lord Sorin's monthly court was due to convene. Once he settled into the guild, he immediately went to his office and began his investigation. Then after looking over the newest information he was given, he sent for a courier.

Within moments, the courier was at his door. "You sent for me, my lord?"

Reivn looked up. "Yes. Take this letter to Lord Sorin at once. You need not wait for a response." He handed the courier the sealed letter. "Oh, one more thing…"

The Courier paused in the doorway. "Yes, my lord?"

"Do not tell anyone of my arrival," Reivn commanded and dismissed him.

The courier bowed and left.

By the time Reivn had prepared the assignments for his men, Lunitar, who had long been the Commander of his Enforcers, was finished assigning the men their quarters, and had returned to the Warlord's office.

Reivn handed him the lists he would need. "Take the team to these locations," he ordered. "Acquire any available information on these people. I need to know their identities before court."

Lunitar bowed. "When we finish, shall I report in or stay on site and await further orders?"

Before answering, Reivn pulled out another report and quickly read it. Then he looked up, "Return here once you have finished with this. I have something else I need you to do, and the matter will not keep for long."

Lunitar frowned. "May I ask what the mission is, my lord?"

Reivn picked up the report and handed it to his son. "Your sister has run away again. I need you to find her and take her home. I cannot leave here to hunt her down, and her behavior will get her killed if it comes to the attention of the Council."

"I will find her, father. Was there anything else?" Lunitar glanced at the report in his hand.

Reivn shook his head. "No. Say nothing to the others of your mission concerning Mariah. They know better than to question me."

Lunitar nodded and bowed. "As you wish." Then he saluted and walked out.

Reivn got up and walked to the window. His irritation growing, he stared out into the night. *Wherever and whoever you are, you cannot hide from me.*

The Enforcers searched the city for almost a week to locate their quarries hiding places, but they found very little. The unknowns were well hidden, and this worried him. Reivn knew the Shokou Azuma had, at the very least, watched the three. *If they are affiliated with the Eastern Lords, then surely trouble is brewing. There has never been this many of them in one city before.*

The Shokou Azuma were one of two collectives of tribes claiming independence from the great powers that fought the endless war driving much of their society. Through the last few centuries, however, the Eastern Lords had exhibited enough quiet involvement to give rise to the suspicions they had an agenda of their own. That boded ill for Alliance territories.

Reivn had dealt with their kind in the past and did not look forward to dealing with them again. *Judging by what we've found so far, it's probable the unknowns are Shokou Azuma as well, perhaps a deliberate plant to gain access to Lord Sorin's throne*. In frustration, he summoned Gideon and Lunitar back from the hunt.

Gideon arrived first. "You sent for me?"

"Take this report to the Council immediately. I think these three may be Shokou Azuma. That brings the headcount to roughly six or more," Reivn growled. "We never allow more than two... three at the most. This bodes ill for their intent, and the Council must be notified."

Gideon nodded. "Anything else?"

"Yes, let them know the Principatus raids have recently increased." Reivn frowned at the thought. "I'm going to have to be nearby until things cool down again. Ask if they have any specific orders on the matter."

"Yes, my lord." Gideon bowed again, then headed out. He passed Lunitar in the hallway, and the two exchanged silent nods before Lunitar entered Reivn's office.

Reivn looked up from his notes. "Ah… good. I've been waiting for you."

Lunitar bowed. "You asked to see me, my lord?"

Reivn sat back. "Yes. Change of plans. Send one of our most trusted to find your sister in your stead. This issue with the unknowns requires direct handling and I need you here."

"I can dispatch someone now if you wish," Lunitar reported. "I have already completed my nightly reports." He waited, knowing there could be more orders forthcoming.

With a sigh, Reivn began digging through the papers on his desk. "Then make it so. The last thing we need now is for an incident to shed poor light on this family. I have enough to contend with concerning the hunt for Valfort and my duties here."

Lunitar agreed. "It would not be the best of timing," he agreed. "I will have him notify me the moment Mariah is found." Then with a shake of his head, he walked out.

Reivn finished going over the information they had gathered. Then realizing it would soon be dawn, he went down to his chambers to sleep.

The night of the monthly court arrived. When Reivn got to the stately mansion, he dispatched his enforcers around the property. Once they were in position, he went in and headed for the grand ballroom. When he reached the doors, he paused briefly. *Time to find out the truth.*

In the grand hall, the whispered discussions continued while the Prince sat quietly talking with the man beside him. The double doors at the end of the room opened and Reivn strode in, his importance evident as the heralds scrambled to announce his arrival.

*Very important*, Angelique observed as the Prince got to his feet, staring at the newcomer as he approached. She eyed the arrival with curiosity. He was tall, chiseled, and muscular, with a handsome tan complexion. His ebon hair was loose and fell across his back in disarray. He wore a black tunic emblazoned with twin crimson dragons. His black cloak billowed out behind him as he moved.

Kuromoto tapped her on the shoulder. "This ought to be interesting," he whispered in her ear.

"Why?" Angelique asked quietly.

"I don't think Prince Sorin was expecting him," he replied. "He only comes when one of the Tenets has been broken. His name is Lord Reivn Draegon. He is a Council Warlord."

More curious than ever, she stared at Reivn, who now stood speaking to the Prince.

Sorin's expression was grave as he invited Reivn to join him. He accepted and sat in the chair on the Prince's right. Then they sat conversing quietly as the room around them fell silent.

Angelique turned to ask another question, but then a herald announced that court had begun. Her attention was drawn back to the throne, and she watched as three guests went forward to speak with the Prince and visiting Warlord. They were talking so low she could not hear them. She focused her senses to catch what was being said.

"Forget it, Angelique," Kuromoto whispered. "You will not hear them unless they desire you to. We are next."

She looked at him in surprise. "For what?"

He pulled a scroll from within his robe and got up. "...to introduce you to their Prince. It is customary to show respect in this way." He helped Angelique with her chair, then took her arm and led her forward. Blake and Armand followed them in silence.

Unhappy at this new turn of events, Blake was very much on his guard, staying where he could see everything Kuromoto did.

Angelique nervously pulled on the front of her gown. *I have not been face to face with royalty since my mortal years. Please God, do not let me offend the Prince in some way.* For years, they had hidden from the world and never discovered the existence of this society. Now she was going to meet one of its rulers. She tried to appear as calm as possible, but she was terrified. When they reached the Prince, she curtsied low, waiting for his permission to right herself. "Your majesty…"

"Rise. I want to see your face," Sorin commanded in thick, accented English. "What is your name and what brings you into my territory?"

Angelique rose and shyly gazed up at him, unsure how to answer.

Kuromoto squeezed her arm and stepped forward. "My Lord, may I introduce the Comtesse Angelique Marie De Legare and her protégés, Blake Sinclair…the Duke of Kent, and Lord Armand Girard. They are newly arrived in America, having come from the south pacific. They are of my tribe, great lord, so I respectfully claim the right to speak on their behalf." He bowed, and then backed up to stand by her side again.

The Prince cast a glance at Reivn.

With a stone-cold expression, Reivn eyed them carefully.

Sorin frowned. "Lord Kuromoto, just how many more of your tribe should we expect? I was not aware of any decision from the Council recently to change their views on the Shokou Azuma." As he spoke, his eyes never left Angelique or her children.

Kuromoto bowed again. "There has been no change in our state of affairs, Prince Sorin. We are, however, trying to forge a negotiation toward this end." He waved his hand toward her. "These three are not involved in our politics." He pointed at Angelique. "I knew her some time ago. She was in need of help and became family. Surely you would not begrudge a man the presence of his family?"

The room fell deathly quiet. Sorin stared at them in silence, deep in thought. *If I grant them freedom here, it could be disastrous, yet to outright deny them could start a tribal war.* Finally, he nodded. "Very well. I will allow them to remain for now, but they must swear loyalty to me and our laws. Lady, you and yours approach and state to the crown where your allegiance lies." He held out his hand, his signet ring glinting in the candlelight.

"I serve you, my Lord, as I loyally served the crown of France in the past. I swear I will learn and obey your laws, as will my family. I swear this on my honor." She curtsied, and then kissed his ring as she remembered her father doing long ago. Then she stepped back and raised her eyes to meet his.

Blake and Armand followed her example, believing this to be much as the courts of England and France had been.

Reivn telepathied Sorin. *The Shokou Azuma never swear themselves to the Alliance. Something is amiss here...*

Sorin made no outward indication he had heard, but he answered Reivn. *They definitely bear watching. I sense absolutely nothing from her. A Haka Kami perhaps? They are the most secretive and deadliest of the Eastern sects.*

His eyes shifting to look over the girl again, Reivn responded. *I do not yet know. If she is, I will uncover the truth. Dismiss her for now.*

"You may stay... for now." Sorin waved Angelique and her companions on.

The group was quiet as they walked back to their seats, memories of the past and thoughts of the future blending together in a jumble of mixed emotions. Finally, Angelique stopped and turned to Kuromoto, full of questions. "Is it always so... intense? He seemed to dislike our presence. Why?"

"Those in power always mistrust those from foreign shores. Our tribe has never been accepted by the Alliance. Now, you must excuse me. I have other matters to see to." Kuromoto bowed and walked away, leaving her standing alone in the middle of the room.

Formal court went on for another hour while the Prince handled the business of those in his territory. Then he declared the remainder of the night to be a social affair.

After formalities had concluded, Angelique walked the room, seeking solitude. When she passed by the open doors to the gardens, she overheard soft voices outside. She moved closer and listened, hoping to learn more about this place she now called home. Her eyes widened when she heard the conversation unfold. She recognized one of the two voices and it caused her stomach to knot in fear.

"If you do it tonight, then we have the perfect alibi. The newcomers will be suspected, and we would suffer no losses. Just take the passage to the room and wait for my signal." Kuromoto paused. "This will render him unconscious. Then you can cut out his heart. Feast on it if you wish, but bring me his ring as proof."

She strained to hear them more clearly. *Who are they planning to kill?* she wondered. Their next words answered her question.

"What if Prince Sorin suspects us? He will have his guard cut us down before I can even get close enough to poison him, much less kill him."

Kuromoto answered his unknown accomplice. "I will keep him distracted with the Comtesse until you are in place. I noticed how he looked at her. Now... we must go our separate ways. Someone will notice one of us is missing and start asking questions."

Angelique moved as quickly as she could without drawing attention to herself and scurried away from the doors. Then she pretended to be admiring the décor of the room. Kuromoto and his companion barely cast a glance her way when they walked past. She carefully studied the stranger, realizing he was the same one she had seen Kuromoto talking to earlier that evening.

*What are we going to do?* she wondered. *This will get us all killed.* She looked hastily around until she spotted Blake and Armand chatting with a couple of guests. Then she headed toward them. She jumped when someone grabbed her arm.

"What's the matter, Angelique? You have are quite pale. Are you ill?" Kuromoto stared at her in apparent concern.

Angelique wondered if he suspected that she knew. "I am just nervous being around so many of our kind. I've never done anything like this before." Putting on an innocent face, she smiled.

He relaxed his grip and glanced first at Blake, and then over at the Prince. Then he smiled. "I want to take you to Prince Sorin when he's done talking with his staff. I am sure he has more questions for you."

Angelique played along. "I will join you in a few minutes. I need to speak to Blake privately. We've quarreled tonight." She tried to look as though this saddened her. Her charade worked.

Kuromoto smiled at her. "Then go. Take care of your problem. I will join you when you are finished. There is still time."

She watched his back as he walked away. She was worried. *I have to tell Blake and Armand*, she decided and hurried across the room.

Blake looked up when she approached. Seeing her face, he quickly pulled her off to the side where no one would hear them. "What's wrong? You look scared to death."

She whispered so no one could hear her. "We have a very serious problem. Where's Armand? I need to talk to you both right now!"

Moments later, she stood quietly explaining what she had heard. Blake was not at all surprised to hear Kuromoto was planning to murder the

Prince. "I knew there was something not right about him! And he is planning to use us as bait! I should have killed him when I had the chance!"

Angelique put her hand on his arm and shot him a warning look. "Be careful, Blake. You are getting too angry. Someone will hear you. We need to figure out what we are going to do. We just gave our loyalty to the Prince! We cannot allow this to happen!"

Armand tapped her arm and the three of them fell silent as one of the patrons passed within earshot. "You must be careful, Angelique. Many of the guests are asking questions about you."

She stared at him. "About me? Why?"

Armand shrugged. "I don't know. No one is talking. I overheard it in conversation, but when I asked, they avoided the question."

With a groan, she buried her face against Blake's chest. "Oh! What are we going to do?"

Blake put his arms around her. "Don't worry, love. We're going to be just fine. I think we need to talk to Lord Sorin… now." He took her hand and dragged her across the room. Then he began waving his hand at the Prince. "My Lord, a moment!"

She protested, trying to pull away. "Blake, what are you doing?"

He grinned at her. "Improvising! Just play along. We need an excuse to get close to the Prince without Kuromoto suspecting us." He continued pushing forward. "Your highness! Lord Sorin! A moment, please! I have a wonderful announcement and a request of your majesty!"

Sorin turned from his conversation to see what the commotion was about. Upon seeing the couple moving rapidly toward him, he held up his hand to the guards. Immediately they converged on the two and restrained them.

Blake would not give up. "Your majesty, she has just consented to be my wife! Please, I would ask that you bless our union and perform the ceremony! In England, it is tradition to have a formal ceremony! I do not wish to dishonor my bride!"

At the back of the room, Armand watched in amazement. Blake's performance had been flawless, and most of the guests were shouting their congratulations. He shook his head. *That took guts.* He could not help but wish it was he who stood at her side.

Sorin motioned for his guards to let them approach. His eyes told Blake he would cut them down if they made one wrong move.

Blake bowed respectfully, and then lowered his voice. "Your highness, you are in grave danger. My lady discovered a plot against you. They are planning to murder you."

Sorin frowned. "What is this?" he asked. "What are you saying? What do you mean?"

Angelique cringed inwardly and dropped into a deep curtsy. "Please my Lord, you must believe me! I overheard Kuromoto and another man talking on the veranda! They weren't aware of my presence! They spoke of a passage behind the throne and a private room!" she paused, nauseated at the images her mind threw at her. "They spoke of cutting your heart out!"

Reivn leaned forward, his eyes on her. "I will speak with her alone!"

The prince waved his hand and Angelique was escorted to the doors the prince had entered from earlier that night. The guards restrained Blake and he watched helplessly. *What have I done?* he wondered fearfully. He stopped struggling, his shoulders sagging as he admitted defeat. "Your highness, she is innocent of any wrongdoing! If one of us must die, then take my life for hers!"

Sorin glared at him. "Be silent! Lord Reivn is merely going to question her. You will await his return!"

When they were alone, Angelique stood fearfully before Reivn. She knew only what she had been told. *He intends to kill me.*

Reivn looked down at her, a serious expression on his face. "You are from the East, yet you look of the West and betray your brethren with news of a plot against our Prince. Why?"

She held her chin up in defiance, refusing to show her fear. "It was my duty to the crown."

Amused by her answer, Reivn merely circled around behind her and cupped his hand around her neck. "Not good enough. I could destroy you right now and none would question it. You do not hold the protection of the throne. Now…answer the question!"

Realizing the truth behind his words, she replied, "I have been a member of the aristocracy for over three hundred years, my lord. What blue blood do you know that does not follow a royal banner? I have no memory of the Easterners before here, or any of your other tribes for that matter. I did not even know of the existence of your society until I traveled here from the Caribbean." While he silently digested her answer, she studied his face. He was rugged and good-looking, and appeared noble-born. She suspected from his long, dark hair and accent that he was from somewhere in Romania.

He interrupted her thoughts. "I will search your mind. If you permit me to do so unchallenged, it will be painless. Resist me and you will regret it." Without waiting for a response, he cupped her head in his hand and reached out with his mind.

Immediately invasive, she could feel his presence inside her. Her memories raced forward as though being ripped from her at super speed, and everything she had been through over the last three hundred years replayed itself as he searched for the information he sought. "Please... don't make me see this again," she begged.

*What are you so afraid of, Angelique?* Reivn whispered in her thoughts, his voice echoing in her head. *If you are innocent, then you have nothing to fear. I will not harm you.*

Angelique tried to pull away and pain ripped through her as an iron grip held her, her mind unable to break free. She cried out.

He spoke into her mind again, trying to calm her. *You have magic and knowledge. Why do you refuse to accept your nature?*

Terrified, she fought him as his invasion drove further, until her agony grew to unbearable levels. As he searched her mind, the image of a familiar face appeared. In shock, he withdrew from her with sudden deliberation.

She dropped unconscious into his arms.
"It would appear there is more to you than meets the eye." He picked her up. "Foolish child," he muttered softly, carrying her to the sofa where he gently laid her down. "It would not have hurt if you had just let me see the proof of your innocence unchallenged."

He stared down at her and frowned. With cold deliberation, he crossed the room, threw open the door, and signaled the guards. "Stay with her... and bring those two fools back here with her. They have no doubt given her up for dead already!" He was surprised at the contempt in his own voice. Annoyed with himself for the second time, he left the room without a backward glance. *This problem needs to be handled first. The other must wait.* With that in mind, Reivn returned to the grand hall, leaving all thought of the girl in the room behind him aside.

## Chapter Fourteen
## Guest or Prisoner

*A wise man once said that everything happens for a reason. You may not always see it when you first face the situation, but if you look hard enough it is indeed there. These unidentified young... why are the Shokou Azuma so interested in them? I feel the two are somehow linked, and yet there is no ascertainable connection. They have joined the Eastern Lords, but I do not believe they are truly of Eastern origin. All three are of European blood, and it is exceedingly rare for the Shokou Azuma to make children outside the Orient. The chance of this many in existence in one place is almost impossible.*

*I spoke at length with Sorin after my men and I arrived in Atlantic City, and he knew I planned the late entrance to court. If I am right, my sudden appearance caught at least the newcomers off guard. I have not yet ordered their extermination, as I first intend to find out as much about them as possible. I want to know who they are. Not spies surely, but what then? They do not appear to be young, but I have never heard of any Elders not listed in the tribal genealogy books. Gideon has reported what little information I have to the Council, but there is more here.*

*Our hold on North America has strengthened considerably in the last two decades, and our enemies are growing. I warned Sorin of the possibility of an attack, and the tribal Prefects have all been alerted. Still, their young are not as strong as their Elders. Even now, I am seeking possible ways to use new weapons and techniques to our advantage. Defending our territory was never more important than now. God help us all if we go to war with the Easterners as well...*

*Lord Reivn Draegon*

\* \* \* \* \*

Later that night, Angelique awoke to Blake sitting beside her, holding his head in his hands. Armand was a few feet away, staring at the fire burning in the hearth. Four guards stood near the doors, watching them silently.

She touched Blake's hand. "What happened?"

With a start, he looked up. "Thank God! You're awake! It's been hours since..." He wrapped his arms around her, his voice hoarse with worry.

Armand joined them and waited until Blake calmed down. "There has been all kinds of commotion out there, but we don't know anything yet."

She looked up at him and frowned. "No one has come in to question you? Did they catch Lord Kuromoto? And what of Takara and Akihana?

At each name, they shook their heads silently. They had been in the room under guard since Reivn had emerged from his interrogation of Angelique and had neither been spoken to nor given any information.

Then she sat up and discovered how much her head hurt from her encounter with Reivn. She moaned in pain.

Blake tried to help her when she got up from the sofa, but she shook him off. Then in agitation, she walked up to one of the guards. "I don't know your name or what your orders are, but I want to see someone with the authority to speak with me. If this is not possible then I demand to know why we are being held and on what charge. If I am not accused of any crime, then I wish to return to my own lair."

The guard eyed her for a second, then turned and left the room.

He was back minutes later and resumed his position. "You will be seen shortly." He said, ignoring any further attempts to converse with him.

Annoyed and wanting answers, Angelique walked over and sat back down.

Blake paced back and forth, his thoughts dark. Then he stopped and glanced at Armand, who had retreated to the hearth again.

Finally, Angelique broke the silence. "We can expect punishment unless we can somehow prove Kuromoto's treachery. He may have been acting alone. If so, then our own people may hunt him. The problem is we have no idea where to find them."

Blake frowned. "We need to find out if anyone here knows how to contact the Shokou Azuma. It may be the only way to protect ourselves at this point."

Their conversation ended abruptly when the door opened, and three men walked in.

Angelique and Blake got up.

One was the man who had entered with the Prince during court. Now Angelique stared at him. He was tall and well cut, with long light brown hair and hazel eyes. The other two men she did not recognize.

One of them approached. "I am Lord Lunitar Draegon. My companions are Lord Gareth Sutherland, the High Chancellor of this territory, and Franz von Thalberg. I apologize for the length of time you have been detained, but we had to be sure."

Angelique curtsied, and then studied them carefully.

Of Germanic origin, Franz was stocky and of medium height. His blonde hair was a mass of unkempt curls that fell in his face, and his tanned complexion spoke of sun-filled years before his awakening. His eyes carried a smile, though he presently wore a more serious expression.

The man talking to her was tall and well built, with a chiseled physique and long white hair. The respect the other two gave him told her he was the one to worry about. "Sure of what, my Lord?" she asked, turning her attention back to him and boldly meeting his eyes.

Lunitar met her gaze with a steely-eyed expression. "…sure that the plot you overheard was of factual content and not a trap. You have done a great service this night and on behalf of Lord Reivn and the Alliance, I thank you."

Angelique hesitated. "If we are not in any trouble, then why are we being detained?"

"For your safety and that of others," Lunitar replied, motioning for her to take a seat. "You have revealed a plot to kill a territory Prince, which is an act of treason. The question is... how did you come by this information?"

Gareth walked over and joined Armand by the fire, listening in silence.

Franz sat down in a chair not far from the door, and he too, was quiet.

"We explained that to Lord Reivn before he interrogated Angelique!" Blake growled. "She overheard Kuromoto plotting against the Prince during court. Why do you question this?"

Lunitar glanced at Blake before continuing. "Why you were so opportunistically placed to overhear said conversation?"

Angelique started to answer, but Blake silenced her. "I was not! Only the lady was, and that only because she was exploring the room. She has never been here before and thought the architecture beautiful enough to warrant a closer look! Is that illegal?"

Lunitar looked first at Angelique, and then at Blake. "Who is the Elder here?"

Angelique put her hand on Blake's arm and silenced him. "I am, my lord. He and Armand usually protect me, so he is used to answering such questions."

"Very well. Then I will have the rest of this conversation with you alone," Lunitar stated, frowning at Blake and his blatant irregularity of protocol. "As by your prodigy's admission, you have first-hand knowledge of tonight's events. This brings me back to my original statement… you were detained for your protection and the protection of others."

Confused now, Angelique turned and glanced at Blake. "Should not Blake be the one you speak with since he usually handles all our affairs?"

Lunitar sighed in irritation. "Tonight, Blake will not be handling your affairs or answering questions. Speak truthfully, for your answers will determine whether you are guest or prisoner."

Angelique involuntarily shuddered, and her eyes widened. "I don't understand! We have obeyed every directive given us since our arrival! I have always been loyal to the crown, even when France was in a state of revolution!"

From near the door, a snort rose as Franz tried to muffle his laughter.

Gareth had also turned around, raising an eyebrow at her comment.

Lunitar gaped at her in disbelief. "What?" He shook his head. "Do you have any idea where you are and how much trouble you could be in?"

Angelique glared at him. "Yes, I understand! We betrayed our tribe tonight and they may well hunt us because of it, but shouldn't loyalty to the crown come first? Treason is treason, regardless of the family from whence it originates. As I'm sure you know, this is not the first time an aristocrat has turned in one of their own to preserve the sanctity of the throne and their own name among the court!"

Lunitar frowned. "Well, it is safe to assume you know absolutely nothing of the Alliance or the potential danger you face. You speak as if you're dealing with the old… aristocracy, I guess. The Prince I speak of is a territory Prince of the Alliance, not of any national affiliation. He rules this territory, but he also serves a more powerful entity known as the Alliance Council."

Blake stood fuming behind her. He growled at Lunitar. "Is it not the same thing? A crown is a crown, whether it is in France or a much wider area, such as the church holds, ruling over many countries with their religious laws!"

Lunitar's gaze did not leave Angelique, but he drew his blade so fast on Blake she barely saw it, stopping at his neck and leaving a shallow cut that wept droplets of blood. "I told you he will not answer for you tonight. Next time, I will not stop. All three of you sit down… now."

In shock, Angelique grabbed Blake's arm and pulled him down to the sofa with her. Armand, walked over and sat down beside her as well, gazing at Lunitar boldly.

Blake glared at Lunitar, his anger rising.

Worried one of them would further anger the man, Angelique placed a hand on each of them, asking them to calm themselves through her gentle touch. Then she turned her attention back to Lunitar. "My apologies, my lord. None of us seeks to offend you. We are still new to your society and have not yet had time to learn your ways. I do not understand why Blake cannot speak his mind. He is my equal as is Armand. We have been thus since we were children."

"It is apparent you have not noticed that the world you now exist in is far different and much more dangerous than that of your childhood," he replied, keeping his own temper in check. "Let me explain to you how our world operates, and exactly what transpired tonight."

Angelique and her companions spent the next half hour listening to what had happened after their revelation. They also heard for the first time the truth behind the Council, their laws and how the tribes came to terms of peace.

Amazed at all the things Kuromoto had not told her, Angelique asked dozens of questions.

Lunitar answered each one patiently, amazed at how little she and her children knew. Then the question came around to how Blake and Armand had offended Lunitar when the conversation had first begun. "By speaking out of turn, Blake was actually being what is considered rude because he is your prodigy and you his master," he explained. "As such, in all official capacities, it is the senior ranked who speaks and the lesser ranked who remain silent unless asked to do otherwise. During social periods and equal interaction they can speak freely, provided they are released to their own and not still in your thrall."

Angelique dropped her gaze in embarrassment. "I am terribly sorry we offended you. We were not aware of that particular custom. In fact, it was only hinted at when we first met Lord Kuromoto. For tonight, he merely stated he would speak on our behalf when we first met your Prince. He never explained that this was a rule here. Had any of us known... we would have followed protocol and shown the decorum this society demands. We are all from the aristocracy, albeit that of the human world, but we do understand the need for rules. As for their being released... I'm not sure I understand your meaning."

Gareth gasped and turned to stare at them in shock.

Franz shook his head and put a finger to his lips.

Lunitar looked at her in surprise. "You court death in more ways than you know. Have you released them or not?"

Angelique frowned. "I don't understand the question. They have been with me since their change, but they have always been free to travel where they will, if that's what you mean. They simply chose to remain with me."

Lunitar laughed outright at her explanation. "I do not mean to be rude, but how have you three survived this long being this ignorant?"

Franz chuckled in amusement and Lunitar shot him a dark look.

Gareth feigned a cough to smother his laughter behind his hand and focused on the fire, knowing any further interruption would merely irritate Lord Reivn's son.

Angelique glared at Lunitar indignantly. "Forgive my boldness, my lord, but I am hardly ignorant! I am a well-educated woman!"

"It is good to know you are educated," Lunitar stated, sobering immediately when he realized she truly did not understand what he meant. "Understand that by not being trained yourself, it is easy for you to misstep and be put to death. By not training your thralls and releasing them, they have the same potential. You could be put to death for their lack of training. You should also know that Blake's glaring at me is an open challenge, and gives me the right to kill him, as well as your other companion with his unspoken ill will. And though competent they may be, they are sorely outmatched, and I am about the average you will meet."

Angelique sat back and stared at him in confusion. "But I just told you they have been free since their first night with me. I do not make them stay. That was their choice. Are you telling me they must leave me to be considered free in their own right? Moreover, they were trained. We all were... by Lord Kuromoto."

Lunitar sighed and shook his head. "The fact we are having this conversation at all tells me you are not properly trained. Any fledgling or thrall knows all we have discussed and more. So, considering this latest information, we will continue to detain you for your own protection."

Angelique interrupted him. "Our training was with our own tribe. Perhaps the Eastern Lords do not require the differences you mentioned. Lord Kuromoto was quite thorough in teaching us healing herbs and how to use our sight, hearing, and speed. He even had Blake and Armand trained in the ways of the sword, though they already knew it well."

Gareth turned and opened his mouth to speak, but Lunitar shot him a warning look. So, he walked over to Franz, where he began conversing in whispered tones, so as not to interrupt the ongoing interrogation.

Lunitar turned his attention back to Angelique. "It is not my intention to insult you or belittle your training, but you must understand. I was able to mark Blake in the blink of an eye, and I am considered merely an adequate swordsman."

Franz snickered and glanced knowingly at Gareth.

Lunitar ignored them and continued. "My skills lie more heavily in the arcane. I have been well trained by my sire. and I know better than to approach a Prince in the manner you did. You were lucky you weren't executed then. Had my father's enforcers been in charge, you wouldn't have gotten within three feet of the throne. There is a lot more to training than just the sword or herbs. Albeit they are important, protocol is just as much so, and it is in that you seriously lack. As you have seen, in our world ignorance of this nature can be a death sentence."

Angelique caught her breath. "If this is true, then what must we do to learn the rest of your ways? Surely there is some way we can prove ourselves."

Lunitar got up. "All in good time. For now, it is almost dawn. I need to report to his lordship and attend to the rest of my duties. I promise you that you can discuss this more tomorrow night. I believe Lord Gareth can offer you a place of safety for the day."

Gareth walked over. "I can, my lord. We will give them safe haven tonight. Franz will escort them down to the day-chambers and get them settled in."

Angelique looked warily at them. "Then are we guests? Or are we still being detained? I would like to think we have proved our loyalty and are free to go tomorrow after sunset."

Lunitar walked to the door, then stopped to answer her. "That is for Lord Reivn to decide. For the moment, just accept that it is enough you have survived the night. Go and rest. This will all be settled soon enough. We will let you call yourselves guests of the crown tonight."

"Thank you." Angelique curtsied and accepted his offer, nodding to Blake.

After bidding Lunitar and Gareth a respectful good day, they followed Franz through the doors and down the hall. From there they went down a staircase until they came to a wide underground corridor lit only by candlelight. Here there were rows of doors, each thick and well-made of heavy oak, and fitted with a custom lock.

Franz stopped before one of these and turned. "I will put you in here," he stated to Angelique in thickly accented English. He motioned toward the door.

"I am staying with her," Blake stated, pulling her close.

Franz smiled. "If we were going to harm her, we would have done so already. You are safe here." Opening the door for them, he handed Blake the key. "Lock it if you wish. Most of us here don't bother. It makes it more difficult for the servants to get in at dusk to attend your needs." He bowed and motioned for Armand to follow him.

After looking at Blake and Angelique for a second, Armand followed him to the next door.

Franz opened the door and handed Armand his key, then bid them all a good day and disappeared into a room further down the hall.

Armand shrugged and went into his room, closing and locking the door behind him. Then he settled onto the bed and wearily closed his eyes.

Angelique and Blake had already settled into each other's arms. Angelique felt safe in his arms, but her mind wandered. She thought about how worried he had been when she had revived earlier. *God, we should have married years ago. He loves me so much...*

Blake caught her gaze and kissed her softly. His own thoughts were drastically different from hers. They were shadowed by the fact he now knew this society's existence spanned the world over. *What it means for us is there is no place we will ever be safe if we turn away from these people we are now a part of.* He knew they needed to learn a completely new way of survival or die. He fought off sleep long after Angelique and lay watching her. He was still thinking of her when he finally drifted into sleep.

When they rose the following evening, they were surprised to find Genevieve waiting for them. "Ruben is in the other room with Armand. We were brought here in the Prince's own Limousine," Genevieve explained. "I have never ridden in one before. It was exciting." Rushing to help her mistress, she prattled on about their retrieval from Kuromoto's lair. "None of them had returned when we left, so I hope it won't be a problem later."

Angelique listened absent-mindedly to Genevieve's chatter, her mind on the night ahead.

Blake walked over and kissed her cheek. "It's going to be fine, but if you continue to scowl like that you will chase away any allies as well as enemies. Calm yourself."

Angelique tried to relax. "I wonder who will be speaking with us." She tried not to let fear edge into her voice.

He got up and wrapped his arms around her. "You have a singular thought process, my love," he laughed. "I told you, we will be fine. If they had any intention of killing us, they would have already done so. They have had plenty of opportunities."

"What if they were just waiting until they found Kuromoto?" she blurted out. "He did say he was going to blame it on us! I don't want to have to try and fight our way out! There's too many of them! And what of the Shokou Azuma? Will they hunt us as traitors?" Agitated, she tried to pull away, but he held her fast.

"Come on, Angelique." He kissed her forehead. "You've toughed it out with worse situations than this before."

She gaped at him. "What? When have we ever had a situation this bad before?"

Blake hugged her, laughing again. "Last night when we were out cold… it would have been a lot harder to run."

A sound interrupted them, and they turned to see Franz quietly waiting to speak to them. "I could not help but overhear the end of your conversation, and I apologize for the intrusion. His Lordship, Prince Sorin, requests your presence in his private study. Rest assured, my Lady. You are in no danger. His Lordship does not hold you responsible for the actions of Kuromoto or his co-conspirators. Please, when you are ready, I will take you to him." He bowed respectfully and stepped out to wait in the hall.

After exchanging quick glances, they joined him.

Armand was already waiting, and the three of them followed Franz in silence to the waiting Prince's private quarters.

The hall led to a set of winding stairs going further downward.

To their surprise, Franz held up his hand and mumbled something incoherent. Instantly, a ball of light appeared in the palm of his hand. Then he moved forward and down into the gloom.

Uncertain as to their fate, they followed him down into the darkness and the unknown...

## Chapter Fifteen
## New Beginnings

*Events have played out we had not even guessed at and I am, for once, pleased with the results. Whatever the plans of the Shokou Azuma, the new arrivals did not join them. They turned on Kuromoto, showing remarkable loyalty to the crown. Perhaps this is why the Shokou Azuma do not usually make children of European people. They do not hold to the same ideas as those born in Eastern lands.*

*I have made a discovery so incredible it defies explanation, but I am not yet sure what it means. I have much to consider. If I am right, this could change everything. The newcomers' demeanor and attitude all show an amazing devotion to the throne I would not have thought possible. I must find out more about them. I plan to see to it they do not leave here anytime soon, if ever. This is a most opportune circumstance, and it may open doors we have never before been able to breach.*

*We sent a hunting party to collect Kuromoto and his followers, but they returned empty-handed. This is dangerous for the lady and her kin. Kuromoto will not so easily forgive their betrayal. I must use this to my advantage. In putting them under the protection of the throne here, it will give me time to seek the information I want from them.*

*The woman Angelique, the face I saw in her mind... his face. God, could it be? And if it is true, then what of Council law? She saved the life of a prince tonight. Can I repay this with giving her death? I need answers now... before Gideon returns with the Council's orders. I need to know the truth...*

*Lord Reivn Draegon*

* * * * *

Later that night Angelique, Blake and Armand left Prince Sorin's study to return to the hotel they had originally stayed in. They had been released with the agreement not to leave the territory, and to appear at the next court. In the meantime, they were to familiarize themselves with their new society. Their minds reeled at the information revealed to them. Each of them realized a new way of life had intruded into their secluded world... one that would never let them go. They left the manor in silence... completely unaware they were being watched.

Lunitar kept his distance so they would be oblivious to his presence. His orders were clear... keep an eye on them until the questions surrounding them were answered.

They were quiet on the drive back, until Angelique could not take it anymore. "I am amazed this society has existed for so many centuries," she said uneasily. "...and yet somehow we managed to never be a part of it until now."

Blake shrugged. "Luck I guess...if you can call it that. There is so much about our kind we don't know. Even the knowledge we have of our power is limited. There are many things we need to learn, and learn fast, if we are to survive."

Armand stared out the window, his thoughts very dark.

Angelique looked at him and sighed. "I spoke to Franz before we left. He wants to teach us."

Armand turned around. "Has either one of you thought about how much like a dictatorship this society seems to be? It's as though their laws are the only way you are allowed to live and there's nothing else."

Blake looked at him sharply. "Careful, Armand! Statements like that border on treason and will get us killed. We don't really know enough about this society yet to make that judgment. Has it occurred to you the reason they are giving us a crash course in their laws is so that we don't follow in Kuromoto's footsteps?"

Angelique stared at them in fright. "Don't you understand? Did you listen to anything we were told? Our kind are everywhere! Some are so old and powerful we can't even sense what they are unless they want us to!"

Armand put his arm around her to comfort her.

Blake glanced at the driver, frowned, and telepathied them. *Keep it down. We don't want the driver to hear.* Then he reached across the seat and put his hand on her knee. "I'm not going to let anything happen to you. We are protected for now, and perhaps in time we will be accepted."

They arrived at the hotel and settled in. All their belongings had been sent there with Ruben and Genevieve, who were waiting in their rooms.

Ruben greeted them with worried looks. "What happened? Did they capture Kuromoto and the others? No one said a word when they brought us here! They treated us more like property..." His voice trailed off when he saw their faces. Silence filled the room

Angelique sat down on the bed. "We talked extensively with Lord Sorin about last night's events. Kuromoto was questioned by the Prince about the plot he and his co-conspirators planned. But then Akihana and Takara rescued him by something called shadow-walking. We don't know what that is, but it does mean they escaped."

"When the Warlord went to the warehouse, they found it boarded up and empty," Blake added. "There was no sign of the palace, or Kuromoto and the others. The warehouse looked as though it hadn't been used in years. Don't ask me to explain that because I can't."

Angelique reached out and caught his hand, silencing him. "We have learned a great deal about this society we've become a part of. Everyone has their place here. We will win ours too. I am weary. Blake please..."

He helped her up.

Bidding the others goodnight, they left for their own room.

Once they were alone, Blake wrapped his arms around Angelique and pulled her close, his mind racing ahead. "If we are going to stay here, then I should travel back to Europe to deal with our estates. It has been awhile since we have returned home. Even though the descendants are still loyal to our secrets, I do not wish to strain the relationship by staying away too long."

Angelique buried her face against his chest, so he scooped her up and carried her to the bed. "Let's forget it tonight. There is time enough to talk tomorrow. For now, you need rest. I can..." Blake stopped as she pulled him on top of her, wrapping her arms around his neck.

"Hold me?" she whispered.

Blake whispered his love as they passed precious moments intertwined in each other's arms. He saw her as no one else would. She was gentle, delicate and vulnerable, and needed his protection to survive. He did not see the killer that had become a part of her. He could not. To him, she was still the innocent girl he loved in his youth. Her eyes, however, betrayed the truth, telling a much different story for those who cared to see. Behind their veil was the drive to survive that is the eternal part of every Vampyre.

Angelique was desperate to cling to the past, but things had changed for them all. Her fear for the future was that this war of tribes would bring death to their family. "What if Kuromoto retaliates for our betrayal, Blake?" she asked. "What are you going to do if they come after you? If you go back to England now, you'll be a target. The three of us have been able to survive together, but it's been years since any of us traveled alone. Who will watch your back?"

Blake hugged her tight. "I will be fine, and I'll be back before you know it. If we learned nothing else tonight, we know Vampyre law is harsh and that it exists in England as it does here. That enables us to travel without fear." He kissed her again. "Now sleep, love."

In the adjacent room, Armand was talking with Ruben. He had rightly guessed that Blake would want to travel back to England, leaving the rest of them behind. "We've always gone together, but now it makes more sense to stay and learn all we can. But I am worried he may be too over-confident. One of us should travel with him just to keep an eye on him."

Ruben agreed. "I can go. That will leave you free to watch over the ladies. I'd feel better knowing they were not alone."

They both knew the philosophy of safety in numbers was a true one, and neither had any intention of leaving the others to their own devices to survive. After deciding to discuss the matter with Blake later, the two got up to deal with their nightly routine.

Ruben went to get Blake and Angelique, aware they may have forgotten the time.

Armand headed down to the lobby. Feeding would not be difficult. There were plenty of guests in the hotel. *Someone's going to wake up in the morning blaming the beds for a bad night's sleep,* he half-joked to himself. He had time to look around, so he explored the layout and security of the building. By taking careful note of the cameras' placements, he knew exactly which rooms to avoid. When Angelique and Blake finally joined him, he told them all they needed to know to keep their activities a secret.

After they fed, they all gathered in Angelique's room.

Angelique was against Blake's leaving. "I don't want us to be separated!" she argued. "It isn't safe, and I don't want to lose you again!"

Blake was firm about his plans. "I need to go to the estates to take care of business, love. Then I will return. Don't worry so."

Not wanting Angelique to get more upset, Ruben interrupted. "I have things I need to do at the chateau as well, so I'd like to travel with you, Blake. It's more convenient if we are together and it gives us the chance to watch each other's backs."

Angelique frowned. "You know very well this isn't a good idea. Until they find Kuromoto, we should all stay together!"

Blake smiled at her. "You're beautiful when you're angry, did you know that?"

In response, she merely glared at him.

With the departure date set, they settled in for the day. Ruben began his watch and Armand left for his room after saying a quick goodnight.

Once they were alone, Angelique curled up to Blake. He wrapped his arms around her as she drifted into slumber. She did not even hear him when he kissed her forehead and whispered, "Goodnight love, I'll see you in your dreams. I love you too."

They awakened that night to a messenger waiting for Angelique with an invitation from Franz. She accepted and quickly dressed for the occasion.

Blake decided to escort her, so she would not be alone. "Perhaps he wants to know more about us," he suggested with a smile. "It's not unusual to exchange information in a social visit. In the old-world style, remember?" He was not as convinced as he pretended, but he did not want her to worry. *Besides*, he reminded himself, *that's why I'm going to be there.*

Two hours later, Blake and Angelique stepped from the car and climbed the staircase to the main doors of the building. Angelique grew apprehensive as they approached and hesitated.

Before she could change her mind, the doors opened, and Franz stepped out to greet them. "My friends! I did not expect you both, but you are most welcome! Please come in!" He walked inside, hiding his apprehension. Reivn's orders had been very clear. *How am I supposed to get some of her blood without raising Blake's suspicions?* "I took the liberty of having a meal prepared. Then we'll walk in the gardens."

Angelique interrupted nervously. "A meal? But we don't…"

Franz's laughter kept her from finishing her sentence. "You really were out of touch with our world. Had you even met any others like us before now?" He stopped to look at them.

Blake and Angelique both shook their heads.

"We stayed as far away from populated areas as possible, only taking a few human servants where we lived, so we could feed while they slept." She paused. "We never killed. We felt it too risky, and I have never wanted to do so. Even with Kuromoto, we did not try food, only the Sake' he was so fond of. All feeding was just that."

Blake sensed she was uneasy and squeezed her hand.

There was an uncomfortable moment where it seemed as if Franz were judging their responses, but then he shrugged. Then with a smile, he led them inside.

Franz pushed open at pair of double doors, then stepped aside to reveal a great dining hall. The table was set for a banquet and wine was poured. "Come," he invited, "and experience what it is to eat food again." He walked in and sat down. Then he picked up a fork and helped himself to a roast. "Sit. Eat. The meat is rare, and the rest is laced with blood. It will probably taste odd at first, because you haven't tried this since your change, but it won't hurt you."

Angelique stared at the food in front of her. She was afraid they would cause her pain. Finally, she settled on some roast and wine, and timidly began to eat.

Blake dug in, eager to taste the foods he had missed for so long. The blood did not bother him. After exploring the selections on the table, he ended up trying everything.

After a few minutes, Franz paused eating. He waved his fork in the air as he began to ask questions. "So, tell me… where are you from? France? You sound French. Are you French?"

Angelique nodded.

"I knew it!" he declared exuberantly and smacked the table, waving his fork. He chuckled merrily. "And you…" he pointed at Blake. "You are English, no?"

Blake looked up. "Yes, from the Kent region." He could not help but like this jovial and boisterous man. "What about you? Where are you from? You sound as though you are of Germanic origin."

Franz grinned broadly. Thumping his chest, he said proudly, "I am the son of Wilhelm von Thalberg. I am also a master of magic, a grandson of Mastric. We call ourselves Mastrics in his honor. Our tribe is difficult to understand, so I won't bore you with stories of our greatness."

Angelique was both intrigued and repulsed by the man's obvious arrogance and lack of manners, but her curiosity about their society made her ignore it in favor of more knowledge. "Will you tell us more about the tribes? It's all quite confusing to me," she stated politely.

For the next two hours, the three exchanged stories. Then Angelique mentioned her ten years of lost memory and how the only information she had been able to obtain had been from Kuromoto. "And we all know how reliable a source he turned out to be," she finished.

Franz smiled, delighted he had found a way to fulfill Lord Reivn's orders. "I could maybe restore them… for a small price."

"What could I possibly give you that you don't already have?" she asked in surprise.

Putting his fork down, he gazed over the table at her. "The offer is simple. I know of a potent spell that could aid against our enemies, but it uses Eastern blood. You say you are from the Eastern tribes. If you will exchange a small portion of your blood for me to use in the spell, I will use my magic to help restore your missing memories."

Angelique hesitated. *Sharing my blood could be dangerous. What if he uses it against me?* She listened thoughtfully as Franz and Blake discussed the matter. Finally, she decided it was worth the risk.

Franz produced two vials... one for him to use, and the other to aid in retrieving her lost memories.

Angelique filled them and handed them back.

Blake hoped this would finally give her some answers. He knew her missing memories bothered her.

After dining, they strolled out to the gardens, talking until it was almost dawn. They learned of the tribes and their creators, the blood that made them different, and the birthrights each could wield.

When they left that night Franz promised to teach them more about their world, and both Angelique and Blake believed they had made a friend.

The next few nights were spent at Franz's, talking about their past and his. They learned more about their society's laws, and their darker nature.

Angelique was eager to regain her memories and often asked if there was any progress.

Then one night, Franz sat her down to talk. "I need more of your blood," he explained. "...because the spell didn't work the first time."

"How can a spell fail when you're a master of magic?" she asked in confusion.

He shrugged nonchalantly. "Who knows? Magic is not an exacting science. It takes a great deal of skill and practice, and even then, it sometimes fails."

Assuming he knew more than she did on the matter, Angelique gave him another vial.

Franz kissed her hand. "Now I must get to work. I will not be able to see you for a while, but remember the Royal Court is due to gather again soon. So until then, my lady, farewell." He bowed and waited until she was out of sight. Then he headed to his laboratory, stripped off his jacket and shirt, and donned his black robe. Quickly summoning the spirals, he conjured the blue flames that always lit his workroom. *I must be sure before I report back to Lord Reivn*, he reminded himself.

He retrieved the vial that held her blood from his jacket's pocket. Then opening it, he began to manipulate the Spirals to learn the secrets of her blood once more. The truth he sought came forth again and he sank to the floor, head in hands as his own past laughed at him from the shadows. He leaned against the wall in despair, remaining there until dawn forced him into sleep.

When night came and he awoke, Franz sat deep in thought for a long time. When he could no longer delay the inevitable, he got up, changed his clothing, and went in search of Lord Reivn.

Reivn was in his study at the Prince's mansion drafting a letter. Lunitar had sent news of Mariah's successful return. On his orders, Captain of the Dragon Guard had found her and taken her back to the Keep. Now he was awaiting further instructions from Reivn.

> *Lunitar,*
> *Send word to Draegonstorm that your sister is to be kept under guard until I return home. She tends to be rebellious and this presents a problem for our family. I will explain when I see you. Until then, be sure she is well-guarded. Do not let her leave again.*
> *Lord Reivn Draegon*

He handed the letter to a courier to deliver to Lunitar, who was still keeping distant watch over their three visitors, when Franz arrived.

Franz waited until the courier left. Then he approached Reivn with a heavy heart. "I have done as you asked, my lord."

Reivn motioned for him to take a seat. "What do you have for me?"

Franz walked forward, cringing inwardly at the question. "I checked her blood. As you suspected, she is indeed a Mastric."

Reivn frowned. "I was aware she was a Mastric from the moment I walked through her mind. What I wanted to know is whose line spawned her?"

With a heavy sigh, Franz sat down. *There will be no hiding this from him.* Slowly he began to recant what he had learned.

Unaware of the events involving Franz, Angelique arose that evening full of hope. *Only one more night until Royal Court,* she reminded herself. "This time will be different. We have friends and we've been accepted." She looked up and smiled when Blake walked into the room.

"I will be leaving for England after court. I did not plan to leave until next month, but I received a letter from the estate. A problem has developed that needs my immediate attention." Blake walked over and sat next to her. "I'm sorry. I know this isn't what you want. I'll make it up to you when I return, I promise." He wrapped his arms around her.

Knowing there was no changing his mind, she buried her head against his shoulder.

Blake knew she would not cry this time because her pride would not allow it. He thought about the pressing situation developing at their estates. It had been years since they last traveled home. *I am needed in England,* he telepathied. "The families are having difficulties with local bank changes. There are questions that have arisen about funds transferred from our previous banks because of our lengthy history of wealth. Bank managers are suspicious there are illegal activities involved with the money. I need to meet with them as the present Duke to clear up the problem." *A little convincing with my talents should help in their persuasion that all is well,* he added silently. He spent the rest of the night holding her and trying to ease her mind about the coming separation. Night came again, and they awakened in each other's arms. As they prepared for Royal Court, nothing more of his pending trip was mentioned.

When they arrived at the Prince's mansion, Angelique and her companions were again surprised at how many Immortals could exist undetected in one city.

Angelique put her hand into Blake's for reassurance as they walked in. They quickly found their seats, and then sat and conversed quietly while waiting for the Prince's entrance. Franz was not there and many of the other Vampyres were actively avoiding them. Worried about the looks they received, Angelique wondered if it was due to the events at their last court.

Lord Sorin finally entered and took his seat on the throne. Lord Gareth was with him, and so was Franz. The three of them sat quietly talking while Sorin's guards kept everyone away. Long minutes passed, and they ignored the many people trying to get their attention, until Sorin finally gave the signal and court began.

The room quieted and everyone took their seats. Court proceeded as normal, and individual business was handled one at a time. When their turn came, Angelique, Blake and Armand went forward to greet the Prince.

Lord Sorin silently telepathied Reivn, who waited in the hall, and the doors at the other end of the room burst open.

All eyes turned to see who had arrived. They were surprised to see Lord Reivn storm into the room, his black cloak billowing out behind him. He strode purposefully toward Angelique and her companions, who stood staring in utter surprise at his arrival. Lunitar and another man walked in behind him, their expressions grim.

"I must insist on stepping in, Lord Sorin!" Reivn announced, his expression foreboding.

The Prince did not appear at all surprised by the sudden intrusion. He merely nodded and stepped down, signaling for Reivn to take the throne in his stead.

Angelique feared a trap and backed away, but Lunitar and his companion had moved behind them and prevented her retreat.

Reivn's voice rose so the entire court could hear him. "Approach the throne, Comtesse, and bring your children!"

She realized there was no escape and raised her eyes to meet his. Then lifting her chin proudly, she walked forward with Blake and Armand. She curtsied and then stood before him, but her eyes betrayed her fear.

"Comtesse Angelique Marie De Legare, it has been brought to my attention that you are not who you say you are! When you came to this city, you were introduced to this court as belonging to the Eastern tribes. This has proven false!" Reivn leveled his eyes on her.

She stared at him in confusion. "My Lord, I don't know what you mean. We were told…"

Reivn held up his hand. "Silence! Franz used your blood and discovered something most unexpected. Blood does not lie! In lieu of this,

I petitioned the Mastrics Council and though skeptical, they have granted me permission to take you into my custody."

Feeling helpless to save herself, she stopped Blake when he tried to step in front of her. *No*, she silently telepathied. *Do not interfere.* Then she dropped to her knees in front of Reivn and bowed her head in surrender. "If I am to be arrested, my Lord, I would ask only that my children be allowed to leave in peace. They will cause you no trouble. You have my word."

Reivn got up and descended the steps to stand in front of her. Then he took her chin in his hand and lifted her face to meet his eyes. "Do you not know what you are?" he asked quietly.

Angelique stared at him, too afraid to speak. She knew he could destroy her, and feared Blake and Armand would die with her.

Reivn gazed into her eyes, as though searching for the answer. "All right," he finally conceded. "I asked the Council to give you to me because I found good in you, and I believe your sincerity." He looked up and loudly addressed the room. "Angelique and her kin are in fact, members of my tribe and my family. They are Mastrics. By the law, I claim right of guardianship over her and her children." Then he looked down at her and whispered. "Do not make me regret my choice. You are the child of a Renegade and by our laws, you and yours should be destroyed. I asked the Council to let me teach you, but if you betray me, I will kill you myself."

Lunitar looked up sharply and drew a deep intake of breath, listening in stunned silence. *Father,* he telepathied. *You know I would never question your authority or your decisions, but what kind of dangerous game are we playing?*

*Not now!* Reivn glanced at his son in passing and pulled Angelique to her feet. Then he turned to the audience. "Please welcome Lady Angelique and her sons. She is indeed one of us and is entitled to all the rights and protection of the throne."

Angelique paled when she realized everyone was staring at her, suspicion in their eyes. Feeling the room spin, her knees buckled.

Before Reivn could react, Blake had moved to her side and caught her. Undaunted, he met Reivn's gaze boldly. "You could have warned her first! You didn't have to frighten her!"

Reivn's eyes narrowed. Instantly, an invisible shield went up around the small group, cloaking their conversation from the rest of the room. "Hold your tongue! You are in no position to challenge me. The laws neither bend nor break for any reason or anyone. She is no child, but she is of Renegade blood, as are you. If I did not think her innocent, she would already be dead!"

Blake stared at him, the truth of his words sinking in. Sensing the dangerous nature of the man before him, he fell silent. He did not like the way Reivn had looked at Angelique when their eyes met and liked even less the idea that they were now in his custody.

Reivn chuckled, recognizing Blake's discomfort. "Do not worry," he whispered, "I like my solitude." Then he dropped the shield and raised his voice again, so everyone would hear. "Lord Lunitar, take her and her companions to one of the rooms down the hall. She needs time to recover. They may return when she is feeling more herself. Franz, well done." Then he turned to Sorin, "My Lord, the throne is yours again. Thank you."

Franz bowed to Reivn without a word, avoiding his gaze.

Lunitar waited while Blake lifted Angelique into his arms and then led them out.

As Reivn stepped down, he stared at the retreating trio, deep in thought. *"What is it about this girl? She is a Renegade, and yet her lack of knowledge makes her as innocent as a newborn. Is it really possible she has no idea who she is?"* Disturbed by his own thoughts, he walked out onto the terrace. He had seen Armand take a position opposite Blake's, flanking him when they were led from the room. *Two very young, very brave and extremely foolish men... I wonder if they know just how weak they truly are.* Shaking his head, he turned and walked out into the night.

## Chapter Sixteen
## The Novice and the Master

*Time has once again shown me that patience in all matters is indeed
rewarded. We have killed many young in the past, but this one is different.
I believe she has no idea what she actually is, nor does she know anything
of our race or society... nothing. She is a clean slate ready to be written
on... clay to be molded into the perfect creation. But her fate was decided
the night she was taken from her home. The Council will want her
destroyed like all the others and yet... if I succeed in training her as one of
us, perhaps I could prove to them that not all children created by our
enemies have to join them in their fate.*

*She is a rare flower, innocent to the truth of our ways, but the power
that sits deep within her is incredible... almost my equal. If allowed to
keep her, I will see to her schooling myself. First, I must be absolutely sure
of my suspicions. One mistake could cost me my own head as well as hers.
Mastric will not lightly take my request as it is, particularly if she is who I
think she is. Valfort wounded him deeply when he took Elena's life and
that pain may bleed over to any who are his spawn.*

*With the whole world on fire and the war with the Principatus so
heated, she won't easily gain acceptance. If word gets out whose child she
truly is, many will shun her, and others will try to kill her. It would be
better if none know her lineage. Then she would have a chance to become
accepted and respected. If I claim her as my own, then that would be even
more of a possibility, but then I would also forfeit my life if she betrays us.
Mastric will not tolerate or allow another such betrayal among us. His
wrath would be swift and brutal. I must tread carefully here...*

*Lord Reivn Draegon*

\* \* \* \* \*

After the night of Reivn shocking revelation, Angelique and her family
were relocated to the Mastric's guild under his watchful eyes. Once there,
other Mastrics began teaching them about the laws of the Alliance and
their tribe. They also learned about the magic they each carried... the
power of their own birthright: The Mystic Spirals.

Angelique had never even suspected she was capable of that kind of
power, and at times it frightened her.

Armand grew troubled as his knowledge of Alliance law grew. Although he kept his thoughts to himself, the others sensed the change. But though worried, they said nothing, wondering if this festering resentment would grow to fruition and become open rebellion.

Blake took to his training quickly and he soon began to wield his power with finesse; a natural with magic. However, several weeks after their training began, he approached Reivn, feeling he had delayed the trip to England as long as he could. Ruben was to travel with him and had already prepared for their departure.

Reivn was reluctant to let Blake go, concerned about keeping a tight rein on his protégés. However, after a long discussion, he finally agreed on a four-month time allowance for Blake to return to England to tend to their affairs. But they would have to travel by ship because Blake had not yet mastered the portal spell, so Reivn forbade its use.

The night of their departure, Angelique and Armand rode with them to the docks.

Angelique threw her arms around Blake and sobbed. "Please don't go! We haven't been apart in ages! I'm so afraid! I will be lost without you!"

Blake pulled her close and kissed her forehead. Then he gently brushed the stray hair from her cheeks. "Love, you mustn't. If anyone saw the blood on your face…" his voice trailed into silence as he saw the pain in her eyes. "Please don't cry. I'll be back before you know it, and Lord Reivn will probably work you so hard you won't even notice my absence."

Angelique buried her face in his chest.

Armand stood nearby, watching in grim silence. *This is foolish! No good can come of this!* In frustration, he strode back to the car and leaned against it to wait for Angelique.

Angelique watched the ship until it disappeared on the horizon. She felt her whole world was leaving with him and sent him one last thought. *Please come back soon. Don't forget me.*

Standing on the deck of the ship next to Ruben, Blake smiled when her mind touched his. His answer was simple. *I promise.*

She was still standing there when Armand came looking for her, so he gently put his arm around her and led her to the car. On the ride home, the only sound to be heard was her soft sobs.

Months slowly passed. Angelique's power gradually grew as she learned to harness her magic, and she was rapidly winning over the other Guild residents with her charm and good nature. Armand never ventured far from her, worried about her continued safety.

Reivn was pleased with her progress. He saw the natural talent in her and often trained her himself, discussing the skills she would eventually master. He would take her on long walks near the river, where they could talk in peace, and it was during one of these that he told her of his own past. "I have lived countless centuries and seen many things. When I was human, the Romans enslaved my people. Many were conscripted as soldiers, myself among them. It was there Mastric found me and made me his blood servant. I served in the mortal world for centuries as his eyes and ears, under one human ruler after another. I fought their wars, advised on affairs of state, and shared their fates on many battlefields." He paused and glanced up at the stars.

"It was when I served Vlad that things changed. We fought a hopeless war trying to free our people from the tyranny of the Ottoman Empire. Our army was vastly outnumbered, and many of our own nobles could not be trusted. We set up an ambush in the Borgau pass, but the reports on their movements were wrong. We were outnumbered and had to retreat or risk defeat, so we fled to Tirgoviste, where we stood our ground. It was a slaughter. They were too many and we were not enough. I fell that day. That was when Mastric awakened me. He is an Ancient and my progenitor." Reivn lifted her chin to meet his gaze. "No one knows how long the Ancients have existed or the truth of their beginnings." Letting her go, he turned to stare at the river. "But we do know that centuries ago two of them betrayed the others, and then hid in the Caribbean while they grew in strength and numbers. A great war began. Over time many have joined their ranks, and they have slowly overrun one territory after another."

Angelique's eyes widened. "A war between our kind?"

He paused and glanced at her. "Yes, and as a Warlord, my job is to prevent breaches in this region's security. Many have died because of inside infiltration, much like what happened with you and Kuromoto. That is why we had to be sure about you. I hunt and kill Renegades... and their children. I am judge, jury, and executioner."

She had been listening quietly, but now she was curious. "Then why teach me? Why not just destroy me?"

He gazed at her, contemplating his answer. "When I searched your mind, I found no hint of the Renegades' teachings. I did find the gap in your memories, but could not see whether they were blocked or erased. It did not pertain to the situation, so I left it alone. Everything else I found in you was purely innocent of their doctrines."

She frowned. "That doesn't explain why you took on my training."

Reivn smiled at her. "I approached our Council on your behalf because of the sincerity with which you revealed the plot against Sorin, betraying the one you believed to be your Elder. It is rare for any tribe to betray one of their own."

He glanced down at her and their eyes met. "However, the betrayal of who you thought was your Elder is also why our Council did not want to give you that chance. For you to live, I had to take full responsibility for you and your children."

Angelique gasped. "But... doesn't that mean you will die if we fail you? By claiming responsibility for us, you also declared us your children! Aren't creators responsible for the actions of their children until they are released?"

Putting his hands behind his back, he stared at the river in silence. "You do not miss a thing, do you?" He turned and gazed at her in admiration. "Yes, I am taking a risk, but I believe in you. You also know if you betrayed us, I would destroy you myself." Then he frowned. "I saw an image of your creator. Do you know him?"

A shadow crossed her features and she shook her head. "No. I only saw him twice... the first when he made me, and the second right before I ran away. One of his people was teaching me, but we were attacked before he could do more." She turned away, unable to meet his eyes. "Is my blood considered...tainted? I never knew who or what..." She did not finish her thought.

Realizing how uncomfortable she was, Reivn steered the conversation in a different direction. "Perhaps Blake will return soon. You miss him, do you not?"

Angelique nodded, relieved he was no longer asking about her past.

"You realize he looks on you as helpless?" he continued, hoping to touch on another important subject.

"I know," she admitted quietly.

Reivn frowned. "If he does not learn that you are stronger than he and able to protect yourself, he is going to get himself killed trying to defend you."

Angelique looked away, afraid to meet his eyes.

He gently lifted her chin to meet his gaze. "Angelique, why are you so repulsed by what you are?" Unable to look away, her eyes met his. He was stunned by the grief he saw there. "Why can you not accept what you have become? There is no shame in being what we are... It is how we survive. We only take what we need from mortal kind. I have watched how you starve yourself." Reivn took her shoulders and shook her slightly. "It is a dangerous practice. You could easily lose control and in desperate need for blood, kill the very person you are trying to protect."

Angelique fought back tears and tried to pull away, unwilling to let him see any further into her soul. "What about blood-laced meals? Can't they sustain you?"

"Somewhat," he answered, letting her go. "The problem is those who feed only through laced foods grow weak and cannot readily defend themselves. Those who indulge in laced meals also hunt. They only feast on food to indulge their decadent side."

A tear trickled down her cheek. "I never wanted any of this..." she whispered, thinking he wouldn't hear.

He gently wiped it away. "Who made you, angel of the night?"

"I have to go..." she stuttered and backed away. "Goodnight, my Lord." Then she turned and fled back to the Guild.

He watched her go in silence.

His words rang in her ears. She knew he was right. Fear of her creator had taught her to hide to survive. Reivn's attempts to help her embrace her nature frightened her. She ran to her room, seeking solace. But when she opened her door, a figure rose from the chair and she screamed.

Blake quickly walked over and pulled her into an embrace. "It's me, love. I'm sorry. I did not mean to startle you. I got in a little while ago and wanted to surprise you."

Angelique threw her arms around him. "Oh Blake, I have missed you!" she cried. She showered him with kisses, failing to notice his expression. When he did not respond, she stopped. "What's wrong?"

He looked down at her. "Have you?"

"You know I have!" she replied happily. "Why would you ask that?"

Blake held her at arm's length. "You've spent a great deal of time with Lord Reivn in my absence. Is that because of training, or because you didn't want to be alone?"

Angelique angrily pulled away. "How could you ask me that? After all this time, how could you even think such a thing?"

He immediately regretted his accusation when he saw her expression and pulled her into his arms again. "I'm sorry, love. I should not have doubted you. It's just been a long few months. I couldn't wait to get home." He kissed the tip of her nose. "I got jealous when I heard you were with him. Please, forgive me."

She began to cry. Reivn's words and Blake's accusations coupled with all she had learned the past few months overwhelmed her.

Blake lifted her gently and carried her to the bed. Then he settled down next to her. Regretting his harsh words, he held her while she cried herself to sleep. Long after the sun rose, he fought the inevitable. *The thought of losing her still scares me. Maybe it's time to make things more permanent.* His decision made, he finally let sleep claim him.

At dusk the following night, Angelique awoke first. She quietly pulled away and stared at him as though seeing him for the first time. Her conversation with Reivn filled her thoughts. *Lord Reivn is right! He is too protective. I am hurting him by letting him fight my battles.* Her mind wandered until his voice brought her back to the present.

"Angelique? Are you alright?" Blake stretched to rid his muscles of the stiff ache of slumber.

Angelique smiled at him. "I'm fine. I didn't want to wake you."

His eyes filled with worry. "You're not upset about last night?"

She laughed at his expression, suddenly seeing him as almost childlike in his affection. "Of course not! Now get up! Lord Reivn is expecting us."

Blake pulled her down and into his arms. "I love you, Angelique. Marry me?"

Angelique stared at him in surprise. "What did you say?"

"All these years, we never finished what we planned our whole lives to do. Why not?" He grinned, trying to look like the boy she loved in their youth.

"I love you too, Blake, but why the sudden change? This isn't because of last night?" She watched his eyes, knowing he could not hide the truth from her.

Her question did not sway him. "You are all I ever wanted, and I fear losing you to this dark world." He paused. "I hurt you last night, and it was because of my own insecurity. I want you to be my wife. Forgive me, my love, but that side of me is still very human."

Angelique hugged him, too emotional to say anything.

Blake gently moved back and gazed at her. "What do you say? Isn't it time we married?"

She pulled away and got up, her thoughts in turmoil. *What of Reivn's warning?* She wanted to marry him. She always had, but not because of fear. *Still, Blake has loved me all these years, remaining at my side even when he could have hated me for turning him.* Finally, she turned to look at him. He had gotten out of bed and stood waiting, a lost expression on his face. Her heart melted at the sight. "Of course, I will!"

Blake grabbed her and whirled her around, whooping for joy.

"Blake," Angelique squealed, "put me down!"

He let her go and reached into his pocket, pulling out a small velvet box. "You have the ring I gave you the night our parents announced our engagement, but I thought this was more appropriate. I bought it in England while I was away."

She stared at him in amazement. "You thought about this in England?"

He shrugged. "I was hoping we could start over when I came home. I really missed you."

Later that night they met with Reivn, but Angelique could not concentrate on their discussion. She kept staring at Blake. The change in him was remarkable. He was happy. She could only guess what the future held for them now.

Time passed in a bustle of activity as Angelique maintained her studies and made plans for their wedding. She saw very little of Armand, whose duties kept him busy, but she was content to spend the end of each night alone with Blake. Reivn had forbade them to attend court for several months to give them time to adjust to their new lives. There were also no lessons with Reivn, so her time was free after her training each night.

One night, Blake received another letter from his estates in Kent. Another child had been born and they were requesting he come for the traditional ceremony to name the child as heir to the estate. Before he even told Angelique, he knew what she would say. He was also worried about Reivn's involvement with her. He had seen how the Warlord's eyes followed her, yet to all appearances there was no attraction in them, only curiosity.

In truth, Reivn was still trying to figure out why he had claimed Angelique and her children as his protégés. All other Renegade young he found were destroyed instantly, no questions asked. Yet she was walking the halls of his guild. He had stopped walking with her because he recognized the anger in Blake and did not wish to cause Angelique any pain by dividing them. He already knew they would never turn from Council law. They were too content.

When Blake did approach Angelique about returning to England, she was devastated.

"How can you even think about leaving again?" she cried. "Our wedding day is growing close and we still have so much to do! You can't leave now!"

He put his arms around her, trying to calm her. "We've been through these ceremonies over titles and land before. You know we must be present for these. It's how we keep the families loyal and on good terms. We do not need to make enemies of them. It could ruin us." He kissed her forehead and his tone softened. "I promised I would not leave again unless necessary. It won't be for long, I swear. This is important, and you know it."

Angelique leaned her head against his chest in defeat. "All I ever wanted was you, not this life we exist in every night."

Blake played with her hair, noticing for the millionth time how her copper curls reflected the light. "I'm sorry. I must do this, but I'll be back before you know it." He kissed her gently and whispered. "I love you with all my heart."

A tear slipped down her cheek and she looked up. "I hate this," she cried, angrily wiping it away. "I feel lost in the dark when I'm alone! For three years, I lived in fear, hovering on the brink of insanity! I don't even know how I remembered you! I am afraid I'll lose it again! That's why I was willing to train with Reivn!"

He kissed her eyes, then her cheeks, and finally her lips. "Hush, love. It will be all right." Picking her up, he carried her to the bed. Then he covered her body with his own. "You are so beautiful. Do you honestly believe I could leave you for any longer than I must? I'd worry about someone trying to steal you in my absence." In the hours that followed, their passion and emotions charged the fiery intimacy they shared.

To Angelique this was goodbye, and the moment was bittersweet. His whispers only served to grieve her more, reminding her she would once again be alone for many nights to come. Long after their passion was spent, she lay thinking quietly in his arms, unaware that Blake's thoughts were not so different.

Blake stared up at the ceiling. *I wonder if she realizes how lonely the last trip was, with only Ruben to talk to and an empty bed at dawn.* He knew his departure this time would be far more difficult than the last.

The night he left, Angelique watched him sail away, her heart inexplicably filled with fear. Not wanting to appear foolish or weak, she had said nothing to him. *Stop it. You cling to him like a child. Lord Reivn warned you about your foolishness.*

Ruben walked her to the car in silence, knowing she was distraught. His thoughts were far darker. His knowledge of the last trip included things she had not been told, and he was worried. *After his last voyage, he knows he shouldn't be doing this alone.*

There had been much talk of hunters in Europe, and many of the Vampyres were moving to underground havens as they dug into the earth for safety. Hunters had always been around, but their technology had grown more advanced, making their prey more vulnerable and the hunt less difficult. Now it was the Vampyre's turn to fear the hunter, and Europe had been rank with that fear. Ruben knew Blake would be cautious, but for her sake, he hoped it was enough.

The nights passed slowly for Angelique. Reivn's duties kept him busy, so she often found herself wandering the gardens alone. Her reputation in the tribe was flourishing and she had gained substantial respect among those in the guild. To her surprise, many of them now bowed in recognition when she passed them in the halls.

Then two weeks after Blake's departure, she received a summons from Reivn. Curious as to the nature of this visit, Angelique hurriedly completed her tasks. When she finally approached his office door, her hands shook. She knew he had been avoiding her and it worried her. *Did I do something wrong?*

His voice harsh, Reivn's voice echoed from within. "Come!"

Angelique calmly entered as he got up from his desk.

"Good, you're here." He motioned for her to sit down. "I have been hearing many good things about you. Your reputation has grown considerably." He paused. "I have thought about this a great deal and have concluded that you need reassignment."

She stared at him in shock, thinking he meant for her to leave.

Before she could say anything, Reivn held up his hand. "I am not sending you anywhere." He walked over and sat down beside her. "I want to make you tribal Prefect for this territory."

Angelique gaped at him in amazement. "But I don't know enough about the laws yet to sit in any seat of power! I haven't even had the time to learn about all of my own abilities yet!"

"I am confident you can handle our affairs with great efficiency, and I will help you learn what you do not yet know." He went to his desk and began to write.

She shook her head in protest. "I'm not ready!"

Abruptly, Reivn looked up, his eyes dark. "I am not giving you a choice."

Hours later, Angelique sat in her room staring at the parchment in her hand, stunned by what had transpired, but there it was in ink, the handwriting as bold as the man who had written it.

> *Let it be known that by the authority of the Mastric's Warlord,*
> *Lady Angelique is appointed as tribal Prefect and selected*
> *Regent of the Mastrics tribe in Atlantic City.*
> *Done this day by my hand,*
> *Lord Reivn Draegon*

Angelique stared at the letter. *Why is he doing this? How can I possibly do what he wants without endangering lives? He knows I am still a novice. What is he thinking?* Troubled and filled with doubt, she settled down to sleep. Her thoughts turned to Blake, and she wondered how he would react. When she finally drifted into slumber, her memories of his touch warmed her.

Toward sunset, Angelique's dreams were shattered by a soul-rending scream, and she sat up, jolted awake by its intense agony. Looking at the clock, she was surprised to see that night had not yet come. *Why am I awake?* she wondered. Then she remembered the scream. *What was that?* She quickly showered and dressed. Disturbed by her dream's intensity, she could not shake the feeling something was wrong, and she began to pace the room.

By the time the sun hit the horizon, she was already headed to Reivn's quarters. She hesitated at his door, but the scream still echoed in her mind, so she cast aside her doubt and knocked.

"Come." Reivn's voice answered.

Angelique opened the door and found herself standing in darkness. "My Lord Reivn? I'm sorry for disturbing your rest, but I urgently need to speak with you."

Candles flared, bathing the room in a soft glow. She jumped in fright.

Reivn was standing a few feet from her, clad only in a pair of breeches.

*I must start keeping my senses alert*, she reminded herself, annoyed.

His chest, burnished from his years in the sun, was bare save for small wisps of black hair.

Angelique averted her eyes in embarrassment. Other than Blake, she had never seen another man half-naked and Reivn was beautiful to her. Having no desire to let him hear her thoughts, she closed her eyes and focused on the scream.

"You wished to speak with me?" Reivn was staring at her expectantly.

She began to tell him what had awakened her, careful not to meet his gaze.

Amused, he watched her silently and listened. His expression changed to concern when she told him of the scream. He caught her chin and lifted it until she met his gaze. "Are you sure? Was it just a dream or did you actually hear it?"

Angelique stammered, "yes, I'm sure! It felt real! Why are you angry?"

Reivn let her go and hit the intercom on the wall. "Send for Lunitar immediately! When he arrives, send him to my chambers!"

She stood still as death, fearing she had done something wrong.

When Reivn saw her expression, he almost laughed in spite of how serious the situation was. "You are in no trouble, Angelique. But I believe one of your own could be." Seeing the confused look on her face, he continued. "What you felt was a pull on your blood and the bond we all share with our kin. I think you felt the pain one of your children was experiencing. The question is who and where."

Angelique turned ashen. *That was why I felt as though something was wrong*, she realized. Sending an immediate question to Armand, he responded. Ruben and Genevieve likewise were tired, but well. *That leaves* "Blake!" she blurted out his name. Desperation filled her as she tried to telepathy him over the tremendous distance between them.

He took her shoulders and shook her. "Pay attention to what I am telling you! I have been speaking to you for the last five minutes and you have not heard one word I said!"

Angelique stared at him in shock. "I…I'm sorry. I tried to…" she trailed into silence.

Reivn nodded in understanding. "I know. You tried to contact him. Even I cannot cover that great a distance. Only the Ancients have that much mental skill. Calm yourself. I am sending an officer to make sure he is safe. Do you trust me?"

She nodded, unable to voice her fears. When he stripped off the breeches to don his clothes, she did not even flinch, barely noticing his nudity for those brief moments while he changed.

When Lunitar arrived, he opened the door himself.

Lunitar bowed respectfully. "You sent for me, my Lord?"

Reivn nodded and quickly gave him instructions. "Use the portal and find Blake Sinclair! I believe he is in danger! Secure what information you can and bring him back if you find him!"

Angelique listened quietly. Her fear for Blake was so great her mind was a mass of jumbled thoughts, none of them clear.

Lunitar bowed again. "Yes, my lord."

After Lunitar had gone, Reivn turned to her. "Let us walk together while we wait for news. It is better than sitting alone."

She followed him without a word. She could not think past Blake and what would happen if she lost him…

## Chapter Seventeen
## Severed bonds

*By God, I have done it! I managed to convince the Mastric's Council to let me train a Renegade's child! I was reminded of the law and told if I do this and they betray us, I will forfeit my own life. It matters not. I finally have the chance to show that perhaps not all Principatus young need be destroyed just for the blood in their veins. God give me the strength and the wisdom to see this through to its end.*

*Now that I have claimed Angelique and her young as my own, the real work begins. I do not yet know what my brother taught her, or how much she knows of our war. What I did see is a intense amount of loyalty to the prince and his court. I believe this is more than likely due to her aristocratic upbringing. Loyalty to the throne was a tradition in her time and now it may help keep her alive. Still, I will have to watch her every move, as well as those of her children.*

*Blake is an angry one. If any of these three were to give me trouble, it would be him. Angelique allows him to lead her around, ever playing the maid and he, her protector. The fool does not realize she could crush him with a thought. I am at a loss with her on that one. Even after all the years she has been one of us, she still seems to be fighting her natural instincts.*

*Moving them to the Guild under the watchful eyes of other tribe members was easy. However, getting them past all the resentment will be much harder. Armand and Blake carry more of this than Angelique does, but even she still looks at me with guarded eyes. She does not trust so easily, and she fears me. I will have to tread carefully if I am to win her confidence...*

*Lord Reivn Draegon*

\* \* \* \* \*

Angelique had just finished her nightly routine when Reivn came and got her. "Angelique, walk with me," he stated.

She wanted to be present when Lunitar returned and followed him into the garden. They strolled down the path in silence toward the park they so often frequented, and she glanced up at Reivn, anxious to hear what he had to say.

His expression was grim.

She cleared her throat to break the stillness. "Has there been any word yet?" Hope and fear filled her gaze.

Reivn stopped walking and turned to her. "Lunitar returned half an hour ago."

Angelique froze. "Then he found Blake and he's all right?" His silence unnerved her.

He paused, reluctant to tell her the truth.

Seeing his expression, she shook her head. "Please...tell me he's alive." she whispered.

In response, Reivn offered her a box wrapped in a black cloth, and then waited, knowing she had to discover the truth for herself.

Afraid of its contents, Angelique accepted it. It was a large jeweled box, the opening of which was sealed with wax. She reached out with her mind to discover its contents, and then in anguish, almost dropped it to the ground. "Oh, my God, no!"

It was filled with Blake's ashes.

She dropped to her knees in shock, and tears ran down her cheeks.

Reivn quietly left her side, letting her have a few minutes alone.

She wanted to scream. She wanted to demand all she had lost be given back. She wanted Blake. Agonizing pain filled her heart as she realized he was never coming back. Overwhelmed and frightened, she broke down and sobbed like a lost child.

Blake's body had been burnt to ash, and what little could be retrieved had been stored in the box and brought back.

Her tears falling unheeded, Angelique's mind turned to why. She got up and looked around. Reivn was waiting for her not far away. She joined him, and they walked together in silence. She had never felt more alone, even in her mentor's company. Somehow, she had already known, but now that she had proof, her grief was overwhelming. She had seen who murdered Blake in the vision. Now she wept openly, tears of blood pouring down her face.

Reivn reached out and wiped her cheek.

It was too much. She fell to her knees. "You are the law!" she sobbed. "I demand justice! I claim the right of vengeance against those who murdered him!"

He lifted his hand to touch the top of her head as she covered her face and cried. But then he lowered it again as he listened to her sobs fill the night. Something about her moved his ancient heart. He did not want to refuse her, but Alliance law was strict, and her passionate plea was exactly the type of emotion they were taught to control. "Such raw emotions are usually frowned upon. I know your attachment to Blake was a strong one that went back to the time before your awakening, but you must contain your grief." He gazed down at her, compassion filling him. "You must come to terms with what you are. Let your ties to the human world go. You will have your vengeance. Not by my hand, but by your own."

Her eyes betrayed her inner conflict when she got up, but she tried to mask her emotions.

Reivn was not fooled by the sudden change. He merely shook his head, a hint of a smile crossing his face. "This is not the first time you have refused my counsel, Angelique. There is great strength in you, far beyond what you want to acknowledge even to yourself."

Angelique took a step back and stared at him in silence, her green eyes growing sad again.

He ignored her expression and continued. "You have denied yourself far too long and now can no longer do so. I am again extending your duties to our tribe. Keeping you busy may fill the void you feel and will help you grow stronger, which you need to be. The Atlantic City guild will not be your only responsibility. This region has other guilds. I am adding them to your duties."

Angelique looked up and shook her head, prepared to argue.

Reivn glared at her and continued. "You need not worry about your background. The Council is well-aware of your origins. Because you serve the tribe and Council so loyally and are under my protection, none question your motives or actions."

Unable to meet his gaze, she looked away.

He caught her chin and turned her back to face him. "You will have your revenge, Angelique. That I promise you." Then he kissed her forehead gently and walked away.

Angelique stared after him in confusion, as tears pouring down her face.

Reivn appeared as composed as ever, but his thoughts were a mass of confused anger. His fury at seeing the grief that losing one of his protégés caused was a far cry from peaceful. His own feelings concerning the matter also bothered him and his thoughts were in turmoil.

She wiped her eyes and got up. When she joined him, she was quiet.

They went down to the river's edge and stood side by side staring at the water, each lost in their own thoughts. Finally, Reivn spoke up. "You saw his final moments, correct?"

Angelique silently nodded.

"Then you know who his attackers were." he stated gently.

She nodded again, unable to choke out the words.

He turned to gaze at her. "You will be given the manpower to hunt them down to the last man and the leave to do so if you wish it."

Angelique met his eyes. "It won't bring him back," she whispered. "Besides which, as you have so painstakingly pointed out on numerous occasions, I have neither the skills nor the training to achieve such a goal." Her eyes mirrored the pain she felt.

Reivn sighed in resignation. "Very well. When the time is right, I will help you find them. However, right now I want to share a story with you. Perhaps it will help you understand that loss in this dark world of ours happens without warning and can come from anywhere." He hesitated, considering his choice of words. "There was once a man who loved a beautiful and bewitching woman. She belonged to the tribe of dark Egypt, yet to him, it mattered not for she was as radiant as the night." He closed his eyes, allowing himself to remember.

"Go on," she whispered.

Reivn seemed to be lost in the past and his voice echoed with memory. "He brought her among his people and made her his equal, but he did not truly know her heart. It was as black as the raven locks of her hair. One night while he laid injured and unconscious, she rose against him. Now the son of this lord was standing watch, having seen the darkness in her. So when she set to her evil task, he came between them. The son managed to drive her from the fortress, and she disappeared. For long years, the man thought her dead and mourned her. But then he discovered her betrayal and the fatal mistake he had made."

Angelique realized he was telling his own story and a tear slipped down her cheek.

He caught it with his finger. "Is this for me? Do not cry for me." She shuddered at his icy tone, but he ignored her and continued. "Before she fled into the night, she tainted his blood by planting something evil deep in his heart. Her betrayal taught him the meaning of hate and mistrust, and how to be as cold as ice. He locked his emotion away, allowing only logic, reason, and duty to govern him."

Angelique impulsively touched his arm, finding shared pain in his tale.

Reivn looked down at her and smiled. "You see? You are entirely too gentle, your heart too easily touched. This makes you vulnerable. You must learn to embrace the darkness."

She averted her eyes, realizing she had overstepped her bounds. "I…I'm sorry, I thought this was your story. I cannot think of you as cold, only alone."

He turned abruptly and walked away. Then he stopped and looked over his shoulder at her. "That is why you are weak," he said grimly. "You give pity when none is needed. You must harden your heart. Our world is one of darkness and damnation, Angelique. There is no room in it for gentleness and forgiveness. You will not find redemption or retribution in the shadows. Goodnight."

Angelique stared after him in mute shock. *He must have been deeply hurt by her*, she concluded.


Angelique walked back to the Guild, staring down absent-mindedly at the box in her hands. She could think of nothing but the news she had received of Blake, and Reivn's story. Feeling more lost than ever, she headed to her room, where she could grieve in private. She was so distracted, she did not see Armand, and screamed when she ran into him.

Armand reached out to steady her, catching the box when it fell from her hands.

"Armand!" she cried. "You scared me half to death! Don't sneak up on me like that!"

He smiled at her in amusement. "I wasn't the one a million miles away. Where were you?"

His question brought back the news of Blake's death and her expression changed.

He wrapped his free hand around her. "What's wrong, Mon Chere? Has something happened?"

Angelique nodded, that familiar lump working its way into her throat. Then she burst into tears and buried her face against his chest.

Concerned now, Armand pulled away and held her at arms' length. "What is it?"

"It was Blake. He…" She choked out the words and pointed at the box, unable to say more.

Armand stared at the box, suddenly understanding what she was trying to tell him. "God..." he breathed. "Oh, God! When? How?"

She recounted what she knew until too distraught to speak further, she could only lean against him sobbing.

He closed his eyes and held her close. Fury at Blake's loss tore at him, but he said nothing. Instead, he offered her comfort while silently seething over what had happened. Finally, he handed her the box and picked her up. Then he carried her the rest of the way to her room, telepathing Ruben and Genevieve to meet them there.

Once there, Armand laid Angelique on her bed. Then he let Genevieve care for her while he quietly told Ruben what he knew. "I have to know more, for her sake. Otherwise, for her the grief will never end. He was her whole world! We need to know what happened so she can have some measure of peace! Promise me you will care for her until I return!"

Ruben took him by the shoulders. "We have been friends a long time, Armand. I have always watched over them and you. Do not do this. What if something happens to you too? It will break her. You know that! We'll figure out something together, but if you go off alone there are no guarantees of your coming back."

Armand angrily shook him off. "This is something I have to do! I vowed long ago to watch over them both! I failed him! I am not going to fail her! I need to do this...for her sake!" He pointed to Angelique and Ruben followed his gaze.

Angelique laid sobbing on the bed, her tears staining the sheets red. Genevieve was fussing over her and trying to wash her face, insisting she rest.

"She isn't like the rest of them!" Ruben growled. "She isn't dark or fierce... not brutal nor even a hunter! She is more like a lost child than anything. If you leave her now, how will she survive?" He blocked Armand's view of her as he spoke. "Think of her, Armand! She is going to need all of us! Please... don't do this!"

Armand gripped Ruben's shoulders, his eyes filled with pain. "I have to go. Look after her for me. Tell her I'm sorry. I'm sorry for all of it." Then without another word, he turned and left.

Angelique cried out in her sleep and Ruben turned to look at her. "Don't worry, Armand," he whispered. "I'll watch over her." He walked over and pulled the blanket around her still, cold form. What he had said of her was indeed true and it worried him. She was far too gentle for their dark existence. Armand and Blake had been her shields and now they were both gone. Stepping over to the window, he pulled aside the curtain and looked out.

In the driveway below, Armand glanced up from the car.

"Good luck, my friend," Ruben murmured.

Armand seemed to hear him. He looked up and waved goodbye.

Ruben stood at the window until Armand's car was out of sight.

Reivn's mood was chaotic. He had flown across the trees to his office balcony. Then he shifted back to human form and went inside. He began pacing back and forth in agitation as the image of red curls and green eyes stared back at him from the recesses of his mind. Finally, he headed down to the portal chamber in irritation.

The guard on duty snapped to attention and saluted. "My lord?"

"I am going to Draegonstorm. I will return tomorrow night." Reivn walked over to the portal. "Talianakarnae vraa Leviste Draegonstorm!" he commanded. The soft glow of magic filled the room and he stepped through. The portal snapped closed behind him, instantly transporting him to the portal in the bowels of his Keep.

When he emerged, a member of the Black Guard scrambled to his feet. "My Lord! We weren't expecting you! Welcome home!"

Reivn held up his hand. "Thank you, but I am not staying. Where is Lunitar?"

"He is most likely in the library, my lord," the guard answered. "He returned hours ago."

Reivn nodded. "Good. Then he is dealing with matters here. Return to your station."

The guard saluted. "Yes, sir!"

Still agitated, Reivn made his way to his private quarters, Then he telepathied the captain of his Dragon guard. *Bring Reyna to my chambers.*

By the time the captain arrived with her, Reivn had bathed and donned a robe. He sat deep in thought, staring at the flames in the fireplace, until he heard the door open.

Soft footsteps approached and a gentle voice asked, "You sent for me, my lord?"

Reivn did not move. "Come here, Reyna," he answered quietly. "I have need of your comforts tonight. I have waited too long since my last visit."

"Yes, my lord." Reyna lowered her gaze and knelt at his feet, awaiting his commands.

He reached down and tenderly stroked her dark hair. Then he caught her scent and closed his eyes. His hunger quickly arose and brought forth his fangs, but he held back, wanting to enjoy her. "Of all my women, you please me the most."

She nodded, staring at the floor. "It is my duty, my lord."

Reivn frowned and looked down. "I would hope it is more than a duty by now. I desire you to be happy here with me. I gave you my word I would not hurt you. I claim my right from you, nothing more. Am I not gentle with you? Do I not care for your needs? You live in comfort and want for nothing."

"You are good to me, my lord," Reyna admitted quietly.

He reached down and lifted her chin, so their eyes met. "You do belong to me, but I care for my finer things and you, my fragile flower, are quite fine."

"Thank you, my lord," she whispered. He owned her, and in their world, she was his to command. To disobey meant death by law.

Reivn got up and gently pulled her to her feet. Then he pulled her blouse free from her shoulders, baring them to his gaze. "My hunger is awake," he growled. "I have need of your tender hands and a measure of peace." He leaned forward and bit into her flesh, pulling her into his arms. As he drank, he freed himself of his robe. Then running his hands down the length of her slender form, he finished removing her clothes. With an impatient growl, he picked her up and carried her to his bed. Then laying her down, he joined her and kissed her gently. "I am hungry for you," he whispered against her cheek. Then he bit into her neck and drank again.

Reyna flinched when his fangs sank in and whimpered. Unconsciously putting her hands against his chest, she stifled a cry as she struggled beneath him.

He caught her hands and lifted them above her head, holding them against the pillows with ease. "Do not fight me, child. I will never harm you. The night will eventually come when you will grow used to this. Then you will give yourself to me freely."

Shivering slightly, she closed her eyes as tears slipped down her cheeks, but she made no sound when he slipped into her.

Reivn gently kissed her tears away. "My sweet flower... relax. Soon you will welcome this."

Hours passed as he lost himself in his desire for her, until his passion and thirst were sated. The sun had begun to climb the horizon when he finally closed his eyes to sleep.

The following evening when Reivn awoke, he kissed her gently on the forehead and left her to her slumber. When he finished bathing and dressing, he slipped out quietly, closing the door softly behind him. He knew the guards would see her safely to her quarters. He had other matters that could not wait. He headed back through the portal to Atlantic City to find Angelique.

Angelique had awakened from slumber to find Armand was absent and had left her to explain it to their new master. "What do you mean he's gone? Gone where?" She cornered Ruben, demanding an answer. "Please tell me he didn't go after Blake's killers!"

Ruben shook his head, frustrated he could not say something that would ease her mind. "My lady, I wish I could tell you what he was planning. The only thing he said was that he wanted to find out exactly what had happened."

She pulled at her hair in desperation and began pacing the room. "What is he thinking? He's going to get himself killed!" She turned and grabbed his arm. "When exactly did he leave?"

He never had the chance to answer.

Reivn stood in the doorway, watching them with an irritated expression. "I have already sent someone to find him, Angelique. He is a hothead, and running off like this will indeed get him killed. We need to talk. I will wait for you downstairs." He left them staring at each other in silence and made his way down the hall to the stairwell.

Angelique sighed in exasperation. "Now we have a bigger problem." She threw her cloak around her shoulders. "I'd best not keep him waiting," she grumbled. She picked up the box Blake's ashes were in and slipped it into the pouch at her side. Then she hurried out the door.

Ruben stared after her in frustration.

Genevieve came in from the adjoining room and saw the look on his face. With a sigh, she wrapped her arms around him and leaned her head against his chest. "She is not mad at you," she stated quietly. "She is afraid...for him. She misses Blake terribly and fears Armand will meet the same end. There is no helping this. What is to happen will happen. It is fate's way of keeping a balance. She loved Blake. Armand loves her. She mourns for Blake and it pains Armand to see it. He is handling his grief in his own way."

Ruben looked down in surprise. "What makes you say that?"

"Say what?" She glanced up at him.

He scratched his head in confusion. "That Armand loves her..."

With a smile, Genevieve began to tidy the room. "Because you used to look at me the same as he does her," she laughed and handed him the broom. "Now, get to work!"

Reivn was waiting at the foot of the stairs. He held out his hand to Angelique as she descended them to join him.

Angelique took his hand and curtsied. "You wished to see me, my Lord?"

He did not answer, instead guiding her into the garden and along the pathway in silence until they reached the river's edge. Finally, he stopped and turned to her, his eyes troubled. "I would like to ask your forgiveness for my anger last night. I was not myself." He paused. "For many years I have been trying to overcome something my wife did. It has had some painful side effects. Part of it is that I no longer gain sustenance feeding off mortals. I must feed from other Vampyres for that. That is more than a challenge, due to the nature of how I must do so. The other night, you awoke my hunger. My apologies if I offended you."

She stared at him in complete surprise. "I...it's..." Embarrassed, she fell quiet.

Reivn mistook her stammering and ensuing silence for anger and turned to go.

Angelique reached out and tentatively caught his arm. "I'm sorry too," she whispered. "I should not have intruded on your privacy. You are right. I do not always think when I speak." Then looking down, she laughed softly. "It's gotten me into trouble in the past. Forgive me?"

Reivn lifted her chin to meet his gaze. "Then we will start over. If you will forgive my temper, I will forgive your impulsiveness. Agreed?"

Angelique nodded silently. His eyes softened, and she impulsively swept her hair to the side, baring her throat for him.

Visibly shaken by the offer, he averted his eyes and fought the urge that rose once again.

Thinking he was trying to be polite, she reached for his hand, intent on reassuring him.

"No, my lady!" Reivn's voice sounded pained. "You do not know what you offer! I cannot take advantage of such innocence. Forgive me, I must go." He turned abruptly and hastened toward the guild. Then to her astonishment, he transformed into a Raven and flew out of sight.

Angelique watched him go in confusion, trying to understand what had just happened. There was no one in sight, so she walked along the river's edge to clear her head. For the first time since her change, she felt no fear. Instead, she felt an odd sense of unity with the darkness around her. Blake's absence was keenly felt, and her footsteps led her to the spot they had last been together. She realized her old life was gone. In its place, a new one had begun. She pulled the jeweled box from its place at her side, drew her dagger and cut the seal. Opening it, she held it out and released Blake's ashes. Then she dropped the box into the water below. She stared at the water where it had fallen. "I swear I will find the ones who did this, and they will pay with their lives. Part of me will always be with you, my love. Be at peace."

When Angelique made her way back to the guild, she did not notice the change in her step. In the absence of fear, there was only grace, and all hint of the child she had been was gone. Now she was a Vampyre at one with the night, and her mission was vengeance.

She slipped through the halls quietly, seeking solitude. Her thoughts turned to Armand. She hoped for his sake it was Reivn who found him first. She remembered what Reivn had told her. Dealing with hunters had never been easy. She had learned through her studies that the fighting and slaughter had been going on long before her parent's time. *Blake's death was needless...* she thought angrily. *There was no cause for it... no reason other than unbridled hatred.* Her mind racing, she paced back and forth across her room like a caged animal. "I will show them what it is to fear the night!" When she fell finally asleep later that night, she was still making plans.

The next evening, Angelique was surprised to find a letter on her bedside table. Sealed with the Draegon crest, she did not have to guess who the author was. Fearing it was about Armand, she hurriedly broke the seal.

*My dear Lady Angelique,*
    *I wish to thank you for your offer last night. Even with my strength of will, you provoked my hunger on many levels. If I ever*

*entertained doubts of your being one of our tribe, they are gone now. You truly are an enchantress. I refused you due to my nature of feeding. My trouble resides in the necessity of only feeding from my lovers. The kiss of an Elder is also much more powerful than that of other Vampyres and leaves a lasting effect. I know you were not aware of any of this, so I could not accept. Please forgive me.*

*Until we meet again,*
*Lord Reivn Draegon*

The letter was stamped inside with his personal sigil... the twin combatant dragons.

Angelique stared at it for a long time before finally shaking herself into motion. She quickly dressed and hurried to begin her duties, she hoped to hear some news of Armand. But her mentor was nowhere to be found. In frustration, she started her nightly routine, as she listened for his return. She rarely spoke to other residents in the guild. Only Reivn, or those that reported the guild's activities or city events ever sought her out. Most Mastrics kept to themselves, preferring the company of their studies and their magic. The hours went by, and only the low chanting of spell-casting could be heard deep in the Guild, but there were no footsteps to herald Reivn's return. The night came and went with no sign of him and she wondered if he had gone after Armand himself. She hoped that answer would miraculously come as it had the night Blake died, but only the sound of daylight's beginning greeted her when she settled into bed.

For several nights, Angelique had no word of either Armand or Reivn. Curiosity about his absence filled her along with the fear that perhaps he was hunting Armand as a Renegade. *Nonsense*, she chided herself. *He gave me his word that he would help me.*

Then one night a letter arrived from Lord Sorin. It was an invitation to join the other Prefects at a tribal meeting. It went on to explain that this happened every six months to maintain peace. Angelique noted it was to be in two days' time at the Prince's mansion and began arranging for other Mastrics to cover the Guild's needs while she was gone.

Nervous about meeting the other Prefects, Angelique was quiet when she arrived at the hall. She lifted her chin and walked in with as much dignity as she could muster. But when she looked around, she realized only a few others had arrived, so she wandered around the room to take in some of the exquisite statuary and artwork she had previously been too preoccupied to notice. A polite cough behind her got her attention and she spun around.

Reivn smiled. "Good evening, Angelique. I trust you are well?"

Angelique curtsied. "Of course, my lord. I trust your trip was a pleasant one?"

Offering her his arm, he nodded. "I had pressing business in the Sahara. I apologize for my absence, but it was last minute."

She turned and walked with him, completely unaware they were being watched.

Reivn knew the other Prefects were watching them. He wanted them to realize she was under his protection. Smiling down at her, he could almost hear the tongues wagging with their gossip and chuckled at the thought.

"What's so funny," Angelique gazed up at him in complete innocence of what was passing among the room's other occupants.

He glanced down at her. "You really need to be out in our society more. To be as unobservant as you are in a room full of killers is dangerous. The other tribes are as ruthless as we are in their dealings, so you must constantly be aware of your surroundings."

The puzzled look on her face caused him to laugh. "They have been watching the two of us since I first took your arm, no doubt speculating you are my new lover."

Angelique stopped and stared at him open-mouthed. "That's disgusting!" Then she blushed profusely when she realized what she had just said. "I don't mean you, my Lord, but rather that they would make such vulgar accusations! It would be quite improper of me to… to…"

Patting her hand, Reivn could not help but chuckle at the expression on her face.

Indignant that he should laugh at her, she was about to say something rude when the trumpets blared, heralding the arrival of Lord Sorin and his escorts. "We'll talk of this later," she muttered, as they moved toward the table that had been set for all the Prefects to meet as equals.

# BLOOD FEUD

## Chapter Eighteen
## The Power of the Throne

*An awakening to oneself is a powerful and frightening thing. It does not always bring the most pleasant of realizations. I am concerned about Angelique. My brother should never have taken such a rare flower and turned her. She is too gentle in her ways and too delicate a thing to be exposed to the violence of the night. I do not fear she will betray me. I fear she will be destroyed by her own lack of inner fortitude. She holds incredible amounts of power, but in such raw form. And so untrained... how did she manage to survive this long without discovery or destruction? She is far more fortunate than she knows...*

*Valfort has vanished again. I know he is somewhere here in America. He has been since before the revolutionary war. I am worried what activities he may be involved with. None of us has heard any more of him since his arrival here. He knows I am here and yet has spent years in silence, hidden away somewhere unknown. What is he waiting for? I know him too well to believe he has given up his torment of me. His hatred runs far too deep for that. I suspect once he discovers I have taken Angelique as my own, his fury will be as a mad thing is, uncontrollable and dangerous. Whether he cares for her well-being or not, he will not like that his greatest enemy has claimed one of his own making.*

*Who knows... perhaps this will be the fire that ignites the explosion in him. I want him to face me. He has been running far too long. This should have been settled between us centuries ago. I will remain vigilant and continue to teach his creation, now my own progeny, and we shall see what comes from this. What may come, I will be ready...*

*Lord Reivn Draegon*

\* \* \* \* \*

Deep in the Sahara at Polusporta fortress, discussions of a much different nature were taking place. Victus and several other Council members were having a heated debate.

Armenia paced the room angrily. "I do not care what his reports say, Victus! You should never have agreed to it! What if she is tainting his thoughts? She should be destroyed!"

"Sit down, Armenia," Victus ordered, tired of her tirade.

Thylacinos unfolded himself from the corner. "She's right, you know. Our laws have always called for the destruction of the renegade's children and she should have been no exception. We allowed her to live and yet he has still not brought her before us. Why, one may ask?"

Victus tapped his fingers on the arm of his throne, his patience beginning to wear thin. "Armenia, Thylacinos... sit down!" he commanded again.

Armenia glared at Victus, but she complied and silently took her seat.

Thylacinos growled and strolled over to his throne. Then he dropped to the floor in front of it and stretched out. "As you wish."

Once they were seated, Victus let his presence fill the room. "I spoke with Mastric two nights ago, and he is investigating the delay. Lord Reivn has always been loyal to this Council. Making an enemy of him is not wise. He is powerful in his own right and is his father's right hand in most of their tribe's affairs. We are already dealing with one Elder's betrayal. We gave Reivn permission to claim her as his child. So now we must handle her as we would any other newborn. We must also remember he is a Warlord. It is possible other matters have kept him away."

Armenia scowled. "You are too lenient with him, Victus. He may be Mastric's son, but as a Warlord of this Council, his duties far exceed those of lesser children. As for the girl, she is no newborn, and the blood that runs through her veins is not Reivn's. She is of Valfort's line and has already lived over three hundred years. Let's not forget Valfort has eluded the hunters for centuries now. He has also helped the Renegades grow in strength and organization. If she is working for him, then by being beside Reivn, she is in the most dangerous position possible. Imagine how losing another of Mastric's children could affect this Council and our power."

Victus' eyes narrowed. "You forget your place! We are equals here, but I am still your king. I know what a dangerous game this is. However, this will allow Lord Reivn to prove his continued loyalty after that incident involving his wife. Have you forgotten how long it has taken for him to heal from the last of the Daemon taint?"

Galatia had been listening silently, but now she leaned forward. "Knowing of the recent problems we encountered with Mastric, I realize you are trying to avoid insulting him. But I feel perhaps Armenia is right this time. I have spoken to Serena about Reivn's progress. She removed the Daemon seed long ago, but he has remained distant and cold even toward his own son. Not even Mastric knows what he is thinking. If there is even the smallest chance this girl was corrupted by Renegade teachings, then can we really trust this? We should not leave this solely in Mastric's hands. If he has another agenda…"

A shadow stirred and Mastric stepped from its core. "Your vote of confidence is touching, Galatia." Moving to his throne, he sat down and gazed at her from beneath the shadows of his hood. "I have already received news from Reivn and know the reason for his delay. He wanted to give the girl time to adjust and learn more of our society. She knew next to nothing of our laws or her own power. He has been training her and plans to present her when she is more aware of what is expected of her."

Armenia stared at him. "He is training her? You mean he is giving her more power! Before this Council has even recognized her? We know nothing of her other than what he told us, and yet she is gaining knowledge that will make her even more dangerous! Who authorized that?"

Mastric turned on her, the glyph on his forehead growing in brilliance as his anger rose. "I did! She is of my tribe and when you allowed him to claim her, by law she gained the same rights as any other member of my line! He is well within his right as her master to train her! We do this with every child, and she is no exception. He approached the Mastrics Council and I with his intentions and I allowed it! You dare to challenge this?"

Victus held up his hands. "Peace! Peace!" He knew the Council could not afford another fight between its members. They had been in danger of breaking more than once. He turned to Armenia. "Mastric is well within the perimeter of our laws, Armenia. Do not forget the girl saved the life of a Prince. If she is learning our laws, she is also learning to be loyal. However, I do understand your concerns, so we will address this matter to satisfy those concerns. Send word to Lord Reivn. Tell him he has had ample time to prepare her for introduction to this Council. She is to be presented within a fortnight or her life is forfeit."

Armenia snapped her fingers and a courier scurried forward. "Take a dispatch to Lord Reivn Draegon in Atlantic City. Tell him he is to present his new protégé to us within a fortnight, or they are both subject to punishment. Remind him of his duty to this Council and the oath he took to serve. Perhaps that will shake him from his sojourn."

The courier bowed and hurried away.

Armenia rose from her seat and left the throne room, her visage dark as she headed to her lair in the lower level of Polusporta.

Thylacinos chuckled as he watched her go. "She is displeased with you, Victus. She wanted blood tonight. Still with Mastric's son, who knows? There may yet be blood. This should prove to be most amusing. I told you when you agreed to it that I thought it a bad idea, now we shall see who was right. In the meantime, I am hungry. I too, shall bid you goodnight. I am for the hunt." Uncurling from the floor, he dropped to all fours and shifted into a wolf. Then he opened a portal and leaped through, knowing it would take him into the heart of forest terrain where he would hunt with the wolves that dwelt there.

Mastric was silent until they were gone. "Victus, I would speak with you when you are finished here. I will be in my laboratory. Do not keep me waiting too long," he stated coldly. Then he vanished in a swirl of black mist.

As soon as they were alone, Galatia's expression changed. "How long?"

Victus glanced at her and his blood stirred. He turned away. "How long for what?"

"You know very well for what. Why do you keep yourself from me?" She stared at him in frustration, her porcelain features uncharacteristically bitter.

He got up and went to her. "I am doing what is best for our people, Galatia." He took her hand and pulled her to her feet. She was a radiant beauty worshiped by many as a Goddess, but to him, she was a rare and delicate flower.

"How is our being separated aiding our people? Do you truly believe they care if we have a liaison?" She moved closer, so he could smell the musk of her perfume.

Trying to ignore the desire he felt for her, he remained aloof. "Do you not imagine it would cause mistrust with the others if they believed I showed you favor? The balance here sits on the edge of a knife. The war, our people, and our very survival depends on our unity. I cannot risk rifting these halls, even for you."

He turned to walk away, but Galatia grabbed his arm. "And what of me, Victus? What of what I want? At least see me when we are alone… like now."

Victus kept his back to her. His desire was growing and with it his thirst. "I know of your desire, as it is also mine. I could not ever forget your heart. However, in spite of how either of us desires more, I am bound by duty to do what is right. The burdens of leadership were handed to me, and the trust that I would not fail any of our brethren with it. I gave them all my word that I would be fair, look on them as equals, and never betray them, Galatia. I must not ever break that vow. To ensure the balance is maintained, I cannot think of myself before my people. I can only give what little of me may remain when my duties are done. If you can get to my chamber unseen, then meet me there in one hour." Not waiting for an answer, he walked out, heading for Mastric's laboratory.

Galatia stood staring at the doors well after he was gone, until her thoughts turned to his chamber. Then she slipped behind Victus throne and stepped through the portal. When she stepped out and into the hall outside his lair, it was deserted. She quickly slipped into his room and closed the door quietly behind her.

The chamber lay in darkness, but at her command, the candles flared and bathed its interior in a golden glow.

Victus walked the halls in an agitated state. When he got to Mastric's laboratory door, he hesitated, arm upraised to knock.

"Come in, Victus," Mastric bade him, opening the door with a wave his hand.

Victus strode into the room. "I should have known you would be watching," he stated simply and sat down. "What are you studying?"

Mastric remained bent over a book and did not look up. "Soul research. The ancient magic of the Egyptian mages... it is fascinating."

Nodding in agreement, Victus sat back. "I have read their works as well, but I do not believe you asked me here to discuss Egyptian ideology. What's on your mind?"

"I want my son left alone." His voice emotionless and unyielding, Mastric continued to read as he spoke. "His unwavering loyalty has never been in question in Chambers, nor should it be. He is by far, not only more loyal than any child the lot of you have created, but more powerful as well. I have tested him many times and he has never failed me. I have been grooming him for some time now to deal with certain issues within my own tribe that none others are capable of, and I have plans for him. I will allow neither you nor any of those sods above to disrupt them."

Victus contemplated this for a second before answering. "If he does not respond to our summons, he is subject to punishment. That has always been our law. Though powerful, your son is no exception any more than are mine. I cannot yield in this matter."

Mastric looked up, slamming the book closed. "Then perhaps I shall not keep to myself what I know of you and Galatia. What would the others say if they knew how much you favor her?"

Stunned, Victus stared at him. "Are you mad? That could shatter the Alliance! You would risk the validity of the whole Council for the protection of one child?"

"You rule because I allow it. Do not ever forget that," Mastric reminded him coldly. "You may have the birthright that aids you when ruling over the rest of our brethren, but as you are well-aware, it has never had any hold over me. I do not often enforce my will on our pathetic little gathering of Immortals, but I will have my way in this. My son is of great import to my plans and I would indeed destroy our pathetic Council for him. We both know the Council merely hangs together by a thread, and that they often scheme against each other, and against me when it suits them. I will be the knife that cuts the cord if necessary. So my son will be left alone. Go through the motions if you must, but there it is." Mastric stood. "I will leave you now to your decision and your rendezvous. She waits in your chambers."

Victus got up. "Mastric, wait!"

The master of magic turned. "Yes?"

"How do I know you will keep your silence if I agree to do as you ask?" Victus' eyes demanded an answer, the cold fury in them mixed with fear.

Mastric's smile was hidden beneath his hood. "You don't. Good night, brother."

Victus watched him go, his disturbing words echoing in the silence. Finally, he headed for the sanctity of his lair, knowing Galatia was there.

Galatia lounged in his bed, her half-naked form enticing him to her side.

He undressed and joined her. "This is only for one night. This can never happen again."

She smiled and purred like a cat in his embrace. "Why not?"

He doused the light with a word and whispered in her ear. "Because I am king."

## Chapter Nineteen
## The Daemon's Daughter

*Angelique never ceases to amaze me. Blake's death deeply wounded her, and she struggles to accept it. Yet every night I see changes as she grows. I am pleased my faith in her was not unfounded. Armand, however, is another matter. His disappearance only confirms my suspicions about his anger. I know he may have intended to avenge his friend, but all he will do is find himself among our enemies as an ally or as a tool for their amusement. Either way, this cannot end well. My greatest fear is that his bloodline will be discovered and Valfort will find him. If that happens, it could lead him to Angelique, and she is too vulnerable to resist him right now.*

*Sending the enforcers out risks Armand's life, but if I do not find him quickly, I risk hers and my own as well. I do not think she realizes what a foolish thing he has done. There are those among the Ancients that already want my head, and this would merely seal my fate. I have long thought malcontent festered in his breast. For Angelique's sake, I hope I am wrong in this. If he has joined the Renegades, avoiding the Council's wrath will prove impossible.*

*Valfort has still not revealed his whereabouts, but I now know he is not far away. I recently received word he was in Philadelphia, right in the heart of Principatus territory. For now, he is out of my reach. The Renegades have a far stronger hold on their territories here than in Europe and gaining entrance to them is much more difficult. I do, however, have eyes on him, and I trust the one I sent to watch him. Valfort will be none the wiser, and my youngest son will finally be able to show his mettle...*

*Lord Reivn Draegon*

\* \* \* \* \*

Valfort sat brooding in the main chamber of his underground lair, staring at the fire in silence. His work in America had been finished long ago, yet he had stayed on rather than returning to Europe, distracted by other matters. *Damn him for taking her! I knew I should not have left finding her to that sod, Justin! Now Reivn has her! But why did he not destroy her?*

"My lord?" a young girl interrupted from the door. "Forgive the disturbance, but your presence has been requested at the rave tonight. Magister Dominick asked for you personally. What shall I tell him?"

He growled at her, a dangerous glint in his eye. "What the hell does the bastard want now? I have done more than enough to settle him here and he has more power than he ever dreamed of! I have my own matters that need to be seen to and they have waited long enough!"

She shrugged her shoulders. "I'm sorry sir, but he didn't say. All he told me was that it was a matter of great importance."

With a sigh of annoyance, he nodded. "Very well. I'll be there, but this needs to stop! I did not leave one tyrant only to serve another! I am my own master!"

She bowed respectfully and ducked out the door, leaving him alone once more.

Valfort shook his head and got up, knowing it would take time to prepare. Raves were a vicious experience even at their best, created by Principatus leaders solely to incite the rabble into a frenzy for Alliance blood. Warped and twisted magic would flow through the crowd, as would blood-laced drugs and a few sacrificial lambs. *Lambs… I have never understood why they would call a herd that. Those bumbling, brainwashed human fools resemble nothing close to the grace of their namesake.* He frowned as he walked back to his room. His children were somewhere nearby. He could feel them, but they actively avoided him.

When Valfort reached his room, Tommy was waiting for him. "Which outfit would you like, master?" the boy asked. His expression was blank as he waited.

"I will decide that after I have bathed and done the ritual. You know what to do. Ready my bath and be quick." Valfort dropped onto his bed and lay back, his mood worsened by the fact Tommy had been ready for him. He wanted to beat the boy.

Tommy quickly prepared the bath and laid out Valfort's robes. Vicious scar lines marred the boy's once handsome face. His nimble fingers showed signs of repeated breakage and were twisted and uncharacteristically gnarled for such a youthful body. He barely noticed the change in his appearance though. He had long existed for one purpose only: to serve his master.

Within the hour, Valfort had bathed, donned his robes and disappeared into his laboratory to conjure the necessary protective magic. When he was finished, he quickly changed into the clothing Tommy fetched for him. Then he headed out to a waiting car.

"Where to, my lord?" the driver asked.

Valfort sat back and glanced at his pocket watch. Then he hit the intercom. "To the rave at Club Diamonds."

Kaelan nodded, put the car in gear and turned down the drive. He knew Valfort's reputation too well to disturb him.

Valfort stared out the window. *This had better be important. I have my own plans, and this is going to take more time than I am willing to spare.*

The rave had already begun when Valfort arrived. He had Kaelan drive him close to the entrance. "Wait for me. I won't be long," he ordered as he got out of the car. "Oh..." he paused. "What is your name?"

Kaelan bowed. "I am Kaelan, my lord."

Valfort laughed. "A rather lofty name. I like it! Any family?"

"No sir," Kaelan answered. "I have no one. I've been serving the Magister since I got here."

With a grin, Valfort turned around. "Not anymore. Now you work for me."

Kaelan bowed again. "Thank you, my lord. I'm honored."

Valfort laughed again and walked away. "We shall see," he called back. Then he headed to the front gate. It was packed with the culled, eager to pass their tests and gain their marks. He could hear the shouting and loud music from the parking lot. He scowled and pushed his way through the crowd at the front door, shoving people aside until he got to the security men at the entrance. A guard looked up at the intrusion. His eyes registered recognition, and he quickly ushered Valfort in.

A fresh band had just begun to play when Valfort entered the warehouse. Shouts went up as the sea of bodies started to move to the furiously pulsating rhythm. A laser lightshow flashed neon colors of green, blue and purple across the crowd, transforming the frenzy below into a Mephisto's ballet of twisted forms. The music shook the building, the bass beat sending a pulse that vibrated its very foundation. Every alcove along the edges of the dance floor was filled with young progeny openly feeding on human unfortunates that had come looking for a party and had instead found death. Needles filled with blood-laced drugs were openly passed around and injected. Hundreds danced with wild abandon, packed onto the dance floor like sardines in a can.

Valfort pushed past young ones high on their own depravity, heading toward the side of the room and a platform where the Magisters conducted their twisted rituals. Annoyed at the number of those he considered fools around him, he searched for the quickest way through. Then to his right, he caught sight of a woman with ebony hair spilling down her back. Unlike the rest of the writhing crowd, she stood unmoving, and stared at him. Their eyes met and she smiled, her seductive eyes beckoning him forward. Dressed in a black leather bodysuit that revealed every curve, and six-inch heels, she provoked his thirst on many levels. He quickly glanced over at the Magister on the platform. He was still busy. *Perhaps just a few minutes*, he thought and looked for the woman again, but she had disappeared. He growled. "Curse the rotten bastard... I could have amused myself with that one for hours." He pushed his way over to the stage. "Dominick! You wanted to speak with me?" he yelled above the din.

Dominick waved at him. "Be right with you!" he shouted. "Just let me finish here!"

Valfort frowned and leaned against the edge of the stage. He searched the crowd for the mysterious woman and sighed in resignation when he failed to find her.

"Let's go somewhere a little quieter!" Dominick yelled when he walked over. "Follow me!"

The two pushed through the noisy crowd to the back of the warehouse until they reached a door that led to the offices above. Closing it behind them, Valfort shook his head. The music could still be heard, but it was muffled enough to have a normal conversation. "Tell me, Dominick," he growled as they ascended to the second level of the building. "How do you have any hearing left after doing this every week? I find it highly irritating."

Dominick laughed and opened the office door. Then he stepped aside and let Valfort enter.

After cautiously looking around, Valfort walked in and sat down. Then he looked at Dominick, expecting an answer.

"The young are thirsty for action. It keeps them tamed until we are ready for them to die... for the cause of course." Dominick added hurriedly and cleared his throat.

Valfort stared at him in disgust. "Of course," he stated dryly. "Now... you wanted to talk?"

Dominick nodded and quickly drew some papers from a drawer. "I received these yesterday. It's new information about your quarry. I knew you'd want them immediately." Handing the papers over, he waited while Valfort read them. "I also need a favor from you."

Valfort looked up. "What is it this time?"

"Would you make a few young for the cause? We could really use their abilities..." he stopped at Valfort's icy stare.

Valfort stood up and glared at him. "I've told you I will not allow any of my young to be a part of this sycophantic crowd. My children have better uses than this and they serve me. If you want the assistance of one of my blood, you will come to me. It's costly yes, but you can afford it with the money you draw in from these idiots here." He turned to go, but Dominick's voice stopped him, and his eyes narrowed.

"We need them to wage better war against the alliance. Their magical uses far outweigh..." Dominick stopped, his hands trembling.

Valfort spun around in cold rage. "...Outweigh what exactly, Dominick? My search? You should be thankful for that rivalry because it keeps him away from your doorstep! Otherwise, he'd be hunting you and all your useless breed! The matter is closed!" He turned to leave, shaking his head. "One of these days you will learn I serve no one."

Dominick sat gripping the desk in fear long after the door had closed.

Fuming inwardly, Valfort pushed his way back through the still swarming crowd as he slowly headed for the exit.

*Leaving so soon?* a feminine voice whispered in his mind.

He spun around, looking for the source. Standing behind him was his mystery woman. *Well, I could stay awhile if I had reason to*, he telepathied with a grin.

The woman smiled. "Are you sure you want my company? There are not too many who are up to that challenge. They say I am dangerous."

Valfort stepped closer and gazed down at her. "I'm dangerous too. Would you like to find out just how dangerous, little girl?"

"You are either very brave or very foolish. Not even my father calls me little girl." She laughed and caught his hair between her fingers. Then she yanked his head down to hers and kissed him full on the lips. "Oh, you are going to be fun."

Growling like a feral animal, he wrapped his arms around her and devoured her kiss with his own. Then he asked, "What is your name, beautiful?"

She smiled again, her eyes cold and hungry. "I am Alora Leopold."

"And I am yours," he muttered against her lips.

She laughed and omitted a sound akin to a starving beast. Then she gripped his hair tighter and tore open his neck, feasting on his blood.

Feeling her fangs sink into him, he pulled her closer and let her take him. As she drank her fill, he let out a rumble of satisfaction.

Finally, she let him go and closed his wound. "You really aren't afraid of me. Intriguing. I think we have much to talk about though. Your blood gave me far more than I imagined it would. This meeting is fortuitous."

He frowned and pulled away. "Why should my blood be of any importance to you?"

She curled her arm into his and began walking toward the entrance with him. "Because we share a common enemy."

"Interesting. Then perhaps this trip was a lucrative one after all," he replied. They crossed the parking lot and climbed into his car. "Where to, my sweet?"

Alora smiled and leaned against him. "Let's go to your place. You and I have much to discuss. By this time tomorrow you will be my new best friend."

Valfort stared for a minute at the window separating the driver's seat from the rear cabin, knowing it's specially treated glass did not allow even an Immortal to eavesdrop on the Limo's interior. Finally, he tapped the intercom. "Home, driver." Then he looked at her curiously. "I'll bite, sweetness. What's on your mind?" he settled back, waiting for an answer. *She is obviously not without power, but what possible use could she be?*

"You are related to the one who drove me from my home. I tried to kill him, but his son got in the way. I have been gathering the strength to take him down, but he has managed to evade every attempt I've made thus far." She frowned, putting on the airs of a petulant child.

He took the bait. "Tell me who hurt you and I will make them suffer. They will bleed until they run dry and you shall feast on their bones!"

She sighed, her eyes taking on a dangerous glow. "Lord Reivn Draegon and his sons. You hate him almost as much as I do, so it would benefit us both to work together in bringing about his destruction. Oh... and yes. I got all that by drinking from you."

Valfort snarled and pushed her off. "How dare you presume to know so much of me! You may have gotten fragments of my past, but know nothing of what you speak!"

"Oh, but I do. My birthright is far different from yours, wizard! I can see right through to your very soul if I choose! I offer you an alliance that would benefit us both. When our pact is complete, you can go your separate way. Apart we may not accomplish what we seek, but together we will destroy him! Join me!" Her eyes were devoid of any warmth and moved as though watching her prey. It chilled him to the core. He contemplated her offer in silence for a minute, weighing the odds. Finally, he nodded. "Very well. I will join you long enough to bring Reivn to his knees. He has something I very much want. Then we go our separate ways."

Alora's icy purr filled the Limo's interior. "I'll bet. I want him hanging on my walls. An alliance then… you get your prize and I get mine. Between the two of us, we will destroy him."

Valfort scoffed at her last statement. "He's not that easy to break, my dear. I've been trying for years to do so. I even tried to convince him to join me once."

"It's very clear to me that you have never met anyone who thinks with anything other than the brain of a cockroach!" She growled. "Has it not occurred to you that perhaps you have just not offered the right incentives? Give him what he wants most, and he'll come around faster than you can say Daemon!" At that, she threw her head back and laughed.

He stared at her, his brow furrowed as he mulled over the idea. "Then you have a plan?"

She sat straight up and stared at him, her laughter gone. "You bet I do…"

# BLOOD FEUD

## Chapter Twenty
## Council Law

*My enforcers have retrieved vital information on Armand's recent whereabouts, and I am closing in on his location. I search now only because she begs it of me, but there is little chance of saving him. Council law can be stretched only so far. I have delayed my reports to their halls far too long. If I do not find him soon, I will have no choice but to deal swift death when he is found or forfeit my own life. How can I tell this to Angelique?*

*Duty in conflict with honor... how do I resolve such a thing? If I kill Armand, I will lose her loyalty to hatred. In her mind, she is still living the life she left behind centuries ago. Until she accepts our ways, she will never understand my hunting Armand even if he has betrayed us.*

*Angelique has surprised me with her devotion to her assigned tasks. She is eager to please and seeks to gain my respect. So why does she trouble my thoughts thus? I cannot seem to take one step but what I find myself dealing with her in some way. Conversation with her often turns to verbal battle and yet, in the end, I find myself giving in to her. She is as bewitching a woman as I have ever met, and she covets my soul, I think. How has such innocence survived for so many centuries untouched by the darkness of our curse? I look upon her face, still so tied to her humanity, and I cannot help but wonder what Valfort saw that fateful night he found and made her anew. Was she truly only a buffer for him or was there more to his claiming her? I would request of the Council that I be allowed to return to hunting him, but they will only deny me. Always it is this Godforsaken war, the drive behind which escapes me. And now with my own protégé disappearing, I have fallen under their shadow of doubt.*

*Lord Reivn Draegon*

\* \* \* \* \*

The meeting of Prefects lasted three days. During that time, Angelique learned how seriously she needed to take her duties. Reivn remained beside her throughout her stay and rode home with her afterward. She knew he was merely protecting her, but was still annoyed so many had assumed they were lovers. When she got home, she jumped back into her duties with zeal to put that memory behind her.

The week following their return, she awoke to a letter from Reivn, but this time it was not personal. Horrified, she sank into a chair as she scanned its contents. She read it a second time and then a third, not wanting to accept what it said.

> *My Lady,*
>
> *It is with the deepest regret I must inform you that your child, Armand Philippe Girard, has renounced his allegiance to the Council. He has joined a Renegade force heading south. Upon direct order of the Council, a blood hunt has been called on him. Forgive me. I do not believe I can save him. I wanted to tell you this grievous news before others could. Unless I can prove him innocent, he is a marked man, even if he does return on his own. If I cannot, then all our lives are in danger. I am sorry.*
>
> > *Your servant as ever,*
> > *Lord Reivn Draegon*

Angelique dropped the letter and ran from her room down the hall to Reivn's quarters. Desperate to speak with him, she ignored curious stares. She burst in unannounced and froze when she saw him standing with his back to her, clad only with a towel around his waist.

Reivn turned around and met her gaze, his expression sympathetic. " So you read the letter. I have no choice. I am sorry."

Closing the distance between them, Angelique slapped him across the face. "You're sorry? You said you would help find him! You've had him sentenced to death and for what? Because he left without your permission? How could you?" she raised her hand to strike him again.

He caught her hand and pinned it behind her. Then he pulled her close. "Stop it, Angelique! You do not know what you are saying! He attacked and killed innocent people in cold blood, revealing himself and endangering us all!"

Stunned by his accusations, she stared up at him in disbelief. "Armand would never do such a thing!" She beat her free hand against his chest and screamed. "He has always valued human life! He would never kill anyone that way!"

Reivn let her go and turned to a small wood box sitting on his table. "We tracked him to Europe and then back here, but we lost him in Philadelphia. It is what he did in Europe that has condemned him. He attacked a small Rrom Kumpania. He was traveling with two others whose names we do not yet know, and he and his companions killed every man, woman, and child they found. This box holds the eyes of one of those who were slaughtered that night. Using your magic, you can see what he saw before he was killed." He opened the box and held it out to her.

Angelique hesitated, staring at it in fear. She knew if she saw Armand, he would be beyond any salvation. "Promise you will find out the truth before you kill him. If he did this, there must have been a reason. Armand is not a killer."

He did not answer. He gazed at her expectantly and waited.

Looking down at the box again, she slowly picked up the dead man's eyes and closed her own, willing forth the Mystic Spirals. Then she watched the horrible scene unfold.

Everywhere around her, people were running and screaming in terror. She sensed confusion and fear. The man, whose name she discovered was Verne, ran for a gun. She could see burning wagons as he rushed to save women and children, their cries cut short as they were cut down.

"No..." Angelique cried, drawn into the man's memory. "Not that way... run!" Lost in the vision, she felt his agony as his people died in front of him. Then she saw who hunted them. Bloodlust had twisted his face almost beyond recognition. *He looks as though he's enjoying himself...* she thought in panic. He dodged back and forth, killing with no mercy.

The man whose eyes were guiding her was shooting. She could feel the vibrations when his gun fired. Verne ran out of ammunition and glanced down to reload. When he looked up, a face that was unmistakable snarled at him and he was cut down. Then the vision went black.

Angelique let go of the vision and lifted her eyes to meet Reivn's. "It wasn't Armand," she whispered. "It couldn't have been. He's never been like that. This is very wrong. If you just give me some time, I promise I will find out the truth. Please, my Lord, I beg of you..."

Reivn took Verne's eyes from her and placed them back in the box without a word.

"Please," she cried again. Fear for Armand drove her beyond caring about propriety or the Alliance and their laws.

He walked over and took her hand. "I cannot promise you anything, but I will try to investigate a little further. Understand that if I do not deal with him swiftly, the Council will summarily order my execution, as well as any who are my proteges. That means you. There are no doubts as to your loyalty yet. Do not give a reason for there to be."

She snatched her hand away and stepped backward. "Why? Would you hunt me next? I am his maker, after all. Isn't that the law?"

Reivn sighed and closed the distance between them. "I tire of this, Angelique. You have been a part of our world for several hundred years, yet you still act like a child. I have taught you our laws. You released him a long time ago. That removes your responsibility, but it does not remove mine. I claimed you both. I will not let injustice befall you, or him if he is innocent. But with those images I find it difficult to believe he is." He wrapped his arms around her and pulled her close. Then he leaned against her cheek and whispered in her ear. "Do you love him?"

Taken aback by the question, Angelique tried to pull away, but he held her fast. "Of course, I love him! He has been with me for many years!"

He shook his head and smiled. "Very nice evasion. I could get used to dueling with you this way. I asked if you love him. Now answer the question."

His face was so near hers that she could feel his breath. She shook her head vehemently. "I knew what you meant! He is as much my brother as he is the child I created! What affair is it of yours anyway?" Forming as indignant a look as she could, she raised her chin in defiance.

"It's not," Reivn answered, releasing her so suddenly that she lost her balance and landed quite abruptly on the floor. "I can promise you nothing, but I will try to find out what I can."

Angelique's cheeks turned crimson. She got up angrily and turned to go.

"Angelique," he continued. "Do not come here uninvited again or you may be embarrassed, as I prefer to sleep without clothes. I do not wish to offend you further. Good night."

Attempting to recover her dignity, she yelled at him. "I am sorry you have had to put up with me, but you did insist on taking us into your tutelage! How quickly you forgot that!"

"I have not forgotten who offered me her blood, or who has walked with me every night I asked!" he shot back, angry now. "I did not choose for this to happen! Contrary to your belief, there are powers even I must bow my head to."

Angelique fled in shame at his words, tears stinging her face. She knew she was being unfair and that he did not want this either. Fear of losing Armand had driven her to do the unthinkable. She had intruded in his private lair without good cause and then insulted him. He had every right to be angry. *I'm such a fool*, she chided herself. *I am making an enemy of the only one that can actually help me.* She ran to her rooms, his words still ringing in her ears.

From the shadows, Ruben watched her until she closed her door, then returned to his own room. Worry creased his brow. "She needs to stop before she gets herself killed," he mumbled.

Genevieve squeezed his hand affectionately, closing the door behind them. "She'll learn. She's no fool. She is just young by nature. So many things to learn the hard way and all at the same time… it must be horrible for her to have to handle so much, so suddenly."

"You are right of course," he admitted, smiling at her. "We will aid where we can, and pray Armand is not what they think. She is not ready to lose him too." The door clicked softly as the latch slid into place and the hall was silent once more.

Completely unaware they had seen her, Angelique dropped onto her bed, mental anguish causing a fatigue she had never felt before. Turning her thoughts again to the images she had seen, she closed her eyes and spent the remainder of the night trying to see that face clearer. It was so distorted that at first, she found it hard to believe it could possibly be Armand. But as she replayed it in her mind, though twisted with the lust for blood, to her dismay the identity was unmistakable. She was still trying to solve what had happened when she slipped into slumber.

Perhaps it was the devotion she had for those she called family, perhaps the power of her blood, but she felt him calling to her. There was no anger or rage... only incredible pain, ongoing and terrible. Armand was reaching out to her and begging for help. Unlike the single scream she felt when Blake died, this was a continuous stream of cries, and when she awoke, she could still hear them. *Armand*, she telepathied with as much strength as she could muster, *I don't know where you are or what's happened, but I swear I'll find you.*

As the lethargy from sleep faded so did his voice, but Angelique was sure it had not been a dream. She prayed he had heard her wherever he was. Rushing to complete her duties, she kept thinking of how best to find him. She had access to the guild's resources, but was not sure where to begin. Then she remembered Reivn's promise to help her and considered asking him. She was worried he might not give her the chance to find out the truth, however. In frustration, she wandered into her office, seeking seclusion. But no matter how much she argued with herself, her answer always returned to the mentor who had already taught her so much. Finally, she picked up a pen and paper, and wrote a letter to Reivn. When she sealed it, she sat debating whether or not to throw it on the fire. A knock at her door interrupted her thoughts. "Come in," she answered, trying to sound as calm as possible.

A courier stuck his head in, clearing his throat politely. "My Lady? I have a letter for you. I was asked to deliver it immediately."

Angelique got up and stepped around the side of the desk. "Who is it from?"

"From Lord Reivn, my Lady." He handed it over, then bowed and turned to leave.

"Wait," she called. "I have a letter for him as well. Will you see that he gets it?"

The courier smiled. "I'll see to it at once." He took the envelope, bowed again and left the room.

She turned her attention to the message in her hands, opened it and began to read.

> *Lady Angelique,*
>
> *Please forgive my anger. I do not doubt your loyalty to the Alliance or our tribe. I believe you to be a woman of the old blood and noble ways. I shall continue to support you as a tribal Prefect for our tribe and will add to your training in the arts. As far as your child, I can only say I will offer what assistance I am able to without endangering either myself or any in my charge. I do not wish to jeopardize any of the lives of those under me. It means far more to me than you know. My healer, Serena, urges me to move forward with existence and to hold on to the gentler side of my heart. I told you once what my feeding requires and what is usually involved. Yet you seem determined to offer it still. So if*

*this is truly your wish, I will accept. Again, I must warn you of the potent effect my feeding has on my donors. I admit this would please me greatly, but you do not know what catching the Dragon's eye entails. As for putting up with you, I am an old teacher and all my students have done well. With your natural power, you shall also prosper in the learning. In addition to your magical training, it is time you began working with others of our tribe in this territory.*

*Until Anon,*
*Lord Reivn Draegon*

Angelique smiled and walked to the window. Clouds covered the moon, so though her view of the garden was perfect, it was shrouded in shadows. She focused her senses and looked closer.

Reivn was there, absently brushing his hand across the tops of the roses as he strolled down the path. Then the courier she had spoken to approached, handed him her message and disappeared, leaving him alone once more.

Opening the balcony door, she levitated down to the ground. Then she picked up the edge of her gown and silently made her way toward him. She smiled. *I wonder if he knows I'm here.*

In response, she received a tap on her shoulder. Startled, she turned around.

"We really need to work on your awareness skills," Reivn chuckled, offering her his arm. "So, about helping you find Armand..."

Countless nights passed with no word as to Armand's whereabouts, and Angelique began to give up hope. Reivn and his enforcers were actively searching, but it seemed as if Armand had simply disappeared. She spent most of her time with Reivn, learning her duties as Prefect, meeting other Mastrics in the territory, and honing her skills. The loss of both Blake and Armand had driven her to delve into their world with zeal, determined no further harm would befall her family. She kept Ruben and Genevieve within the safety of the Guild. Her own trips were planned and were only for tribal business or her responsibilities as Prefect. She was determined to find Armand and avenge Blake's murder.

One night while Angelique was finishing her tasks, Reivn came to her laboratory.

He stood quietly waiting until she was done, then bowed when she turned to him. "I am sorry I interrupted you, but we need to talk," he explained. "It is time you went before our Council, so they can formally accept you. You would have done so upon your creation, but because your creator is a Renegade, it never happened. So, we leave for the Sahara tomorrow night."

She stared at him open-mouthed. "What of my duties? And my search for Armand? And my family... I can't be away from them!"

He sighed and gripped her shoulders. "It is expected of you. We will not be gone longer than a couple of nights, but we are going." He turned and walked out, leaving her to her thoughts.

They left the following night. Angelique had expected to leave by car, but instead found herself following Reivn to the lowest level of the Guild. She stared at him, a question in her eyes.

He smiled. "We are using the portals. It is time you learn to use them. Would you not agree?"

She nodded. She had learned of the magical gate system when she had first arrived.

He pulled her onto a stone dais in the center of the room. Then he chanted, "Talianakarnae vraa Leviste Polusporta!" The room shimmered and disappeared in a brilliant flash of light.

All around them was a seemingly endless vortex of color. With a start, Angelique realized it continuously shifted and altered in appearance and glanced worriedly up at Reivn. He remained undisturbed, however, so she relaxed.

Seconds later, Reivn and Angelique stepped out into a chamber that annexed a beautifully ornate great hall. It had the appearance of a fortress built during the height of the Roman Empire and was a palace unlike any she had ever seen. Gems encrusted the walls of solid marble, and the high, arched ceilings complimented the immense columns that rose to thirty feet in height.

When they left the chamber, two guards greeted them and led the way toward a chamber where nine empty thrones sat in a half circle. When they stopped, Reivn knelt down on his left knee, crossed his right fist across his chest in salute and bowed his head.

Glancing over at him in surprise, Angelique hurried to curtsy and bent her head low, wondering why they did this to an empty room. Then a voice flooded the room with its commanding presence, and it filled Angelique with fear.

"Welcome, Lord Reivn. Stand and be recognized."

Reivn got up and took her arm, gently guiding her to a standing position beside him.

When she looked up, she was surprised to see every chair but one was occupied. Lowering her eyes respectfully, she glanced sideways at Reivn and wondered what to do next.

The Ancients observed her in silence with critical eyes.

Reivn waited quietly, as the Council looked over their latest newcomer.

"Let her come before us," Victus finally commanded.

A simple enough request, yet Angelique felt her legs threatening to give way. Fear filled her heart. She willed herself to move and stepped closer, feeling the raw power that emanated from these beings in front of her.

When she was only a few paces from the base of Victus' throne, he held up his hand. "That is close enough," he commanded. The Ancient gazed at her intently, sizing her up for several minutes. "Raise your eyes to me, girl."

When Angelique obeyed, she felt him enter her mind. Her instinct to resist rose to the surface, but Victus quelled it, crushing her will instantly. A fine sheen of blood began to cover her skin, as he went deeper, seeing things she could not remember and uncovering the darkest details of her past. Tense moments of silence passed while he continued his exploration, until she began slipping into unconsciousness from the strain. Finally, he withdrew, releasing his grip on her mind and senses.

Angelique dropped to the floor the moment he let her go.

Reivn caught her, and then grimly looked up at the Ancient. "My Lord Victus, I would ask what you found." Lifting her into his arms, he waited.

"She has many hidden memories that were of great interest to me. It would appear the Eastern Lord, Kuromoto, took her many years ago. He planned to corrupt one of the larger domains in Europe using her as the trap. It was he who wiped her mind to prevent her from remembering." Victus stopped, silently sending the images of what he had seen to his colleagues. "She is totally unaware of how she was used. If she is guilty of any crime, it would be the lack of knowledge she has about our world, and though she is a child of the Renegade Valfort, she is remarkably loyal to our ways. So…" Victus paused and looked at the others, but they remained silent. "We will accept her. She is henceforth recognized as a member of the Alliance. Continue teaching her, Lord Reivn. You have the permission of this Council to do so."

Reivn bowed to them and backed away slowly, taking her with him.

Still unconscious from her experience, Angelique did not hear anything that was said, as he carried her from the room.

Once they had left the throne room, Reivn hastened to a side room with her. He gently laid her on the bed and then sat staring at her as night turned to day. He fought off sleep, struggling to sort his thoughts until he finally drifted into slumber and dreamed of the copper-haired beauty.

When Reivn awakened the following night, his eyes were immediately drawn to the bed.

Angelique's copper hair slid across the pillows and she stirred. Her eyes fluttered open to greet the night. Then she moaned when pain surfaced. She tried to sit up, but yesterday's meeting with the Ancients was still too fresh.

Without hesitation, Reivn moved to her side and took her hand to help her up.

She looked up at him in confusion. "What are you doing in here?"

He knew she was unaware of where they were and thought herself in her room at the guild. "We're still in the Sahara, remember? You're weak, here…" He opened his wrist and held it to her lips. "Drink. You need it."

Still shaking from yesterday's strain, Angelique did not argue. She gripped his arm to steady herself and then began to feed. His ancient and potent blood burned like liquid fire going down her throat, and a rush of strength flowed through her being.

"When you are feeling better, I will take you home," Reivn told her gently.

It struck her how odd this statement sounded, for she had never considered any place but St. Etienne home. She looked up to find he was watching her, his thoughts unreadable. Their eyes met, and she froze, suddenly feeling very vulnerable. "My Lord?" she whispered, her voice barely audible in the silence.

Reivn reached out and gently pulled her to her feet. Then he wrapped an arm around her, drawing her closer. Without a word, he swept her hair back, revealing the pale skin of her neck.

They stood gazing at each other in silence, until finally, he bent his head and bit into her, drinking only a few drops.

She gasped when his teeth punctured her flesh, but did not resist.

Her scent intoxicated him, and he buried his fangs deeper, desiring to possess all of her. Completely unaware his curse had shifted his need onto her, he knew only that his intense yearning for her blood was irresistible. He closed his eyes, reveling in the potency of the connection, unwilling to let it go. When he finally gathered his senses and pulled away, she collapsed in his arms, ashen white. The realization he had taken too much shocked him. He knew he could not feed her again so soon or the bond between their blood would seal itself, joining them together, and he would not readily submit her to that against her will. He immediately summoned a servant. Then he stood holding her and staring at her until the servant arrived.

When the man walked in, Reivn grabbed his arm without hesitation, extended his fangs and tore it open. Then he held it to her lips, forcing the fluid down her throat.

Her color slowly returned.

Reivn stopped before he took too much, closed the man's wound and sent him away. Then he turned his attention to the unconscious woman in his arms. He eased her back on the bed and sat down beside her, resting his head in his hands and berating himself. Once he saw her color had finally returned, he picked her up and carried her back through the portal. His thoughts were in turmoil when he returned her to her chambers in the Guild, where she could recover. *I am a fool*! He bitterly chastised himself, angry for losing control and ashamed of his weakness. There had been no invitation this time and he had taken from her. He gently laid her on her bed and covered her with a blanket, brushing wisps of curls from her brow. Then he doused the lights and left the room, leaving her to sleep.

Reivn returned to the portal chamber and growled out the command to take him home. "Talianakarnae vraa Leviste Draegonstorm!" The portal came alive and he stepped through.

The sergeant of the Black Guard that was on duty saluted him. "Welcome home, my lord."

Reivn barely acknowledged his presence. He stormed down the hall to his private chambers.

The Dragon Guard officer posted outside his room snapped to attention as he approached.

Reivn snapped, "Fetch Reyna and ensure I am not disturbed."

The guard bowed and hurried off.

Reivn slammed the door behind him and began to pace the room. His turbulent state only increased as he thought of the copper curls and green eyes that haunted him from the shadows. Within minutes, there was a knock at the door. "Come!" he commanded.

Reyna timidly entered the room. "You sent for me, my lord?"

His agitation apparent, he walked over and grabbed her. Then pulling her into his arms, he sank his fangs into her neck. He drank almost savagely in a vain attempt to cure the thirst that burned in his veins. Then he picked her up and carried her to his bed. "Tend to me, my beautiful flower," he growled. "My need for you tonight is insatiable. Make me forget what I feel. I want to lose myself from all thought for awhile."

With shaking hands, Reyna obeyed and began to undress him, keenly aware of his mood. When she finished, she removed her own clothing. Then she obediently laid back on the bed.

He dropped down beside her, desire consuming him. All thoughts of control disappeared, and he pinned her arms above her. Then with a bestial snarl he sank his fangs in again, devouring her blood as he drove himself into her with desperate and painful need.

A slight whimper escaped her, and she closed her eyes, as his ferocity grew. When he finally freed her hands, she kept them above her, clinging tightly to the pillows beneath her head.

Reivn explored her body, the curse he endured wresting away the last remnants of his self-control. Beyond the point of no return, he struggled to subdue the urges that drove him, but could not bring his hunger to bay. The remainder of that night he used her again and again, his thirst so insatiable that no matter how he tried to quench it, it would not abate. Alora's curse had once more turned his body against him, and the only woman that could fulfill that need was untouchable. Tortured by his inexorable thirst and driven almost mad with a desire he could not satisfy, he was relentless.

Finally, Reyna slipped into unconsciousness beneath him.

He gasped and rolled away, some part of him recognizing even in his frenzied state that she could not safely withstand any more. He laid there, shaking and staring at the ceiling, his hunger gnawing at him, mingled with something else he could not fathom. Finally he closed his eyes, gulping in air and fighting the urge to attempt satisfying himself with her one last time. He knew now that she could no longer help him. The image of emerald green eyes flooded his mind and his fangs throbbed as though he had not fed at all. The wretched curse had done its work well. He opened his eyes and he screamed... one long, agonizing sound. When his lungs were empty, he sucked in air and then glanced at the unconscious girl beside him. Seeing the condition he had left her in only served to further his anguish and he sat up, drawing his knees to his chest and leaning on them in despair. He sat there until the sun rose over the horizon and he felt sleep tugging at his consciousness. Finally he dropped back on the bed. Then he turned to stare at Reyna again, watching over her until he slipped into an uneasy sleep.

# BLOOD FEUD

## Chapter Twenty-One
## The Dragon's Eye

*Atlantic City is in jeopardy. The Eastern lords attempted to murder not only Lord Sorin, but those in his staff as well. This could not have come at a more difficult time. The rumors of another Renegade attack have been filtering in from almost every outlying Principatus territory. This region is at serious risk of total anarchy if we lose the Prince right now. I have warned him and posted extra security details. I hope it is enough. I have my men scouring the city for any sign of the Easterners. The men I sent are too few, but I cannot afford to spare any others with the threat of another attack. Even the Guild does not presently have enough men. If the Principatus launches an assault on this city anytime soon, we may not hold our borders. I dispatched letters to the Council as soon as I received the reports, but it could be days before any serious reinforcements arrive. We are on our own until then.*

*Another discouraging situation has arisen as well, and this one I cannot easily solve. I overstepped my boundaries when I took sustenance from Angelique. I know not what possessed me to touch her. And yet... it did not sicken me, as it has with others I have not mated with. I believe Alora's curse is somehow the cause of this. It has drawn Angelique inside its net. Now she, and certainly Reyna, must loathe and fear me for what I did. God, I am such a fool! In taking what was not mine I may have lost her faith in me, as well as her loyalty. With any other, I could say this was no great thing, but with Angelique, I could not fathom saying our goodbyes. She touches my heart like no other and warms it in a way I have not felt since my human years. Does she feel it too?*

*Lord Reivn Draegon*

\* \* \* \* \*

Angelique awoke that night to raging thirst and sent for a servant before she even dressed. As she shook off sleep, she remembered the events of the previous night. Her first thought was Reivn and the words in his letters. He had promised her he would not touch her. *What happened?* she wondered as she walked down the darkened halls to her lab. She thought over the previous night's events. *I caused him to lose control somehow,* she thought in frustration. *He would never have done this unprovoked. I need to speak with him.* Her mind made up, she headed to his office.

To Angelique's surprise, it was locked, and there was no light shining from beneath the door. Thinking he had not left his rooms yet, she made her way there, but they were also empty. She turned away in confusion, walking right into another of the Guild's residents. "Oh, excuse me," she muttered, her thoughts still on last night.

The woman smiled. "You seem lost. Are you okay?"

Angelique nodded, not wanting to talk to anyone. She started to walk away when she remembered something Reivn had written in one of his letters. "Wait," she called to the retreating figure.

The woman stopped and turned around.

"Are you Serena?" Angelique asked.

"I am," Serena replied.

Angelique sighed. "Do you know where I can find Lord Reivn?"

"That might prove to be difficult at the moment," Serena answered. "He left for Draegonstorm and is not expected to return for a while. I spoke with him last night."

Stunned, Angelique stared at her. "Thank you," she finally muttered and walked away. *Why did he leave?* she wondered in confusion. *Is he that upset with me?* Jumping as a hand touched her arm, she spun around.

Serena had followed her. "Is something wrong?" she inquired politely.

Angelique started to shake her head when she realized just how much she needed to talk to someone, so she nodded and began to tell the Cleric everything that had transpired since her arrival. She poured out her frustration and pain in a torrent of words that would not stop.

Putting her arm around Angelique, Serena guided her to a quiet room where they could sit and while away the hours.

The two women talked for hours and quickly became good friends. Angelique shared many things with Serena that night. Serena was much older and wiser and had given her a great deal to think about.

Angelique realized during the conversation that she was approaching her troubles as though she were still human and a youthful, unmarried woman. Serena had explained to her in ways she never heard before exactly how dangerous this really was, and she knew now she had to change, or the rest of her family would suffer Blake's fate. When she returned to her rooms, the greatest thing she wanted was to set things right with Reivn. *But how, when he's not here and no one knows when he will return?* Silent contemplation preoccupied the rest of her night until sleep finally claimed her.

When Angelique slept that day, she again heard Armand's voice crying out in agony. Pain overwhelmed her as she felt his tortured presence deep inside her mind.

*Find me*, Armand begged. *Please find me!*

At sunset, she woke screaming, "Armand!" Her face was covered in a fine sheen of blood, sweat out while dreaming. She was disoriented for a moment. Then she remembered the dream. "Oh, God!" she cried, realizing they must have touched minds a second time. She threw off the covers and jumped up. "I have to find him! He's in trouble! I just know it!"

Angelique quickly washed and dressed, and then hurried to her office and sent for a courier. By the time the man arrived, she had already drafted a letter to Reivn, telling him what she knew. "Lord Reivn must get this dispatch immediately! It is an urgent matter that cannot wait! I'm going to need his help!"

As soon as the courier left, she went looking for Serena.

Serena was in the library talking with a gentleman.

Without waiting for an introduction, Angelique began to tell her about the vision.

"It's possible Armand is trapped somewhere in Renegade territory. They frequently capture and torture…" Serena fell silent when she saw Angelique's horrified expression.

The gentleman at Serena's side cleared his throat. "My lady, we have not met. My name is Duncan Campbell. Perhaps I can help." He began gently explaining to her just what Serena meant. He knew if their suspicions were right, getting Armand back would be difficult. Trying not to frighten her, he briefly told her about the Renegade's war against the Ancients and how determined they were to wipe out both humanity and the old ways. "The Renegades never accepted the universal agreement among the nine that took place centuries ago. It was made to preserve and protect our life and society from the rest of the world. However, the Principatus believe the world is one big feeding ground to do with as they please… a sort of Gods among men syndrome. They seek to destroy all mankind. This sort of thinking led to rebellion and the murder of some of our first Elders. Many of us believe that is what started the war that has now lasted several thousand years."

Duncan paused and took Angelique's hand. "Many innocent people have fallen victim to this conflict, and many others have…" he glanced at

Serena, who nodded for him to continue. "Well, they have been taken by our enemies and tortured, mutilated or worse. The Renegades use their magic to twist the existence of those unlucky captives, bending not only their bodies, but their minds as well. Not many of those taken ever return."

Angelique's expression froze, fear preventing her from asking the obvious question.

Duncan nodded in understanding. "Yes. I'm afraid it is possible. For the kind of agony you described to be in one of our kind, something terrible has to have happened. We have a much higher tolerance for pain than mere humanity does. Observe…" Without warning, he pulled a knife from his pocket and sliced open her hand, letting it go so she could see it.

Angelique winced when he cut her, but the pain disappeared almost instantly, and she was fine. Licking her hand to close the wound, she stared at it thoughtfully, seeing Armand's face as it had been in her dreams. Then she looked up. "What can I do? How do I find him? How can I help him when I don't even know where to begin looking?"

Duncan shrugged. "It may already be too late for him. I do not know. But we can see about contacting some of my associates in Philadelphia. If anyone can find out about your Armand, it would be them and with relatively little risk."

Serena walked over to Angelique and firmly gripped her hand. "Angelique, you must be strong for him now. If you fall apart, all hope for his survival would be lost. There is strength in you. I see it. You were not chosen as our Prefect because Lord Reivn loves you. He sees your strength and knows you will survive to be a good leader."

Angelique turned to stare at her. "What…what did you say?"

Duncan interrupted them. "Serena, I'm afraid I must be off. I have private matters to settle before dawn."

Serena pulled Angelique toward the door as Duncan prepared to leave, and they walked him to the front entrance.

Angelique's thoughts were on Armand, and she sent him a silent message that she prayed he would hear. *Please hold on. I will find you.*

Her fear that Reivn would destroy him the moment he was found was shadowed only by the fact that if they did not find him soon, he would be killed for certain. She also wondered about Serena's statement. "Lord Reivn loves you," she had said. *Can that be true?* she wondered. *Why did he not tell me?*

Their arrival at Angelique's office was met with a message for her. The seal on the front told her it was from Reivn and she immediately tore it open.

*Come to my study as soon as you get this.*
*Your servant, Lord Reivn Draegon*

Angelique turned to Serena. "Lord Reivn has returned and wishes to speak to me. I'll join you later." Not waiting for a response, she hurried down the hall. Light shining from under his door confirmed his presence, and after taking a moment to tidy herself, she calmly knocked.

Reivn opened the door immediately and stood there staring at her.

"My Lord," she whispered, remembering the last time they had seen each other.

He remembered too and abruptly retreated to the other side of the desk, not trusting himself to be near her. "I received your message and came immediately. Are you sure?"

Angelique nodded, her emotions chaotic beneath the calm visage she wore.

Reivn was silent for a moment before he finally asked, "Will you let me walk inside your mind to see what you saw as you slept?"

She involuntarily took a step back, afraid of what else he might see. Her earlier thoughts were not ones she was ready to share.

Reivn came around the desk to stand in front of her, believing her afraid of him. Grabbing her by the shoulders, he gritted his teeth and held back the fury at himself. "I will not hurt you, I promise! I should not have...taken from you as I did when last I saw you. Forgive me, please." Then he realized he held her in an iron grip and let go, backing away. "I swear to you, it will not happen again."

Shocked by his sudden outburst, Angelique stared at him.

He would not meet her eyes, instead turning to gaze out the window at the gardens they were both so fond of.

"My Lord, please. It wasn't... isn't you. I didn't want you to see...to hear my..." Frustrated, she reached out and touched his arm.

Reivn turned to gaze at her, his eyes troubled.

"I trust you, my Lord," Angelique whispered. "You have been good to me. It isn't you. My thoughts have been very confused lately. I didn't want you to see them."

Without a word, he took her hand and led her to the French doors. He threw his own cloak over her shoulders and they stepped out into the gardens. Then they walked together in silence while he turned some unknown thought over in his head. She jumped when he finally started to speak, causing him to smile. "I left to look into some serious matters I recently learned of. It would seem Kuromoto has hired assassins to eliminate Lord Sorin, Lord Gareth, myself, and you for interfering with his plans. I needed information on the eastern tribes from my fortress library. I did not leave because of you." He stopped and faced her. "I... enjoy your company and very much regret having offended you by drinking from you during our stay in the Sahara."

Angelique giggled at the look on his face. "It did not offend or upset me, my Lord. I thought I had in some way offended you. So you see, we have both been victims of a misunderstanding. It would seem we need to start over...again."

Now it was Reivn's turn to be surprised. "You are an amazing woman, Angelique. You can charm even a Dragon into submitting to your gentle ways. I am at your service, my lady." He bowed to her and smiled, and then offered his arm.

They walked on to the river until they reached a boulder that was large enough for them both to sit on. Then they sat and talked for hours about the Renegades, the Ancients, and the future of all the tribes. Finally, talk turned to Armand, and to her surprise, Reivn was more than willing to aid in the search. "May I suggest we not notify the Council of Armand's whereabouts until we are able to solve the situation completely?"

Angelique threw her arms around his neck. "Oh, thank you! Thank you so much!"

Caught off guard, he held her for a moment before pulling away. His face was a mask to the chaos that stirred within. He glanced down at her and drew a sharp intake of breath. The moon had emerged from the clouds and in its soft light, her copper hair gleamed in brilliant hues of red and gold and her eyes reflected shades of deep emerald green. His heart stirred, and his thirst with it. On impulse, he caressed her cheek. Then a slight breeze carried wisps of curls across her cheek and he caught one between his fingers. Like woven silk, it yielded to his touch. He played with it absently, staring at the river.

She glanced up at him shyly, wondering what he was thinking.

Reivn looked down at that moment, and seeing her gaze, bent his head and brushed his lips against hers gently. She timidly returned his kiss as his arms found their way around her, pulling her close. Aware only of each other, all other thoughts vanished.

Finally, he pulled away and helped her to her feet. Sweeping her hair aside, he tilted her chin upward and gazed down at her in silence. The question in his eyes needed no explanation.

Angelique silently nodded.

Reivn pulled her into his arms again and held her close as he bit into her neck and drank. Then she leaned against him, resting her head on his chest while he closed the wound. But he was not finished. He knew what he wanted and gently lifted her chin until their eyes met. Then he tore open his wrist with his fangs and silently held it up for her to drink.

She hesitated only a second before she bent her head and fed. His blood was potent and sweet, and as she drank, a fire began to burn in her veins. It filled her need and sealed the bond between them. When she was done, she closed his wound. Then she leaned back into his embrace, content to while away the night.

Neither cared how long they stood there. Their minds were not on the coming nights. The bond of blood that had begun was flooding them both with emotions and sensations they could not control. Afraid to break the moment, each waited for the other to move or speak.

Finally, dawn began to creep over the horizon. Reivn lifted her into his arms and levitated skyward, carrying her across the gardens to the balcony outside her rooms. When they landed, he carefully set her down. "Goodnight, my angel," he whispered against her lips, as he kissed her. Then he disappeared over the balcony's edge.

Angelique watched the ground below, hoping to catch sight of him. When it was obvious he was indeed gone, she wandered inside, lost in her thoughts as she remembered the feel of his kiss. *This is so different from anything I knew with Blake.*

The idea caused her to be ashamed, thinking herself disloyal to Blake's memory. Yet she could not deny the truth. Still dwelling on the night's events, she lay down and curled up to a pillow. Its softness against her cheek gave her comfort as she slipped into slumber. Her dreams that day were far different.

Two nights later the territory was plunged into chaos. Lord Sorin had been murdered. The assassins had even torn his chambers apart to find and destroy his organs, which had been painstakingly removed by a Council representative and handed back to him for safe keeping. Minutes after the discovery of Sorin's ashes, they discovered that Lord Gareth and the rest of the Prince's officers had been assassinated as well. In response to the crisis, the Council summoned Reivn to the Sahara. There he was ordered to place Atlantic City and its surrounding territory under martial law, taking the throne himself until a new Prince could be appointed.

Angelique was terrified. She was certain those who had killed Sorin and his officers had been the Eastern Lords.

Reivn feared they would come for Angelique next and assigned extra guards at the Guild as a precaution before leaving for the Sahara. Even then, he worried it would not be enough to stop Kuromoto. He forbade her to go outside and ordered Serena to safeguard her in his absence.

Shadowed by memories of Gareth's kindness on their last meeting, Angelique sat in one of the parlors, staring at the flames in the hearth.

Serena walked in and sat down beside her. "Are you all right?"

Angelique shrugged. "I don't know. I thought that my having revealed the Shokou Azuma's plans would prevent them from getting to Lord Sorin. Nothing I did made a difference."

"This isn't your fault, Angelique." Serena touched her shoulder, trying to comfort her. "The Alliance was defending their borders long before you were even born. Kuromoto merely saw you as a pawn and tried to use you to get close to Sorin. If you had not been there, he would have come up with some other plan. That is just the ruthlessness of our world."

A soft sob escaped Angelique. "I know you are right, but somehow I still feel responsible for their deaths. Oh Serena, how could this happen?"

Serena wrapped her arms around Angelique and hugged her. "I wish I had the answer you were looking for."

As the nights passed, the territory slowly quieted. Angelique was inundated with letters from the other tribes asking her to take part in the selection of a new ruler. Her responses reflected the unrest that was prevalent in every Prefect's mind, even though she agreed to meet for the purpose of resolution. When she received the date, she sent a message to Reivn with the details. Three weeks had already passed since she had last seen him, and his absence was keenly felt. She missed him. She also wanted to discuss the upcoming meeting. She was expected to vote on a subject she knew nothing about, and it worried her.

The following night, Angelique awoke with a start. Immediately her thoughts went to Reivn. She had drafted several letters to him and promptly thrown them into the fire, frustrated for not saying more during their last meeting. Her own confusion left her torn, and she worried her silence would be misunderstood. She mourned the past she had lost, and yet wanted the possible future that lay before her. When she could no longer avoid the night, she began to move through what had now become a monotonous routine. She went down to her office, and had just begun to write her reports to the Council when a knock interrupted the silence.

Reivn's courier looked in to see if she was there, waving a letter at her and grinning broadly. "Is this what you've been waiting for, my lady?"

Angelique frowned at him as she took it and tried to appear annoyed, but she failed, and he walked out laughing. Tearing it open, she sat back down in her chair and read.

> *My Sweet Angel,*
>
> *You have my deepest gratitude for that beautiful night by the river. I am amazed I was not caught by the dawn while lost in you. I must also extend my joy at the offer of your blood. Truly no wine in all of France can compare. As long as your offer stands, I shall gladly accept. You were right. We do have the same sorrows and passions. I have finally found a measure of peace. Please allow me to comfort you so you may find the strength to do the same. As Merlin once said, "Rest in the arms of the Dragon." This may seem somewhat forward, but in my centuries of existence, my experience has taught me to act swiftly or lose everything. This territory may presently be a crown to be claimed, but you are truly one of its brightest gems.*
>
> *As for this domain, it shall not fall. The Prefects may squabble all they like. I have consolidated my power and position temporarily on the throne. They will follow when I have need of them. I have done this before and shall no doubt have to do so again. Trust in that.*
>
> *Until we meet again my sweet Angel,*
> *Lord Reivn Draegon*

A soft smile crossed Angelique's features as she folded the letter and tucked it into her desk drawer. She got up and walked to the window, hoping he was in the garden. The moon was hidden behind the clouds, shrouding the path below in darkness. Staring down into the courtyard, it looked empty. She was about to turn away when her attention was caught by sudden movement as a hint of moonlight broke through, illuminating the roses at the bottom of the walk. She peered out into the night. The absence of crickets and other night creatures told her someone was there. She telepathied Reivn, *Is it you in the garden beyond my window?*

Reivn answered almost at once. *I am still at the mansion, meeting with some of the Prefects. The garden was ordered off-limits until... my God! Angel! Get out of there!* His telepathy changed to urgency as he realized she was in danger.

Angelique sent an immediate alert to the guards and turned to leave the office. But two black-clad figures were already moving up the hall toward her. She quickly closed the door and locked it. Her only chance was to flee through the doors of the balcony and down to the garden. She turned off the lights and moved swiftly and silently to the doors, cracking one open to gaze out. Then seeing no one, she wrapped her cloak around her and slipped out into the night. She stayed in the shadows and moved carefully along the path, heading toward the river.

A shout filled the air and four figures emerged from the shadows.

Angelique began to run. Behind her, the number grew to six. They quickly gained on her and cut off her escape. Surrounded now, she could see the glint of steel in their hands. She summoned the spirals in an attempt to defend herself and hurled a fireball at her nearest attacker. It engulfed him in flames.

"Is that all you've got, Mastric?" the assassin asked. With a laugh, he used his own magic and extinguished the inferno before it did any real damage. Then behind her, a second assailant threw a net over her head.

Angelique instantly felt her magic dissipate, dampened by a spell cast on the net. It forced her to the ground with its weight... more magic conjured by her captors. Her attackers closed in.

The realization that she was trapped hit her hard, and she closed her eyes, waiting for the blow that would end her.

Screams suddenly erupted around her and her captors began to scatter.

Angelique was stunned and opened her eyes.

A large crimson dragon moved through her attackers, its huge talons ripping into them while its fiery breath reduced them to ash.

Terrified, she fought to push the net off, but she was hopelessly tangled in its heavy coils. Even her claws could not cut through it. She was still struggling when the dragon approached. She stared in fright for a second as it slowly began to transform. Finally, she screamed in terror.

"Use your eyes, Angelique. You can see even in the darkest night when you do. You know that. Quell your fear and use your power. See me," the figure commanded.

Doing as the voice commanded, she focused and then looked up again.

Reivn stood in front of her, now in clear vision. He pulled the net off of her and helped her up. "I am sorry. I did not mean to further frighten you. But you need to use your senses more. Those assassins could not have caught you off guard were you using what is so much a part of you. You know how to fight, but you must also use your instincts. They were able to hit you with this." He held up the net as he spoke, "because you were not using your senses to stay alert. I want to begin teaching you with practice fighting. I will not risk your safety like this again."

He stopped his tirade when he saw her face and pulled her into his arms, holding her close. "I know you were frightened, but believe what I am telling you, angel. You can fight off attacks like this. You just need to be prepared."

She buried her face against his chest. "You called me angel again. You do care."

Instead of responding, he picked her up and walked down to the boulder where they had spent their last evening together. Then he set her down gently and pulled her cloak closed around her. He tilted her face up to meet his. "Yes, I do." Softly brushing his lips across her forehead, he smiled. "I think I have fallen in love with you, my lovely Comtesse. But I must warn you. To be loved by a Draegon is a dangerous thing." Reivn bent his head and kissed her again, this time with more passion. When he finally pulled away, he cupped her chin in his hand and looked deep into her eyes. "I thought I was going to lose you tonight. I begin to understand the depth of your emotion for your friend Armand. I do not want to lose you. I must confess my own selfish desire in this, as I have not felt this alive in centuries. You are more precious to me than my own soul."

Angelique looked down, embarrassed by his declaration, but delighted too. Her fright from the attack gone, she was content to remain in his arms.

To her surprise, he pulled away and held her at arm's length. "I cannot stay. I am needed back at the mansion. I was in Council there when you called me. Forgive me, but I must go."

Footsteps running down the path interrupted their conversation and Reivn turned to meet the newcomer, prepared to do battle if necessary.

"Angelique," Serena cried out, appearing around the bushes as she ran into the light. "Are you all right? We heard the commotion from the Guild, and when we couldn't find you anywhere, we feared the worst." She stopped when she saw their faces, realizing she had interrupted something important. "I'm sorry. I didn't mean to intrude. My Lord," she apologized, addressing Reivn directly. "I wasn't aware you had returned to the Guild. I wasn't informed…"

Reivn held up his hand and smiled. "I have not returned, Serena. I only came to deal with the intruders. I must return to the throne."

Serena stared at him in absolute amazement. "Yes, my lord. Of course. Goodnight." Without another word, she turned and disappeared down the path. She wanted to catch the others before they were disturbed again.

Angelique giggled, and he looked down at her. "And just what is so amusing?"

With a laugh, she gazed up at him. "I don't think she's used to seeing you smile."

A short while later, as Angelique was walking back to her chambers, Serena caught up to her. "It's really quite remarkable, you know."

Angelique glanced sideways at her companion in curiosity. "What is?"

Serena stopped and gazed at her. "The change in him," she explained. "You brought him back to life. You are just what he needed." Not waiting for a response, Serena walked away, leaving Angelique to stare after her.

Angelique headed to her room, thinking about what Serena had said. She remembered how Reivn had been during their first few meetings and realized Serena was right. He had changed. She smiled as she thought of his declaration earlier that evening. Then she remembered his last comment. *His throne*, she thought. *My God, he has become Prince.*

Though assigned to the throne as a temporary measure to protect the territory, Reivn had still become a territory ruler. The thought shook her when she remembered what had happened to Lord Sorin. That thought stayed with her even when she closed her eyes to sleep.

The following night Angelique left for the gathering of Prefects. An array of thoughts ran through her head, most of which centered on what would happen at the meeting. She knew it was for the preservation of the territory and an attempt to recover from the loss of its leader. There were other nearby domains and other Princes, but they could not solve the problem here. The territories were divided strategically to enable their protection, and each was controlled by an appointed Prince or Regent. The letter she had received had even stated that a Prince from a neighboring territory would be in attendance just for the selection of his new peer.

The mansion was a bustle of activity when Angelique arrived, and several people greeted her. She was now a respected member of the court and many looked at her with admiration.

Reivn spotted her when she walked in and called out to her from where he stood a few feet away. He was talking with a rather tall man.

Angelique made her way across the room to join them, this time very aware of the eyes that watched her. She was also listening with her senses and could hear much of the whispered talk. She knew they were talking about her, so she merely lifted her chin and walked on. When she reached him, she held out her hand in proper greeting.

Reivn bowed and kissed the hand she offered, his eyes sparkling with amusement. He knew she was watching her surroundings this time, and it pleased him. "Lady Angelique, may I present the Prince of Wilmington, Jonathan Davenport. Jonathan, this is the Mastric's Prefect for Atlantic City, the Comtesse Angelique De Legare. She is the one I mentioned."

As she curtsied low, Angelique raised her eyes in curiosity to take in the man before her. He was of medium build with shockingly blonde hair and brilliant blue eyes. His boyish face exuded a likeable charm and gave the illusion of innocence when underneath, he was a seasoned ruler and a good one at that. "It is a pleasure to make your acquaintance, my lord."

Jonathan chuckled and shook his head. "Please, no formalities. I get that all the time in my own domain. Tonight, I just want to be an observer and another face in the crowd. I only came in case my friend here…" he paused to slap Reivn on the back, "needed my help. A sad business, Sorin being killed like that… and Gareth too. What a mess!"

Angelique glanced at Reivn and almost burst into laughter at the indignant look on his face. She quickly placed her hand on his arm and smiled. "Not that he really needs the help, of course, but it's always good to have a friend on hand to watch your back." She did not have the chance to say anything more because one of the other Prefects walked up to inform Reivn that everyone had arrived.

"Thank you," Reivn stated and turned to them. "Time to get this meeting started."

Jonathan did not miss Angelique's eyes as they followed Reivn to the throne, and he smiled. Politely offering her his arm, he escorted her to her chair. The debate over the throne had begun.

Reivn stared across the room at Angelique. He listened to the arguing with only half an ear as his mind drifted to future possibilities.

Completely unaware of Reivn's thoughts, Angelique smiled at him. Then she dropped right back into the discussion with her peers.

After hours of debate, the final decision was that each candidate would be brought before the Prefects to prove their worth by reciting the Council's Tenets, and the book of laws. The Prefects would adjourn for three days to allow them time to bring all the elects to the hall, and Reivn set the date accordingly. Then he made his way across the room to Angelique and held out his hand.

Angelique got up and placed her hand in his, aware of the whispers throughout the room. "Are you sure this is a good idea... being so openly affectionate toward me, I mean?"

She had spoken softly so no one else would hear, but Reivn chuckled without concern. "I want them to know I have claimed you as my own, so they will all think twice before issuing you a challenge of any kind. They know you stand under my protection. I told you, I am the master of my domain and for now, that includes you. Come."

Painfully aware that all eyes were on them, Angelique allowed him to lead her across the room and through the double doors leading to the Prince's hall and his private lair.

## Chapter Twenty-Two
## The Viper Pit

*I have known the true face of evil and have seen the writhing things that can crawl from the darkest places of the world to steal away your soul. When you fall prey to them, it forever damns not only you, but also those luckless enough to cross their path when they come for you. I fear the curse I bear is one such taint, carried in a vow I made so foolishly all those centuries ago. I watch the darkness knowing she is out there… waiting to strike at me again.*

*A wise man once told me that you must think through every action for a hundred years before making your decision. He claimed that such a task is the path of righteous men. Have I then fallen so completely from grace I cannot find my way back to the endeavors of good men? I feel the shadow that hangs over me, and yet cannot place its source. Even while I pursue what keeps my honor before me, I feel it to be a travesty of terms.*

*I feel her eyes on me like the stab of an icy chill that lays into your spine on an early winter's morn. Would that I had struck her down when I had the chance. Now I fear her strength has grown and I will find myself equally well matched in the arcane. Still, she has a long arm indeed if she can stretch across the ocean to challenge me here. Egypt has become the dwelling place of devils and only the ones that lie hidden deep beneath its sands can combat such foul creatures. As long as she remains in that forsaken place, my vigilance can be more tempered, leaving room for other things. Learning to live made foremost in my mind by the gentle hands that minister to me, I marvel at the difference that has opened my eyes…*

*Lord Reivn Draegon*

\* \* \* \* \*

"This isn't going to work! He's too smart for that!" Valfort put down the basin he was holding and moved to the window, and then stared down into the street below. Philadelphia was teeming with activity even at this late hour.

Alora glared at him. "Shut up and get back over here! You know damned well where his vulnerability lies! He is forever playing the hero when in truth he is as much a monster as we are. He merely justifies his kills by calling it the Council's will! Now he must look reality in the eyes, Ceros. Don't you see?"

Valfort laughed at her. "He is a Warlord! You really think he would so easily be fooled? Even if you do manage to catch his attention, what could you possibly use for bait?"

"This…" Alora turned to the door and called out. "Bruno? Bring him!"

A moment later two Renegades entered carrying an unconscious man. They dropped him on the floor near her and left as silently as they came.

She knelt down next to her prisoner and pushed the hair from his face. "Welcome to my home, Armand." Then she smiled and looked up at Valfort. "Do you know him? He is the son of the lost daughter you seek. If Reivn truly favors her line, then he and his enforcers will come looking for this pathetic creature. Reivn will think he has turned traitor. We have already baited the line with the decoy I turned loose to kill those gypsies in England."

Valfort gazed at the unconscious man thoughtfully. "How did you acquire him?"

Alora laughed. "The foolish boy came into Philadelphia by himself to catch a flight to England. I recognized the fact that he wasn't a Renegade and had him followed. I had no idea who he actually was until we took him, but he is a find, isn't he?"

Valfort snorted in disgust, giving Armand a nudge with his boot. "A find? He is weak and of little value. This is how you plan to get close to Reivn? He isn't going to bargain for anyone, Alora! I've seen him give men up for dead on a battlefield just to secure a victory! He will not be fooled by this at all!" He paced back and forth in irritation.

Alora watched him in amusement. "You really do not know him well at all, Ceros. His greatest weaknesses are his honor and his compassion. If we draw those out of him, he will forget himself and play right into our hands. So calm down. I made sure his enforcers caught our decoy, so they knew without a doubt it wasn't this pathetic child. We just need to finish our plans. This is nothing more than a game of chess and it's our move. Trust me. It will be checkmate for him. Now hold the basin."

Valfort scowled and picked up the bowl, holding it up again as she began her casting. He watched in silence. Before him, the water turned black and began to spin.

She skillfully summoned the dark magic she so masterfully wielded, and then stared at the blackened water when Reivn appeared. She studied him for awhile, noting his activities and where he went. "This is going to be such a delightful game."

Valfort shook his head. "This isn't a game, Alora."

"Isn't it?" Alora laughed at him. She quickly closed the vision and pushed the basin away. "I look forward to matching wits with him. Once he is mine, you can take back your child." She looked up at him then. "Then this partnership is over. I get what I want, and you get her."

Valfort growled, his eyes taking on a dangerous look. "Do not forget you promised me some time with Reivn once he is caught as well. I have my own score to settle. Then I can begin working on my plans again." He put the basin down on the table and walked over to a nearby desk covered with papers and maps. "I have been in this cursed country far too long. I owe my father a visit and it is long overdue."

She glanced up at his words and snickered. "That is who you are going after? Well, your lifespan is going to come to a sudden and brutal end. That is one I will not help you with, although..." She fell silent for a moment as a thought crossed her head. Then she said, "You know, you should wait. There are other ways to handle him. Yes indeed, there are ways..." She drifted into silence as she mulled over the possibilities of gaining control of so powerful a being.

Valfort ignored her and scoured the map, searching for key locations near enough to his target to begin setting up a base. Finally, he pushed it away. "Bah! There is time enough for this later. I have need of some sport. Tommy!" he called. He began to tap his fingers impatiently when the boy did not appear. "Tommy!" he bellowed again, getting up.

The boy came running in and dropped to his knees, bowing his head to the floor in front of Valfort. "Forgive me, master, I did not hear you."

Valfort frowned and stared at him. "Tommy, how long have you served me now?"

The youth looked up, fear in his eyes. "Over two hundred years, master."

Valfort walked over and stood in front of him, crossing his arms angrily. "And in all that time, have I ever tolerated mistakes?"

Trembling now, Tommy closed his eyes. "No, master."

Valfort glared at him. "Then what makes you think I would accept one now? Get up!"

Clearly terrified, the boy slowly stood. "I'm sorry, master," he stuttered. "I swear I will do better from now on."

"No," Valfort replied calmly. "You won't." He grabbed Tommy by the throat and tore it open. Then he drained the boy completely. When he was done, he dropped the lifeless body to the floor and turned to Alora. "Good help is so hard to find these days."

Alora laughed. "There are a million more right outside that window... pick one or pick twenty, it matters not. They breed like cattle. You could kill and replace them by the dozen every day and would still never run out."

Valfort went to the window and stared down into the street again. As he watched the passersby, he assessed each one, looking for one that captured his interest. Finally, he yanked the curtain closed again. "There is nothing on the streets tonight. How long is this going to take?"

Alora went over to Armand, who still lay unconscious, bound and helpless on the floor. She grabbed his arm and lifted him, inspecting his face carefully. "He's still out cold, but by the time we get him across town and into the chamber, he'll be awake. Are you ready to go? Take everything you want with you. We aren't coming back here."

Valfort went to the table and gathered his paperwork. Then he stuffed it into his coat and turned around. "Let's get this over with then. I want to hunt tonight."

She grabbed Armand's bound arms and dragged him out the door and down the back stairs.

Within the hour, they were safely ensconced in the dungeons built beneath an abandoned building deep in the city. The ancient reinforced walls were made of stone and mortar. Their haven was well hidden from the eyes of the mortal world. It was one of many old hiding places their kind had created to protect themselves from discovery. The bloodstains on the floors and walls echoed of a shady history and gave an eerie feel to the atmosphere. The stench of old blood and death were everywhere, causing Valfort to wrinkle his nose in distaste.

Alora smiled as she fastened shackles around Armand's wrists and then hung him from chains that were attached to the ceiling. "You don't appreciate the scent of death, Ceros? That truly surprises me. I would have thought a man with your lust for killing would enjoy the fruits of his labor. The smell here is merely a reminder of past enjoyments we have had."

He gave a disgusted snort. "I enjoy my kills, Alora, but unlike you, I do not wallow in the filth of the aftermath. Your love of corpulent entrails lying about as decorations is nothing short of depraved. I find it disgusting. Let us finish with this, so I may be on my way."

She walked past Armand's unconscious form and drew close to Valfort. Then she glared at him. "I might learn to watch my tongue if I were you. Someone might cut it out while you are sleeping or maybe even when you are awake. A wise man once said that the man who has no allies cannot afford more enemies. Now enough foolishness! He's coming around."

Valfort stepped over to the wall to watch.

Armand groaned and began to move his head, awareness slowly coming to him. Finally, he realized he was hanging from chains and looked up, as he attempted to free himself.

Alora snickered and stepped from the shadows.

Shaking his head in an attempt to focus, Armand stared at her. "Who are you? What do you want with me?" he demanded.

"It speaks," she taunted, smiling sarcastically. "Don't worry boy. I want nothing from you whatsoever... well, not from you directly. I am fishing, you see, and you are the bait. I'm really going to enjoy this."

Armand struggled with his chains. "What the Hell is this about? Who are you people?"

Alora stepped in front of him and laughed. Then she brushed the hair from his eyes. "I am your host and your captor. I am your worst nightmare. Now..." She walked over and picked up a fillet knife from a table in the corner and then turned to him. "Shall we begin?"

Leaning against the wall, Valfort watched with disinterest while she tore away Armand's shirt and began to slowly skin him.

Armand's screams filled the chamber.

Her eyes glowing with pleasure in the torchlight, Alora licked the blood spatter from her lips. She reveled in his pain and continued methodically until her prisoner lost consciousness.

Hours later, Valfort followed Alora from the last of the chambers and another of her victims... a young girl of six years.

Fully covered in gore, Alora was half crazed with bloodlust and laughing hysterically. She made her way to a shower well-hidden behind a wall.

Irritated, he stood there watching while she cleaned off the mess. "Why are you bothering with that? You'll only cover yourself again come sundown. It'll be dawn soon, and I have yet to get to the streets for my own satisfaction!"

"Will you stop whining?" she growled. "I thought of you. There are a couple of girls in the apartment above us where you will stay tonight. I cannot go above looking like I just came from a slaughterhouse." She smiled at the thought.

He shook his head and laughed in spite of himself. "You did just come from a slaughterhouse. What was the body count? Eleven? Twelve? And there will be more tomorrow night."

Alora grinned. "Whatever is the matter with you? I'll give you your turn, but this is my playground, so I make the rules. I was having too much fun tonight to let you step in. You know how it is when you're excited... you tend to forget yourself. I'll do better tomorrow, I promise."

Growling his displeasure, Valfort turned and headed for the stairs. "I'll wait for you above, my sweet. I am going to find those playthings you got for me. My appetite beckons."

"I will be in the upper chambers when you're done. I have no need to hunt," Alora scoffed. "I can feast on my pets here and gain infinitely more than you do from your pathetic excursions."

He scowled and headed up the steps without a word. Her laughter stung his ears and only further soured his mood as it followed him.

The next night the dungeons were again filled with screams of agony. Alora took her time with each one, dreaming up new cruelties to outdo her old ones. Her laughter and screeches of delight followed the eventual submission to death, as she slaughtered one after another. Finally, she returned to Armand's room. She grinned and slowly closed the door behind her. "I'm going to take my time tonight, Armand. I want you to know that. I will spend the rest of my night with you, just so you aren't alone."

Armand looked up, his eyes filling with hate. "It matters not what you do to me. I will never give you what you want."

Alora purred and ran her fingers over his chest. "You already have."

"You haven't told me what you want with me, how you know me or who you even are," he spat through gritted teeth.

Circling around to face him, she smirked. "I am so sorry. I shall have to rectify that immediately. What's your favorite color?"

Armand stared at her in disbelief. "What?"

"Your favorite color... what is it?" She was laughing at him now.

He closed his eyes and shook his head. "You did not go to all this trouble to ask me trivial things. What is it you really want?"

She swept her fingers across his chest again slowly, this time extending her claws and digging them into his newly grown skin. "I'll tell you what my favorite color is. Can you guess? It is blood red."

The searing white-hot pain ripped through Armand from the new wounds and he threw his head back, gasping for air as though deprived from his lungs. He thought of the hours to come and a shudder passed over him.

Purring low, she moved up close to his face. "You like that, Armand? That is good. What shall we discuss then, you and I? We have all night and I love good conversation."

He lifted his eyes to meet hers. "Go to Hell!"

Alora's laughter chilled him to the core. "I'm not ready to go home yet, boy, but I'll do my best to bring it here, so you can taste of its pleasures."

Already torn and battered from the previous day's torture, Armand had endured healing from her to renew his flesh and the nerves within, but they were still raw. The new wounds screamed now, sending waves of pain battering against his senses. "You're insane!" he gasped.

She smiled and picked up the knife from the table. Then she moved around behind him. "Perhaps, but should you really be saying things like that to me? I am the one with the knife. Maybe you should try to be more gentlemanlike. Yes... a more subtle approach." She casually began to carve runes deep into the newly grown flesh on his back. "Don't you think?"

Unable to even lift his head, Armand cried as the pain washed over him in torrents and crushed his resolve until he could think of nothing but the agony.

Alora put the knife down and walked up to him to stroke his cheek. "Don't cry, Armand. It didn't hurt my feelings. I was just teasing. Come... smile for me." She lifted his chin and pushed the corners of his mouth up into a smile. "Not a very good one, you know. One would almost believe you didn't want to see me. That would hurt my feelings."

Because he could no longer hold it up, Armand's head rolled almost sideways when she let go. He closed his eyes and tried to focus on enduring what was to come.

She stroked his hair for a moment, matting it with his own blood as she gripped it and stared up into his eyes. "Such a handsome face... I think I want to keep it for my collection. What do you say?" She grinned and began to slowly skin the side of his face with her claws, cutting the flesh from around his eyes with razor sharp precision. Broken sobs passed through his lips as she peeled away the skin, leaving exposed muscle and tissue. When she finally let go of him, his head flopped forward as he struggled to remain conscious.

"You know the problem with you, Armand? You're just like all the other men out there... always assuming we ladies actually want something from you." Alora cackled at the very idea. "Unfortunately for you, I do want something. I want screams. I want screams of delicious agony. I want your suffering to bathe my ears in wicked torment. I want you to bleed for me as I rip the flesh from your bones, heal you and rip it from you again just so I can listen to you break into fragmented little pieces." She lifted the meaty flesh that was his chin, so she could look into his eyes. "And as I drive you further and further into the void, I am going to watch when the beast begins to devour your soul. That is what I want from you."

Almost a gasp, Armand answered her. "You! You crawled out of Hell's pits! You have laid claim to something you could never understand."

Alora leaned in close to him. "And what exactly is it I don't understand, Armand dear?"

"Love," he whispered. "I was on a mission of mercy. Now it is as beyond me as you are beyond salvation."

She moved around behind him. "Love... it's such an over-rated emotion. It restricts you and turns you into a blithering idiot. Hate is so much better. When you hate, there is no limitation to you. Think about it. Would you really want to dance like a Marionette on strings for some witless wonder just because it is female? Oh, wait... I forgot. You do."

Armand snarled. "You know nothing of which you speak!"

Valfort slipped quietly into the room and leaned against the wall, listening intently.

Alora smiled at Valfort and then continued her ministrations on Armand. "Oh, but I do. Your maker is Angelique, daughter of Valfort. Her father wants her back. Sad, pathetic little boy. She doesn't love you, does she? She has already chosen another, even while your brother's bones are still warm in the earth. How fickle and totally delightful!" With a laugh, she picked up a jar of acid from the table and poured it across the wounds on his back.

A scream grew from deep inside Armand, until it pushed its way to the surface and poured forth. He hung barely conscious, only vaguely aware his captors were still in the room.

A look of sheer delight on her face, she whispered in his ear. "Think of her, Armand. You need her… you love her. She will save you from all this. Her very presence can give you peace."

"No…" Armand gasped.

She smiled. "You know you want her. Her beautiful red hair and soft, pale skin… the very vision of the angel you have compared her to for so long. You can see her in your mind this very moment, her smile and laughter filling you with longing."

He tried to shut out her words, but his heart betrayed him. "Do not do this!" he cried.

Seeing his resolve crumble, Alora pushed further, knowing she had already won. "Say her name, Armand... Angelique. Tell me, can you feel her presence? Call to her. She can hear you."

A sob escaped his throat, her words pulling at his memories. He could see Angelique sleeping in peaceful repose. "Oh, God!" he wept, no longer able to hold the images away.

Alora turned to Valfort. "Do it now!"

Valfort stepped over and grabbed both sides of Armand's head. Projecting all his power into the injured man, it flowed outward and into the sleeping girl in his thoughts.

Alora waited until she was sure Armand was closely connected to Angelique and then struck hard, tearing open his belly with her claws. Then she gutted him slowly.

In the heart of the Guild, Angelique's eyes snapped open and she was fully aware when Armand threw his head back and screamed…

# BLOOD FEUD

## Chapter Twenty-Three
## Behind Enemy Lines

*The long debate continues. It would seem none of the tribes can readily agree on a decision without some difficulty. While they argue, I must continue to safeguard this territory, which would fall into chaos without leadership to guide them. The aggravation the tribes presently throw at me is only somewhat abated by the knowledge the Council will not wait forever. They will appoint their own choice if the decision is not made soon. Each of the tribal leaders vies for more power and their arguments grasp like living fingers at this throne they covet so much. Many of them do not think of the inherent dangers this seat represents. The young infants they bring forth as candidates cannot hold such a potent position without falling prey to foul play as Sorin did. There is a man I will miss. He was a great leader and a good friend.*

*There was a time when had anyone told me I would find such peace amidst the turmoil that befell this city when Lord Sorin died, I would have scoffed at them. I generally suspend my own emotions during such occasions. The young often whisper my name when I pass by. Their words always carry an edge of fear and only a few will even look me in the eyes. Such is my reputation. But it is different this time. Angelique demands my time and attention as no other has ever dared in our dark world and yet, I cannot find fault with her. Her presence fills me with such hunger that I find myself wanting to linger at her side long after the night has begun. I watch her while she sleeps until sleep claims me, and then her fair countenance fills my dreams. If not for the origins of her blood I would easily believe an angel walked among us here, so gentle is her nature. Why she distracts me so, I cannot say...*

*Lord Reivn Draegon*

\* \* \* \* \*

The next few weeks were a flurry of activities as the Prince-elects arrived. Angelique only saw Reivn each night after the debates finished and they retired to his lair. Though the entire assembly of tribal leaders was under the impression they were lovers, he had respectfully kept his distance. He took a chair each night, leaving her the bed and her privacy. She would lay with her back to him each night, pretending to be asleep, listening to him move around the room before settling for the day's rest.

Angelique finally argued with him one night about the ideas the other Prefects had of them because of her presence in his rooms.

Reivn's response quelled her opposition quickly. "I did not bring you to my rooms to set their meddling tongues wagging, nor do I presently care what they whisper in the shadows. Their gossip does not concern me. Your safety does! I brought you here for your own protection! Kuromoto will not quit at one attempt or even two. Do not test me on this, Angelique! I will not put your safety at risk for your pride!" He paced back and forth, clearly angry now.

Annoyed with herself for not realizing the reason for his actions to begin with, she plopped down on the bed more like a petulant child than the woman she was.

He crossed the room to where she sat and dragged her to her feet, staring into her eyes. "Do you understand how much danger you are in, angel? He took a walk inside your mind. He programmed you all those years ago, and because he had you for all those years, he knows you better than I do! The only thing he cannot predict is me! These meetings have gone on too long, but they will be ending soon. Then I can put you back within the protective walls of the Guild." He pulled her into his arms and held her close.

Angelique laid her head against his chest, taking in the faint scent of the dragon's blood oil he wore. The collar of his shirt hung open, revealing the wisps of the black hair on his chest in the soft light that filled the room.

Reivn held her in silence for a moment before he drew away again. He gazed at her steadily. "Please do not be angry. There are many things about this world you have yet to learn. Save your stubbornness for the enemies of our society, not for those of us who would see you do well." He kissed her forehead, let go of her, and began to pace the room again. "Kuromoto was spotted within city limits by my enforcers, but before they could catch him he stepped into the shadows and disappeared again. The birthright of some Shokou Azuma gives them the ability to step into the astral plains. It makes them difficult to hunt."

He took her by the shoulders. Then he met her gaze and sighed. "This is why he is such a dangerous enemy. Some of the power he uses comes from the darkness itself. We never accepted the Eastern tribes for that reason. They follow their own path, not our laws. Their power is very dark and often unholy." He started pacing again, as he spoke. "There are those among us who serve God on a higher level than mankind. My devotion to

God gives me strength in battle against evil and aids me even in my blackest hours. There are many of our kind that have such a gift. This is also why so many fear me."

The scent of her hair caught his attention, distracting him.

Angelique thought he was waiting for a response and quickly answered. "I am sorry, Lord Reivn. I... wasn't thinking about what could happen with Kuromoto. I thought that was finished. I will do as you ask in the future. Forgive me."

Unable to resist the temptation any longer, he reached out and pulled her to him. Then he kissed her passionately. When he released her moments later, he sat down on the bed and then pulled her down beside him. "I wanted to tell you something else. I found out some information about Armand. We located him in Philadelphia. The initial reports were that he was running with a group of Renegades in Europe. One of my enforcers spotted who we thought to be him transforming into another face. Does Armand have the power of transformation?"

Surprised at the question, she shook her head. "He never learned to use anything like that."

Reivn seemed relieved. "This means the one using his face is a fraud; a duplicate set to mislead us. I believe if we find him again, he will lead us to Armand, whom I now think must be a prisoner somewhere in that damned city. Do not worry, I will find him." He patted her hand reassuringly, as he noted her silence and continued. "As soon as I am freed up from the accursed problem here, I will be heading to Philadelphia with several of my enforcers to try and locate his whereabouts and bring him home if possible."

Angelique's eyes brightened and she jumped up in excitement. "I'm coming with you!"

He shook his head. "Not this time, angel. Philadelphia is dangerous territory. I have to watch my own back. Trying to protect you as well could cost us both our lives. I promise I will get him back. I am not going to let an innocent man die. Trust in that."

Though frustrated with her lack of ability, she understood and finally agreed she would wait for their return.

They talked long into the night and Angelique told him about the dreams, detailing everything she could remember that might aid him in his search. When dawn approached and they settled in for the night, Reivn tucked her down and pulled the blankets over her. Then he kissed her forehead. "Goodnight, angel. Rest well."

As he turned away, Angelique reached up and caught his hand. "Wait," she begged. "Please don't go... I want you to stay."

Reivn sat down next to her and brushed a lock of hair from her cheek, looking down at her with a serious expression. "Do you understand what it is you are offering me? I cannot lightly take what you offer."

Angelique stared at him, her emerald eyes glistening in the light. "You cannot or will not?"

He looked away briefly before turning to meet her steady gaze with equally intense eyes. "I cannot. The curse my wife put on me all those years ago complicates everything."

"You still need to feed," she reminded him. "You have not done so for several nights now... not since we were last together. Was it not you who told me to heed that need so as not to risk losing control?"

Reivn stared down at her in surprise, his thirst and desire growing rapidly. "I think you will find I have a great deal of control. Are you sure this is what you want? I have never lightly taken a lady of breeding to my bed, nor do I take lightly the invitation you now offer."

Angelique smiled softly. "I know. I am not afraid."

He contemplated her offer in silence for a minute. Then he slid off his boots and climbed under the covers next to her. As he wrapped his arms around her, a low rumble formed in his throat.

She sighed in contentment and laid her head on his chest, playing with the black wisps of hair poking out the front of his shirt.

Reivn's desire grew rapidly at her teasing. Then he growled and captured her mouth in a kiss. Without warning, he shifted and rolled on top of her, his weight melding into her until they were one. Then he began to blaze a trail of kisses down to the hollow at the base of her throat, where he sank his fangs in.

Angelique gasped at the ferocity with which he fed.

His hunger took over. He reached behind her and undid the laces of her dress. Then with a single command, he doused the lights. He quickly rid her of her clothing and then shed his own.

The passion between them blazed far into the night and he met her desire in ways she had never known. In the aftermath of the fire that burned between them, they fell asleep in each other's arms as the first rays of dawn crossed over the horizon.

Angelique awoke with a thirst far greater than usual. With a content moan, she reached for him only to discover the bed was empty. She turned over and found him staring out at the night, the window curtain pulled aside. "Reivn?" Her soft voice filled the quiet room.

Reivn turned and walked over to the bed. "I am here. I did not wish to wake you. I was a bit... demanding last night. How do you feel?" He sat down next to her and took her hand.

She smiled up at him. "You did not hurt me, beloved. I am hungry, but happy."

Relief filled his features. He leaned over and kissed her. "You never cease to amaze me," he whispered. Then he tactfully changed the subject. "I was just thinking about the events taking place this evening. The new Prince will be chosen. That means I leave for Philadelphia soon."

Angelique sat up hurriedly, and then realized with some embarrassment that she was still naked. She blushed profusely and tried to cover herself with a sheet.

Reivn smiled in amusement and reached over, pulling the sheet from her hands. "A body as beautiful as yours is nothing to cover in shame. Your shyness is refreshing and only proves you to be a true lady. But you need not hide from me…not anymore."

Timidity replaced her embarrassment, and she struggled to hold on to the sheet.

He teasingly ran his free hand down the small of her back, tracing her spine with his fingertips.

At his touch, she shivered with desire.

Reivn chuckled and handed her a robe that was lying on the foot of the bed. "You are so provocatively beautiful, angel. I could happily pass the night here with you." Then he kissed her forehead and got up. "Unfortunately, our presence is required in the main hall. Tonight the new Prince will be selected. If the Council approves, he will be endorsed within a fortnight."

He brushed his lips against hers and pulled the robe around her. "I will leave you to get dressed. I'll be back in a little while." He turned and walked out.

Angelique quickly showered and dressed for the evening. She was humming to herself as she moved around the room and did not realize he had returned until she looked up to find him leaning against the doorframe.

Reivn smiled at her in amusement. "You were a million miles away. Are you ready?"

Embarrassed now, she nodded and joined him. "Yes," she whispered shyly.

He offered her his arm and the two made their way to the main hall together.


The decision that night was almost unanimous. The Prefects selected Edward Leon De Schaul to assume the throne, provided the Council's approval was given. He was of Victulian lineage, and as such, was thought to be the best choice because of his knowledge of Alliance law. Some of the Prefects doubted him because a few of his contacts were shady, but as he was not the first Prince-elect to have them, it was ignored.

The debate with the Prefects had lasted most of the night. During the entirety of their heated arguing, Angelique could not help stealing glances at Reivn, who looked as bored as she was.

When the meeting was finally over and the weary Prefects were heading to their lairs for the last time, a courier hailed Reivn. He took the message and dismissed the man, and then opened it and quickly scanned its contents. Immediately he signaled two of his Dragon Guard to wait until the hall was empty and then meet him in his private office. After sending Angelique back to his room with a third Guard, he went to his office to wait.

Angelique wondered what was amiss and paced back and forth while the Guard stood in front of the door, blocking her exit. Agitated and worried, she waited for two hours until Reivn strode into the room.

Reivn threw his coat on a nearby chair and crossed the room to where she stood waiting.

The guard slipped away quietly, closing the door behind him.

Picking her up, Reivn spun her around and kissed her. "I have news! We caught Kuromoto and hiding in a warehouse. He has been taken to the Council to be dealt with for his treachery! The Council will never release him, and once you testify, they will have enough evidence to condemn him. He will not be able to harm you again."

Angelique threw her arms around his neck in relief. "Oh, that's wonderful! Does this mean I can resume my regular duties now?"

"Not quite. We must go to the Council halls to attend the court proceedings. There are going to be repercussions with the Shokou Azuma for his execution. You must testify, and my knowing the details of his trial will be helpful to dissuade future problems with them." He set her down and began to strip off his formal clothes to replace them with a long robe.

She watched him shyly, fascinated by this man she had come to love. His confidence amazed her. She had never experienced anything like it. Every time she had coupled with Blake, it had always been modest and in the dark.

When Reivn noticed her eyes on him, he walked over and kissed her nose playfully. Then he led her to a chair near the window. "We are going home tomorrow night. I plan on leaving for Philadelphia immediately after. I have already sent for Lunitar and my other enforcers. I want to start the search for Armand as soon as possible."

Angelique looked down, unable to meet his gaze. "I wish I could go with you. I feel his presence and I know I could help find him."

Lifting her chin so she would look at him, he shook his head. "I understand your desire to help, angel. But as I said before, going with me is too dangerous. However, I do have a way you can help. I want you to allow Serena to put you into a deep sleep. While you are asleep, I will link our minds and follow the trail Armand leaves. You would have the ability to guide me from the safety of the guild. Can you do that?"

A determined look crossed Angelique's features, and she nodded. "Yes, I can. But what of the Council proceedings with Kuromoto?"

Reivn laughed. "They will not start without us and they know I have a mission to do first. Kuromoto will stay imprisoned until we get there. I want to find Armand and get him safely home first, which I can do with your help."

"I would die if I thought it would help him," she cried.

He scowled at her outburst. "I would never let that happen," he mumbled.

Angelique had been too distracted by her own thoughts to hear him. She looked up with a frown. "What was that?"

"I said it would not be necessary," Reivn answered somewhat gruffly. He got up and strode to the window. "Dawn is coming. We should be settling in. Tomorrow is going to be a very busy night." He walked over and caught her by the hand. Then he slid his hand around to undo her dress, as he sank his fangs into her neck.

They returned to the Guild the following night and immediately prepared to begin the search for Armand. Within the hour, they were ready. Reivn looked up at the windows where Angelique was watching he and his enforcers load the truck they would be traveling in. He knew she was afraid. *Do not worry, angel. We will find him,* he telepathied.

Angelique moved into the darkness of the room. Her bottom lip quivered as his words rang in her ears... *do not worry*. They frightened her. They were the same words Blake had said the last time she had seen him alive. Her fear was not just that they would not find Armand. It was also that he would disappear as Blake had.

She turned to find Reivn walking toward her, Lunitar behind him. "Please trust me?" he asked. "I cannot leave you like this... not when I know you are afraid. I am stronger than any others you have met. It will be all right." He pulled her close and gently stroked her hair.

Standing behind him, Lunitar raised an eyebrow, somewhat surprised at the affection his father showed her.

Angelique shivered involuntarily.

Reivn kissed her forehead and smiled, knowing her thoughts. "I am far more powerful then Blake was, and by far more familiar with our world. Now come. Serena awaits us in my rooms." He picked her up and walked to the door, indicating for Lunitar to open it.

Lunitar said nothing, but he did as his father commanded.

Reivn carried her down the hall to his private quarters.

Lunitar followed them in worried silence.

Serena met them at the door to his chambers.

Walking over to the bed, Reivn put Angelique down. Then he sat down next to her. "I have to go, angel. It is time for you to sleep."

Serena began to weave her enchantment over Angelique and Reivn joined her, casting the spell that would bind their minds together.

Lunitar watched disapprovingly.

Angelique held tightly to Reivn's hand, afraid to let him go. As her eyes closed, the last thing she saw was his face when he kissed her goodbye.

Once she was asleep, Reivn got up and hastily made his down to the waiting truck.

Lunitar followed him, glancing around to be sure they were alone. Then he cleared his throat. "If I may be so bold, father, you risk much."

Reivn slowed his steps. "How so?"

"You once told me that distraction in our world is an invitation to death, and you father, are very distracted," Lunitar stated quietly.

Turning to gaze at his son, Reivn frowned. "I am doing what is necessary to find one of my own. Why do you challenge this?"

Lunitar stared at his father. "What do you mean one of your own? The girl up in that room is not of our blood. Is the one we are hunting for?"

Reivn shook his head. "No, they are not my own creations, but they are my protégés. If they betray the Alliance, as their master my life would also be forfeit."

"Judging by your actions with the lady, it appears much has occurred since last we spoke," Lunitar stated, shaking his head. "I will do as you command, but I am concerned that you may be too distracted by her. This is uncharacteristic of you and could lead to a fatal error."

His eyes flashing dangerously, Reivn growled. "I risk nothing but the time I am losing while dealing with this foolishness. She is already in the bond and if I do not join with her, the trail will be lost. If you wish to discuss this further, we will do so after our quarry has been found."

Lunitar bowed. "As you command."

The two left the building and got into the waiting SUV. They immediately pulled away from the curb and headed out into the night.

Reivn closed his eyes and slipped into the bond he had forged with Angelique.

Angelique could see nothing clearly. Everything was shrouded in darkness. "Hello?" she shouted. Her voice was muffled even to her own hearing. She called out in fear. "Reivn?"

Reivn's voice answered. "I am right here with you, angel."

She looked around, but she could not see him. "Where are you? Reivn please, I'm afraid! Don't leave me alone here!"

An ethereal image appeared before her. "I am right here. You are in your own mind, angel. This is what you have made of it. You cannot see anything because you are not focusing on any one place or thing." He smiled. "That is why I am here... to guide you. I want you to focus on Armand and those dreams. Can you do that? Think of Armand and listen for his voice. It will come to you again, but you must look for him."

Angelique turned her thoughts to Armand. Almost immediately, she heard his voice again.

"Angelique, please help me! No! Don't come! They'll kill you!"

She followed the sound of his voice through the darkness.

"It's a trap! The pain… make it stop! Please no more! Angelique, I failed you! Help me!"

As she drew closer to the source, she could see images beginning to take shape. First roads and then buildings began to appear.

"Agh! Help me! The pain!"

The agony Armand felt tore at her soul, and she called out to him. "Armand! We're coming! Please don't give up! Tell me where to find you!" The images were gaining clarity as she moved out of her own mind and fully into Armand's, the blood they shared guiding her.

Reivn followed, his ethereal spirit the minute part of him that held the bond with her. His connection to her guided him while she sought her child through the images her blood was gathering. "That's it, angel! You are getting closer! Keep going! You can lead us right to him!" he whispered in the silence of the truck's interior.

Lunitar stared at Reivn, concern filling his features.

The link Angelique shared with Armand pulled at her, showing her the path leading straight to him. She could see the streets he was carried through in the dead of night, reliving the moments he had been captured. Following the visions, she felt as though she were walking the streets of Philadelphia herself.

Reivn and his party raced through the night toward Philadelphia, following the trail she showed them. "We need to hurry, or we will lose her! She made contact with him a lot sooner than I expected!" He fell silent and turned inward to his bond with her again, and then mumbled to himself. "Damn, she's good!"

*And strong,* Lunitar thought in concern. He began to reach into the spirals, slowly preparing himself for the coming battle.

It had been too risky for the party to use magic to travel to the city. The Renegades would have picked up their trail. So they were traveling in an SUV. They had left as soon as Angelique was asleep, and in the hour it had taken her to become aware of her own mind, they had gotten into Philadelphia. Now they were searching for the roads she showed them.

Reivn sensed that she was already moving through back alleys. "Stay with me, angel! Do not lose me or I cannot help him!"

Lunitar looked up sharply at his father's words. Then he turned to the other enforcers and began quietly discussing the possible scenarios they could run into at their destination.

Reivn ignored them and continued to guide Angelique through their link. "Angel, do not go too far ahead. Keep close and lead me to him."

Angelique heard his voice and turned, but he was nowhere in sight. "Reivn? Where are you?"

He turned his concentration to her. "I am here."

He appeared before her again and she relaxed. Then the urgency to find her child took over and she returned to the hunt. "We're getting close! I can feel his presence! We need to hurry!" She reached out for Armand and an image briefly flashed before her.

Armand hung in chains in a darkened room, burns covering his body. Mutilated and bleeding from dozens of wounds, he was too weak to hold his weight off the torn flesh of his wrists any longer. His hair was matted with blood and clung to his forehead as it dried and crusted over where his eyes had once been. He hovered half-conscious near death, his agony too great even for an immortal. Begging for his torture to end, he asked only for release.

Angelique could hear the laughter that met his pleas.

Serena sat at Angelique's bedside wiping the sheen of blood from her patient's skin. Then she tended the IV that kept a steady blood flow into Angelique's arm, as her patient continued to use her own to find Armand. Serena checked her watch and silently prayed Reivn would be successful. They were running out of time.

The risk had increased when the mental connection between creator and child was forged. If Armand died while Angelique was linked to him, they could lose her too. The connection between Angelique and Reivn would soon break as well, leaving him to hunt blindly, and leaving her helpless and trapped in the consciousness of a dying man.

Serena got up and began to pace the room, stopping every so often to check the still figure on the bed. She waited impatiently for word that the mission had been a success.

Angelique cried when she saw Armand's condition, trying to touch him and reassure him in some way, but as fast as the image appeared, it faded again. His voice continued in the back of her mind, screaming in the darkness. She returned to the visions that flooded her thoughts and tried to pay attention to the landmarks and street signs emerging from the darkness, wanting to leave a trail Reivn could find. Ahead of her, she saw where the Renegades had carried Armand through the last alleyway to a door hidden from mortal eyes. She watched when they opened it with a security code and dragged him into the building. She slipped through and followed them down a staircase to the lower levels, where she found herself standing in a dungeon. The cells had been carved from solid rock beneath the streets. Now she could hear what Armand had picked up in his unconscious state... the moans of other victims.

Reivn watched the street signs, as they grew closer to their goal. On the back roads, they slowed their pace, unable to move any faster than the scattered traffic on the late-night city streets. Then he would shift back to his inner mind again to follow Angelique.

Angelique tried in vain to see Armand's captors, who were only shadowed visages as they hoisted him up in shackles hanging from heavy chains. The shackles bit into the tender flesh of his wrists, tearing them from the sheer weight of his body as he hung suspended in the air. She stared in mute horror when they began to skin him and burn the open wounds. His shirt had been torn away and his breeches were soaked in blood that ran down to pool on the floor beneath him. The scenes flashed before her quickly, several nights seen in mere seconds. Finally, his captors gouged out his eyes and gutted him. His screams filled her mind, and she wept, unable to touch the vision before her.

When Reivn and his party finally found the alley holding the entrance to the dungeons, he could see the image that filled her thoughts. It was the same one that had flashed through her mind almost an hour before. He saw Armand hovering near death. He punched in the code Angelique had sent him and carefully pushed open the door. Without a sound, he slipped inside.

Lunitar quickly joined him, followed by the other enforcers.

A quick search revealed four Renegade guards sitting in the main room. They were playing cards and chewing occasionally on a young girl that lay half-dead on a dirty mat on the floor.

Silent and swift, Reivn, Lunitar and the other men slipped into an attack position surrounding the door. Then Reivn picked up a stone and pitched it across the room, hitting the far wall.

The distraction worked. One of the guards wandered to the door and looked out. "I'm gonna check it out, Frankie! Don't look at my cards while I'm gone!" The man shuffled off in the direction the noise had come from, not seeing the men hidden in the shadows.

The second the man moved out of sight of those still in the room, Lunitar decapitated him. Catching the body before it hit the floor, he quickly and quietly pulled it back around the corner and out of sight.

Reivn changed his voice to sound like the dead guard and called out to the men inside. "Yo, Frankie, you got to come see this."

Inside the room, the sound of movement told them their prey was indeed heading their way. "What is it, Jose? You find something'?"

Reivn faded into the shadows and responded to the man at the door. "I just found something all right. You coming or not?" Disgusted at these street thugs turned Immortal, he thought again how stupid the Renegades were, turning these people into cannon fodder for their senseless war. *They could have at least turned those with intelligence or who could think and speak as though they were*, he thought. He turned his attention back to the man who was peering out into the dark hall trying to see his partner.

"Hey, Jose! Where you at, man?" Frankie called.

Reivn let out a whistle and Frankie lumbered toward him, muttering under his breath. *Now!* Reivn telepathied and grabbed the surprised guard by his throat. The enforcer beside him immediately impaled their captive on a steel spike. *This is too easy*, he sent to Lunitar. *We have not met with any real resistance yet. Stay alert!*

Giving the signal to move on the room, Reivn waited as another of his men changed his appearance to look like the dead guard. Once the transformation was complete, the enforcer moved casually into the room. One of the other Renegades looked up as he passed. "What was it, Frankie? What'd he find?"

Reivn's enforcer ignored the man's question, quickly noted that the girl on the floor was already dead and cleared his throat. Then in a rush, he grabbed the guard closest to him.

*Go!* Reivn sent to the others waiting beside him.

Lunitar moved in as the remaining Renegade ran for the door and struck him down. The guard's head hit the floor and he quickly finished the job, destroying the man's heart.

While Lunitar and his enforcers burned the dead bodies, Reivn reached out with his mind to find Angelique again.

She stood sobbing in the gray haze that again covered her senses, unwilling to see any more.

Reivn gently told her they found him. "Go home, angel. I will be there soon." Then in a silent message to Serena, his command was simple. *Wake her, Serena. She has had enough. I will not risk her safety further. When she wakes, tell her we found him.*

The team slipped from the room, moving silently down the staircase and into the corridor, noting the many doors that covered both sides of the long, desolate hall.

Reivn counted them, searching for the one he knew held Armand. Once he confirmed there were no guards, he ripped the door from its hinges. In the dark interior of the room, he found the pathetic figure of Armand hanging from his chains. He growled and moved swiftly into the room. Then he freed the young man's broken body, catching him and easing him down gently. One look at the damage wrought by their enemies was enough. "Every room! Search for any other prisoners! Do it now!"

Lunitar had entered behind Reivn and stood staring at the battered unconscious form in his father's arms in disgust. The level of brutality the man had suffered was unthinkable.

The other enforcers moved down the length of the corridor ripping the doors open one at a time. Each room was filled with gruesome discoveries, but none were alive.

After Reivn took note of the extent of Armand's injuries, he handed the unconscious man to Lunitar and joined the search. He ripped through the doors in fury. When he reached the last one, he tore it from the wall and entered the chamber. Inside, a woman hanging from the ceiling by chains groaned. *I have a live one!* he sent to Lunitar. *Bring Armand! It is time to go!* He circled around the woman to see her face and found himself staring at the past.

"Help me…" she begged.

Without hesitation, he summoned the spirals and broke her chains, catching her in his arms when she fell. He gave the word and his entire team teleported themselves back to the guild. He followed, bearing her in his arms.

When they arrived at the guild, Reivn was abrupt in his orders. "Lunitar, take Armand to his chambers and send for Serena at once! He needs immediate attention! I will be in my old quarters in the south wing if needed!" Then he turned his attention to the woman he carried. Ignoring Lunitar's stunned expression, he headed to a part of the guild that had not been used for time uncounted. At his command, the torches in the hall flared and lit the way, as he moved swiftly to a room layered in dust. He kicked the door open and growled out a cleansing spell. It instantly cleared the room from the dirt and dust that hung like a cloud in the air. He laid her on the bed and stared at her broken body in silence.

Serena was still tending to Angelique when she received word they had returned. She had brought the Elder out of her magically induced slumber the moment she received Reivn's order and had then allowed her to fall into a natural sleep. Confident in Angelique's well-being, she immediately headed for Armand's chambers to see what she could do for him.

Lunitar waited at Armand's bedside for her, his curiosity only serving to further his anger at his father's reckless and confusing behavior. He wanted answers.

When Serena joined him, she was curious as to where Reivn had disappeared to and was surprised when none of the enforcers would answer her questions. She turned to look at Lunitar, who sat staring at Armand in silence, his expression troubled. "My Lord?" she inquired quietly. "Is his lordship safely returned?"

"He has safely returned. He has a charge in the South wing. You are to see to Armand," Lunitar stated coldly.

Surprised by his answer, she nodded slowly. After assessing the seriousness of Armand's injuries, she began her work. There was too much damage for her to put him completely back together. He would be healing for some time to come.

Lunitar sat watching her in silence, his thoughts elsewhere.

When Serena finally finished what healing she could, she looked up. "What happened out there?" she asked.

"To be honest I'm not entirely sure," Lunitar answered. "I don't know that I'm ready to put words to it. How's the patient?" he asked, changing the subject.

Serena shook her head. "It's too soon to tell. He took a great deal of damage over several nights at least. It has had a profound impact on his ability to heal. A fever has already set in, so now we must wait to see if he is strong enough to survive it. I can tell you the loss of his eyes is permanent. He was healed that way."

Lunitar frowned and got up. "I see. I must look into a few things. If there's anything you need to help him, let me know." Without another word, he went in search of his father.

Serena stared after him for long moments before settling in to watch over Armand.

Lunitar walked down to the south wing, disturbed by the thoughts running through his head. *Why the south wing? He hasn't used it since Gideon drove Alora away. Who is the woman he brought back and why here?* His thoughts in turmoil, he made his way down the dusty old corridor until he reached the one room he knew well.

The door was closed and locked, and light radiated from beneath its sturdy frame.

Lunitar stared down at the soft glow in dismay and dread filled his heart. Fear for his father slowly crept into his mind and he knocked on the door.

"Go away!" Reivn demanded from within.

Lunitar sighed and tried again. "My lord, I must speak with you on an urgent matter."

The locks snapped out of place and the door was thrown open. Reivn stood in the opening, glaring at him in cold fury. However, it was his haggard appearance that startled Lunitar.

Reivn snarled at him. "What is so important it cannot wait?"

Lunitar tried to gaze past Reivn to see who lay within. "Permission to speak freely, my lord?"

Shifting his stance slightly, Reivn effectively blocked the view to the room's interior. "Speak and be quick about it."

"I will speak, and I will be quick," Lunitar stated. "Have you lost your mind? Tonight, you single-handedly threatened the safety of this family, the security of the Alliance and the lives of your men so you could rescue a child. That is not something you usually do." Lunitar paused. "You normally delegate such matters. I have never seen you needlessly and recklessly charge into enemy territory searching for someone. You send others to do that."

Reivn stepped into the hall and slammed the door behind him. Then he glared at Lunitar. "As with all things, there are exceptions to the rule and this situation necessitated that exception. The child you refer to is from a Renegade line, as is the young woman that sleeps in the room upstairs. The Council gave them to my charge, and if I fail to keep them under control, then I forfeit my life with theirs."

Lunitar nodded. "Understood," he answered. "But what wards were in those rooms you charged into? What traps were laid? None that I found. Don't you find that odd? They took the time to torture the man in a location with only four guards present. There were how many captives, including those we found dead? You charged me with the safety of this family and that includes you. My sworn duty is also to protect the Alliance. If you find me so incompetent and incapable of rescuing one individual, then you will have my resignation in the morning."

"That will not be necessary." Reivn stared at his son, a pained look on his face. "You do not understand. I gave my word that I would find him. This was not done for duty, but for..." he stopped and closed his eyes, realizing what he had been about to say and who lay just beyond the door. His shoulders dropped. "I cannot discuss this now. I have work to do."

"Very well, father. Just understand you are more important than you could possibly believe... not only to the Alliance, but to this family as well." Lunitar met his father's gaze. "...and to me. You do what you have to, and I will do what I have to do to protect this family, even if I have to protect them from themselves."

Reivn stared at his son, his eyes troubled. "Then protect her. As long as she lives, so do I."

Lunitar was astonished, but he masked it. "On my honor and life. By your leave, my lord."

Reivn waved him away and turned back to the door, then stopped. "Lunitar," he whispered.

Lunitar turned around. "Yes, father?"

"She's back," Reivn's voice was barely audible, but his meaning was unmistakable.

Lunitar stood there for a moment in shock. Then he slowly nodded. "Understood," he answered calmly and walked away.

Watching until his son was out of sight, Reivn settled in to watch over the unconscious woman that occupied the bed. Finally, he began to work on healing her wounds. Ignoring the scar on her chest, he worked for hours, a strange expression on his face. One wound at a time, he restored her body until she lay somewhat whole again before him. When he finally finished, he dropped into a chair in exhaustion. Sleep found him quickly.

As dawn broke the horizon, a hush settled over the guild. The blood servants silently walking the halls to protect their masters. The woman sequestered with Reivn remained unconscious throughout the day, while her wounds finished healing. By the time the sun would next set, they would merely be a memory. The day passed and dusk fell once more. One by one the immortals awakened.

Deep in the bowels of the guild, Reivn opened his eyes with a start and looked around.

"Hello, husband," the voice was icy soft.

Reivn's heart went cold and he turned around. "Why did you come back?" he asked grimly.

Alora smiled. "I had thought husband, that it would have been obvious. I have come home…"

## Chapter Twenty-Four
## The Face of Evil

*There is no greater void than the emptiness of a love denied. It festers in your heart like a bleeding wound that never closes, sitting heavy upon your chest until the pain becomes so unbearable it begins to break your spirit. For such an illness, there is only one cure. How then does one go about seeking redemption from the seeming eternity of a love lost? Is it better to have loved and lost then, or to never have known what a wonderful thing that love could have been, given the chance to be seen through to its glorious finish?*

*The one constant in this bitter world of ours is change. The more we strive to stay as we would have our lives be, the more fate thrashes us down to our raw core, ripping up the fabric of our imagined destinies almost before they begin, and leaving in her wake the rent fabric of another dream undone. This is the only true destiny... the knowledge that fate will forever torment us with the poisonous barbs she laces into the coils of our very souls. We are damned by the very nature of what it is to be human. Make no mistake, no matter the blood that races in our veins, we are still, measure for measure, tied to the weakness of our mortal kin.*

*This is the birthright given us by the Ancients, who knew that to survive we would have to hold on to that fragile bond with our mortal connection. With all the pain we gain from its touch, it still reminds us we are destined to be a part of their salvation. There is a knowing, an understanding, a sympathy if you will, for the suffering they endure from the moment they draw their first breath to the last time they close their eyes to their short lives. God, there is no more terrible curse than to endure for an eternity what destroys them in so short a span of time...*

*Lord Reivn Draegon*

\* \* \* \* \*

Angelique awoke to pain in her head and slowly sat up.

Sitting across from her, Lunitar looked up and breathed a sigh of relief.

Serena had been standing next to the bed. Now she offered Angelique a cup. "Drink this. You will feel better. Don't worry, it's laced with blood."

Angelique took the drink without argument and downed its contents. Then she frowned when its bitter taste assaulted her. "Ugh, what was that?" she asked in disgust.

Serena smiled. "A healing draught. Among other things, I use alchemy potions. They are quite effective in helping to heal our kind."

Lunitar got up and walked over to the bed. "Do you remember me? I'm Lord Reivn's son. I've been charged with the task of seeing to your well-being and safety."

Angelique looked up. "I'm at your service, my lord."

Ignoring her, Lunitar turned to Serena. "Is she well enough to travel?"

Serena stared at him in surprise. "She cannot leave the Guild, my lord. She is appointed Prefect here and must return to her duties as soon as she is able."

"Son of a!" Lunitar snapped. "I'm gone for a few months and everything around here changes!" Glancing at his charge, he frowned and covered his eyes, giving a frustrated laugh. "Very well, as a Prefect..." Then he dropped his hand and stared at Serena. "Wait a minute... she's an Elder?"

Serena nodded and giggled slightly. "She is just like the rest of your family... only far gentler than some. I suppose his lordship felt this would toughen her a bit and stretch her skills."

Angelique interrupted the two of them. "You could just ask me directly, you know."

Lunitar sighed in resignation. "If father has claimed her as a member of the family, then she is a member of the family." He glanced down at Angelique. "You are right, I could ask you directly, but I'm not going to." Then he turned back to Serena. "There's no easy way to say this, but someone that we both know has an affinity for darker things has returned."

Serena's eyes widened. She gave him a warning glance, looked at Angelique, and then slightly shook her head. "I have to check on my other patient," she whispered and turned to go.

As Serena turned to walk away, Angelique grabbed her arm. "Wait," she begged, "what of Lord Reivn? Did they come back? Did they find Armand? Please tell me."

Serena paused, not sure how to explain what had happened. "Yes, his lordship did return with Armand... and one other."

Angelique looked up, saw the expression on Serena's face and grew fearful. "Armand's alive? He will recover?"

"It may take a long time for his mind, but his body will for the most part recover," Serena explained. "I have to go now. I will check in later. You are ordered to rest tonight." She left them alone and headed down the hall to Armand's quarters.

Angelique sat in silence for a moment, and then turned to look at Lunitar. "Have I offended you in some way?"

Lunitar thought about his answer before he replied. "No." He gazed at her intently, hard lines crossing his features. "Are you loyal to my father?"

"Lord Reivn?" She stared at him in confusion. "Yes… with all my heart! Why wouldn't I be? I love him."

"Then understand this," he replied, staring her down. "No matter how strongly you may feel toward him, it is but a mere fraction in comparison to the love and loyalty I bear him. I will destroy you if you bring him harm. That being said, I will also fiercely protect you if you bring him happiness."

Tears slipped down Angelique's cheeks and she looked away. "I would rather die than bring him any pain. I have never loved anyone as I do him. He has filled my life with a joy I never imagined possible. I cannot breathe without him."

Lunitar stared at her in surprise. "Then know you have more than one Draegon who will die for you, my lady."

Angelique dropped back on the bed again and closed her eyes, trying to shut out the sounds of the night. They called to her senses like a moth to the flame. "Why are you here?" she asked suddenly. "Where is he?" She looked up at him, waiting for an answer. Her thoughts on Serena's behavior, she wondered why her friend had been so aloof. It was not like Serena not to speak her mind and it worried her. *I wonder what she isn't telling me,* she mused.

A knock at her door interrupted any response Lunitar may have given.

She called out. "Come in!" Reivn entered and she sat up, happy to see him. "My love, I was so worried! No one told me…" She fell silent when she saw his face.

His expression grave, Reivn pulled her into his arms and held her close. He did not speak for several minutes. Finally, he let go of her and backed up.

Seeing his face, Lunitar moved away, letting him speak with her alone.

"What is it? What's wrong?" Her eyes filled with fear at his behavior.

Reivn stared at her, silently going over the events of the evening again before speaking. "Angel...I have been challenged on one of our laws and must appear before the Council. I have to go. There is no choice. I am sorry. I had hoped it would be different."

Angelique stared at him in alarm. "What are you talking about?"

Reivn's shoulders sagged as though in defeat. "Alora has returned." He walked out without another word, leaving her more worried than before.

Milling his words over in her head, Angelique grew frustrated. *Alora?* She stared at the door, stunned and confused.

Lunitar sat in silence for a moment, taking it all in. Finally, he cleared his throat, got up, and walked over to the bed to sit at her side. "You must be truly special. That man has been my father for over five hundred years and we have known each other for twice that long. In all that time, you could place all the outward emotion he has ever shown in a thimble. Yet in less than a couple of months, you brought out a side of him I have never seen. He named you aptly, for an angel you must be to bring about that miracle."

Angelique turned her eyes away, a soft sob escaping her. "I don't understand what is happening, but it scares me. I know he must often leave on business, but this was so different. He was so... aloof. Did I in some way anger him?"

"No," he answered. "It was nothing you have done. It is the current circumstances in which we find ourselves that has him frustrated. As much as it frightens me to say this, and I do not frighten easily, I do not believe there is anything you could do that would anger him."

At that, she turned over. "Oh no. That's not true. You should have seen how upset he was with me after the attack here on the Guild. When the assassins came, they caught me. But he killed them. Then he chastised me for not being more aware of my own surroundings." She smiled and laughed a little. "It has become almost a game between us when we are alone, but in public, he is most insistent of my being more alert."

Lunitar stared down at her with mixed emotions. "As I said, I do not think you are capable of angering him. What he showed you was not anger. It was love and concern. You will learn the difference with him when you have spent more time amongst us."

"I've been around for over three hundred years, my lord," Angelique reminded him. "It was only your society that I recently discovered. Prior to that, it was just me and my children, but that does not mean I do not understand him."

Running his hand through his hair, Lunitar sighed in exasperation. "By your age, it appears you are perhaps an Elder in your own right, but we really need to work on your knowledge. Concerning my father, I was referring more to my family and time amongst us as such."

Angelique sat up, her copper hair falling over one shoulder. "I know I still have much to learn. I have been reading in between my duties here at the guild, but some of what I have read has confused me somewhat. Reivn was going to begin teaching me more when he returned from finding Armand. Now I'm not sure when we will be doing that."

Lunitar smiled and tucked the blankets around her. "Well, your doctor has ordered you to stay in bed tonight. So, I will go to our library and get some books. We can read together awhile, and I will do my best to answer your questions. Fortunately for you, I am second only to my father in the Draegon line as far as knowledge of our laws. My brothers call me the bookworm."

She frowned. "It isn't entirely the laws I'm confused about, although there are some that are beyond my complete understanding. The whole warrior or healer class idea has me confused. I've also only just begun the journey into learning about the spirals and don't quite understand how it affects our abilities."

He chuckled and gazed at her in amusement. "I can help you with that as well. I am a warrior like my father, but Serena is a healer and I'm willing to guess you are as well."

Angelique shook her head. "I'm not sure about that. I apparently have quite a knack for fire, lightning and other forms of destructive magic, but I can heal too… quite well actually."

Lunitar stared at her in surprise. "You believe you are both? You are most likely incorrect. That gift is exceedingly rare. However, if true, it would be up to you which you choose to be."

"I think I'd like to learn as much as possible about both," she answered after a moment's silence. "It would be nice to read awhile, and I would definitely welcome any knowledge you wish to share. Sometimes studying alone can be downright boring. It's so much more fun when sharing it with someone." She smiled. "I won't run away. I promise."

He got up and headed to the door. "Then I will be back shortly," he replied.

For the next three nights, Lunitar and Angelique read together after they finished their nightly routines and he found himself liking her spirit and thirst for knowledge. In between their study sessions, however, no one else would talk to her and every question she asked was met with silence. Finally, she cornered Serena, unable to take it anymore. "Tell me what has happened! Why is everyone avoiding me?"

Lunitar cleared his throat uncomfortably and gazed at Serena in frustration. "She needs to know sooner or later. It may as well be now."

Looking from one to the other of them, Serena realized he was right and sighed. "Sit down, Angelique. This will not be easy to hear." She waited until Angelique had settled before she continued. "When Lord Reivn found Armand in Philadelphia, he found many other victims' bodies. Only one other was alive, so he also rescued her and brought her here."

Serena paused and looked up at Lunitar. He nodded, so she continued. "You must understand, Angelique, she was so badly injured that he was not certain... until three nights ago, when she awakened. She exercised the rights of Council law, so he is at Draegonstorm with her. To disobey would have brought a sentence of death on his head. Do you understand?"

Angelique shook her head. "No, I don't! What law? What did he do?"

Serena stared at her. "You really don't know, do you?" When Angelique shook her head again, Serena sat down next to her. Then she glanced up at Lunitar. "Perhaps you should explain," she stated.

Lunitar sighed and joined them. "The laws on the right of marriage and of claimance... they state that when you marry, it is for eternity. There can only be one unity, one alliance unless death takes one from the other. The humans have this thing they call divorce, but amongst our kind, there is no such thing. The sharing of power between two of our kind, one to another is too dangerous. If one of our kind were to marry many times and take power from each tribe, then that one would become unstoppable and almost as powerful as the Ancients. So, it is forbidden."

Angelique appeared puzzled. "What does that have to do with Lord Reivn?"

Serena looked down, not wanting to see her friend's face when she answered. "Alora is Lord Reivn's wife and she has declared the right of claimance."

Angelique paled visibly, choking sounds slipping from her as she gasped for air. She stared at Serena and Lunitar in shock for a mere second before bolting for the door to the gardens.

Lunitar glanced at Serena. "I'm out of my depth here," he stated uncomfortably.

Serena stared after Angelique's retreating figure. "This is very difficult for her. She needs to digest what she heard. Give her some time."

Angelique wandered the garden. *His wife! His wife? He told me about her and how horrible she was. How could this happen?* Feeling eyes on her, she turned.

Reivn stood a few feet away. "You were not keeping watch again, angel," he admonished gently. He fell into step beside her. "I need to talk to you. Will you walk with me?"

Angelique nodded, so they continued down the path toward the river. They were silent as they made their way toward the water and their favorite place.

"I do not know where to start. I am deeply in love with you and that will never change, but…" Reivn stopped, taking hold of her arm and turning her to meet his gaze. "I am bound by our laws. I have been a Warlord for the Council for centuries. If I break with them now, they will kill us both. She petitioned the Council and I was ordered to bind myself to her once more." He stared at her, his eyes reflecting his grief. "Please forgive me. I never meant for this to happen."

Unable to hide the pain in her eyes, she stood stiff and unmoving as she tried to absorb it all, but the pain was too much. Tears began to run down her cheeks.

He pulled her into his arms and held her tight, unwilling to let go. Closing his eyes, he fell silent and gently stroked her hair in an effort to comfort her. The air around them stilled as her sobs filled the night.

Hours passed as they stood in each other's arms, both knowing this was the last time they would be together. When the sun finally began to hint it would soon be upon them, Reivn pulled a ring from his finger. "Take it. It is my family's crest. As long as you wear it, no one will dare harm you. I will be returning to my fortress soon. If you have need of me, send this ring. I will know you are in danger and I will come for you." He gripped her shoulders. "Promise me you will do this! Promise me, angel!"

Angelique nodded, unable to speak for fear tears would fall again.

He pulled her into his arms and held her close. "Remember me, angel. I will always love you." He bent his head and claimed her mouth, his own pain pouring into the ferocity of his kiss.

The sorrow drowning her was even more intense than the grief she had felt over Blake's death. When he finally let her go, she walked slowly back to the guild, wanting to be alone.

He was still standing there long after she vanished from sight.

The next evening when Angelique awakened, she knew instinctively he was gone. She made her way to his offices and found them dark and the doors locked. She turned away to perform those responsibilities to which she was assigned with listless duty. The first part of the night passed slowly while she finished her tasks and closed up her lab. Then she wandered toward the wing Armand slept in. Serena had advised against seeing him, but she could wait no longer.

Lunitar and Serena were just coming out of Armand's quarters when she approached.

Serena held up her hand. "You really shouldn't be here."

Angelique did not flinch. "He's all I have left, Serena. I will see him... now."

Serena glanced at Lunitar, then bowed to her and sighed, recognizing her authority. "As you wish, my lady. I must warn you that when you see him it will come as a great shock. You have not yet seen violence like this in our world." She opened the door and stood aside.

Angelique hesitated for the briefest of seconds and steeled herself for what she would see. Then she walked in, followed by Lunitar and Serena. A vicious snarl greeted her, and she stared.

Armand was chained to the bed. His face was twisted with rage, the holes where his eyes had once been now sunken and empty. He strained against the magical chains that bound him, thrashing about and snapping at the air more like a rabid animal than the man he was.

Frozen where she stood, Angelique jumped when Serena touched her arm. "I told you it would be difficult."

Angelique stared at Armand in horror. "What's wrong with him?"

Serena glanced at the patient she had been caring for. "The torture they subjected him to triggered a rare fever that only our kind contracts. It causes a sort of insanity to occur as the fever hits the brain. I do not know if he'll survive it. These first few nights are the most crucial."

Angelique paled considerably, this latest news just too much. "What are his chances?"

Serena shook her head. "Not good. I have been treating him with both my magic and potions, but they are not enough. Our healing ability is almost powerless against this kind of illness because it is caused by our own blood."

Angelique looked away, the sheer horror on her face evident as she fought back tears. She grabbed Lunitar's arm for support. "No! He can't die! I can't lose all of them! Please God... not all of them," she whispered.

Lunitar gripped her hand firmly. "It looks worse than it is sometimes. There have been some who have survived the fever," he told her quietly.

She clung to him, as she tried to pull herself together.

Ignoring them, Serena began to whisper soothingly to Armand. His snarls turned to whimpers and he settled down, crying out as some image came to him that they could not see. She sat next to him, wiping the sheen of blood from his brow and stroking his hair as though he were a small child.

Angelique let go of Lunitar and slowly approached the bed. "I want to help him, Serena. What can I do?"

Serena looked up. "Sit with him and talk to him about the past. Try to help him remember who he is. This is important if we are not to completely lose him to the beast that rages within the fever in his brain."

Angelique nodded. "I would give my own life to save him," she choked out and stared at Armand, who lay mumbling and lost in the horrors only his mind could see.

Serena got up slowly and moved aside so Angelique could sit down.

Angelique began to speak softly of the memories they had shared for over a century of St. Etienne and Blake. A tear made its way down her cheek when she got no response.

The whimpering continued, as Armand wandered in his own twisted insanity.

"Keep talking to him," Serena encouraged. "He can hear you. You are a voice in the darkness. It will be his beacon, slowly guiding him back...if we can."

Angelique nodded slowly and turned back to Armand, wiping away her tears. Taking a deep breath, she started again.

Lunitar nodded in satisfaction and left the room. He wanted to check on his father and home. He knew Gideon and Moventius had to be warned about Alora's return. As it was, it would be impossible to warn Kaelan. He was still on assignment and his whereabouts were unknown.

In spite of Lunitar's warning, Reivn's return to the Keep was met with shock when Alora stepped from the portal behind him. Moventius and Gideon had expected their father, but not the dark creature he had married so long ago.

Gideon was unable to believe his eyes. "Father?" he asked, the question in his voice obvious.

Reivn ignored him, his mood as dark as Alora's raven-colored hair.

Lunitar cleared his throat and stepped forward. "Hello, Alora. I see you have rejoined my father." He bowed to her stiffly, his discomfort apparent. Then he turned to Reivn. "Father, it is good to have you home. We have all missed you."

Nodding to him, Reivn muttered something unintelligible and left the room, not waiting for Alora as he headed for his office, desperately needing to be alone.

Alora smiled coldly at the three men in front of her. Her eyes settling on Gideon, the smile vanished, and a veiled threat passed between them.

Gideon met Alora's gaze with a steely-eyed expression. "How did you manage it?" he asked, his tone challenging her.

She smiled. "I am his wife, child. I had every right to return to his side."

Lunitar moved to stand beside his brother. "Just so we're clear, Alora... my father is well-loved and well-protected. It is obvious you have forced this union upon him according to the law, and that he is anything but happy about it. Step wrong and we will intervene on his behalf, so it would be ill-advised to attempt any further antics such as those done in the past."

Alora stepped forward and stared at Lunitar, her eyes black pools of mystery. "Are you threatening me, boy?" she asked coldly.

"Not at all," Lunitar replied, meeting her gaze with an equally intense glare. "I am merely stating that my father does not ever stand alone. My brothers and I will always be watching."

She laughed and headed to the door. "So noted. Thank you for the warning."

Gideon growled and stepped forward, but Moventius caught his arm. "No..."

Lunitar stepped in front of him. "Now is not the time, brother," he stated. "For now, we watch and wait."

Gideon's eyes followed her, full of hatred and unease. Then the three of them left the portal chamber, going their separate ways to digest this newest turn of events.

After pacing his office like a madman for several hours, Reivn finally sent for Lunitar. He was still walking back and forth in agitation when Lunitar entered.

"Father, you are obviously quite upset. Would you care to talk?" Lunitar asked quietly.

Reivn stopped and turned to stare at his son. His eyes were filled with desperation.

Lunitar stared in shock. "What is wrong, father?"

Reivn hesitated, and opened his mouth as if to say something, then closed it again and quickly masked his expression. *He and my other children do not need to know of the curse. It will only serve to endanger them all when they become too angry to control themselves.* Realizing he had momentarily lost control of his own emotions in front of his son, he changed the subject. "I was merely… thinking. I sent for you to ask about Mariah."

"She is in her quarters under guard, and none have spoken with her as you ordered." Lunitar replied, noting the change in his demeanor. Concerned, he decided to stay close and learn more about the circumstances surrounding his father's distress.

Reivn remained distracted and waved his hand, dismissing his son without another word.

Lunitar bowed and stepped from the room, but he did not venture far. Instead, he slipped into the shadows where he could watch over Reivn from a distance.

Reivn waited until he believed Lunitar was gone, his emotions in turmoil. He stared at the fire, seeing copper curls in the flames, until he shook himself from his thoughts in frustration. Cursing under his breath, he headed for Mariah's quarters. *It is time I talked with my errant daughter. I need to make plans to marry her child off before Alora has the girl killed…*

Lunitar followed his father in silence, staying well away to avoid detection. Concern for Reivn's behavior drove him enough that he was willing to risk his father's wrath if caught.

Mariah sat on the floor of her room, staring at the wall while she played with her hair. In agitation, she was pulling small clusters free from her head to float to the floor beneath her.

Reivn had silently unlocked the door and stood observing her for a moment before walking in. "Mariah. We need to talk."

She looked up, her eyes flashing in rebellion. "I don't want to talk to you. I don't want to see you! Why did you have him bring me back here? I wasn't causing any trouble!" Her voice drifted through the open door into the hall where Lunitar stood listening in silence.

Reivn sighed in annoyance. "I am weary of your childishness. You were brought home because you belong here. You are my daughter and as such need to learn the dignity of what becoming a Draegon entails. You have been one of us far too long for this behavior to be allowed to continue unchecked. Would you have preferred a Prince or magistrate find you and reign you in using far harsher means?"

She tossed her hair back and glared at him. "I would have preferred you left me as I was! What happens to me now scarcely matters! You made me an outcast among my own people and stole my life a long time ago! Why even try to pretend you care about me now?"

Reivn growled and reaching down, he grabbed her wrists and yanked her to her feet. "I would not have kept you alive had I not cared! When Alora gave you to me, you were supposed to die! I kept you because your fire sparked something in me that I had not felt since before my turning! You should learn a little respect, my dear!" He dragged her across the room and dumped her into a chair. "I did not come here to listen to yet another forked tongue, so keep it behind your teeth or I will remove it!"

Lunitar frowned at his father's harsh words, shocked by his anger. Inching closer, he continued to listen, worry creasing his brow.

Mariah shrunk back in fear from Reivn when she saw the cold fury in his eyes. "Why didn't you just kill me?"

Reivn sat down opposite the dark-haired gypsy and gazed at her. "Because of what I saw in you... freedom that could not be tamed," he answered. "It reminded me of myself long ago. You have a passion for life in you that I could not bring myself to extinguish. I wanted to see it burn eternal and watch it blossom into the rare flower you have become."

"So, I was a pet? A toy? You did not even once ask me what I wanted!" She spat at him, her anger slowly returning. "Now I am nothing more than a shadow that haunts these halls! I do not belong here! I do not belong with my own people! I do not even belong to your tribe! What am I supposed to feel if not anger? You took everything from me!"

In the hall beyond the room, Lunitar shook his head in frustration. He knew Mariah was still bitter over her turning. But he felt there was more that had yet to be explained. He stood still as death listening to the conversation, hoping for answers.

Reivn sighed in exasperation. "Stupid girl! Had I not claimed you, you would have been destroyed and those you made with you! That is in fact why I am here! Your child is in danger! Alora has returned, and she will suffer no rival in my court, least of all those in my house!"

Mariah glared at him. "I don't have the power to save her. What do you expect me to do?"

"I want your consent to marry her to one of my officers. She will be safe once she is no longer under my ownership," he explained.

Mariah stared at him, her own emotions buried deep beneath the surface. "You are asking me? Since when have I had any say so over anything that happened to them or me? You claimed them almost from the moment I made them! Can I protest? Would you free them? Or is this merely a formality so your wife knows you are clearing your stables?"

Reivn reached over and slapped her, knocking her from her seat. "Keep your fury for the men you scorn, child, and remember to whom you speak! I was trying to give you the courtesy of having a voice in her fate. However, I see now I have wasted my time in coming here." He got up and stared down at her in anger. "I will do what must be done. I see no further need to keep you behind these walls. You have my permission to go where you will, but do not expect me to run to your rescue should you find yourself at the mercy of a Prince. I release you."

Mariah got up slowly, looking stunned. "I… yes, my lord," she whispered.

Lunitar decided it was time to go and swiftly teleported to his own quarters, not wanting his father to catch him eavesdropping.

Reivn stared at Mariah for a moment longer before walking out, leaving her door open behind him. She was still standing there when he rounded the corner of the hallway, heading for his own rooms. At his door, he growled at the guard on duty. "Fetch Reyna at once." Then he shut the door and began to pace the room, deep in thought while he waited for his slave.

Minutes later, Reyna arrived. "You sent for me, my lord?" Her voice was soft and hesitant.

Reivn took her hand and pulled her into his arms. "I am hungry tonight and it will take far more than blood to satisfy my thirst."

Reyna lowered her gaze. "I live to serve."

He kissed her gently, stroking her dark hair and inhaling the vanilla scent that rose from her soft skin. Then he gently pulled off her blouse. He let it slip to the floor while he slid his hands down her hips, entranced again by her provocative curves. His hunger rose quickly, and he stripped away her skirt, so she stood naked before him. Her bared flesh was beautifully illuminated by the torchlight.

She closed her eyes and let him guide her.

Reivn took her hand and led her to the bed. then after removing his own clothes, he laid down, pulling her down beside him. "There have been too many nights of war in recent months, and the peace I gain when with you is fleeting. I always look forward to you, my beautiful flower. You remain as innocent as the night I first took you. That is a rare gift indeed." Growling as his thirst awakened, he rolled on top of her and sank his fangs into her flesh while he claimed her body with his own.

Reyna submitted without a sound. She stared at the ceiling, willing her mind to another time and place she could scarcely remember anymore.

He was gentle, but demanding in his ministrations, taking what was his by law. But in spite of his pleasure in her, his thirst remained unquenchable. In frustration, he finally dropped down to lie beside her again. "You have served me well, but the time has come to change that. I am giving you in marriage to a member of this house."

"M... marriage, my lord?" Reyna stammered. She fought back the fear that rose at his words.

Reivn stroked her cheek and smiled. "He is my brother. You shall make him a wonderful wife." He caught her expression and smiled. "Fear not. It is a great honor, Reyna. You will no longer be a slave, but a lady of our noble house."

Reyna looked away, afraid if she met his eyes he would see the dread she could not hide. "I... thank you, my lord. I live to serve."

Reivn wearily closed his eyes, confident Alora would no longer be a threat to her. He had tried to be as gentle as possible breaking the news to her. Now his thoughts grew dark as he turned his mind to the nights ahead. Feeding would be far more difficult without the herd he had so painstakingly cultivated over the years. *Still... better to send them on than to let Alora slaughter them like cattle,* he mused in silence. *At least I have a small store of collected blood in my laboratory. It will keep me for a short while, but I am going to have to find a way to end the curse soon or it will weaken me too much.* Finally, his agitation rose again, and he got up. "Return to your quarters until you are sent for by my son. You will not see me again." Without waiting for a response, he showered and stormed from his room, headed in the direction of his office. *Gideon, my office... now!*

Lunitar sat on the edge of his bed trying to digest much of what he had heard. He had more questions than answers and this fact frustrated him. *Mariah was a gift?* he mused, stunned at the revelation. *And what is bothering my father so? What is he so afraid of? He has more than enough power to deal with Alora, so why does she hold such sway over him? I need to know more. It is the only way I can help and perhaps the only way I can keep him safe in light of her return.* In agitation, he got up and went to the Commonroom in search of Gideon.

Gideon arrived at Reivn's office to find the door wide open and Reivn seated behind the desk waiting impatiently. "You took long enough! I have a job for you that needs doing forthwith."

"Father?" Gideon's response echoed with worry.

Reivn frowned. "My herd needs to be dispersed immediately. They are going to different locations and owners post haste. I want you to see to their safe deliveries."

Gideon gaped at his father in surprise. "All of them, my lord?"

"All of them," Reivn affirmed. "I have particular people that will take on a few, but others are merely to be given over to the care of close colleagues of mine. You can tell them it is a gift in recognition of their loyalty to me on the battlefield. That should sufficiently stroke their egos and satisfy the curiosity of any who ask as to why."

Gideon frowned. "I do not understand. You have kept them for..."

Reivn rose from his desk with a snarl. "Do not question me! That is how you lost my favor to begin with! The fact I need to continuously remind you of that has become tedious at best!"

Gideon involuntarily took a step back, startled by his father's response. He dropped to one knee immediately. "My apologies, my lord. I am yours to command as always. Forgive me. Is there a list of names to whom I shall deliver your charges? If so, I will begin tending to the task the moment I leave this room."

Reivn handed him a list. "There is one with whom you can deal with right here in the Keep and it will resolve not only this issue, but another as well. Take Reyna to Adam and offer her to him as a wife and gift from me. That dissolves my responsibility for her and will likewise settle the present matter I have with him."

Gideon nodded. "I shall do so at once." He glanced up at his father, awaiting further orders, but Reivn had already turned away to focus on something else.

"Why are you still here?" Reivn growled over his shoulder.

Gideon got up and bowed. "I was just leaving, my lord."

Expecting to see Gideon, Lunitar had arrived at the Commonroom to find it empty. But as he turned to leave, he came face to face with Alora.

She smiled coldly at him. "Well, if it isn't the little scholar."

Lunitar gazed at her emotionless. "Good day," he replied and stepped around her to continue on his way.

Alora laughed. "You are as much a coward as your father is... not even the courtesy of polite conversation. How droll! No words for your mother?"

Lunitar turned around. "You are not my mother, and polite conversation would imply that I want to converse with you. I do not. So again, good day," he said and left the room. In the hallway, he passed a man that bore a striking resemblance to Reivn.

The man ignored him in passing and kept going.

Lunitar turned to stare at the retreating figure. *Who the hell was that? That was definitely not father and yet the resemblance is uncanny...* He frowned. *Father must at least be aware of him, otherwise, he would not be here... not even with Alora's presence.* Making a mental note to find out more about the mysterious stranger, Lunitar made his way to the library.

He still wanted to speak to Gideon, but needed time to think. He did not get very far.

*Lunitar, come to my office at once. I am sending you on assignment.* Reivn's telepathy was brief and direct, leaving no room for anything other than a quick response.

*On my way*, Lunitar answered. Minutes later, he stood in front of his father's desk waiting, while Reivn penned out his orders. "May I ask what the assignment is, my lord?"

Reivn looked up and handed him the finished paperwork. "It's all there. You are to leave at once. Be vigilant and do not leave your post unless I personally send for you. So that you know it is indeed me that summons you, a code is written in your orders that only you and I shall know. Now go and be swift. I can trust no other with this. Do not fail me."

Disturbed by his father's words, he looked down at the sealed documents, wondering about their content. "I will see it done, father," he said. Then he bowed and turned to go.

Reivn called him back. "Lunitar."

Lunitar turned around. "Yes, father?"

"Do not let your guard down, not even for a second. Should anything happen to me, then the leadership of this family will fall to your shoulders. Stay safe and Godspeed, my son." Then he whispered, "Protect her well."

Lunitar bowed again. His father's last comment had told him all he needed to know. Bypassing the need to take anything with him, he made his way to the portal immediately, knowing where his trip would take him even before he opened the orders in his hand. He was headed to Atlantic City to guard the one person Reivn could not...

# BLOOD FEUD

## Chapter Twenty-Five
## The Guardian

*Were I in Hell I would know better peace than I do now. I have been sitting here this last hour, watching the wood in the hearth burn, with no desire to move or expedite the execution of my nightly reports, for it is the only respite I have from her. God, but she is relentless! It is not enough for her that I have emptied my house of those I needed to feed. She wants me to feed from her. I know the potential danger this presents and have avoided it these last four months. But the hunger is beginning to take its toll. I feel the weakness creeping into my body. Soon I will have no choice but to find some sort of resolution. My blood stores are expended, and with no donors here to refill them, I am out of any resources I had left. Now I play a dangerous game. I dare not let my sons know. It would start a war they cannot win against her and would run the risk of wiping out my bloodline.*

*I sent Lunitar away for this very reason. He is the most observant of my sons. I could not have hidden my present state from him for long. So he was sent where he can do the most good... guarding my beloved angel. She still has so much to learn, and he is a scholar of the arcane. I doubt he would leave her to her own resources once he learns of her lack of knowledge. By bringing them together, it will keep them both where they are out of harm's way and still serve real purpose. I envy him his freedom. The two of them are very much alike in their thirst for learning, and he will be with her when I cannot be. I fear he will realize what a rare flower he has in his hands, and I do not want him to see her through my eyes. I cannot... will not... share her with any other. And again, a fool's desire. Alora will never set me free...*

*Lord Reivn Draegon*

\* \* \* \* \*

Within moments, Lunitar stood in the portal chamber in Atlantic City. With a sigh, he headed above to find the object of his assignment. He found her sitting in her office.

Angelique looked up at him in surprise. "My lord, to what do I owe the honor of this visit?"

Lunitar walked in and sat down. "I am here on assignment for my father, so I thought we could get to know each other better in light of the affection my father now holds for you."

She smiled softly and blushed. "He sent you, didn't he?" she asked matter-of-factly.

"Well, I can see there won't be any fooling you, so yes," Lunitar answered. "He is concerned for your safety and the fact he sent me speaks volumes."

Angelique's eyes clouded over at the mention of her safety. "It's because of her," she stated more than asked. "She has him by the throat because of Council law and levies it against him to control his every move." Her voice grew bitter with hatred. "I want to kill her."

He nodded in understanding. "Know that you are not alone in that sentiment. Also, be aware she is far more powerful than you and I combined. Taking her down is no easy task, and even Lord Reivn would be hard pressed to accomplish such a feat. For now, we must endure what cannot be changed. So let us look to things here until the time comes to change it."

She sat back, sadness filling her features. "I used to look forward to the nightly routine, knowing he would be there. Now it just seems like endless monotony."

"Then let's turn this tedium to our advantage and find a solution to our current problem," Lunitar stated. "Would you do me the honor of giving me a tour of the Guild and helping me get to know its operations better? Last time I was here I did not get that opportunity."

Angelique got up and joined him. "It would be my honor. If you are to be with us a while, then you will also need quarters of your own to stay in."

He nodded in agreement. Noting how fragile she appeared, he briefly wondered how he could possibly protect her if Alora came crawling from the darkness to take her life. He got up and opened the door for her. "After you, my lady."

She blushed slightly and moved past him. "Angelique would be best, don't you think? The other sounds so... formal."

Lunitar chuckled and shook his head. "You started it by addressing me as my lord."

Angelique laughed. "You are his son, are you not? It seemed the logical way to address you."

He chuckled, liking her pleasant demeanor. "Well, you are a Guild Prefect working directly under my father's command, so the same could be said about you. I'll make you a deal, you call me Lunitar and I'll call you Angelique."

She giggled and nodded. "Agreed. Lunitar... Is that a proper way to address each other in the presence of others though? Or should we just keep that for when we are one on one?"

Lunitar laughed then. "You are a Guild Prefect and I am Lord Reivn's son. I doubt anyone would question how we address each other. But for propriety's sake, I believe you are correct."

"Well, at least I'm getting more familiar with the nuances of our society. There's so much to remember. Your father often teases..." Angelique stopped, realizing what she said. "I mean he used to tease me about not watching out for myself. It just takes a little getting used to."

"You told me that before," Lunitar interjected. "Father is correct. Ours is a dark society and we must be ever vigilant. How is it you survived so many years and still don't know this?"

She stopped walking and turned to gaze at him. Her eyes were a mass of unreadable thoughts. "Well, I spent the last three hundred years before here living in the Caribbean islands. There were few if any of our kind, so there were no rules except to survive."

"Then if I may ask and please believe I really am not trying to be rude," he stated. "Why are you a Prefect when you are still this unskilled? That's almost setting you up for failure."

She dropped her gaze. "Please stop apologizing. If we are to be friends, then we need to agree on the ability to speak our minds without the threat of insult from the other. I understand your confusion as it was also mine when your father assigned me to this position." She paused before continuing. "Lord Reivn wanted me to take this position because I was training directly under him and he was personally teaching me. But, since he left, I have felt very inferior and am afraid I may not be able to live up to the expectations of the other Prefects in this city."

"I see." Lunitar sighed and then smiled at her. "First we must agree to speak with candor in private. Second, I will try to teach you what I know of the position you hold. You must understand that your position is a very political one, and that the political battlefield is by far the deadliest and bloodiest in our world."

Angelique nodded. "Much like the courts of Louis the fourteenth, I'd imagine. I remember those days too well, as I believe I mentioned before.

He chuckled, remembering their first conversation. "Yes. You were a member of the aristocracy. That knowledge should actually help while learning to maneuver your way through the quagmire of intrigue that filters through the political social circles here."

"I was a Comtesse in my country and went to court on more than one occasion with my father, so yes. I do understand political jousting." She sighed. "Even the ladies at court were subject to its brutality in those days."

Lunitar ran his hand through his hair and frowned. "Well, for all our power and knowledge, we still have not left the dark ages with political intrigue. Is it safe to assume that you are still lacking in the knowledge of your birthright as well?"

Angelique slowly nodded. "My birthright? You mean my magic?"

"For a Mastric the birthright is magic, or more specifically, mastery of the Mystic Spirals," Lunitar explained. "Not all birthrights are the same."

She laughed at his remark. "I know that for the most part. I'm still trying to sort out who is who and what tribe possesses what in the way of power. So far, I know the Victulians are the ruling class and the Thylacinians are the most animalistic of the tribes. How am I doing?"

They reached the library doors and he opened them for her. "Not bad. Only seven to go."

"You definitely sound like him. He teases me too," Angelique laughed. "What about the other tribes?"

Lunitar pulled out a chair at one of the tables for her to sit down. Then he walked around, absent-mindedly pulling old tomes from the shelves and putting them on the table in front of her. "Well, you are correct about the Victulians and the Thylacinians. As you know, there are nine tribes that comprise the Alliance. Do you know the names of the other seven?"

She nodded. "I believe so... The Armenians, the Galatians, the Sargonians, the Dracanas, the Mithranians, the Epochians and the Mastrics are the others. I've met someone from almost every tribe so far, although I get a little confused at times as to what tribe some come from."

"Well, that's good... meeting others I mean, because that's a primary role of a Prefect," he stated, smiling. "That's important to not only our tribe, but to foster relationships with the other tribes on behalf of our own."

Angelique listened intently before answering him. "As Lord Reivn explained it, a Prefect's job is to represent their own tribe's interests in the political arena within each territory. That is to ensure we don't lose ground to another of the tribes, as it could jeopardize our own strength and standing within the territory or cost us the respect of our fellow tribes."

Lunitar gazed at her in admiration. He saw that he had a good pupil in her and grinned. "You are correct. Now, what are the names of the Council members from each of the tribes?"

She hesitated for a second, thinking hard. Finally, she replied, "I believe our tribe is named after its progenitor, Mastric. The Victulian Council member would be our King, Victus. Then there is Thylacinos of the Thylacinians of course, and Galatia of the Galatians. I'm afraid I don't quite yet know the others. They were present when I was brought before them, but they did not speak. They simply waited while Victus determined whether or not I would be allowed to join the Alliance." She shuddered at the memory.

"You are correct about Victus, Mastric, Thylacinos and Galatia," Lunitar explained. "So… four of the nine. Let's flesh out the rest for you. For the Epochians, it is Chronos. For the Dracanas, it is Silvanus. The Sargonians are from Sharrukin, the Mithranians from Mithras, and finally there are the Armenians. Armenia is their progenitor. They are the Guardians of all our collective knowledge." He paused. "That is the Council of nine, also known as the Ancients. It would probably be a good idea if you also knew the identities of the Warlords and the first-generation Elders. It wouldn't hurt to know who the second-generation Elders are as well."

Angelique nodded in agreement. "That is what your father said, because they are my peers. He told me it was important to know those who are on my level of creation."

Lunitar turned to stare at her, somewhat confused. "You are a second-generation Elder?"

She glanced up. "I am. Is that bad?"

He shook his head. "Not at all. It's just one more name I need to add to my list, though it does confuse me. Just who is your sire?"

Angelique paled and looked away. "He is not around."

Lunitar sat down across from her. "I thought we agreed not to be guarded or easily offended," he reminded her gently.

She looked up in embarrassment. "We did. I'm sorry. It's just that I don't think he is well liked. His name is Ceros."

"As in Ceros Valfort?" he asked incredulously.

Angelique nodded and dropped her gaze. "Your father said I should not speak of it since he has claimed me as his own protégé now. He told me it would be dangerous for people to know."

Lunitar closed his eyes and sat back as he digested the information. *So, she is not just of Valfort's line. She is his daughter.* He looked up. "Lord Reivn is correct. That is indeed dangerous information." Without hesitation, he put up a ward to prevent any eavesdropping. Then he continued. "Do you know who Ceros Valfort is?"

Looking uncomfortable, she shook her head slowly. "I remember very little of him. I know he took me from my home against my will and turned me, then abandoned me to my own fate, but little more. Lord Reivn refuses to speak of it with me."

"Well, I will not refuse to talk about it," he answered firmly. "You need to know just how dangerous he is. But after we discuss it, don't ever speak of it again." He paused. "Valfort was the first child of Mastric himself. In fact, he was the first child ever created by any of the Ancients. He is the oldest of the Elders and the true measure of his power's potential remains unknown. More importantly, he is a Renegade."

At the mention of the Renegades, Angelique looked up nervously. "I… I know that. Lord Reivn was going to hunt down Armand when he left because he thought Armand had joined that fight. I'm afraid I was rather rude to your father when he told me. We argued about it because I wanted to know if he would hunt me too."

Lunitar stopped her. "You have to understand exactly who and what the Renegades or the Principatus, as they call themselves, are. Valfort betrayed Mastric and in doing so, the Alliance as well. When you said you went before the Council and they allowed you to join the Alliance, you need to realize they did not just allow you to join the Alliance. They allowed you to continue to live, and to my knowledge, you are the first that has ever been given that courtesy. Every other Renegade or their spawn are killed on sight."

She shuddered and paled. "I don't understand. Why would they let me live if no other before me has ever been allowed to do so?"

He shrugged. "My guess? My father asked a favor of my grandfather or my grandfather finds you a curiosity, or a combination thereof. Either way, you'll notice the common denominator is my grandfather. Learn that lesson well."

Angelique frowned. "If Valfort is Mastric's son, wouldn't that also make me his grandchild as well?"

"For the most part, yes," Lunitar answered. "However, when one becomes a Renegade, there is a rite that is performed that severs the blood ties. It changes everything from their genetic markers to the way they access their power. It even alters their birthright. So in your case, no. You are not directly tied to my grandfather's line. Your direct line goes no further than Valfort."

She shook her head. "What you are telling me frightens me to a level I cannot fathom. I have felt him on the edge of my mind at times, as though he is searching for me. There are even times I can almost hear him trying to beckon me to his side and it terrifies me. He terrifies me. The first time I felt truly safe was after your father took me under his wing and claimed me as his own. Before that, I was always looking over my shoulder."

He nodded in understanding. "There are spells you can learn that will prevent him from tracking you. However, the easiest thing to do is to establish a blood bond with my father and fully accept him. That will mask you better than any spell."

Angelique relaxed a little when she heard that. "He and I have already done that several times. I offered him my own blood, and he not only accepted, but gave me his own in return."

Lunitar's eyes widened in surprise, and he whispered under his breath. "You are important to him." Then he said, "From now on, if anyone asks who your sire is, you tell them Lord Reivn, because for all intents and purposes he is. This is not only through the bond you share, but also because he made you his protégé. In the eyes of the law that makes him your sire."

She nodded. "I promised your father I would say nothing to anyone. I've already broken that oath by telling you. Please don't tell him?"

"Your secret is safe," he promised. "But if he ever asks me directly, I will not lie to him."

Angelique dropped her gaze. "Then I pray he never asks. I love him more than my own life. I fear losing him to this hateful world we live in. I know he is a powerful man, but I don't care. I love him for who he is when he is with me and I don't want to jeopardize that for anything." Then she looked up. "Lunitar, I would die for him."

Lunitar smiled gently. "In that, you and I both agree. Now as I said, we will never speak of this again. Let us move on to a better topic. One near and dear to my heart… the Spirals."

Over the next four months, Angelique spent her nights caring for Armand, tending to her Guild duties and joining Lunitar in her studies. She learned how to feed Armand and give him his draughts. She sang to him and read him books. Though he never gave any sign of recognition, she refused to quit, her zeal to heal him stronger even than Serena's. Even in his madness, Armand began to trust her, and his rage lessened. He knew her voice when she entered.

Lunitar would frequently accompany her to Armand's rooms and sit with her through the long hours. They would often study together there, while Armand slept.

One night as Angelique tended Armand, a Courier barged in. Armand shrieked and sank his teeth into her arm, tearing it open. "You fool," she screamed at the messenger. "Get out!"

The man waved a letter at her. "It's from Lord Reivn. He's requesting an audience with you."

She ran to the door. "Give it to me," she ordered and took it from him. Then with a brief glance at the seal, she quickly tore it open.

> *My Lady,*
> *I hope you are well. I have recently been informed of your hardship with Armand and it grieves me. I pray for his recovery. I have in my possession an archaic scroll that may aid him. Its magic comes from the bloodline known as the Mesenetere. They have divided themselves into four tribes. This scroll was created by the tribe among them called 'the Manu' or children of the water. Their magic healing is far more potent than any other in the world. Because of the origin of his illness, there is no guarantee, but it at least offers you hope. I will be traveling back to the Americas with my wife in a couple of nights. I request an audience with you to discuss important business. I will give you the scroll then. I await your response. Remember what I told you upon our last meeting, as that has not changed. Until then my lady, I am forever your servant.*
>
> *Lord Reivn Draegon*

Angelique slowly put down the letter, staring into space until Armand's snarls brought her back to the present. She moved to his side and began speaking softly, trying to calm him. His growling changed to whimpers, and she reached out her hand and brushed his hair from his eyes, smiling down at him.

"A... Angelique?" Armand whispered hoarsely and fell asleep.

It was the first time in four months he had recognized her. She fought back tears and stood up slowly, backing out of the room. Then she closed the door and ran down the hall to Serena's quarters yelling. "Serena, come quickly! He knew me! He knew me!"

People began looking out their doors at the commotion.

Lunitar heard the shouting and immediately teleported into the hallway from his room. Then he turned in the direction of her voice and hastened to join her.

Serena opened her door to see who was making all the noise. "What's going on?" she asked when she saw Angelique.

Lunitar joined them, his concern rising when he saw Angelique's arm.

"He recognized me! That means he's getting better doesn't it?" Angelique could barely contain her excitement.

Serena stepped into the hall and closed her door. "He actually spoke your name?"

Angelique nodded. "Yes! Just now, when a courier upset him, and he bit me! I was finishing getting him settled and..."

She did not have the chance to finish as Serena cut her off. "He bit you? Breaking the skin? Oh, God!"

Lunitar knew the danger she faced. He wasted no time. He wrapped his arms around both women and teleported them directly to the infirmary.

Serena grabbed Angelique's hand and dragged her over to the medical cabinets. "I've got to give you the serum at once to fight the infection! He has a rare fever, remember? You can contract it through a bite!" She grabbed a vial and filled a syringe, then turned to Lunitar. "I'm going to inject this directly into her heart. It's the only way. Once the contagion reaches her heart, it will transfer to her brain and she'll contract the fever. I need you to hold her."

Lunitar moved behind Angelique and caught her arms. Then he pulled them up and restrained them above her head. "I'm sorry, but this is for your own good."

Angelique struggled with him, fear overcoming her reason as she tried to pull away. "No," she cried, her voice filling with panic.

Lunitar kept her firmly in his grip and spoke softly, trying to calm her down. "If we lose you to the fever, how can you help Armand? Just close your eyes and hold on to me."

Realizing he was right, Angelique locked her hands in his and fearfully shut her eyes.

When he saw she was ready, he nodded to Serena.

Serena plunged the long-needled syringe into Angelique's chest, injecting the bluish serum deep into her heart.

Angelique screamed in pain and her knees buckled, as a searing fire exploded in her chest.

Lunitar scooped her into his arms and carried her over to one of the empty beds. Then he carefully laid her down and sat down beside her.

Serena walked to the bed. "The pain will pass soon. What you feel is the syrum attacking the infection and rendering it harmless. Had I been with Armand when the fever first began, I could have done this for him too." She gazed at Angelique in concern. "How do you feel?"

"Like a dagger went through my chest," Angelique managed to gasp. "What was that?"

"You don't want to know. Just suffice it to say you'll be fine. But be more careful next time. Armand has a long way to go before he will no longer be a threat to anyone." Serena smiled at her and closed the wound on her arm. "Now tell me what happened. What did the courier want?"

Angelique quickly told them everything she knew.

Lunitar made silent note of every detail, hoping for news of his father.

Serena listened in silence until Angelique mentioned the scroll. "A scroll of the Manu? They are considered more legend than reality. The possession of such a scroll is rare indeed."

Lunitar frowned. "Lord Reivn has seen and done far more than either of us in his time. If he offers it, then it is real."

Serena smiled at Angelique's worried expression. "He's right, Angelique. Come. If you are feeling better, let's go check on Armand. You have a letter to write."

Angelique looked at her, puzzled.

Serena grinned. "Well you aren't going to give up a chance to see him, are you?" Laughing, she took Angelique's hand and helped her up.

Lunitar stepped over and stopped them. "Before we go to check on Armand, further precautions must be taken to ensure this does not happen again."

Angelique turned to look at him. "What do mean?"

"Well, first we need to establish two checkpoints that need to be cleared before anyone can enter Armand's quarters, to avoid startling him again since he is prone to that," Lunitar stated calmly. "And other than when he is being given medication or fed, a bite guard needs to be put on him to prevent any further incidents."

Angelique stared at him. "A bite guard? You mean a muzzle? No! He's not an animal!"

Lunitar reached over and picked up the syringe, and then held it up to her face. "How many more times do you want this jabbed into your heart?"

Angelique flinched at the sight of the needle and took a step back. "I don't, but we've managed all this time..."

Serena interrupted her. "Angelique, perhaps you should listen to Lord Lunitar. He has dealt with many things in our world."

Angelique glared at Serena. "We're talking about one of your patients, Serena! He's sick, not rabid! I can't believe you would actually agree to this! He's already chained to his bed! It hasn't seemed to bother you before! Why now?"

Lunitar stepped in. "You say he's not rabid. Then what did we just cure you of, if not something akin to rabies? You are correct. Armand is not an animal, but as long as he is acting like one, he presents a very real danger. I am under orders to protect you, my lady, and that includes from your own hard-headedness. Your choice here is that either he is muzzled, or you are to refrain from entering his rooms until he has fully recovered."

Angelique's jaw dropped, and she stared at Lunitar in shock. "You wouldn't really do that... would you?" she finished quietly.

Lunitar's gaze hardened. "I will answer your question with another question. What do you think my father would do? Once you've answered that then ask yourself if you believe me to be any different than he is."

Angelique looked away, knowing what the answer would be. "You argue with logic I cannot defend against. I know Lord Reivn would never allow me to put myself in danger. That is why he sent you in the first place. Nevertheless, please reconsider this? Muzzling Armand, I mean. It just seems so... cruel."

"This is only until he regains a stronger measure of control," Lunitar reassured her. "Even you must admit that he is more animal than man at this point."

Angelique's lower lip trembled. "It's just so hard to think of him that way. I am not sure I can do this. What if he hates me for it later?"

Serena interrupted her then. "He'll hate himself a whole lot more if he hurts you in any way."

Lunitar stopped her. "I'm pretty sure he's not even aware of what is going on, so I doubt he even has the capacity at present to hate anyone for what must be done."

"God I can't do this…" Angelique sank onto the bed and covered her face with her hands as the tears began to fall. "Everything has gone so wrong. I just don't think I can do this alone. Reivn was right when he told Blake I am weak. I have no idea how to survive in this world."

Serena sat down beside her. "That is why we are here, Angelique. You are not and never were alone. We can teach you what you need to know, but you have to trust our judgment about things you do not understand."

"My father and I both warned you that ours is a cruel world." Lunitar reminded her. "I am truly sorry you have to learn it this way, but as Serena said, we're here to help. It is far better than being suspended from a wall in a dungeon bathed in the flames of wrath."

Angelique looked up in confusion. "What are you talking about?"

Lunitar sighed then. "It is one of the ways Mastrics are trained to focus mentally… by being forced to endure excruciating pain until they can shut it out and still focus on casting."

Serena closed her eyes in silence for a moment, remembering her own training at the hands of Galatia. It had been infinitely worse. She shuddered slightly.

Angelique stared at Lunitar. "Reivn would never do that! He is a good and kind man!"

"No, he is a just and honorable man," Lunitar corrected her. "And he did do that to me to ensure I learned how to survive. You still have much to learn."

## Chapter Twenty-Six
### The Altar of Sacrifice

*I have condemned myself. This union she has revisited on me will be my undoing. Her power is beyond my control and she has weakened me. The curse she placed on me all those years ago is taking its toll. I am slowly starving. Without the essence of the lovers I fed from, I can gain no sustenance and she knows it. Every night that passes, I feel the need that has grown to desperate levels and yet I must continue to somehow subdue it. If I feed from her as she wishes, I risk sealing my fate and letting her gain total control.*

*What I would not give to be with my angel... her soft copper hair gleaming in the moonlight, as it did the many nights we walked together. However, if I am successful, she will no longer remember us as I do. Her life will go on and she will be free of the grief I caused her. Lunitar will look after her, of that, I am certain. Perhaps in time, he will find in her the same beauty I have and will claim her as a mate. Then at least I could rest easy in the knowledge she found happiness with one who is worthy of such a precious gem. The scholar in him will find a most worthy pupil and her desire to learn could be the bridge that unites them through a shared love.*

*I am such a fool. I read the words I write and even as I write them, I can only laugh at my foolishness. I cannot imagine letting him have her and yet I cannot have her myself. I envy every moment he spends with her, every word she speaks and every smile she gives. I could order him to take her as his own, but my heart will not allow me to do so. To give her to another man in that way, even to my own son, is more than I could ever endure. How do I let her go when I know all I have ever desired in this world waits for me in her arms?*

*Lord Reivn Draegon*

\* \* \* \* \*

Pacing the floor of her office, Angelique watched the clock as the minutes ticked by. *God, he is taking forever. When will he be here?* Her thoughts a jumble, she played with her skirt and smoothed it for the hundredth time since awakening that night. Then resuming her pacing, she glanced at the clock again.

"Hello, angel."

Spinning around, she came face to face with Reivn.

He frowned. "You were not..."

Angelique cut him off with a nervous laugh. "I know, watching out for myself, right? I knew you would be here, so I wasn't worried. I know everyone else's footsteps here." Looking up at him, she smiled wistfully. "You look pale. Have you been ill?"

Reivn stared at her, his eyes troubled. "I am fine. I need to discuss the trip to the Sahara for Kuromoto's trial. It is next week. You will have to travel alone. I will be meeting you there."

She nodded, her eyes taking in his pallor. "I can manage as long as I have the date, my lord."

"Why are you being so formal?" he asked, the agitation in his voice growing.

Taken aback by the question, she froze. "I didn't want to offend you. I was just..."

Reivn growled and slammed the door behind him. He was across the room in three long strides. "God, I have missed you!" he moaned and pulled her into his arms. Without hesitation, he brushed her hair back and sank his fangs into her neck, half-starved and desperate to feel the bond with her again. He drank ravenously, his need and desire taking complete control. The months of denying himself sustenance took its toll as he succumbed to his thirst.

Angelique gasped at the ferocious appetite with which he fed. She could feel the blood being pulled from her veins at a rate that frightened her.

From his room down the hall, Lunitar felt her fear, and he looked up from his books. "Something's wrong," he growled and got up. In his mind, he searched for its source and felt his father's presence. It was bestial and almost violent.

With savage thirst, Reivn dug his fangs deeper, tearing her throat to increase the blood flow.

Angelique cried out. She knew he had lost control and had no idea how to stop him.

Lunitar realized what his father's state of mind was in and wasted no time. He teleported to Angelique's office. He was shocked by the sight that greeted him.

Reivn was so overcome by his need to feed, he was barely recognizable, and Angelique stood pale and afraid, held fast by the iron grip he had on her.

"Father! Stop!" Lunitar yelled and crossed the room. He grabbed Reivn's arm, trying to pull him off her.

Reivn growled and shoved him away. His eyes had glazed over, and the beast had taken control. The scent of her blood filled his senses and only served to drive him further into the frenzied state to which he had succumbed.

Lunitar knew she was in trouble. He summoned the spirals and wrapped its tendrils around Reivn as magical restraints. Then using the tendrils, he pulled his father from Angelique and immobilized him. "Father, you need to regain control before you kill her!"

Angelique was shaking badly, and barely able to stand. She closed the wound on her neck and allowed herself to sink to the floor. Then she leaned against the wall for support and stared at Reivn in despair. Trembling from head to toe, she drew her knees up and hugged them close.

Reivn struggled against the bonds that held him, his thirst not yet gone. He snarled at Lunitar. Then he turned his gaze on Angelique. Almost immediately the rage disappeared. "My God! Angelique..." Sheer horror crossed his features and he stared at her. "What have I done?"

Lunitar cautiously released Reivn and stepped closer. "Are you all right, father?"

Reivn turned to his son and his eyes filled with grief. "It was not me you should have had to protect her from..." he whispered. "Please forgive me."

Angelique looked up, trying not to show the pain she was in. "This was not your fault. This is that woman's doing. Had she not forced herself on you again, you would not be in such a state." Her voice trailed off and she fell silent, too weak to say more.

Reivn dropped to his knees beside her and opened his own neck. "Feed, angel. You desperately need it. I took far too much."

Lunitar raised an eyebrow and put his hand on Reivn's shoulder. "Are you sure that is wise, father? You have obviously not been feeding properly yourself, so you need every drop of blood you have. I can see to it she has sustenance. I have fed well tonight."

Reivn looked up. "She must take at least enough to renew the bond we share. She needs that protection. Only then will I allow you to take care of the rest." He nodded to Angelique.

Obediently, she sank her fangs into his neck and drank, her body trembling with need. The moment she felt the bond with him strengthen again, she licked his wound closed and pulled away. She had barely taken a pint, and her hunger was far from satisfied after what he had taken from her. "The bond is renewed," she whispered.

Reivn reluctantly let her go and stepped back, knowing she needed more.

Lunitar knelt down beside her and opened his wrist, offering it to her. "Drink, my lady. Take what you need. I will restore myself after."

Angelique glanced up at Reivn and he nodded.

"Drink, angel," he whispered.

Closing her eyes, Angelique began to suck down the blood that flowed from Lunitar's veins. She shook from both need and the emotions that tore at her as the image of Reivn only moments before drifted through her mind. Minutes passed in tense silence while she fed. Finally, she pulled away and licked closed Lunitar's wound.

Lunitar slowly stood up and turned to gaze at his father. He felt something Angelique had not. He felt her presence in his mind and realized that just as a child links to their Sire with their first feeding, she had somehow been linked to him as well. It disturbed him. He dared not voice what he knew to his father and counseled himself to keep silent.

Reivn was staring at him, his eyes filled with an almost unreadable envy. "Thank you," he whispered hoarsely. "I am still adjusting to the changes in my life. It has been... difficult. This was an unexpected side effect. It will not happen again."

Lunitar gazed at his father in understanding. "I gave you my word I would protect her, father, and to that I hold. I am honored with the trust you have given me. If need be, it would be my life for hers. In that, I give you my solemn vow. No matter what the present circumstances are, she is my mother, for I know how dearly she holds your heart and you hers."

Reivn bowed his head slightly, acknowledging his son's revelation. "That is why I chose you as her guardian. You are my son in all things and know me far better than most. You have proven tonight that I chose well."

"And I will always endeavor not to betray that trust, father," Lunitar replied quietly, slightly shaken by his father's admission and praise.

Reivn turned to Angelique. "And you, angel... can you forgive me?"

Angelique got up. Then she walked over and took his hand in hers. "There is nothing to forgive, beloved. This was not your fault. Were I to have my way, you would feed from me every dusk and dawn and we would never be separated. I love you."

Reivn pulled her into his arms and kissed her passionately as he held her close. He only let her go when a knock at the door interrupted their reverie.

Straightening her skirts when Reivn backed away, Angelique called out. "Enter."

The door opened and a beautiful woman with waist-length black hair walked in. She was dressed head to toe in black. Her cold eyes settled on Angelique and she smiled. "Good evening. I do hope I'm not interrupting anything?" she purred and looked expectantly at Reivn.

Lunitar's eyes grew cold when he recognized the newcomer.

Angelique realized who the woman was, and a sick feeling formed in her stomach.

Reivn growled at the intruder. "I told you to wait in my rooms! This is Mastrics business!"

Alora snickered and sat down in a chair near the fire. "Indeed. I can see what kind of business you are conducting. Your aura still lingers on her." She gazed intently at Angelique. "So, this is my rival?" she hissed. "How sweet and young, although I just don't see the appeal. Really Reivn, you could have picked something more... well, just more." She glanced at Reivn, who stood quietly staring at the fire and laughed.

Lunitar growled. "You have no business here, Alora. These offices are reserved for Mastrics Prefects and higher-ranking officers... not for the likes of you. Even with all your vaunted knowledge, you cannot tell the difference between my father's aura and mine."

Alora snickered. "You think me a fool, child? I can smell his scent still lingering on her lips! I think you try too hard to defend what passes for honor in your father. I could call him out before the Council now for his betrayal and none would question it!" Then she glared at Angelique. "You'd best understand, my dear. I have returned to my husband's side and I intend to stay. He is not and never was yours. You might have been a pleasant distraction, but that is over now. Stay on a business level in your dealings with him or answer to me."

Reivn spun around. "You overstep your bounds! You have no authority here and Council laws forbid threatening another of our kind! If you attempt to harm her, I will kill you myself!"

Angelique tried to approach the chair Alora sat in, but Lunitar quickly slid between them and pushed her back a couple of steps. "You don't want to do that. Leave it to his lordship."

Angelique shook Lunitar off and tried to get past him. "It's all right, my Lord. I would welcome the challenge. If it freed Reivn from her iron grip, I would gladly destroy her."

Alora laughed, her eyes glinting dangerously. "Well, she has spirit. Too bad that is not enough. Reivn, tell your pet to get back in line or I'll put her there myself."

Grabbing Angelique's arm, Reivn pulled her away from Alora. "Both of you stop it! I forbid it as Warlord Prefect! Alora, you may have forced claimance on me, but that will not protect you if you break the law! Back down now! Angelique, you also know our laws! Step back from this! She is trying to goad you into a fight you cannot win!"

Angelique glared at him, angry now. "She walked into my office insulting and threatening me! Why should I step back?"

Alora got up and walked out, her laughter filling the hall.

Reivn took Angelique by the shoulders and shook her. "I can fight my own battles, angel! You are no match for her! I will not have her take the life of the only woman I love…" He stopped, realizing what he had said.

Lunitar looked away, clearing his throat uncomfortably. Then he knelt and stoked the fire.

"I am sorry," Reivn continued after a minute. "I should not have brought her here. Now she has seen you, and you are a target." Reaching into his breast coat pocket, he pulled out a piece of ancient parchment. "Here is the scroll I promised. Take it to Serena. She will know how to use it." Then he looked over at Lunitar. "Alora will be on the hunt now. You know what to do."

Lunitar nodded and stood up. "I do, my lord. Is it possible to give Angelique a leave of absence from her duties as Prefect? She is a sitting target here."

Reivn shook his head in frustration. "No. The law is very clear with that. She has only been in office a short time and has not yet fully gained the knowledge of what her duties entail. That coupled with her already unsteady acceptance from the Council would put her in even greater danger and I will not risk that. This is why I assigned you to guard her. Your familiarity with battle and defense are an asset to a situation I cannot yet control. I may also need ready access to her again at some point if I cannot contain my hunger."

Lunitar raised an eyebrow at his father's last remark. "What of your herd at Draegonstorm? Can you not use them for sustenance?"

Reivn stared at the fire, his thoughts on the hurried dispatch of the young women he recently had living within the fortress. "There is no herd, Lunitar. They are gone by Alora's demand. I believe she seeks to weaken me or force me to feed from her tainted blood, but I will not yield to her foul intentions any further than what has already been done."

Lunitar's eyes widened in shock and he stared at his father. "Do you mean to tell me you haven't fed in over four months?"

"Prior to tonight, the last time I fed was the night I sent you here," Reivn answered somewhat reluctantly. He glanced at Angelique. "I have barely been able to leave Alora's side, but what I find her trailing behind me everywhere I go. I have not had a moment's peace since her return."

Angelique sat down quietly, trying to digest everything Reivn said and finding she could not voice her own thoughts.

Lunitar shook his head in disbelief. "That explains a great deal. Alora is right. She could take you before the Council. You have fed from your herd since she was driven from the fortress, and without that sustenance, she will gain the upper hand. Why would you allow her to deny you what is yours by right of law? I know you do not feed from humans anymore, so how are you going to feed?"

"From me... as often as he is able," Angelique interjected, getting up. She had quickly realized that for whatever reason, Reivn had not told Lunitar his secret. "I don't care what the consequences are. I would rather die beside him than leave him to suffer alone."

Reivn did not answer. He stood staring at the flames in the hearth, deep in thought.

Lunitar sighed. "I understand your sentiment, Angelique, but there is a bigger picture you need to consider. Lord Reivn is the Warlord Prefect. That means he is the Commander of all nine Warlords and all the Alliance forces. If Alora incapacitates him through starvation or some other means, it could cripple the Alliance and shift the balance of the war. Through her actions against him alone, she could bring the Alliance to its knees."

Angelique turned to Reivn. "Is this true?" she whispered.

Reivn nodded. "I never wanted the position of Prefect and in fact tried to resign my rank as a Warlord, but the Council does not let you decide your own fate. They govern us all with an iron grip that allows no yielding unless it is to their will. I did not tell you the full measure of my title and position because I did not wish to worry you with such things."

"I understood when you first fed from me there was some need in you to drink from our kind, but can you not also drink from humans? Could you not simply feed while on assignment?" Angelique asked in confusion.

Reivn shook his head and turned to look at her. "Not long after I married Alora, she caught me in a compromised moment when I was unconscious following one of our battles with the Principatus. She placed a Daemon seed in my chest. She intended to awaken that seed, so she could take total control of me." He paused and glanced at Lunitar. "That much you know. What you did not know was that during that incident, she also cursed me with a spell only her kind can create. She condemned me to feed only from the lovers I take from amongst our race. I gain no sustenance from any other source."

A sob escaped Angelique and she sank back into the chair. "My God... she is trying to kill you. You can't just not feed. You will grow too weak to defend yourself."

Lunitar stared in shock at his father. "Now I understand. Why did you not tell me? Father, we need to figure out how to keep you from starving."

Reivn turned to gaze at his son. "No, Lunitar. Your job is to protect Angelique. I will deal with Alora. This must run its course. She loves her dark ways too much to leave them aside forever. Sooner or later she will step wrong and when she does, I will be waiting."

"As you command, my lord," Lunitar bowed reluctantly. "Though I will do what I can to watch your back as well."

Reivn shot him a warning look. "I will pretend I did not hear that, as it is in direct violation of the orders I gave you when you left Draegonstorm."

Lunitar bowed. "Thank you, my lord. By your leave, I will return to my duties."

Reivn walked over and embraced his son unexpectedly. "Take care neither she nor you come to any harm," he whispered before pulling away.

Lunitar returned his embrace. "I will, father. I give you my word."

Reivn watched in silence as Lunitar left the office. Then he walked over to Angelique and pulled her to her feet. He kissed her forehead and turned to go. "You will always hold all that is best in me. Do not forget that. Watch your back. If anything happens, send my ring." Without another word, he left, closing the door behind him and leaving her to her own thoughts.

Staring at the door in silence, Angelique moved her fingers over the scroll in her hand. She could feel the magic mixed into the very fabric from which it was made. "I love you too, Reivn," she whispered to the empty room. When she looked down, the ring he had placed on her finger caught her eye. It glinted in the firelight and as she stared at it, she could almost feel his presence. She sat down at her desk, put her head in her hands, and began to sob uncontrollably. All the pain she had bottled up for four months coming out in a flood of tears.

Lunitar headed to his own quarters after leaving Angelique's office. He needed time to think. Pacing back and forth, he went over everything in his head. Then he paused for a moment and reached out with his feelings, searching for Angelique to test the new bond he shared with her. Almost immediately, he felt her pain. He realized with a start that she was grieving Reivn's loss to almost dangerous levels. After making a mental note to work with her on that, he set it aside and turned to how best to protect her. Finally, he decided to take a walk around the Guild to determine exactly what its defense capabilities were. He swiftly changed his clothes and headed out again, a look of determination on his face. He knew Angelique was still in her office, so he made his way to her quarter's first, intent on checking them for access points before she returned. Once he finished there, he headed for the lowest level of the Guild and the old south wing where only a small handful had chosen to dwell.

Reivn went to his chambers where he knew Alora awaited his return. His thoughts darkened as he turned over in his head the conversation in Angelique's office, and his fury grew. By the time he reached his quarters, his mood was blacker than his hair. He threw open the doors and stormed in to find Alora lounging on his bed. "Get up, you foul witch! We are going to talk about this right now!"

Alora looked up when he crossed the room and laughed. "I don't think I've ever seen you this angry. So, I will humor you." She got up and walked over to a nearby chair, then sat down and looked up at him expectantly. "What do you wish to talk about?" she asked sweetly.

"You know damned well what I want to talk about!" Reivn snarled at her. "You are going to stay away from Angelique! I cleared my herd to meet your demands and have granted you almost every wish you have asked for since your return! You will do this for me!"

Alora's eyes flashed red and she got up. "You dare to tell me what to do?" she growled at him, her voice growing angrier with every word. "You may once have held more power than me, Reivn, but those days are gone! I am my father's daughter and I have come fully into my own! I can crush you with a word! If you try to control me, I will destroy your entire bloodline from the lowest to the ones you hold dearest! Don't think I do not know of the secrets you keep even from your own sons! I have walked in your mind a thousand times while you slept, and I know you! Do you hear me? I know you!"

Reivn leapt at her and grabbed her by the throat. Then he slammed her into the far wall and pinned her there. "Do not dare threaten my family, Alora. I will rip your soul from that body of yours and feed it to the dark things you keep as pets! I am not yours to command!"

Lunitar stood in the hall in grim silence. He had heard Alora's voice the second he left the stairwell and had hastened toward the sound, fearing for Reivn's life. Now he stood listening to their conversation. He had never heard his father this angry before and it worried him.

Alora grabbed Reivn's hands and burned them with dark energy. "Get your hands off me! I may not command you, but you do not control me either! Let me remind you that I know you cannot sustain yourself any other way than a woman's embrace! If you want me to leave Angelique alone, then you will not only couple with me, you will feed from me and give me my due as your wife!"

Lunitar turned and stared at the door in apprehension. Reivn's safety relied on his answer.

Reivn snarled at Alora and dropped her to the floor. "What are you about, Alora? I know you do not desire me as a woman does! You are little more than another Hellspawn Daemon from the pit! Your heart is incapable of anything but deceit and hatred! What is it you want?"

"What makes you think I do not crave the touch of a man or to hear his words of affection? Even my father loved Pandora and held her dear to him!" Alora spat at him. "And he was the first fallen from grace!"

Lunitar's eyes widened and he shook slightly, realizing to whom Alora referenced.

The hall was deathly silent. Finally, Reivn spoke. "If I do what you ask, Alora, will you leave those I love... including Angelique... in peace? If I bed you and feed from you... you must agree to leave them alone."

Alora smiled and got up. "Are we negotiating? I could entertain the idea, but you must first show me how genuine your offer is. Furthermore, you would have to agree to give our son more freedom than what he has now. You gave him a wife, but little else."

Lunitar shifted uncomfortably when he heard Reivn. *He's going to give in to try and protect the family.* A gut-wrenching fear slowly began to form in his heart.

"You can call it negotiating if you want. I will call it what it is: blackmail. You are using our laws to force me into a corner," Reivn snarled, his hatred of her abundantly apparent in the tone of his voice. "You are below my contempt, but I give you my word. As long as you leave my family alone and I do mean all my family, I will give you what you want with me and me alone. This includes Angelique and any of her young. She is mine and shares the same bond with me that all young have with their masters."

Alora smiled. "A strategic move on your part, my pet. If not for your obvious desire for her, I wouldn't care much either way. I don't see her as being part of the equation for too long. After all, she is not really your daughter, is she?"

Reivn looked up sharply at the reference. "That is none of your business! Leave her alone, Alora! I'm warning you!"

"Or what, my love? Or what exactly?" Alora laughed at him. "You will not raise a finger to me. Your Council forbids it, remember? After all, it was you who pulled me from that horrible dungeon where I was tortured, and it was you who brought me home and healed me."

"You planned all of it," Reivn growled, the anger in his voice turning to cold steel. "You planned it knowing I would come for Armand, and you set me up."

Alora feigned a hurt expression. "Husband, you wound me! How could I possibly chain myself up and damage myself that badly? I was near death if you remember. Why would I risk my life in such a way?"

Reivn growled. "You had help! I'd stake my life on it!"

Laughing now, Alora walked over to Reivn and took his hand. "Come. Entertain me. I am hungry. Be good and I will forget that the reason Moventius is your son is because you killed his mother. Otherwise, I may have to tell the young man what his so-called father actually did. Then we shall see if he still feels the same about you."

Lunitar stood listening in stunned silence. In one night alone, he had learned far more about his father's past than in all the years he had served him.

Reivn allowed Alora to push him back onto the bed. Then she drove her fangs into his chest with a snarl and began sucking on his heart's blood. He yelled as the pain hit him. Then he fell silent, willing the pain away while she continued to feed.

Feeling nauseous from the knowledge that Alora had such a tight grip on his father, Lunitar slipped quietly away, unwilling to hear any more. With grim purpose, he made his way up to the library to spend a day in research. After casting a spell to stay awake, he turned to finding some way to save Reivn from the grips of the she-devil that had collared him so tightly.

Reivn lay beneath Alora, letting her crawl over him while she ripped the clothes from his body. Then she sat astride him, purring like a hungry cat, as she raked her claws down his bare skin, slicing it open and licking the surface to lap up the blood before reclosing the wounds. He closed his eyes in revulsion and shut out the pain, instead trying to focus on a copper-haired angel that laid two floors above, dreaming of happier nights.

## Chapter Twenty-Seven
## Awakening

*I am undone. She now knows Angelique and will kill her if I do not submit to her will. How can I lead my people and keep them safe when I am nothing more than a puppet to her evil? She knows I would do anything to keep my own safe, and she has seen the one thing I sought so desperately to hide... my heart's desire. Dear God... my angel... she is in more danger now than she has ever been. I have to find a way out of this before Alora kills us all. My sons, my daughter, even my soul will be devoured by her if I cannot find some weakness... some way to defeat her that will not drag me outside the perimeters of the law. She knows I will not violate the laws I serve and uses this against me to tighten the noose around my neck.*

*Lord, shed your grace on my son and lend him your wisdom and strength, for the journey he embarked on tonight is a road few if any ever travel without losing themselves to the darkness. He does not know the full measure of what evil he now must face. She will kill him and anyone else that stands between her and her chosen mark. Her hatred runs too deep. I know not yet what her true purpose was in seeking me out in marriage all those centuries ago, but I do know now it was not because she desired me. No... she wants something far greater than even I can yield. I am but a means to whatever end. A devil has come to the Dragon's den, and the dragon lies, stripped of power, in chains. Only a miracle can save us now. I can only pray Alora steps wrong and misses her target when she strikes. Then and only then will I have the one shot I need at breaking the iron yoke she has placed on my shoulders. I must be ready. If by the grace of God, she misses her target, I cannot and must not miss mine...*

*Lord Reivn Draegon*

\* \* \* \* \*

Angelique remained in her office crying until she was numb. When her tears were finally spent, she went looking for Serena with the Manu scroll in hand. Her face was drawn and white. She finally found the healer in her Alchemy lab and knocked.

Almost immediately, Serena stuck her head out the door. "Angelique. What's the matter? You look terrible. What happened? You saw Lord Reivn, right?"

Angelique nodded and began to tell her about the confrontation with Alora.

Serena frowned. "That witch! She makes a habit of hurting people. One thing is for sure," she put her hand on Angelique's arm. "Now she'll be after you. And any person she deems an enemy usually winds up dead. You'd best be on your guard from now on."

Angelique handed her the scroll and changed the subject, having secretly already determined to be ready for Alora if she came. "This is the scroll he promised me. He said you would know how to use it. Can you read this?"

Serena opened it and looked it over with interest. "It's written in Hieratic, although a much different form than I'm used to seeing. Still, I will be able to read it. Fascinating..." Walking into her lab, she almost forgot Angelique was there until she looked up. "Well, come on. If you're going to learn anything about the ancient languages, this is as good a place as any to start. Besides, I've heard from Duncan and I have information you will find very interesting."

Angelique followed, her interest peaked by the scroll.

They spent the rest of the night translating the historic artifact and chatting with each other. One symbol at a time, Angelique began to learn the archaic language in front of her and Serena proved to be as patient a teacher as she was a healer. They finished shortly before dawn, and before they went to their own rooms, they agreed that as soon as their duties were completed the next evening, they would attempt to use the scroll on Armand.

Angelique flew through her tasks the following night, eager to get to Armand. When she entered the corridor leading to Armand's quarters, Serena was just coming from her own labs.

Serena nodded to her reassuringly.

When they passed through the checkpoints and entered Armand's room, they found him awake. He whined, indicating he was hungry. Angelique quickly fetched some blood bags. Then she took off his bite guard and fed him, while Serena prepared the scroll for use.

As she sat next to him, Angelique whispered. "Come back to me, Armand. I really need you now. You are and have always been my greatest friend."

Much to her surprise, Armand grabbed her hand and squeezed it. His head lifted toward her for a moment, recognition crossing his features. Then it was gone again, and his hand fell away.

She quickly joined Serena to prepare for the ritual. Then they began to cast as they had discussed in the lab, focusing all their magic on the scroll in front of them.

The scroll started to shimmer. Then one by one, the hieratic symbols floated up from the page. Each one hovered in a brilliant fiery hue for a second, before flying to Armand, embedding itself on his forehead, and disappearing into him. Armand began to shake as the magic overtook him, rising off the bed to hover in the air. He cried out in agony from the pain that was ripping through him, until it became more than he could bear, and he passed out.

Angelique closed her eyes to shut out the image of his suffering and concentrated on the magic. Finishing the spell as the last of the symbols left the scroll, she and Serena sealed it and ceased their demand on the spirals.

Armand slowly floated back down to the bed.

Wanting to see if the scroll worked, Angelique hurried to his side and reached for him, anxious to awaken him.

Serena grabbed her hand and stopped her. "Not yet," she commanded. "Wait until he revives on his own. You might interrupt any lingering magic."

Even as she spoke, Armand's back arched up off the bed and he let out an agonizing scream. Liquid fire erupted from his chest, dissipating in the air above him. Then it passed and though unconscious once more, he seemed to relax as though the pain was gone.

Serena watched him for a few more minutes, waiting until she was convinced the scroll had finished with him.

In frustration, Angelique walked back over to the scroll, wondering what else they should look for. Then she cried out, getting Serena's attention. "Look," she exclaimed, holding up the scroll. "All the symbols are back! I think it worked!"

Serena took the scroll from her and opened it the rest of the way. Every symbol had returned to its place, restoring the scroll to its original form. Handing it back to Angelique, she smiled. "This is obviously more than a mere spell. I believe Lord Reivn gave this artifact to you. Lock it away in your labs. You might need it again someday." She glanced at her friend. "Watch over Armand for awhile. I think he will be fine, but you should stay just to be sure."

As she opened the door to leave, Angelique called her back. "Wait a moment! You never told me what Duncan said. You told me last night you had news."

Serena walked over and sat back down. "He actually had a great deal to say. It would seem the men who grabbed Armand were hired to take him. What we don't know yet is why or by whom. Duncan is digging a little deeper, but I told him to be cautious. There is treachery here and we don't know yet who else is involved."

Angelique sat listening in silence, turning the events over in her head. She was silent a moment before speaking. "If no one knows who or why Armand was targeted, he could still be in danger. I am going to ask Lunitar to heighten security around the Guild until further notice. No one should enter or leave without my knowing it." She got up and began to pace the room. "Also, I am assigning a second guard to watch this room. No one but you, Lunitar or I should come in here. I want to meet with Duncan as soon as possible. Tell him I will pay whatever is necessary to ensure getting the answers we need."

Serena nodded in agreement. "I will inform Jim, our chief of security, and ask him to send another guard at once. Stay with Armand. I know how important he is to you. We will talk later."

Angelique shook her head. "No, I need to talk to Lunitar, and it can't wait. I'll come back here after I'm done." She telepathied Lunitar. *Please join me in my office. I have urgent news.*

*On my way,* Lunitar answered her and immediately teleported to the hall outside the small office. He was waiting when she arrived. "You called?"

Angelique nodded, her expression one of obvious concern. "Yes. I have news about Armand's recent abduction. He could still be in danger."

Lunitar sat down opposite her and leaned forward. "Tell me what you know."

"Serena got word from Duncan... the Armenian in this area." She sat back, fidgeting with her hands nervously, worried now. "He has been digging into the matter using some of his contacts in Philadelphia. He found out that the ones who took Armand were apparently hired to do so, but for what reason remains unknown. This concerns me because in his present condition he is far too vulnerable."

He frowned. This news unsettled him. "Prior to your introduction into our society, who if anyone did you come into contact with?"

She shook her head. "No one of any significance, just a few that spent their time looking over their shoulders. They were running from someone, but I never learned who."

"What I am trying to figure out is what he knows or who he injured to bring about this vendetta," he explained calmly, his brow furrowed. "In order for him to be tortured to that level, there must be something, because that is extreme even by our standards."

She stared at him in frustration, shaking her head again. "Lunitar, I'm telling you we knew no one. The last person of any note or power any of us had contact with was the last time I saw Valfort before I made my escape. From that time until we came to this city and met Kuromoto, we remained to ourselves and trusted no one with our secret."

Lunitar leaned back in aggravation. "And we do not yet know what if any questions that may have been asked of him. This presents a problem not easily solved."

"I know," Angelique whispered, nodding her head. "What of his safety here? I sent word to double the security on his room, but what of the Guild to ensure no chance of the same person getting to him again? We need answers and until he can talk, there's no way of getting them."

He thought quietly for a moment before answering. "I don't know that we need to increase the security of the entire Guild. But increasing the security around his room was definitely a good idea, at least until we know more."

She got up and paced the room worriedly. "I had Serena contact our Chief of Security. The scroll did as Reivn said it would, so hopefully Armand will wake soon. Then maybe he can provide us with some answers. I am planning on returning to his room when you and I are done here. Perhaps you should just come with me."

"Perhaps," Lunitar agreed. He opened the door for her.

Angelique joined him, and the two headed back to Armand's chambers together.

When they arrived, she turned her attention to Armand, mulling over who he could have as an enemy. Walking to the window, she stared out into the night and analyzed what she knew. Armand was jovial and carefree. He rarely offended anybody. For someone to go to that much trouble, they had to have a serious grudge against him.

Lunitar stood gazing at Armand in silent contemplation, gauging the progress of the man's healing. To his surprise, the man slowly turned his head and touched the bite guard on his face.

Angelique was still at the window when Armand's voice broke the silence. "Angelique?"

She spun around and stared at the bed. "Armand," she whispered, crossing the room swiftly.

Lunitar breathed a small sigh of relief. "Welcome back to the land of the living," he stated and cautiously unfastened the bite guard, pulling it free from Armand's head.

Armand lay on his back touching his eye sockets. His hand shook when he felt the emptiness within. After a moment, he pushed himself slowly up to lean on his elbow and half sitting, he turned his face toward them. "Boy, do I feel like hell." His voice trembled when he spoke. "What happened? I don't remember much after being attacked."

Angelique slipped her hand in his. "It's a long story. Are you able to talk a bit?"

Armand groaned and nodded. "I feel as though I've been in a shipwreck, but I think I can manage." When she sat down on the edge of his bed, he held up his shackled wrists and touched the chain. "Do I want to know?"

Lunitar sighed. "You were having a little trouble identifying friend from foe."

Armand frowned. "Not sure what you mean, sir? Uh, Lord Lunitar... correct?"

"That is correct," Lunitar answered and pulled up a chair. "What I mean is you were lashing out at whoever came near you, hence the need for the restraints and bite guard."

"Are you kidding me?" Armand's expression registered disbelief. "I doubt I could hurt anyone right now. I'm in too much pain from my ah... adventure."

Lunitar looked at Angelique. "Do I tell him or will you? He should be told now, because eventually he would find out either way."

Armand cleared his throat. "Tell me what? What is going on?"

"Don't worry about it. I'll remove those chains for you," Angelique stated, averting her eyes. She got up, walked over and grabbed the keys.

She stared at them for a brief second before returning to Armand's side. Then undoing his chains, she helped him to sit up. "You have been very ill. I'm glad you're finally awake."

"Well, since you don't want to address the topic, I will," Lunitar interrupted, giving her a stern look before turning to Armand again. "You were abducted and brutally tortured over a period of some considerable time, hence the pain you feel and the condition you find yourself in. During the healing process, which was afforded you because of my father's efforts to find you, you were delirious with a very dangerous fever. During your delirium, you lashed out and did injury to the lady here."

Angelique looked up sharply. "You didn't need to tell him that."

Lunitar disagreed and shook his head. "On the contrary, he needed to know. He is not a child to be coddled."

She glared at him. "No, he isn't, but he's only just awakened. You could have given him some time to at least get used to what has happened before..."

Armand cut her off by putting his hand on her arm. "Angelique, it's okay. The man is right. I need to know everything that happened, not just the good things. I don't even know how long I was gone or how long I've been here and out of it."

"You've been gone a long time," Angelique replied softly, looking away. The sight of his empty eyes hurt her in a way she could not fathom.

Lunitar leaned forward." I know you've been through a terrible ordeal, Armand, but do you remember anything... anything at all?"

Armand laid back and felt his eye sockets and face, trying to discern the damage in silence, while he thought for a moment. "I don't remember much, but what I do remember is bizarre. They tortured me, reveling in my pain. But they never asked me any pertinent questions, not even when I asked her what she wanted. She laughed at me. Then they forced me to think of Angelique, insisting I remember her. They knew about her. At some point I must have passed out, because I don't remember anything after that."

Lunitar frowned. "You used the words they. How many?"

Armand shook his head. "Only two I think, though there could have been more. I heard a lot of screams, but I only ever saw the two."

"You saw them? What did they look like?" Lunitar asked, eagerly pressing him for more information.

Armand turned his head toward Lunitar. "I wish I could say, but one was always in the shadows. The other one... well, she was beautiful, but twisted. She seemed to be the one in charge, but she must have been insane with the things she kept saying."

Lunitar sat back and listened carefully. "Go on," he replied, motioning for Angelique to remain silent.

Armand shuddered slightly, remembering. "She told me her favorite color and said she wanted to hear me scream. She acted as though I were entertaining a lady... courting her even. I asked what she wanted, and she said nothing. She just wanted me to bleed. Nothing made sense."

Lunitar sat quietly a moment, absorbing what Armand told him. Then he asked, "Did you hear any names mentioned?"

Armand shook his head. "None. The only thing I know is that they were trying to set up someone they want to harm, and that the man there was bent on linking with me when my thoughts turned to Angelique. I don't know what they wanted or who they were. As I said, none of it makes any sense. They mocked me, but never tried to get anything from me."

Lunitar frowned. This was not what he had expected to hear.

Armand touched his empty eye sockets again. "I don't suppose they will come back?"

Angelique averted her gaze from the painful sight and whispered, "No."

Armand nodded and fell silent, as he absorbed the information. "Well..." he finally answered, trying to sound cheerful, "at least I will finally get you to spend more time with me. Guess it was a rather drastic way to accomplish that but...." His voice trailed off at her continued silence. "Don't worry, love. It will be all right. I'll figure out... something."

Lunitar got up and put the chair back in its proper place. "Well, where she is, I shall be for a number of reasons. One will be to help you see again by using your birthright. It will not be vision as you know it, but with proper training, it is far more effective than normal sight. The other reason is to ensure her safety and yours."

Armand nodded and sat up slowly. "Well, that would only be until I can get on my feet again. Then I can watch over her as I always have."

"Then when you are ready, I will help get you back to operating at full capacity again," Lunitar told him. "I will leave you two to get reacquainted. If you will excuse me," he bowed and walked out. But he stopped just outside the door and listened to ensure all was well within.

Unable to hold back any longer, Angelique began to cry the moment Lunitar left. "Oh, Armand... I have needed you so badly. Now you're here, but with everything that has happened, I don't even know where to start anymore! It's all such a mess!"

Armand reached out and felt around until he found her hand. Then he patted it reassuringly. "Well I'm back and I have plenty of time, so start talking."

Angelique sat next to him and wiped her tears, trying to figure out where to begin. The last six months had done so much to change her. Realizing she was no longer the innocent girl he had tried to defend six months ago, but a strong Vampyre who stood as a leader among her tribe, she knew she had a lot to tell him. "I guess I should start with what happened after you left to find Blake's killers." She paused, looking at him. "That was six months ago..."

# BLOOD FEUD

## Chapter Twenty-Eight
## Right of Claimance

*So small a thing, her eyes… so much do they carry her soul in them that I could lose myself in their depths forever. I find it an irony that fate will give you so wonderful a gift only to snatch it away with such brutality, leaving your wounds raw and ulcerated. I made this fate for myself, for it was my foolish acceptance of Alora's union so long ago that brought me to this. How can I ask my angel to suffer with me? I have but to close my eyes and I can see her as she was that last night together. I would give my heart, my soul, even my last breath to hold her one more time. If it is the same for her, how deeply the pain must tear at her. No, I cannot ask her to suffer for me.*

*It has taken forever for me to finish the spell, but at least with this, she will, at last, find a measure of the peace she once knew. I will miss that sparkle in her eyes, the way she would hurry to meet me each night, and the soft scent of her hair when she lay in my arms. I have found myself bereft, my arms so painfully empty since my return to the fortress. Draegonstorm has become my torment. These empty halls have shown me the truth of my own existence…*

*It is a terrible thing to discover that what once made you alive died in you long ago, so gradually you never even noticed when your heart grew numb. Then she came and taught me what it was to feel, reawakening passion in me. I was so dead before her. How can I go back to that empty existence now that I know what it is to feel such incredible joy? It was as though I have never before truly drawn a breath, and now the air I need is denied my lungs as I fight to hold on to that fragile pulse of life.*

*Lord Reivn Draegon*

\* \* \* \* \*

Two days after Armand revived, Lunitar received a package. It was sealed with the familiar crest of his father, with orders to deliver it to Angelique. When he did not see the code his father had put in his previous orders, he grew concerned. Wanting to ensure its authenticity before handing it over, he summoned the spirals and carefully opened the letter without breaking the seal, He scanned its contents and quickly realized it was not meant for his eyes, so he resealed it. Then he went in search of Angelique. He found her in her office. "This came for you tonight," he stated gently and quickly turned it over to her. Then he waited while she tore it open.

Angelique's hands shook slightly when she saw the parchment inside. There were two scrolls wrapped in silk, with a letter tucked in beside them. She pulled out the letter and read it, and then sank to the floor, tears pouring down her face.

*My Dearest Angel,*

*I have returned to the fortress. It is better we are not near each other lest I forget myself again. My foolish alliance with Alora all those years ago was a costly one. I have never truly known what love could be until you. Forgive me, for I would not leave you with so much pain.*

*Enclosed in this package are two scrolls I have created for you. The first scroll is a new protective spell for the Guild. Considering the events of the past six months, I did not want to leave you unprotected. Please gather the items listed and add the vial of my blood still sitting in your lab when you cast it. This will seal the spell, protecting you and all within the Guild. It is a very potent spell, keeping the Guild safe from most intruders, both human and supernatural. I have been working on perfecting it these last six months.*

*The second scroll I must explain to you. It is a spell of forgetting. It would only be selected memories, not everything. I poured all the memories we share of each other into it. Please know I never wished you any suffering. I wish only joy for you. She will never release me and unless she breaks our laws, I am bound to her for eternity. Though I do not fear her, I am wary. I know her ability to hate, and she will destroy you before she will allow you to share any part of me. I cannot leave knowing you are alone. This way perhaps you will at least be able to find love again. I will carry the memories of you into my final days and when I die my thoughts will be of you as the last blade stroke falls. Your beautiful face, your sweet voice, the red-gold hues of your hair and the love you were always so willing to give will be my last breath.*

*I have recently gotten wind of the location of a much-wanted traitor to the Council and will be leaving soon on that*

*assignment. That is all I can tell you. Please use the scroll and set
yourself free. When I see you again, you would know me, but
would bear no memory of ever loving me. Only one heart needs to
break. This was my doing. Please allow me to carry this burden
alone. I would give my immortal soul to see you smile again. Alora
is Ancient and even I do not know the full extent of her power. I
will say no more. Forgive me.*
*Your loyal and ever faithful,*<br>*Lord Reivn Draegon*

Angelique looked up when she finished, unable to speak.

The incredible amount of grief on her face tore at Lunitar's heart and
he dropped his gaze, letting her grieve in peace. "You know he is only
trying to protect you," he told her quietly.

A sob rose from her and she shook her head vehemently. "I don't care!
I cannot do it! I could never do it! I would rather die a thousand times over
than do this!"

"Then don't," he replied. "It wouldn't be the first time someone that
loves him defied his orders for good reason."

Shaking from overwhelming sorrow, she stared at the letter in her
hands, as her tears stained the page red. "It does not matter if she comes
for me. I cannot forget what I shared with him. He gave me breath when I
could not breathe. He taught me everything I know. He could have killed
me and chose instead to love me. How could I ever let that go?" She knew
Reivn was right about the laws and Alora, but she did not want to let go.
She thought of the first time she had laid eyes on him in Lord Sorin's
court. She remembered his entrance, the pride in his footsteps…or had it
been power? She did not know. *How can I forget the night he first carried
me over the balcony? I can still feel his kiss.* "How can I forget? I've never
felt more alive than I do when I'm with you," she whispered and glanced
down at the ring on her finger, remembering his face.

Lunitar saw her look down and followed her gaze. He stared at the
ring and his eyes widened as he recognized his father's coveted crest. Even
he had not yet been granted that privilege. It was the symbol of the Order
for which his father had fought, died, and been resurrected. That crest was
the icon of what all the Draegons stood for, and thus far, only Reivn
himself wore. To see it on her finger was monumental and shook him to

the core. Its presence spoke volumes of the love Reivn bore her, and how much he cherished her existence.

Angelique got up and slowly went to the fireplace. She read the scrolls briefly, deciphering which one she wanted. The second scroll was indeed a scroll of forgetting, as Reivn had promised. She stared at it for a second, and then slowly put it in the flames, searing her hand while she held it to ensure it caught. She barely noticed the pain. "If you want me to pretend I don't love you, I will try, but my heart will never forget. It is etched into my memories forever," she whispered in the silence of the room.

"Well, my lady, it appears we are both committed to a course of action now," Lunitar stated quietly. He walked over and took her hand. As he turned it over gently, he healed it and let her go again. Then he turned to stare at the fire as it consumed the scroll. The flames turned first green, then blue. He watched in mute silence. *So much magic...* he thought, shocked with the realization of just how much magic she had destroyed with that scroll.

Angelique stepped back as the flames flared and turned purple, scarlet and finally black, watching the scroll crumble and turn to ash.

Lunitar turned and left quietly, giving her the room and the privacy to grieve. He knew there would be time later to talk more.

She was still staring at the fire when a knock came.

Armand cracked open the door. "Angelique? Are you there?" He caught her scent and smiled. "Didn't you hear me? I have been knocking for the last five minutes. Are you okay?"

She sighed and turned to him. He was getting around better every day. "I'm fine Armand. I was just deep in thought. I have much to do in the next few nights. I am sending Ruben and Genevieve to St. Etienne to stay. The Guild may fall under an attack of some kind and it's better they aren't here if that happens." She grabbed the remaining scroll, tucked it into her pouch and joined him. Then they headed to the west wing together. Within hours, they had Ruben and Genevieve prepared to leave. While Armand helped them pack where he could, she had taken the time to write the necessary letters for their safe passage. She had also given them an introduction letter for the local Prince of that region, requesting they be under the protection of the crown.

When all their preparations were finished and Armand had said his goodbyes, Angelique walked Ruben and Genevieve down to the portal room she had traveled from with Reivn. One of many things he had taught her was how to portal travel. "Talianakarnae vraa Leviste St. Etienne!" She uttered the command masterfully and opened the doorway. Then she took them safely through.

In the library, Lunitar looked up from his studies, startled when he felt Angelique's sudden absence. He immediately teleported to the portal chamber. The remnants of the spiral's magic still hung thick in the air. He used his aegis sight and read the residual magic to pinpoint her whereabouts. *France? What in God's name?* Heaving a sigh of frustration, he opened the portal and followed their trail.

Angelique had just left Ruben and Genevieve at the gates of her old estate. She said goodbye, then stood for a moment staring at the historic bastion that had once been her home. Memories flooded back. She turned and walked across the field toward an old cemetery that stood half buried with overgrowth.

Lunitar followed and watched her from a distance, sensing her need to have a few minutes alone. He glanced around at the beautiful landscape and realized this must have been her home once. Staring at it, his understanding of her grew. She had never known hardship until her awakening. The concept had been completely foreign to her. He sighed and patiently followed her through old cemetery gates to an ancient tomb half-covered with vines. He stopped far enough away he could hear her, but where he would not be seen if she to turn around.

Angelique wandered past the old headstones until she reached her parents' tomb. "Hello, mama, papa. I am sorry I have not visited you for so long. I know now that you can hear me. It may be a long time before I join you... much longer than I thought. Blake is there now somewhere. If you see him, tell him how much I miss him. Tell him I said thank you for all the love he gave to me. My world has become so complicated... and cold. You never told me, papa. I wish you were here now. I feel so alone. Is it always like this? Being in love?" She glanced up at the horizon and realized it was time to leave. "I have to go now. The sun will rise soon. But I promise I shall see you both again one day."

Following the path back to the Chateau, she saw Lunitar waiting for her and slowed her steps. "You followed me," she stated simply.

He shrugged. "You did not think a Prefect could leave the Guild unannounced, did you?"

She frowned. "I had something I needed to do, and it could not wait. I planned on returning immediately afterward."

Lunitar frowned at her nonchalant attitude. "I'm sure Armand said the same thing right before he was abducted." Without waiting for a response, he spoke the command. "Talianakarnae vraa Leviste Atlantic City!" The portal opened once more.

She turned to gaze at her home one last time. Ruben was watching her from the door. She waved farewell and then stepped through the portal with Lunitar.

Armand stood in the portal room waiting for her, knowing she would feel alone when she came back. Surprised to find Lunitar with her, he smiled. "My lord, thank you for accompanying her. I wasn't aware you were going."

Lunitar chuckled. "Neither was she, but she should have realized I would not let her leave unguarded. Now I will return to my studies. If you will excuse me..." He left them and headed back to the library, deep in thought.

Angelique watched him walk away. "I should have known he would follow me. He is very much like his father." Then she changed the subject. "Ruben and Genevieve are safely installed at St. Etienne. The letters they have will ensure their residency."

Armand smiled. "I do not doubt it. You have always been thorough when you set out to do something."

"I'm going to miss them, Armand. So much has changed. Sometimes I wonder where it is all leading us." She looked sad and fell silent.

Understanding filled Armand's features and he rested his hand on her shoulder as he tried to comfort her. Then they walked to her office in silence, where they said goodnight and headed to their separate rooms to sleep.

The following night when Angelique awoke, she hurried to shower and dress. She planned to cast the spell Reivn had sent for the protection of the entire Guild. When she left her rooms, she headed to her laboratory to prepare. *This is not a spell like most of those we cast. It needs various items added to it to make it permanent.* Pulling the list from her pocket, she began collecting the needed vials from the shelves. *Daemon tincture, Wolf's bane. Wow, some of these contents I barely even understand.* The last vial she retrieved was that of Reivn's own blood. Once she finished gathering the ingredients, she put them in the pouch at her side. Then she slipped a dagger on her belt in preparation for beginning her nightly rounds.

Making her way to Serena's room, Angelique knocked on the door. A voice within answered, so she entered quietly.

Soft, sheer drapes covered the walls. The entire room was bathed in candlelight and the rich smell of incense gave the room a serene atmosphere. An encircled, canopied pit strewn with soft blankets and huge pillows echoing Roman decor occupied the room's center. Sheer drapes that hung around it created the illusion that a fine mist surrounded the entirety of the pit.

Serena parted the curtains and peeked out. "Welcome to my quarters, do you like them?"

Angelique smiled, accepting the hand that reached out to pull her in. "It's beautiful," she sighed. She dropped down opposite Serena and laid back, staring at the drapery above them. "How do you always manage to create such peace around you?"

Serena rolled over to look at her. "It's not easy, but I refuse to let what we are pull me so much into the darkness that I succumb to it. This is where I come to escape the world."

Deep in thought, Angelique fell silent.

"What's wrong?" Serena asked. "You didn't come here to visit. You usually leave that for later, at my labs."

Angelique looked up, her eyes filled with sorrow. "I received a letter from Reivn. He wants me to erase my memories of our love as though they never existed. How can I do that?"

Serena took her friend's hand and squeezed it. "You can't, I know. I once loved someone too, but a liaison of any kind was forbidden by the Ancient that commands me."

Angelique stared at Serena in surprise. "I'm so sorry. I did not know."

Serena smiled. "I have learned to live with it. Eventually, you will too."

Angelique's eyes flooded with tears. "I don't know what to do," she sobbed. "I miss Reivn terribly and I'm powerless to do anything about it. I've lost him, Serena."

Serena slid over beside her to try and comfort her. "Come now. It will be alright. The pain will dull with time, I promise, and I'll be here to help you through this every step of the way." Lifting Angelique's head gently into her lap, she gently stroked her hair and let her cry.

Through her tears, Angelique tried to tell her about the other scroll and how important it was, but her words came out as more of a garbled mess than anything that made sense.

Serena shushed her. "You can tell me what you need to when you're calmer. Now rest for awhile." With a slight wave of her hand, she quietly put Angelique into a deep sleep. Then she went in search of Armand. She found him sitting on a garden bench in the night air. "Armand?"

Armand turned in her direction. "Hello, Serena. I knew it was you. What can I do for you?"

"I want to talk to you about Angelique. She isn't handling Reivn's loss very well," she explained, sitting down beside him.

He nodded. "I know. I felt her grief through our shared blood. She still hasn't learned how to not project her feelings when she's emotional. I always know when something grieves her. But I don't know how to ease it. She has lost so much in such a short time."

Serena sighed. "Yes, she has, and she is very vulnerable right now. I was trying to think of ways we can keep her mind off the present situation to give her time to heal. Any ideas?"

Armand sat quietly for a moment. Finally, he replied, "I think the best way to walk her through this is to find ways she can help others. She has always been compassionate and is at her best when tending to them. It may well be a good time to teach her more about the cleric's healing abilities. Who knows, she might take to them better than she has the fighting."

Thinking of the possibilities, Serena slowly nodded. "You know, that's not a bad idea. She hasn't truly found her own niche in our magic yet. Perhaps she is more of a healer than a fighter. After all, when those assassins came for her, she would have died had it not been for Lord Reivn's timely intervention."

"Assassins? What assassins?" Armand asked, concern crossing his features.

Serena frowned. "She should have told you. Kuromoto sent assassins to kill her. They almost succeeded. Had Lord Reivn not come as quickly as he did, they would have."

Armand shifted in his seat. "I should never have left her. She has never really been able to adjust to this life. Now I know why she said she needed me so badly when I awoke."

Putting her hand on his shoulder, Serena gave it a gentle squeeze. "Do not dwell on what cannot be changed. She is safe and that is what matters. I will talk to her about learning the Clerics ways when she awakes. I put her to sleep for a bit. I wanted to calm her mind."

Armand nodded again. "I think it's an excellent idea."

Serena smiled. "You are a strong-willed man, Armand, and a survivor. I knew that despite your loss you would be all right."

"I can only blame myself for leaving here as I did. I made myself a target. Do you know, they never even asked me any questions?" Bitterness crept into his words and he fell silent.

Serena sighed. "Many Renegades thrive on that type of behavior. It's why they are so dangerous, especially to our human brethren. Don't let their cruelty make you into what they are. You have to cleave to the light, or the darkness will consume you. I have to go, but I leave you with this thought. If we let the beast within us control who we are, then everything our fight has stood for all these centuries will have served no purpose. We fight to defend our mortal cousins, so they are safe from what threatens to destroy them. Find your comfort in that. Good night." She walked away, leaving Armand to digest what she had said.

Serena went back inside and was heading to the lower level of the Guild when a servant caught up to her and told her Duncan had arrived. She went to the main hall to greet him and found him talking with Lunitar. She quietly told them of the events earlier that night.

Lunitar listened with concern, knowing Angelique had already proven she was unique. "She has taken my father's loss hard. The amount of grief she feels is dangerous."

Duncan stared at them in alarm. "How stable is she? You know our blood is more potent than a human's and our emotions with it. If she's never experienced anything this traumatic before, she could lose control."

Serena nodded. "I put her to sleep about an hour ago. Only an Ancient or higher Elder has the power to wake from that deep a slumber anytime soon… and I doubt she's one of those."

Duncan raised an eyebrow. "You still don't know her bloodline?"

"No," Serena shook her head. "Lord Reivn hasn't given that information to anyone. The only thing I do know about her is that she is indeed a Mastric and has a remarkable amount of untouched power inside her. Whether she is a warrior or cleric remains unknown."

Lunitar cleared his throat uncomfortably and frowned. "I think it safe to assume she is at least among the second generation of Elders, if not the first. So, we should leave nothing to chance. Not knowing her Sire is not nearly as important as recognizing the power level she is capable of wielding. It would be prudent to keep an eye on her until she gets past the extreme grief she is exhibiting now."

Duncan frowned, deep in thought. *And yet she has become a tribal Prefect in this area. There is far more to the lady than meets the eye. This will bear watching.* "I agree," he answered. "She is the Mastrics Prefect here. We cannot afford to lose her."

Angelique woke herself to find she was alone. Then her memory came flooding back and she broke into fresh tears. "I don't want to lose him, not like this! Alora will fill him with hatred until his soul turns as cold as his blade!" She left Serena's rooms and wandered the halls aimlessly. Finally, she found her way to her office. Her emotions were beginning to spiral like a whirlwind in her heart. She entered the office and ran to the French doors, pulling aside the drapes that shut out the light. Then she stepped out onto the balcony, looking up in desperation. "God, please don't let this happen! Please..." she sobbed, sagging against the railing. From her vantage point, she could see a faint glimpse of the river where they had so often walked together, and her grief overtook her. She levitated over the edge and down to the ground below without a sound. The wind captured the folds of her gown, wrapping them around her as she staggered down the path. Just ahead, she could see the boulder by the river's edge where they had talked, and she remembered how Reivn had first spoken of his love. Going to it, she sank to her knees and wept. Her hands shook, as tears stained the ground red. *I need you... Why did this happen? I do not want to live without you.*

In a moment's despair, she reached down and opened the pouch at her side. Her fingers found the vial of Daemon tincture. Pulling it out, she opened the top and drank, frowning at the smell of its contents. The poison hit her almost immediately and she doubled over in pain.

In the main hall, Lunitar suddenly looked up from their conversation. "Something's wrong!" he growled. Not waiting for an answer, he teleported to Serena's chambers only to find them empty. He was just exiting them when Serena and Duncan came running down the hall.

"Someone saw her in the gardens! I think I know where she went!" Serena exclaimed, grabbing his hand to pull him after her as she ran for the upper levels and the garden path.

Angelique struggled to pull herself upright. Fumbling at her side, her hands trembled violently as she slid her dagger from its sheath. The first rays of light were fast approaching. In the distance, she thought she heard Reivn call her name. "I'm coming..." she whispered. Then she closed her eyes and plunged the dagger into her heart. She crumpled to the ground. In a daze, she stared up at the stars, as her blood flowed unheeded from the wound. The earth beneath her grew cold and she felt the first of the morning air wash across her face. She became aware of the mist crossing the water. The sun would soon rise. She smiled softly and closed her eyes.

"She's over here!" Duncan yelled when the flashlight's rays briefly touched her copper curls and pale face. Lunitar and Serena joined him, as they rushed to her side.

Angelique was very near death.

Lunitar knelt down beside her and quickly realized the danger she was in. "Dear God, what have you done?" he whispered.

"If we don't get her inside quickly, she's going to die before I have time to do anything," Serena cried frantically. "But we can't take her back to the Guild! Too many there will know, and she will be vulnerable! Duncan, we need to take her to your lair! We have just enough time to beat the dawn!"

Lunitar picked up Angelique's now unconscious body and carried her to Duncan's nearby car. "Go!" he yelled, as he jumped in. They raced away, trying to outrun the dawn.

Duncan mulled over the night's events as he drove them to his lair. Alora's sudden return certainly had been unexpected and about now unwelcome. He knew the stories of her dark God's chaotic ruthlessness all too well. Glancing back at Angelique's still form lying next to Lunitar, he frowned and wondered what this would mean for the gentle Prefect of the Mastrics tribe. "Angelique should never have been turned by your tribe. She is much more akin to the aristocrats than the Wizards," he stated bluntly.

Lunitar disagreed. "I do not think she would have worked well in their ranks. They are often too lofty to allow such a child to survive among them. They would have eaten her alive."

Serena nodded in agreement. "They use everyone and if they believe you are an asset they need, it does not matter who or what you are."

Duncan sighed. "At least there are those among you who do still have honor, they are just too few and not outspoken enough to really instigate a change in your tribe's politics."

His companions were spared having to answer, as they had arrived at Duncan's lair. Lunitar pulled Angelique from the car. Then he followed Duncan and Serena. They rushed inside just as the sun broke on the horizon.

Lunitar was alarmed at her condition, afraid they may have already lost her. He cradled her gently in his arms as he carried her to one of the small bedchambers, and then carefully laid her on the bed. "Don't you give up. Your time with father is not over... not yet. This is only a bump in the road. Stay with me."

Serena chased him out. "I need to begin at once! I'll call you when she wakes."

Without argument, Lunitar left the room. Then joining Duncan, he started pacing.

Inside the room, the battle to save Angelique had begun. Serena turned all her attention to the fallen Prefect, worried she might not be successful. *Lord Reivn will not take the news of her death well if I fail.* She forced herself to stop thinking about anything but her abilities. After casting a waking spell on herself, she called forth the power deep in her core, determined this was one fight she would not lose.

Hours went by and the two men continued to pace, forcing back the natural sleep of day while they waited for Serena to emerge from her seclusion.

Lunitar was more agitated than he had ever been. He repeatedly turned to stare at the door that kept him from knowing what was happening. *Father will never forgive me if she dies...* No sound came from within, and the silence was unnerving. He was still moving back and forth long after Duncan had collapsed and let sleep claim him.

In the room, Serena was fighting a desperate battle. The poison racing through Angelique's system was slowly killing her, and the absence of blood in her body only hastened it. She forced down her fear and renewed her efforts. Angelique was slowly fading and the only thing preventing her from dying was the healer's power. *Lord of light, please help me pull her back from the darkness!* she prayed in desperation, hoping she would be heard.

Hours passed and night returned. Duncan awoke and got up. Seeing that Lunitar was still pacing and now haggard in appearance worried him. He began to fear the worst when he realized Serena still had not emerged from the room. The light radiating from under the door was intense and finally, he could stand it no longer. He broke the silence. "Have you heard anything at all?"

Lunitar shook his head. "Not one sound all night," he growled and glanced again at the door. Determined to find out what was happening, he moved quietly to the door and cracked it open. A wondrous sight met his eyes and he stared, unable to turn from the vision before him.

Serena stood over the still form of Angelique, her body aglow with powerful magic. Above her was a radiant being of pure light, with brilliant wings that spanned almost half the length of the room. The angel above her was pulling the putrid taint from the dying Elder's body. Serena seemed completely unaware of the creature that continued to aid her while she fought to bring Angelique back from the edge of the abyss.

Lunitar watched for a long time, unable to turn away.

The angel was slowly destroying the swirling black vortex that was rising from Angelique. Then the blackness coming from the Prefect suddenly ceased and the entity disappeared. Serena collapsed to the floor.

Angelique was unconscious and fragile, but alive.

Lunitar slipped in, picked Serena up and settled her down next to Angelique. Relieved, he left the room and joined Duncan. "She will live," he stated and sat down. "If you don't mind, I'd like to wait here until Serena revives." He closed his eyes wearily.

"Of course." Duncan sat down and began to browse over documents he had been researching. They were both still sitting there when dawn came, and sleep claimed them once more.

When Lunitar and Duncan awoke shortly after night had fallen yet again, it was to find the two women were still asleep. Their need for blood was very apparent, so Lunitar slipped out to collect a few willing donors. He arrived back in record time, carrying two sleeping figures. He concentrated on Serena first. "Wake up, my lady. We need you," he whispered as he gently pushed the man's wrist into Serena's mouth. Letting the donor bleed just enough to refill her without causing permanent harm, he closed the wound and laid the unconscious man on the floor. Then he turned to the second donor and Angelique. "I don't have enough here to revive Angelique. She's lost too much blood," he told Duncan. "This will get her out of immediate danger, but it will be a while yet before she wakes." Once he finished giving her what he could from the donor, he put the unconscious human next to the other one and went back to the bed. "I know my father has not given his permission in this one, but it is necessary if you are to regain your strength," he whispered. Then with grim purpose, he opened his own wrist and pushed it into Angelique's mouth to give her more potent sustenance that could replenish her strength and healing at a faster rate. When he finished, he stared down at her. *Her grief drove her to try and take her own life. I was afraid this would happen.* His thoughts filling the silence, he gathered the two humans to release them where they would safely revive on their own.

When Lunitar returned, Duncan was sitting at Serena's side waiting for her to wake. He joined the concerned Armenian, but they did not have long to wait.

Serena opened her eyes and groaned. "How long was I out? Angelique?"

"Only a day," Duncan answered and smiled at her. "And she's alive."

Then she gripped her stomach and rolled onto her side, moaning as a wave of pain ripped through her. Without warning, her body rejected the blood she had been given, and she covered the floor with its remnants. Heaving uncontrollably, her body finally emptied itself, and she lay back trembling.

Lunitar stared at her in concern. *I have never seen such a violent reaction to blood before… did she overtax herself? Or did I accidentally give her tainted blood? Either way, she still needs sustenance,* he thought to himself. With a frown, he opened his wrist and offered it to her.

Still only half-conscious, Serena took what he offered without argument. Her bite was delicate across his flesh, like the wings of a butterfly brushing against his skin.

Lunitar gave her as much as he could spare, then pulled away. He watched her with concern, waiting for her to fully regain consciousness.

Duncan buzzed around, cleaning the mess up and periodically glancing at the bed.

Finally becoming aware of her surroundings, Serena looked around. Then she slowly sat up. "I guess that took more out of me than I thought it would. I'm sorry if I frightened anyone."

"I'm just relieved you are recovering," Lunitar stated quietly, breathing a sigh of relief.

Duncan smiled and helped her up. Then he led her out to the sitting room, where the three of them could sit down together to discuss recent events.

Serena quietly discussed the situation with them, all the while listening out for her patient. She mentioned Reivn and Angelique's bond, and then continued with Alora's return.

Duncan frowned at the mention of Alora's name. "That woman doesn't have a good bone in her body. She's up to something. I found out a little more about the Philadelphia incident." He picked up the documents he had been going over. "It seems there was more to Armand's capture then we knew. He was a means of getting to Lord Reivn. I don't yet know for certain who was behind it, but I have my suspicions considering who else he found there.

Lunitar growled. "If there is any truth to that, then Angelique is in serious danger. Alora will kill her to be certain nothing stands in the way of whatever she is planning. Even if she was not behind Armand's abduction and it was one of Reivn's other enemies, then they know of her."

Serena got up and paced the room, thinking hard. "While she is unconscious she's easy prey, especially at the guild. It's the first place someone would look for her."

Duncan sat quiet, absorbing all they said. Finally, he looked up. "Why not leave her here for a while? At least until she is somewhat recovered. No one knows of my lair except for you two. I can take care of her and she'll be well hidden."

Serena gazed at him with uncertainty, but Lunitar nodded, liking the idea.

Duncan reassured her. "I will be digging further to find out who was behind everything."

"I think for now we should assume it was indeed Alora that set up the abduction," Lunitar replied, walking over to the bedroom door and checking on Angelique. Then he turned around. "With the vulnerable state she is in, we can't afford to take any chances."

Duncan agreed. "If you take her back to the Guild, you're right. Here, on the other hand, we tilt the balance in our favor."

Serena looked at Duncan in surprise. "Duncan, this attack was against the Mastrics. Are you sure you want to put yourself at risk like this."

Reaching over, Duncan took her hand. "My love for you has never changed, Serena. You are all in danger, so I am already involved. Now," he stated, standing up. "Unless Lunitar has any objections, it's settled. She can stay here. You can stop in as often as you wish."

Lunitar nodded. "Angelique is staying here until she recovers. When she is well enough, I'm going to have a talk with her. She needs to leave the killing to our enemies. God knows we have enough of those. I'm going to Draegonstorm to report to Lord Reivn. Then I'll be back."

Lunitar and Serena left a short while later, and Duncan returned to the parlor to read.

Though unconscious, Angelique was fighting a battle of her own. She was beginning to discover hidden power she never even knew she had. Then in the darkest part of her mind, she found the beast. The nature of every Vampyre is to kill. The drive for blood is strong and can pull them away from their humanity. The core of every Vampyre holds a curse as ancient as the earth itself. In her mind, she could see Mastric, the father of her tribe, and he beckoned to her. She could see their bloodline back to the beginning. Hazy images that made no sense flooded her mind as she resisted the call of the beast. She looked around in terrified despair, running from what relentlessly pursued her. Just when she thought she could run no further, a brilliant figure with white wings would appear for the briefest of seconds and renew her hope. Oddly familiar, she could only call out to the darkness in her mind. She was alone...

## Chapter Twenty-Nine
## Old Vendettas

*Even Aristotle surmised that keeping oneself occupied in discordant times would make for clearer thinking. I learned not long ago that Valfort has returned to London for reasons as of yet unknown. North America is my assigned position, yet I find myself here at my Keep with Alora, and the walls are closing in around me. I frequently find myself thinking of someone else…*

*I have petitioned the Council to let me go on the hunt again for this very reason. Annie is a strong Warlord even by Galatian standards and she can cover the North American continent for a while without jeopardizing the region. If I am hunting Valfort, I can distance myself from Alora for a short time and there is no law she can levy against me to stop that. The added advantage of ensuring that Valfort dies is in freeing Angelique from the danger he presents to her. If all I can do for her is to protect her from harm at a distance, then I will see it done.*

*My enforcers will meet my son and I in England and from there we begin our search. I sent the necessary dispatches to Jack as well. I look forward to seeing him again. He is one of the few I know that has always been forthright with me and does not cater to my power. I respect that in a man. Then again, he is one of the few who walks as my equal. I envy him the freedom he has to move about the world as he does. That is one luxury a Warlord is not afforded. I go where I am needed. Council law deals too much in absolutes, and while I understand the necessity for such strict rule, I find myself as much bound as any other by the cruelty it sometimes ushers forth. The love I bear my own has no weight where Council ruling is concerned. I dare not to hope. It has forsaken me.*

*Lord Reivn Draegon*

\* \* \* \* \*

Reivn took in his surroundings. From this vantage point, he could see almost every door on the street. After taking careful note of the locations his men had chosen, he turned and began to pace the room. "If we hope to trap Valfort successfully this time, Jack needs to get here soon. Valfort will not go down without a fight." He moved to the window again and his agitation grew.

Lunitar watched Reivn in silence. He had returned home to find that his father had largely secluded himself in his laboratory to avoid Alora's company. Then the news of Angelique's near demise had shaken Reivn into action, resulting in a trip to the Council, and a return to England for the renewed hunt of Mastric's vile firstborn. They had only been in London for two nights and both were already tired of watching their target.

Reivn briefly thought of the copper-haired woman lying unconscious on the other side of the world, and a twinge of pain passed through him. If he fed at all, it was from Alora. His hunger would only be mildly satiated, and that only if she allowed it to be by manipulating his curse. His thirst for the woman he truly loved plagued him to an extent he found increasingly difficult to ignore. He turned his attention back to watching the street below in a vain attempt to forget his own suffering. Finally, he spotted a familiar figure headed their way.

Jack entered through the back of the building and took the steps two at a time. He knew Reivn had been waiting for him, and his own desire to finally catch Valfort had his nerves on edge. The many years he had spent chasing the traitor had worn heavily on him as each encounter had ended in failure. He reached the door and lifted his hand to knock, but it flew open before he could.

Lunitar reached out to shake hands with Jack as he entered. "You must be Jack Dunn. It's good to meet you at last. My father has spoken of you often."

Jack grinned. "So, you are Lunitar. It's always a pleasure to meet a son of his. The old bastard is telling stories again, huh? Nothing too bad I hope. Reivn, old boy... how are you?" he looked past Lunitar to where Reivn stood staring down at the street.

"You are late," Reivn answered without turning around. "Valfort has been using the house on the left end of the street to shelter in. I believe he has more children there as well." He moved aside, allowing Jack to get a good look.

Jack's expression turned grim as he took note of the heavy traffic below. "This will be difficult to cover up if we fail," he cautioned. "When were you reassigned the hunt?"

Ignoring the sudden pang he felt, Reivn frowned. "I asked for the assignment. Annie is in America at the moment, so they could afford me the time."

Jack raised an eyebrow. "You asked to hunt Valfort again? Why?"

Lunitar shook his head silently, trying to warn Jack not to touch on such a sensitive subject, but Jack ignored him.

Reivn turned around. "Let's just call it a vested interest and leave it at that." Changing the subject, he moved to a table in the center of the room. "This is how I want to do this tonight..."

For the next hour, they poured over the floor plan of the target house and all the access points to any manholes or entrances in that area of the street.

Jack frowned and sat back, frustrated. "There aren't too many ways in or out, and if he has a portal set up in there, we may lose him again. I have been chasing him for two centuries and I'm tired of his running. I want to finish this."

Lunitar glanced up at his father, noting his mood. "This has been a long and hard hunt for both of you. I haven't been involved more than two nights and already I want to see this done with. I imagine the desire to finally end this is far greater for you.

Reivn nodded in agreement and rubbed his chin thoughtfully. "I know he has continuously been able to keep one step ahead of us. I am sure he already knows we are here. If not, then we are just plain lucky. I also have my suspicions about how he is getting his information, but we play this by ear. Are your men here yet?"

"They're outside, preparing for the attack. We have about three hours before dawn. We need to move." Jack got up as he spoke.

Lunitar rose and grabbed his weapons in preparation to leave.

Reivn joined him and strapped on his sword. His dark expression caught Jack's eye as he turned to grab his coat.

Jack frowned. "Are you going to tell me what this is about, or do I have to guess?"

Looking up from his preparations, Reivn shook his head. "It's routine."

Lunitar looked up sharply at his father's comment and raised an eyebrow, but said nothing.

"You're not very good at lying, old friend," Jack pointed out, noting Lunitar's reaction. "You forget how long we rode together. This is far more than just the hunt it was for you before. What's changed?"

Reivn scowled at him. "Damn it, Jack! Must you always pry?"

Smirking now, Lunitar walked out and closed the door, heading downstairs and leaving Reivn and Jack to talk in peace.

"Only where my friends are concerned," Jack shot back, unyielding.

Sighing in defeat, Reivn gazed at him. "I took responsibility for one of his… children… and she is under my protection. I fear he will try to reclaim her, and I will not let that happen."

Though his expression had given no hint, Jack saw in his eyes what was not said. "You love her, don't you?" he asked unexpectedly, catching Reivn off guard.

A shadow briefly crossed Reivn's features before he masked it again, but he did not answer.

Jack saw it and nodded. "We'll get him, my friend. We'll get him."

Reivn headed to the door. But when he opened it, he came face to face with a familiar countenance. "Look out!" he yelled as he dodged a fireball that flew at him. It hit the far wall, instantly exploding into a mass of flames that quickly began to consume the room.

"Looking for me, little brother?" Valfort snarled, his lips curling back in a sneer.

Jack drew his guns and began shooting, peppering the stairwell with bullets.

*He is in the building! Get up here now!* Reivn sent to Lunitar and his men. He heard screams from elsewhere in the building and realized nearby humans were already aware of the fighting. He rolled as he crashed into the floor, the edge of his coat singed where his brother's attack had barely missed him. "Damn!" he cursed and recovered his footing. He quickly doused the fire with his magic. Then he ran after their quarry. "He's on the move!"

Jack ran for the door, kicking the table out of his way as he followed.

Valfort was already down the three flights of steps and heading for the back of the building.

The sound of rapid footsteps rose from somewhere below as Lunitar and the rest of the hunting party rushed to join the fight.

Reivn leapt over the edge of the banister, landing on the floor a few feet from Valfort and blocking his escape. "Not this time!" he snarled.

The door next to them opened unexpectedly and a frightened face peered out. A young girl no more than fifteen stared at them. "What…" she began, but Valfort already had her by the throat. Her terrified screams filled the hallway.

Jack jumped over their heads, landing behind Valfort. "Let her go, you bastard!" he roared.

Valfort glared at him, his eyes taking on a dangerous hue. "Move out of my way, or the little lady here is going to know what our world is all about!" He licked the girl's cheek and she shuddered, grabbing desperately at the hand around her throat, her brown eyes filled with terror. She hung from his hand, immobilized by fear. Her soft wavy hair was braided, and Valfort pulled on these, exposing her throat.

"Help me!" she choked out.

Lunitar had ran up the stairs behind Reivn, stopping in his tracks when he saw the scene before him. Then intent on charging Valfort, he took a step forward and summed the spirals.

Reivn stopped Lunitar with a single motion. Then he growled, "If you hurt her…"

Valfort laughed. "You'll what, little brother? You were never able to best me! You're weak!"

Lunitar stepped forward. "Lord Reivn doesn't have to defeat you. I will gladly do it for him!"

Reivn stopped him again. "Hold, Lunitar. He is mine."

"That's right, Reivn. Hold back your pup," Valfort grinned. "This building is filled with witnesses. What are the chances there isn't a resistor among them?"

Jack shifted his stance, ready to pounce at a moment's notice. Behind him, the rest of the enforcers filled the hall, blocking Valfort's exit.

"You have preyed on innocent children for too long! Let her go!" Reivn spat back.

Valfort slid a razor-sharp nail across the girl's neck, just barely cutting the skin. Then he grinned. "I like her!" He licked at the blood that seeped from the wound, testing it. Then he smiled, the evil expression on his face angering his adversaries even further.

Reivn stared with hatred at Valfort. "You've spent centuries putting innocence between us, yet you call me weak. Put her down and fight me. Then we will see who is weak!" he challenged.

"Perhaps some other time," Valfort laughed.

"Take him!" At Reivn's command, Lunitar, Jack and the enforcers closed in.

Valfort vanished swiftly from sight before they could grab him, taking the girl with him. Her screams faded as they disappeared.

"Find him now!" Reivn yelled, "I want the girl back intact! This ends tonight!"

Lunitar immediately dispatched his men. Then he turned to his father in concern.

Jack looked sharply at Reivn. The Warlord had never lost control of his temper on a hunt before. Shaking his head, he made silent note of it and followed as Reivn and Lunitar headed for the house across the street. Crashing in the front door, they swarmed the upper levels of the building, separating to search the second and third floors.

Jack pushed through a bedroom door in the back of the house and cursed aloud, calling to Reivn before moving to the bed that occupied the room.

Reivn and Lunitar came at a run, entering just in time to see Jack shove his wrist into the girl's mouth.

Reivn yelled "No!" Then he quickly crossing the room.

The girl had slipped into unconsciousness, and her pallor was slowly turning to a healthier glow as Jack fed her.

"What have you done?" Reivn whispered hoarsely.

Lunitar swiftly shut the door to prevent the men waiting outside from hearing anything. Then he moved cautiously across the room to join his father and Jack.

Jack licked his wound closed and carefully picked her up. "I saved her. She did not deserve any of this. He took her blood and left her for dead. I gave life back to her."

Reivn glared at him. "You turned a child! Jack, you know the law!"

Lunitar took a step back, recognizing Reivn's authority.

"Would you rather I had let her life expire while your brother yet again makes his escape?" Jack challenged.

Falling silent, Reivn stared at the girl in Jack's arms. She was pretty, with brown braids that fell almost to her waist. Her features showed strength and her body was nearly full-grown. Perhaps she could still survive if taught how to fight. "Where would you take her?"

"I don't know. She is strong and her will to live fierce. I couldn't just let her die." Jack wanted him to understand, but he would not beg. He stared at Reivn and waited, knowing he defied the Council's will.

For tense moments, the room was silent as Reivn stood assessing the situation, his thoughts traveling back to another youthful face that had once stood before him in strength and defiance.

Lunitar cleared his throat and stepped forward. "My lord," he ventured. "Perhaps with training, she will indeed be able to survive. Her body is almost full-grown, although she will always be smaller than most."

Reivn turned and looked at his son, then back at Jack who stood holding the unconscious girl in his arms. Finally, he nodded. "I will, of course, have to report this to the Council. However, since she was the last one to see Valfort, the information she had was very necessary and we could not allow her to die. You did what was necessary," he amended.

Jack caught his meaning and smiled.

Lunitar glanced down to hide the amused grin on his face. Then straightening his expression, he looked up. "Congratulations, Jack. It's a girl!" he laughed as he headed to the door.

"For the love of God, Lunitar! Do not encourage him!" Reivn scowled.

Lunitar chuckled and walked out to talk to their men and get reports.

Jack grinned. "Good to see we're still square. I owe you one." The girl in his arms stirred and opened her eyes. "Hello, beautiful. Do you have a name?" he asked her gently.

Her eyes widened as she remembered Valfort and she struggled to get out of Jack's arms. "Who are you people?" she asked, trying to wiggle free.

"Give me your name and I'll tell you all I can," Jack stated.

She looked around at them. "My name is Lissa," she finally answered.

Jack smiled at her. "Lissa, I'm Jack Dunn. I'll be looking after you for a while. Where are your mom and dad?"

Squirming uncomfortably, she looked around. "I... live by myself. I don't have parents."

"She is a runaway," Reivn observed. "Whose place was that you were living in?"

Lissa stared up at him. "My friend's house. Long as I did what he wanted, he let me stay. I'll be okay mister, really. Can I just go?"

Her eyes bore into Jack's soul and he realized she was one of the many kids that were misused on the streets every day. He smiled reassuringly at her. "Lissa, your luck just changed for the better it seems. You'll never have to do those sorts of things again."

Lunitar came back in at that moment. "We've located a possible trail, my lord. If we leave now we stand a good chance of finding him."

With a nod, Reivn turned to Jack. "She'll have to come with us. We can fetch her things later."

Lissa looked down in embarrassment. "I don't really have anything."

Jack set her down. "Can you walk?" he asked her. "We have to catch this guy, so he doesn't hurt anyone else."

Lissa smiled at him. "I can."

Without hesitation, the group headed for the door, their new charge obediently following them. Jack kept a close watch on her when they climbed into the waiting vehicle. "If you get hungry or tired, just tell me," he instructed her.

Looking across at them, Lunitar suppressed a smile and turned to look out the window.

They drove into the night, their thoughts a mix of the hunt ahead and the life left behind.

The trail led them to Heathrow airport. To search without arousing too much suspicion, the group took two limousines. When they drove into the terminal, it was filled with people.

Reivn spotted a couple of police officers and quickly tucked his sword under his coat. "We cannot follow him here," he growled. "There are too many people around."

Jack agreed and unstrapped his holsters, tucking them under the seat. "Let me find out where he's flying. I'll rendezvous with you in about half an hour. Head for the top floor of the parking garage and wait for me there." Without another word, he jumped from the car and headed toward the entrance of the busy building.

Reivn telepathied his men in the second car. *Have your driver follow us.* Then he opened the window separating them from the driver and instructed him to take them to the garage.

Lunitar looked over at him and silently asked, *what are your plans to follow Valfort?*

*We will decide that when Jack returns. For now, we wait,* Reivn answered.

Lunitar did not respond and Reivn settled back, staring out the window as they passed the terminals and pulled into the parking lot.

Wide-eyed with fascination, Lissa was staring out the window. "Are we going to fly?" she asked. When he did not answer, she turned and looked at him. "I've never flown before."

"No, we do not generally travel that way. It is too risky for our kind." Reivn glanced out the window in general disinterest and the interior of the car fell silent.

Minutes passed by in silence. Then Lissa sighed. "I'm sorry," she apologized.

"For what?" Reivn stared at her in confusion.

Lissa shrugged. "You tell me," she insisted. "You're the one who's mad at me."

"What?" he asked in surprise. "I am not angry with you."

Lunitar covered his mouth, so his father would not see his smirk, and pretended to busy himself taking note of their location.

"Then why won't you talk to me?" she asked, her brown eyes staring up at him.

Reivn scowled at her. "There is nothing to talk about."

Rolling her eyes at him, Lissa crossed her arms. "Make up something. What's your name?"

He stared at her in amazement. "I am Warlord to the Council of the nine tribes, Lord Reivn Christof Dimitri Draegon."

She groaned. "Can I just call you Reivn? That would be easier."

Unable to suppress his laughter, Lunitar dove out of the car the moment it stopped and strode back to update his men on their plans.

"Certainly not! You are too young to show such disrespect to an Elder. Lord Reivn will do fine," Reivn told her and cleared his throat uncomfortably, hoping Jack would return soon.

At that moment, Jack appeared around a corner and headed for the car.

"Look, he's back!" Lissa exclaimed, pointing out the window.

Tapping the driver's window, Reivn sighed in relief.

Lunitar spotted Jack as he crossed the lot and hastened back to the car.

Jack climbed in beside them and was greeted with a smile from Lissa. "Lord Reivn's mad at me," she stated emphatically and stared out the window.

Jack glanced at Reivn, one eyebrow raised, and Lunitar burst into laughter.

Reivn glared at his son, and then frowned at Jack. "Do not ask."

Grinning ear to ear, Jack leaned back in his seat.

"Where is Valfort headed?" Reivn asked, changing the subject.

Jack smiled. "We're going back to the good ole United States. He's headed for Philadelphia."

# BLOOD FEUD

## Chapter Thirty
## Evil Unveiled

*There comes a moment in life, no matter how much time has passed, when they realize the deepest of truths... Regardless of the dark days in which you live or what battles you must face, you cannot live without the love of another... not just anyone, but the one that connects to your soul. The deepest of all grief comes with the loss of that one connection, and an empty hole sits in your breast that threatens to destroy you with every memory. There are no tears to be shed that can quell the pain... no words of comfort to give solace in the quiet cold hours before dawn. The grief I now feel in knowing my angel is forever beyond my reach only serves to further eat away at the edges of the light remaining in me. I now understand that we only truly fall when we suffer this loss and slip into a darkness beyond the reach of any salvation.*

*The law serves a purpose, as does my honor and the honor of those within my heart. But there comes a time when need outweighs the honor in a man, and he finds that to truly be happy, he must seek what his heart desires to fulfill the empty void that has taken over rational thought.*

*Then again, is not happiness or the need of it rational? The world is filled with grief, war, hatred and the cruel fate that awaits us all in the end. Does not happiness exist to contend with these dark things? Does not love come to give those whose lives are so burdened down by the selfish grappling of others for control over our existence the strength of will to see it through? Love is not selfish in the very nature of its definition. Those who force their will on you to suit their own selfish desire are not doing so because they love you. They do so because they fear losing that power over you.*

*Lord Reivn Draegon*

\* \* \* \* \*

Angelique awoke to strange surroundings. Then the pain hit her, and she rolled onto her side. "Oh, everything hurts," she moaned. She tried to get up and fell off the bed to the floor. Her vision was blurry and distorted, and the room seemed to move beneath her. "Help..." she cried, grabbing the edge of the sheets in a vain attempt to pull herself up.

From nowhere, a pair of hands picked her up and settled her back in bed. "You're safe here, my lady. Rest now. You are not yet fully healed."

Duncan spoke softly, soothing her fear as he pulled the covers over her once more.

The last thing she saw was his familiar face looking down at her. Then her eyes closed again, and she drifted into unconsciousness.

*Damn*, Duncan frowned. *I had hoped she would stay awake this time.* He gently brushed her hair from her face and then slipped quietly from the room, leaving the door half-open to listen for her. "Two weeks and little change," he muttered as he sat down at his desk. He picked up his journal and thumbed through the pages, reading the other entries about her brief awakenings. Agitated, he picked up the phone and quickly dialed Serena's number.

At the other end of the line, a gentle voice answered.

He smiled, recognizing her soft accent. "She awoke again, but not long enough to talk. She's still very weak. It could be days or even weeks before she's well enough to return to the Guild."

There was a pause on the other end and then a sigh. "Well, I guess I'll have to come see her myself and see if I can help her along. Don't worry. I'll be there soon."

"That's a good idea. You know how much I enjoy your visits. I'll see you when you get here." Duncan hung up the phone in relief and turned to his other tasks. Confident that Serena would bring Angelique around, he began humming to himself as he worked, pleased that his charge was finally on the mend.

Alora put the receiver down and looked over at Serena's unconscious body. She snickered. "Thank you, Serena. That was almost too easy. Consider yourself lucky I didn't kill you. Were it not for the obvious alarm it would raise, you would already be dead. However, you won't revive for quite awhile. Enjoy the headache I've left you, because your friend Duncan will not have that luxury. By the time they find what's left of him, I'll be long gone." She laughed and summoned her magic from the pool of chaos, altering her face and body into Serena's likeness. Then she went to the closet and carefully picked through Serena's clothes until she found what she was looking for... a dress she knew Duncan would recognize. She smiled when she put it on, thinking how she would tear her prey apart. When she finished, she walked out of the Guild and climbed into Serena's car.

Alora followed the images she had pulled from Serena's mind and drove to Duncan's. "Hello, precious pet," she purred to herself when Duncan opened the hidden door and revealed his lair. Then she slid out of the car and beamed up at him. "Duncan dear, I'm glad to see you. How is our patient since we talked? Any changes?" She walked up to him, hugged him tight and kissed his cheek. Then she tucked her hand into his arm as she had seen Serena do when she dug through the Paladin's mind.

Duncan looked down at her in surprise. "Uh, Serena? Are you feeling all right?"

Alora laughed and pulled him closer as they went inside. "I'm fine, Duncan. Why do you ask? Do I look ill or something?"

He chuckled and shook his head. "No, but you haven't shown affection like this since Galatia forbade..."

Shrugging it off, she laughed again and closed the door behind them. "Well, perhaps I just missed you too much. I needed this," she smiled, moving closer to him.

Duncan nodded, staring at her in confusion. "Won't you get into trouble for this?"

"Perhaps, but I can't ignore my feelings forever," Alora lied, wrapping her arms around his neck. She stood on her tiptoes and nibbled his ear, teasing him playfully.

He closed his eyes and moaned. "Serena, we shouldn't..." He caught her arms and gently lifted them off him, holding her at arm's length.

She pouted and lifted her eyes to him, pleading for his attention like a desperate lover. "It's been so long, and I am so lonely. I do not care if I get into trouble. It's worth every moment I get to spend with you. Please...make love to me."

Unable to deny Serena the love he bore her anymore, Duncan picked Alora up and carried her to his room, completely taken in by her deception. She in every way looked, sounded and even smelled like Serena, and he was undone. He laid her on his bed and gently undressed her. Then removing his own clothes, he slipped down to lie atop her. He captured her mouth with his own, kissing her deeply as his desire took over.

Beneath him, Alora writhed in pleasure, delighted he had been so completely fooled. She let him claim her and reveled in the knowledge that she had taken what Serena could not. She smiled and closed her eyes, allowing herself to enjoy his attention until his passion was spent.

He laid his head against her chest and closed his eyes. "I don't know what made you decide to let me have you, Serena, but I don't think I care either. I have wanted this too much."

Alora laughed. "I can believe that. Creatures such as we are with such powerful emotions as love... or hate... should not deny ourselves what we desire most. It's unnatural."

"Serena, what is wrong with you?" He gazed down at her in concern. "No matter how much I love you, we both know this can't happen. You could be crucified for this one night alone. No matter how we feel, this is forbidden by your master's command."

Alora rolled over, pushed him onto his back and straddled him. "I answer to no one but myself where my desires are concerned. That arrogant tripe sitting on her throne in Polusporta... she herself lies like a prostrate whore beneath the king in the dawn hours under the sands of the Sahara. Why should I allow such a creature to govern my own desires?"

Duncan tried to push her off, her words disturbing him greatly. "Such words are treason."

She shoved him back down and pinned his arms above him. Then she smiled, her gaze turning cold. "Look into my eyes, Duncan. They'll show you how serious I am." Her eyes changed to a deep golden hue, taking on a serpentine appearance and she began to mesmerize him. Once she knew he was fully in her power, she snickered. "Meet all the power of Dark Egypt, my pet. Let me show you what happens when you cross a real Ancient's path." She slammed her claws into his chest and ripped his heart from him.

Duncan's eyes widened in shock for the briefest of seconds before the vacant expression of death crossed his features and his body went limp.

She raised his heart to her lips and sucked on it, savoring the young guardian's flavor. "Ah..." she sighed. "Your blood is sweet indeed. I had forgotten how good an Armenian could taste. It's too bad you were not older. At least then your blood would have served a purpose."

Alora climbed off his body and went to clean the blood from her naked frame before donning some of his clothing. Then she went to the door behind which Angelique lay in sleep and pushed it open. She moved silently into the room... a killer stalking her prey. Then she approached the bed and stared down at Angelique with hatred. She let her face change back to the one she used so often, the face Reivn knew. "And here you are… Valfort's defenseless, useless child whose deluded dreams give false vision to her very existence. How pathetic you are. Reivn should have known he could never hide you from me. Now your soul is mine! I will feast on you and leave your empty husk to rot, while the maggots devour what's left of you!" She drew a jeweled dagger from her side and prepared to strike, aiming for Angelique's heart. The steel flashed in the candlelight as her hand flew downward, its gem pulsing when it sensed the soul of its target.

Before the dagger could strike its mark, Angelique's hand shot up and grabbed Alora's wrist, stopping it mid-air. "You didn't think I would be that easy to kill, did you?" She opened her eyes and stared up at her attacker.

Alora snarled at her and struggled to force the blade down.

Angelique fought with her until she managed to push the blade away. Then she quickly sat up. "My father is Ceros Valfort, first son of Mastric and an Ancient in his own right. I have awakened to the night and to my blood. I know now who I am and where to find my power."

"You're nothing but a brazen brat that is too young to fathom what I am! You will never be a match for me!" Alora growled. She raised her other hand and extended her claws, intent on ripping Angelique's heart out as she had Duncan's.

Angelique grabbed Alora's other hand and struggled to hold on. She called on her newfound power and instinctively ignited spheres of blue flames in her palms of her hands.

Seared and burnt, Alora refused to back down. She transformed her fingers into snakes, growing them longer and thinner as she changed her blood to poison. "Let's see how well you defend against Hellspawn!" She snapped at Angelique, but found only empty air.

Angelique had transformed into mist and moved away. *We will meet again, Alora,* she telepathied as she floated from of the room.

Alora grabbed the blanket from the bed and raced for the front door. "Oh, no you don't!" she screamed and stuffed it into the crack, cutting off Angelique's escape.

Angelique reformed in the parlor a few feet away. "You want me to fight? Then come and get me! I will not let you destroy Lord Reivn!" She drew from her magic, sparked her hands and shot energy bolts across the room, hitting Alora in the chest.

Alora screamed in rage and transformed into a giant Cobra more than twenty feet in length. Then she raised her head and spewed acidic poison.

Dodging the venom, Angelique backed into the hall. She reached into the spirals again and shot a fireball at Alora, engulfing her in flames.

Alora countered it and doused the fire almost before it started, but not before it singed her skin. "You'll pay for that!" Slithering after Angelique, she caught her by the ankle and wrapped her giant coils around the fleeing woman, twisting tightly.

Somewhere inside Angelique, the sound of crushing bones rose, accompanied by excruciating pain. She gasped and struggled to free herself.

Alora seized the opportunity. She sank her fangs deep into Angelique's neck and pumped her poison through the wound, sure of victory.

Angelique closed her eyes and forced herself to concentrate on her magic. The spirals obeyed and a shield of energy enveloped her, crackling and lighting up the room as it grew in strength.

The jolt caught Alora off guard and she loosened her coils slightly.

Angelique looked around in desperation seeking a way to even the odds. Almost immediately, she spotted the water pipes that ran overhead. She used everything she had left and forcefully twisted the metal with her magic, splitting them and pulling them free from the ceiling. Water sprayed from the pipes and soaked them both. The electrical shock that followed ripped through them.

It was too much for Alora. She let go and ran for the door. "This is far from over!" she screamed and fled into the night.

Angelique collapsed and laid trying to let the pain pass enough to sit up. She had no idea where she was. When she could finally get up, she began to look around until she found Duncan's body, which lay face down on the bed. She turned him over and gasped. The gaping hole in his chest told her all she needed to know. *He must have been watching over me*, she realized. She covered him with a sheet and left him there while she searched for clues as to what had happened after she lost consciousness in the park. Then on his desk, she found his journal and began to read.

*April 4th: No change since yesterday. Serena did all she could last night, but the amount of Daemon venom running through her has greatly slowed her healing.*

*April 5<sup>th</sup>: I feel useless. There is not much I can do except feed her. I gave her some of my blood to strengthen her. It will at least help her some.*
*April 7<sup>th</sup>: She is mending. Her wound shows visible improvement. Serena is pleased with her progress and hopes she can return to the Guild soon.*
*April 13<sup>th</sup>: Angelique woke briefly tonight. She remains stable, although still unconscious. I remain optimistic about her recovery.*
*April 17<sup>th</sup>: She continues to try and wake, but her body is not ready. She fell out of bed tonight, and then slipped into unconsciousness again. No further injury...*

Angelique closed the book and sat down. "I'm sorry, Duncan," she whispered softly. She picked up the phone and started to dial the Guild, then changed her mind and hung up. Instead, she closed her eyes and called out to Reivn, focusing on his face and the presence she had felt when he was with her before. *Reivn, I need your help. Alora was here and killed Duncan. I don't know where Serena is or even where I am, but I'm alone. Alora is wounded, but still lives.*

She wondered if he had even heard her. She sat and stared at Duncan's body in silence until finally, she could no longer wait. She was beginning to feel severely ill. Weak from her battle with Alora, she needed to feed and could not risk the dawn. She glanced at his body again and frowned. "I will be back to give you a proper burial, but I need to make sure Serena and the others are safe first."

Angelique left him where he lay and staggered out into the night. In looking around, she quickly realized nothing was familiar to her. She looked up at the moon, recalling the direction it stood in the sky when she was on her balcony. Her vision blurring slightly, she turned and began to walk in the opposing direction.

Minutes after Angelique left, a car pulled up. Serena and Reivn jumped out, Lunitar and his enforcers right behind them. "Wait here!" Reivn ordered his men. Then he turned and ran for the door. "Angel!" Throwing it open, he called for her again. "Angel! Where are you?"

Lunitar quickly assessed the situation, then moved swiftly into the lair to join his father in searching the interior.

Serena entered behind them to find Duncan's lair as silent as a tomb. She lit the torch that hung just inside the door and then gasped when she saw the body on the bed. "Oh God!" she cried out and rushed over, ripping off the sheet. "No! Oh, Duncan, not you!" She laid her head on him and wept, her tears mingling with the blood that already covered him.

Reivn searched room by room, calling Angelique's name. Not finding her, he returned to the front hall where Lunitar waited. "I need to find Angelique before Alora does."

Lunitar walked into the bedroom and to Serena's side. Then he gently pulled her to her feet. "Come, Serena, we can't help him. We will see to him after we find my mother."

Silently exchanging glances, they headed out the door to the waiting enforcers.

"Angelique is not here!" Reivn growled. "Spread out! Find her!" He transformed into a raven and immediately took to the air, searching the roads and surrounding areas.

Lunitar joined his men and quickly moved into the surrounding woods, searching for any sign of the missing woman. "Look everywhere. Leave nothing to chance," he commanded.

Reivn's frustration grew as area after area proved to be empty, and he opened his mind in desperation, calling out to Angelique silently.

A whisper touched his mind in response. *Reivn, you heard me. There is a man in that place. Duncan. He's...*

Reivn interrupted impatiently. *Where are you?*

In moments, images of a nearby location flooded his mind. *Here, I'm here.*

He recognized the landscape and headed in that direction, sending a message back to Serena and Lunitar. *I found her! She is here!*

He swooped down and landed by Angelique, noting she was not surprised by his sudden arrival. "Angel, are you hurt?" He spun her around and froze when she shifted form. He found himself staring at Alora. "Where is she?" He snarled. "What have you done with her?"

Alora sneered at him. "Your precious little pet? Do you think me so foolish as to give you my greatest bargaining tool? If you kill me, you'll never find her! Sweet, innocent girl... she put up a good fight. Better than that stupid child you left to watch over her."

Reivn took a step toward her. "I'm warning you, Alora, touch one hair on her head and..."

Alora cut him off. "Oh, I've already done that. I told you she put up a good fight, but in the end, I always win. You know that, don't you? Now are we going to negotiate or is she going to die?" She stood smugly in front of him. "You had best decide quickly. She won't last long."

Reivn snarled and attacked.

Alora bared her fangs and met him head on, the fires of hatred blazing in her eyes.

Reivn summoned the spirals and hit Alora with everything he had. She responded in kind and the field exploded in a haze of fire, lightning and dark magic.

They were so intensely locked in battle that neither one noticed the new arrivals in the clearing... Angelique on one side, Serena and Lunitar on the other.

Angelique began staggering toward the battling Ancients.

Serena saw her and immediately sent a silent warning. *No, Angelique. This is not your fight. This must be settled between them now. She has broken our laws. I sense you are injured. Come around them and join me.*

Angelique moved sluggishly around the edge of the clearing as the poison finally overtook her, but she kept her eyes on the battle that raged unheeded before her.

Lunitar barely noticed the woman headed their way. He was too focused on the fighting. He stood on edge as he watched his father and Alora tear into each other. He was prepared to defend Reivn if necessary and moved to where he could get to his father's side quickly.

First Reivn and then Alora struck blow after blow as magic exploded and blood flowed, covering the grass with its dark essence. Their hatred deepened by recent events, they fought furiously to end each other's existence.

Angelique finally reached Serena and fell into her friend's arms. The poison was shutting down her system, and she collapsed.

"Angelique!" Serena exclaimed in alarm.

Reivn spun around at Serena's cry. "Angel?"

Alora took the opportunity and hit him again, forcing him to defend himself.

Lunitar turned when he heard the Cleric and rushed to join them. "Let me take her," he insisted, sweeping Angelique up as though she were no more than a small child in his arms.

Serena wasted no time in summoning the spirals. Reaching deep into Angelique, she began to search for the source of the problem.

Holding Angelique in his arms, Lunitar stared at her for a moment. Then he glanced up again to the battle still raging before them. *She is the reason*, he realized and looked down at her again. He quickly sent Reivn a telepathy. *I have Angelique. I am taking her and Serena to safety. Please be careful... and do what you must.*

Serena questioned Angelique, worry filling her voice. "What happened? Can you speak?"

"Poisoned..." Angelique choked out. Then she lost consciousness.

Alarmed now, Lunitar gazed at the woman in his arms. "Hold on," he whispered to her. Then he looked at Serena. "Take my arm. We're leaving."

Serena quickly grasped his arm and nodded. Within seconds, the three vanished from sight as Lunitar teleported them away.

## Chapter Thirty-One
## Draegonstorm

*Fate is a cruel taskmaster, but every once in a rare lifetime it sees fit to grant a prayer of the heart. I have vanquished the Daemoness for now, and in doing so have been liberated from the law binding me to her. I am free to follow my own desires. I can only hope my angel still feels about me as she once did. If Alora killed in her what I found so untouched and pure...*

*Angelique once again surprised me and indeed, I am thankful for it this time. She held her own against Alora long enough to save her own life, despite the poison in her veins. I dare not think of what I would have found had she still been unconscious when Alora discovered her. She is one loss I simply could not have accepted. She awakened a part of me I thought long dead and gave me back my life. The darkness in which I dwelt for so long has been touched by a light so rare I never dreamt I would ever see its like.*

*Watching over her as she heals, I have had much time to contemplate recent events. I have a new perspective to not only my past and present, but my overall existence as well. Have I been isolated so long from the pulse of life that I have forgotten the need to feel as I do now? She has washed away the emptiness of the void in which I dwelt. She has breathed love into my soul and taught me that compassion is not beyond my reach. Were I only worthy of such a gentle creature, but the blood on my hands will never wash away, and my deeds, no matter who ordered them, have left their mark on me. Perhaps she is an angel sent to show me that even my sins can be forgiven, and that redemption can be won even for the wicked...*

*Lord Reivn Draegon*

\* \* \* \* \*

"I am not leaving until... shh. She is waking up..."

Their voices seemed muffled and distant to Angelique, and she tried to open her eyes. Her lids felt heavy, and her vision was blurry and distorted. Someone leaned over her and was talking, but she could not make out who. Her body felt numb. She could not lift her arms or legs. In fact, she could not move at all. *My body*, she thought fuzzily. *What's wrong with me?*

Reivn knelt at her bedside and bowed his head. "Thank you, God," he choked out. "Thank you for giving her back to me." He held her hand and gazed at her, tears staining his cheeks.

Lunitar stared in shock at his father, seeing a total stranger before him. For all the centuries of knowing Reivn, he had never seen him filled with such emotion. *Such unbridled emotion... the love he has for her. My God... if she were to die it would destroy him. I must speak to Gideon. We must protect her at all costs.*

Gradually Angelique's vision focused. Then seeing Reivn, she smiled weakly.

Reivn forced himself to calm and quickly wiped his face. Then he got up and sat on the edge of the bed and pulled her into his arms. He kissed her gently. "Rest, angel. You did well."

Angelique closed her eyes again, briefly wondering where Alora was. Then she realized she did not care. Reivn was, for the moment, at her side.

Serena walked over and gently rested her hand on his shoulder. "She'll be alright in a day or two, my Lord. The poison partially atrophied her limbs, but that will heal. We were fortunate we found her when we did. A slow acting poison is more difficult to diagnose, but she already knew what it was. If she hadn't told me, I don't think..." She did not finish her statement.

"Let's not dwell on that. Instead, we should focus on what is at hand. She is safe and will mend." Lunitar gave her a warning look and shook his head.

Serena caught his meaning and fell silent.

Reivn leaned over and kissed Angelique's forehead. Then he turned to Serena. "Send a dispatch to the Council concerning Alora's betrayal and demise. By law, I am now free. Inform them I must delay my trip to Delaware and sign my name to it. And please, send for Gideon."

Serena nodded and left the room.

Reivn gently moved a stray lock of hair from Angelique's eyes. "My beautiful Angel... I can see we are going to have to work on communication. You should have listened." Then he bent over, brushed a kiss across her lips and whispered, "But I am glad you did not."

Lunitar cleared his throat, reminding Reivn of his presence. "Father was there anything else you needed tonight?"

Reivn wearily shook his head and looked up. His eyes echoed his fatigue... and something else. "No... no. You did well, my son. You brought her home."

Lunitar turned to leave and then paused for a moment. "Sleep well, father. Our family is safe tonight." Then without another word, he slipped out and closed the door behind him.

Reivn leaned back against the headboard and closed his eyes, replaying the battle with Alora in his mind. His wounds still hurt. He rubbed his side where Serena had partially closed and then bandaged a rather large hole earlier that evening. *Alora is dead for now, but she will be back*, he reminded himself. *She is of Daemonic lineage, so resurrection is still possible. God help us all when she returns.* Exhaustion finally overtook him, and he fell asleep.

The daystar rose and only the soft footfalls of servants going about their daily duties disturbed the silence while their masters slumbered. When the sun finally set, sounds of the Guild's residents stirring from their slumber slowly began to fill the halls.

Reivn opened his eyes. "Se aprinde!" he commanded, and the candles flickered to life. Then he looked down at Angelique.

Angelique's eyes fluttered open. "You are here," she whispered. You're alive and... Alora?"

The silence that followed was deafening as he remembered the previous night's battle. "She will trouble us no more. Though it is possible for her to be resurrected, she is finished here. Her death satisfies Council law and gives me my freedom." He waited for condemnation that did not come and marveled at what he saw in her eyes. Then in frustration, he got up and paced the room. "You almost died! Why did you not follow the letter's instructions? Woman, you seem to make a habit of being headstrong and disobedient! How can I protect you if you do not listen?"

She sat up, turning red in the face. "I never asked for your protection! As to obedience, you don't own me! I am neither your woman nor your wife!"

He crossed the room and, pulled her up into his arms. "I intend to change that," he growled, lifting her chin so their eyes met. "I will never let anyone come between us again. I swear it!"

Her desire, denied for so long, finally crushed her resolve, and she melded into his embrace.

He stretched out beside her and pulled her close, his relief at her acceptance of him filling him so completely, it rendered him speechless.

Afraid to damage the fragile threads of renewed joy, neither one spoke. They were content to just hold each other, lost in their own thoughts in the silence.

Lunitar made his way to the library when he woke. He had never had the opportunity to peruse the Atlantic City Guild's vast collection before. Worried about his father's statements concerning Alora's possible return, he wanted to research the subject to see if there was a way to prevent its occurrence. When he walked in the door, he stood gaping at the number of books in front of him. Rows and rows of bookshelves filled the room, each one laden with tomes of the arcane. A slow smile spread across his face and he began to wander around, reading titles and browsing through the wealth of knowledge before him. Finally, a book captured his interest, and pulling it down, he settled into a chair to read.

Hours later a courier walked in to find him deeply engrossed in his studies. "My lord Lunitar, I have a message for his Lordship, but I was told he did not want to be disturbed. I was instructed to bring it to you."

Lunitar sighed as he put the book down. "It's ok. I'll take it."

The man bowed and handed him the letter. "It's from the Council, my lord. It's urgent."

Lunitar immediately broke the seal and opened it. Then after briefly reading it, he looked up. "I'll take this to his Lordship myself. Thank you."

The courier bowed again and left.

Lunitar headed down the hall to the room Reivn presently occupied with Angelique.

Reivn was still lounging in bed holding her when the knock came and Lunitar's voice shook them from their reverie. "My Lord, I hate to disturb you, but a dispatch has come from the Council. We are to leave immediately."

Reivn sighed and got up to open the door. When he looked out, Lunitar handed him the letter. Quickly scanning its contents, his eyes turned dark and a frown crossed his features. "I'll join you in my study in ten minutes. Meet me there." Then he turned to Angelique and kissed her gently. "Duty calls. I have to go. There are matters I left unfinished that need my attention. But do not worry. I will be back soon. I have absolutely no intention of leaving you alone ever again. You might get other ideas."

Angelique sat on the edge of the bed and watched silently as he dressed. Finally she asked, "You're not in trouble, are you? They won't take you away again... will they?"

Reivn walked over and sat down beside her. Then he took her hand. "This is just an assignment, angel. I give you my word I will come back." He kissed her and got up to go.

"Reivn, wait!" she cried as he opened the door.

Eyebrow raised, he turned around. "Yes?"

"What is the assignment this time?" she asked.

He smiled. "We found your father..." He left without another word.

She stared after him in amazement. Then she realized what he had said. She ran to the door and threw it open, intent on asking what he meant, but the hall was empty. "Reivn!" she called, but no one answered. He was already gone.

Angelique paced back and forth until frustration drove her to find Serena.

Serena was in the library talking with Armand when Angelique finally found her. Armand lifted his head when she approached and they both fell silent.

"What are you two up to?" Their silence made Angelique suspect they were talking about her, and quite possibly the mission Reivn was on.

Serena smiled at her. "What would make you think we were up to anything?"

Angelique frowned at her. "You two are never cloistered here like this, so is there something you should be telling me?"

Armand shook his head and mouthed a silent *no* to Serena.

Angelique did not miss it. "Please tell me what is going on? Lord Reivn just left, saying something about going after my father. Now I find the two of you in a conversation I'm apparently not supposed to hear. I am the Mastrics Prefect charged with the care of this territory! I'm supposed to know what is happening here, so start talking!"

Looking guilty, Armand turned his head in her direction.

Serena sighed. "I'm sorry, Angelique. You are right, you should know. I just did not want you to worry. Lord Reivn told me who created you and why your power is so strong when you are still so untrained by our standards. Your true creator is Lord Ceros Valfort. He is Mastric's oldest son. He betrayed the Council centuries ago when he murdered Elena and went Renegade."

Angelique stared at her in shock. Lunitar had told her some of this, but not all of it.

"He is far older and more powerful than most Renegades," Serena explained. "He has been known to aid them, although he apparently claims no official affiliation with them."

Shaking her head, Angelique backed up. "Please don't tell me any more!"

"You need to know this," Serena continued. "Lord Reivn has been hunting him for centuries. You escaped the carnage Valfort left in his wake by accident. He wants you back, Angelique. Lord Reivn hunts him to protect you. It's a fight he might not return from."

Shaking now, Angelique dropped into a nearby chair. "What are you saying, Serena? Reivn can defeat anyone. He's powerful."

Serena shook her head. "Yes, he's powerful and a son of Mastric, but weaker than Valfort. Valfort was the first. Lord Reivn isn't as old as he is. Valfort will kill him if given the chance."

Angelique jumped up and ran for the door, but Armand caught her. She struggled to free herself. "Let go of me, Armand! I must stop him! I can't let him die for me!"

Armand kept a firm grip on her. "No, Angelique! You cannot stop this! It's beyond your power to do so. It was the Council's edict and Lord Reivn's choice!" He tried reasoning with her. "You can't interfere. Council laws forbid it."

Angelique saw the determination on both their faces and knew they would not let her leave. Defeated, she stopped fighting him. "Fine. I promise not to try and leave, but I'll be watching every moment for his return."

Armand cautiously let her go and stood by in case she tried to run.

But Angelique faced them in surrender. "He will return, you'll see. I know he will."

When she turned to go, Serena stopped her. "You must go into hiding if he fails. That is what we were discussing. Lord Reivn does not want you falling into Valfort's hands."

Shaking her off, Angelique ran from the room, seeking solitude. *I cannot tell them how afraid I am that Reivn may have gone to his death.* She could not put those thoughts into words, afraid they would come true if she did. Heading for the garden, she walked alone for hours. She hoped to hear a welcome voice call her name, but none came. When dawn finally approached, she reluctantly made her way back inside and headed to her rooms.

The day passed in tomblike silence. Not even the servants disturbed the stillness.

Then the sun set, and Angelique's eyes snapped open, her ears hearing only the dead calm. *It's quiet*, she thought. *Too quiet... why?* She leapt off the bed, getting herself together quickly. Then she ran from the room and down the hall almost before tying the laces of her gown. When she got to Serena's room, she broke the silence of the halls and banged on the door. "Serena, wake up! Something's wrong!" She got no answer, so she pushed the door open and went inside.

Serena was nowhere to be found.

Angelique quickly left the room and headed for Serena's lab, passing right by Reivn's private quarters. She was almost to the lab when she realized there had been light coming from under Reivn's door. Running back, she threw it open.

Serena was inside, looking through some of Reivn's wardrobes.

"What are you doing? Why are you going through his clothes?" Angelique cried.

Serena continued her search. "Lord Reivn needs some of his things," she answered, her tone subdued. "His son is here to fetch them. I'm merely getting what was asked for."

Picking up the list sitting on the table, Angelique read it and gasped. "Most of these items are healing spells. Why does he need these? I want to speak to his son!"

A wolf by the fire loped over to her and licked her hand.

Serena turned. "This is his son, Moventius. Lord Lunitar did not trust sending anyone else. He did not want Lord Reivn's whereabouts known."

Moventius shifted to human form and bowed. "My lady," he stated softly.

Angelique stared at Moventius as though he were a ghost and sat down on the edge of the bed. "Oh God, he is in trouble. I must go to him, Serena. He needs me now. The battle is over. If he is injured and in need of healing, then I must be there to care for him. You can't go because there are too many here who need you. As Prefect, I can appoint someone else to care for the Guild and its necessities in my absence. Please don't argue with me on this. I…"

Serena touched a finger to her lips and silenced her. "I think you should go," she interrupted. "There is no better medicine than love, and he loves you. Your presence alone will be good for him." She glanced up at Moventius for affirmation.

He nodded. "Aye... quickly go gather some of your things. You can send for more later."

Angelique sat gaping at them both until Serena grabbed her arm and pulled her to her feet. "Go! He needs you now!" she insisted, shoving Angelique toward the door.

Finally shaken into action, Angelique rushed back to her room and gathered her immediate needs. She threw them into a small travel sack, then sent for a servant and had him take the bag down to Reivn's rooms. Looking around one last time, she snuffed out the candles and hurried to join Serena for last minute instructions as to the Guild's care.

Armand was in the hall outside Reivn's quarters talking with Serena when she arrived, and he smiled at her. "Here we go again. At least this time you're not going to get into trouble. Don't worry about anything here at the Guild. Serena knows what to do and I'm going to help her."

He walked over and gave her a hug. "Life is changing again for us, only this time, I think for you it will be better. I'll miss you."

Angelique smiled at him. "And I you."

Serena touched her arm gently. "Moventius has already left. It's time to go," she stated.

Armand swung the bag over his shoulder, and they headed to the portal chamber. The portal was open and waiting. He put her bag into its core, amazingly adept at locating its center.

Then Angelique stepped in and waved goodbye as she disappeared, transported to Reivn's fortress and the unknown.

Angelique stepped into a room lit only by torches.

An unfamiliar voice greeted her. "Who are you and what are you doing here? Speak and be swift about it!"

Shading her eyes from the light in front of her, Angelique could make out a figure standing a few feet away. "I am Lady Angelique, from the Atlantic City Guild. I am here to help Lord Reivn. Will you take me to him?"

The figure moved and she saw his face. He bore a strong resemblance to Reivn. Handsome and dark, his hair was of medium length, falling into his eyes. They gave him a veiled and mysterious appearance. "You are Angelique? My brother told me about you. I am Gideon. I am also Reivn's son. My father has called out your name in his more lucid moments. Come."

Angelique followed him quietly, wondering just how badly injured Reivn was. Unable to keep silent, she caught his arm. "You said he is not lucid. Does he suffer from the fever?" she asked, trying to keep her voice steady.

Gideon spoke quietly as he led her through the halls, his deliberate calm unnerving. "Lord Reivn is merely not in any condition to greet anyone at present." He waved his hand at what she thought were stone gargoyles, "These are what greet newcomers presently."

One of the gargoyles moved, startling her as its eyes watched her silently.

"You are lucky it was not them that found you in his lab," he stated bluntly.

She frowned. "His laboratory? Shouldn't we have arrived in a portal chamber?"

He did not answer. Instead, he reached into the spirals and invoked their magic.

She followed him down the hallway as torches flared, lighting the old stone walls in a shade of deep gold. "This place, what is it? Where are we?"

Gideon slowed his pace, moving beside her as they walked. "You are in Reivn's Keep, named Draegonstorm…our ancestral home. It is an ancient fortress from another age. We are deep in the Australian wilds, beyond the reach of most of humanity. The Keep has stood for centuries now, a testament to my father's power. This way…" He opened an aged oak door, its heavy wrought iron hinges groaning as he opened it.

The room was bathed in the soft glow of candles. In its center stood a huge canopied bed, draped with black velvet curtains held back by gold tasseled ties. It was not the bed itself that caught her eyes. It was the figure in it. She dropped her cloak and stared down in horror.

Lying unconscious, Reivn was a mass of horrifying wounds, abrasions, burns, and bruises. A dried trickle of blood ran from the edge of his mouth down the side of his cheek to the back of his head, indicating that he had either fed or bled.

Angelique turned to Gideon. Her eyes carried a question she dared not voice.

Gideon nodded. "My father bleeds internally, my lady," he told her and turned to go.

She caught his arm and stopped him. "Wait! Has no one tried to help him? Don't you know any healing magic?"

He shook his head. "My brother has not yet returned from the Council's chambers, and I am personally forbidden to assist in this matter. It is my father's law here. I will fetch fresh blood. He is near death. There is a poison in his blood that is slowly killing him, but perhaps you are the one who can save him." He left before she could ask anything further.

Angelique found herself with more questions than answers. *Why can't he help in healing his father? What law is he referring to?* Her thoughts wandered while she moved around the room, looking for what she would need. Finally finding a jug, she filled it with fresh water, took it to the fire and poured it into a pot she found hanging there. Then she stoked the fire higher and waited until the water was steaming hot. She carried it to the washbasin, poured it, and soaked a cloth lying nearby. When she went back to the bed, she gently began washing the blood from Reivn's face, noting the discoloration that prevailed around his mouth and throat. Then she pulled the covers back. She cried at what she found.

His chest had suffered a grievous wound and his innards were partially exposed. She could see there was serious damage inside.

*Oh, Serena, I wish you were here. I don't know if I can do this,* Angelique thought as she reached her hand carefully into his chest, casting the first of many healing spells as she began to weave his inner organs back together.

Gideon brought some much-needed sustenance and quietly left.

Exhausted from what healing she had already done, Angelique fed from the blood he left, strengthening herself in preparation for the silent battle ahead. Then she slit her wrist and pushed it into Reivn's mouth, forcing the fluid into him.

It met with little success, as there was no response. However, the sun was rising. They were safe enough in the darkness of his lair, but she feared he would grow weaker as the day lengthened. She knew that to survive injuries like his, he needed to feed, and he had taken precious little.

Angelique took a cushion from a chair and lay down on the floor, unwilling to risk moving Reivn by sharing the bed with him. She did not hear the door open or the footsteps that entered, nor did she feel the blanket Gideon covered her with before he left the room.

The fire crackled and burned down to embers in the silence as they slept.

When night drew near and Angelique awoke again, it was to a cold room. Quickly lighting the fire, she turned back Reivn. She recalled the poisons Serena had taught her how to treat. She knew if she was to rid Reivn of the poison, she had to drain the tainted blood from him and slowly replace it. This would bring him even closer to death, and she feared failure. But she knew of no other way to save him. She began to drain his blood and the poison in it from his system. When Reivn grew as low on it as she dared allow, Angelique tore her wrist open. Knowing he could not feed on his own, she held his head back and forced her blood down his throat. She did not care how much he took and fed him until she grew weak. Then she sent for Gideon and fresh supplies.

Lunitar had hurried back to the Keep after reporting to the Council, his first concern to find out just how bad his father's injuries were. He headed for Reivn's chambers, prepared to do what healing he could with what few skills he had. He chastised himself for following the warrior's path instead of the Clerics. He was mildly alarmed when he approached the door and saw no guards. Then hearing chanting coming from within, he threw them open and strode in. He looked around, his eyes almost immediately settling on Angelique, who even now worked feverishly over Reivn. The scene before him told him everything he needed to know. Reivn was potentially lying on his deathbed. He stared in shock for a moment before moving swiftly to her side. "Dear God! I did not know he was this bad! How can I help?"

Angelique looked up, her pallor visibly paled. "He needs blood desperately. I've been giving him all I can, but it just isn't enough. We have to rid his body of the poison and that means slowly bleeding it out of him and replacing it. It's the only chance we have of saving him."

Without hesitation, Lunitar sat down and opened his own wrist, lifting his father's head and forcing his blood into the dying Warlord's mouth. He whispered so faintly Angelique could barely hear. "They cannot have you. They can have me in your place. Our people need you to survive." He reached into the spirals with his mind, infusing his blood with magic to target the poison that threatened to take Reivn's life.

Angelique reached up and gently touched his hand. "If you die in his place, he will never forgive himself or any other that allowed it to happen. I know him, and he values the lives of those he loves far more than his own. This is not the way. We must work together."

He looked up at her. "Who do you think I learned this from? Those of us who love and follow him value his life far more than our own."

She nodded. "I can see that. The love you bear him is in every word you speak and every action you take. However, between us, we can save him and neither of us has to die. I don't know how long it will take, but I do believe we can succeed. What we really need is more blood to feed on or we will be too weak to complete what he needs to recover fully."

Lunitar listened in grim silence. Then he nodded, realizing the truth in what she said. After thinking a moment, he closed his eyes and sent a silent summons to one of his enforcers.

Within minutes, the officer knocked on the door and entered. "You sent for me, my lord?"

Lunitar nodded. "Our Lord is in dire need of blood. Ask all those not on duty to spare all they can. Tell those who are on duty to prepare for a long watch. No one outside of Draegonstorm is to know. He must be protected at all costs until he recovers."

The enforcer bowed and disappeared. Before long members of the guard, officers, enforcers, and even servants began arriving to offer their blood to aid the dying Warlord.

Angelique stared at them, tears in her eyes. Then she whispered, "...there are so many."

Lunitar glanced over at her before accepting the first of those to offer their blood. "You are right. None outside of this fortress know how well-loved and respected my father truly is. Any here would gladly lay down their lives for him. Welcome to the family."

## Chapter Thirty-Two
## Rally to the Banners

*Four weeks have passed and still you lay there. Father, open your eyes. This family is not yet ready to lose you and I am not yet ready to lead. I know you believe in me, and I will always endeavor to be worthy of that trust, but I am not you. They will not look to me as they do you. Please don't leave me here to rebuild their fading hope. I see it every night in their faces when they come, willing to bleed out their last drops if it means resurrecting you from the abyss where you sleep. I have never been afraid before. Yet now I find myself dreading the outcome if we somehow fail you.*

*Your young protégé works feverishly over you. She is still so untrained and yet so willing to do whatever it takes to help you. That kind of devotion cannot be forced. You garnered that love in her, just as she instilled it in you. Surely you did not find yourself such a welcome happiness only to leave it here to wither without you? You could not have saved her from death only to yield yourself to its touch. Father, even for us, fate is just not that cruel.*

*The hours are relentless, only serving to remind me just how many nights have passed since you fell. We have kept this secret within the walls of the Keep and in the Council chambers at Polusporta, but that will not protect us if you leave. Each time I look down at your pale face and see how much you have faded, I fear I will return to find you gone, and I dread facing our world without your guidance and friendship. The truth is... I cannot fathom what will become of all of us should you perish. Wake up, father... please?*

*~ Lunitar ~*

\* \* \* \* \*

Each night as Angelique fed from the many people offering their wrists, the desperation of wanting Reivn to live and her own dire need for sustenance pushed her to forget her aversion to the process. She became a vessel to channel life-giving fluid to him at an impressive rate.

Lunitar also fed his father every night. But mindful of the curse that still plagued Reivn, there was the added concern that the blood might not actually help him. In an effort to prevent that from being a problem, he infused his own healing magic into all the blood he gave.

They worked together, repeatedly bleeding Reivn, feeding on donors and then repeating the process to slowly dilute the poison in his system.

Angelique continued to work on healing Reivn's wounds until she reached the edge of her endurance. Her hands began to show telltale signs of overuse as burns appeared and exhaustion overcame her. She refused to stop, and disregarding her injuries, she kept going.

Lunitar saw her rapid deterioration and caught her hands, pulling them away when she reached out to start again. "My lady, heed your own advice. You need to rest. He will make it through the night." Then Lunitar closed his eyes and telepathied Gideon, calling to his brother for help. *Gideon, I need you here now, father's rules be damned. I will accept full responsibility for this when he has recovered. His survival is far more important than his pride, and it is far better to accept his wrath than to deal with his funeral.*

Moments of tense silence passed before Gideon finally answered. *I hope you know what you are doing. I'm on my way.* When he walked in, those still present turned and stared.

Lunitar cleared his throat to get everyone's attention and then spoke. "In lieu of Lord Reivn's condition, I am assuming command. Now clear the room."

While those in the room left in silence, Gideon slowly approached the bed.

Angelique stood to leave as well, a somewhat pained expression on her face.

"My lady, you are excluded from that command. You are the chief healer here and your presence is sorely needed," Lunitar insisted, stopping her. Then he telepathied her and added, *and your love for him is needed even more. I should also remind you that the only blood that will actually nourish him is yours. Our blood will merely help dilute the poison from his system.*

Angelique nodded and sat back down, her relief apparent. Then she reached over and took Reivn's hand. "Please come back to me," she whispered. "I cannot live without you."

Hearing her, Lunitar looked sharply at Gideon and the two exchanged silent glances. Lunitar nodded to his brother, a brief smile passing over his features.

Gideon did not respond. He waited for Lunitar to move, and then sat down beside his father in silence. He gazed down at Reivn for a moment, his eyes dark with worry. Then opening his own wrist, he lifted Reivn's head and began to feed him.

This method of treatment continued for three weeks as Angelique, Lunitar, and Gideon slowly diluted and finally rid Reivn's system of the poison. Nevertheless, the Warlord's unconscious state continued even after his system was cleared. They feared the worst.

Lunitar began to worry Angelique would sacrifice her own life trying to save Reivn's. She had grown weaker and continuously remained pale. Concerned for both her and the effect her death would have on his father, he kept a close watch on her and insisted she feed more.

In spite of his efforts, Angelique would take enough blood from donors to stabilize herself, but then give most of it to Reivn. She slept on the floor by day and refused to leave his side at night. She was determined to keep him alive. She even bathed in the room, using the washbasin and a cloth after heating fresh water by the fire. Serena had sent clothes from the Guild, and Lunitar brought them to her, hoping to entice her to go to the baths. But she would not hear of it. She worked over him obsessively and only rested when her body gave in from sheer exhaustion.

Lunitar joined her every night to aid where he could. Knowing his father was primarily out of danger, his concern turned to Angelique and how little blood she was keeping for herself.

By the fourth week, when Reivn still had not regained consciousness, Lunitar decided it was time to search for other possibilities as to the cause and headed to the library. He and Angelique had finished washing and feeding Reivn. Now she watched him go, wondering what more she could do. She had closed most of Reivn's wounds, leaving only a few minor ones to heal on their own. They had also rid him of the poison, yet he would not wake. Feeling helpless, she heated water to bathe. Then she locked the door, stripped off her clothes, and began to wash. The warm water soothed her aching body, and she closed her eyes.

A sound rose from the bed and Reivn moved slightly.

Immediately, she forgot what she was doing and rushed to his side. Sitting down beside him, she wiped his brow. Then he opened his eyes and she cried, "Oh my God, you're awake!"

His eyes slowly focused and he became aware of her presence. "Angel... What are you doing here?" he asked.

"I… you needed me." She knew it sounded weak, but she was too relieved to care.

He tried to sit up and groaned. "God my muscles are stiff. How long…" He stopped when he caught sight of her. Then he smiled. "Well, this is a rather different way of greeting me."

Blushing profusely as she realized she was still naked, she reached for a blanket.

His hand closed over hers gently, stopping her. "Too late for that…" He pulled her to him and kissed her, hungry for the pale beauty that had filled his dreams. Then he pulled her under the covers and wrapped the blankets around them. "How long have you been here?"

Angelique rested her head on his shoulder and relief flooded her senses. "Over Four weeks," she whispered. "You almost died. We had to drain you repeatedly to dilute the poison in your blood and then we had to replace it."

Reivn leaned back to look at her. "We?"

She nodded. "Lunitar and others, many donating their blood to help keep you alive."

"Is that why you are so pale, beloved?" he asked her with a frown. "Because you have been feeding me and not keeping back enough for yourself?"

She blushed. "I gave you as much as I could and only kept enough to sustain me. I was more concerned about your survival than my own state of being."

"Always my angel," he said and smiled. He ran his hand gently down her back, caressing her soft skin and causing her to shiver. "Are you cold, beloved?" he asked tenderly.

"No," Angelique answered softly. "I'm happy." Her fingers tracing his scars, she followed them softly with her lips, trying to kiss away the memory of him lying so near death.

Reivn growled with desire and turned her on her back, slipping on top of her and pinning her hands to the pillows as he kissed her neck. Then he began to tease her with soft caresses.

Her skin on fire with desire, she whimpered as he continued to torment her with his touch.

He moved slowly and deliberately as he claimed her, delighting in her every cry. When their passion was finally sated, they lay wrapped in each other's embrace, content to be together in the late silent hours of the night.

A knock at the door interrupted their reverie and Angelique moved to grab her clothes. But Reivn caught her hand and pulled her back under the blankets. Then he raised his hand, summoned the spirals, and issued a command. The bolt lifted and settled at the door's side . "Come," he commanded, the authority in his voice apparent as he spoke.

Lunitar pushed the door open and walked in, followed by Gideon.

"Thank God. Welcome back, father." Lunitar bowed." Your nurse wouldn't leave your side... ah... even now I see."

Angelique blushed and moved closer to Reivn, trying in vain to hide under the covers.

Reivn chuckled and pulled her closer. "Do you approve of this one?"

Lunitar smiled. "She has already proven herself a valued member of this family, so yes. I do approve. Seeing you happy is a most welcome change."

Gideon shifted his stance uncomfortably and nodded his approval as well. "Her devotion to you is quite obvious. It is good to see you happy."

An awkward silence fell between Reivn and Gideon.

Angelique looked from one to the other, wondering at the obvious distance between the two. She knew Gideon was very loyal to his father and could not understand the apparent rift.

Lunitar cleared his throat. "My lord, while you were recovering, Gideon and I tended to any business that arose. There are matters I need to discuss with you once you have fully healed.

Concern crossed Reivn's features. "What of Gabriel?" he asked.

"There has been no change, father. He remains chained below. He is still refusing to bow his head to you." Gideon dropped his gaze as he answered.

Reivn growled. "It has been too long. He should have accepted his fate by now."

Lunitar raised an eyebrow, but remained silent. Then he excused himself to return to the library and his studies.

Gideon looked uncomfortable. He finally cleared his throat. "Father, why do you trust Gabriel? Can you not see how much he hates you?"

Reivn shook his head. "Nonsense. He is just angry. The passions of his blood make it harder for him than it was for us. He will come around eventually."

Angelique could keep quiet no longer. "Who on earth are you talking about?"

Reivn smiled at her. "My oldest son, Gabriel. We have been at odds for some years. He is angry with me. He will get past it."

At that, Gideon shook his head in exasperation. "As you say. With your permission, I will take my leave. Good night, my lord." He bowed and left, closing the door behind him.

Angelique stared after him. "Why is Gideon so upset?"

"He is over-zealous in his service," Reivn stated, and then added, "and he thinks there are conspiracies in every corner. But Gabriel is just difficult."

She was worried about Gideon, but knew better than to challenge him, so she changed the subject. "The man in that place where I fought Alora... It was Duncan."

He sat up and tested his side, pleased with its progress. "I know. He and Serena were...close friends. He was one of the Guardians."

She shifted her position to look at him better. "A Guardian? You mean an Armenian?"

Reivn nodded. "That is correct... one of the tribes you have not really dealt with yet. They serve as keepers of knowledge. He was one of their younger members and no match for Alora."

Angelique dropped her gaze at the mention of his wife. "Lunitar has actually been teaching me about the tribes. Anyway... how did Alora know where I was?"

"Alora went to the Guild and attacked Serena. Fortunately, she did not kill her, but she did dig through her mind to get information about your condition and whereabouts." He frowned. "When you called to me, I went to the Guild expecting to find you and found Serena instead. I revived her, and we came after you. But Alora got to you first."

She lay silently absorbing what he said, and then remembered her promise to Duncan. "Reivn, I promised to go back and give him a proper burial. I feel I owe it to him."

He shook his head. "Do not worry. It was taken care of that night. I could not leave him there, not after he helped you. Serena cleaned out his lair. She took his private journals to her lab at the Guild and notified the Guardians of his death. His sire was not very happy and listed a grievance with the Council against Alora."

She wriggled out of his arms and sat up. "What about Alora? Won't she be angry with you for having me here?"

Reivn pulled her back down and kissed her. "I told you she is gone. I destroyed her that night. Though there is a way she can return, she will never do so here. Her death finished any vows between us. Does that put your mind at ease?"

Angelique curled closer to him, content that they were together.

But he pulled away and held her at arm's length, looking her in the eyes. "Why did you not do as I asked in the letter? For that matter, what was this insanity that you tried taking your own life? Thank God Lunitar and Serena found you!" She tried to look away, but he caught her chin in his hand, and turned her back to face him. "I could not have lived with your death. That was why I sent you that scroll in the first place. I did not want to lose you, but did not wish for you to suffer either. What made you disobey me?"

She shifted positions and dropped her gaze. "I couldn't do it. My memories were all I had left. As for the park, I do not know what came over me. I just wanted to be with you and the thought of never seeing you again was too much to bear." Tears began to trail down her cheeks.

Reivn caught one in his hand. "I am sorry, beloved. I never meant for this to happen. I fell in love with you and in my selfishness, did not think of what would happen if Alora were to return. Forgive me?" He pulled her into his arms and held her close.

Angelique smiled and whispered. "There's nothing to forgive. I love you, Reivn Draegon."

His need for her rose and he kissed her, igniting her desire again. Then they lost themselves in each other, as the candles faded. When their passion was finally spent, they fell asleep in each other's embrace and did not wake until dusk had again covered the horizon.

Reivn got up, wincing when he stood. His wounds were still tender. Then he grinned at her worried expression. "A little pain is good. It lets you know you are still alive. Anyhow, I have duties to take care of. I have been down for four weeks and there is much I need to do."

Angelique reached out and took his hand. "What of your injuries? They need to finish healing. You shouldn't be out of bed yet."

He turned around. "Angel, there are many things I do that you do not yet know about. Many of the responsibilities I have cannot wait. I am the right hand of the Council, their executioner, and their voice in the field. I would like nothing better than to stay here with you, but I do not have that luxury. I was in the middle of several investigations when I got news of your father's whereabouts and his intent."

She lay silent until he mentioned Valfort. "Was your fight with Alora the reason you were so badly injured fighting Valfort?"

He sat down next to her and shook his head. "No, angel. He is stronger than I am. The reason I survived is because another Warlord aided me. Her power combined with my own managed to back him down, but he ran before we could finish the job."

Fear crept into her eyes. "He's not going to come after me, is he?"

He shook his head. "No. He is on the run from the Council and in hiding. You are safe here." He got up and finished dressing. Then he smiled. "My lady, would you like a tour of my Keep?"

She giggled and pulled on a robe. "Only if I can bathe first."

Walking over to one of the wardrobes, he pulled out clothes for them both and draped them over his arm. "Then we will start our tour with the baths."

She laughed again, warmth filling her as they walked from the room hand in hand. A single whisper echoed in the hall outside. "Who's going to bathe who?"

## Chapter Thirty-Three
### Secrets and Sacrifice

*There are times when I find myself wondering what fate has planned for me, and whether or not it is something I want or am even willing to accept. But there are also times, even in all this darkness we dwell in, when the light pierces the shadows to shed its purity on my soul, breathing into it new life and the desire to go on for a little longer. I never understood how important a part love could play in one's world, because I had never experienced the full measure of that emotion... until now.*

*Recognizing that your own soul is mirrored in the depths of one another is not only a life-altering experience, it can be a soul-shattering one as well. With that love and all its power to draw you in comes the reality that if lost, it can crush you at an infinite level and leave you in the dust in despair. I never imagined it could be like this... this desperate yearning... this... need I have. It pulls at my heart every time I hear her voice. The idea of never knowing her love again fills me with a desperate fear I cannot shake. I tried to break the hold it has on me, only to find that in those final moments when I should have said goodbye, I could not deny what my heart wanted... and it did not want to let go.*

*What would life be for me if I could not hear her laughter, share her desires, be the one to make her smile. I admit the idea of even letting another man be near her, much less touch her, causes an envy in me that I dare not recognize, for the power it wields could destroy less honorable men. The love I bear her is that which would annihilate an entire nation in an effort to protect her. It is the stirrings of a Dragon when its heart awakes...*

*Lord Reivn Draegon*

\* \* \* \* \*

"Kaelan!" Valfort stumbled through the door to the underground lair. "Damn him, where is he? Kaelan!" he yelled again. Still not receiving an answer, he made his way toward the basement where Kaelan's quarters were.

Kaelan had his back to the door. He had just finished his cloaking spell when Valfort barged in. Alarmed by the unexpected intrusion, he kept his back to the angry Elder until the glyph on his forehead completely faded from sight. It would have been a dead giveaway.

Valfort growled and staggered toward him. Sniffing the room, he stared at Kaelan in suspicion and tried to turn him around. "Doing magic, Kaelan? What do you Victuliates know of magic? Your command of the spirals is pathetic at best! You should be worrying about more important matters, such as serving me when I call you!"

Kaelan turned around, feigning an expression of concern. "My lord, I apologize. I did not hear you return. What happened? You've been gone for weeks."

Growling in irritation, Valfort made for the lair's upper level. "I was away on business!" Then he glanced at Kaelan slyly. "What sort of magic were you trying to do? Surely you weren't fool enough to try something beyond your ability?"

Kaelan shrugged. "I was attempting a new protection spell in case you didn't return, sir."

Valfort snorted in contempt. "A protection spell? Ha! It's a good thing I came in when I did! You couldn't pull one of those off even if you were a Mastric! Leave the magic to me from now on." The threat apparent, he coldly stared at Kaelan before turning to walk away.

Kaelan stared after him, worried that Valfort knew more than he was letting on.

Ignoring Kaelan's discomfort, Valfort headed to his room. He knew the man would follow. He dropped onto his bed and began stripping off his clothes, most of which were half-burnt and covered in dried blood and dirt.

Kaelan hurried in. "My lord, what did happen to you?"

Valfort growled and shot him a deadly look. "Never you mind! I need to finish healing! Get me fresh blood and be quick! That is if you aren't too busy playing with things beyond you."

Kaelan looked up sharply at Valfort's words. "I don't try to do any real casting, my lord. I don't possess that kind of skill. I apologize if it disturbed you. I will get you something to eat."

Suspicious even of his own shadow, Valfort gazed at him intently. "I see many things in you Kaelan, but subservience has never been a role you've looked comfortable in. It is not in your Victuliate nature. But you still do not want to make me angry. You wouldn't live to tell the tale to your successor. Now get me sustenance!"

Kaelan nodded and backed out of the room. He was worried. *It is way too dangerous to stay here. Valfort suspects something, I'm sure of it.*

Making his way down to the street, he hesitated, thinking hard. Then his decision made, he headed for the car.

After Kaelan was gone, Valfort laid back on the bed, thinking of the four weeks he had spent in the ground while the worst of his wounds slowly healed. "Reivn is going to pay dearly for this. If he thinks I am so easily defeated, he is sadly mistaken. I will take back what is mine, and then I will cut out her heart for her miserable betrayal. Damn them both!"

Turning his focus inward, Valfort closed his eyes and slipped into a subconscious state. Then he detached his soul and guided it to the spirit pool of the Mystic Spirals. He slowly waded into the brilliant blue hues of magic that radiated from the pool. First his legs and then his waist disappeared beneath the surface. When the pain began, he ignored it and forged ahead, forcing himself to absorb more of the potent magic, while letting his body burn from the agony of overload. The surface rose to meet his chest and he stopped, hovering in the pool at that depth. Pain flooded his senses, but he forced it from his mind. He focused on the pure magic that was pouring through every fiber of his being until he began to shake. Finally, unable to withstand anymore, he shot up and out of the pool, gasping at the agony he felt.

Valfort's eyes snapped open and he let out a long, slow breath. Then he looked down. His wounds were almost completely healed. *I went in further this time. Mastric will have his rival soon. Then we shall see who the true master of the spirals is.* He grinned at the thought and slowly got up. "Kaelan, where the hell are you?" he yelled down the empty hallway.

Grumbling about incompetence, Valfort went to his desk and began to shuffle through the papers that were strewn about. Then he spotted a sealed letter among them, the stamp of the Elders on it. He picked it up and turned it over. "What do they want this time?" He tore it open and read the note, then snarled in rage when he saw Reivn's name. "Damn it all!" he crumpled up the letter and threw it on the floor. "Damn him for the bane he is! How could this happen? She is stronger than he is by far and yet it did not stop him! Now I'm going to have to waste time retrieving her soul from Tartarus! I swear if it's the last thing I do, I am going to gut him and feed him his own entrails!"

Going to his closet, he pulled out new clothes and headed for the shower, his thoughts on Alora. *She will be a long time recovering from this. It will take months to find a suitable body and craft it to her needs for her to use when I bring her back. This is going to slow my plans considerably. I need to talk to the Elders. I cannot have them interrupting my summoning ritual.*

His mind on Alora and the defeats they had both recently suffered, Valfort allowed the water to soothe his irritation while he washed off the last remnants of his battle with Reivn and the Warlord that had aided him. *Leshye should never have interfered. I would have left her alone. Now she's going to answer for her actions. She will be harder to kill than those other sods. Still, if I can get her alone with a few Daemons, they should make short work of her.*

Valfort quickly dried and dressed, and then laid back down. He closed his eyes to wait for Kaelan, noting how slow he was. His suspicions rose once more, and he decided he would have to dig deeper into Kaelan's background. He was still waiting when he drifted into sleep.

Kaelan drove at top speed away from Valfort's lair, but instead of driving into central Philadelphia, he headed toward Atlantic City. He checked his watch again to be sure there was still time to get to his destination before dawn. *It was too dangerous to stay on assignment watching Valfort. I know how he got those marks he bore. I must speak with father.* His mind raced as he drove on, heading for the Alliance border. Though it was only an hour away, he worried he would be caught before reaching his destination. He kept a close eye on the rearview mirror until he had crossed into Alliance territory. Finally, he arrived at the Atlantic City guild and presented himself at the gate.

The sentries looked Kaelan over with suspicion and then restrained him as an intruder. Then they quickly dispatched a message to Serena.

Kaelan struggled with the guard holding him. "Release me! I am a member of this guild! On what grounds do you hold me?" *Where is my father? He must know I'm in the city by now.*

Serena interrupted his thoughts when she approached and held out her hand. "Kaelan, welcome back. I'm sorry about the guards, but we've had intruders recently and had to double our security. These new men don't yet know who you are. Why are you here though? I thought you were to be gone for months yet. What's happened?"

"The situation got too dangerous. I was nearly exposed and risked discovery if I remained there. My father's orders included forbidding me to take that risk, so I had to leave." Kaelan jerked his arms away from the guards and scowled at them.

Serena sighed and held up her hand again, backing the guards off. "He's one of us," she told them. Then she turned to Kaelan. "Your father isn't here right now. I am not even sure where to begin when it comes to recent events. Come with me. I'll get you settled into your old rooms. Then I'll tell you everything that's happened."

Somewhat agitated, he followed her. "I need to get a message to my father. This information cannot wait. It concerns Valfort. He survived the recent fight and is back in Philadelphia."

"Once he is able to accept information, you can do that. However, when I received my last communiqué from Draegonstorm, he was still unconscious. Lady Angelique is with him and working on him even as we speak, but it may be days yet before he awakens." Serena turned away, so he would not see the worry in her eyes.

Kaelan caught her arm and pulled her around. "Just how bad is he?"

She sighed. "It's bad, Kaelan. There is a chance he won't pull through this time."

He stared at her in shock. "Are you certain of this?"

She nodded. "I sent Angelique because she more so than any other holds his heart. If anyone can pull him through, she can."

He closed the distance between them instantly. "What do you mean? Who is she? Is she a skilled healer? Does she know what to do?"

"Your brother can explain about her and your father. She knows much about healing. The biggest problem she faces is the poison in his system. It is presently the source of our greatest concern. I have taught her how to manage poisons and I'm hoping what she has learned is enough. There is little else that can be done." Serena stared up at his angry face. "He needed her at his side. She is far better for him now than any medicine. Even my skills can't replace the power of the love he bears her."

Kaelan let her go. "My father has never loved anyone like that. I have never even heard of this woman you speak of. I will be going to the Keep as soon as you finish briefing me. Father needs me, and I should be on hand when he does wake."

She shook her head and put her hand on his chest, stopping him. "And what do you think you can do? You're not a healer, Kaelan! You are warrior caste. All your skills are based on fighting. You can do what... basic healing at best? Leave this to her. She is an anomaly and can do both because of her blood. That's an almost unheard-of skill. That coupled with her love for him and her determination not to lose him makes her the best person for the job."

He pushed her off and stormed past her. "I don't even know who she is! Besides, I may not be a healer, but I can still lend my strength or... something!" Spinning around, he glared angrily at her. "Come on! He's my father! How can you ask me to just sit here and wait for news?"

"The same way the rest of us do, Kaelan... one night at a time." She took his hand. "Come on. You can re-familiarize yourself with your surroundings while you wait."

Kaelan's shoulders sagged in defeat. "Fine. I'll wait, but only for a few more days. Then I'm heading home to see for myself how he fares and anyone who gets in my way will regret it."

Serena did not answer. Instead, she led him inside and took him down to his old rooms.

A thick layer of dust covered the room. It had remained undisturbed since his departure. Cobwebs layered the ceiling and walls, and the white sheets that had been draped across the furniture had grayed. Kaelan shook his head silently and looked around, remembering the first time his father had brought him here. Reivn had seen to it he had every comfort. He whispered a spell and magic blew through the room, instantly wiping away all the dust and dirt. Within moments, it was clean again. He nodded in satisfaction. Then he turned to Serena. "It will be dawn in a few hours. I know you still have things to do, and I need rest. Please let me know if you hear anything."

Serena nodded and squeezed his hand. "I will, I promise. Good night, Kaelan."

He watched her as she headed down the hall, then closed his door and sank into a chair in exhaustion. He closed his eyes to sleep, his mind on a distant fortress and the battle being waged there for Reivn's life. *Live father...*

Serena headed back to her own chambers and slipped into her bed. She stared at the ceiling, praying silently that Angelique would indeed be successful. There had been no word for over three weeks and hope was fading in the hearts of many within the guild.

The day passed in silence and dusk fell once more. In Philadelphia, Valfort opened his eyes, sleep still weighing heavy on him as darkness fell. His body screamed to be fed. Then he remembered the night before. "Kaelan..." he growled. Weak from lack of blood, he sat up and swung his legs over the side of the bed. "Why didn't he come back last night?"

He stood up and held his head as waves of dizziness washed over him. *Feeding first then...* he groaned. He went to his office and sat down at the desk. Then fishing around for a specific card, he finally picked up the phone. He dialed the number and leaned back in his chair.

A soft feminine voice answered on the other end.

Valfort smiled. "Yes. I am one of your sponsored clients. I need two of your finest tonight." He gave the address and hung up the phone. Then he snuffed out the candles with a single command. "Seliataprinde falan!" Shrouded in darkness, he leaned back in his chair and closed his eyes. He did not have long to wait.

A voice called out. "Hello?"

"I'm upstairs, second door on the left, and I'm growing impatient," Valfort growled.

Quick footsteps came up the stairs as the girls hurried to find him, anxious to make their money. They slipped through the open door into the dark room. Then the door closed behind them. Within moments, both girls were drained of blood and dead on the floor.

Valfort gathered their bodies and took them down to the crematorium in the basement, shoving them into the flames once it reached the right temperature. Then without further thought, he headed back to his room. Within the hour, he was clean again and ready to leave. "Kaelan's luck is holding only because I have to focus on Alora first," he muttered as he went down the stairs to the front door. "But I'll find where that bastard went. He won't be hard to find and I'm long overdue some amusement." He flagged down a cab.

The driver glanced over his shoulder. "Where to, sir?"

Valfort gave him the address and sat back in silence. They drove across the city to the docks, coming to a stop in front of a warehouse. Then he paid the driver and waved him on before punching a security code into the keypad. When he got inside, he went down to the lower levels and his laboratory. He quickly gathered what he needed, and then donned his robes. The room was deathly silent, as images slowly appeared in a mist in front of him, and he observed Kaelan in silence. Then his eyes grew dark when he realized where the youth had gone. "So, you have gone to the

Alliance. I should have known. Enjoy your brief respite from my presence, boy. Next time you see me, it will be the last thing you see."

With a wave of his hand, Valfort dissipated the spell and began to pace the room. He read the Magistrate's letter again. Then he growled. "It would seem I have to give Reivn a reprieve. Months of seclusion to bring her back… he will indeed pay for this in blood."

He shuffled through the different ingredients he had stored in cabinets around the room. Then he exploded. "Damn Reivn! For every night in seclusion, I will deal him a blow to the soul! I will bleed his family first, and when he is finally broken, I will rip it from him!" Closing his eyes, he sighed. *Finding a suitable host body alone could take months. Time to hunt…* He cast aside his robes and headed out into the streets with a purpose, his sharp eyes careful to observe every passing female in sight. His long vigil had begun.

## Chapter Thirty-Four
## The Code of the Warlord

*As I sit in silent contemplation of recent events, I have come to realize we are all merely pawns on a chessboard for the twisted pleasure of fate. It is such irony that the very thing that brings us to defend humanity can also cause us to destroy all we love. In war, there is no perfect decision... go left or go right, leave or destroy. Either way, you do not know the outcome until it has played itself out to the bitter end. Mortal men in their sixty or so years can never truly grow beyond the stages of a child. They thrive too much on war and wish too much for the destruction of other men. This is folly and only brings about their own ruin. And yet, are we any different? We wage war against our brethren in the Principatus and seek to destroy each other entirely and the why has gotten lost, if indeed it was ever truly known. I have loyally followed the Council's will in all things and have led our armies to many victories, but to what end? It seems the more we war, the more we must continue to do so. Now there is a veiled threat from the Eastern Lords. Will we begin another war then?*

*My angel is still so new to all this. She learns stoically and follows my lead, but I see the innocence slowly disappearing from her eyes and it torments me. I know she must grow in our ways and learn to defend herself, but to watch while her youthful innocence slowly falls away grieves me greatly. I wish there was another way, a way that would preserve her as she is. I intend to give her as much power as possible to shield her from others of our tribe and society. Ranking does offer that privilege and with it, some semblance of protection. That at least will give her some immunity from the barbaric behavior we deal with every night.*

*Lord Reivn Draegon*

\* \* \* \* \*

The night Reivn revived, he resumed his duties. The first thing he did was to send out two messages. The first was to Serena to assure her of his status. The second was to the Council requesting a trial date for Kuromoto.

Angelique was with him when the response arrived.

He read the letter and frowned. "We are required to attend immediately, as they feel the trial has waited long enough. I will be glad to be done with it. With the trial behind us, we can focus on other matters that are more important than the life of this easterner. We leave tonight."

They knew the length of their stay depended on the Council's whim, so they prepared for an extended trip. They were packed and ready within the hour.

Reivn opened the portal and nodded to Angelique.

Angelique followed silently, barely concealing her agitation.

When they arrived, they were greeted and escorted to separate rooms. Angelique settled in quickly and was ready when Reivn joined her to await the summons. Finally, they were sent for, and they walked to the throne room together.

The Ancients sat on their thrones like primordial Gods ready to pass judgment on a lesser creature infested with the disease of destruction. Victus waved them in. Then Kuromoto was brought forth and the trial began.

Reivn and Angelique stepped forward. Then they bowed in silence.

"Welcome Lord Reivn," Victus greeted. The chamber echoed with his presence. "You and your protégé know why you are here, so let us get started."

Reivn bowed again, and then tactfully positioned himself between Kuromoto and his protégé.

Victus rose from his throne and stepped down from the Dais. Then he stood in front of Kuromoto, the fury in his eyes growing as he exuded his power over the bound easterner. "Lord Kuromoto, you are accused of the murders of Prince Sorin Mandrulano and his advisors in the Alliance court of the Atlantic City territory. You have been brought before us that judgment may be rendered. What say you to this charge?"

Kuromoto looked around at the assembly until his gaze fell on Angelique and his shrewd eyes narrowed. "So, the words of a traitor are believed among this honored Council now? Must I remind you of the treaty with the Eastern Lords? This will not be taken lightly."

Victus turned and resumed his seat on the central throne. Then his voice filled the great hall. "We already know the true origins of Lady Angelique's bloodline. She is not and never was one of yours. Your lies will not help you here." He sat quietly for a moment, allowing his revelation to sink in. "Lord Reivn, Lady Angelique, you are here to bear witness against the accused. Lady Angelique, can you identify him as the one responsible for the planning and execution of the deaths of our honored Prince and his staff?"

Angelique glanced at Reivn before raising her eyes to Victus and slowly nodding. "Yes, my Lord. He is the one I heard speaking of the Prince's murder. He planned to use me and my children as his pawns."

Victus turned to Reivn. "Lord Reivn, what did you find when you investigated her claims that night?"

Reivn glanced at Kuromoto in disgust. "I found Kuromoto in this lady's mind. It was also Kuromoto and his companions my enforcers and I had to chase down following the deaths of the Atlantic City nobility. As per the Council's mandates, upon his capture, I brought him here to be tried by Council law. There is no doubt in my mind. He is guilty, my Lord."

Victus eyed Kuromoto silently for a moment before speaking. "What was the purpose of your attack on an Alliance territory?" he finally asked. "Are your Lords preparing for war again? Speak and you may yet find your life of some worth to this throne."

Kuromoto stared at the Ancients. "I am not yours to judge, my lords. I do not hold to your Council or your laws. I answer only to the Shokou Azuma."

"You're not in the East now, Kuromoto, and your lords cannot aid you here. You are a prisoner on trial for the assassination of one of our princes and his entire senior staff." Victus narrowed his gaze as he spoke. "You were accepted there as an honored guest and you left as a murderous enemy. You can either tell us what we want to know, or we can extract it under much suffering from your mind. We care not, as you are already condemned by the measure of your own actions and the evidence presented against you. Your death is already assured. It is merely the matter of how you die that is your choice. Tell us what we want to know, redeem your honor and receive a quick death, or die slowly in shame and in agonizing pain."

Kuromoto shook his head. "I am no fool, Victus. I know you will pick me apart like vultures. Much like rain in the mountains of my home transforms to snow when the winds change, your charade must stop here. Its continuation merely dishonors us both."

"This from the impostor who would claim a daughter of my line as his own..." Mastric got up. "You are right, Kuromoto," he answered in a deadly tone. "It stops now." In a flash, he was at Kuromoto's side. "There is a far more efficient way to get the answers we seek." He reached out with his power to enshroud the easterner's mind and soul.

Angelique watched in horror as Kuromoto's face contorted in agonizing pain. Then he screamed when Mastric ripped through him, collecting all the eastern lord knew.

Thylacinos stretched and got up from his spot at the base of his throne, chuckling to himself. "Every once in a while, Mastric... just every once in a while... we actually see eye to eye." Then after flashing a toothy grin, he walked out.

Reivn bowed to Victus, ignoring the scene beside him. "My lords, it would seem my father has found a much more effective way to deal with this murderer. I trust you no longer need our presence? If so, then I ask permission to depart as I have other pressing matters to see to."

Victus briefly glanced at Mastric and Kuromoto. Then he waved to Reivn in response. "You have leave to go. The trial is obviously at an end."

Taking Angelique silently by the arm, Reivn led her out quickly, making for their assigned rooms. "Gather your things. We are leaving immediately."

Angelique caught his hand as he turned to go. "Wait. What about Takara and Akihana? They were kind to me. What will happen to them?"

Reivn gazed down at her for a moment before answering. "You must understand the necessity of the harsh laws by which we live. The power our kind wields, if allowed to go unchecked, would destroy all... man and Immortal alike."

She looked down. "They are to die then?" she asked quietly.

He hesitated. "One will die. The other will be sent back to the East as a warning to their lords that the Alliance still guards its borders. Theirs was an act of war. It will be answered likewise." Leaving her to collect her bags, he went to his own room and gathered his belongings in record time. Angelique was waiting for him when he returned to retrieve her.

They headed to the portal together to return to Atlantic City. Reivn pulled her in with him and as they faded from sight, he told the guard, "deliver our bags later."

When they arrived, Reivn sorted through the business that had piled up at the Guild, teaching Angelique how to manage the daily issues that arose. Then upon learning Kaelan had returned, Reivn immediately sent for him.

Kaelan's reunion with Reivn was short-lived. They disappeared into his office so Kaelan could give his report.

Reivn listened in grim silence while Kaelan relayed all he knew of Valfort's activities.

"Father, you do realize Valfort has primarily targeted you among all the Mastrics to destroy? He hates you as no other." Kaelan frowned, remembering Valfort's fury.

Reivn sighed. "Yes, I know. He sees me as the reason he fell from grace in Mastric's eyes. He refuses to see it that was his own continued rebellion against my father's wishes that caused him to lose favor. He murdered Elena in cold blood. She was the gentlest and most cherished among my brethren, and he only did so to target Mastric directly."

Confused, Kaelan stared at him. "I don't understand, father. How would killing her be any different than any other of Mastric's own?"

"Mastric loved her more than any other. She was his chosen mate." Reivn frowned at the memory of her death. "In killing her, Valfort took a direct stab at him. A dangerous move on his part, because now Mastric will hunt him to the end of time if need be."

Kaelan nodded. "True that and you with him, judging by how long you've been on the hunt. Speaking of assignments, what will my assignment be now that I'm finished in Philadelphia?"

Reivn walked to the window and stared out at the garden, deep in thought. Finally, he turned around. "I want you to return home. It has been too long since our family has been together, so I am sending all of you back to the Keep."

"Moventius and Lunitar as well, father? It's been years now. It would be good to see them again." Kaelan smiled at the thought.

Reivn nodded. "Yes. Gideon is there as we speak. I think we shall join them. Our family's duties have kept us all away far longer than I anticipated. You leave first thing tomorrow night."

In his excitement at the thought of returning home, Kaelan forgot to ask his father about the mysterious Angelique that Serena had spoken of. He bowed and exited quickly, anticipation putting a bounce in his step at the thought of seeing his brothers again.

Reivn watched him go, and then turned to write the necessary letters.

Kaelan left the following sunset. He cheerfully said farewell to his father before stepping through the portal to home. His exuberance quickly turned to disappointment when he found out neither Lunitar nor Moventius were at the Keep. Both had left after Reivn's recovery to handle matters of their own and had not yet returned. He joined Gideon in the common room to wait for his older brothers and began pacing back and forth, stopping every few minutes to listen for footsteps in the hall before resuming his impatient vigil. Finally, he ran his hands through his short, dark blonde hair and growled. "What is taking them so long?"

Gideon watched him from a chair nearby. "They won't be here any sooner for your pacing, Kaelan. They will arrive when they arrive. Relax."

Grumbling, Kaelan looked at him. "It has been two years since I saw Moventius last and even longer with Lunitar. Father summoned them last night. They should be here by now!"

"I understand your concern, but wasting needless energy isn't going to bring them home any sooner. Come… sit down and play a game of chess with me. We will pass the time together." Gideon turned the board in front of him and reset the pieces.

Kaelan reluctantly walked over and dropped into the chair opposite Gideon. "You need to loosen up a bit, Gid. You're way too tightly wound." Slight build and good looks gave him boyish charm, complimenting the twenty-three years of age at the time of his turning.

Gideon sighed. "It was my letting my guard down that almost cost father his life. I am as I need to be. It would do you well to exercise a little more self-control yourself."

"Let him alone," a voice interrupted gruffly from the doorway and both men looked up.

"Mo!" Kaelan grinned and jumped up." God, it's good to see you! How are you?"

Moventius crossed the room and picked Kaelan up in a bear hug. His long, dark brown hair was a mass of mangy tangles. Towering over Kaelan, his huge muscular structure complimented his Wolven heritage. Laughing, he finally put his brother down. "Little brother! You didn't even hear me coming. I've been well. And you?"

Returning his hug, Kaelan chuckled. "I am good. And the only reason I didn't hear you was that Gid was talking."

Gideon got up as Moventius turned around and shook his hand. "Welcome back, Mo."

"It's good to be back. I haven't been here in ages. I've been quite busy these last two years trying to reestablish friendships with the Wolvens. I've had little success so far. They still don't want to trust Vampyres, especially not a Mastric." Moventius sighed and shook his head. *My kin are far more stubborn than Vampyres and if not for father, they would not be even considering an alliance at all.*

The sound of a throat clearing drifted in from the doorway and Lunitar walked in. "Well, we're just going to have to change that. Father never said it would be easy, but it is a necessity. Having them as an enemy only means another front from which to watch our back. There are few of us they will talk to, but you are their kind, Mo, so they are more willing to listen."

Gideon smiled. "You never change. Welcome home, Lunitar."

Lunitar glanced over at him. "Was I supposed to?"

Kaelan briefly hugged Lunitar. "So here we all are. How long has it been?"

"With the exception of two nights recently, it's been two and a half years for me," Moventius stated and walked over to greet Lunitar. "Well, most of us are here. Has anyone heard from or seen Mariah? I haven't talked to her since her last fight with father, right before I left."

Lunitar nodded. "She ran away again, and I brought her back. Then she was confined to her quarters until father spoke with her. Now, who knows where she is. I was also on assignment. I've been delivering the necessary letters to the warriors father sent for, so I was not here to keep an eye on her."

Gideon looked up. "Sent for?"

Kaelan's confused expression caused Lunitar to sigh. "He's going to have them permanently assigned here to the Keep. There is little in defensibility at present and we are a major hub for the Alliance. Do not forget that father is Prince of this territory. Now, he plans on expanding it. I have been working on those plans for months now."

"Wow... when were you going to tell me?" Kaelan grumbled. "I'm always the last to know."

Gideon snorted. "That's because you are always away, Kaelan. You play emissary while the rest of us are assigned to deal with larger matters."

Kaelan glared at him, rising from his chair. "I've been in Philadelphia watching Valfort! That's hardly playing messenger! I was risking my neck out there!"

Lunitar put his hand on Kaelan's shoulder, pushing him gently back into his seat. "Sit down. We've all risked our lives at some point on assignment; Moventius with the Wolvens, Gideon at father's side for the better part of his years, you in Valfort's camp and myself dealing with other matters. No one is discounting your ability, little brother. Calm down."

Moventius scratched his head. "Where's father? He said he would be meeting us here."

Gideon nodded, getting up. "He'll return once he has finished handling his affairs."

Moventius nodded and dropped into a chair near the fire. "No doubt. Well, since we have the time, perhaps we can share stories of some of our recent adventures."

Gideon cleared his throat uncomfortably and shook his head. "I need to go check on Gabriel. I'll be back later." Without waiting for an answer, he disappeared out the door.

Kaelan stared after him. "So, father still hasn't released either one of them. Gabriel is still in chains and Gideon might as well be."

"Now isn't the time for such observations, Kaelan," Lunitar admonished quietly. "The time will come to speak with father of this, but that time is not now. I'm heading to my quarters to get settled in. If anyone needs me, that's where I'll be."

Kaelan sighed and leaned back in his chair when Lunitar left.

Moventius sat down opposite him. "Come on little brother. Let's play for awhile and catch up on old times."

Kaelan turned back to the chess game and nodded.

Within minutes, the Commonroom was filled with laughter and conversation as they renewed an age-old bond.

Reivn and Angelique arrived shortly after his sons, and he immediately made her residency at the fortress permanent. He had appointed Serena as the new Prefect of the East American territories, leaving her to care for the Atlantic City guild and its surrounding domains.

Angelique was immediately swept up in a whirlwind of activity settling into her new life. She would often sit with Reivn and one or more of his sons, learning of the family history and the man she loved. As she learned more about Reivn's work for the Alliance Council, she finally began to understand that his service to the Council was absolute. He was frequently called to their great halls for consultation on one matter or another, and each time, she would wait anxiously for news that would take him once more into battle. When he returned to tell her the trip had been one of politics, she would again breathe relief.

After one such night, Reivn led her out to the balcony down the hall from their chambers. "I want to talk to you."

Angelique smiled at him nervously, afraid he brought news she dreaded to hear.

He put his arm around her and stared out over the vast expanse of the mountains that shielded their fortress. "This place…" he waved his hand toward the mountains. "This is our sanctuary, our haven from the outside world. It is one of the few bastions that still stand from historic times. There are many of our kind that do not have such a safe haven."

Taking her hand, he turned her to face him. "I was once mortal just as you were. I was a knight and warrior from my earliest days. My people fell to the Romans and were enslaved. Along with many of our other warriors, I was conscripted to fight for them and would have died had Mastric not found me and made me his blood servant. I served as his eyes and ears in the human world for centuries. I served in many places, but for the most part, he kept me near my homeland. In one thousand four hundred and thirty-three, I was inducted into a society known as the Order of the Dragon, a collective group of the noblest and most honorable warriors and kings known to the old world. I fought beside countless princes from not only my country, but also many others. I even stood beside Vlad Dracul, father of the one now known as Dracula."

His voice took on a distant tone, and his eyes filled with memory. "Our goal was a common one… to unify the people of our countries, bringing education, prosperity, freedom and peace to the nations of the known world, much like Alexander the Great dreamed of doing in his time. There were many warlike nations that stood against us in those days, seeking to destroy the Order. The Ottoman Empire was among these, and though Vlad once had an alliance with them, he led the rebellion against them. The Christian world demanded he stand beside them or be excommunicated. It was then that many of the Order fell. It was the Immortals that ultimately saved us from being completely destroyed."

Reivn paused and stared out at the mountains' vast expanse, remembering the bloodshed and conflict.

"Vlad, who was my lifelong friend, was murdered before the Council could claim him, but his son, Wladislaus Dragwlya, joined us in immortality before the Turks could finish him. Ironically, a priest saw him when he left his coffin in the monastery, and the legends that named him Dracula were born that survive to this day. Romania has been his domain in our world since that time. There were others from the Order that were saved as well, King Alphonse of Aragon and Stefan of Serbia among them. You will not find this story in the history books today, for history is written by the victors. Most of the truth surrounding our cause has been buried for centuries by the lies of our enemies. They twisted the stories of the Order and its members into goals of greed, power, and corruption. The truth of our original purpose is now known only to those of us that survived the bloodshed."

He touched her cheek as she stood silently listening to his tale. "I am telling you this, so you can understand the code I live by, the code I taught my sons and in fact all those under my banners to follow."

She shivered and he took her arm, leading her back inside. As they walked, he continued. "Centuries before I was even born, a great war began between the tribes. The confrontation of Mysia was named for the land in which the rifting took place. It was there the Council first formed the Alliance and took control of Polusporta fortress, driving the Renegades from its halls forever. However, it was not until after Agamemnon burned Troy in 1250BC that the Council decided it was no longer safe to keep Polusporta in Mysia. They decided to move the fortress to the Sahara where they have since remained, safely hidden from mortal eyes. The great expanse of sand and heat makes it easy for the Ancients to keep our existence a secret there." Kissing her forehead, he smiled. "Have I confused you yet?"

Angelique giggled and shook her head. "No… It's incredible! Tell me more?"

They walked into the common room and Reivn led her to a sofa to sit down. Then he continued. "After the alliance between the tribes was formed, the Council had to lay the groundwork for our society. They built the hierarchy as we know it from the ancient practices in Rome and Greece." Reivn paused. "Each territory has its own Prince or magistrate, and they are governed directly by the Council of the nine tribes. Each of the tribes also set up their own hierarchies according to their needs and ideals. The Council I serve first and foremost is our own. I hold the position as Mastric's right hand and enforcer, as my men do under me. However, I am also Warlord Prefect for the Alliance Council and am responsible for dealing with any particularly dangerous Renegades that surface."

She started tickling his ear and laughed when he batted her hand away. "You little minx, are you trying to entice me to taste of you again?"

She wrapped her arms around his neck. "Yes. Enough talk for now. It's hard to remember it all anyway. There's so much to learn. It's giving me a headache."

He shook his head in exasperation. "It is important that you do learn all this, angel. The history of our people has been passed from one to another over the centuries and written in the arcane and historic tomes stored in Polusporta's library. By doing this, each of us knows who we are. I do not know when our kind first began or where we came from, but it is whispered that our Sires do, and they keep that truth buried behind those walls. You are the daughter of Mastric's firstborn son. You may one day be responsible for carrying the story of our people."

That sobering thought lingering in her mind, Angelique laid her head on his chest. "I know it's important, beloved, but some of it frightens me. As a girl, I grew up afraid of the legends about Daemons and darkness. Superstitions governed much of my country at the time. Now you tell me that we, meaning Immortals, have existed as a people since ancient times."

Pulling her closer, Reivn kissed her before answering. "I know you aren't completely at ease with our society yet, because you were hidden from the world for so long. But believe me when I say not all of us are evil." Cupping her chin in his hand, he gazed into her eyes. "Can you say I am evil? My faith in God is stronger now than it was in my mortal life. Our change enhances everything, birthing power even in something as incorporeal as faith. My faith now aids me when I fight those that serve the darkness."

Reivn turned her around, lifted his hand, and touched the crucifix still on her neck. "If I had bargained with the darker side of our existence, I could not touch this. Our curse is what keeps us on the edge of the abyss and many of us strive for redemption. However, some prefer to climb into the abyss to play. They are the reason we must defend ourselves and humanity."

Angelique's expression grew sad and she looked away, unable to meet his eyes. "Is that all we are… that and nothing more? Good or evil, no chance of ever walking in the light again?"

He frowned. "It's not that simple, angel. No one knows exactly where our curse comes from, but its nature is also the source of our power. There are some, including myself, who believe that by finding redemption in ourselves, we will also find a way to break the hold it has on us. No angel, we are not just of the darkness. We feel. Like this…" he caressed her cheek softly. "We see, hear, taste and sense everything stronger than mere mortals. Our emotions are also more intense than mortals. That is the reason you succumbed to madness in your grief when you and I were apart, and the reason Armand became so violently ill with the fever."

Angelique shook her head, trying to understand. "Are you saying we may one day be able to reclaim the light, no longer needing blood to survive?"

Reivn got up and pulled her to her feet. "I am saying there is a slight chance, but no one knows for certain. Now come, it is time to rest. Daybreak is coming, and I am hungry for you."

Taking her hand, they left the Commonroom and walked back to their chamber.

Dawn was just beginning to creep over the horizon when he closed the door behind them. He lifted her into his arms and gently carried her to the bed. "Remember those intense emotions I was telling you about?" he asked, smiling as he laid her down. "You are about to experience them." Chuckling as he joined her, he whispered, "Seliataprinde falan," and the torches went out.

## Chapter Thirty-Five
## The City That Never Sleeps

*I managed to gain the Council's permission to raise Angelique in the ranks again, to where she will be working side by side with me. It was merely a matter of pointing out how much she has already learned of our plans and the fact she is still being hunted by her maker. Now I can keep her at arm's length where I can protect her from Valfort's reach. I will not ever let what happened with Alora be repeated. She has become more precious to me than life itself.*

*Lunitar thinks I do not see his disapproving eyes, nor does he feel I think with any clarity of thought where she is concerned. He is perhaps correct concerning my favor toward her, but I intend to see to her training as well. She will one day be a formidable opponent in her own right, given the time to develop the potential I have seen in her. She is the one thing Valfort did right. In her, he created a magnificent creature, not hindered by the bond the rest of our tribe shares, but unique, and able to tap into both the warrior caste and the Paladin's way. This means having a healer with our war parties that is a warrior herself. She is still timid and unsure of her own ability, but that will pass given the time to develop her confidence and skills.*

*Valfort has fallen silent since my battle with him, and no news has come in recent nights as to his whereabouts. I fear what this means for myself and my angel. I am not fool enough to believe he was defeated, or that he will slink back into the pit where he has chosen to dwell. I sense there is far more to his recent attack than met the eye, and I will be ever vigilant in awaiting his return. I will also be watching for Alora's foul presence on the horizon. I know she is not gone for good. It is only a matter of time...*

*Lord Reivn Draegon*

\* \* \* \* \*

When Reivn and Angelique woke the following night, it was to find a courier waiting with an important message from New York.

After reading the letter, Reivn sent for his sons, and then quickly dressed and headed for his private office.

Angelique followed in worried silence.

Gideon, Lunitar, Moventius and Kaelan arrived minutes later, concern showing on their faces. They listened grimly while Reivn told them the letter's contents. "The Magistrate in New York is requesting help. An Immortal named Cyrus Darien entered the city some months ago, under the guise of one of the nine tribes. No one knew him, but Lord Moravini still welcomed him and gave him the crown's protection. Shortly after his arrival, things began to happen."

Lunitar listened in grim silence.

Moventius glanced at Gideon and frowned as a silent thought crossed his mind.

Kaelan shook his head and closed his eyes. "So much for being home," he whispered.

Reivn tapped his fingers impatiently and glanced up at the courier. "What sort of things? This letter does not explain. What exactly is the problem?"

Shifting nervously, the courier stammered out, "He's suspected of killing several people, but we have no proof. He's really good at covering his tracks. Even the Magistrate's security men haven't been able to catch him. They respectfully request your assistance."

Reivn stared at the letter, thinking for a moment before he answered. Finally, he looked up. "Tell your Magistrate I will be there tomorrow night."

The courier bowed and scurried from the room like a frightened rabbit.

Gideon, Lunitar, and Moventius quietly awaited orders, but Kaelan frowned. "Father?"

Angelique voiced what they were all thinking. "You're leaving again?"

Reivn nodded and looked at her. "Yes, and you are coming with me."

Lunitar looked up sharply, concern crossing his features at his father's statement.

Reivn ignored his son's gaze and finished. "Tell the servants to prepare what we need. We leave at dusk tomorrow."

Angelique threw her arms around him and kissed him happily. Then she ran from the room to make the necessary preparations.

Impatient now, Kaelan spoke. "Would you let us accompany you? You may need our aid."

"Not all of you. I will take Lunitar and Moventius with me. Gideon needs to be here to care for Gabriel and you have only just returned. Stay. I will not be gone long." Reivn glanced at Gideon, who was silently heading for the door. "Gideon, you have said nothing, yet you do not appear to approve," he growled.

Gideon stopped and shook his head. "It isn't my place to approve or disapprove, father. I will never question your judgment." Turning once more, he left the room.

Seeing the annoyed expression on Reivn's face, Moventius draped his arm around Kaelan's shoulders. "Come on, little brother. Let's head to the Commonroom for a drink before I go pack. I can't leave you and Gideon to have all the fun while I'm gone."

Kaelan grumbled and followed Moventius as he headed out the door.

Lunitar waited until he and Reivn were alone. "Permission to speak freely, my lord?"

Reivn turned around. "We are at home and you are my second. There is no necessity for such formalities here. You can speak plainly. What is on your mind?"

Concern once more crossing his features, Lunitar gazed intently at his father. "Is it wise to take Lady Angelique into such a potentially dangerous situation with so little training? New York isn't Alliance territory and Lord Moravini is unpredictable at best."

Reivn frowned. "She will be safe enough with me and she needs to begin learning the responsibilities of her new position. She was just made a Mastric Ambassador. That way, she can work directly for me."

"A position that in all honesty she isn't ready for," Lunitar stated calmly.

Reivn growled at him. "Under any other circumstance I would agree with you, but this is different. She is under my direct tutelage. She could have no better teacher."

Lunitar realized there was no point in arguing, and he bowed. "I stand corrected, father," he replied quietly. "I will go prepare." He turned and left, his thoughts on the coming trip far different from his father's... and far more dangerous.

Reivn got up. Going to the fire, he put in another two logs and stoked it higher. Then he sat in the chair in front of the hearth and leaned back, trying to relax. *Cyrus Darien*. He stared into the flames, trying to remember where he had heard that name before. Mulling over what little he knew, he sat long into the night. Just before dawn, he returned to their shared chambers to find Angelique patiently waiting for him.

"Where were you all night?" she asked in curiosity.

He was silent while he changed. Then he walked to the bed and sat down beside her. "There is something about this case that disturbs me. The name sounds familiar, but I cannot recall from where. I feel I should know it."

She wrapped her arms around him. "It will probably come to you soon enough. In the meantime, I know the perfect way to occupy your thoughts."

Hungry with desire Reivn laid back, pulling her with him. "I hope, my sweet Comtesse, that you will occupy more than just my thoughts."

Angelique simply smiled and whispered, "I thought you would never ask."

When they finally slipped into the sleep of day, she was still wrapped in his arms.

When Reivn opened his eyes again as the sun set the following night, he laid silently watching her while she slept and smiled. Her pale beauty was almost ethereal in the soft candlelight. He waited quietly for her to awaken.

Finally, her eyes fluttered open. "Beloved?"

He pulled her closer. "I swear you have put a spell on me. You really are an enchanting creature." Reivn kissed her nose. "However, if I do not get up, we will not be leaving tonight either. Time is of the essence. The change in the time zone makes traveling by portal difficult. You should remember that from the trip to the Sahara."

She groaned and got up. Then she snatched his robe and threw it around her shoulders.

"Woman! Give me that!" He made a grab for it, but she dodged his grasp.

With a laugh, she began moving about the room to gather her things. "I thought you didn't mind being naked," she teased.

"I do not, but it is going to be difficult to explain why I am walking to the baths this way." In response, his robe hit him in the face as she raced out the door in her dressing gown, her laughter filling the hallway.

An hour later, Reivn and Angelique joined Lunitar and Moventius in the portal room. Reivn opened the portal and they stepped through to New York's Guild.

A young Mastric was waiting for them when they arrived. "Good evening, my Lord. I was instructed to take you to your quarters. I'll have to make arrangements for your men as we weren't expecting them. Our Prefect would have met you, but he isn't here at present. If you'll come with me..." holding up the torch, he turned and walked away.

Reivn took Angelique's arm and they followed.

Lunitar and Moventius exchanged glances before joining their father and heading down the hall with their guide. Once Reivn and Angelique were settled, Lunitar and Moventius disappeared to prepare for the meeting with the magistrate.

Once they were alone, Reivn caught Angelique's hand and pulled her down beside him on the bed. "I need to talk to you," he began. "I planned on waiting to tell you, but in view of our assignment here, it is time you knew. I sent a letter to the Council last week, requesting your promotion to the rank of Ambassador. The response came last night." He kissed her forehead. "Congratulations, angel. Tonight, you are here on official business for the Mastrics Council."

Angelique stared at him, stunned the Council would even consider such a request, much less grant it. "I'm not qualified!"

Laughing at her expression, Reivn swung her around in his arms. "You will be traveling with me. I can give you all the help you need." He grinned and kissed her again.

She shook her head. "I don't think I can do this."

He took her hand and pulled her into his embrace. "In a position of leadership and power, you must appear impenetrable on the outside to command the respect of those around you. Remember I am an executor of the law. People fear me because they believe my heart cold and my soul black. Save your gentle side for when we are alone. Now... it is time. We must first meet with the Guild Prefect, and then with the Magistrate of this territory. Best face, angel..."

The meeting with the Mastrics Elder went well. Reivn and Angelique handled business with quick efficiency while his sons stood watch. Angelique was surprised at the response she got from the other Mastrics and quickly realized what a heavy title 'Ambassador' was. Reivn had informed her there were only four Ambassadors for each of the nine tribes: two that served as liaisons between the Councils and two that served in the field. "The world is your assignment, angel..." he had said. Now she understood. These people looked to her to mediate inner tribal disputes and other matters requiring a higher power's interference to resolve. When they left the Guild to head for the Magistrate's Manor on the outskirts of the city, she sat quietly thinking about her new responsibilities.

Reivn tapped her shoulder. "You were a million miles away. Did you hear anything I said?"

Lunitar suppressed a chuckle as he watched them from his seat and Moventius elbowed him, grinning from ear to ear.

She shook her head, staring at Reivn in confusion.

Reivn smiled again. "I said you did well back there. They feared you. Well done."

She smiled at him. "I wish I was as confident in myself as you are in me. It wasn't difficult to be distant or cold, but I was quaking in my shoes. I felt they could see right through me."

Reivn laughed. "They cannot do that unless you allow them to. We all have that ability, but unless they wanted to challenge your power they were not going to see anything other than a confident and cold ambassador that is here on business."

Moventius laughed. "As a Draegon, we tend to inspire that reaction. You'll get used to it."

Lunitar smiled at his father's expression, but remained silent and watched the roads. His thoughts were far different from theirs. He was worried.

Angelique stared out the window at the stores and people bustling on the streets at such a late hour. "Doesn't this city ever sleep?"

Reivn glanced out at the familiar sight. "Not New York. It is referred to as the city that never sleeps. The Council has wanted to add it to our territories for a long time, but the Magistrate holding it is powerful. Not too many are willing to challenge him for the throne."

Chuckling, Moventius leaned forward in his seat. "What my father means is that none have lived long enough to try."

Angelique looked at Reivn in alarm.

Her expression made him smile. "He is not of the nine tribes, but rather of a bit of an enigma… a rare independent bloodline. Their kind are unusual, and are almost never part of the Alliance. He is strong enough that he and his kin have maintained their independence through the centuries, merely working with us for the common good. They do not hold to our laws, but they do not agree with the Renegades either, so they maintain their distance from both sides."

"Then why are we here?" she asked. "We have no jurisdiction here, surely?"

Reivn shook his head. "Under normal circumstances, the only jurisdiction we have is with our own Guild here. However, the Magistrate himself has requested our help in this matter. That gives us temporary jurisdiction. Ah, here we are…"

Lunitar stared at the building as they approached. *Why did they ask specifically for my father? There are three Warlords in a closer vicinity than he was.*

Gazing out the window as they slowly pulled through traffic to the curb, Angelique could see nothing but a tall building, the front of which was decorated more like a gothic cathedral than a business or private building.

When the car pulled to a stop, Lunitar opened the door and got out, followed by Moventius. The two quickly took protective stances on either side of the car, making an obvious show of security for the occupants within.

Angelique's expression caused Reivn to laugh. "We always hide a building's true purpose from the eyes of mortal men. In the mortal world, this place is known as a privately-owned business by a wealthy, eccentric entrepreneur. So, we play the part of wealthy business associates. In this way, we blend into the human world better. None of us tries to draw attention of an unwanted nature. Come." Climbing out of the vehicle, he offered her his hand.

Angelique stared at the building as she joined him, amazed at the structure that to her seemed to climb right into the sky itself. "It's incredible," she whispered.

Lunitar and Moventius immediately flanked them.

"My lord…" Lunitar spoke briskly, as two security men approached them from the entrance.

Reivn nodded to Lunitar and tucked Angelique's arm in his. Then they followed the guards quietly until safely indoors. When they stepped into the elevator, he squeezed her hand reassuringly. *Remember you are an Ambassador*, he telepathied. Then they stepped out into an immense and lavishly decorated reception hall.

Four guards stood by a set of enormous double doors, gilded and glowing in the soft light. One of them stopped both Lunitar and Moventius, and then patted them down for weapons. Seeing each only had the one allowed weapon, he nodded to his companions and stepped aside.

Angelique followed Reivn's example and barely acknowledged the guards' presence when they were issued through the doors into the great room beyond.

A voice greeted them from within, but no one could be seen. "Well you have come at last, Lord Reivn, and brought your men too, I see." A man stepped from the shadows. "I was, however, not expecting any other guests. Who is your lovely companion?"

Reivn bowed briefly and following his cue, she curtsied and answered his query. "I am the Ambassador for the Mastric's tribe my lord. I accompanied Lord Reivn to see if I could assist in any way with this evil that plagues your domain."

Reivn smiled. "May I present the Lady Angelique? My lady, this is Lord Moravini."

The man walked over and kissed her hand. "Well spoken. She's beautiful, my lord. A nice choice, but is she skilled? Our situation here may put her in the line of fire."

Angelique looked up. "Pardon monsieur, but shouldn't you be asking me that question? His lordship does not speak for me."

The magistrate stared at her quietly for a moment, a look of sheer amusement on his face. Then he turned and walked across the room, motioning for them to follow. "I can see you have backbone, my lady. That pleases me. Welcome..." he waved his hand and the lights rose, bathing the room in their soft glow. "...to New York."

Lunitar moved first, keeping a respectful distance between himself and the Magistrate, while making sure to be in a defensible position should they be attacked.

Moventius let Reivn and Angelique pass, and hung back so he could intercept any possible attack that would come from behind.

Reivn nodded his approval to Angelique when she glanced his way and she fought the smile that threatened to break across her face. *I pleased him*, she thought in delight.

Moravini waved them to the sofas that sat in the center of the room. Then seating himself, he looked at them expectantly.

Reivn guided her over to the sofa opposite Moravini. Then he sat down next to her.

Lunitar and Moventius moved into positions flanking them on either side.

Reivn immediately turned to the matter at hand. "Lord Moravini, you said there was a problem with someone called Cyrus Darien. What have your people discovered thus far?"

Moravini smiled. "Right to business, as usual. Have you no time for a polite exchange or civil conversation about the outside world?"

Reivn leaned forward, a serious expression on his face. "That name has been plaguing me since your courier first spoke it. I know it from somewhere."

Shifting in his seat, Moravini smirked at their obvious formality. "Please, call me Stefan. Lord Moravini is so formal. As to your question, I would not know as to what reference you might be thinking. I know nothing of the man's history prior to his appearance in this territory. How is the Sahara this time of year? I'm told it is rather hot."

Lunitar's gaze shifted from the room directly to the magistrate, suspicion in his eyes. Then he glanced at Moventius, but said nothing.

Moventius nodded almost imperceptibly.

Despite his growing irritation, Reivn responded diplomatically. "The weather there is not my concern. The safety of your city is. Please tell me what you know about Cyrus."

Moravini realized his questions would get nowhere, so he leaned forward and took on a more serious tone. "He came here about six months ago and presented himself. We do not have the same customs as your Council, as you well know. He was only required to appear here…" he waved his hand at the room. "I do not hold a formal court. It is a waste of time." He got up and went to a liquor cabinet. "May I offer you a drink, Lord Reivn? My lady?"

Reivn and Angelique both nodded.

Moravini poured a dark red liquid into three glasses. As he handed them their drinks, he began recounting the events of recent months. "At first, he seemed a friendly fellow and moved around getting to know everyone. Then the disappearances started. Young and weak Immortals just vanished without a trace."

Reivn's interest peaked and he listened intently. "Go on."

Moravini got up and began to pace, growing irritated as he continued the tale. "We weren't able to find out who was responsible for several months, but last month we had a lucky break. A hybrid from the Wolvens came into the city looking for aid for some of his people. They had been attacked in an alley." He paused. "I gave them sanctuary in my home. Their attacker obviously thought the fellow was alone, because when his companions jumped from the shadows to give him aid, it surprised the man, who then ran. One of the Wolvens positively identified Cyrus as the assailant."

Stopping mid-stride Moravini turned to them. "My people went to bring him in for questioning, but only one came back and he died before we could get any information. I have since sent three different war parties into his lair. Each time their numbers have been nearly massacred. That..." he looked hard at Reivn, "is why I called you."

Reivn leaned back, staring at Moravini while he contemplated their next move.

Angelique sat silently gazing at Moravini, not sure what to say.

"If he is truly responsible for all these crimes against the tribes, then we must hunt him and destroy him," Reivn finally stated. "However, we must have proof first. You said those who went missing never turned up, correct?"

Moravini nodded. "Not one."

Reivn frowned. "Then it would seem we must first investigate from a different angle, hopefully bringing something to light that will allow us to solve this situation. Have any of the survivors told you anything? What is in his lair that is so deadly to our kind? Surely, he did not kill all of them by himself. Perhaps there are more you do not know about?"

"Or worse," Angelique whispered as she listened.

Reivn looked over at her. "What are you thinking, Ambassador?"

Angelique sat thinking for a moment before answering. "If he's as dark as he appears to be, then perhaps he uses Daemons to aid him. I will install myself here at the Guild as a new Cleric, temporarily of course. Perhaps if I use myself to give him a tempting target, we can draw him out into the open. There's a good chance he would get careless. One mistake is all we need to catch him, correct?"

Lunitar frowned, not liking where the conversation was going, but he maintained the outward silence his duties demanded. Instead, he telepathied Reivn. *My lord, if she is used as bait she will be directly in harm's way. She may have good intention, but there is no way she is prepared for this. If someone must be the bait, then allow me to do it.*

Shaking his head in Lunitar's direction, Reivn stared at Angelique in surprise. "I do not think it would be wise to put someone so valuable in harm's way. What if we were not able to get to you in time? We could not afford your disappearance."

Angelique shook her head, adamant in her choice. "He would suspect anyone else. I'm still new to this position and most still think me relatively naïve. That makes me the perfect choice. You can put necessary people in place to protect me, but I am the best option if you want to succeed in drawing him out of hiding."

The room was deathly quiet for long moments until Reivn reluctantly nodded. "Very well."

Moravini bowed. "It's a good plan, my Lady. Let's hope it works, for all our sakes."

Reivn helped Angelique up and signaled his sons. "We should return to the Guild and begin putting plans in motion. Good night, Stefan. We will speak more when this begins to unfold. We will see ourselves out." Taking Angelique's arm, he guided her to the doors.

Moventius walked ahead and opened the elevator. Then he stood waiting for Reivn, Angelique, and Lunitar. Then the four exited the building to their waiting car in silence.

Angelique grew more afraid with every step, wondering if she had made the right choice. Reivn's silence only served to worry her that this trip could quite possibly be her last.

Once they finally reached the Guild, Reivn specifically asked for separate rooms. Then he, Lunitar and Moventius disappeared, leaving her at her door.

Heading to his temporary office, Reivn had barely closed the door behind his sons when Lunitar spoke up. "Father, if I may?"

Reivn sat down. "I figured you would," he answered, rather agitated.

Moventius looked from one to the other, then shook his head and sat down.

"Well, it is pointless to recant the decision to go forward with this plan. I understand why you chose to do it, but do we truly have the resources to provide adequate protection for Lady Angelique during this..." Lunitar paused and frowned, "scenario," he finished. "Do we even know what this man looks like? More importantly, do we truly want a renegade loose inside the guild? We need more intel if we are to successfully execute this mission."

Reivn sighed. "I understand your frustration, as it is my own as well. She was impetuous in offering herself up, but I had little choice but to accept or diminish her position. I intend to ask Lucian for aid. He has a safehouse for the Thylacinians here in New York. He holds it as part of our strength here to discourage Renegades who would challenge Moravini."

Moventius leaned forward then. "What about asking him for Grimel? He helped you in the hunt for Valfort. I'm sure he would help with this as well."

Reivn got up and began pacing. "There are many loyal to our cause I could call in, but too great a change in our numbers would be noticed by someone who has already been clever enough to outsmart a magistrate that has thus far held this domain since its creation."

Lunitar stood thinking for a moment. "Then I request to be assigned as aid to the Ambassador," he finally replied. "That would put me in constant close proximity to her and I have work I can do here in the library. This would not noticeably change our numbers, but it would still allow for her protection should she need it."

Reivn turned to his son, his thoughts on Angelique. "That is actually not a bad idea. I can send Moventius to find Grimel and bring him here. I would then be free to distance myself so as not to arouse suspicion. She will not like it, but I think it is the best way. I can publicly claim her as my pupil, making her appear younger than the Elder she actually is."

Moventius smiled. "Finding Grimel will be easy, father. I spend enough time with my Thylacinian brothers that they will no doubt be able to direct me right to him."

Lunitar sighed reluctantly and nodded. "Agreed then, father. I'll see to making the necessary arrangements tonight. Will you be staying on at the Guild as well?"

Reivn shook his head. "No. That would be too obvious. I will instead remove myself to Atlantic City. I will be near enough to respond, but not so near as to draw unnecessary attention."

Scratching his head, Moventius interrupted. "Father, what do you want me to do after I bring Grimel back this way?"

"You can head back to the Keep and let Gideon know we will be in New York for a while. Then just try to keep your brother out of trouble. We do not know how long this mission will take, so I need you to watch over things at home."

Lunitar frowned and stated, "If there is nothing else father, I'd like to remove myself to begin making the necessary arrangements."

Reivn nodded. "You may go. I will explain matters to Angelique tonight. I am leaving at dusk tomorrow."

Moventius got up. "I'll head out tonight then and begin tracking Grimel down. Good luck, Luni." Then he grinned and walked out.

Lunitar followed and headed toward the Guild's library, needing time to think.

After they left, Reivn sat for some time in the office mulling over the coming nights. Thinking of the danger Angelique had unknowingly placed herself in, he began to form a plan in his mind. Shortly before dawn, he finally headed for Angelique's chambers.

Angelique was listening to the comings and goings of those around her as they went about their nightly business. When the halls finally quieted, she got up to prepare for bed.

"You were not watching again," Reivn reprimanded her quietly from behind.

She spun around in sudden fright. "Oh! Beloved, you startled me! I was..."

He crossed the room quickly and caught her in his arms. "...Not guarding yourself. I know. How many times must I remind you to do this, even in your lair?"

She sighed and curled into his arms. "I was just caught up in thought. I'm sorry."

Reivn lifted her chin so her eyes met his. "This is precisely why your willingness to put yourself out as bait scares me. You do not always watch yourself, you are not yet well-enough trained and you are too willing to become a target to catch this man. We do not yet even know who he is or what he is capable of. Please, angel, remember to watch yourself. I cannot always be there."

"You are right. I'm sorry. I did not think and in this new position, there is no room for mistakes. I will try to do better," Angelique answered softly.

He held her close. "I could not imagine losing you. Do not put that kind of fear in me. It is crippling. A single moment of distraction can lead to both our deaths, especially here in the field. At least in this territory, we have backup if needed. This is the home of Lucian, the Thylacinian Warlord. So, he can be here to aid us within minutes."

She looked up. "Will I need to meet him?"

"You probably will. I have not seen him much of late, as we have both been busy with our assignments, but we Warlords do aid each other when necessary. It is where some of our strength lies." Reivn smiled down at her. "Now it is almost dawn. Come. We need rest."

Angelique smiled and took him by the hand, leading him to the bed.

Halfway there, he swung her into his arms and carried her the remaining distance, growling low. "It is after all my favorite time of the day."

## Chapter Thirty-Six
## A Dangerous Game

*A new enemy has crawled from the corners of the pit before the dust has even settled on Alora's rotting corpse. At least the she-witch will not return for some time to come. Even with all her power, coming back from Tartarus will take months at best. With any due luck, this new threat will be short and concise to deal with, and we will be back to dealing with greater issues involving the war instead of chasing traitors.*

*Cyrus Darien... the name rings in my ears and I cannot place it. It is like a forgotten memory that washes over you with the familiarity of a relic long since tucked away from use, but which still reminds you of its presence. Where have I heard that name? It has echoed in my head since I first learned of it and taunts me like a nightmare from which I cannot wake. I am certain I know it, and yet cannot find in my memory where it hides.*

*My angel's zeal for her new position both impresses and frightens me. She risks far more than I believe she truly recognizes in her desire to help capture this murderer. She has taken well to being an ambassador, but she still has so much to learn. I am glad of Lunitar's presence, for I find it difficult to be stern with her when I am teaching her our ways. I find myself wanting instead to make her smile, not doing things that make her cry. She will be my undoing.*

*I have summoned my family home. By the time I return to the Keep, the rest will have arrived. It is time I see them again. Gideon remains there with Kaelan and Moventius, caring for Gabriel. Having the others home will be a pleasant sojourn from duty and a welcome repast. It has been too long since last I saw them, and the halls of the keep have been quiet and empty.*

*Lord Reivn Draegon*

\* \* \* \* \*

Within hours, Reivn, Angelique, and Lunitar had laid the groundwork to catch Cyrus. Then Reivn left for Atlantic City and Angelique settled in at the Guild. She met with its Prefect, Jacob Lowry, and told him their plan. Then after several nights catching up on the city's recent events, they were ready to set it in motion.

Reivn had decided he and Angelique would argue publicly. This would draw the attention of Vampyre society and set tongues wagging, which was sure to reach the right ears.

On the appointed night, Angelique was driven to one of the prominent underground clubs. She entered with ease, using the membership card purchased by Jacob earlier in the week. He had also gone to some of New York's finest shops and purchased her a stylish miniskirt and a crop top, much more risqué than she was used to, but appropriate for the club she was attending. Impressed with its interior layout, she looked around. Here was a place royalty could be entertained in style. Burgundy plush carpets and black marble walls adorned its vast interior. A members-only club for Immortals, 'The Sanguine Rose' was used to visitors. Its fame in their society enticed Immortals to travel from all over the world. Its entertainers were top billing and the cuisine was tailored to their kind. The Galatian owner, Ryanne McAllister, prided herself on having one of the classiest clubs in the world.

Angelique had caught the attention of several young men the second she walked in the door. She moved to the bar, calmly ordered wine and then stood watching the dance floor, making it obvious she was alone. Her curiosity over the dancing styles that so vastly differed from what she was used to almost made her forget why she was there.

Her attention snapped to the present when a young man walked up and introduced himself, his smile genuine as he eyed her beauty. "I'm Randall. What's your name, baby?"

Returning his smile, she introduced herself. "Angelique. I just recently came to the city, but I'm really more of a country girl though."

Randall looked her up and down and whistled, causing her to blush. "You sure don't look like a country girl. Those are some of the hottest threads I've seen around here in a while. Lana's gonna be jealous 'cause the guys got a new face to look at tonight." He glanced at the stage, "I got to go for now. We're on soon, but I'll come find you after the show. Stick around, honey. You can party with the band later." Kissing her hand, Randall disappeared into the crowd.

*This place is very strange*, she thought. The stage spotlight turning on caught her attention, and she watched with interest as a beautiful woman walked out and began talking.

The woman's voice echoed through the whole club. "Welcome to the Sanguine Rose, ladies and gentlemen. Put your hands together and welcome *Phantasm*."

The stage went dark and the crowd started screaming enthusiastically. Then the first strains of music began to pour from the stage and fog spilled over its edges, filling the front of the dance floor. It reminded Angelique of the old cathedrals when the boy's choirs sang Mozart at mass. She felt a thrill of anticipation waiting to see what would happen next. Then the lights flared and the band, decked out in black leather, broke out singing the first rock music she had ever heard. Like a wave flowing across the ocean, the crowd began to dance to its rhythm. She found herself tapping her foot as she watched, fascinated with the whole experience.

Seated at the drums, Randall played across them enthusiastically with his sticks. The lead singer danced across the stage, energy pouring from her and infecting the crowd with her excitement. The girl at the keys lifted her hands and started clapping. Then she waved to the audience to do the same and they followed along, shouting their delight.

Someone grabbed Angelique by the hand, and she found herself among the sea of faces on the dance floor. "Wait," she yelled, trying to get her unknown companion to stop. "I don't know how to do this!" Her voice was drowned out by the music and the screaming of the crowd. She stood staring at her new companion wondering how she could avoid embarrassment.

He grabbed her arm and pulled her close, yelling in her ear. "Just go with the flow, love! You'll get the hang of it!" Smiling at her encouragingly, he started moving with the music.

Angelique watched him for a moment. Then she began to sway, trying to feel the rhythm. He nodded, screaming out his encouragement as she laughed at herself. Soon she was dancing with her companion, whose name she still did not know, and moving with the rest of the crowd as though she had been doing it for years. Another song started, and she signaled to her new friend that she wanted to sit down.

He took her hand and led her off the dance floor. Then leading her to the bar, he got her a drink. After getting his own, he guided her to a table in the lounge area. "What's your name?"

Angelique could not hear him over the music and crowd. She shook her head. "What?"

He leaned toward her. "Your name?" he asked again.

"Angelique," she shouted in his ear.

With a grin, he held his hand out to her. "Grimel! It's a pleasure. With anybody?"

She shook her head again and smiled.

"Cool," he responded and turned to watch the crowd still on the dance floor.

Now Angelique had a chance to examine her new friend up close. His long, light brown hair was almost to his waist. He was dressed in a jade baroque-styled silk shirt and a pair of black European slacks. The scruff on his face gave him the appearance of a rugged outdoorsman though, and his eyes were almost wolf-like. His fingernails were longer and sharper than any human's, and his ears moved as he listened to the sounds around them.

Grimel turned with a chuckle. "Are you through examining me yet?" He smiled playfully. The music had momentarily softened, and she could hear his Australian accent. "You know if I looked you over that way, you would consider me fresh. I hope you like what you see, but don't worry. I won't tell Reivn."

Angelique's jaw dropped in shock. "You... he... just who are you anyway?" she demanded.

He grinned and leaned on his elbow, gazing at her. "Lucian sent me, at Lord Reivn's request. I'm your insurance policy. The Warlord Prefect doesn't want you to get hurt. So I'm here to watch your back without blowing your cover."

Sitting back, she rolled her eyes in exasperation. "I should have known," she mumbled.

He tapped her arm. When she looked up, he motioned her closer. "I'm supposed to flirt with you and act like there's an interest here. That gives you two a reason to fight. Lunitar is here too, just to be sure you're safe. And yes, I know the plan."

She stared at him, not attempting to answer.


The band finished, and the crowd went crazy chanting their name. "Phantasm! Phantasm!" Then music pulsed through the club again as the DJ started playing tunes and the club-goers began swaying to another song.

Angelique glanced at her companion, who seemed content to watch rather than participate. "Is it always like this here?"

Grimel nodded and laughed. "Don't get out much, do you? Yeah, the clubs are always like this. It seems like a living thing all its own sometimes. Looks like our man is here." He carefully motioned toward the entrance with his eyes.

Angelique followed his gaze and saw Reivn walking in, dressed in a black silk shirt and a pair of matching dress pants. She did not get a chance to see much more.

Grimel grabbed her hand and dragged her back to the dance floor. Then he put his arms around her and ground against her while they danced.

"What are you doing?" she hissed between clenched teeth, afraid someone would hear.

"Just play along!" Grimel's expression told her he knew what he was doing, so she relaxed a little, trying to go with the flow of the music. It was not until voices around them grew loud enough to be heard over the music that she realized people had stopped dancing and were staring at someone.

Angelique half-turned and saw Reivn hovering above their heads. A shield of brilliant blue energy radiated from his body as he moved slowly over the crowd. It was obvious he was searching for someone, and she quickly realized it was her.

"Boy, he doesn't ever do anything subtly, does he?" Grimel groaned.

She turned to her companion. "Did you really expect him to? There are no humans here. He is well-known the world over, and many fear his power. I think it's a great way to gain the attention we need to pull this off." She did not have the chance to say anymore.

Reivn's voice echoed like thunder through the club, drowning out the music. "I should have known I would find you here!" He descended to the floor and spun her around to face him.

"Following me again?" Angelique sassed, trying to sound angry. "Why can't you just leave me alone!" His roar caused even her to jump despite the fact she knew it was an act, and she briefly wondered if she had gone too far.

"You dare?" he snarled. "You belong to me! I will not allow you to display yourself in such a disgraceful manner!"

Grimel stepped forward and interrupted. "Now wait one minute, mate. The lady and I were just having a bit of fun. There's no harm done."

Reivn turned and snarled at him. "Step back and do not interfere! This is Mastrics business! Do you even know who I am?"

Grimel stepped in front of Angelique and bared his fangs. "I know who you are and quite frankly don't care! I say the lady stays if she wants to! You got a problem with that then come and get her!" Openly challenging Reivn, he extended his claws and fangs, and snarled.

The crowd pushed back as the air began to crackle with energy, clearing the floor mere seconds before Reivn attacked, his magic exploding into a ball of pure energy.

Angelique screamed. Not sure if it was still an act, she stood frozen with fear until someone grabbed her hand and pulled her clear.

"Boy, you sure do have a way of getting attention, don't you?" Randall grinned at her. "Well, looks like somebody's going to be toast tonight. Hope your new friend likes singed fur. That's the Mastric's Warlord and your friend is just plain crazy."

Fireworks exploded when magic met fists and the two men collided in mid-air. The smoke that filled the room blocked onlookers' vision and the two opponents were lost in its thickness. Growls and enraged snarls caused the club-goers to move back even further.

In the excitement and tension, no one noticed Lunitar move closer to Angelique. He watched her from behind and observed those near her with a critical eye.

Grimel came flying out of the smoke and landed on the floor at Angelique's feet, bleeding from several wounds. "Be right back, love," he grinned. Then he got up and dove back in again.

To her astonishment, he looked like he was enjoying himself.

A second later, it was Reivn's turn. He landed with an unceremonious thud on the floor in front of her. Then after briefly looking at her, he jumped back in.

Lunitar moved closer to Angelique, prepared to grab her if anything went wrong, and watched the fight in silence. Finally, he telepathied Reivn. *You have drawn the attention you needed, my lord. Perhaps now is a good time to stop this.* His concern was rising over the crowd. He knew it would be difficult to get them to safety if the number of people continued to grow.

Security had converged on the spot and stopped the music. Now they stood trying to figure out how to stop the two fighting Elders. The magic had ceased, and the two men were just tearing into each other and snarling in rage. Both were wounded and bleeding, but neither seemed to notice as the fighting continued.

Ryanne came down from her office, her attention drawn by the cessation of music. She froze when she saw the two rolling around on her dance floor, staining the wood with their blood as they fought. Then moving toward them quickly, she screamed out over the crowd. "Stop this! Stop it at once! How dare you do this in my club! Stop or I'll order my people to open fire!" As she spoke, her security team drew their weapons.

Grimel backed away from Reivn and put his hands in the air. "Hey! No problem. I can take a hint." Then pointing at the Warlord, he growled, "This isn't over. I'll be seeing you again!"

Reivn responded by taking one more shot at him and cuffing him on the jaw. The room echoed as several triggers cocked in the deadly silence that followed.

Grimel grinned at Angelique. Then he ran for the door and disappeared into the night.

Reivn turned angry eyes on Ryanne. "This was a matter of claimance. He interfered with my protégée, whom I came to collect." He pointed at Angelique, who stood staring at him, speechless. "I will take my leave for now. I will send you payment for the damages."

Ryanne nodded in acceptance, satisfied that the situation was resolved. "I would appreciate if this didn't come to my club again. You are both welcome of course, but save the battles for an arena, not my dance floors."

When Reivn grabbed Angelique's hand, Randall whispered in her ear, "I'll see you again, sweetheart, but next time leave the boss at home."

Waiting until Reivn and Angelique were safely out the door, Lunitar nodded in satisfaction. Then he slipped into the shadows and teleported back to the Guild to await their arrival.

Outside, Angelique was issued into a waiting Limo. She turned to Reivn. "What were you thinking? You should have known me better than that!"

She was cut off abruptly when Reivn, still bleeding from a cut on his mouth, claimed hers in a kiss. "You are beautiful, do you know that?" He tapped on the window separating them from the front seats as they drove away. Then he smiled.

She stared at him in confusion.

The window lowered and to her surprise, Grimel sat in the front passenger seat. "Hello," he grinned, waving at her.

Angelique stared at him. "You mean this was…"

Reivn laughed and finished for her. "Yes, angel. It had to be believable, so I had to catch you off guard. It was more realistic that way."

She was stunned. "But you actually injured each other!"

Reivn put his fingers to her lips to calm her. "Who among us do you know that fights and does not draw blood? If we had not injured each other, they would have seen right through us."

Grimel grinned. "Besides, I like a good scrap now and then."

*Oh*, her mouth formed the word silently.

Reivn sat back holding his side. Blood seeped through his fingers.

Grimel looked similarly uncomfortable. Glancing back at the wounded Warlord, he grimaced when he saw the wound. "Sorry about that, mate. Hope I wasn't too rough on you."

Reivn smiled, despite the pain. "No more than I on you. That was a good fight."

Nodding in agreement, Grimel sat back exhausted, and they rode back to the Guild in silence.

At the Guild, Angelique was very quiet as she cleaned and healed Reivn's wounds. When she finished, he caught her hand. "What is wrong, angel?"

She sat down next to him. "I never realized our world was so dark. I mean, even after the attack in Atlantic City, it never occurred to me it would always be so violent. You were so different. I don't think I want to see that side of you again. You frightened me."

Reivn squeezed her hand. "You must understand... this is what we are. But my anger will never be with you. Tonight was only for onlookers' benefits. It was an act, angel." He pulled her down to lay with him, cradling her in his arms.

Angelique laid silent, her mind playing out the scene at the club again. She realized then just how powerful the man beside her must be to command such attention from the crowds.

He was playing with a lock of her hair, lost in his own thoughts.

"Reivn?" her soft voice brought him back to the present.

He looked down at her. "Yes, angel?"

She glanced up at him. "I'm glad you're on my side."

He pulled her closer and kissed her. Then he whispered, "Selianaprinde falan," and snuffed out the lights.

## Chapter Thirty-Seven
## Warlord's Conclave

*There are times in our lives when events we did not expect shape the most important aspects of our future, and we can neither stop them nor run from them. We can only embrace them, even when knowing they may each in turn be that final, crushing vortex of adversity that finishes what we have worked so hard to build. The young and stout of heart often act without thinking, their impetuous decisions only serving to further fuel chaos rather than offering a solution to a situation of great difficulty. I cannot shield those I love from any storm if they willingly step out into its fury, and I fear this may be the case now.*

*My angel's heart is in the right place, but she is nowhere near ready to take on such a formidable foe as Cyrus. She is brave, and honorable to a fault, but she does not know where honor ends and wisdom begins. Now all I can do is support her and pray that should she need help, those around me are fast enough and skilled enough to get to her side if I am not be able to do so. The risk to her own life is immeasurable. We go against an unknown foe who has God knows how many allies lying in wait to kill us all, and she offered herself up as a lamb. Why? If she seeks to please me, she could have done so through much safer means. Never before have I been so lost as I am with her. With any other, discipline is as easy as opening my eyes, but with her, I cannot bring myself to say or do anything that would take the joy from those emerald eyes. This action of hers unsettles me in a way I cannot fathom, and I fear for her. God help me... I fear for her, and I am never am afraid...*

*Lord Reivn Draegon*

\* \* \* \* \*

The next evening Jacob was waiting for Reivn and Angelique when they emerged from her quarters. "Well, your plan was certainly successful. This just arrived for the lady." He handed her a bouquet of roses and a card.

Angelique ripped open the card and read.

*I have not met anyone with beauty as radiant as yours in a long time. These roses pale in comparison. I hope to become closely acquainted in the future. You know where to find me. I look forward to seeing you again. Randall.*

Reivn snorted when he read the letter over her shoulder. "As if I would ever let a Galatian court you! Or anyone else for that matter… you are mine."

She giggled when he walked away and handed the roses to Jacob. "Will you see to it these find their way into a vase? I think the main office is a good place, not my private quarters."

"No problem," Jacob replied, watching as the two headed toward the laboratories. He smiled when Angelique caught up to Reivn and slid her hand into his.

"You know I will not share you with anyone, not even for this assignment. Perhaps you should explain that to your new admirer," Reivn growled.

Angelique kissed his cheek, her eyes sparkling with pleasure. "My love, you shouldn't worry so. My eyes see no one but you. I had already planned on telling my new friend I wasn't available. Now, what's on the schedule for tonight?"

He wrapped his arms around her and smiled. "Stage two." Her expression made him laugh, his voice filling the hallway. "Tonight, we meet with the other Warlords that are joining us to deal with this. The Galatian Warlord, Annie Aquila, arrived last night. Lucian is here as well. He's the Thylacinian Warlord. I also invited Jack Dunn to join us. He is an Epochian, which will come in useful, and he is also an old friend."

Angelique frowned, as some thought distracted her.

"What is wrong, angel?" he asked, seeing her confused expression as they entered her lab.

She walked over to the table and picked up the notes she had made the previous night. "I was wondering about the Epochians. I've never met one before."

Reivn laughed and joined her. "Angel, there are several tribes you are still not familiar with. Do not worry. The more you intermingle with our world on a global scale like this, the more you will learn. Epochians are among the oldest of us, but like ours, their tribe is very secretive. They are masters of time, manipulating it at will. How much truth there is to this, few know for certain. But I do know Jack is a warrior few can best."

A short while later, Angelique found herself greeting a tall gentleman who reminded her of the men she had seen in movies about the old west. He wore a long black duster and a cowboy hat draped down to hide his eyes.

When Jack shook her hand, she caught a glimmer of metal from either side of his waist. *He wears guns like a cowboy too.* She smiled at him, and then turned her attention to the Galatian woman beside him.

The only similarity between Annie Aquila and the other Galatians Angelique had met was her skin. It was milk white and translucent. Instead of fine silks and lace, she was dressed in a black, leather full-length bodysuit under her trench coat. She wore black kidskin gloves, and when she shook Angelique's hand, the grips on the underside revealed their purpose.

Lunitar walked in, followed by a fierce looking man over six feet in height. The newcomer's face was almost wolf-like and his eyes were a golden hue. Angelique rightly guessed he must be Lucian, the Thylacinian Warlord, and she curtsied when he approached. Reivn welcomed them into the meeting room as they gathered around the table.

Moravini had also arrived and been seated, while his two guards stood behind him. Now he patiently waited for Reivn to begin.

Grimel was pacing back and forth, somewhat less patient than the company he was with. Lucian strode over to his younger brother. "Grimel! I hear you've been scrapping with Lord Reivn," he chuckled.

Grimel grinned and embraced Lucian. "Well, I couldn't let a Mastric best me, now could I?" he laughed. "I gave as good as I got."

Reivn nodded and rubbed his side, where he still felt the effects of the previous night's fight.

Lunitar joined his father. *Three Warlords, three Elders and a magistrate, father?*

Reivn glanced up. *I am creating the right insurance policy to protect our own.*

Lunitar did not answer. He moved to Reivn's left and took his place behind his father. Then he turned his attention to their guests, looking each one over carefully.

Reivn motioned for everyone to be seated. "Thank you all for coming. This is an urgent matter that cannot be ignored. This enemy is powerful and presents a threat to our entire community. He must be stopped before more humans discover our existence."

Jack looked up. "It must be serious for you to have summoned so many of us."

Annie sat back and stared at Reivn with a serious expression. "Tell us what you know, Lord Reivn. You have everyone's undivided attention."

Reivn nodded in her direction. "Thank you, Annie. My Ambassador and I began laying a trap for Cyrus last night with a little help from Grimel. We sent out a message that let him know there are powerful Ancients in the city, some of us with unskilled protégés in tow. We offered something better than the weak to devour. The hope is that he will take the bait. If he comes after one of us, the others will know immediately. We need to be near enough to each other to respond at a moment's notice. He cannot take all of us on at once. He's not strong enough."

Grimel spoke up then. "Lucian has already authorized the use of any weaponry and supplies we may need from his headquarters here."

"Yes, and my men will join us if needed," Lucian added.

"Good. We will need any you can spare," Reivn answered.

Jack cleared his throat and tapped his finger on the table.

Reivn turned to look at him. "Jack, you wanted to say something?"

Jack's fingers stilled. He spoke without looking up, so his eyes remained hidden beneath the brim of his hat. "Exactly which of us is to be the bait? I'm game, but I'm too well known... you, Lucian and Annie too."

Reivn nodded. "I was coming to that. My Ambassador will be our bait." He pointed to Angelique. "She looks young and pretty and yet is powerful enough to fight in her own right."

Behind him, Lunitar frowned in disapproval, but said nothing.

Annie's undignified snort caused Reivn to scowl. "Her? She looks like she's barely out of diapers, although I agree with the pretty part. She's definitely got that down."

Angelique opened her mouth to respond, but a silent warning from Reivn caused her to close it again quickly.

"Enough," Reivn growled. "We are wasting precious time. Annie, please refrain from hurling insults at my Ambassador. She got the position because of her ability to handle herself."

Jack got up and headed to the door. Then he stopped and looked over his shoulder. "I'm sorry, Lord Reivn, but if you expect me to be a part of this, then I train her my way. I have seen enough senseless death." Without another word, he turned and walked out. His voice drifted back down the hall. "You know where to find me."

An approving smirk crossed Lunitar's face and he dropped his gaze to hide it.

Reivn sighed in annoyance.

Annie spoke up. "He's right. The extra training will only help her. Besides, then one of us is right in the vicinity should our quarry come calling. I wouldn't want to lay any bets on who's going to win if she's alone. I know about Cyrus."

"What can you tell me?" Reivn asked. "His name plagues me from somewhere familiar, but I cannot place it." He frowned and sat down, crossing his arms in front of him as though interrogating a prisoner instead of talking to an ally.

The rest of the assembly sat back and listened with interest.

Annie smiled and leaned on her hand. "To begin with, he's far older than you know…"

The conversation lasted for an hour. Then Reivn, Angelique, and Lunitar said their goodbyes. Then they headed for the office of the Guild, discussing Annie's revelation about Cyrus.

"Wait, Reivn. What are you saying? His reputation here doesn't hint anything like that." Angelique stated. "They haven't found any of the victims' bodies."

He stopped and turned to look at her. "They won't either. If he is the same Cyrus from Achaemenia, then he is a ruthless killer. He hid his atrocities behind the guise of being a generous and benevolent ruler in his day. Hidden from sight he tortured and murdered thousands of innocent victims during his reign."

Lunitar spoke up then. "If he is indeed who they believe him to be and he is a Martulian, then he is far more dangerous than the evidence suggests. When we do find him, we need to take him down quickly to prevent him from jumping into another body to escape.

Angelique frowned. "But they claim he worked with Daemons and prayed to them. There's no evidence of that here."

Shaking his head, Reivn took her by the shoulders. "Angel, sometimes you scare me with your naivety. I think you would find good in the devil himself if given the opportunity. The Alliance considers dealing with Daemons a crime and kills anyone that does so. If he is consorting with them, he will not reveal that to even the youngest among us. You see, unlike the humans who in reality only play at worship, for us, it is very real. Our powers allow us to move among the Gods themselves, actually using our magic to unleash them on earth."

Lunitar shook his head in concern. "This is why you are not well-suited as bait, my lady. You are too inexperienced. That makes you a danger to yourself and those around you. I think training with Jack would be beneficial and would give you a differing view from what you have already learned among our own tribe."

Her shoulders sagging in defeat, Angelique frowned. "I just don't like the idea of condemning someone I've never met to death without being absolutely sure he's guilty."

Reivn pulled her into his arms and kissed her. Then he smiled. "Compassion is not a crime, angel, but blindness is. You must never turn a blind eye to the wrongdoings of any of our kind."

"Please listen to him, my lady," Lunitar added. "Though most of us seek a way to find redemption, there are those who like the darkness and prefer the company of Daemons to that of God. They endanger us all. As my father said, keep your compassion, but open your eyes. My eyes were closed once, and it cost me dearly. I would not see the same become true of you."

Angelique sighed and nodded in understanding.

Reivn stared at Lunitar as though to say something. Then changing his mind, he turned back to Angelique. "It will not be long before Cyrus will leave a calling card," he reminded them. "We must finish our plans tonight. Tomorrow, you'll be meeting with Jack for a while."

Lunitar agreed. "Time is indeed short and if we are not ready, any one of us could pay for it with our life, so there is no room for errors."

The following night, Jack arrived at the Guild shortly after sunset. He stood staring at the painting that hung over the fireplace in the parlor while he waited for Angelique to appear.

Spotting Jack when he passed the doorway, Lunitar walked in and joined him. "Hello, Jack."

Jack turned around and smiled. "How are you?"

"I am well, thank you," Lunitar replied. "I wonder if we might speak plainly for a moment."

Jack smiled. "Is there any other way? What's on your mind?"

Lunitar sighed. "The same thing that's on yours, I'd imagine. Angelique's inability to defend herself is a threat to both herself and to my father as well. Her learning is paramount not only to our success, but to the survival of my father's sanity. His love for her is far deeper than I have ever seen before. I fear losing her would be the end of him."

Jack contemplated his response for a moment before answering. "That is possible, but I have a suspicion you didn't stop in here just to voice the obvious, so what did you have in mind?"

"I want to help with her training," Lunitar answered. "I have worked with her before, so she knows me well enough to know I am quite adept at combat magic. Unlike my father, I will not take it easy on her while she is learning. The physical training I will leave in your hands, but I'd like to be included when you begin schooling her on the spirals."

Jack smiled. "I like the way you think. I will be starting her with the physical portion of her training, but when I'm ready to start her magical training, I'll pull you in to work with her as well. Two teachers from different aspects... excellent."

Lunitar agreed. "I'll wait to hear from you. In the meantime, I'll be continuing my own research in the library. I look forward to working with you again." He shook Jack's hand, then walked out, leaving Jack to wait for Angelique alone.

When Angelique arrived, it was to discover Jack did not approve of her mode of dress. "First we cover the basics. When you know you are going into a fight, you need to dress accordingly." Jack touched the sleeve of her gown. "A gown will only hold you back and could mean the difference between living or dying. If you don't care for modern clothes that much, then a pair of breeches, a shirt, and coat with a good pair of boots is acceptable." Taking her hand, he pulled her toward the parlor door.

"Where are we going?" Angelique asked nervously.

"To get you outfitted better. There's a tailor for our kind not too far from here, and his shop is open all night. Come on." He dragged her after him.

She tried to pull free. "I should not leave the Guild without Reivn's knowledge!" she argued. She was still protesting when they got outside. Then she stopped when she laid eyes on his transportation. "Oh no! I'm not going on that thing!"

He walked over to his motorcycle and climbed on. "It's called a Harley and you can either get on the easy way or I'll put you on the hard way. Give me any more trouble and I'll turn you over my knee and spank you like the royal brat you're behaving as! Now get on!"

Her cheeks flaming red, she scowled profusely and hiked her skirts above her knees. Gathering them closely around her, she climbed on behind him.

"Hold on tight," he told her, tucking her skirt hems under him on the seat. Then he revved the engine and pulled away.

She screamed when they lurched forward and grabbed his waist, clinging to him in fright. "This isn't safe," she screeched.

"I know," he yelled back. The last thing the guards at the Guild heard as they disappeared down the road was his laughter.

The tailor's shop was discreetly hidden in an alleyway in China town. After they parked, Jack pulled her with him behind the building and knocked three times.

An old oriental merchant with long, white braided hair opened the door. "Ah, Master Jack, why you come see me so soon? What you need, new shirt? Fix your coat? Pretty girl. Not your type though." He shuffled into the shop interior and motioned for them to follow.

Jack took hold of her arm and pulled her behind him. "I want you to outfit her for me. Put her in breeches, a shirt, a suitable coat, and boots. She's my newest pupil and needs to learn how to fight. I'll be back in one hour. Oh, and Li, you know what to do if she argues with you."

When Jack returned, an indignant Angelique was sitting in new clothes tailored to Jack's specifications. She held her gown on her lap, wrapped in brown paper. The scowl on her face told Jack she had indeed argued with Li and had been firmly put in her place by the old man.

Chuckling as he walked in, Jack paid the tailor and then held his hand out to Angelique.

She ignored his offer and stiffly got up. Mustering as much pride as she could, she walked out to the waiting motorcycle.

"I'm going to assume she was a bit argumentative?" Jack asked with a grin.

Li wiped his hands off and shook his head. "Nope. No trouble. Just a little lesson in self-discipline. She is feisty. I like that in a woman! You bring her to visit again?"

Jack's loud laughter could be heard half a block away. "If she doesn't behave, I'll be sure to bring her by for tea. Thank you, old friend."

Li bowed and smiled as Jack walked back to the bike and a furious Angelique.

Jack took the package from her and stuffed it into his saddlebag. Then mounting the bike in front of her, he pulled away from the curb and sped back to the Guild.

When they pulled up in front of the building, Reivn himself came down the steps to greet them. "Where have the two of you been?"

Angelique smiled to herself. *Now he'll answer for this.*

Jack stepped off the bike and shook Reivn's hand. "I took her to the tailor and had her outfitted properly for battle. She can't wear a gown if she's going to defend herself. She was resistant to the idea at first, but she came around."

To Angelique's horror, Reivn nodded his approval and he looked her outfit over with a critical eye. "The arena is ready down below. Take as much time as you need."

Bristling with indignation, Angelique jumped off the bike. "Don't I have any say in this? I'm not a puppet, you know!"

Reivn turned around, looking at her with both amusement and curiosity. "You had another idea for training, angel? I trust Jack and I know how well he will teach you. His methods are a little rough around the edges, but his students always learn a lot. That is what I am counting on."

He moved closer and lifted her chin to meet his eyes, noting she was dangerously close to tears. "I want you to stay alive through this. The better prepared you are, the less chance of you disappearing from my world. This is for your own good. Do this for me?"

When she met his eyes, she saw how afraid he was of losing her and slowly nodded.

Jack stood quietly leaning against the wall while Reivn and Angelique talked, patiently waiting for his student. His quiet observations told him much. Angelique was naïve, pampered, spoiled and used to having her way. He knew that to toughen her up, he was going to have to be hard on her. *At least Reivn recognizes this*, he thought as he watched them together. *He obviously prizes her above all others, judging by his actions.*

Finally, Reivn and Angelique finished talking and walked over to him.

Jack straightened up when they approached, touched his hand to his hat and nodded to Reivn. "I trust she is ready to work?"

With Reivn's affirmation, she knew she was defeated. Angrily she brushed past them both and made her way inside.

Reivn exchanged looks with Jack and silently sent him a message. *She will not be easy, you know. She is very proud.*

Jack responded. *She must learn though, or she won't survive. She has the will, now let her learn the skill. I'll be very hard on her. Let her cry on your shoulder at daybreak.*

As Jack headed into the building, he overheard Reivn whisper "Good luck."

Angelique stood waiting in the arena, agitated and angry. *Why should someone from another tribe be allowed to teach me anything?* she fumed.

"…Because you're a petulant child who knows little of our ways."

She turned to find Jack standing a few feet away. "How did you… oh never mind!" Angrily she strode over to the seats by the door and plopped down.

Jack walked over to her. "We really can't start this way. Come, first we need to finish your grooming." He held out his hand, but Angelique ignored it.

Shock ran through her as he grabbed her and yanked her to her feet. Then he propped his booted foot on the edge of the chair and dropped her over his knee. When his hand came down across her backside, she screamed and kicked her feet, but he held her fast. He repeated the motion several more times until tears ran down her cheeks.

Finally, he stood her back up and looked at her harshly. "You are a spoiled brat and there's no room in our world for that! You'll get Reivn killed trying to protect you. If you truly wish to stand as an equal at his side, then you'll take your training seriously! This isn't the aristocracy of medieval Europe and it's a hell of a lot more brutal! If you want to stay alive, then you need to learn to be far more resourceful than you are now."

Turning her around, he began to brush her hair while he spoke, producing a brush from the folds of his coat. "You are intelligent, but very childlike in our ways. Were you already better trained, I would have had a difficult time putting you over my knee as I did just now. Believe me when I say the day will come when no one would ever dare try such a thing. Now," he stated firmly, as he finished pulling her hair into a braid, "Are you ready to learn?"

## Chapter Thirty-Eight
## The Gathering Storm

*Angelique's training proceeds well. Jack has managed to do what I could not. She did indeed need a firm hand. These last few weeks she has cried many times in my arms at sunrise. I see the change in her. She grows more confident with each passing day. The darkness that has claimed us all has finally bled through her innocence and her eyes have taken on a new look. My sweet angel, how I wish I could have preserved you as you were.*

*Laying the trap for Cyrus was easy, but hunting him is going to be far more difficult. I have considered sending Lunitar home. His presence here is important, but I will not risk his life in those tunnels. The size and layout of Cyrus' lair is still unknown. It could run half the breadth of this city. I will not risk taking more than I have to into his net. If he is the Cyrus legends speak of, he could be as dangerous as Alora and as difficult to take down. There is no telling what we will face once we go in. It is enough that I must risk my angel to lure him out, I will not do so with my son as well. At least with only her here, I can more readily protect her. I had hoped to let my children revel in their reunion. It has been years since my children last saw each other. Yet now we must deal with this threat instead of returning home.*

*Jacob and the rest of the Guild here have been very accommodating. This is particularly true of a cleric named Rosalind. She tries hard to see to our comforts. I told Jacob she is to be promoted to Paladin level and become a leader among the clerics. Their caste could use a competent leader and she is very efficient in her duties. She reminds me in many ways of Elena, as she used to be all those centuries ago...*

*Lord Reivn Draegon*

\* \* \* \* \*

Over the next few weeks, Angelique's nights were filled with endless lessons and drills.

Jack began with the art of swordplay, teaching her to use first a western, then an eastern style blade. He taught her to parry and defend against attackers, and she would get whacked with the flat side of the blade each time she missed. "Come on, Countess, strike me!" he taunted her, driving her harder with every move.

Angelique spun around, trying to strike back only to be countered again.

"Move faster, more control on your blade!" he commanded.

Angelique refused to admit defeat and tried again. She missed and got swatted for her trouble.

Jack moved swiftly around behind her and into a defensive stance. "Again! Come at me!"

She charged him again only to be smacked once more when she missed.

Her training repeated this way over and over until she could not just hold her own, but could out-maneuver him. When she had mastered the western blades, she moved on to the eastern ones. Then it began anew, but this time she was ready and picked up the style differences quickly. Before long, she had become a master of blades, turning them into an extension of herself.

Then her training turned to more modern warfare and firearms, and Jack quickly discovered it would be more difficult to teach her because she had an anachronistic view of their use. Nevertheless, she learned how to aim, fire and reload in record time. He taught her about various ammunitions that could effectively kill the different races of Immortals, and how some bullets could carry fast-working poisons. However, learning to recognize different guns was very frustrating to her. "They all look alike!" she complained each time she got one wrong.

At this point, the other half of Angelique's training time was spent learning magic. Jack included Lunitar for this, as promised.

Angelique objected until she saw Lunitar was a master at his craft. Then she gave in and eagerly followed directions, learning to use the spirals in ways she never imagined. During some of these sessions, Reivn would also join them.

All the skills she had previously learned had dealt with more benign forms of magic, not the use of magic in combat. Now she proved to be quite adept at it. She found she could summon lightning and focus it on a specific target, either hitting it with one immense strike or splitting it into as many as five separate bolts to hit multiple targets at once. She realized this was the power she had inadvertently tapped into when she had fought Alora.

Through Lunitar and Reivn, Angelique also learned more about fire manipulation. Now she could not only throw the fireballs she had used against Alora. She could consume a target in flames or cause a form of spontaneous combustion. She also learned to magically douse the flames when they began to burn. When the last of her fire abilities emerged, it proved to be a firestorm that rained molten flames down on any area she targeted. During her first attempt, she set the Guild on fire, and Lunitar had to hurriedly put it out to prevent any serious damage.

Then Angelique discovered that the mist she had transformed into during her fight with Alora had also not been instinct, but a controllable power. She also found she could take on the forms of a wolf or Hawke. She could read energies left by people on things they touched, seeing into the past as though she had been there. This was how she had been able to see Blake's last moments, and the gypsy's. She could connect with those of her own blood through her dreams, as she had done with Armand. She learned that magic was limitless, as long as you dedicated the time to studying it. By the time they were through with her lessons, she had almost mastered the Spirals, and was almost equal to Lunitar.

One night, when Angelique got to the arena, she found Jack quietly conversing with Lunitar.

"Aren't we going to train tonight?" she asked them curiously.

Looking up, Jack smiled. "And what else exactly do you think I can teach you? You have done remarkably well and are ready to go on your own now. I've already notified Reivn. I just came by long enough to give you a gift. It's on the table over there." Then he propped his foot against the wall and waited.

She walked over and stared down at the cloth that covered something large.

"Go on," he answered.

She slowly pulled the cloth away and gasped at the beautiful katana that lay resting on its side. Intertwined twin dragons formed the handle and the hilt was shaped into flames, allowing the dragons to nest in them. She stared at it in amazement. "Where did you get this?"

Jack looked up. "I had it made for you. It will serve you well. Safeguard yourself, Angelique. I don't want to attend your funeral." He turned to leave, nodding to Lunitar as he passed.

She called out. "Jack, wait!"

Jack stopped and turned around.

"Thank you," she blushed and smiled at him.

"You're welcome," he responded. Then he tilted his hat to her and disappeared.

Angelique stared after him, still holding the sword in her hands.

Lunitar walked up to her. "This is one of the rarest moments of your life, so cherish it. Not only is that one of the finest blades I have ever seen, it is a gift from a man who rarely if ever bequeaths one. It would seem you have gained his respect and his friendship, just as you have gained mine... a feat not easily done when it comes to my father."

Angelique turned to look at him. "I am not really that special you know... more of a spoiled child finally learning to take her first steps alone. I should have done this long ago."

"You say you are not special, my lady," Lunitar began. "You could not be more wrong in that assessment, for you turned a Warlord's heart back into that of a man's. Guard yourself carefully, for now you truly are its keeper."

She stared at him. "Is it true I can get him killed? How could he possibly fall?"

He sighed. "You can get him killed through his love for you. He will do anything to protect you and I do mean anything, including sacrificing himself to save you."

Realization crossed her features. "You mean like what almost happened to Armand. I understand. My learning doesn't stop here then. I need to spend time studying on my own."

"Correct. On that note, here is my gift to you." He handed her a leather-bound tome.

Angelique took it carefully and stared down at it. "What is this?"

Lunitar smiled. "This tome contains copies of some of the most powerful spells known to our tribe. Many of the tribes have magic, but none as powerful as ours. Use it wisely and well."

Blushing slightly, she hugged the book and then kissed his cheek. "Thank you," she exclaimed, unable to contain her delight. "I will begin reading it tonight."

He chuckled. "Then I will leave you to your studies and bid you good night."

A short while later, after Angelique had changed her clothes, she went to Reivn's office.

Looking up when she entered, Reivn smiled at her. "I got Jack's message a little while ago. How does it feel to be free?"

She blushed and looked down. "All those nights I cried in your arms seem rather silly now. I've learned so much these past weeks. I don't even feel like the same person."

He got up, walked over, and put his arms around her. "Believe me, you are still the same person, just better. I have a surprise for you." He went to the couch and picked up his cloak. Then he put it around her and took her arm. "Come with me."

He led her down to his lab, opened the portal and teleported them both to the Atlantic City Guild. Serena and Armand were waiting for them.

Serena hugged her friend. "We have missed you so much!"

Armand stood by quietly waiting. Then she hugged him and he smiled. "Welcome back."

They talked for a while in the parlor, catching up on the last few months. Finally, Reivn stood up, and helped Angelique to her feet. Then he looked at Serena. "Would you excuse us?"

"Of course, my lord," Serena answered with a smile.

They said their goodbyes. Then Reivn led Angelique down the hall to his office, which had been locked for many months. After he closed the door behind them, he walked over and opened the French doors to the garden. A soft warm breeze blew in, carrying the fragrance of the roses she loved so much. He smiled and took her hand, then stepped out into the night air with her.

They walked down the path to the river and the boulder where they had shared their first moments together. The they sat down and stared at the water in silence.

Reivn sat watching the gentle waves cresting on the river's edge as the tide rose.

Waiting silently, Angelique wondered what was so important.

After a few moments, he stood and turned to face her. Dropping to one knee, he took her hand and kissed her palm. "I have loved you almost since the first time I laid eyes on you, yet there has always been something keeping us apart. The last obstacle was removed when Alora died. That left a doorway to happiness open for us both. I ask you now, Angelique, if you would have me as your husband, to walk at your side in all things and to love you throughout eternity until our final death." He pulled out a small black velvet box and opened it to reveal an exquisite blood red garnet mounted on woven filigree strands of gold.

Angelique was speechless. She reached out and touched his cheek, nodding her consent.

Reivn carefully took the ring from its box and slipped it on her finger. Then he stood and pulled her into his arms. "I love you, angel," he whispered and held her close.

They stood holding each other until a voice from the path called them back to reality. "Lord Reivn? Are you there? I have a message from New York! They said it was urgent!"

Reivn and Angelique looked at each other in dismay, and then quickly joined the courier.

He waved as they approached and handed a sealed message to each of them. The seal on both was that of Jacob Lowry, the New York guild's Prefect.

"This can't be good. We both got one," Angelique observed as they headed back to the Guild.

When they entered Reivn's office, they stopped to open their letters.

He sat down and stared at the hearth in silence.

She finally put down her own message. "Oh God, how is that possible? So fast? And with no warning? We must find her. It was supposed to be me." Then picking up her letter, she read it one more time.

*Dear Sirs,*

*This is to inform you that Cyrus has claimed yet another victim, this time my second here at the Guild. Rosalind was tending to her duties in my office and found some errands she wanted to run. She left a message that she had gone, but never returned. Consequently, she never arrived at any of her destinations either. A search of the city has turned up nothing. She vanished without a trace, just like all his other victims. Please help.*

*Your servant,*

*Jacob Lowry*

Angelique met Reivn's eyes across the desk.

His expression told her he believed they were too late, and that Rosalind was already dead.

"I want to go look for her," she insisted, looking at him. "…even if it means going down into his lair. We can't just abandon her for dead! I can't do that!"

He did not even look up. "Do not worry," he growled, his voice as cold as steel. "We will not." Throwing his letter into the fire, he walked to the door. "You'll want to tell Armand and Serena our news before we leave. Hurry. I'll wait for you in the lab."

When they stepped back through the portal into New York half an hour later, Jacob was waiting for them. There was no trace of his lighthearted nature, and the worry on his face told them there had been no word. "Rosalind was attentive to everyone with unwavering devotion, but when it came to socializing, she was always shy. She never spoke to anyone other than me really." His agitation was very apparent.

They walked to his office in silence.

Reivn's eyes took on a dangerous look while he listened to Jacob talk of Rosalind.

Angelique listened quietly and realized that Jacob must have feelings for her. *She's not dead yet. I refuse to give her up for dead,* she thought.

They briefly discussed the situation and Reivn decided they were going into Cyrus' lair with a war party. He immediately summoned Lunitar. Then he sent out dispatches to Lord Moravini, Annie, Jack, Grimel and Lucian, along with several other well-known warriors within the city's limits. The dispatches called for a war Council later that night with full attendance while they planned the attack. The responses came back quickly. Everyone felt the same outrage. They all knew Rosalind.

Reivn was ready by the time everyone arrived. He had amassed all the information available on the New York tunnel systems, as well as the reports on Cyrus' hidden lair. The trains that ran underground hid a myriad of lairs that had been built into the very stone of their tunnels. Cyrus' lair was under one of the main lines. "The entrance is a man-hole cover disguised to look as though it was sealed shut," Reivn told them. "That is our way in. Once inside, we divide into two parties, one to find him, the other to find her."

Annie tapped on the table, gaining their attention. "Our intel reported that last time a team went down there, communication even through telepathy was impossible. Cyrus's bargains with the beasts of the pit have afforded him much power. We'll have no contact with each other. Do you have a plan to keep us aware of whether or not the other team is still alive?"

Reivn gazed at the faces around the room. "Long ago I created a spell that when used, is cast on two stones. It creates a beacon on each that links to its companion stone. I can tie all our essences to them. If each party carries one, then we will know each other is alive. If every member tied to their particular stone dies, then so does the stone's signature and the companion stone will cease to give off its glow. A child's spell really, but in this case quite useful."

Lucian spoke up then, concern on his face. "How are we setting up our parties? We should keep an equal number of our most skilled in both groups. Dividing our forces too unevenly would make a target Cyrus is sure to take advantage of."

Reivn nodded. "I agree. Magic will also come into play if he has loosed Daemons in his halls. In truth, we do not really know what to expect other than a poor reception to our presence. Stay alert. Make sure you have plenty of ammunition and weaponry at your disposal. Lord Moravini, what supplies can you provide?"

Moravini shrugged. "I can pretty much supply whatever you need. I have a substantial arsenal here, older weapons as well as newer ones. Just give me a shopping list."

"I also have a well-supplied arsenal in my tower," Lucian added. "We can get what we need from there and grab a few of my people to take with us as extra firepower."

Lunitar spoke up. "I would recommend leaving some of that extra fire power at the entrance of the lair. When things turn bad, he may try to run. They most likely would not be able to stop him, but the delay they provide could help us catch him. I also think we need to have at least one competent scent tracker with each party."

Jack smiled. "I think Grimel and Lucian are more than qualified, although I can't speak for the younger pups," he chuckled when he finished.

Lucian growled. "They are more than qualified as well! Grimel and I will be going with opposite parties to lend our strength to the pack."

Reivn dropped a notepad next to Jack. "Fill it out. Pass it around. Make sure everyone has their name and supply needs on that list. We leave at dusk tomorrow night. Lord Moravini, Lucian, please see to it your people have all the supplies we need here by the end of tonight. If we have any chance of saving Rosalind, there is no time to waste. That is all."

The room filled with the sounds of talking as many of them began making lists of supplies and trading information.

Reivn leaned back, waiting for the noise to die down.

Lunitar walked over and joined his father. "My Lord, may I assume you and I are to go with separate groups so they each have a skilled master of the spirals?"

Before Reivn could answer, Jack hailed him from across the room and made his way toward them. "Lord Reivn, do you have a minute?"

Reivn nodded and motioned toward a seat.

Lunitar stood guard while the two of them talked.

Jack sat down, leaned forward and spoke in low tones. "I don't think Angelique should be in your party. The two of you are among the best magic users here. If you are both in the same party, the other party would be left at a disadvantage."

Reivn did not answer, instead pointing at those still milling around the room. "Have you looked around at all of them?" he asked quietly.

Jack sighed. "I have."

"Half of them will not come back from this," Reivn stated. "I do not want her among them."

"My lord, if I may?" Lunitar interrupted.

Reivn frowned and nodded.

Lunitar glanced meaningfully at Jack before speaking. "Your group will be searching for Cyrus while the other group is searching for Rosalind," he explained to Reivn. "If you send me with the second group, they would have both a Mastric's warrior and a healer if Angelique is with us. Whereas my healing skills are rudimentary, Angelique can handle just about any injury Rosalind has sustained during her captivity."

Jack nodded again in agreement. "Reivn, I'll go with them and watch her back. We need you in separate parties to keep as many alive as possible. You know I am right. She is remarkable... an anomaly. She surpassed even Lunitar's magical ability. You two are the only chance we have of pulling this off with minimal losses."

Knowing there was little point in arguing the matter further, Reivn reluctantly agreed.

Completely unaware of the pact just made between the three men, Angelique was moving around the room gathering warrior's names and supply needs listed for the coming night.

Reivn watched her, amazed with her composure despite the coming danger. S*he does not really understand what we face*, he thought, missing what Jack said completely. A tap on his arm snapped him out of it and he turned around.

"You didn't hear a word I said," Jack sighed. "It's just as well she won't be with you. That would get you both killed. Don't worry, it'll keep. Spend some time with her tonight. Who knows what tomorrow will bring." Jack stood up to leave. "See you tomorrow night."

Lunitar leaned over and shook his hand. "Until tomorrow, my friend."

Reivn frowned when Jack walked away. "He takes me for an idiot," he growled.

"Well, father, you did seem distracted," Lunitar hid a smile. Then he rose. "By your leave?" At Reivn's nod, he walked away. Then he overheard Reivn growl. "I was not distracted."

When everyone finally left, Reivn swept Angelique into his arms and carried her to their quarters, kicking the door closed behind them. He took her to the bed and gently put her down, dropping down next to her. Then he kissed her forehead and pulled her to him. "Tonight angel, no barriers between us." Too troubled to say any more, he pinned her beneath him and began to blaze a trail of kisses down her neck, consumed once more in his desire for her. "God, you are so beautiful!" he whispered. "You fill me with a thirst I do not understand!" He spoke so softly she almost did not hear him.

Angelique wrapped her arms around his neck and pulled him closer, enticing him to drink.

He needed no invitation and bit into her neck, drowning in the sensations her blood gave him. As he drank, he lifted her up and pulled her free of her gown.

She teased him and slowly undid the ties of his shirt, sending fire racing through him.

Quickly shedding the rest of his attire, he slowly ran his finger down her back, burning a trail on her skin with his touch and causing her to shiver with excitement. "My beautiful angel," he growled softly. "Tonight, there is only us."

In the early hours before morning, when their passion was finally spent, Angelique curled into his arms and wept.

Reivn tried to comfort her. "Shush, my love. It will be all right."

She buried her face in his chest. "I'm afraid this might be the last... afraid that you..."

He pulled her closer and held her tight. "Do not be afraid. Fear can cripple you. I have fought in numerous wars and led my warriors to battle many times. This one will be no different. I will always come home. Trust in that."

"I can't help it," she sobbed. "What if..."

He put his fingers to her lips and kissed her tears. "Do not dwell on what if. It will only distract you from the task ahead. Let us just enjoy tonight and let tomorrow take care of itself." Raising his hand, he whispered "Selianaprinde Falan" and doused the torches. Then he reached for her again.

# BLOOD FEUD

## Chapter Thirty-Nine
## The Road to Hell

*Valfort has gone to ground again and now finding him must wait. I have another to hunt. Cyrus Darien... the new name of fear in New York. Among the young, fear is normal and even healthy, but when among the Elders, what does it say? His greatest power thus far is his ability to instill fear in those that had none. I am not among them. In the face of this new evil, I have but one purpose... to hunt and destroy him, and to bring home those who may yet live. Then we will bury the dead and honor them as we always have.*

*When this is over, I have my own plans to make. I will let nothing else come between us. God knows she deserves better than I, but she accepts me as I am, and I love her for it. Through her, I see the world as never before. How did I ever exist in the darkness alone? After centuries of fighting and killing, she shines like a star before me, lighting the way to my own redemption. I know not why, but God saw fit to grant me a new beginning. Until she found me, I had given myself to the cold, relentless night. I never dreamed there was more to our dark existence than emptiness and death. Yet she has awakened something deep within my soul. Yes, when this battle is over, I intend to take her and return home. Draegonstorm has been empty for too long and the surrounding territories have grown wild in my absence. It is high time I take my sons and daughters home and assemble the Honor Guard as it once was. It is time I retire as Warlord and reclaim my throne as Prince of Australia. It is time to reforge the Order. I feel the change in the wind. It is time for the Dragon to awaken...*

*Lord Reivn Draegon*

\* \* \* \* \*

When the war party began to gather the next night, Reivn stood counting their numbers and silently dividing them into two groups. Most had been around a long time and he knew them each by face and name. His frown darkened when he saw some of the younger, weaker Vampyres appear prepared for battle. Looking around, he caught sight of Jack and waved to get his attention.

Jack joined him. "You called?"

"What are they doing here?" He pointed to the young group, standing off to one side.

Jack followed Reivn's eyes to the small bunch milling around and prepping their weapons. "You'll have to talk to Lucian about that one. They're his people."

Reivn nodded and looked for the Thylacinian Warlord. He spotted Lucian a few feet away and walked over to him. "Lucian, why are your young ones here?"

Lucian grinned. "They are vicious fighters, though still relatively young. But they have all gone on campaigns before. They're Thylacinians, so you won't be able to dissuade them."

Reivn rolled his eyes in disgust. He had dealt with Thylacinians before. He knew they did not recognize any authority other than from their own ranks. They considered themselves independent of the other tribes and worried about their own first. Grimel was a Thylacinian, but he was under contract and his interest was money. He stared at the group, trying to figure out what their interest in this hunt was. It was not long before he got his answer.

Grimel walked in and immediately joined them, bringing three others with him.

Reivn walked over to them. "Grimel, may I have a word?"

Grimel grinned and shook his hand. "Sure thing! What's on your mind, mate?"

Reivn pulled him off to the side. "What are your people doing here? Do they realize how dangerous this mission is? They could be killed."

Grimel nodded. "They know, and it doesn't matter. Our code has always been that it is better to die with honor in battle than on the outskirts in shame. They are here because they choose to be. Some of our own people disappeared because of Cyrus. They want revenge."

Reivn gave him a sharp look.

Grimel ignored it. "Come on," he chuckled. "I have some people I want you to meet."

They walked back over to the group that stood waiting to leave. Grimel motioned to the three that had come in with him.

"I want you to meet some of my tribesmen. Bram, Morgan, Hawke, allow me to introduce the Mastrics Warlord, Reivn Draegon. Lord Reivn, these are two of my sons and my daughter. They will be going with us."

Reivn shook hands with each in turn, noting the features they wore. They were obviously Elders and bore the marks of creatures that had run in the wilds too long. Their ears were elongated and slightly pointed, their fangs longer and their claws rougher hewn and more bestial than other Vampyres. Their hair was thicker and coarser than a human's, and each had the scent of the predators they ran with instead of the selective odors of the other tribes. *This is what comes of feeding from animals for too long*, Reivn thought as he greeted them.

The rest of the war party had assembled, so Reivn moved to the center of the room where Annie, Jack, Lucian and Lunitar waited. His eyes settled for a moment on Lunitar and a flash of guilt crossed his features for not sending his son home. But Lunitar was one of his commanding officers and a powerful Mastric as well. His skills were needed in the coming battle. Silently reminding himself of that fact, Reivn turned his attention back to the group.

Lunitar had glanced up and seen his father's expression. He telepathied Reivn. *Father, do not worry about Angelique or myself. I will ensure we are both safe. You do the same. Good hunting.*

Reivn met his son's eyes and nodded.

Angelique stood silently watching as everyone prepared for the coming hunt.

Seeing her expression, Grimel joined her and squeezed her shoulder encouragingly.

"Okay, people! Quiet down and listen!" Jack's voice filled the room.

Everyone fell silent and turned to face Reivn.

Reivn nodded to Jack and then looked around. "As you all know, we are going into Cyrus' lair to find and hopefully retrieve the Mastric's Elder Rosalind, along with any other possible survivors we find. We also plan to stop Cyrus from committing further crimes. Now... I have divided you into two groups. One group goes with Annie, Grimel and I, the other with Jack, Lucian, Lunitar, and Angelique."

Angelique looked up sharply, wondering why she was not going with him.

Reivn saw her expression and ignored it. "All right, the following people are with me..."

Within the hour, the two teams were moving along the subway lines into the tunnel that would take them to Cyrus' lair. They were careful to avoid human contact and the trains. They had entered the underground railway through a secret passage below Moravini's building, in the lair of an Elder Armenian who protected its existence from humankind.

Reivn had avoided Angelique so she could not argue her position in the other group. Now she was moving away from him, following Lunitar and Jack through the tunnels.

Noting the expression on her face, Jack joined her as they walked. "It was my idea, you know. We needed a skilled healer with us in case Rosalind is injured. You, Reivn and Lunitar were the only Mastrics to come. Reivn wasn't keen on the idea, but he saw the sense behind it."

Lunitar overheard Jack and joined them. "He's correct, my lady. Though my father and I are both powerful, neither of us possess the skill level necessary to heal the injuries sustained while trying to reach the hostages, nor any injuries to the hostages themselves. Even with all your skills, we may still be carrying some out with us."

Angelique sighed. "I know. I'm still not sure I am ready for this since I have never been tested in battle, but I do see the sense in what you are saying."

"Did you study the spells I gave you?" Lunitar asked quietly.

She nodded again. "Yes, I did. I read and reread them all carefully. Why?"

He sighed. "Those are powerful spells. If you know them, you will do fine." He glanced at Jack as he spoke. "You were trained well and the warrior, or healer, within you will emerge."

She was silent the rest of the way to their destination.

They reached Cyrus' lair undetected and slipped down through the manhole quickly.

Angelique looked around and found Reivn quickly.

Reivn met her gaze for a moment, masking his fear. Then they went in separate directions and he waved. *Be careful*, echoed in her mind when his silent message reached her.

Angelique watched his group depart. They were so quiet that she heard nothing even with her keen senses. When they had completely disappeared from sight, she turned to follow her own team. Carefully glancing around the corner and into the hall, she found nothing but carved stone and torches hanging on the walls.

*Let's go*, Lunitar telepathied the others. "Se aprinde!" he commanded. The torches flared, lighting their way.

Jack kept careful vigilance, watching for possible traps in the walls, floor, and ceilings.

Lucian followed them, shifting into wolf form and keeping close to the ground. He took the lead beside Jack, his potent sense of smell aiding them as they moved into the dark unknown.

Reaching into the small pouch at her side, Angelique felt for the enchanted stone Reivn had given her. It pulsed in her hand, reassuring her that he was safe.

Jack's hand shot out suddenly, signaling for everyone to stop.

Lucian lifted his gaze and stared down the dark hall. Then he let out a low growl.

Lunitar quickly grabbed Angelique's arm. *Wait,* he telepathied.

Angelique froze in her steps and looked at him, a question on her face.

Lunitar pointed at Jack, who was staring down the hall. Then he motioned a silent warning to those behind him.

Following Jack's gaze, Angelique saw nothing at first. Then her own heightened senses made out a black shape hiding in the shadows.

*It's a Daemon,* Lucian telepathied.

The team raised their weapons and waited for the signal.

When they were ready, Lunitar raised an invisibility shield, hiding their presence long enough to get them close.

The group moved soundlessly down the passage until they were right in front of the beast.

The Daemon stood over twenty feet in height. The acrid smell of charred flesh filled the air. Black ooze dripped from its mouth and claws. When they drew close, it sensed their presence and rose to its full height, spreading massive wings to block the hall. Then it roared out a challenge to its attackers.

Everyone scattered and in seconds, total chaos filled the hall.

Jack opened fire on the creature, pelting its leathery hide with armor-piercing incendiary bullets. But they barely pierced its thick, rough hide.

Lucian and his warriors attacked with both swords and claws, but these made little more than superficial cuts. Then the rest of the party got into the fight, trying to take the beast down.

Lunitar dove deep into his magic, first casting light in front of the beast to temporarily blind it. Then careful not to hit his comrades, he unleashed lightning to try and slow it down.

Angelique stood riveted to the ground with fear. She had never seen anything like the monster in front of them, and she was terrified.

Jack saw her and then realized the Daemon did too. It was moving toward her like a God toward a sacrificial lamb. He screamed her name. "Angelique! Snap out of it! Use your magic! Fight, damn it! Fight!"

Lunitar heard Jack's cries and turned around. When he saw her standing as still as a statue, he moved swiftly to her side and erected an invisible barrier to shield her.

A few feet away, Grimel's daughter Hawke saw what was happening. She moved swiftly to Angelique's side and smacked her hard, almost knocking her to the ground.

Angelique recoiled instantly and angrily spun around.

Hawke merely pointed at the beast bearing down on them.

Angelique realized with shock that the girl was trying to snap her out of it. She immediately turned her attention back to the battle. Then with a deep breath, she summoned the spirals. Her hands sparked, and then exploded into a deadly lightning bolt that struck the beast in the chest.

The Daemon roared in fury, the gaping hole in its chest smoldering where it was hit.

For a moment, Lunitar was stunned. Then he shook himself and telepathied the party. *Angelique has breached its armor. Focus on that spot.*

Jack wasted no time. He drew his sword and yelled for the rest of them to follow.

Lucian shifted back to human form. Then he swiftly drew his sword and ran up the wall at inhuman speed. He gained enough momentum to get up and over the Daemon, and he slashed out one of its eyes as he passed over it.

The rest of the group needed no invitation and doubled their efforts. Angelique and Lunitar unleashed a steady barrage of lightning to lay down cover fire.

Two Thylacinians leapt for the Daemon's back. The first one, named Lynx, managed to drive his blade into the Daemon's wing. Then he rode it down as his dagger ripped through the beast's thick hide. But the other Thylacinian missed her mark. She hit the ground hard inches away from their target and was momentarily stunned.

The Daemon was screaming in pain and rage, as it swung at its attackers. Now it made a grab for the girl on the ground.

"Watch out!" Lucian's warning came too late.

The beast caught her by the throat and ripped it open. The young girl gurgled as blood flowed from the deep wound and she struggled to free herself. But the Daemon was too powerful. It plunged its claws into her chest and crushed her heart. Then it dropped her lifeless body.

Horrified at the Thylacinian's brutal death, Angelique screamed angrily and shot another lightning bolt into the Daemon's chest.

It turned on her with a vengeance.

Members of the team moved in and blocked its advance. Then an Armenian landed a good blow with his blade, cutting into the hole in the beast's belly and opening it further.

The Daemon roared in pain when its innards were exposed and swung its immense claws down on him.

The man hit the wall hard and fell to the ground.

Lucian howled, calling to his kinsmen. They followed his lead and jumped in front of their fallen comrade to defend him.

The Daemon shrieked and clawed at them as their bullets tore into it. It razors found their mark, sending one of them flying backward.

The man got up with a snarl and jumped back into the fight, ignoring the blood seeping from his shoulder.

Aiming for the opening the Armenian had made bigger, Lunitar sent a fireball into its innards, setting them ablaze.

Jack saw the opportunity and signaled the team to move in for the kill. Then he yelled. "Finish it!"

Angelique saw Lunitar's attack and followed his example. Within seconds, the Daemon's innards began to shrivel as the flames burned hotter within its belly.

Jack let out a war cry, leapt into the air, and drove his blade deep into the monster's throat.

Lucian drove his sword into the monster's chest, drawing its rage while Lynx aimed for its other eye.

The beast thrashed around wildly trying to fend off its attackers. It caught a Victulian moving in on it from the left and cut him almost in half with its razor-sharp claws. The man fell to the floor, bleeding profusely from his exposed innards.

Angelique saw him go down. She immediately forgot about her own safety and dropped to her knees, and then crawled over to heal the fallen Victulian, who was still alive. She carefully tucked his insides back in, trying to close the wound to prevent further blood loss. Although shaking from the pain, the man suddenly raised his gun and shot passed her as the beast bore down on them both. Then he lost consciousness.

Lunitar instantly saw the danger Angelique was in and tried to get the beast's attention to lure it away from her and the man she was trying to save. He focused his power on the Daemon's existing wounds and hurled fireballs at it as fast as he could create them.

Several party members jumped in to intercept the monster when it continued toward the helpless two on the floor.

The beast whirled around again to meet their renewed attack.

Jack leapt onto its back and began a steady climb upwards.

Taking advantage of the distraction, Lucian grabbed both the Victulian and Angelique and dragged them both to safety. As soon as they were clear, he turned back to the fight.

The warriors struggled to keep the monster busy to try and give Jack time to inch his way up the Daemon's back.

Jack's progress up was slow. The beast kept trying to shake him off, and he had to repeatedly dodge its claws. Then he would hold on tight as the creature slammed into the wall. Finally, he reached the top and drove his blade down through its skull and into its brain. The Daemon collapsed as life finally left its body and Jack rode it to the ground.

Scattered around the hall, the warriors waited a moment to be sure it was dead. Then one by one, they sat down or laid on the floor, drained from the fight. Some leaned against the walls for support, while others just laid where they landed.

Angelique looked around in stunned silence. A Thylacinian girl was dead and several others were seriously injured, the Victulian severely enough to be evacuated to the surface. Then Jack groaned, drawing her attention. She turned and cried out when she saw he was hurt. "Jack!"

Blood was pouring down his arm, but he pushed away her attempts to help him. Ripping his sleeve off, he tied it around his wound. "Take care of the others first," he insisted.

Angelique nodded and walked away, still shaken by the sheer brutality she had just witnessed. Numbly, she began healing the worst of some of the wounds.

Lunitar grinned when he saw Jack's refusal and walked over to them. Then he cast a minor healing spell to close Jack's wound. "Quit showing off for the ladies, Jack. There's time enough for that later." He chuckled and smiled at Angelique, trying to lighten the mood.

"Fair enough," Jack laughed. Then he began getting everyone organized. He directed two of their party members to evacuate the Victulian to Moravini's people, who were stationed above. The remaining warriors waited until they had disappeared back toward the entrance before they moved on to the tunnel leading downward.

Angelique turned around. "What was that thing?" Her voice shook.

Lucian joined her. "That was almost as bad as it gets. That thing was a Daemon warrior. Fortunately for us, it was not a black angel. If it had been, our losses would have been far greater, if we survived the encounter at all. As it is, we've lost some of our strength."

Angelique stared at him. "I didn't realize they could actually come into our world like that. I thought Reivn was merely using them as a metaphor of what evil we could face."

"There's something you need to learn about our world, my lady," Lunitar responded, as he picked up the fallen Thylacinian's weapons. "When you are in training and the Warlord speaks, it's the truth. It is not a facsimile of what could happen. You had best be prepared to move or lose your life. And if you freeze at our next encounter, I will repeat what Jack did to you in the training room if we survive the fight. You do not have the luxury of hesitation anymore."

Leaning over to pick up the other weapons that lay on the floor, Jack never even looked in their direction. Instead, he pulled a torch from the wall and moved forward. "If we are lucky, Daemon warriors will be the worst of what we find down here," he growled. "We all need to be ready to fight. The losses we had here were unnecessary."

Ashamed, Angelique fell silent and followed him.


At the end of the hall, Lunitar disarmed a door sealed with heavy magic.

The group entered the small room behind it. It was furnished scantily and stank of age, as though it had been abandoned for some time. Then a quick search of the room revealed a door hidden behind an enormous wardrobe.

Lucian pulled it away from the wall, and then nodded to Lunitar.

Lunitar stepped forward and broke the seal. Then he carefully opened the door.

The room beyond smelled of old, dead blood.

Jack carefully held forth the torch and peered into the room.

The sight before them sickened Angelique.

Bodies hung upside down from the ceiling on meat hooks, throats cut and blood drained. Many had holes in their chest where their hearts had once been. Some were mutilated beyond recognition. The group walked through the room staring in silence at the horror around them. Then Lynx howled in anguish, reaching for a young girl hanging above him. "No!" he cried. His voice broke as he desperately tried to lift her down.

Lunitar levitated upward and carefully dislodged the young girl's lifeless remains. Then he lowered her into Lynx' arms and floated back down in grim silence.

Lynx dropped to his knees, holding her body in his arms and howling in anguish. He brushed the matted hair away from his sister's face and wept at the vacant expression in her eyes. "We can't leave them here!" he cried, the pain in his voice filling the room around them.

Lucian placed his hand on the man's shoulder. "Come on, Lynx. We can't help them now. We will come back for the bodies when it's over and Cyrus is dead."

Angelique felt for the enchanted stone in her pouch again, reassuring herself that Reivn and his group were still alive somewhere in the bowels of this den of evil.

Lynx held the body of his sister for a minute longer before reluctantly easing her to the floor. Then he got up and made his way to the door on the other side of the room. "Let's go find this bastard and show him what true pain is!"

No one said a word as they left the sad scene behind them in grim silence.

Over the next five hours, they fought Daemons and all manner of other unnatural creatures as they made their way from room to room. One by one their warriors fell, and their numbers dropped by half. They came across more bodies in a chamber of ritual sacrifice that was bathed in the blood of those Cyrus had killed. But they found no sign of Rosalind.

Lucian scouted each room in turn, then telepathied his findings to the team before entry, so they were not caught off guard again.

Despite being further injured, Jack stayed near Angelique and Lunitar to ensure their safety.

Angelique was also wounded, but still adamantly stood her ground to defeat each creature they faced.

At her side, Lunitar, though physically uninjured, was beginning to feel the pain of repeatedly delving into the spiral's magic without rest. But he refused to let any of them see it, knowing they heavily depended on him.

The war party finished clearing the hallway and pushed deeper into the lair. Then they came across what appeared to be a great arena. The room was shrouded in shadows.

Lucian took the lead, his senses alert.

Keeping their ranks close, the group entered the room cautiously.

Jack watched their flank, and entered last, his keen eyes watching the hall behind them.

Sudden laughter echoed off the walls and the group formed a protective circle, carefully covering each other as they looked around.

The laughter vanished and the voice taunted them. "Have you come to try and kill me? How amusing that I instill such fear. Fools! Neither you nor your friends elsewhere in my house will leave here alive! Come then, children! Come and claim me, if you dare!"

The party moved carefully along the walls to avoid becoming open targets. Then one of their men screamed as he disappeared, dragged into the wall by a hand from the shadows.

Lucian yelled. "Get away from the walls."

"Tana Arovite!" Lunitar shouted, quickly conjuring the shield around them. *Stay close to me*, he telepathied.

Angelique frantically looked around, seeking a way to even the odds. Finally, she spotted a wooden support beam that ran around the entirety of the room's ceiling. She summoned the spirals. "Se aprinde!" she cried, directing the magic to ignite the dry wood. It instantly flooded the room with light from the flames.

"Clever little witch," Cyrus called out. "You've doused my shadows! However, it is a minor inconvenience, at best! I have other tricks to amuse myself with."

The floor beneath one of their women vanished. She screamed and dropped into the hole before anyone could grab her. The floor instantly reappeared and closed off any chance of helping her.

With a cruel laugh, Cyrus taunted them. "Thank you! I will enjoy her later! Who's next?"

Jack telepathied Lucian, Lunitar and Angelique. *Above us on the beams, do you see him?*

Lunitar nodded. He had spotted Cyrus hiding above them as well.

Angelique slowly glanced up, hoping their quarry would not notice. She barely caught sight of movement on the ceiling beams high above them. *I see him*, she answered.

Jack moved closer to them. *Can you hit him with your magic from here?*

Angelique tried to gauge the distance. *I can try.*

Jack smiled and sent her one last message. *It's all we've got and it's better than being picked off here one at a time.*

Lunitar sent back, *I will stop him. You hit him... now!* He erected a magical barrier in front of Cyrus, momentarily halting his movement.

Angelique narrowed her eyes and sent a lightning bolt surging toward Cyrus. It exploded against his chest and knocked him backward off the beam.

Cyrus plummeted to the ground and hit the floor with a sickening thud. He immediately rolled sideways to avoid blows from Lucian and Lynx. Then he jumped to his feet and uttered a command, and fire rained down on them.

The party scattered, dodging the balls of flame that pelted the ground around them.

Lunitar yelled, "To me!" Then he cast a magical force field around them to deflect the blaze.

Angelique countered Cyrus' flames, shooting out a firestorm of her own.

Cyrus hissed at her as he quelled the flames that engulfed him. "Well done for a whelp," he sneered. "Try to defend from this!" He laughed and waved his hand, opening a hole beneath her.

Caught off guard, Angelique fell through. She barely managed to grab the edge in time.

"Hold on!" Jack yelled and dove to catch her. Grabbing her arm, he started to pull her up when the hole began to widen, and the ground started to disappear beneath him.

Lunitar shouted a warning. "Watch out!"

Jack backed up quickly, dragging her with him.

Lucian grabbed them both and pulled them to safety.

As Angelique stood back up, she spun around in anger. "My turn," she snarled at Cyrus, surprising even Jack and Lunitar with her vehemence. She summoned another lightning bolt, hitting him hard and sending him flying backward.

The rest of the party took her cue and attacked.

Cyrus doused the torches with magic and called forth the shadows again, commanding them to rip into his attackers.

Lunitar immediately dropped the shield and turned his attention back to their enemy. "So you don't like fire? Then how about this?" He encased Cyrus' legs in solid ice.

Angelique shot Cyrus a second time, and then hit the torches with fire, lighting them again and driving back the shadows.

The party surrounded Cyrus and attacked with a vengeance.

Cyrus threw spell after spell at them, seriously wounding some and draining the power of others as they used their own magic to defend themselves. But the team scored hit after hit, slowly weakening him, until finally, they moved in for the kill.

Just as they dealt Cyrus the final blow, he pooled the remainder of his strength and cast his most powerful spell, jumping his soul from his dying body into Lynx. Then before anyone realized what he had done, Cyrus disappeared through a wall in his stolen body, leaving the Thylacinian's soul trapped in his abandoned dying shell.

Jack dropped down next the body in which Lynx was now imprisoned and held his hand.

Lynx stared up at him, struggling to hold on. He coughed, and blood trickled down the side of his face from the internal damage to the body he was now in. "Please... my sister... Take her home... for me..." Anything further was choked out by blood as his life faded.

"He's gone," Lucian stated quietly. "And Cyrus has escaped."

Lunitar walked over and stood by the body. "We need to ensure he can never reclaim this body," he stated.

Jack nodded slowly in agreement.

Lunitar whispered a quick prayer, and then ignited the still body on the floor.

Battle-worn and weary, Jack got up and turned to the others who stood quietly by. "Let's finish our search and go home. I'm sick of this place."

# BLOOD FEUD

## Chapter Forty
## A Night to Remember

*Grief is such a terrible emotion… I see it in the faces all around me, as those here try to put their losses behind them from the senseless killing. Despair on the faces of those that have lost partners or young, I watch them and yet can feel naught but relief that my angel was not among them. Even the near loss of Grimel only slightly dampens my heart. He is a warrior, and much like myself, is prepared to lay down his life for the fight.*

*Cyrus ran, but at least those here are safe. I need to turn my attention back to the problem of the Principatus and Valfort. I imagine by now he is working on resurrecting Alora from her long sleep in Hell. If I cannot find him before he succeeds, then I must be ready for them when they return. The vendetta he pursues with me and mine is not yet over. I only pray I have time to locate him before he can complete his endeavor to bring her back. If she returns, Angelique will be in far more danger than she has ever been before. I will not allow them to use her against me.*

*I sent in my request to be relieved as Warlord to both Mastric and the Council recently. They have not yet answered my letters. The offer I have given in return I cannot see them as refusing. They are largely greedy in their desires. I will remain as their Commander-In-Chief, but I will use my own fortress as the main base of operations from which to wage their war. They would have the territories there secured in the name of the Alliance and I would have my freedom.*

*It has been centuries since I was able to stay in any one location for longer than a month or so, without traveling elsewhere on another assignment. I look forward to evenings in my own home with my beautiful angel at my side…*

*Lord Reivn Draegon*

\* \* \* \* \*

Angelique stood silently trying to reach Reivn. The stone still glowed, so she knew they were alive, but she wanted to tell him what had happened. She was still as death, concentrating on him, and then she heard his voice.

"Angel?"

She jumped as someone touched her arm and spun around.

Reivn stared at her, worry crossing his weary features. Behind him, stood less than half his party, several severely injured among them.

Angelique threw her arms around him and began to cry.

Lunitar gazed at his father in relief. But his heart sank when he looked over Reivn's shoulder.

Several of Reivn's group were carrying bodies, among them Rosalind's. Torn apart and emptied as many of the others had been, her pale face was battered, and told of the suffering Cyrus had inflicted on her before she had finally, mercifully died.

Angelique saw them too and stared in shock.

"We were not fast enough," Reivn stated quietly. "Our losses were far greater than I feared and far more tragic."

He moved aside and Angelique caught sight of Bram, holding Grimel in his arms. The old Thylacinian appeared lifeless, the gaping holes in his chest and side bleeding profusely.

"Is he...?" Angelique could not bring herself to ask that dreadful question.

Reivn shook his head, the lines on his face creased with weariness. "He lives... for now."

Lunitar stood by in silence, his hands behind his back to hide the burns he had endured from the spirals.

Lucian walked over. "Cyrus got away and we've lost half the party. I say we clean out this place, burn it and bring the bodies home for proper funerals according to their tribe's traditions."

Reivn agreed. "We found a portal to hell back there and shut it down. That was how he brought the Daemon warriors here. I think we got them all, so let us level this place."

Jack and Annie agreed and began rallying others to collect the bodies they had found.

It took the remainder of the night to gather the dead and bring them back to the Guardian's lair where they could be identified and delivered to their tribes for burial. By dawn, four hundred and sixty-seven bodies had been collected. The lair was finally empty. However, there was no time to return to their own sanctuaries, so everyone gathered in the Guardian's haven to rest until nightfall.

Reivn pulled Angelique down next to him on the floor and held her close.

While other were collecting the dead, Angelique had spent the remainder of the night working on the wounded, and she was exhausted.

Reivn knew she would desperately need to feed when she woke, as would they all. He kissed her forehead. Then he closed his eyes and quietly whispered as he drifted into sleep. "I'm proud of you, angel. You did well tonight."

Lunitar sat leaning against a wall nearby, watching them, and waiting for them to sleep. He was worried. *Cyrus may somehow return and strike us down while we sleep. Someone needs to keep watch.* Once his father had drifted into slumber, he closed his own eyes and cast a final spell for the night. He summoned the flames of wrath, an excruciatingly painful blue fire that would engulf him, but leave his body unharmed. This spell was known to all Mastrics, as it was vital in the training period to teach self-discipline. It was also often used as punishment for young ones that refused to be obedient to their Elders. It would keep him awake. Wincing as the pain set in, he sat back and settled in to keep watch through the night.

Shortly before anyone awoke the following evening, Lunitar stood up and groaned from the agony his body still endured. Quelling the spell around him, he took a slow deep breath as the flames subsided and the pain slowly vanished. Then after allowing himself a minute to fully recover, he began walking around and waking those still in slumber.

"Lunitar, a word?" Reivn stated from behind him.

Lunitar turned to find his father awake and gazing at him intently. "As you wish, my lord."

Reivn motioned for Lunitar to join him in a corner, where they could talk in private. "I understood the intent behind your actions. However, I find it a bit extreme to put yourself through such an ordeal on top of the strain you felt from our battles below. Perhaps a different approach would be wiser in the future."

Lunitar met his father's gaze without fear. "What approach would that be, father. Everyone was exhausted from the night's encounter and there was no one to stand watch. I would not allow a creature such as Cyrus to come amongst us while we slept or allow one more to die. There has been too much of that already. The butcher's bill was far too expensive this venture. Better one tired Mastric than any more lost beyond recall." He kept his hands behind his back, where Reivn could not see them as he spoke.

Reivn frowned and reached out, pulling one of Lunitar's arms forward to expose his hand. "Did you think I would not notice? You forget how well I know you. I trained you and raised you in our ranks. You have been at my side far too long to be able to hide such things from me."

"It was not as much to hide, father, as to relieve the strain on an already burdened mind. I promised you long ago I would never deceive you. Nor would I ever hurt you." Lunitar shifted his gaze for a moment to Angelique, who was across the room helping others that still felt the strain of the previous night's war. "That does not mean I will not do what I can to protect you or our family. You are as important to me and our family as she now is to you."

Reivn stood silent for a moment, contemplating his answer. Finally, he replied, "I have never questioned your ideas or judgment, merely the execution and punishment you are willing to inflict on yourself in order to aid others. I had erected both a warning spell and an awakening spell on this place last night. Any movement or magic occurring in this lair instantly alerted me. That is how I knew what you had done."

Lunitar sighed. "Well-noted for future, father, but I still prefer a pair of eyes over magic."

Reivn put a hand on Lunitar's shoulder. "And I still prefer a son to a burnt-out corpse. Delving so deeply into the spirals that it burns you..." he indicated Lunitar's hands as he spoke. "...may have been necessary during the fighting, but not as much here. Your body must stay ready for the next encounter we will face. This kind of damage only weakens you."

"Understood, father," Lunitar acquiesced.

Reivn turned to look around at everyone who was now up and moving. "See Serena about your hands when she gets here. She has the unique ability to heal even that harsh of a wound."

Lunitar bowed. "Yes, my lord."

The two men joined the others preparing to head home. Angelique had just finished the last of the healing she could do. Working together to get the stragglers on their way, Reivn, Lunitar, and Angelique finally returned to the Guild. Lucian, Jack, and Annie had taken their leave to go back to their own duties within New York City, and Lunitar retreated to his quarters to rest.

After settling Angelique in to rest, Reivn filled in Jacob and sent a dispatch to Serena, requesting immediate aid.

Grimel hovered between life and death, and he remained unconscious. Reivn had him taken to the guild's infirmary to await Serena with the other casualties that still needed attention. When she finally arrived, she began working feverishly over those with the worst of the injuries. Her presence was quickly felt as nights passed in the endless task of healing the survivors.

The evenings that followed were difficult as the New York Immortals recovered from their losses. Cyrus' lair had been cleaned out and all traces of it destroyed. The bodies of his victims were one by one burned, erasing all evidence of their existence, and the city's Immortals fell into silent mourning for the dead.

Reivn and Angelique assisted where they could and took care of the funerals of those unfortunate souls no one could identify. The dead among the Mastrics were fewer than most, but still counted heavily in number.

In the underground crypt where the dead were traditionally burned, Angelique stood silently watching as Rosalind's body turned to ash. She wanted revenge. Reivn had tried to comfort her, but for her there was none, nor would there be until Cyrus had been found and put to death.

After the funerals were over, Angelique wanted to plan the search for Cyrus. She found Reivn in his office talking with Lunitar. They looked up when she entered and fell silent. "Are we going home soon? I want to help catch Cyrus. I thought we could plan it while your enforcers hunt for new leads," she stated.

To her surprise, Reivn shook his head. "I want to remain in New York for a time. I have an important matter to see to," he explained, glancing at Lunitar.

Lunitar smiled, silently waiting for them to finish their discussion.

"Anything I can help with?" she asked, frowning at his illusive answer.

Reivn shook his head. "Not this time. I do not want you hunting Cyrus anyway. Leave him to me. Your duty lies in helping Jacob restore operations here. He will need a new Paladin."

"I suppose." She looked from Reivn to Lunitar, who was staring at the fire. "I can see I'm interrupting the two of you, so if you'll excuse me…"

Reivn nodded, and then waited until she was gone. Then he smiled. "Three weeks will be all I need. Send for your brothers and sister, and for the rest of the family as well. Also, retrieve our dress uniforms. We will need them."

Lunitar smiled at his father's enthusiasm. "I will see to it, father. Everything will be ready on time. I am curious about one thing, however. What other family is expected?"

Reivn chuckled. "Our family extends beyond just you and your siblings. Jack's daughter, Lissa, will be here too. Gideon knows them all."

Lunitar raised an eyebrow. "Very well. I will be sure to speak with him and make the necessary arrangements. Will that be all, father?"

Reivn leaned back and gazed at his son, his eyes full of hope. "For now."

"Then I will take my leave and say goodnight." Lunitar stood up.

"Of course. Good night, my son." Reivn answered, looking down at the list on his desk.

Lunitar bowed and left. As he walked down the hall, he was still smiling.

As Angelique walked away from Reivn's office, her mind was racing. She could not stop thinking about Rosalind. Finally, she decided to begin the search for Cyrus anyway, and hastened to restore the operations at the Guild so she could finish the task quickly. She wanted to start planning.

For many nights, she did not see much of Reivn except at dawn when they slept. It was then that Immortals began arriving and taking up temporary lodgings in safe havens around the city. She kept a close watch on them in case Cyrus had disguised himself and was trying to slip back in. She had the names of any that arrived almost before Moravini himself knew of their presence.

Then one night, he pulled her aside. "News has reached me of how closely you watch the comings and goings of our kind here. I knew you would make a fine ambassador, and now you have surpassed even my expectations." He kissed her forehead and turned to go, but at the door, he stopped. "By the way, you should start thinking about a gown. I can arrange the rest, but gowns of that sort are not in my area of expertise. I will see you later tonight." He left her speechless, staring after him.

She spent the rest of the night trying to figure out what he meant. She contacted people she knew he had met with only to be told she had to speak to him directly. By the time she got to their room that night, she was beside herself with curiosity. "What did you mean when you said I needed to think about a gown? Our wedding isn't..." she was cut off as he kissed her.

"For at least another week," he interrupted, finishing the statement for her.

"I'm being serious!" She expected him to laugh.

Instead, Reivn sat quiet, a serious expression on his face.

Angelique stared at him. "You're not joking...are you?"

"The rest of our family arrives tomorrow." He got up, pulled her into his arms, and kissed her. "I have never been more serious in my life. The last few months have shown me just how precious you are to me, and I do not want to let the moment pass to be able to call you mine. We have waited long enough. You do still want to marry me, do you not?"

She sighed and smiled at him. "I couldn't want anything more. It's just that Cyrus..."

He touched her lips gently, shushing her. "Cyrus, Valfort, even Alora... they are precisely why we should marry now. There will always be an enemy seeking to disrupt our lives. I am not going to give them what they want. Say yes, angel."

She silently agreed. Her eyes glistened with happy tears that threatened to come forth.

Angelique spent the next few nights shopping for the perfect gown with Serena, but she found nothing that appealed to her. Finally, they hired a seamstress to make it, styling it much more seventeenth century than anything she had been able to find. A rich crimson accented with spun gold, the gown had a dropped neck and lengthy train, and promised to be exquisite.

She quickly learned that most of the Immortals arriving in the city were in fact there for the wedding. Even an Elder from the Mastrics Council had come to witness the event. Reivn not only knew them, he had invited them.

The night of the wedding finally arrived. The main ceremony was to be at Lord Moravini's mansion, in a rather large family chapel, and the banquet afterward would be in his sumptuous ballroom. Serena was as excited as Angelique. She had acquired his permission to hire a decorator and had turned the entire place into a medieval palace.

Angelique had asked Serena and Genevieve to stand as her ladies in waiting. There would also be two young women Reivn had brought from Draegonstorm, neither of whom she had yet met. She greeted them with enthusiasm when he explained they were his granddaughters, Reyna and Anya, from his daughter Mariah.

Reivn insisted that Jack, Lunitar, Moventius, and Kaelan stand with him. But when Lunitar was told of his intentions, he pulled Reivn aside quietly. "Father, I realize you and Gideon don't see eye to eye, but he has always stood by you loyally. He deserves to be included in this, so I wish to bow out in his favor."

Reivn frowned at him. "I do not want you bowing out of my wedding. I asked you because I choose to have you stand at my side."

"Begging your pardon, father, but I would not feel right doing so while Gideon remained on the outside." Lunitar stood his ground and gazed intently at his father, daring his anger.

Glaring at his son for a moment, Reivn finally gave in. "Fine. I will include Gideon in the party, but you will still likewise do so. I will make the necessary arrangements."

Lunitar nodded, but he was not finished. "What of a partner for him? Whom will you ask?"

Reivn shook his head. "I am not sure. He is halfway around the world and still working on his own assignment. I do not even know if he will be able to get here in time."

"If you summon him, he will come," Lunitar answered. "May I suggest Lissa join the wedding party? She would finish out the number nicely."

Irritated now, Reivn growled. "Make it so."

Lunitar bowed. "Thank you, father. I'll send for them immediately."

Reivn watched him go in silence, then sighed and turned back to the wedding plans.

The day before the wedding Serena had refused to let Reivn sleep next to Angelique, insisting he instead take rooms at Moravini's stronghold with the other male members of the wedding party.

Reivn's brother Germineau, a priest from the Mastrics own Council, was to be performing the ceremony. He was among the most respected members of their society and an advisor to Mastric himself. Upon hearing Serena, he insisted Reivn stay with him in his own suite.

When night fell, there was much activity at the Guild. Serena and Genevieve wept as they helped Angelique get dressed and did her hair.

Armand had the honor of giving her away and was waiting in the main hall for them to emerge from Angelique's room. His thoughts were on Blake. *Part of me wishes you were the groom. I miss you, brother*, he thought and turned to the empty stairwell for the thousandth time.

Then Angelique descended the stairs escorted by the other ladies.

Armand gasped at the mental image Serena sent to him. Angelique had never looked more radiant than she did now, and he realized she truly was in love with Reivn. Smiling at her, Armand took her hand and escorted her to the waiting limo.

The ride to Moravini's was filled with excited chatter. Armand was grateful for it since no one noticed his silence. He was thinking about Blake, Angelique and Reivn, and how the last year had played itself out. He realized that had Blake lived, Angelique would never have been as happy. The love she bore Reivn was a woman's, but her love for Blake had been that of a dear friend. Somewhere during that ride, he finally found the peace within himself he had been searching for all those years, and he sat back, enjoying the happy sounds filling the car.

Reivn entered the chapel with his men and stood listening as the first strains of music by the orchestra floated down from the balcony. When Gideon told him the bridal party had arrived, his heart filled with anticipation. Now he stood impatiently waiting for her to enter. Jack stood at his side, followed by Lunitar, Moventius, Kaelan and finally Gideon. Each wore the gold-trimmed black and crimson dress uniforms of the Dragon Guard... and Reivn's personal colors.

Germineau stood, bible in hand, in front of the altar, ready to officiate. The room was filled with friends and well-wishers from all over the world.

Genevieve entered first, walking slowly down the aisle, followed by Lissa and then Anya. Behind them came Reyna and finally Serena. Each stopped in front of Germineau and curtsied respectfully to the Elder. Then they moved to their positions as the music announced the bride's entrance. All eyes turned to the giant oak doors and the guests rose to their feet.

Out in the hall, Armand squeezed Angelique's arm lovingly. "Are you ready?" he asked.

Angelique hugged him one last time and nodded. Then she turned as the doors opened. Her eyes sought Reivn's as she walked down the aisle on Armand's arm. She could see the pride, joy, and love that poured from him as she approached, and she smiled, her own joy filling her to the core and bursting forth with radiant light.

Standing beside Reivn, Jack grinned and nudged Lunitar.

Reivn bowed and took Angelique's hand, as Armand stepped back. Then the two faced Germineau.

The old priest smiled and began. "Friends, kinsmen, children, we are here to celebrate a timeless renewal of life and tradition…"

Angelique wandered in her mind to St. Etienne and her beginnings. *My life is complete*, she realized. *I have become who I was meant to be.* The rest of the ceremony passed by in a blur until Reivn lifted her veil, draping it down her back.

Jack presented a goblet to Germineau who then held it forth to the two of them.

Following tradition, Reivn ceremoniously held up his wrist, allowing the priest to puncture a vein and bleed him into it. Then Germineau turned to Angelique and she did the same. When the goblet was full of their mingled blood, Germineau blessed it and cast a spell of binding on it, joining their blood irreversibly. Then he offered it to them to drink.

Reivn held the goblet while she drank.

The priest declared, "This grail begins their union. The two are now one under the law."

Angelique took it and held it for Reivn.

When it was emptied and set aside, Germineau held out his hand. "The rings, please." Jack and Serena handed them over. "I bless these rings with the holy light of our father of fathers. Let them hold you bound one to the other until you meet your fate."

He handed one ring to Angelique and the other to Reivn.

As Reivn slid the ring on her index finger, as was the custom, he spoke the ancient vows of their people. "I will love you and cherish you always, honor you and call you my equal when we are alone and respect you when under the eyes of others. You are mine, my life, my own. My soul and heart will recognize you until the day fate separates us once more."

Angelique repeated their vows, slipping his ring on him.

Nodding in satisfaction, Germineau raised his hands over their heads and began to pray. "May God shine his light on you for the eternities to come, may the light conquer the darkness and your wings finally spread to carry you home. I pronounce you whole. Amen."

Angelique turned to Reivn, her eyes tearing up as she gazed at him.

He smiled and pulled her into his arms, kissing her while the crowd applauded.

A tap on Reivn's arm reminded him they were still in front of an audience. "Ahem, Lord Reivn? The announcement?" Germineau smiled.

Jack choked back his laughter. Moventius elbowed Kaelan with a huge grin, while Lunitar chuckled and shook his head. Even Gideon had a smile on his face.

Hearing them, Reivn reluctantly let her go and turned with her to face their guests.

Germineau raised his hands one last time and announced, "ladies and gentlemen, I give you Lord and Lady Draegon, joined for all eternity, amen."

The entire room stood and applauded as Reivn and Angelique made their way down the aisle. Their bridal party joined them, pairing up as they walked behind the bride and groom.

Serena shyly took Jack's arm, walking with him behind Reivn and Angelique, her eyes shining with joy for her dearest friend.

Lunitar offered Reyna his arm, looking down at her with a smile, but she kept her eyes to the floor, refusing to look up as she walked beside him.

Behind them, Moventius towered over Anya's lithe and small figure, looking almost out of place with his slight scruff, his Wolven blood showing in his features. Anya looked uncomfortably at the crowd and clung to him nervously.

Kaelan followed his brother, blushing furiously as he escorted Lissa on his arm. But Lissa ignored him and smiled profusely when they walked by the curious onlookers.

Gideon was the last to file down the aisle with Genevieve. His mood was a stark contrast to the lighthearted attitude the rest of the party exhibited, yet he made little effort to hide it. The girl on his arm was merely a blood servant and had no real place among them. Having to escort her was blatant insult even to a child, and he was no child. He ignored her nervous glances and went through the necessary motions until they were free of their duties.

Moravini had set a bountiful feast for the reception in his formal dining hall, which was adjacent to the ballroom, and had invited all to attend. Beautifully set, the tables had been strategically arranged to place the bride and groom in the front of the room.

Reivn and Angelique stood together as guests filed by, giving their blessings and congratulations to the couple. Then they were finally seated, and the festivities began.

During dinner, a beautiful young girl was brought in to dance. The dark-eyed gypsy danced around the hall, charming the entire ensemble with her grace until the music wound to a close. Then she stood breathless before them until Reivn waved her forward. She approached, her chin tilted up proudly as she curtsied.

Reivn smiled and introduced her. "Angel, this is my daughter, Mariah. Tonight, she has pleased me," he added, gazing at the girl.

Angelique greeted her warmly. "I'm happy to meet you. You are my daughter now too."

Mariah said nothing. Her eyes glinted in the light, as she looked expectantly at Reivn, who nodded. Then turning on heel, she almost ran from the room.

Puzzled over her sudden exit, Angelique turned to question him, but other guests drew her attention back to the celebration.

The remainder of the evening was spent in feasting and dancing. Quarters had been prepared for all the guests in the lower portion of the building and as they retired one by one, the room slowly quieted down until only the wedding party and Moravini remained.

Their host shook hands with Reivn, and then kissed Angelique's cheek, excusing himself.

Moventius approached them next. He hugged Reivn. "Father, she is beautiful, and I wish you both happiness." Then he looked at Angelique. "Welcome to our family, mother."

Her eyes widened in surprise and she stared at him as he walked away.

Kaelan and Gideon approached them together and while Gideon bowed, Kaelan hugged Reivn warmly. "It's good to see you happy, father." He grinned. "And welcome to you, my lady. I think you will like it among us."

Gideon gave him a shove to move him on, and then kissed Angelique's hand. "Congratulations mother… father. I am happy for you," he stated stiffly. Then he turned to go.

"Wait" Angelique put her hand on his arm.

Gideon turned around. "Yes, my lady?"

Stepping forward, Angelique hugged him warmly. "You are my son now, so I hope we will be friends. You helped me a great deal when I first got to Draegonstorm. Thank you."

Gideon bowed again. "No need to thank me. It was my duty, my lady. Good night." Turning abruptly, he walked away, leaving her speechless at his response.

Lunitar was the last to approach. "Father… mother, congratulations. It is good to see you both so happy." Hugging Angelique, he whispered in her ear, "You look radiant, mother."

Angelique blushed and smiled.

Lunitar stepped back and shook his father's hand. "I'll take my leave now, so you can enjoy the rest of your evening alone." Then he wandered from the hall out into the gardens of Moravini's sumptuous home, deep in thought. Absent-mindedly walking the path, he stopped and turned when he heard a sharp intake of breath.

Reyna stood a few feet behind him, staring at him in fright. She was dressed head to toe in Rrom clothing except for the shoes she was wearing, which were plain black boots.

He approached her, hoping to try and get her to talk to him. Her silence during the wedding had bothered him. Then a flash of red at her feet caught his attention and he glanced down.

Around her ankle, a band of red shown in the dark, carrying an almost angry glow. He frowned, recognizing the signature of dark magic it held, and looked up again to speak to her.

The terror in her eyes caused him to pause, and before he could regain his composure, she fled, leaving him to stare after her in confusion. Disturbed by her actions, he decided to find out more about the silent young woman who had held his arm so gingerly. Heading back inside, he went to Gideon's room.

Gideon glanced up as Lunitar walked in. "What's wrong?"

Lunitar pulled up a chair opposite Gideon and sat down. "Tell me what you know of Mariah's daughter?"

"Which one?" Gideon asked, raising an eyebrow.

Frowning, Lunitar leaned forward. "The one I escorted at the wedding tonight... Lady Reyna. She seemed very uncomfortable."

Gideon shrugged. "She's been that way as long as I can remember."

Not satisfied, Lunitar leaned back in his chair and stared at his brother. "Then tell me what you know about her."

"Well," Gideon sighed, scratching his head for a moment. "I know father used to keep a tight leash on her until she was married. Now we hardly see her."

Lunitar tapped his fingers in irritation. "You're being vague, Gideon. Explain. Where is she from? Where does she live? Who is she married to?"

Gideon frowned, staring at him puzzled. "Why the sudden interest in Reyna?"

"Because the girl I escorted earlier and just saw in the garden was filled with fear, and that's not something I'm accustomed to seeing here. Now tell me everything you know." Lunitar sat back and folded his hands in front of him, gazing intensely at Gideon.

Gideon sighed again. "I can only tell you what I know, and that is not much."

Lunitar simply nodded. "I have plenty of time."

Back in the hall, Reivn and Angelique had finished talking with the last of the guests.

Angelique looked around. The hall was empty except for a few lingering friends that remained. Serena had discreetly left, taking Lissa and Genevieve with her, and Reyna and Anya had slipped away the moment they were allowed. But before she could explore the remaining faces, Reivn lifted her into his arms.

Smiling at those still around them, he bid them goodnight and turned to the doors. "Come, my love... my wife. I think it is time we were alone..."

## Chapter Forty-One
## Hunt for the Daemon Master

*I have sent out enforcers again. Any sense of where Valfort could be at present was lost and we are hunting blind. Sadly, there is little time to search for him, because the Principatus are gathering in numbers again, not far from Atlantic City. This concerns me greatly since there is not enough manpower in that region to defend the territory adequately if attacked. The Council has summoned me to discuss the growing threat, but somehow, I feel their meetings are a futile attempt to control a situation that has already grown far beyond what can be quelled. The Renegades are as many in number, and in some regions, outnumber us a hundred to one. It is clear our strategies at this point must be in defending our borders rather than on wiping out a growing sect that has declared itself independent of Council law.*

*I want Angelique to go home to Draegonstorm while I deal with this turmoil. As things heat up, the cities on the front will become far more dangerous than my Keep will ever be. My sons can protect her there and penetrating the magic defending those walls is far greater a challenge than most Renegades can successfully manage.*

*I intend to mention my desire to step down as Warlord when I go to Polusporta. I have still heard nothing of my request and I grow impatient. There are others who can take up the mantle in my stead... many that are worthy of such a title. I have not known the peace of staying in one location for any length of time for centuries now, and I long for some measure of that peace. I envy those with lesser duties who while away their nights in the solitude of their laboratories. I want to be among them once more, lost in magic of my own making...*

*Lord Reivn Draegon*

\* \* \* \* \*

The nights following the wedding were busy for Reivn and his family. Gideon and Moventius returned home to deal with matters at the Keep, and Kaelan was sent with them to prepare for another assignment. Mariah had left right after the wedding and no one knew where she was. Lunitar alone remained in New York with Reivn and Angelique to help deal with any remaining affairs. He was so busy he was still working when the dawn rose each day.

One night, Lord Moravini sent word about a build-up in the Renegade forces on Long Island. Reivn and Lunitar met with him, and the three men spent several nights discussing the restructure of the domain's forces in preparation for an attack.

While they were away, Angelique received word that Cyrus had been seen in the mid-west territories. She immediately sent out dispatches to try and track him down. She spent hours poring over maps and ancient texts on Texas and Mexico, trying to figure out where he was headed. When daybreak came each morning, she joined Reivn in their quarters, frustrated and weary. Their intimacy brought a certain measure of peace, but they both longed for more.

Then one morning just before dawn, as they lay in bed together in the soft glow of candlelight, he told her he had been summoned to Polusporta.

"I don't want you to leave. More and more I feel this dark world of ours stealing you away from me." She fell quiet, crying softly in his arms.

Reivn played with a lock of her copper curls, wrapping it absently around his finger while his mind wandered to the nights ahead. He knew he would be gone for weeks or even months this time, because the war with the Renegades was growing, and not just in North America. "If tonight is all we can have, angel, then I will spend it lost in you. Forgive me, beloved. This is not what I thought would transpire with the Council. I must go. My duties cannot be ignored, nor will battles be won here in your arms." He knew the separation would be hard on her. "I want you to return to the Keep. You will be safe there and can still do your duties. I will get word to you as often as possible as to my whereabouts."

Angelique laid her head on his chest, her tears falling softly against his skin. "I'll go, but I want to complete my work here first. I can't leave Jacob to finish settling the Guild alone. Rosalind's loss was a big one to them."

He sighed. "Only as long as you promise to cease your search for Cyrus. He is far more dangerous than you know." Then he kissed her forehead. "I am leaving Lunitar here to travel back with you. While he waits, he can work on reorganizing the arcane library downstairs."

She did not respond. Her mind was on the coming nights. She was still deep in thought when she closed her eyes to sleep.

Reivn left the following evening.

His kiss still lingering on her lips, Angelique left the portal room and went to her office, returning to the task of tracking Cyrus. Reivn had cautioned her before he left, worried her obsession with Cyrus was consuming her, but she wanted to find him. The image of Rosalind's broken body still burned in her mind.

Lunitar walked in, interrupting her thoughts. "May I speak with you, my lady?" he asked.

Angelique nodded, sliding a book over the lists she had written concerning her search. "Yes, of course... Come in. What can I do for you?"

He sat down across from her. "My lady... mother." He cleared his throat. "I have completed my task in the library, and it is once more in order. I was informed that you would be returning to the Keep with me. I was planning to leave first thing after sunset tomorrow. Are your duties here concluded or should I postpone our departure?"

She walked over to the fire and stared down at its burning embers. "I still have a few things here I need to see to, so I'll need more time."

"We are expected back at the Keep soon, but I think we can postpone it for a day." He raised an eyebrow when his response seemed to agitate her.

She turned around. "I need at least two. Jacob still has need of me and the new Paladin has not yet arrived."

Lunitar sighed. "I understand. Then I will send word to the Keep, and to father, as well, telling them both of our delay."

Angelique walked back to her desk and sat down again, but refrained from touching anything as she looked up. "Was there anything else you needed?" she asked pointedly.

"Permission to speak candidly," he asked quietly. He got up and stood in front of her desk.

She frowned. "You were not doing so before?"

He met her gaze with a steely-eyed expression. "No. I was not, my lady."

She folded her hands in her lap to keep them from shaking. "Then please do so now."

"I know not what you are up to, but I have my suspicions. If I am correct, then you seek a dangerous quarry, and not one to be handled either lightly or alone." He glanced down at her desk and the book with the papers jutting out from beneath it. "Any individual that gives Lord Reivn cause to take notice should be a matter of great concern. Be careful what you seek. You may well find it. Do you remember our last hunt? How many powerful warriors went against Cyrus? And he still held us off long enough to escape. You are a Draegon now and fall under the family's protection. In other words, I will do whatever is necessary to protect you as I would my father, even if it means protecting you from yourself."

Angelique put her hand on the book and stood up. "Believe me when I say I am doing my duties as an Ambassador to this tribe and serving the people in it. I appreciate the candor and honesty with which you speak. I will keep your warnings in mind."

"Thank you for your time, my lady. Good night." Lunitar bowed and turned to go.

She sat back down. "Good night."

He paused and turned around. "Rest well, mother." Then he left, and she returned to work.

Hours later, she was still in her office digging through more ancient archives when a knock interrupted her thoughts. Her irritation disappeared when Jack poked his head in. "Am I disturbing you?" he asked, "I intercepted this message from your courier and thought you might want it." He waved a sealed scroll at Angelique.

She frowned. "You mean you took it from my courier to find out what was in it. He had already returned from his last run."

He feigned a hurt look. "What? You would accuse me of such a thing? I am wounded, Angelique. How could you..." Her book flying at him cut him off and he dodged.

"Why are you really here and what is your obvious interest in my activities?" she growled.

Jack chuckled, closing the door behind him and tossing the scroll to her. "Well officially, I'm here as a favor to Reivn to make sure you're safe. I also wanted to see how Grimel's recovery is progressing." He bent over and picked the book up from the floor where it had landed. Then he handed it back to her. "Unofficially, I'm here to help you hunt down that filth. I have never let a target walk away before, and I don't intend to start now. So," he bent over and gazed at the map she had marked with information about Cyrus' whereabouts, "what have you got?"

All her thoughts turned to the hunt and she leaned over, pointing out various recent sightings and their locations on the map before them.

"Judging by the recent reports I've received, it looks like he's heading for Mexico. The problem is, I cannot figure out where or why. There are numerous places there that are shrouded in mystery. Much of the territories there are either Wolven sanctuaries, unclaimed, or the Renegades have taken them." She went to the bookshelves and pulled down an old tome. "I found this downstairs in the arcane library, buried under a pile of other books. It mentions a primordial race of Gods that were worshiped throughout Mexico by ancient civilizations. There are several references to a blood God. I don't know if they are connected to our kind or not. The references are not very detailed. They only give sketchy information at best. In counting the number of locations mentioned, there are thirty-three such places he could be going, and that's assuming he continues on his present course." She turned to look at him, worry creasing her brow. "It's not going to be easy to find him."

Jack pulled off his hat and dropped into a chair opposite the desk, scratching the goatee on his chin thoughtfully. "Well, I can ask some of the Wolvens in that area to start sniffing around, pardon the pun. They don't usually have much to do with our kind, but we do work together from time to time. Cyrus is a danger to all the races. I know once they hear what has happened, they aren't going to want him anywhere near their sanctuaries."

Angelique sat down and stared at the map, deep in thought. "If they find out where he is, then we shouldn't leave it to chance. We need to take a small team and go after him ourselves."

Reaching into his pocket, he pulled out a toothpick and started chewing on it. Then he sat back and stared at the fire, lost in thought.

She was also watching the flames in the hearth, mulling over the problem.

Silence reigned in the room as long minutes passed until finally, he looked up. "I think we should ask Annie to join us. She is an excellent fighter, even if her tastes are somewhat eccentric. Anyway, her sexual preferences don't bother me one way or the other. I just know that in a fight I can't think of too many other people I would want at my back. She's good and we need her."

Angelique agreed. "We will definitely need skilled fighters and I can't ask Lunitar. He would not approve of this. I cannot ask Reivn either. He would never agree to it. So, that limits our options a little."

Jack frowned. "We are going to need one or two more at least," he told her, tossing the toothpick into the flames. "If we need to separate for any reason, there should be more than one person for each group, it's safer that way."

She began tapping her finger on the desk, trying to think of someone strong and skilled enough to risk taking along.

Their answer came from an unexpected source.

The scroll sitting in front of her was still unopened. She realized as much and picked it up. When she broke the seal and read it, she gave a shout, jolting Jack from his silent musings as he looked up in alarm. "That's it! Why didn't I think of this before?"

Sitting bolt upright, he gaped at her. "What is it?" he asked, somewhat alarmed.

She tossed the letter to him. "Ruben is arriving tonight for a visit. He's the perfect choice! He was turned on his own request by one of the Mastrics in France, and he and his wife serve the Guild there now. He is trained in the eastern fighting techniques and a really good shot, better than I am! And," she smiled, leaning toward him, "he's one hundred percent loyal to me."

Jack shook his head in exasperation. "It's not up to me, Angie, this is your call. I'm just along for the ride. Now," he stood and dusted off his hat. "May I suggest we assemble the team tonight and begin the briefing? I can contact the Wolvens and Annie if you take care of the PR work." He looked up from putting on his gloves to find Angelique looking at him with a puzzled expression. "What?" he asked.

Angelique blushed. "I was wondering what PR meant."

He laughed and turned to go. "I'll be back tonight after I handle my end of this." As he walked out, he chuckled again and called over his shoulder. "It means public relations, Angie." His laughter rang out in the halls.

She stood staring at the door, feeling very foolish. "I knew that," she mumbled.

Later that night, Annie arrived fully armed. Ruben joined them from his newly assigned quarters, dressed for battle. Having followed Angelique's instructions, they had both prepped for the trip, carrying extra supplies and ammunition.

Angelique was still briefing them when Jack arrived. He dropped a rather large knapsack beside the door and sat down, nodding to them in greeting. "My contact got hold of the chieftain of a local tribe near Mexico City and he's going to pass the word to the other tribes there. By the time we get there, I guarantee they will have something for us. I also contracted a completely custom outfitted trailer and two jungle SUV's for the trip." He pulled off his hat, playing with it as he continued. "The trailer is set up for a trip through even the hottest sunshine and deep terrain. We have two blood-bound drivers…both mine, and two humans going along for daytime duties. They can also double as emergency food supplies if we need them. The laws on killing don't apply out there."

Angelique frowned, a grim look on her face.

Jack leaned over and shook Annie's hand. "Welcome aboard. What do think of our plans?"

Licking her lips, Annie smiled at him. "I think I'm going to like the company, love the fighting and have a story to tell when I get back. I love it! However, I do think we need one more person with us. I'll talk to him after we're done here, if you don't mind."

Jack spoke up before anyone else could answer. "We also have at least one Wolven going with us as a guide if we have to go into unknown territory."

Angelique nodded in satisfaction, confident that this time Cyrus was not going to escape. "We leave in two days. You can store your supplies here until we go. If you need lodgings, you are also welcome to stay here. Annie, get in touch with your friend quickly. He'll need time to prepare and that's the one thing we don't have much of."

Annie grinned. "So, the girl is a woman after all. No worries, we'll be ready."

When they were finished discussing the plan, Annie and Jack left to see to their affairs.

Once they were alone, Ruben turned to Angelique. "I knew it was a good idea to come for a visit. I had this nagging feeling I was needed." Walking over, he hugged her. "I'm glad you asked me to come with you. Someone's got to watch your back."

Angelique nodded. "I am lucky you decided to accept the turning, although I wish Genevieve had too. I am worried about her safety."

"She plans to, once I am completely finished my training. She wants it to be me, so our bond can be as close as you and Lord Reivn are." Ruben smiled then. "She is delighted that you are finally so happy."

Angelique giggled. "I suspect she knew how I felt about Reivn before I did. She cried right through my wedding night. Now, I asked for your help because of your skill with a blade, your skill with magic and your ability to fight. But I cannot promise you will survive the coming battle. I am not sure any of us will. The better our team, the better a chance we have."

He smiled. "Don't worry. I won't let you down."

Within two nights, their small group was prepared to leave.

Annie arrived with a tall and muscular man dressed in buckskin pants and a white shirt. "This is Shaman. He's a Blackfoot Indian. He's been one of us since the first settlements invaded their lands. He already knows the mission. I explained it last night and he's ready."

Angelique shook his hand, introducing him to the rest of the team. She liked the look of him. Though he did not smile, his eyes were sincere and missed nothing. Turning to the rest of the group, she announced, "We need to move quickly. To protect this mission, I cannot allow word of our departure to get out too soon."

After seeing to last minute equipment needs, the team followed Angelique down to the lab. She had used portal travel enough that she was not worried about its success now. But before she opened it, she erected a temporary barrier spell that would prevent anyone in the Guild from sensing its use. She knew it would dissipate in minutes, but it would give them enough time to pass through unnoticed. She glanced around nervously. "Time to go," she stated. "If anyone wants to opt out, now would be a good time."

Each of them looked at her expectantly and waited.

In relief, Angelique nodded and opened the portal. Then one by one, they stepped through into Austin, Texas carrying their supplies.

An elderly man was waiting for them. "Welcome, Ambassador. We just received your message last night, but your rooms are ready. If you will come with me?"

The team followed without a word, mentally preparing for the task ahead. Then after settling into their rooms, they met again to go over the plans for the coming hunt before retiring to sleep.

The moment Angelique's barrier spell dropped, Lunitar felt her absence, and looked up from his book in concern. "Mother... what are you up to?" he muttered. Curious as to her whereabouts, he left the library and headed to the Guild Prefect's office at a brisk pace. He knocked and then quickly entered when he got a response from within. "I was hoping I would catch you here. Have you seen the Ambassador tonight? I finished with the library and wanted to offer my help to expedite the completion of her duties here. We plan to head home soon."

Jacob looked up from pulling on his boots. "I heard she was going to be taking care of a few things in the city and then returning later."

With a sigh of frustration, Lunitar turned to go. "I'll check with the Captain of the Guard to see if he knows where she is. Thank you."

Jacob nodded and followed him from the room. "I need to find our Paladin anyway. He was supposed to meet me an hour ago. I promised to teach him some new magic."

"The new Paladin? I was told he had not arrived yet," Lunitar stated and shook his head. "If you will excuse me, I need to look into a few things."

Jacob watched him walk off in confusion. Then he turned and headed the opposite direction.

Lunitar went down to the Guild Commander's office, his mind working over the possibilities. In agitation, he opened the door and stepped into the room.

The Captain seated behind the desk glanced up at the intrusion, and immediately straightened in his seat. "Lord Draegon... how may I help you?"

"Do you know where I might find Lady Angelique?" Lunitar stared at him in frustration.

The captain nodded. "That I do. Last night Jack Dunn mentioned she was going with him on a mission. He didn't give me any details, but did mention it was research... something about an old tome she wanted to learn more about. He said they would be back in a day or two."

Lunitar slowly nodded, digesting the information. "Then she is in no danger?"

"He gave no indication they were going anywhere dangerous," the captain answered. "Surely he would have told me if there was? Why? Has something happened?"

Lunitar shook his head. "No, I suppose not. If you don't mind, however, I'm going to remain here and wait for her. Lord Reivn assigned me as an escort to see her safely home."

The captain smiled. "Of course, my lord. I understand. Unless his lordship assigns you elsewhere, a few days shouldn't hurt anything. I'll notify Jacob immediately."

Lunitar bowed. "Thank you. If you will excuse me, I need to make the necessary arrangements."

The captain saluted him, and then returned to his work.

With new purpose in his stride, Lunitar turned and headed to the upper levels of the Guild to find a courier. Had he known the truth concerning Angelique's mission, his footsteps would have led him in a far different direction.

When sunset came the following night, Angelique and her companions had the SUVs and trailer loaded in record time. Then after a quick check on the small refrigerator to be sure their blood stores would keep during the journey, Jack signaled her. He had communicated with his Wolven contact the first night the plan set in motion, and now knew where they were going. They would be heading across the border into Mexico and would have to travel by both night and day to reach Mexico City in time to rendezvous with their guide. To quicken their pace, the blood-servants traveling with them would handle the driving during the daylight hours, when their masters were forced to retreat from the sun.

The team got on the road and drove through the night. They made good time and only stopped long enough to refuel. At dawn, they pulled off the highway so the Immortals could retire, giving the driving over to their servants. Then they were back on the road. The day passed without incident and come sunset they had reached the border. Angelique hypnotized the patrol officer when he stopped them to see their papers, and then smiled when he turned to the other officers and gave the okay. The group drove on, determined to make their destination on time. Little had been said during the trip. Their thoughts lay on the coming battle ahead.

They would reach the city's outskirts before dusk if they continued their present pace. So when morning finally approached, Angelique gave the servants last-minute instructions. True to the trust placed in them, the servants maintained good time. By nightfall, they were almost to the rendezvous point. Not knowing what to expect, they strapped on their weapons, refusing to go into unknown territory unarmed.

The team finally arrived at a rundown hotel that looked as though it had been abandoned for years. A man was leaning against the doorframe wearing a somewhat worn duster and a western hat that hung over his eyes, hiding his face.

Jack signaled for the others to wait while he and Angelique cautiously approached. "Excuse me," Jack called out, waiting for him to move. "Can you tell me where to find Nicholas?"

The man lifted one corner of the hat up to gaze at them. "You found him." Then without another word, he turned and went inside.

Exchanging glances, Jack and Angelique followed him into the building. The interior was dark, and the windows were boarded up and painted black to block out the light. The moment the door closed behind them, they were jumped and pulled to the ground, their hands restrained, and their mouths gagged. Angelique could feel the fur on her captors and realized they must be in their true Wolven forms rather than their human ones. Their strength outmatched her own, and no matter how she struggled, she could not break free. Their captors waited until she and Jack stopped fighting, and then hauled them both to their feet. A spotlight turned on, shining in their faces and blinding them. Then the man they had met outside spoke. "Who are you?"

Jack snarled when the gag was pulled from his mouth. "We are supposed to rendezvous with Nicholas! He is to be our guide through Mexico! Your own tribe arranged this with us! Talk to your chief about it! He can confirm who we are!"

The man frowned. "How do we know you're not renegade spies trying to set us up? Too many of us have already died because of their relentlessness. Can you prove who you are?"

Jack struggled with his captors and tried to break free, but those that held him only twisted his arms tighter behind him, causing him to wince in pain. "I have contact papers with the chieftain's own mark on it! It's in my right inside pocket! Ungh! I also wear the mark of respect on my inner wrist! We are comrades in the same battle!"

One of the Wolvens restraining him lifted the sleeve of his duster to search his arm and growled when he saw the mark. They immediately untied Jack, but blocked his escape.

Grabbing the paper from his coat, Jack tossed it to their captor. Then he grabbed hold of one of the Wolvens that still held Angelique. "Let her go! She is the Ambassador to the Mastric's tribe! If she is injured here, it will bring a war with the Mastrics to your people!"

Then the man spoke. "Release her. They are who they say they are."

The spotlight went out and soft lights came on, allowing them to see their captors. The man they had seen outside came toward them. "I apologize for the rough treatment, but we couldn't take any chances. The Renegades have been finding our sanctuaries and slaughtering us by the dozens. They are trying to drive us from our home, so they can claim the territory. They think it will tip your war in their favor. We had to be sure."

Unnerved but unharmed, Angelique brushed herself off.

Jack rubbed the soreness from his wrists and gazed intently at the man. "Are you Nicholas?" he demanded to know.

The man shook Jack's hand with a firm grip. "Nicholas Skyfire, at your service."

"I'm Jack Dunn and this is Lady Angelique Draegon," Jack motioned toward the door. "The rest of our party is waiting outside. I suggest we bring them in, so we can discuss the hunt."

Nicholas signaled one of his men, and he disappeared without a sound, returning moments later with the rest of Angelique's group.

After a round of introductions, they opened the maps and got to work. The Wolvens had indeed located Cyrus and his heading was fairly obvious. He was headed into the dense jungle terrain of the Yucatan. He was only a day ahead of them, but he was moving at a fair clip, as though there was some urgency to reach his destination.

"What worries us," Nicholas continued, looking up at the assembled faces, "is the location he seems to be headed for. The jungle holds many things best forgotten, but some more than others." He walked over to a run-down cabinet and pulled out some old papers. "There is an Aztec temple buried deep in the Yucatan jungle known as Mitlamiquiztli, or in our tongue, place of death. The legend says an ancient blood God there demanded sacrifice from the Aztec peoples. If they did not journey to this place once a month with ten new victims for their God, he would take brutal vengeance on them and slaughter whole villages while they slept. That sounds like the work of a suckhead to me."

Jack frowned at the derogatory reference to their kind, but said nothing.

However, Annie looked up from the maps. "Now wait one damn minute, furball! Your kind has done bad things to ours as well! So, don't be so rude! You never know when one of us is going to have to watch your back!"

Jack held up his hand. "Enough, Annie! This problem with Cyrus is too important to let personal feelings get in the way. The man does have cause to hate our kind. They're fighting their own battle here against the Renegades." Turning back to Nicholas, he sighed when the Wolven nodded in his direction. "Please continue," he added, sitting down in a dusty old chair.

Angelique wrinkled her nose in disgust when she saw the dirty furniture.

Nicholas pulled out a wad of tobacco and chewed on it. "Supposedly it's an old suckhead, I mean Vampyre." He glanced at Annie and she scowled, but said nothing. With a sigh, he explained. "This one is from a tribe even your kind doesn't really know much about. The story goes something like this... One of the Vampyre Ancients broke away from the others, drowning himself in blood and corruption. He struck deals with Daemons and changed the blood of he and his children, making them more monster than man. They hid themselves to avoid destruction until they could gain enough power to stand alone against the other tribes."

Nicholas stopped and spat the tobacco across the room, hitting a small spittoon on the floor. Then he continued. "That's the direction Cyrus is headed. Supposedly, it's been quiet in there for centuries and the temple has been left alone for that reason. Many of us fear there is something or someone sleeping inside. Any reason why this Cyrus would want to go there?"

Silence filled the room as each retreated to their own thoughts.

Angelique frowned, trying to figure out what Cyrus could possibly be looking for.

"I know what he wants," Shaman stated quietly.

Everyone gaped at him in surprise. Not used to him speaking, it even caught Annie off guard.

"He wants new body," Shaman continued.

Jack contemplated this for a moment and then slowly nodded. "You could be right. He did make a jump into one of our people during the battle with him. The body he took was a weak one. Perhaps he intends to take the sleeping Ancient by surprise. It's far-fetched, but if the Ancient has been asleep for centuries then it's bound to be weak, making it easy prey for Cyrus."

Nicholas growled. "Do you realize what you're saying? Assuming you are right about this, such an act would make him as powerful as the Ancients of your Council! He would go on a killing spree that would never end! He wouldn't stop with your kind, either! He would kill us too, and the Fae! Even the Dragons would be at risk if he found a way into their world!"

Angelique interrupted him as she stood and held her hands up between them. "Wait a minute! We can't be sure that's his intention! We don't know if he is aware of any legends surrounding that area. Maybe he isn't doing anything other than attempting to hide!"

Nicholas scoffed at her. "My God, you are naïve! If there ever was an Ancient in that temple, you can be sure he not only knows about it, but intends to take its power!"

Angelique looked around. "Perhaps. Either way, I do think if there is an Ancient still resting within that temple, then we need to destroy it before Cyrus finds it!" As she gazed the faces around her, they each nodded in agreement.

Jack winked at her, showing his approval, but she ignored him.

Impatient with all the talk, Annie stood up. "Then why are we still sitting here? Every minute we waste puts him closer to that pyramid and further away from us! Let's move out!"

Stalking out, she did not notice Nicholas' eyes on her. "Is she always so passionate?"

Jack shrugged nonchalantly and snickered. "Why don't you ask her yourself?"

Back in New York, Lunitar was worried. It had been two nights with no word from Angelique or Jack. He wandered from the library where he had spent the last two nights in his studies. He was so deep in thought, he did not hear his name called.

"Lunitar!" Moventius caught up to him. "Didn't you hear me?"

Lunitar looked up, confused. "No, I'm sorry. I was… thinking."

Moventius chuckled and shook his head. "Come out of your studies a little, brother. The world awaits you. I came from the Keep tonight because I wanted to know if you were interested in a few rounds in the arena. I've been working on my magic a bit and was hoping to see how well it would stand against a Mastric's. Outside of father, you and Gideon are the only ones I know well enough to trust. What do you say?"

"I am actually in the process of trying to locate Angelique. She isn't in her rooms and hasn't been there for two nights," Lunitar stated in concern.

Moventius merely grinned. "She is probably dealing with Mastric's business. She is the Ambassador, you know. At least she takes her position seriously and does the job well. Father will no doubt be proud of her."

Lunitar sighed. "Perhaps, but I intend to be sure before I stop inquiring on her whereabouts."

"I'm sure she's fine. It's not unusual for any of us to be gone at times. Jack isn't around either. He left two nights ago." Moventius chuckled. "You worry too much. She is well-trained."

Lunitar stopped and faced his brother. "Yes, I know. I assisted in her training. She left with Jack, but that does not explain the length of their absence. Even our best-trained sometimes cross paths with someone stronger. Think of father's run-ins with Valfort and Alora."

Moventius sighed and rested his hand on Lunitar's shoulder. "She is the Mastric's Ambassador, Lunitar. That comes with great responsibilities to the tribe, regardless of the danger. If she is on an assignment, then she is doing her job. Talk to whomever you must and if she has gone on an important mission, let it go and head back to the Keep. She knows the way home." Without another word, Moventius walked off toward the gathering hall.

Lunitar stood in silence, watching him go and contemplating his words.

# BLOOD FEUD

## Chapter Forty-Two
## The War Council

*War... I detest the very word. We kill the Renegades and they kill us. Blow after blow is exchanged as we stain the ground red with our blood. We are awash in the sin of slaughter. The Principatus bargains with Daemons and unleashes them on the world, where they devour all that is pure and righteous. If we do not fight, the innocent die or worse, are taken by their new allies and used as vessels. If we do fight, we lose many valuable people on the field of battle. There is no perfect answer, only the question of what is right. Do we then leave the humans to their fate or step in front of them, defending their innocent lives?*

*When I was human, I once learned from a Roman what it means to pray, and that God hears us and sees all that transpires from his seat in Heaven. I have long prayed he would send his angels to combat the evil unleashed by our brethren who dwell in the pit to play. If only there was some way to even the odds and stop them before they unleash far greater an evil than even they can command. It is a foolish prayer, for God does not look with favor on the damned creatures of the darkest places in this world. His light is so far beyond us that we cannot stand its gaze without burning the flesh from our very bones.*

*Yet I still have my faith, and it manifests against the creatures from the pit like a glowing flame of hope. Why? Where does this power come from? If God truly has forsaken us, then how is it possible so many of us still feel the burning of faith so strongly within ourselves? Could it be we are somehow still connected to the throne of light? I feel it deep within my core... calling me to remember it. War... it is the evil that drives us ever further into the dark...*

*Lord Reivn Draegon*

\* \* \* \* \*

Reivn sat tapping his fingers on the table. The Council had been in session for three nights and his frustration had grown considerably. Eight of the nine Warlords had assembled to meet with the Council, but one chair remained conspicuously empty. Looking over at Annie's seat, he wondered about her absence for the hundredth time.

Victus rose from his chair, his irritation apparent. "Three nights now and still you give me no answers? Martu and Semerkhet cannot be that difficult to locate! I am weary of your excuses!"

The war was heating up with the Renegades, and the hunt to find the two Ancients that led them had again proved fruitless. The Warlords had returned empty-handed.

Lucian stood to address the Council. "My lords and ladies, I fear you still do not understand the situation here. Speaking for myself and my tribe, we have had all our best trackers out trying to find the trail since you issued the decree. The two you are searching for are well hidden and are not likely to reveal themselves. Their armies are growing in number every night. The cities sitting on the edge of the boundaries between Renegade and Alliance territories in North America have long been under constant attack. Now they are organized and preparing for more than just a few mere skirmishes." His long light brown hair was pulled back, allowing the light to hit his face. The white shirt he wore glowed in the torchlight. His eyes reflected his aggravation. "Finding these Ancients may slow the Renegades down, but it won't stop them. Not anymore."

The man next to him shifted in his seat and cleared his throat. A mass of unkempt brown hair partially covered his eyes. His clothing resembled a devoted bookkeeper's and was covered with ink splotches. Marcus's slight stature misspoke of the strength he carried as a warrior. "I agree with him, my lords. The Renegades have grown too vast in numbers and have their own hierarchy now." He got up and walked over to Lucian. Because of his Armenian blood, his voice had often been heard in the Council halls on such matters. His dark eyes were troubled as he surveyed the room. "If we don't plan our defense of America's Northeast Coast soon, the Renegades will effectively cut off Boston and the rest of the northern territories from Hartford on up. Any of our people still within those areas will be exterminated systematically. Once we have succeeded in securing those locations, then we can resume our search for the two Ancients. It is our duty to defend the front lines. The younger generations cannot defend the northern territories by themselves. They are not strong enough. With our aid, they'll stand a better chance."

Reivn got up, shaking his head. "No, Marcus. If we try to take the younger generations into battle unprepared, then it would be no more than lambs to the slaughter. Too many of our young are not well enough trained to face the things we have been fighting in recent times. In Cyrus' temple alone, we came across Daemon warriors and Incubi by the dozens. The Renegades are freely loosing these monsters on our world. We lost many good people down there."

Thylacinos growled at him. "So we've heard. Many of them were young from my own tribe. And yet you and your charge came safely home."

"We Mastrics were not without our losses!" Reivn argued, almost forgetting whom he was addressing. "All the tribes suffered loss at his hands!"

Thylacinos rose from the floor, baring his teeth as he crossed the room. "Yet Cyrus escaped your grasp!" he snarled.

Reivn gripped the edge of the table in front of him and was about to comment when Mastric held up his hand, silencing him.

Mastric turned his hooded visage in Thylacinos' direction and stared at him. "My son's abilities and power are well known. Some of your Thylacinians were indeed among those dead and yet you recently claimed their superiority over the rest of us. Why then did they lose their lives? Reivn has been fighting on the front lines for over a century now and has held fast the cities in the northern hemisphere. He survives because he is indeed knowledgeable as to their strengths and weaknesses."

Victus interrupted him. "Enough! Arguing amongst ourselves is not going to accomplish anything! If finding our brothers will no longer quell their threat, then we must begin planning a strategic defense and look to the borders of our lands!"

Darius stood up, holding up his hand to be heard. As Warlord for the Victulian tribe and son to Victus, he was well respected among his peers. Though soft-spoken, his words carried much weight. "My lords and ladies, I believe we need not only plan a strategy for defense of the northern territories, but also to restructure ourselves from within as well. The weaknesses in some of the cities on the front lines are too great to be ignored."

Victus nodded in agreement. "So noted, Darius. Reivn, you have long been defending the northern Hemisphere with Annie and Lucian. Would you share your views with this Council?"

Reivn nodded and stood. "The northern territories will indeed fall with what little defenses we presently have. There are not enough experienced warriors in the new world to make a difference. We need more of our

Elders on the frontlines. The young need to be moved back to secondary locations and better trained for combat."

Lucian nodded in agreement. "The Mastrics, Epochians, Mithranians and Thylacinians are among the strongest fighters you have. Use their strength. The Mastrics have spells that can put up barriers to slow the enemy's advance and shield our warriors for a time. The Epochians, aside from being among our greatest warriors, can bend time. If used in correlation with the Mastrics magic, it could be used to fortify any territory's defenses. Our Mithranian brothers are the masters of war. Unleash their fury on the battlefield and let them raze our enemy forces to the ground." He looked around, passion rising in his plea and filling the room. "We Thylacinians have far keener senses than any of the rest of you. We can use that as a defense to keep the perimeters better protected. We also have contacts among Wolven kind. They have no love of the Renegades either and might be convinced to join us."

In the corner, a woman sat forward, shaking her head. Her soft blonde hair was loosely restrained in a ponytail at the base of her neck, and half-hidden under her gaucho hat. She wore a long black trench coat over equally dark pants and a fitted shirt. Resting next to her on the floor lay a matching pair of katanas. Being Warlord of the assassin tribe had left Leshye in the position of playing the strong arm of the Council on many occasions. She was the only appointed bloodhunter among the Warlords and was an expert at hunting down Renegades. Now the Mithranian added her voice to the chamber. "I fail to see how you think that would be helpful, Lucian," she argued. "The Wolvens could turn on us at any time. They cannot be trusted. Better to leave them alone than to involve them in this conflict."

Thylacinos snarled at her. "They have fought beside me many times through the centuries, Mithranian! They have more honor than many of our own! Do not sit in judgment of their kind merely because you have no taste for the bestial!"

Leshye frowned. "I forget nothing, my lord Thylacinos, nor did I intend to offend. However, if we are fighting so difficult a battle with the Renegades, do we really wish to chance adding to our troubles? My concern is for our people and the ability to hold the ground we have."

"Leshye, I see your point, but can we really afford to turn away their help?" Jarod cleared his throat. The dark-haired Rrom leaned forward in his chair. His natural linen shirt hung open almost to the waist, complimenting his dark skin and muscular structure. Brown bloused pants and scuffed black boots finished the appearance, declaring his gypsy heritage to those in the room. He was Silvanus' son and Warlord for the Dracanas, and a well-respected member of their society. "If the threat is as great as Lord Reivn and Lucian suggest, then we are already outnumbered. They may not have the Elders we do, nor the firepower from resources such as the Mastrics and you Mithranians, but they do have Daemons and the magic of the pit to aid them."

To Jarod's right, a young man stood up. Alderion's shockingly blonde hair hung about dark blue eyes and a roughened muscular build. Of Viking descent, the Epochian Warlord carried himself with a presence that commanded attention. He sighed. "That is true Jarod, but this is a decision that must be carefully weighed. Losing the territories in the north would cost us thousands of brethren and all the tribes would suffer. I believe Lord Reivn is right about our young needing serious training. In my visits north, I have seen far too much evidence of their weakness. They are not ready to defend themselves."

Victus scanned the faces of those present until his eyes came to Lazar, the Sargonian Warlord and son to Sharrukin. "You have not said much tonight, Lazar. What of the European front? Is it prepared for such an onslaught?"

Lazar slowly got up. His jet-black hair and eyes, and olive complexion marked him as hailing from the Middle East. He bowed to them before saying a word. "We are not as ill-prepared as our northern brothers, but we are still weak, my lord. Many of our own here have grown decadent and lazy in their ways. They need to awaken their strength again and rally to the cause before death comes to their doors."

Sharrukin agreed. "They do not fight as they did during man's greatest wars. The human's modern ideal of political peace treaties and negotiations has lulled them into self-indulgence."

Galatia frowned. "When there are no wars to fight in, brother, it is indeed hard to remain battle-worthy. For over a century, they have been forced to decay their skills while man grows ever more docile in their ways. When war comes again to man, they will be lambs."

"We are not here to discuss human failing! We are here to discuss the future of our own existence!" Victus retorted angrily. "Sharrukin is right. Many of our people have grown weak. Send notice to all the Elders and tell them to begin training again for battle."

Mastric chuckled. "Only your people have degenerated, Victus. My Mastrics are as ready as ever. They operate within their guilds' hierarchies and discipline is a part of their nightly operation. Among the rest of you, I see only the Mithranians as having learned this."

Victus frowned. "That is perhaps why Lucian suggested we use your tribe as one of our strengths. You cannot deny the fact your tribe holds mastery over the magic flowing through our world. That has always been one of our greatest strengths."

"That and the power of Epochian blades in battle," Chronos added. "We and the Mithranians stand fully prepared to fight. Our tribes have never been weakened by wallowing too much in any luxury. We prefer training arenas to your silk coddled couches."

Mithras stood up and frowned, tired of listening while they argued over what he deemed pointless. "I fail to see how this debate is resolving anything. It is obvious the Renegade problem has grown beyond our control. In my opinion, listening to the Warlords who have fought the war longest is wise, considering the varying reports we have been receiving for many years now. Martu and Semerkhet are neither one without their own resources. Being foolhardy enough to underestimate the situation now could destroy the Alliance completely."

Victus resumed his seat and sat back to listen. He knew the Ancient's knowledge on recent happenings far exceeded his own. The father of the Mithranians moved among his children nightly, leading them in the fight against their enemy.

Making his way slowly around the hall, Mithras gazed at each in turn as he spoke. "We all know their followers have grown much in recent decades and have indeed formed their own society, including ranks equivalent to our Commanders, hunters and emissaries, Lord Chancellors and young. They use the dark forces they allied themselves with centuries ago to fortify both their armies and their defenses." He stopped in front of Reivn and nodded in recognition. "We must look to those of us who have the gift of holy power to combat these evil beings they have unleashed. Organization and planning are the crucial key here."

Chronos gazed intently at Mithras, his mind working. He knew Mithras better than anyone present and knew he was a brilliant tactician. "What did you have in mind, Mithras?" he asked.

Turning to meet Chronos' gaze, Mithras frowned. "This will not be easy. It must be well executed, or we will lose this war. Reivn, Marcus, in your esteemed opinions, what area of the northern hemisphere is the most active location at present?"

Marcus looked to Reivn and then stood. "I believe Lord Reivn has been dealing with the largest amount of activity, my lord Mithras. Despite the many skirmishes we see in California and Texas, it does not compare to the eastern states in America."

Nodding his head in agreement, Reivn stepped around his table to address the Council directly. "The territories in the northern states are very heated right now, from Philadelphia and its surrounding areas on up to the states of Massachusetts and Rhode Island. It appears the Renegades are trying to severe the cords connecting us to our Canadian provinces." He turned to a map on the table, pointing out key locations. "We need to fortify our defenses on the outskirts of these territories to make them less vulnerable. Most of the people we have in these areas are both weak and less skilled. They could not withstand a major attack without help. Even if a thousand Elders fortified these territories, we may not be able to readily hold them."

Mastric leaned forward. "The reports I have received state the Renegades are gathering in far greater numbers than we've ever seen. What kind of truth is there in this? Are they truly generating that massive a strike force?"

Reivn turned to his father and bowed his head in acknowledgement before speaking. "They breed young as cannon fodder with the intent of overwhelming us by sheer numbers. I last got word they have young totaling in the thousands in the areas surrounding Atlantic City on up toward New York. These two territories are both necessary to our foothold on the east coast. The eastern alliance will break if we lose any more ground."

"How do they hide their presence from the humans in that great a number?" Armenia asked, breaking her long silence.

Lucian stood up and stepped around the table to join Reivn. "They don't anymore. Humans go missing without warning, some taken right off the streets in plain sight. The Renegades are dangerous with their carelessness. Soon the whole world will know we exist. Then the war will be with humans and Renegades both and we will be fighting just to survive."

Mithras nodded. "I know the areas around the northern territories have been breeding dangerous levels of Renegades of late. Reports have been arriving almost nightly. However, the problems are widespread throughout the globe. We have seen activity even in remote areas such as Australia. The northern hemisphere is merely the center of their focus for now."

Victus agreed. "Yes. However, their immediate goal seems to be to sever the connection between the United States and Canada. The narrow channel we have between the two ensures the safety of all those that are north of the frontlines. Reivn, how long would it take to train enough of our young to prepare them for such a frontal assault?"

"To train them well enough for that would take several months, my lord, and we would need several of the Warlords to do it. Some of the young require specific training indigenous to their particular tribes." Reivn slowly assessed the group in front of him. "There are other possibilities we could consider if we can amass enough of our Elders to do so."

Thylacinos growled at him. "You talk of gathering power and at the same time claim we are weak. Like your father, you underestimate your brethren."

Mastric turned cold eyes on the Thylacinian Ancient. "You dare? Do not mock me or my son, Thylacinos. I have not seen you in the Americas defending our holdings of late. His assessment of our strengths and weaknesses is not based on arrogance as your boastings are. Mind who you insult and remember I can crush you with one word!"

Victus stood up. "Enough, both of you! If we war amongst ourselves then we stand defenseless in the face of our enemies!"

Mastric turned to Victus. "I will not tolerate the insults of that animal," he replied coldly. "He tends to indulge too much in my affairs and those of my son's."

"You are well aware of the discomfort this Council holds over the ways of the Mastrics. Insulting Thylacinos will not change that." Victus glared at him angrily.

Thylacinos shifted into complete wolf form. He paced the room, staring in bestial hatred at the Mastrics Ancient. "I do not recognize any authority that would claim superiority over me or my kin! This is not over, brother!" he snarled through canine fangs.

"Thylacinos!" Victus called out. "Resume your place at this Council or leave! There is no time for personal grudges here! As we speak, the Lord Chancellors are planning the assault on the eastern territories! If our defenses are not prepared for such an onslaught, the territories, their princes and many of the population there will fall at the hands of our enemies!"

Thylacinos' snarl turned even Victus' head as he spat at Mastric.

With an irritated sigh, the Master of magic lifted his hand and with it, the master of beasts rose off the floor to float in mid-air.

"Put me down!" Thylacinos raged, thrashing about and trying to free himself.

Victus shot a warning look in Mastric's direction.

"Oh, very well…" With a flick of his wrist, Mastric dropped Thylacinos to the ground.

Shaking with rage, the Thylacinian Ancient shifted back to human form and stood up. "I will not sit in chamber with this insult to me and my tribe. When he is gone, I will return!" Without a backward glance, he stormed from the room and out of the fortress, taking to the night. His howls could be heard as he called the desert wolves to the hunt.

"Well, that certainly went well," Galatia scoffed in disgust. "Must you always be so temperamental with him, brother?"

Mastric gazed in her direction, the blackness beneath his hood hiding his expression. "I am not in the habit of tolerating his rampaging fits, Galatia. He is little more than an animal, like those he hunts with tonight. Mindless fury will not win a battle against the Renegades, will it?"

"Enough, Mastric!" Victus stood facing the Lord of magic. "There is cause enough for concern at his leaving! We are weakened without him! If he joins with the Renegades, then…"

"He will no more join them than you or I, Victus," Sharrukin interjected. "I am more concerned he will merely leave this Council and take his tribe with him."

Lucian cleared his throat uncomfortably. "We would not leave you to fight without our strength, but this could divide our younger kin if some follow him and walk out on the Alliance."

Sharrukin nodded. "Indeed, it could. Your tribe is one of our strengths on the front lines. We need him. Mastric, you must make peace with him for all our sakes."

Around the room, heads nodded in agreement and Mastric scowled beneath his robe. "Is that the decision of my brothers and sisters then?" he asked coldly.

Victus nodded. "It is. Make peace or you have no place on this Council. I am sorry, brother, but Sharrukin is right. We need him."

Mastric bowed in mock acquiescence before resuming his seat. "Then it shall be done... for the sake of the Council."

Victus turned his attention to Reivn. "Now... Lord Reivn. If you would continue, you said you had a plan?"

Reivn bowed his head, acknowledging the request. The angst amongst the Ancients worried him. He slowly surveyed the room. "We must retake the territories surrounding our northern borders, loosing the grip the Principatus has on the Americas. If we gather enough of our strongest warriors, it is possible to do so."

Jarod glanced up sharply. "Are you seriously suggesting we attack them?"

"I am indeed, Lord Jarod. It is the last thing they will expect, and it may well give us a needed advantage." Reivn stared at him intently before changing his gaze to others in the room.

Galatia frowned. "You are talking about taking us on the offensive, Reivn. We have always run this war as a defensive campaign, our intent being to end it, not further its fires."

"We have long done far more than that already, my lady." Reivn faced her with his answer. "We have eyes in almost every Principatus city across the globe and we frequently attack their outer fringes, shutting down outposts and safeholds. The only thing we have not done is openly plan an attack on an actual territory thus far. Let us take the fight to them."

Mithras sat back down, listening intently as Reivn spoke and mulling over possibilities.

Victus frowned and leaned forward on his throne. "Yet you recently requested to step down as Warlord. How do you expect we will launch such an assault without our most experienced Commander at the forefront of our armies?"

Reivn lifted his eyes to meet Victus' gaze. "I did not request to step down as Commander of the army, my lords, only as Warlord. I intended to keep my position as Commander and give the campaign against the Principatus my full attention. In this way, I could assure greater numbers of victories and fewer defeats. If I am no longer worried about local matters in the territories, then I can better organize our defenses and attacks against the enemy. I would use the Keep as my main base of operations. If I proclaim that entire area as a legitimate territory again, then it is one more in your arsenal that you can call upon to defend this great nation."

Silvanus scowled. "You do not have the right to declare a territory."

"Wait, Silvanus. I think he may be on to something, although I would revise it somewhat." Mithras stated quietly. "His wife serves as an Ambassador, so they may be able to form a viable defense of that area and reclaim it as legitimate ground. Until now, it has been so wild a country that few wanted to waste resources on it. But this gives us a new advantage in Australia and a second defensible stronghold from which to continue this fight."

Victus frowned. "I would not have him to step down. We can assign a new Warlord to oversee the northeastern territories, true. However, he already leads the Warlords, so let us endow him with a new title. He will be Commander in Chief of the army, and of all the Warlords as well. He would also resume his duties as the Prince of Australia, one of the largest territories in the Alliance… a fitting throne for a prince of his caliber. Your thoughts, my brethren?"

Mastric's smile was hidden beneath his hood. "A fitting task… His knowledge on the field of battle will surely bring further victories. He will of course yield to the will of the Council."

Leshye shoved back her chair and crossed her arms. "Assuming the Council endorses this plan, who would replace him? The Mastric's Warlord has long been a strong influence on keeping the young ones in line and few have Reivn's strength."

"That is my domain, Bloodhunter," Mastric answered her. "I would appoint my son, Demetrius, to become Warlord in his stead. He is older and as skilled as Reivn."

Galatia frowned. "So, you wish him to lead the Warlords as…?"

Victus nodded. "He would become our right hand."

Reivn bowed his head in resignation, not daring to let the Council see his frustration.

"I approve of the idea, Victus," Mithras stated firmly. "He would be in charge of organizing the army and continuing our campaign against the Renegades. And by changing the nature of his duties as a Warlord, then his full attention can be on defending the Alliance."

One by one, the other Council members nodded their assent.

Victus stood and approached Reivn. "Kneel, Lord Reivn."

Reivn lowered his eyes to the floor and his heart sank, as he dropped to one knee.

"I hereby appoint you to the title of Warlord prefect, Commander in Chief of all the armies and Prince of Australia forthwith. Your charge is to lead our Warlords and our armies to continued victory, defending the territories from our enemies. Do you accept this charge?"

Reivn slowly nodded, knowing he had no choice. "I live to serve."

Victus nodded and looked around. Lifting the scepter he held, he laid it on first one and then the other of Reivn's shoulders. "So it shall be henceforth. Rise, Lord Reivn, Warlord Prefect."

Reivn stood up and bowed to the Council in acceptance.

One by one, the other Warlords kissed his crest ring in acceptance of their new leader.

Mastric sat back, eyeing the spectacle in silence. *Everything is going according to plan...*

## Chapter Forty-Three
## Temple of the Blood God

*Confucius once said we may learn wisdom by three methods. First by reflection, which is noblest, second by imitation, which is easiest and third by experience, which is the bitterest. Yet it seems to be through experience we learn the most. When the voice of wisdom speaks, those less experienced too often refuse to listen and find themselves awash in a sea of regret. Is this the only true way any can learn a path... to continually fall and find themselves cut deeper for the experience? Not all experience is for the better. There are some places one should never go, some things one should never see and some events that should never have happened in the first place. If only profound wisdom was so easily given to those we love in order to protect them from the very thing that so often proves most dangerous in their lives... themselves.*

*Even with the best of advice and intentions, one cannot always be sure of the safety of those they love when gone from their sight. My angel... I think of her as I sit in Council chambers and cannot but hope she returned home and left the matter of Cyrus alone. He is far more dangerous than anyone she has ever encountered, and I fear she is obsessed with his demise. It is only the knowledge Lunitar and Jack will keep her from foolishly pursuing him that gives me a measure of peace and keeps me from sending for her here.*

*Is it always like this... this worry I feel for her? Loving someone is a powerful and dangerous thing. It clouds your judgment and makes you weak...*

*Lord Reivn Draegon*

\* \* \* \* \*

At sunset, Angelique's small hunting party reloaded the SUVs and headed toward southern Mexico with Nicholas and two other Wolvens. The rest of Nicholas' men stayed behind to wait for the remainder of their pack.

Nicholas pulled a map from his pocket and began guiding Jack to roads that could give them an edge and gain some ground on Cyrus. He was keeping in constant contact by phone with his people as they tracked the Martulian, staying far enough behind to remain undetected while moving through the jungle terrain.

By dawn the following morning, the group had gained on Cyrus, but they were still not close enough to catch him before he reached the pyramid.

Nicholas approached Angelique and Jack. "I talked to my brothers and we agreed that it would be wise to keep moving to try and gain as much ground as possible."

Jack glanced over at their human companions. "They are exhausted and in need of serious rest. They cannot take another shift of driving."

Nicholas nodded. "I agree. My brothers and I will drive. This terrain is treacherous, and few know how to navigate it well, but this is native soil to us. We know the way. We can keep going as long as the roads hold well enough to pull the trailer."

Angelique sighed. "We will all need rest when this is over. Between the long journey and what I'm sure is a coming battle, this will try our strength to the last."

"Don't worry yourself about me or my own. We can handle ourselves in a fight. We've been defending ourselves from the Renegades for years now, so we're used to this." Nicholas smiled. "Just take care of the team and keep your head down. It gets nasty out here."

After a brief respite allowing them all time for sustenance, the Wolvens picked up the pace while Angelique and her party retired from the daylight. Luck was with them. They were able to stick to fairly well-traveled roads, allowing them to keep going through most of the day.

Not long before sunset, they had to stop. The roads had become too obstructed with overgrowth for them to pull the trailer any further. Nicholas and his brethren waited patiently for sunset. He stared at the trailer where the Immortals lay sleeping, deep in thought. Then he looked up. "We made up some time. Our scouts reported Cyrus was only an hour or so ahead of us and has stopped for the day's passage himself," he told his companions.

"True, but we are in a dead stop now," one of his companions argued. "The H2's can carry their group with ease, but without the trailer, it's going to be hard to get the rest of us on board."

*Not to mention the cargo they'll need to stay alive during the rest of the trip*, Nicholas thought, falling silent as he gazed at the human blood servants hovering near the trailer to listen for their masters. Over the next two hours, he did the equation in his head, until he heard the sound of the trailer door. Glancing skyward, he saw that the sun had indeed finally set.

Jack was the first out, the others not far behind. Approaching Nicholas, he nodded. "How long have we been off the road?"

"Around two hours," Nicholas answered.

Somewhat relieved when he heard it had only been a short while, and that their prey was not far ahead of them, he turned his attention to Nicholas' concern about car space for the crew.

Nicholas frowned. "I don't like leaving anyone behind, but I don't see a way around it."

Nodding in agreement, Jack thought hard. "Without the travel space in the trailer, there isn't going to be enough room for everyone and the necessary equipment too."

"There's no helping it, Jack," Nicholas finally pointed out. "My two and I will have to let you go on alone. You're going to need your servants and that leaves few options."

Jack sighed. "I realize that, but what of you three and the trailer?"

Nicholas looked around. "We can pull the trailer off the road into the woods and disguise it using our own power. It's not like other Immortal's, so it wouldn't be easily recognizable to the Renegades should they come through the area. We'll stay with it until my pack can get out here to pick us up, then we'll take it back to Mexico City."

Jack glanced over at Angelique, who was talking to the servants and working on getting things moved around. "I really wish she was staying with you. If anything happens to her, it will be my life on the line. Reivn is super protective of her."

Nicholas raised an eyebrow. "If I know anything of the Mastrics tribe, it's that they can handle their own pretty well. She is no youngling, so relax. She'll have no trouble handling this."

Jack disagreed. "She may be older, but she wasn't trained until recently. She still has to get used to the idea of how to fight. In our last battle, she froze up and almost got herself killed. I only came with her because I knew she would never leave this alone. She wants this guy pretty bad for killing Rosalind. I understand it because her death hit us all hard."

As the others finished loading their gear into the vehicles, Jack and Nicholas moved out toward the trail, talking about the terrain. Nicholas stared out into the blackness of the jungle around them. "I wish we could do more. We were willing to see this through to the end."

Jack gripped his shoulder. "I know that. You and your brethren are honorable men. It's okay. I have this one. There will be other battles, my friend."

"It will be a tough fight, even with the skilled warriors in your party," Nicholas spoke in low tones, unwilling to worry the others. "You're going to have to keep your eyes open from here on. The roads out here are old and overgrown. There may even be trees in the way."

Jack listened as he drew the lines on his map where the buried roads were supposed to be. "I'll post one of our people on the spotlight as we go, just to be safe."

Nicholas held out his hand. "So, this is goodbye. Good luck, Jack. I hope we meet again. You're not too bad for a suckhead."

Jack grinned and grasped Nicholas' hand in a firm handshake. "Well, you're not so bad for a furball either! You be careful and watch your backs, will you?"

Nicholas nodded silently. He watched Jack walk away and waved goodbye to the others.

Jack drove the lead SUV, taking Angelique, Ruben and two of the servants with him. Annie had the other SUV carrying Shaman and the other two servants. They had pulled the trailer off the road with little trouble, dropping the hitch in record time. When the small party departed, Jack could still see Nicholas in the rearview mirror, finishing the camouflage on the trailer.

The two vehicles moved into the jungle terrain easily, the underbrush not overly dense at first. However, as they pushed on it got thicker, forcing them to slow their pace. Both vehicles had been rigged with military spotlights and these were focused on the trail in front of them.

Jack stopped as the spotlights picked up something beneath some underbrush that had been crushed, as though another vehicle had passed through recently.

Shaman got out to investigate and moments later came back with the answer. "Cyrus has killed again. What you saw was the body of a dead girl."

Jack frowned. "How long?" he asked.

"Maybe an hour. Her body is still warm," Shaman answered.

Jack nodded and signaled to the others. Then he grinned at Angelique. "We've got him!" While he waited for them to get back in the vehicles, he stared at the trail in front of them. "The fool is clearing the road for us. Let's go get the bastard!" When they began moving, he picked up the pace a little, noting they were able to move over the crushed foliage with little difficulty.

Finally, they caught sight of an SUV ahead of them, moving slowly as the creature in front of it moved larger jungle growth out of its way.

"There he is," Jack yelled.

When Angelique's party grew closer to the Cyrus, the beast in front of his vehicle divided into two. Then they worked faster, letting him pick up speed until he moved out of sight again.

The hunting party was not far behind though, and they continued to push forward. The underbrush got thicker, slowing them down and making following the trail even harder.

Jack growled. "If we don't even the odds somehow, we'll lose him again."

"No, we won't. We only need to keep eyes on him. I can do that from the sky. All you have to do is follow me." Grateful of the magic Reivn had taught her, Angelique transformed into a Raven and flew up just over the tree line. She stayed high enough to see the vehicle ahead, but low enough for Jack and Annie to follow her.

Cyrus was moving fast. Small trees and underbrush were torn from their roots and crushed as the creatures cleared the way.

Jack and Annie handled their vehicles with expertise over the rough terrain, and they pushed onward, racing to the distant pyramid that held the sleeping Ancient.

When dawn approached, it was clear to both sides that they would not reach the Aztec city before sunrise, so the chase stopped for the day. Jack's men were both armed and well-trained. They had slept through the night and were prepared to stand watch to protect their masters. No one disturbed them, however, and as darkness fell, the party rose to the sound of the jungle's nocturnal cycle coming to life. They quickly fed, stowed their gear and got back on the trail.

Angelique resumed her Raven form and took flight. She located Cyrus immediately. He was traveling at a rapid pace.

For another hour they chased Cyrus. Now that they were deep in the Yucatan jungle, they could see the magical field blanketing the whole area.

"There's more here than just a temple," Jack observed.

Ruben agreed, but before he could respond, they broke through the underbrush into a clearing and found themselves staring at the pyramid. Set in a clearing in the middle of nowhere, it towered into the night sky… a ghostly structure looming in the darkness.

Cyrus' abandoned vehicle sat just a few feet away.

Angelique landed near it and resumed her human form. Then joining the others, she donned her battle gear.

The party crossed the field silently, moving in a tight formation as they watched the outskirts of the clearing for any surprises. But they reached the bottom of the steps without incident and began the upward climb to the entrance. The jungle around them was quiet and as still as death.

The temple stood three hundred feet high, and each wall was a precise triangle, creating a perfect pyramid. Ornate Aztec symbols adorned the massive stones, depicting the blood God, Tezcatlipoca, with his son, Mictlantecuhtle, whom they called the God of the dead. The Aztecs knew Mictlantecuhtle to be the bearer of sacrificial gifts to Tezcatlipoca and paid homage through human sacrifices. They believed both to be Gods and worshiped them as such.

The group could not help but stare in awe at the images around them as they climbed the steps of the pyramid. Mosaics adorned the walls depicting human sacrifice, with cups held up to fill with blood for their Gods as their victims died. Other scenes portrayed victims tied and left at the door for the Gods to take them to the underworld. By the time the party reached the entrance at the pyramid's top, they were convinced they were dealing with a powerful Immortal and his young. The depictions by the Aztecs left little doubt. The story was written on every stone.

The small group gathered around the entrance and peered into the dark interior, awakening their senses and trying to find Cyrus's trail. But all they found was the scent of old death, crumbling stone, moss, and dirt. Finally, they silently and cautiously entered the ancient temple.

A labyrinth of passageways and corridors holding dozens of chambers awaited them, each with secrets of its own. Originally the temple had been built as a haven, with the intent of worship above and experimental magic below. But over the centuries, the temple had undergone many changes for defense purposes. Secrets of the past had become buried within its walls, and the magic woven into it had taken on a life of its own. Now, somewhere deep inside, evil and its allies waited. The interior looked as though it was untouched by either the elements or time. Everywhere they looked, carvings on the walls depicted Aztecs at work and at worship, with a recurring theme of Priests wearing elaborate headdresses and holding large goblets. The floors, walls and ceiling were made of earth and stone, the air was dry and musty, and the whole structure was blanketed in complete darkness.

Jack lit two torches and handed them to Shaman and Annie. Then he lit another for himself.

When the light hit the floor, it seemed to move, but a closer look revealed thousands of rats scurrying to avoid its brilliance. They moved further into the corridor, noting the small, empty rooms on either side. These alcoves each had only one thing... a single post rising from the center of the floor.

*These must have been where the Aztecs left their live offerings,* Jack telepathied the others.

Angelique shook her head. *I think it's revolting,* she responded.

At the end of the corridor, they found a mosaic of incredible detail made from fine multi-colored stones that depicted the city in its grandest days. In the center was the pyramid, with a dark-haired, dark-skinned man sitting atop it. He was drinking from a golden goblet and the contents pouring from the cup were deep red.

*Wine perhaps, or blood,* Jack telepathied.

The intricacy of the mosaic was far beyond any mortal's skill. Due to the magic it possessed, it was so captivating that it had an almost hypnotic effect.

Angelique shook herself and moved away. "This would easily enslave a human's mind, Jack," she whispered. "It's powerful." She looked down both hallways and frowned.

Jack followed her gaze. *We have to split up,* he sent to the others. *Mark your paths so you can find your way back. We don't know how big this place is or how far down it goes.*

Angelique and Jack took the right corridor. Annie, Ruben, and Shaman went left, moving cautiously. Completely unaware of what awaited them, they slipped into the halls. Without warning, small holes hidden in the ornate carvings on each side of the corridor opened and sharpened darts surprised them with a potentially lethal crossfire.

Annie rolled, dodged and ran for the far end, safely moving past the danger. Ruben followed, magically erecting a shield around himself to deflect the deadly barbs.

Behind them, Shaman caught one in his right arm. But once they were across, he pulled it out without a second thought. Then he tore off his sleeve and tied it around the wound. "Come," he stated. He turned and headed further into the dark interior.

Angelique and Jack also made it safely through their hall, but at the far the end, Jack stopped.

She gasped when she saw a spike had pierced his leg. "You're hurt!" she cried.

"It's a small matter, Angie," he stated calmly, pulling it out and tossing it on the floor. "A minor inconvenience..." he chuckled and closed the wound before they moved on.

When he finished healing himself, they turned to the dark passageway in front of them and began searching for signs of Cyrus or a sleeping Ancient. The first room they found smelled of old death.

Jack entered first, holding his torch high so they could see its interior.

There were six large stone altars positioned around the room. Upon each was the perfectly preserved body of a priest, covered in Aztec ritual clothes and gold jewelry inlaid with precious gems. They appeared to be sleeping, but a closer look revealed puncture wounds on the necks and no blood in the bodies. Their bodies had been preserved by the magic surrounding them. These were Mictlantecuhtle's priests, denied eternity by their master.

Angelique reached out to touch one, but Jack's warning stopped her. "No! Don't touch anything! This room is probably booby-trapped, and we can't risk another fight yet! We need to find the Ancient first... before Cyrus does!"

Angelique backed up, careful not to disturb the bodies. "This place is unnerving," she whispered.

Jack patted her on the shoulder. "I forgot you've never been in a place like this before. It will be okay, I promise. Come on, let's keep moving."

At the door, she stopped and turned. "I can almost feel their presence here," she admitted.

He pulled her into the hall. "That's because they never left."

Neither one saw the wisps that rose from the bodies to watch them as they walked on.

Angelique felt a shiver run down her spine and turned to stare behind her for a moment, then shook her head and hurried to catch up to Jack.

They reached the end of the corridor and found a large room in front of them. All four walls were covered with mosaics depicting Mictlantecuhtle's life. The mosaics here were not as intricate as they had been in the first one they had seen, and these seemed to tell a story. Angelique stepped in to take a closer look.

Jack saw movement in the corner and called out a warning.

An old blood servant, apparently abandoned by another Immortal, charged them from the shadows in a frenzied rage. It was starving and desperate to feed to save itself from death.

Jack sidestepped the mad creature and cut it in half, killing it instantly. Stepping over the body, he wiped his blade off on its shirt and then calmly studied the mosaics.

Angelique walked over and stood beside him. "Can you read those?"

Jack nodded. "As a matter of fact, yes. I have studied many ancient languages, including Egyptian hieratic and Aztec symbolism. This is fascinating. It details the life of their blood God. This last part states their God went to sleep. I'm going to assume that means there is an Immortal in the temple, the lesser acting as sort of a guard for his master. They may already know we're here."

Annie, Shaman and Ruben found a room similar to what Angelique and Jack had, only it was a room where the priests had prepared themselves for the ceremonies in which they sacrificed their victims to Mictlantecuhtle. One wall was made up of highly polished silver, creating a mirror. When it was made, the Ancient Immortal had woven dark magic into it. Anyone who gazed into it would see the darkest side of their existence. Not knowing its power, Annie went over and stood in front of it. A terrifying image appeared before her.

Ruben gasped when he saw the reflection.

But Annie shrugged. "A child's toy. Too bad I don't have more time to play. Nothing important here. Let's go."

When she moved away, Shaman shot a bolt of white-hot flames at it, melting the silver with its intense heat. "Now a toy for no one."

Annie's laughter filled the hall as they moved on.

At the end of their corridor, Shaman found something quite different … a ten-foot wide pit dug into the floor. The hole had been concealed by a powerful illusion. He was leading them and stepped unknowingly onto the illusionary floor. It immediately vanished under him, dropping him into the ten-foot hole. He landed on his feet, but when he touched the bottom it triggered a trap, and a stone block the size of the hole itself plunged toward him from above.

"Shaman, look out!" Annie yelled, diving for the edge of the pit and reaching for his hand.

Time had shifted the pyramid's structure slightly, misaligning the huge block from falling directly into the pit, and it lodged partway down.

Annie grabbed his hand. "Come on, you idiot! It's not going to hold forever!"

As she spoke, it shifted and broke free, continuing its plunge downward. They only just managed to jump clear as the 90-ton block slammed into the pit, crushing everything beneath it.

Shaman got up from where they landed and dusted himself off. "Thank you, Annie."

"Idiot!" Annie growled. "That was a little too close. Let's go."

They crossed the top of the block and continued on. The other side of the corridor had nothing more than small alcoves and a few empty rooms scattered here and there. But the direction of the passageway had turned again, and they were headed back toward the center of the pyramid.

When Annie finally saw light ahead, she frowned and signaled for them to stop. She moved forward to investigate. Then relief showed on her face and she signaled to Shaman and Ruben. When they joined her, she pointed across the open room to the other side.

Jack and Angelique stood across from them. The corridor they had followed had led them there. Jack was silently peering around the corner when he spotted Annie. He motioned for silence and pointed into the room.

The light was coming from within and not from their torches, which had been doused. It was a robing room, much like the one Annie's party had previously come across. There was a mirror on the far wall, carefully placed between two doors. But the torches were freshly lit, suggesting someone else was already there.

Signaling Annie, Jack entered cautiously, Angelique behind him. The group slipped quietly across to the doors on the opposite side. Then a chanting sound filled the air and they froze.

*It sounds like a ritual of some kind*, Angelique telepathied.

*It is*, Jack answered. *They're trying to awaken Tezcatlipoca, their blood God. He's here.* He signaled them to take positions by the two doors as they prepared to enter the room beyond. When they were ready, he nodded.

The group slipped through both doors, hoping to catch whoever was inside by surprise. They were alarmed when they saw there was an archaic blood rite in progress.

Before them on a huge dais, two priests had opened their wrists to feed the sleeping figure of the Ancient lying on the altar. One of them shouted when he spotted the hunting party. Then the sleeper opened his eyes...

# BLOOD FEUD

## Chapter Forty-Four
## The Eastern Alliance

*As I sit here awaiting my father's summons, I cannot but be glad my angel is safely on her way back to Draegonstorm. The mere thought of having her within my father's grasp grips my heart with a fear I cannot fathom. He has promised me her safe keeping and protection from the Council, but I know him too well. He does nothing without a price. What debt will he demand of me this time? What ignoble thing shall pass at my hands just to keep her alive and how far am I willing to go? My conscience battles my heart at every turn now...*

*I prepare once more for war, and more of our kind's blood will stain the earth beneath us. I begin to think the reasons behind our curse are linked to the continuous ravaging of this world's good earth... the destruction with which we so wantonly restructure its face and people. Human history is littered with our vile touch from beneath the shadowed curtain and in their innocence, they do not even defend against it. Only a handful of hunters, those that serve the church, even attempt to stop the violent march across what was once a pure creation. God, when will the bloodshed end? I have been the tip of the Council's sword for centuries and have commanded tens of thousands to their deaths in a march for a victory that will never come.*

*I long for peace and a world in which we can restructure our own way of life, returning to nights as I knew them in Sarmatia so long ago. That life is as far from me now as my own salvation, for with every strike of my blade against a child, who like Angelique, could have been spared and returned to the fold, I condemn my soul to burn.*

*Lord Reivn Draegon*

\* \* \* \* \*

Reivn sat alone in the unlit study waiting in agitation for Mastric to arrive and thought over the meeting that had taken place earlier. He did not have long to wait.

Mastric's fury was apparent in his cold tone when he closed the door. "Why did you not discuss this plan of yours to attack the enemy in their own cities with me? Or worse, this idea of yours to fortify and defend the Atlantic City territory? That city sits on the edge of a blade. When it falls, the Principatus will slaughter any of our kind they find. I will not yield you up in sacrifice to this cause, Reivn. I have greater plans for you."

Reivn bowed his head. "Forgive me, my lord. My resolve causes me to forget myself at times. We need that territory to keep the Eastern Alliance intact. There are many young faces I know too well to stand by while they fall… not while I still draw breath." The deafening silence that followed was unnerving as Reivn stared at his master's back.

Mastric sat thinking, his eyes hollow pools that glistened from under the shadows of his hood. Finally, he turned to his youngest son. "I will let you do this, but only with conditions. You may take offensive in this war, but you are not going to do so alone. I will insist the Council send Jack Dunn and Leshye with you. You will need powerful allies."

Reivn bowed, relieved he would not have to argue the point with his creator. "I am grateful my lord. With the help of Leshye, Jack, my sons and Angelique, I will…"

"I am not yet finished, child!" Mastric snarled, his fangs extending to show his full fury.

Reivn took a step back, then froze as the icy touch of Mastric's magic took ahold of him.

"Now that I have your full attention," Mastric stated coldly, "I will continue. Angelique is to stay at your Keep. Do not involve her in this conflict. The questions that surround her in the Council chambers have not yet abated. If you value her life, you will remember this. Instead, I will send another of my line… Thaddeus Dominici. He can give you the aid you seek. Now leave me! I will send orders for you when all is ready. In the meantime, return to the Americas."

Reivn bowed again before turning abruptly and leaving the room, his pride stinging from Mastric's reprimand. His mind was working furiously by the time he returned to the chambers assigned to him during his visits to the Council halls. *I will have to wait a few hours before I can portal travel to the guild. Damn, but I hate traveling across time zones!* Dropping onto the bed, he closed his eyes and dreamed of his red-haired beauty until a knock at his door roused him from his thoughts. "Come," he answered. The door creaked as it opened, and he looked up in annoyance.

"I hope I'm not disturbing you, but we need to talk." Lucian stood leaning against the doorjamb, waiting until he was invited in.

Reivn motioned him in and sat up. "I am surprised you are still here. With your father having left, I mean." He assessed the man now sitting in front of him. "What can I do for you?"

"I'm going with you. Any battle there will be brutal, and as you said, there are very few Elders there. However, there is something else too," Lucian paused.

His eyes narrowing, Reivn glanced up, wondering if his father had dictated yet another condition of the upcoming campaign.

Lucian sighed and continued. "The Catholic church has sent an expedition into the Eastern United States. All the fighting there has caught their attention and hunters were dispatched to begin extermination. Reivn, my friend, our task just became much more difficult."

"Damn!" Reivn cursed under his breath. "I had hoped to keep this from their eyes!" He got up and began to pace the room. "The border cities already have their hands full with the Renegades. What with the assassination of Lord Sorin and his staff, keeping the factions there together under one banner has been trying at best. For God's sake, even Wilmington's prince reports some repercussions from that loss. These damn Renegades are a disease! We must push them back! We just installed Atlantic City's prince, and he needs time to establish himself."

Lucian nodded in agreement. "At least he has a good staff with him. I already summoned as many of my tribe as could be spared, and I'm moving my own family into Wilmington to be close by. I'm afraid they aren't as numerous as I'd like, but every warrior we can get will be of help in this. I ran into Leshye before I came here. She is already gathering a number of Mithranians and will be returning to the Americas tonight. Are the Mastrics going to send extra help or are they relying on the guilds there to do the fighting?"

"I wish I knew for sure, but my father did not speak of the matter. He merely gave the order to await further instructions. That is what I must do." Reivn's expression spoke volumes of his displeasure. "I should already be in Atlantic City, preparing our warriors for the coming battle, not preparing to take on some coddled boy!"

His curiosity peaked, Lucian glanced sideways at Reivn. "Coddled boy?"

Reivn frowned. "Mastric's grandson. I am to have him with me in place of Angelique. I know nothing of him other than that his creator is my brother, Silas… that and the fact he has supposedly had good training. He was not part of my jurisdiction, so I have never met him."

Lucian chuckled in amusement at Reivn's disgruntled expression. "He is probably far more than a mere boy, Reivn. Mastric is more intelligent than that. You're just upset because it isn't your wife. Believe me, she is far safer away from the fighting, as you are with distance between you. She would distract you. That's a good way to get yourself killed, my friend."

With a growl, Reivn moved angrily across the room to his closet and pulled out his coat. "I have heard that before and not from you! I am aware what you all think! You forget I have seen centuries of battle and am not easily caught off guard! Now, I must see to my traveling arrangements! Good evening!" Not waiting for Lucian to leave, he stormed from the room.

Lucian chuckled. "Damned if that Mastric doesn't have a worse temper than any Thylacinian I know." Shaking his head, he followed Reivn down the corridor.

Deep in the bowels of the fortress, Mastric frowned and withdrew his sight from watching his son. He was in his lab, and still waiting for Thaddeus. His courier had been dispatched immediately after the meeting with Reivn and had not returned. Now his impatience grew, his dark eyes glistening in the torchlight. A spider crawled across the table and he ignored its presence, focusing instead on the wick of a candle. It ignited as his thoughts touched it and he idly played with the flame, causing it to dance as it rose from the wick to hover in the air by his will alone. Another minute passed in silence and he hurled the flame across the table at the spider in annoyance, instantly reducing it to ashes.

Footsteps got his attention, and he focused on the hall. He saw his courier and opened the door with a single thought. "You are late!" he stated, his voice an icy reflection of his anger.

The courier trembled as he stepped into the room. "A thousand pardons, my lord. I had trouble finding him. It took longer than expected to deliver your orders."

Mastric looked beyond him into the hall, knowing it was empty. "Where is he, then? My orders were clear! I told you to return with him, not alone!" His hand barely moved, and the courier lifted off the floor and slammed against the far wall, remaining pinned there. Mastric got up and walked over to stand in front of him. "Answer me or I will end your existence right here!"

"I am here, my lord." A deep voice spoke from behind him.

Mastric turned and came face to face with a tall, dark-haired man, his Roman background obvious in the olive skin and deep brown eyes that met his gaze. "At last, Thaddeus. I have been waiting for you." He dropped the courier and dismissed him with a wave of his hand.

The courier bowed and scurried from the room.

Mastric turned back to his grandson. "I am sending you to Atlantic City with Reivn. I want you to be my eyes and ears. I do not entirely trust my son's thoughts of late. He is besotted over Valfort's daughter, and I am humoring him by allowing him to keep her for now. However, if she should prove a danger to my plans or our Council, contact me immediately. You can rendezvous with Reivn once you reach America's east coast. Here are the necessary documents you will need. You leave immediately."

Thaddeus bowed, accepting the papers without a word. He knew better than to argue and reassignment would be refreshing after so much time with his own father.

Nodding in satisfaction, Mastric dismissed the man and telepathied Reivn. It was short and concise. *Leave for the Americas at dusk. Thaddeus will meet you in Atlantic City. The others will contact you when they arrive in the territory.*

Annoyed beyond words, Reivn stormed back to the room he occupied. "I could have made those arrangements without his interference!" He growled as he prepared to leave. Gathering only what he needed, he strapped one sword to his back and a second to his waist. Then after looking around the room one last time, he headed to the portal chamber. As he stepped into the massive swirling vortex, he closed his eyes, letting the magic carry him to his destination.

Reivn arrived in Atlantic City to chaos and disorderly pandemonium. Many of the different tribes' younger children were scrambling to gather their meager remains and flee the city. Older, more experienced warriors were trying to organize a defensive perimeter to protect against invaders that had begun infiltrating from the Philadelphia strongholds.

Serena and Armand greeted him the moment he stepped from the portal.

"I have never been happier to see you, Lord Reivn," Serena stated, relieved that help had finally arrived. "The Renegades began small raids on the city two nights ago and we have suffered casualties on almost every front here. I've had the healers working overtime."

"So far, it's only been minor skirmishes, whittling away at our defenses. However, it's obvious they are planning a major attack," Armand reported as they followed Reivn to his office.

Reivn scowled. This guild held fond memories for him and the idea of having Renegades invading it greatly angered him. "Serena, send word to evacuate our library to New York or Wilmington! I want all those scrolls and tomes out by morning! Armand, get the weaker Mastrics to the safety of other guilds, as well as any severely wounded! Ignite the Guild's perimeter defenses immediately upon their exodus! Has Thaddeus arrived yet?"

Armand nodded. "He arrived just before you did, my lord. I settled him into his rooms. He should be joining us momentarily."

As if on cue, a knock at the door interrupted them.

"Come!" Reivn ordered briskly.

Thaddeus opened the door and bowed to Reivn as he entered. "Lord Reivn, I am Thaddeus Dominici. I was ordered to join you. I am at your command."

Reivn quickly thought of all he needed to achieve and how soon in order to defend the city. Finally, he looked up. "Gather the strongest of the Mastrics here and prepare them to defend this Guild. I also need to know how many we have. Get me a head count as fast as you can."

Thaddeus bowed. "Consider it done." Then he turned to go.

Reivn called out to him. "Thaddeus... Welcome aboard."

Thaddeus merely nodded and closed the door behind him.

Serena turned to leave too, then stopped. "Is Angelique arriving soon?" she asked.

"No. Mastric ordered me to send her to the Keep," Reivn replied. He began sifting through the paperwork on his desk.

Serena nodded and left the room, relieved her friend was safely out of the way.

Armand followed her, his thoughts on the coming evacuations.

They passed Lucian in the hallway, heading for Reivn's office himself. He knocked, and then pushed the door open and walked in.

Reivn was standing by the French doors and staring out at the garden. *If we lose Atlantic City, we will never walk here together again,* he mused sadly, his thoughts on his wife.

"Am I interrupting?" Lucian asked. He could see Reivn was troubled.

Reivn turned around. "I did not think to have such a fight on my hands so soon. This base has been one of our strongholds for years. Now we must defend it from the coming onslaught. If we lose this city, it may well bring the Eastern Alliance to its knees."

His courier, Girard, interrupted them when he walked in and handed Reivn several letters. "These just came from the sentries on the northeast end of the city, my lord."

Reivn sat down at his desk, tore them open one at a time and quickly read them. Then he looked up. "Are they sure of this?"

"Yes, sir. There aren't too many left." Shifting his stance, Girard looked uncomfortable. "Lord Edward is on his way here now to discuss this with you."

Lucian looked up at the mention of the prince's name. "He's still in the city? Protocol dictates he relocate to a safe location in the event of an attack. Why weren't we notified sooner?"

Girard shifted his glance from one to the other. "Lord Edward himself has been organizing our outer defenses, my lord."

Lucian snorted. "He's still largely inexperienced and new in defending this territory. He hasn't been on the throne long enough to even begin to know how to handle this mess."

Reivn frowned. "We have a bigger problem on our hands, Lucian."

Lucian raised an eyebrow. "What's that?" he asked.

Reivn held up another letter he had opened. "According to this report, most of the outer defenses are already gone," he replied. "The Renegades have been systematically wiping them out. Those still alive have either retreated into the city itself or have fled the territory." Another knock on the door caused him to toss the letters on the desk in frustration. "Damn these interruptions! Girard, just open the door!" he growled impatiently.

Edward was about to knock again when the door opened. "I'm sorry. I wasn't sure anyone was here yet," he stated, entering the room.

Lucian shook his hand. "Lord Edward, I understand you've been trying to organize our defenses. An admirable thought, but you should not be here. Why didn't you follow protocol?"

"My job is to defend this territory and that is what I have been trying to do," Edward explained. "I want to keep this territory intact. I can't do that from another city."

Reivn sighed in exasperation. "This city needed the outer defenses to remain intact! What happened to our sentries posted along the perimeter?"

Edward frowned. "I pulled them into the city to defend it," he answered. Anything further fell silent when he saw Reivn's expression.

"You mean you just handed all the outlying areas to our enemies?" Reivn roared, getting out of his seat. "Have you completely lost your mind?"

Lucian caught his shoulder. "Reivn, don't! It's too late for that! Now we must look to the defense of the city itself! The perimeter can be taken back afterward!"

Growling, Reivn turned his back on Edward. "You incompetent fool! This may cost us the city and many good people with it!" He stood there in angry silence thinking of the preparations being made, trying to find something that would give them an edge. Finally, he turned to Girard. "Have the sentries still guarding the remaining outposts sent any other news that you have not given me yet?" he asked.

Lucian looked up at that, waiting for the answer as well.

"Yes, sir. Reports have come in from all over the city. The attack will happen tonight. I'm sure of it. All our people are saying the same thing… unusual activity on the outskirts. They're going to use the festival to cover their attack." Girard fell silent and waited to be dismissed, knowing there would be no more messages to the Council tonight.

Lucian raised an eyebrow. "Festival?"

Reivn nodded. "It's something the mortals do. They have a parade and fireworks, and there will be people everywhere. That makes it easy for the Renegades to get in without detection."

Lucian shook his head. "And more difficult for us to defend ourselves without discovery. Well, I had hoped we'd have more time, but I guess we'll just have to defeat them now instead of later." He turned to Edward. "We need to get you to a safe location. This city suffered tragic losses with Lords' Sorin and Gareth's deaths. It cannot so soon lose another of its Princes."

Reivn frowned and glared at them both. His silence was unnerving as he calculated the risk of moving the new prince beyond the territory. Finally, he spoke. "Lord Edward, you have one hour to set your affairs in order and gather what you need. I am assuming control of the throne until this is over. You are joining Prince Davenport in Wilmington for your own safety."

Edward stared in fury at the two Warlords. "This is my territory! I should be defending it, not hiding away like some whelp! This is outrageous! I will complain to the Council about this!"

Reivn ignored his remark. "You are running out of time, Edward. Get your things or leave without them. It makes no difference to me. Either way, you are leaving for Wilmington."

Edward stormed from the room growling his displeasure.

Lucian agreed with Reivn and scratched his head. "I'll get one of my Elders to take him. Hawke's a good fighter. He'll be well-protected."

Girard sighed. *It's going to be a long night.* Approaching Lucian, he bowed. "My lord, shall I take the message to her?"

"At once, Girard. Let her know I have a mission for her. Tell her to Head to Edward's mansion." Lucian turned to Reivn when the courier left. "Has Jack arrived yet? We need to meet with both he and Leshye if we are to coordinate this."

Reivn growled in obvious irritation. "Not yet. I received a dispatch from him half an hour ago. He's been held up on another matter. He will be here as soon as he can."

Lucian shook his head. "I should have known. What of Thaddeus? Is he here?"

"He is. I have him organizing the less experienced Mastrics to prepare them for battle." Reivn's thoughts returned to Angelique, who waited patiently for word from him. "Angelique will not like the order to remain at Draegonstorm, but perhaps it is for the best. I am glad I had the foresight to send her home with Lunitar. The Council still mistrusts her, and if something goes wrong, I will be attending her execution and my own as well."

Smiling at Reivn's expression, Lucian slapped his shoulder as they left the room and headed for the security office. "At least she will be safe where she is. Better that than to risk losing her in the coming fight. That was my fear for the new prince. I chose Hawke because she isn't afraid of a scrap and if asked to guard him, she'll die to keep him alive."

Before Reivn could answer, an explosion somewhere in the building rocked its foundation. "Come on!" he yelled and ran in the direction of the noise.

In the woods not far from the Guild, Hawke sat bolt upright when she heard the explosion. Then she caught the sound of footsteps running toward her fast. She rolled over and crouched down, ready to jump on the approaching person. A man crossed the grass in front of her and she leapt, dropping him to the ground and pinning him beneath her.

"Get off me, you idiot! Lucian sent me to find you! Ugh! Get... off!" Girard shoved at her.

She snorted. "Lucian sent you? Why? He knows I'm not a Council lackey." She let him up.

Brushing himself off, he frowned at her. "He needs you to guard the new prince, Lord Edward, and to get him to Jonathan Davenport's in Wilmington. He says you're the best person for the job. You need to report to the prince's manor house immediately."

She stared into the dark, watching a bug crawl up the side of the old oak she had been laying under. "Why me? He must have a dozen or more of us in the city." She knew the answer before she even asked, but she was not feeling cooperative.

He pulled the message from inside his shirt. "He wants you because you're the best there is," he huffed, annoyed. "Here's the letter. I'll tell him you're on your way." Not waiting for an answer, he finished dusting himself off and turned to go.

"Damn it!" she spat out. *Lucian knows me too well.* "Tell him I'll be there!" she shouted at Girard's retreating figure.

Within the hour, she was gazing up at the outline of gates barely visible in the dark. *I should have said no*, she thought as she entered and made her way up the drive. Oddly, there were no lights outside and no security men to greet her. The gardeners, the hired help... all were absent from the great mansion.

Hawke made her way up the front steps, Inside, she found the inner hall destroyed as though it had been sacked. She growled and began to search for her quarry.

Most of the rooms had been torn apart, their valuables stripped and carried off. The shredded remains of the once beautiful house gave her cause to fear for Prince Edward's life. She picked up the pace, the need to find him growing urgent. She crept along in silence, believing the enemy had already arrived and was waiting around the corner to claim her life.

When Hawke reached the second floor, she heard a voice raised in anger. She moved cautiously forward, staying in the shadows while she tried to find its owner. When she drew close to the prince's office, she stopped. Recognizing the voice, she peeked around the corner.

Prince Edward was standing at his desk, his back to the door. He was on the phone deep in conversation, not paying any attention to the door or his own safety.

Hawke was just about to walk in when something he said startled her and she froze.

"I don't give a damn! Kill them all! They can't hold the city with our numbers!" Edward slammed his fist down on the desk. "They're moving me to Wilmington, so get here soon!"

Hawke shifted her position and scanned the hallway, her senses picking up the fresh scent of blood. *He killed everyone here...* she realized, horrified.

Edward snarled, drawing her attention back to the room and the conversation within. "I am sick of your whining! I am the one calling the shots now! Without me, you wouldn't have found the underground passage in the first place! They would have beat you back again!"

Hawke stood in the shadows just outside the door. Her ears, elongated into lupine shape, were stretched forward as she continued to listen.

Unaware of his audience, Edward continued his conversation on the phone. "It's the easiest route into the city! Get your troops through that passage and leave the rest to me!"

The pause in the air hung like a choking fog over the room and she shifted her stance to see if she could hear the person on the other end of the line. *What passage? Damn! Give me something I can use, you bastard!*

"I don't care about the losses! We'll make more when it's over! By the time they figure it out, the city will be ours!" He grew loud, anger making him careless. "What? Of course, the door is open! I did that several nights ago! No, it won't! I already took care of those in the building! They don't suspect a thing! Just make sure your man is here to get me on time!"

Hawke growled involuntarily, and the room went deathly silent. Looking around the corner, her eyes narrowed as she saw the receiver dangling from the phone.

Edward was no longer in sight.

"Damn!" she exclaimed and slipped cautiously into the room.

He stepped from his hiding place and smirked, "Looking for me?"

Realizing she was cornered, Hawke straightened up and stared at him. "Why the betrayal of our people? Don't you realize what will happen if you let the Renegades take control?"

Edward laughed at her. "Foolish girl!" he sneered. "These are not my people and never were! I am Principatus! This territory will be ours in a matter of hours, but you won't live to see it."

"Oh?" she responded nonchalantly.

The laughter froze on his face and his eyes narrowed. He glared at her, his expression deadly. "You know too much."

She stared at him, unflinching. "Then come and get me." Her voice was ice cold as she issued the challenge and her eyes were ferocious.

Edward's hand crackled with lightning and he charged at her, his lips curled back in a sneer. "I will eat your heart, Thylacinian!"

Hawke stood her ground. Just as he reached her, she feigned right and dodged his blow. His electrified hand slammed into the wall behind her. Then she extended her claws as she rose behind him, prepared to fight.

Furious now, he spun around to face her, his hand electrified again. He hit her in the chest and her flesh sizzled from the blow.

Emitting a strangled curse as pain ripped through her, Hawke pushed it from her mind. "Your power is weak compared to a Mastric's, Victulian! I am a Thylacinian! My turn!" She struck hard, her razor-sharp claws ripping through his chest wall. Her hand found its mark and she wrapped her fingers around his heart, tearing it from his body.

Edward's eyes widened in surprise and he made a grab at his chest, trying to stop the blood flow. When he fell, he was still staring with empty eyes at the heart in her hand.

"Game over! You lose!" She crushed the heart in her hand. Then she sagged to the floor as the pain in her scorched chest rose to the surface. Crawling to the wall, she sat back and leaned against it for support, trying to control the excruciating throb that was coursing through her. *Come on, you've been through this before!* she chided herself. *Get a grip. It's just pain!*

She tore open part of her burnt jacket and began to slowly peel away the parts of her shirt that had been melted to her skin. Wincing at the searing pain, she had to stop. She was gasping for breath. "Damn it! I shouldn't have been so careless! I let him get too close..." Finally, she gritted her teeth and finished peeling the rest away. Then she inspected the damage.

The jolt Edward had hit her with had crisped most of her right side. The burnt flesh still smoldered, the acrid odor causing her to wrinkle her nose. Her hand shaking slightly, she began to slowly heal herself with what little skill she had. *I wish I were as adept at healing as the Mastric's clerics. That would prove to be very useful about now.*

A door slamming nearby caught Hawke's attention and she looked up. The rapid footfalls of a young man stopped short when he reached the landing at the top of the stairs and almost fell over her. He looked from her to Edward's body and back at her again. "What have you done?" he cried. "Murderer! Traitor!" He turned and ran.

"Wait! Come back!" she yelled, but he was already gone. "Damn it!" With a growl, she forced herself to stand and then limped over to the steps. *I've got to get to Lucian and report this before anyone else gets the wrong idea.* Worried now, she descended the steps. Her injury slowed her movements and by the time she reached the street, she realized she wouldn't make it across town in her condition. *Where's a cleric when you need one...* She frowned then. *I'll have to find someplace to hole up long enough to heal a bit. Then I've got to find that passage and seal it up again. After that, I'd better find Lucian and tell him what happened.*

At the front gate, Hawke headed for a manhole near the street entrance and lifted the cover off. After making sure she wasn't seen, she jumped down into the sewer. She moved as quickly as she could, trying to put distance between herself and the manor. She was still looking for a decent place to rest when she heard voices ahead of her in the tunnel. Taking shelter in the shadows, she shrank back when she saw the number of Renegades that were coming down the tunnel ahead of her. The attack had already begun...

# BLOOD FEUD

## Chapter Forty-Five
## Secrets Unveiled

*If ever a man is to accomplish truly great things, he must first step out his door and into the wellspring of life. No man can truly move a mountain if he does not start by picking up the first stone. Long have we stayed in the shadows of this war, the Ancients too content to remain as we have ever been. Whereas I believe their intentions are noble, their lack of desire to see this conflict ended disturbs me. If we are to bring the enemy to their knees and finish this, then we need to leave passivity behind and become the aggressor, attacking them in their own territories. They attack on every front, destroying our lairs and murdering our indefensible young and still we sit stagnant, afraid to move beyond the boundaries of our own borders.*

*I was not released from my obligations as Warlord. Instead, they have increased my duties, raising me up as leader among their number. Am I worthy of such a charge? I question their actions at almost every turn and yet they look on me as though I am staunch in my devout leadership. I am not sure I see myself in the same light. The noblest of causes have been seen to completion through total wrongdoing and abhorrent bloodshed. Is there another way, as my angel believes? Has any of us ever truly attempted to seek another solution? Angelique has proven to all that even the child of a Renegade can be shown a better path and that they can rise to greater things among our number. Why then this incessant need to continue the killing?*

*I long for peace or at least the cessation of hostilities with young ones that do not truly know the reasons for this war. Where does wrong truly end and right begin? The lines blur together when you are in the middle of their crossings. God help us all in the nights ahead...*

*Lord Reivn Draegon*

* * * * *

Lunitar stared at the fire in frustration. His patience long gone, he felt impotent with helplessness as the night passed. A knock at the door jolted him from his thoughts. "Come in."

Jacob poked his head in. "I thought I might find you here, Lord Draegon. Still no word? It must have been a longer mission than Lady Angelique anticipated."

"It's been a week, Jacob," Lunitar stated with concern. "So far all I have been able to find out is that she left with Jack. Coincidently, the Warlord Annie left at the same time."

Jacob frowned. "Warlords come and go all the time. Annie was no doubt heading to Polusporta for the War Council with the Ancients. Anyway, how serious a mission can it be? The Ambassador took one of her own with her and he had only just come from France."

Lunitar stared at him. "Your information only lends credence to my suspicions. The more information I find out about the recent comings and goings, the more I am certain she and Jack did not go searching for any arcane tomes. I suspect this was a hunting party and I'm willing to bet it comprises of Angelique, Jack, Annie and this young one from France."

Stepping further into the room, Jacob closed the door behind him. "I'm not so sure about that. Annie had her Native American companion with her. And why would Lady Angelique need a hunting party?"

"Her companion… is he or she a tracker?" Lunitar asked.

Jacob shook his head. "I think he's a warrior and a tracker both. He travels with her on important missions, much like you do with your father. But why would she go with lady Angelique on a mission for an old book? Even for a magical tome, archeological expeditions rarely encompass any combat, and from what I know of Annie, she prefers combat missions. Do you really think she went with the Ambassador?"

Lunitar frowned. "Yes, I believe she did, and with this new information, I think we can both conclude this was no archeological mission. That would also explain why Angelique hid their exit by cloaking the portal's opening. She obviously didn't want any of us to know when they left or where they were headed. I followed the trace from the portal to Austin, and went as far as Mexico City, but the trail vanishes there. She's covered her tracks well… too well in fact."

"Have you contacted Lord Reivn to tell him of her absence?" Jacob asked quietly.

Lunitar shook his head. "Not yet. He sits in a war council at present. If I disturb him before I have something definite to report, I could invoke his wrath and that of the other Warlords, as well as the Ancients down on my head. This is something I have to take care of on my own."

Jacob gazed at him in curiosity. "What do you intend to do then?"

Lunitar sat and thought for a moment. Then he replied, "Moventius has connections to the Wolvens. I'm going to have him contact them to see if they can inquire of their kin in that area where she's gone. I will send word to my father the moment he is out of session."

Jacob nodded. "A good plan, but it will take time to get your answers. If his lordship returns before then, you may find yourself in trouble for prying into the Ambassador's affairs."

Lunitar turned back to stare at the fire. "That is a risk I am willing to take. I gave my father my word I would see to her safety and escort her home. I intend to do just that."

Sighing, Jacob turned to go. "Suit yourself, lad. I hope you don't find yourself facing punishment for your devotion to such a duty."

"If I am punished for following protocol and locating the lady when I have been assigned to protect her, then I will gladly lay down my life in service to my father. I do not lightly take the oath I gave to him," Lunitar stated with conviction.

Jacob nodded and walked out, closing the door once more behind him.

Lunitar fell silent, his thoughts on where to begin his hunt. After moments of quiet contemplation, he went in search of his brother. As he walked down the hall he heard his name and turned to find Moventius trotting after him.

"A little bird told me you were looking for me, brother?" he asked.

Lunitar nodded. "I was indeed. I need your help."

"Name it," Moventius replied with a grin.

Lunitar headed toward the office he had been using, knowing his brother would follow. "I need to locate mother. I know you have contact with Wolvens that can help you do just that."

"You do realize how much trouble you can get us both into, don't you, little brother?" Moventius asked seriously.

Lunitar nodded again. "I do, but I can't shake the feeling something is terribly wrong. She's been gone a week. Far longer than what she told Lowry she would be. There's been no word, no messages... nothing. I would rather face father's wrath for being over-protective than to face his wrath should she get hurt with my failing to prevent it."

Moventius sighed. "Agreed... and I am as concerned as you are, little brother, so I'll help you. If we make father angry, we'll face him together."

For the first time in nights, Lunitar chuckled. "Wall mates? I'd almost rather face a dragon."

Laughter filled the hall as they disappeared around the corner.

Within the hour, Moventius had contacted the Wolvens in Mexico City and gotten their reply. He hurried to rejoin his brother, concern filling his features at the news.

Lunitar was in his room packing a small bag and gathering supplies. He looked up when Moventius burst in the door.

"You were right, Luni!" Moventius growled. "They were in Mexico City! They met with one of the Wolven leaders and then headed into the jungle. From there, nothing more is known!" He dropped into the chair by Lunitar's bed. "Father will be furious about this. That territory is more Renegade and Wolven than Alliance. She has no idea how much danger she's in."

Lunitar frowned, deep in thought. Then he said, "Go back to Draegonstorm and help Gideon oversee Keep operations. That will protect him from father's retribution. I'm going to the Council's halls to seek father's help. I will send word when I can."

Moventius stood up and nodded. At the door, he paused for a moment and turned around. "Stay safe, little brother. You know how to reach me if you need my help." He left Lunitar to ponder over just what he would say to Reivn when he reached Polusporta fortress.

Lunitar bent over his bag once more, double-checking the last of his gear before closing it. *I should have done this four nights ago. Father's rage will be immeasurable.* A knock at his door interrupted his thoughts and he looked up. "Yes?"

Jacob poked his head in. "They told me you were leaving. Heading back home?"

"In a matter of speaking, yes. Just not by the most direct route," Lunitar answered as he finished his packing.

Jacob scratched his head. "You're not going to try to follow the ambassador, are you? You have no way to track her."

Lunitar shook his head. "No, I don't, but my father will know how to find her. There's been no word for over a week now and that is against our strictest protocols. I haven't found anything to indicate something is wrong, but that's also part of the problem. I haven't found anything at all. No trace… nothing. She simply vanished into thin air."

Heaving a sigh, Jacob nodded. "Yes, I know. I've been growing more and more concerned myself. It isn't my place to question her ladyship. However, as her son, you can. I wish you luck, Lord Lunitar. Take care of yourself."

"I will, sir. I promise." Lunitar reached over and shook his hand. "I'll see you again soon."

Within the hour, Lunitar was in the portal chamber and on his way to Polusporta fortress.

The guards registered surprise when he stepped into the hall and hailed him. "Your visit is most unexpected, Lord Draegon. Why have you come?"

Lunitar stopped in front of them. "I need to see my father on a rather urgent matter. I realize I'm interrupting an important meeting, but this can't…"

One of the guards interrupted. "Sir, Lord Reivn left two hours ago for his new assignment."

Frustration edging into his voice, Lunitar ran a hand through his hair. "Do you know where he was headed or what his assignment is?"

The guard shook his head. "I'm sorry, sir. You must speak with a member of the Council on that matter. Our duty is to defend them, not to disclose information discussed in chambers."

"That figures…" Lunitar growled. "Then I humbly request an audience with one or more members of the Council as soon as it can be arranged."

The guard nodded and disappeared to take his request to Victus, who still sat in the throne room speaking in soft tones with Mithras and Chronos.

Lunitar paced the hall while he waited and as minutes passed, he grew more agitated.

"Such impatience in one so young does not show much promise for the success of any task…" Armenia stated, walking up behind him. "What troubles you so, young one. Are you so anxious to come before my brethren that you would wear a rut in the floor with your pacing?"

Lunitar spun around, bowing immediately when he saw who had joined him. "Forgive me, my lady," he replied. "Patience has never been one of my better virtues, I'm afraid."

She laughed. "This I can see. Pray tell why?"

He paused for a moment before answering. "My lady, no disrespect intended, but the news I bear is meant only for my Lord and father. I know of your noble lineage and greatly respect you, but I honor the charge I was given and hold sacred to my oath. Please forgive me."

Armenia stood gazing at him in amusement for a moment. Then she shrugged and turned to go. "Keep your secret then, child of the Dragon," she called over her shoulder. "But know this. Your father is destined for greater things still than a mere Prefect's office. I have seen it."

Momentarily forgetting his purpose for being there, Lunitar stared after her in surprise. Her words rung in his ears. ...*Destined for greater things. Prefect? What is she talking about?*

The guard returned then, interrupting his thoughts. "Lord Victus will see you now, Lord Lunitar. Please come with me."

Lunitar silently followed him into the Council's great hall.

Entering the throne room behind the guard, Lunitar immediately dropped to one knee, placing his right fist over his heart before Victus and the other Ancients still present. Keeping his eyes to the floor, he waited in silence.

Victus looked down at him. "What is it you seek, child?"

"My lords, I came seeking information and my father's counsel on a mission given to me by the same." Lunitar stared at the floor as he spoke, not daring to look up. "It is of the utmost importance I contact him. I merely seek to ask this Council where he has been sent on assignment." Falling quiet, he waited for their answer.

Victus gazed at him in silence.

Chronos glanced at Victus, then back at Lunitar. "The sincerity of your words and the urgency in your tone suggests great troubles, young one. What has you so vexed that you would come seeking your father while he sat in a war Council?"

Lunitar looked up sharply. "Begging the Council's indulgence, my lord, but it is a personal family matter and not one I am comfortable disclosing."

Victus scoffed at his response. "You seriously think you have the right to withhold information from us? Your words are either tremendously bold or tremendously foolish. I can rip that information from you without a second thought."

"Yes, my lord. Of that, I am humbly aware. With respect, however, I must say in my own defense that I do not think it my right to withhold this information. I am merely requesting of those I serve and hold in the highest regard that I be allowed the privilege of doing so." Lunitar again dropped his eyes, silently praying they would press him no further.

Chronos leaned back in his chair, eyeing Lunitar in silence.

Mithras chuckled. "I can see why Reivn picked you, boy. You are loyal to a fault to both your father and family. That is commendable. Perhaps a little more caution on your part would be in order though. Not all are as forgiving as we."

"If your grandfather were here, he would no doubt pick your brain and shackle you to a dungeon wall for daring such a request, and I think that is the reason I will allow your privacy, Lunitar." Victus smiled at the thought. "He has driven Thylacinos from the hall and until all is well, I am not inclined to be so generous of his temperament."

Chronos shook his head. "If Thylacinos does not return to this chamber soon, it could further weaken the Alliance you seek so desperately to protect, boy. Pray he does not further damage the relationship with our brother, but rather seeks to make amends."

Lunitar looked up. "Does my father know of this tragedy, my lords?"

"He does. He was present during the entire exchange. Mastric has been charged with apologizing to Thylacinos and bringing him back forthwith." Victus frowned. "He will not return to sit in chambers here until then."

Slowly rising from the floor, Lunitar could not hide his concern. "I am deeply troubled by this news, my lords. I pray for a quick resolution to the matter, for all our sakes. I am also very grateful for the indulgence you grant me." He bowed again. "May I ask now where my father has been sent on assignment? Perhaps I could be an asset to the completion of his task, freeing him for any further aid we could lend the present situation."

Mithras chuckled. "I should have claimed you as a Mithranian. You are absolutely relentless, young one. He has gone to the Americas… to Atlantic City to be exact. War brews there and he was needed to protect the territory and its new prince."

"Then Atlantic City is my destination as well," Lunitar stated calmly.

Victus held up his hand. "No. The situation there is grave. I want no distractions that will prevent your father from defending that City. Go home. Your news will wait until his return."

Without hesitation, Lunitar dropped again to his knee. "Yes, my lord."

Chronos stood up and walked over to him. "Understand boy, if you disobey and go to your father's side, you will be put to death. There is far more at stake here than private matters between you and your father."

"I do understand, my lord." Lunitar bowed. "I will do as ordered and return home, despite my desire to do otherwise." Bowing again, he backed out of the Hall and turned to head to the portal chambers once more.

"Lunitar wait!" Chronos called after him.

Turning around, Lunitar stood his ground until Chronos caught up to him. "Yes, my lord?"

Chronos put his hand on the younger man's shoulder. "I know the nature of your troubles. Speaking to Reivn about it would only distract him from his present assignment."

Lunitar looked up sharply. "You know about Angelique?"

"I do. My son is with her," Chronos stated simply.

Lunitar frowned. "Then please... tell me what you know?"

Chronos gazed down at him. "Jack, Angelique, and Annie are tracking Cyrus. They followed him to the Yucatan. Their last communiqué was when they met with the Wolvens in Mexico City. I have been waiting for word from them, but it may be a while yet."

"They went after..." Lunitar checked himself, falling silent. "Thank you for the information, my lord. It is as I feared. I had already tracked her as far as Mexico City, but their trail ran cold. This is precisely why I sought my father. He assigned me the task of maintaining the Ambassador's safety. Learning the nature of her mission, I fear I have failed in my duty. My father will be most distressed to hear of this."

Chronos nodded. "I know, and that is precisely why you must wait. Jack is overdue reporting in and I'm assuming that so is Lady Angelique. Do not be too concerned. Both Jack and Annie are capable warriors and I trust them. They will protect her should the need arise."

Lunitar cleared his throat. "My lord, if I may be so bold... their quarry is extremely dangerous. In the New York raid, we had a much larger hunting party and we suffered heavy losses. Granted, he is no longer in his original form, but he still poses a deadly threat."

Chronos sighed. "The situation is indeed a dangerous one. However, it was the decision of one of our Warlords, as well as your Ambassador, to go on that mission. Go home and await your father's return. I will see to it you are notified when I hear from my son again." Turning abruptly, he turned and headed back to the throne room, leaving Lunitar standing in the hallway.

"How am I ever going to explain this to father?" Lunitar asked himself in frustration as he reluctantly headed for the portal chamber... and Draegonstorm.

## Chapter Forty-Six
## The Fall of Atlantic City

*We must hold the cities in America. Much like a house of cards, one false move will send it all crumbling beneath us. We have a tentative hold on them at best. The outer defenses are the greatest reason we have survived thus far. Their alert system has given us an advantage when the Principatus attack our borders. But they do not entirely stop the tide that flows inward, ever seeking to destroy our possession of those territories. Losing even one of them could have potentially devastating results to the Eastern Alliance.*

*So many young have already lost their lives. How many more must do so to satisfy the bloodthirsty desires of our Sires and kin? With every new battle, I see more faces fall before me and each time I pray it is not one of my own. My sons, my daughter... even my angel... I would die before I see them fall to this endless madness, this lust for death. The Principatus is altogether evil and must be stopped. They unleash Daemons on this world and destroy without thought. They awaken the innocent to our presence and damn us to hide in the darkest part of the night. The inquisition is already hunting us, and now the hunters have come here. They will not leave here without kills to satisfy the church. Theirs is a true practice in hypocrisy. God does not want more killing. Only man desires that and the slaughter will not stop until we are all dead.*

*The one true constant is change, good or bad, and it haunts every step we take. New people come into our lives and enrich them with their laughter, their wisdom, and even their tears. Then they are taken from us in one single, agonizing moment. All that they are, all that we love, is stricken from the world in one horrible brutal blow and we are left bereft...*

*Lord Reivn Draegon*

* * * * *

Reivn raced through the halls with Lucian hot on his heels. "That was no minor explosion!" he yelled. "We are under attack!"

Rounding the corner, Thaddeus almost ran into them. "They're attacking all over the city!" He bellowed over the noise of collapsing structure somewhere nearby. They ran for the front of the guild. The sight that met their eyes shook them into action.

The front of the building was gone, blown away by a massive blast. Bodies of Mastrics and other warriors were strewn across the rubble, some dead, and some still breathing.

"We need to get the wounded out of here before the whole roof collapses!" Reivn shouted. He immediately summoned the Spirals and reinforced the damaged section of roof, holding it up by sheer force of will. His only thought was to get the wounded to safety.

Thaddeus was stunned by Reivn's command of the Spirals and stared at him in surprise for a second before being shaken into action. He started levitating debris to free trapped victims.

Lucian began hauling the injured from the rubble, tossing aside broken furniture and chunks of the damaged structure effortlessly.

More Mastrics arrived and started digging into the destruction to rescue the survivors. Several of them combined their power and magic poured from their fingertips, pushing the ceiling back up so they could rescue the fallen.

When Reivn saw the other Mastrics responding to those in need, he grabbed Thaddeus and Lucian. "Come on! They can finish here! We need to rally our troops! This is only the first strike! We must defend the city! Lucian, get your Thylacinians to a good vantage point out there. The Renegades will try to take down the guild first to stop the use of our magic!"

Lucian nodded and ran for the door. His summoning howl echoed through the night and a dozen or more Thylacinians waiting nearby picked up the call. From all over the city, voices joined in unison as their tribe came from their hiding places and rallied in the streets. They were heedless now of the humans that shied away from the strange sights they saw. This was war.

Reivn ran for his office, with Thaddeus at his side. The moment Girard and another courier joined them he barked out their orders. "Girard, find Leshye! Tell her they are coming in from the north! She needs to move in and try to slow them down! Tell her we need time to establish a defensive position!"

Girard nodded and broke off, heading for the underground exit.

Grabbing the arm of the second courier, Reivn growled. "Head to the west end of the city! You will find reinforcements there! Tell them to move inward! The Renegades are already past our outer defenses! Tell them we need them here now!"

Armand came running around the corner with several other Mastrics in tow. "Lord Reivn, these are all that's left here at the guild! The rest are either wounded and being evacuated or are assisting with those being relocated! I can fight! I just have to use senses other than my eyes!"

Reivn had no time to argue. He ordered them to follow Thaddeus to the front of the Guild. "Form a perimeter around the building! Put up your shields and defend this guild long enough for the last of the evacuations to get through the portals. Once the portals are sealed, head to the north end of the city! Rendezvous with Leshye's Company and render what aid you can! We'll join you as soon as we get the rest of our reinforcements in place!"

Thaddeus, Armand, and the others turned and ran back up the hall to the front entrance. The sounds of heavy fighting could already be heard in the streets beyond.

Reivn raced for his quarters, sending Serena a telepathy on the way. *Serena, we are under attack! Make sure our library is secure! We cannot have any of those tomes falling into enemy hands! Then help evacuate the remaining wounded through the portals!*

Serena's quick response reassured him the library had already been moved to the New York guild. *I am assisting with the evacuations as we speak,* she sent back.

When he reached his own quarters, Reivn searched frantically for the items he needed, grabbing precious scrolls and vials, and stuffing them in his jacket. Then he raced to his laboratory to push everything through a portal to safety. Once he finished securing the last of their magic, he closed and sealed the portal. Then he headed to aid Serena with the evacuations.

The shaking of the building every few seconds hastened the actions of those still within the Guild. Serena's team worked frantically to move the remaining wounded. When the last of them were safely away, Reivn ordered Serena and the other clerics to leave as well. Then he ran back upstairs to the front of the building.

When he got out to the street, it was to a full-scale battle between the Renegades and his own people. Hundreds of his soldiers were already fighting to keep the enemy forces from overrunning not only the Guild itself, but the surrounding streets. Drawing his sword, he leapt into the fight, driving his blade deep into the nearest Renegade. "Drive them back!" he yelled.

A few feet away, Grimel fought Renegades struggling to get past him. Snarling with fury, he slashed through them with his razor-sharp claws, his fangs fully extended. He was bleeding from several wounds, but he ignored them as he grappled with his attackers.

Reivn cut through the Renegades and joined Grimel. Then the city's defenders struggled to push back their foes, as they battled for control of the streets. They were completely unaware that the fight was about to take a different turn. While the Alliance forces fought to defend the city above, more Renegades were flooding into the city through an open door in the sewer.

In the city's underground waste system, Hawke was fighting her own battle. She waited until the last renegade passed her, and then followed them undetected at a distance. Her mind was working fast. *I need to find a way to stop them,* she thought to herself. The Renegades were moving fast, headed for key locations in the city.

*They're moving way too fast!* Hawke followed them, taking note of their weapons and looking around as she moved through the tunnels, trying to find something she could use against them. When they passed an enormous ventilation fan built for circulating the air, she caught sight of a gas pipe running parallel to the walls and quickly formed a plan. Slipping up behind the last of the Renegades, she ripped out his throat and took his flamethrower, dropping him to the ground without a sound. Then she yelled at his companions, catching their attention, and raced back toward the fan.

The Renegades took the bait and followed.

As Hawke ran by the gas pipe, she grabbed it and ripped it free, separating a welded seam. Then she left it hanging and raced for the fan when the Renegades chasing her came into sight. She could smell the gas filling the tunnel. Squeezing herself past the fan and into the thin space behind it, she waited until they were almost on top of her. Then she opened fire through the fan's churning blades.

The immense fan blew the flames at her enemies, igniting the gas in a giant fireball that swallowed them in the tunnel. "This is our city!" she yelled, watching them burn. Then ditching the flamethrower, she crawled from her culvert and ran for the nearest manhole to the street.

Hawke emerged from the sewers to realize the fighting had already begun. She stared in shock at the devastated streets of Atlantic City. *My*

*God,* she thought. *They've already broken through.* She quickly hauled herself from the manhole and shoved the cover back into place.

A snarl behind her caused her to spin around. "Where's your mark?" the man barked at her. "You know we're all supposed to wear em! Where's your mark?" He scurried over to where she stood in the fire-lit street.

Shrugging her shoulders, Hawke waved him in closer. "I've got it. Come here and I'll show you," she quipped casually.

He walked over, eyeing Hawke expectantly. She grabbed him with one hand and rammed her other one through his chest. "This is my mark, fool!" She crushed his heart, ignoring the explosion of blood that covered her. Then she dropped the body and made a run for the Alliance-held lines as more enemies began to pour from the tunnel behind her.

Total chaos reigned the streets. From every vantage point, Mastrics hurled down a barrage of fire amid the sea of bodies. The sound of clanging metal and guns filled the night air on every street. Reivn and Grimel fought side-by-side, covering each other's backs, as they tried to cover as many of the weaker warriors as possible. Lucian and Thaddeus had disappeared into the chaotic mass of fighting soldiers.

A shout broke through the noise, and Reivn turned to see a Renegade Martulian summoning shadow beasts and sending them at him full force. Calling on the spirals, Reivn ignited them with fire, returning them to their master in flames.

Two Renegades tackled Grimel, driving him down to the pavement. Roaring in anger, he transformed into an giant-sized Dingo. Then he sank his teeth into one after another, bringing forth shrieks of agony as he tore at their flesh with his savage jaws.

The Alliance was defending themselves from the Principatus on every front. Leshye and her forces had rendezvoused with Reivn's shortly after the fighting began. But now their numbers were dwindling. She wielded her twin Katanas with masterful skill. Yelling to those with her, she swung around to strengthen their left flank, and freed another road behind them. Despite her efforts, however, her squads were falling rapidly. She was still fighting when a group of Renegades overwhelmed her and pulled her to the ground.

Buildings everywhere burned against the night, casting a red-gold glow on the frenzied battle. Screams filled the air, as the warriors of both armies tore each other apart.

Lucian searched for Reivn to try and regroup their forces, which were drastically thinning in number. There were many behind them, lying where they had fallen and bleeding from wounds that desperately needed tending. His eyes stung from smoke and blood, and his side wept crimson from a sword wound. Slashing through enemies, his progress was slow, but he finally spotted Reivn a few yards away. Then he spotted Armand lying on the ground with a gunshot wound in his chest. He was bleeding heavily and would die if unaided. Making a quick choice, Lucian grabbed the injured man's arm and dragged him free of the fighting. He yelled for a cleric and shoved Armand into the girl's hands when she responded. "If he dies, so do you!" he snarled. Then he returned to the fight, leaving her frantically working over Reivn's adopted son.

Thaddeus was also pushing inward when he spotted Reivn and fought his way to the Warlord's side. "We've got to pull back!" he yelled. "We're losing too many!"

Reivn agreed and gave the signal to regroup. Tired and bloodied, their soldiers fell back.

Then the Renegades began to retreat. Shouts filled the air as it seemed like they had given up.

But Reivn could see the Renegade army attempting to regroup for a second attack. His own numbers were severely dwindling. His clerics were already gathering the wounded and pulling them through portals to safety, but there were so many that even at best speeds it would take time to get them all safely away.

"We will hold here and push forward when they come at us again," Reivn instructed his officers. "Gather our troops and prepare for another attack!"

A young captain approached and saluted him. "Sir, the Warlord Leshye was severely injured and had to be removed from the field. She has been taken to the New York Guild."

Frowning, Reivn gave the man his full attention. "Is she expected to live?" he asked.

"I… I'm afraid I don't know my lord," the man answered shakily. His own arm was covered in telltale red that ran from a slash in his upper bicep.

Reivn reached over and inspected the captain's arm. "What is your name?"

"I'm Captain Grant, my lord." The man attempted to salute which only resulted in more blood pouring from his wound.

Reivn pulled him away from the edge of the fighting. "Have a cleric see to your wound. You are losing too much blood. Report to me at Draegonstorm when this is over."

The captain nodded and headed in the direction of the flashing of portals.

Then Thaddeus yelled, "Here they come again!"

Spinning around, Reivn stared in disbelief as he saw the mass of enemy soldiers now charging toward them. Their numbers had almost doubled. "Tighten your ranks! We have to hold them here!" He strode to the front of the line and braced his heel against the street. Then he brought his sword up, summoned the spirals and shaped another fireball in his free hand. "Steady… hold your ground!" he commanded those beside him. He waited until the Renegades got closer. Then he yelled, "Hold the line!"

A moment later the Principatus slammed into them.

Reivn cut into the Renegade numbers relentlessly, ignoring the exhaustion creeping into his arm. He was half-blinded from blood in his eyes. His right leg bled from a fresh wound and his left side was blackened from fire that had scorched him minutes after the fighting resumed. Refusing to leave his men, he ignored the pain and pushed it back with a will of iron. The street filled with bodies, one piling on top of another, but neither side would yield their ground. Any humans in the area had long since fled, their minds unable to comprehend the insanity that had broken loose. Then the echo of cheers went up again and he turned around. Several ranks of Renegades were falling back, leaving the ground free to his men. It appeared they were finally retreating. Breathing a sigh of relief, he turned to Thaddeus. "Tell the men to start gathering the wounded and… Thaddeus?"

A desperate look on his face, Thaddeus was staring past Reivn.

The Warlord followed his gaze.

Lucian approached, carrying the body of Prince Edward.

"What happened?" Reivn growled. "I thought Hawke got him out of the city!"

Laying the body on the pavement, Lucian stood up to face him. "One of the Victulians stopped me on my way back into battle. He told me he had witnessed the Prince's demise. He said it was Hawke who took his heart. She has betrayed us."

Thaddeus interrupted them. "Right now, I think we have a far bigger problem."

Reivn turned and his eyes widened. "They are attacking again!"

Thousands of Renegades were pouring into the streets several blocks behind them. In front of them, still more were joining forces and charging up the street. He quickly realized the city was lost. "We have to get everyone out now or they'll be slaughtered! Give the order to retreat! Save as many of the wounded as possible!"

Lucian joined him, but Thaddeus growled. "There's no way…"

"We save as many as we can!" Reivn repeated. He began grabbing bodies and shoving them through the clerics' portals.

The Renegade forces moved quickly and in moments the outer edges of the streets were filled with screams as the slaughter began.

Working furiously, Reivn, Lucian and Thaddeus continued dragging the wounded to portals. Everyone still standing around them jumped into action, following their example. Finally, the enemy was so close the clerics had to shut the portals for their own safety. Unwilling to abandon so many, Reivn refused to back down and continued picking up the wounded, shoving them into every retreating soldiers' hands.

Lucian and Thaddeus pulled him away by force, retreating to the city's edge and the field above just as the Principatus swept into the street, swarming over those that remained. The Renegades spotted Reivn and gave chase, eager to capture a prize.

Out of nowhere, Grimel leapt in their way. Blocking the Renegades from Reivn's retreating party, he snarled in rage. He flickered and transformed back to human form, letting his claws extend. "Run!" he yelled over his shoulder. Then he disappeared into the sea of bodies, his claws tearing into the flesh of dozens of Renegades as they swarmed over him and pulled him down.

Reivn strained against the grip of his two companions, fighting to get back down to the street. "No! You cannot leave him! We have to go back! There are still men down there! We cannot leave them! We have to go back!" Desperation had taken over reason and he struggled to pull himself free.

"It's too late for that, Reivn! We've lost the city!" Lucian argued. "Come on! You can't help anyone if you join the dead!"

Dragging Reivn after them, they followed the rest of their retreating forces up the side of a hill on the city's outskirts, until they were a safe distance from the slaughter below. Then they let him go, stopping to look back.

Reivn stood on the hill staring down at the burning city.

Smoke rose from dozens of buildings, and sirens in the distance heralded humans racing to put out the fires that besieged the city. The territory had fallen. The Alliance had been forced to pull back, surrendering it to Principatus' control. Grimel had sacrificed himself to save their lives, and Edward lay dead in the smoldering ashes, betrayed by the very one sent to guard him. Bloody remains were being gathered and torched by the victors on the streets below, as were any survivors that had not escaped.

Clenching his fist, Reivn swore to destroy Hawke for her betrayal. In killing Edward, she had shattered the city's leadership, weakening the morale of their warriors as word spread of his demise. He tried to close his ears to the dying screams of those left behind. The Renegades were wasting no time.

"Lord Reivn," Thaddeus began, trying to get his attention.

Reivn did not answer, his fury and grief over the losses refusing to allow him the grace of turning his back on the sight before him.

"Lord Reivn," Thaddeus said again. "We must go! These outskirts will be crawling with Renegades soon and there will be no refuge for us. We must get to safe ground!"

With heavy shoulders, Reivn finally heeded Thaddeus' warning and followed him to a waiting car.

They sped away quickly, heading for shelter outside the territory limits. They would make for New York at dusk.

The following night, Thaddeus and Lucian left for New York. Their wounds were quickly seen to by Serena, who waited there with Jacob to tend the incoming wounded. Then Thaddeus headed to London to report to Mastric. Lucian departed after checking on Armand's condition, needing to seek his father's counsel. So, he said farewell and headed back out into the night.

Reivn headed directly for Draegonstorm. He needed time to think. Giving his personal Guards instructions that he was not to be disturbed, he disappeared into his labs. There were many guilds handling the tragedy, and in the nights to follow, there would be many names listed. His mind on their losses. he could not settle back into his routine. The numbers they had lost troubled him, as did Hawke's betrayal, and he sat staring in silence at the fire as he calculated how to find her. *I wonder if there is any connection to Thylacinos walking out on the Council and this incident.* The fact she was Grimel's daughter disturbed him even more. *I wonder how many more Thylacinians will turn on us.*

When he rose to retire for the day, he failed to notice a note tucked under the edge of a book on his desk, with his name scrolled in Lunitar's hand. His thoughts on the previous night's battle and the loss of so many men, he wanted to avoid the rooms he shared with Angelique. He was not ready to tell her about Grimel. So he wandered toward his old chambers in silence. The Council would get his reports tomorrow and then he would return to his wife's side.

The following night in the Commonroom, Gideon quietly watched Lunitar pace back and forth. "We should have been there. He needed us!" Lunitar growled.

His tone sympathetic, Gideon shook his head. "We wouldn't have made a difference. The Renegades overwhelmed their numbers. Father is alive. Think on that and be thankful."

Lunitar shot him an irritated look. "I shouldn't be tied here while others are out there fighting and dying. I am supposed to be there, damn it! Not hiding here like some weakling child!"

A sound from the door made them both look up. Moventius strode into the room and dropped into a chair near the fire. "It's over now, little brother, so forget it."

"That's easier said than done, Mo!" Lunitar snapped.

Moventius looked up. "Then perhaps you will be happy to know that father returned last night. He spent the rest of last night in his labs and most of tonight as well. You may be able to catch him before he retires… if you hurry."

Lunitar scowled. "Why didn't you tell me earlier? I could have already spoken with him!"

Glancing up, Gideon frowned. "Would you really have wanted to do that in the face of their defeat? It was probably better that you didn't bother him last night. He no doubt needed time to digest all that has occurred. He will take this hard. He always does."

Moventius nodded in agreement. "No doubt. Like any good leader, he truly cares for his people and it grieves him when our losses are so great. The numbers this time were staggering, and many are still unaccounted for."

Lunitar gazed at Moventius, deep in thought at his words. "I have no choice but to speak to him tonight. The matter of our mother can wait no longer. He must know!"

Gideon closed his eyes. "Last time someone told him his wife was missing, it didn't go so well. I hope you have better luck."

Glancing over at Gideon, Moventius sighed. "I'm sorry it turned out that way, Gid. Father's refusal to forgive you is..."

"Is what?" Reivn interrupted, walking in.

Gideon stood up. "...justifiable, father. Welcome home."

Reivn nodded to Gideon before turning to Moventius. "It is good to see you home again, and you as well, Lunitar. However, I have not been able to find Angelique. Do any of you know where she is?"

Lunitar turned around. "In a matter of speaking, Father, but it is urgent that we talk. I was going to leave this until tomorrow night, but seeing as you are here, perhaps now is better."

Moventius shot him a warning look and Gideon turned to stare at the fire in silence.

Slightly irritated with Lunitar's vague statements, Reivn growled. "What is so urgent?"

"Mother is," Lunitar replied.

Reivn narrowed his eyes. "Explain!"

Lunitar turned to face his father. "She left New York claiming she wanted to hunt for an old tome. She hasn't been seen or heard from since and it's been over a week now. She was accompanied by Jack and Annie. When I went to Polusporta to find you, I was told you had already left on assignment. So, I asked for an audience with the Council, seeking information as to your whereabouts. Lord Chronos revealed to me concerning her true mission and ordered me here until you returned. Father, she has gone after Cyrus."

His eyes unreadable, Reivn turned without saying another word and headed for the door.

"Father?" Lunitar called after him.

Reivn's voice filtered in from the hall. "I am going after her. Stay here… all of you!"

Lunitar moved to follow him, but Gideon grabbed his arm. "No," he answered quietly. "We were given an order. Let him go."

Shaking Gideon off, Lunitar glared at him. Then without a word, he walked over to the fire and stared into its flames, thinking hard.

Reivn went quickly to his labs, and within minutes, was using Angelique's blood to trace her. Disturbing images began to form in his mind. He growled and donned his armor, heading for the portals before he even finished fastening on his blades. Within minutes, he was stepping into the chamber. He called on the spirals and opened the portal to Mexico City.

Lunitar stood staring at the fire in silence while his brothers talked, watching the flames dance as he thought of his father and mother.

Moventius glanced over at him. "Stop brooding and come join us for a while, little brother. I am sure father has things well in hand by now." Then he chuckled. "That dark countenance of yours isn't going to bring them home any faster."

Lunitar turned around and scowled fiercely at him. "Don't you think one of us should follow him in case he needs our aid?"

Gideon looked up sharply. "Disobey his orders to stay here? Have you gone completely mad? He would skin us alive. I have felt that punishment before and I don't enjoy intense pain. He told us to stay here and I for one intend to do just that."

Shaking his head in amusement, Moventius turned back to his game of chess with Gideon. "Lunitar, you need to stay away from the libraries and spend more time relaxing, maybe even find a woman. Those books are filling your head with nonsense."

"Books are not nonsense, Moventius," Lunitar chastised. "They are knowledge, and knowledge is power. I merely seek to ensure father is safe. There is no telling what he is going to encounter, but judging by his reaction, it isn't going to be good. She's in some sort of trouble and he's gone to get her alone."

Gideon growled. "Either way it isn't our place to question a direct order given by a Superior. If he decided to take such disobedience far enough, you could be accused of treason."

"If I were disobeying the Warlord, then yes. But that directive was given to us by our father on a family matter. Hypothetically speaking, of course." Irritated, Lunitar frowned as he spoke. "However, I can see your point, so I'll leave it alone for now."

Moventius laughed. "You see? He can learn new tricks."

Gideon gazed at Lunitar for a moment, as though to say something more. Then he changed his mind and looked away.

Turning abruptly, Lunitar headed for the door. "I'll be in my quarters if anyone needs me."

Moventius laughed and shook his head. "He really needs to spend less time in his books. Our world is brutal enough without giving up what few pleasures we do have."

"Let him alone." Gideon chastised. "He loves father deeply and protects him as we do, just in his own way."

Lunitar stood outside the door, listening for a moment, and then turned and headed to his rooms. After quickly donning his armor and weapons, he slipped unseen down to the portal chamber. Then after determining where his father went, he summoned the spirals to open the doorway. Seconds later, he stepped out into the heat of Mexico City. Reaching out with his senses, he caught Reivn's trail. *You're not alone father. I'm on my way...*

# BLOOD FEUD

## Chapter Forty-Seven
## Martyr's Blood

*The fall of Atlantic City is a terrible blow to our cause. Countless good people fell, many of them the wounded we were unable to save during our retreat. As the Renegades overran the city, I was forced to listen to the slaughter of all those we left behind. Though I realize every one of them gave themselves for the cause, I believe those were deaths that could have been avoided.*

*A good friend and ally also lies among the dead. Grimel was the only reason I survived that massacre. We escaped because he sacrificed himself and I will never forget it. I am only glad he did not live to see his daughter's betrayal. Hawke's murder of Edward would have broken his fierce heart. I will avenge this wrong, both for Grimel's honor and justice for Edward.*

*My angel will mourn Grimel. He was a special part of our lives and despite the darkened existence in which we live, we shared many joyous moments together. Many we knew fell on that battlefield, each no less important than the other. So much loss grieves me terribly. I pray all those who have given everything have found peace, and that those of us left behind find a semblance of that peace, as we remember their names and sacrifices.*

*God, when will this war end? Must our legacy always be so bathed in the blood of our kin? I fear for those I love and hold dear… that the night will swallow them as it has so many others. Why must our brethren, now so far removed from their own blood, continue to kill to prove their right to freedom? I must wonder when so much of my kin's blood has stained the earth and undying hatred continues to fuel the fires of war. I pray there will come a day when we at last end the conflict before it makes corpses of us all.*

*Lord Reivn Draegon*

\* \* \* \* \*

"Scatter!" Jack drew his guns, dodging sideways and peppering the dais with bullets.

The priests snarled at the intruders.

Shaman darted around to far side of the dais, tomahawk in hand, waving a silent challenge at the priest near him. Annie followed him, pulling her guns as she ran up the wall. Using her speed as leverage, she propelled herself upward and across, landing on a pedestal near the dais. The second she touched the stone, she rained fire down on the two that protected the waking Ancient.

Angelique stood her ground and called forth the spirals. She focused on the Ancient, not wanting to wait until he was fully awake. At her side, Ruben summoned a lightning bolt that swirled around his hands and body until he hurled it at the waking figure.

Without warning the Ancient sat up and grabbed one of the priests, draining him dry in seconds. As the priest's body crumbled to ashes, he turned on the second man.

The man backed away in fear. Babbling in a primordial tongue, it was obvious to the hunting party that he was begging for his life. His pleas were choked off when the Ancient, Tezcatlipoca, slashed his throat, emptied him and rendered him to dust.

Jack and Annie reigned fire down on the Ancient with new urgency.

Now having fed, Tezcatlipoca slowly stood as his body regenerated from a decayed corpse to that of a healthy man. His vitality restored, he turned his dark eyes on them.

Shaman leapt to the dais screaming a Blackfoot war cry, while Angelique and Ruben shot the Ancient with lightning and fire to cover him.

Their attack did not affect Tezcatlipoca. Growling like a hungry lion, he turned on Shaman.

"Shaman, watch out!" Annie screamed and fired another round, jumping down and running toward the dais.

Shaman managed to land a blow in Tezcatlipoca's spine, but the Ancient ignored it, spun around and backhanded him off the dais, sending him full force into the wall of the chamber.

Angelique hurled a steady barrage of lightning bolts at the powerful Immortal, sending Ruben around behind him to try and hit him from all sides.

Tezcatlipoca's claws extended, and he snarled in rage at his attackers.

Jack closed in, raining steady gunfire on the angry Ancient and making every bullet count.

Shaman picked himself up, blood trickling from the corner of his mouth. Then he leapt for the Ancient again.

Annie joined him, and the two tag-teamed trying to do as much damage as possible.

As the group attacked the would-be God, an ice wall formed in front of him, blocking their bullets and the hits from Shaman's tomahawk.

"Watch out! He has magic!" Jack yelled. He tossed away his empty guns and drew his sword.

Ruben rained fireballs down on the Ancient, but they fizzled when they hit the ice, only slightly melting it before they faded. Undaunted, he continued his assault.

Without warning, the ice dropped and Tezcatlipoca smacked Shaman backward off the dais. Then he grabbed Annie by the throat.

Dropping her weapons, Annie grabbed his arms, fighting to free herself with no success.

Reforming the ice wall, the Ancient sank his fangs into her throat and began to drain her.

Shaman let out a cry and leapt back onto the dais, renewing his attack in fury.

Ruben managed to break through the ice behind Tezcatlipoca with his fireballs, while Angelique continued to hit the Ancient from the other side with lightning bolts, weakening him a little more with each strike. "Don't let up, Ruben!" she shouted. "Shaman! Get Annie!"

Shaman slammed his tomahawk into the ice, crumbling what remained. Then he attacked the Ancient with a vengeance.

Tezcatlipoca dropped Annie to the floor. Then he formed another ice wall, this time completely surrounding himself and trapping Shaman with him.

Shaman circled him, eyeing his enemy. Then he lifted his tomahawk and attacked again.

Jack seized the opportunity and grabbed Annie's arm. He dragged her to safety, laying her as far away from the dais as possible. Then he turned back to try and help Shaman.

A yell from Ruben distracted both Angelique and Jack from the battle. They turned to see Cyrus holding him by the throat. Ruben had been completely immobilized by Cyrus' magic and the Elder was dragging him toward the door.

"Oh, no you don't!" Angelique screamed and shot a lightning bolt directly into Cyrus' chest. He momentarily lost his grip on Ruben, and

Jack leapt forward, grabbing the incapacitated Mastric around the waist. Carrying Ruben with him, he plunged to the ground.

Angelique hit Cyrus again, pouring as much power into her magic as she could.

Annie slowly regained her senses. When she opened her eyes, she saw Cyrus and the two on the floor inches away from him. She lifted her gun and fired until she emptied the chamber.

Cyrus roared in pain and slipped into the shadows before Jack could stop him.

Annie got to her feet, and then spun around when she heard Angelique shout.

"No!" Angelique yelled, letting loose a firestorm, her hands blackening from the strain.

Following her gaze, Annie screamed.

Tezcatlipoca had plunged his hand through Shaman's chest and out his back. He was holding Shaman's heart.

"No!" she shouted, dropping her gun as she ran for the dais. "No! Damn it, Shaman, don't you leave me!" She leapt onto the dais and repeatedly slammed her fists against the ice, watching in helpless horror. Tezcatlipoca let go of Shaman's body and it hit the dais, his blood staining the stone. Enraged, Annie frantically beat on the ice wall, trying to get through it before he could devour Shaman's heart.

Jack jumped up and tackled her, dragging her off the platform.

Angelique attacked the Ancient with renewed fervor, melting the ice surrounding him.

Ruben had gotten to his feet and opened fire, hitting the ice with fireballs of his own.

"Let me go, Jack!" Annie screamed. "Damn you, let me go or I swear I'll kill you!"

Releasing her, Jack turned his attention back to Tezcatlipoca. "We've got to work as a team, Annie!" he yelled. "We can't afford to lose anyone else!"

The Ancient had finished with Shaman's heart and began fighting back, forming ice spikes midair and hurling them at his attackers.

Annie screamed in rage and shoved Jack away. Then she leapt for the dais, claws extended.

Jack dove after her and attacked Tezcatlipoca.

The Ancient was beginning to weaken and knew it. He wasn't closing his wounds as fast and his spells were beginning to lose their potency. The team pushed harder, trying to force him to retreat from the dais. He wouldn't move.

Finally, Annie's knees buckled, and she sank to the floor at the base of the platform, weakened from loss of blood.

Tezcatlipoca tried to grab her.

Jack seized the opportunity, tackled him and knocked him backward off the dais. Wrestling the Ancient to the ground, he found himself trying to dodge razor-sharp claws. His efforts were unsuccessful. The Ancient impaled him, only missing his heart by inches. Gasping at the sudden pain, he screamed.

Angelique saw the chance to hit the Ancient hard and engulfed him in fire, forcing herself to dive deeper into her magic, until her hands began to char. Every time the flames flickered when Tezcatlipoca tried to douse them, she renewed them and hit him again.

Jack pulled himself free of the Ancient's hand and rolled off the dais, hitting the floor hard.

Ruben joined Angelique and was attacking Tezcatlipoca with fire as well.

Finally, it was too much for the weakened Ancient. The centuries of sleep had greatly drained his strength, and without more blood to sustain him, he could no longer fight. The flames consumed him, and he lost consciousness. His body began to crisp, and the flesh burnt away, leaving only bone and the now unprotected inner organs. Then these too began to burn.

Annie dragged herself to her feet and grabbed Shaman's tomahawk from the dais. Then she staggered toward the Ancient's body, falling halfway there. Jack, Angelique, and Ruben watched in silence while she crawled the rest of the way and sank the tomahawk into the Ancient's sizzling heart, destroying it completely. Then falling to the floor, she lay watching the last remnants of his life crumble to dust. "For you," she whispered to the silence of the tomb.

The small group picked up Shaman's body and the badly weakened Warlord, and then slowly made their way out of the pyramid, knowing it would not be safe to sleep within its walls.

Annie was mumbling about Shaman and the dawn. She was badly in need of blood.

Jack was also near the breaking point. And though Ruben had suffered only minor injuries and Angelique only her burns, the amount of power they had used to kill the Ancient had drained their bodies, which now demanded sustenance.

Once they got back to their vehicles, Angelique retrieved the servants and let her companions drain them completely. Then she worked on healing their injuries.

Jack brushed her off when she finished closing up his chest and went to help Annie with the task of preparing Shaman's body for the pyre. He arranged the Indian's body on the pile of wood and stone they had built under the stars.

Shaman had already begun to decay, but Annie wanted to keep an age-old promise. Taking one of the torches, she lit the pyre just before the sun broke the horizon, committing him back to the wind and the Great Spirit the land of his birth called to when a warrior passed. As the flames consumed his body, a mist rose above it, briefly forming a wolf before it disappeared into the first rays of light. At the base of the pyre, Shaman's tomahawk was embedded in the pile of stone, marking it as a holy place where only the dead were welcome.

Annie stood vigil long after the others had walked away, watching until Shaman's body had turned to ash. When she finally turned her back, the wind picked up the ashes and carried them away with the sound of a howling wolf pack welcoming its brother home.

Peace reigned over the field through the day. The four sleeping warriors that had survived the battle heard the whispers of the fallen in their sleep, and for Annie, it brought dreams of tears over secret nights that had been torn away forever.

Angelique arose just before sunset. She had not been weakened as badly as the others the night before. Looking around, the reality of what had happened sank in. Though the rest of the team still slept, she felt their pain. The last hint of light was fading on the horizon and she stared, committing it to memory. Then her decision made, she fed on a little of their remaining blood supplies and prepared to go back inside. She cast one last glance back at the ground where the others lay in sleep and bid them a silent farewell.

With renewed determination, she climbed the temple steps to the entrance. Then at its opening, she reached out with her senses to see deep into the interior of the Ancient stone halls. The only sound she heard was the rats as they scurried away. She silently entered, growing more determined with every step. *No one else will die at his hands.*

Angelique searched every room she passed, but found nothing. Her frustration slowly grew, and she began to question her own abilities. Her anger rose as she continued to find only the silence of a vacant tomb. Finally, she neared the center of the temple where they had destroyed the Ancient the night before. *He must be here somewhere, he was injured and could not have traversed the daylight.* Then she shouted, "Where are you? Come out and face me, you coward! You can murder hundreds, but cannot face me?" Screaming into the darkness, her rage exploded as she challenged him.

From the shadows, a low voice spoke. "Are you so anxious to die then?" Cyrus stepped into view. His smile sent a chill of fear racing down her spine.

"You bastard, you have tortured and murdered hundreds of innocent people!" She stood facing him in sheer defiance. "Tonight, it is you who will die!"

His eyes narrowed, and his voice grew cold. "We shall see. Indeed, we shall see."

Minutes after Angelique had entered the temple, the rest of the party awoke, hungry and worn from the previous nights' battle. Jack quickly realized she was gone and alerted the others. They swiftly fed on what blood they had and raced for the temple entrance.

Annie and Ruben immediately began searching for her, reaching into the dark interior with their senses. Only silence answered them.

Jack tried to make light of it. "She's not exactly weak, you know. I'm fairly sure she can handle herself long enough for us to find her." He did not tell them of his own doubts and focused instead on tracking her.

Ruben frowned and said nothing.

Annie turned to Jack. "Stay here and watch the entrance!" she commanded. "This area is well known to Renegades. We can't afford to be caught off guard." Then motioning for Ruben to follow, she headed down the hall they had traveled the night before, moving at inhuman speed.

Jack took cover behind a partially collapsed column to watch the entrance.

Annie and Ruben wasted no time moving deeper into the Temple's interior. But when they neared the center of the structure, they came face to face with a Daemon blocking the passageway. Rising twelve feet in height with a wingspan that engulfed the corridor, it roared a challenge.

Annie came to a dead stop. "Alright, you monster! You want to play? Come on!" Drawing her guns, she began peppering its leathery hide with bullets.

Ruben moved around to flank the creature, only to jump back as another Daemon came at him from behind the first. "There's another one," he shouted, jumping sideways to avoid its immense claws. Then he joined Annie, trying to drive the first beast backward to block the second one's path. By continuously dodging in and out and coordinating their efforts, they managed to slowly cut the first beast to pieces. The creatures Cyrus had summoned this time were not nearly as powerful as those Reivn had faced in New York.

Ruben had tossed his gun to Annie and pulled out his katana to save any strength he would spend with his magic for Cyrus when they found him.

But Annie spent the bullets quickly, the chambers of both guns clicking empty in minutes. She tossed them aside and willed forth her claws. Then she began a dance with death, moving in and out at incredible speeds, slashing at the beasts with every pass.

When they finally dropped the first Daemon, the second one closed in. Ruben's frustration rose when it attacked. *We need to reach Angelique before she gets herself killed.*

Annie ignored him. She could think of nothing but revenge. The image of Shaman in his last moments haunted her, and it had driven her into a blind rage. She barely noticed each time the Daemon wounded her.

Ruben countered as many blows as possible. He feared Annie wanted to die, and he was unwilling to sacrifice another life. But in his heart, he wondered if Angelique was still alive.

Deep in the temple, Angelique and Cyrus were face to face.

Cyrus circled slowly around her, mocking her. "A mere pitiful girl has come to bring me down. This is amusing, I must say. So what are you waiting for? I am right here."

Angelique kept pace, turning with him as she sized him up.

He came to a stop in front of her. "I wanted the Ancient you killed last night. It was very rude of you to deny me my prize. Where shall I find a powerful enough body now, I wonder..." His eyes leveled on her, his meaning clear. "I know... I'll have yours."

She summoned a fireball and hurled it at him.

He levitated her into the air and threw her against the far wall. Then with one word, the blaze that had covered him flickered and died.

She saw the flames go out as she hit the floor. She got to her feet, wincing at the searing pain of bones broken deep inside her. But she mentally pushed it away and blasted him with a lightning bolt.

The discharge knocked him backward as the current tore through him. The air around him crackled and the acrid smell of charred flesh filled the air. Ignoring the pain, he summoned shadows. They attacked her, tearing her flesh and leaving open wounds.

Pain beginning to overwhelm her senses, she choked out a banishing spell and the shadows vanished. Then she turned and found herself face to face with him.

Cyrus slammed his blade into her side, laughing as he twisted it and drove it in deeper.

Angelique screamed and tried to block the pain, but it forced her to her knees. *No...* "No... NO!" she finally screamed and unleashed a wave of pure kinetic energy.

It hit him hard and he flew backward.

She grabbed the hilt of his dagger and pulled it out, gasping in agony. Then she slowly got to her feet and turned to face him again.

He began to chant, his eyes riveted on her and his expression filled with hatred.

She forced herself to concentrate, and then sent another potent wave of power ripping through him before he could finish his spell.

Searing pain exploded in his head and he fell backward, screaming in pain.

The moment his concentration broke, Angelique gathered her strength and summoned another firestorm, unleashing its fury on him.

Cyrus got up, the pain temporarily slowing him down. Then he snarled in rage when the firestorm engulfed him. He burst into flames, but not before he struck back.

She was thrown into the wall behind her and bound with magical restraints that pinned her to the stone. She struggled to get free, watching him put out the flames covering him. "How long can you keep this up?" she screamed. "I know you're growing weak! It's only a matter of time!"

He lifted his hand and squeezed the air, using the shadows to crush her.

The grip around her tightened and she screamed. Then remembering her encounter with Alora, she closed her eyes. Almost immediately, she transformed into a mist and slipped from his hold. She floated across the room and shifted back to human form.

His eyes followed her, and so did his shadows.

Blood was pouring from Angelique's wounds and her strength was fading, but she knew his was too. *I must not fail...* With determination, she hurled another lightning bolt at him.

Cyrus deflected it this time and it hit her instead, throwing her backward and tearing through her with searing agony. "Hurts, doesn't it?" he snarled from his corner.

Out in the corridor, Ruben and Annie could hear the battle raging between Angelique and Cyrus. But their own strength was slowly waning. They had already killed four Daemons, but were struggling against two more, and their guns had been emptied after the first fight. Ruben was down to his sword and Annie her claws. Both Daemons were badly wounded and kept trying to flank the warriors, but Annie and Ruben kept them herded together.

The beasts roared in anger, slashing at the them with their immense claws.

The black goo that bled from their wounds formed a slick surface on the stones below, and Annie and Ruben had to keep recovering their footing on the slippery substance. But it aided them as well, as the Daemons struggled to stand. Their minds very much on the battle Angelique faced, they both fought hard, determined to get to her before it was too late.

In the inner sanctum, Angelique's strength was deteriorating. *This fight has to end before I am finished*, she realized. It was all or nothing. She changed tactics and attacked him internally, forcing his blood to heat, and using the last of her strength in the power she poured forth.

Cyrus howled in pain as his blood began to boil, finally finishing his body. With his last breath, he muttered one final incantation.

Angelique screamed when she felt the invasion in her mind and fought him as he jumped his soul from his dying body into hers. She desperately tried to block him with her magic, but she was too spent, and only succeeded in maintaining control. She quickly realized if she grew any weaker, he would take over. *I need to get out of here. If I cannot get to Reivn before... oh God! He cannot ever be allowed to get free.* Feebly staggering from the room, she began to make her way back to the temple entrance. Then she spotted Ruben and Annie down the hall.

They had just finished off the last Daemon. Both were badly wounded... Annie so critically she could hardly stand.

Angelique faintly called out to them.

Annie almost fell when she turned, claws out again. Then stabilizing herself, she froze when she saw Angelique, immediately recognizing that the Ambassador was more than just hurt. "How fast do you need to get out of here?" she asked when Angelique joined them.

Angelique opened her mouth, but no sound would come.

Ruben picked her up and nodded to his companion. Drawing what strength she had left, Annie raced down the hall, Ruben hot on her heels, bearing Angelique in his arms.

When they neared the exit, they heard the sounds of heavy fighting. Rounding the corner, they almost fell over Jack, who was crouched down behind a broken column. "Join the party, there's plenty more where they came from!" he yelled, pointing at dead bodies on the floor.

Annie dove behind the rubble next to him. "Jack," she shouted. "We have to get her out of here! I think she's dying!"

Ruben laid Angelique behind the cover of the broken wall and dropped down beside them. "I can't teleport until we're outside! The magic in here prevents it!" He growled in frustration.

Jack grinned. "Then it's time to go!" he yelled and leapt over the rocks. He began pelting the Renegades with bullets and ran for the door.

Ruben followed, cutting through as many as he could to open a path for the two behind him.

Annie gazed at Angelique, who was leaning against the rubble, her eyes closed. "Honey, it's time to go," she said gently.

Angelique's opened her eyes and whispered. "Go... I'll be right behind you."

Annie leaned forward and kissed her. "I can see why he loves you," she smiled. "See you on the other side." With that, she vaulted over the rubble and headed for the door. She tried to clear a path for the woman behind her, killing as many as possible, but bullets and swords hit her from all sides. She finally collapsed when she reached the exit.

Jack stood in the opening badly wounded, trying not to collapse.

"Where is Angelique?" Ruben growled, still hearing a lot of commotion inside. He turned to go back, but Jack grabbed his arm and stopped him.

"She'll make it, but we'll have to run like hell when she does!" Jack gasped. "Those bastards will be hot on her trail, so be ready!"

Before Ruben could respond, Angelique practically fell out the door, tripping over Annie. She grabbed the doorframe, barely able to stand. Then she looked at Ruben. "Teleport them to safety. They need your help."

Ruben looked alarmed. "What about you? You can't stay here!"

Angelique held up her hand and stopped him. "That's an order."

Ruben looked from Annie's unconscious body to Jack, who was leaning against the wall, bleeding from multiple wounds. Then he growled at Angelique. "I can't just leave you!"

Angelique nodded again. "Go," she whispered.

Ruben finally closed his eyes and nodded. He picked up Annie and then grabbed Jack. "I'm sorry," he choked out. Then with one final glance, he vanished with them.

Angelique leaned against the archway, trying to gather her remaining strength. The Renegades inside getting closer. *It's time to move.* She staggered down the side of the temple hoping to get to the vehicles. But her strength failed halfway down the structure, and she fell and slid the rest of the way until she finally reached the bottom.

Behind her, the Renegades poured from the pyramid. Streaming down its sides, they howled in triumph. "There she is! The Ambassador! Don't let her escape!"

Forcing herself to her feet, she tried to make a run for it. Then she froze when more Renegades poured from the woods in front of her. *There's nowhere left to run!* she realized. *I'm trapped*! In resignation, she fell to her knees, prepared to embrace death as the enemy swarmed toward her. Then she closed her eyes and sent a single message. *My love... forgive me.*

## Chapter Forty-Eight
## Dragon Lords

*What do we fight and die for? I believe it is for those we love and want to protect. All that we treasure can be lost in a single terrible moment, and it is that fear that drives us ever forward in this war. We cannot love but that we fight to protect that love and it matters not if it is mother to daughter, husband to wife, or father to son. We would defy our Sires and the very Gods themselves to follow where Angels fear to tread, merely to stand in defense of all we cherish.*

*My angel marches to the very gates of Hell in her quest for revenge against Cyrus. Her heart is right, but not her judgment. The fight I now face will be long and hard, and I cannot guarantee we will all return from the dark depths to which we have gone. I would gladly lay down my life to see her safely home. For me, the night has forever changed, and I cannot go back to the empty existence I knew before her. If I must fight to defend the Alliance from our renegade brothers, then I would do so with her at my side. Then all is bearable.*

*Stand and face your fears, my father once told me. Lift up your chin and show no fear to the enemy, for in fear there is weakness and in weakness there is death. She is my strength. I have something I fight for now that means more to me than anything else I know in this cursed existence, and that is my angel and my family. Truly, her delicate touch and gentle smile are worth fighting and even dying for... far more so than the Ancients who sit on their throne giving orders from behind stale walls where the world does not reach, and life has forgotten them. If I do not return from the road to Hell, then tell her of my love...*

*Lord Reivn Draegon*

\* \* \* \* \*

Reivn sensed he was not alone and slipped into the shadows out of sight. His eyes darting around, he searched for the one trailing him. He did not have long to wait.

A single figure appeared, using the darkness to cover his passage. Obviously tracking someone, he moved slowly but steadily forward.

Reivn waited until the man following him drew close, remaining hidden among the trees. Then he stepped out behind the person and snarled. "Take one more step and I will kill you."

The man put up his hands in surrender.

"Turn around slowly!" Reivn commanded.

The moon slipped from behind the clouds and cast a soft glow on the clearing as the stranger turned around. White hair glistened in the light and a familiar face stared back at him.

"Lunitar! I could have killed you! What are you doing here?" Reivn growled.

Lunitar put his arms down. "I belong at your side. There is no telling what you may face when you reach your destination. I thought you might need a hand."

Reivn struck him across the jaw, knocking him to the ground. "Errant child! You disobeyed a direct order! I should strip the flesh from your bones and leave you for the sun's rays!"

Lunitar got up slowly. "I wasn't given an order by my Warlord. I was given a directive from my father, who was concerned for his family. Am I not allowed the same concerns for those I love? If that is the price you would have me pay for disobedience, I will gladly pay it, but I respectfully request that you allow me to complete this mission with you first."

Reivn growled and raised his hand to strike again, but then he froze when he saw Lunitar's expression. It was one of acceptance and respect.

Lunitar bowed his head and waited.

Reivn lowered his hand. "There is no difference between father and Warlord where the safety of my people is concerned. Remember that, because next time you disobey an order, I will skin you alive and let you spend a week hanging on the walls of my laboratory, suffering the flames of wrath while you contemplate your disobedience."

"I understand, father," Lunitar answered quietly. "When we return to the Keep I will..."

Reivn held up his hand, motioning for silence, his eyes darting past his son to stare into the darkness of the jungle.

Lunitar moved soundlessly next to his father. He felt it too and knew they were not alone.

Reivn crouched down and blended into the shadows, motioning for his son to do the same.

Lunitar ducked down immediately, mingling among the underbrush until he was invisible.

Neither man made a sound as they watched the surrounding forest.

Dozens of people emerged from the trees, moving silently through the jungle. The unknown hunters followed a trail of crushed foliage that revealed telltale evidence of cars having recently passed through.

Reivn and Lunitar watched from their vantage point as more and more people slipped through the underbrush mere feet away. Reivn glanced at Lunitar. *Renegades… they are hunting someone,* he telepathied. *I am guessing it is Angelique's party. We need to get ahead of them.*

Lunitar nodded and turned back to watch them pass. *Overhead... so we can track their movements?* he quietly sent back.

Scanning their surroundings for other possibilities, Reivn finally nodded.

Reivn and Lunitar waited until the last of the Renegades passed them, and then slipped quietly away. Once they were at a safe distance, Reivn transformed into a raven and Lunitar into a falcon. Side by side at high enough altitude to maintain their stealth, they flew ahead of the pack on the ground, watching them as they moved through the jungle below.

Then Lunitar spotted something that made him double back.

*What is it?* Reivn telepathied, circling around to join him.

Lunitar's sharp eyes darted around, searching for what he had seen until he found them again. *There! They have prisoners!* he sent.

Reivn followed his gaze and spotted a small group being dragged through the trees. He could detect the faint smell of blood drifting up from below. *They are wounded, whoever they are. We need to help them and to do that we must get ahead of their captors.*

Lunitar followed his father as they flew ahead of the hunting party below.

Then Reivn landed and shifted back to human form. Drawing his sword, he slipped into the shadows and hid, waiting for them to approach.

Alighting near his father, Lunitar did the same. Then he crouched down in the bushes, his blade in hand. Though he could not see his father, he knew Reivn was somewhere nearby. But not wanting to risk their exposure, he waited. He knew the Renegades were close.

The first of the hunting party emerged from the trees, moving toward them in silence.

Reivn waited until they were almost on top of him. Then he unleashed a barrage of fireballs and chaos erupted, as he and Lunitar attacked.

Several Renegades ran burning through the trees, trying to douse the fire that engulfed them, but their magic was weak and no match for the Mastric's attack. Other Renegades rushed forward, and a hail of bullets rained down on Reivn's position. They hit empty space. The Mastric Warlord had already moved and was now attacking from another location.

Lunitar mirrored his father's tactics, dodging from place to place as he attacked.

More Principatus poured into the area and Reivn turned to hand-to-hand combat, using his magic to supplement the fight. *Sheer numbers alone can overwhelm us. Reserve your strength*, he telepathied Lunitar.

Lunitar joined him and the two fought back to back, defending against the onslaught.

"Put up a shield! We need cover!" Reivn yelled, unleashing a lightning bolt that split in six different directions when it left his fingertips.

Lunitar immediately cast a barrier around them, repelling a hailstorm of bullets. Maintaining the shield with one hand, he wielded his sword with the other, defending himself from any renegade foolish enough to get too close.

Behind him, Reivn continued to be a whirlwind of destruction. He levied lightning and fire at their enemies and drove his sword home whenever one of them came within killing distance.

A few yards away, the Renegades guarding three half-conscious prisoners dropped them to the ground and leapt to the attack.

Reivn saw the now unguarded prisoners and slowly moved toward them.

Lunitar kept pace with him, keeping their shield intact as they inched closer to their quarry. Then he dropped his blade and unleashed fireballs at the Renegades, slowly forging a ring of death around them.

A large cluster of Principatus broke away, disappearing into the darkness of the jungle.

Reivn let them go, focusing on the Renegades still attacking him, and the three injured captives who were lying on the ground nearby.

Lunitar reached deeper into the spirals to strengthen his energy when it began to wane, fortifying his own ability to prolong a spell. Burns appeared on his hands from the sudden surge of magic, and a fine sheen of blood formed on his forehead from the strain.

Reivn was bleeding from several wounds, yet he barely seemed to notice. With his left hand, he kept up the steady pounding of fireballs while with his right he wielded his sword. But the strain was beginning to show on his face.

All around the two Mastrics, bodies were piling up as they continued to defend themselves. Trees burned with intense heat from the flames engulfing those Renegades unfortunate enough to catch one of Reivn's blasts full force. But Lunitar was beginning to pale as he held his ground.

Reivn noticed his son's pallor and tossed Lunitar his own blade.

Lunitar caught the sword and his father's gaze. He immediately dropped the magic and turned to hand-to-hand combat. The loss of blood from fueling his magic had begun to take its toll.

Then a young Renegade got too close, and Lunitar grabbed him and drained him in seconds. Then he decapitated the luckless man in one strike.

Seeing their comrade's fate, the remaining Renegades realized the two Mastrics were winning. They quickly disappeared into the jungle, leaving their captives behind.

Lunitar staggered slightly as they let up the chase.

Seeing him, Reivn grabbed his arm and steadied him.

Once Lunitar could stand on his own again, they went to the half-conscious prisoners lying on the ground.

Lunitar dropped beside them to see how injured they were. His quick inspection revealed grim news. "They are not our kind and they are badly injured. Without aid, they will die."

One of the men reached up and caught Lunitar's hand. "They will kill the ambassador. You must get to her…"

Reivn kneeled down. "Who are you and how do you know of my wife?"

"I am Nicholas. We aided your wife and Jack in their hunt… as far as we could go." Nicholas leaned against a tree, his breathing labored. "We are Wolvens. We have no love of the Renegades. They ambushed us. The rest of those who were with me are dead."

Reivn frowned. "Then you know where my wife was headed?"

Nicholas slowly nodded. "She was after Cyrus. They went to Tzental… to the temple of Tezcatlipoca, the Aztec blood God. He was… one of your kind. She is in danger."

Lunitar closed his eyes in frustration, his fear realized.

"How long ago did they pass through here?" Reivn asked him.

Nicholas shifted so he could better see the Warlord. "Two or three nights ago maybe. I'm not sure how long I was unconscious."

Lunitar watched the surrounding jungle for attackers, but the trees were silent.

Reivn looked up, gazing in the direction the Renegades had disappeared before turning his attention back Nicholas. "Then she's reached the temple?"

Nicholas nodded. "She would have reached it by now. The Renegades found out about her passage somehow. We tried to stop them or at least buy her some time, but there were just too many. They killed the rest of my pack and were forcing us to track her."

"How many are with her, Nicholas? I need to know," Reivn asked abruptly.

Nicholas coughed, blood spilling from his mouth. "There are three others with her beside Jack, two men, and one woman. She also has several blood servants with her."

Reivn took him by the shoulders. "Names... can you give me names?"

"Annie... one of them was called Annie." Nicholas answered. "I don't know the others. We didn't speak much."

Lunitar glanced at Reivn. "The Galatian Warlord."

Reivn nodded. "Most likely. She was conspicuously absent from the war Council." Looking down at Nicholas, who was fighting to stay conscious, he frowned. "Lunitar, you will be taking these men back to the Keep for immediate care. Reyna can help. She is a capable healer."

"Reyna? She is at the Keep?" Lunitar stared in surprise at his father.

Reivn nodded. "Of course. Send one of my personal servants to get her."

Lunitar growled. "What of you father? Surely you don't plan to continue on alone?"

Reivn stood up and faced his son. "I do. And this time you will obey my orders. The lives of these three men are in your hands."

"I understand that father, but you also need someone to watch your back. Can we not open a portal and..." Lunitar stopped short when he saw his father's expression.

Reivn glared at him. "How many times will you defy me? I will deal with the matter ahead. Would you defy a direct order from the Warlord Prefect?"

Lunitar dropped his gaze. "No, my lord. I will see to their safety immediately."

"Good. I will return once I secure the ambassador and her party. Now... you need to go quickly." Reivn leaned down and pulled Nicholas to his feet.

Lunitar opened the portal and moments later, all three injured men were safely away. Looking back at his father before he stepped through himself, he sighed. "Good luck, father."

Reivn nodded in silence and waited until the portal snapped shut before turning back to the jungle and the hunt for his quarry.

The moment Lunitar stepped into Draegonstorm, his presence was known. In the Commonroom, Gideon sat bolt upright. "The Spirals just shifted," he growled.

Moventius did not get the chance to reply, as a cry of alarm rose.

Staring at Moventius for half a second, Gideon jumped up and ran for the door.

Moventius followed him growling. "It's probably another false alarm."

When they reached the doors and looked out, several guards were running past.

Gideon stopped one of them. "What's happened?"

"The portal chamber was activated without notification, sir! Someone's come through!" The guard hurried to join his comrades.

Gideon turned to Moventius. "Very few even know the location key for getting into the Keep! Come on! It may be Alora!"

Moventius snarled at the name and joined him as they rushed down the hall, heading for the bowels of the fortress.

The portal shimmered like a flowering rose. Illuminated for a moment, four figures stepped down from its platform. Then the light faded.

Gideon's eyes widened in shock when he recognized Lunitar, aiding three badly injured men.

Moventius saw them and leapt forward to help. "My God, what happened?"

"They were ambushed by Renegades. We need to get them to the infirmary immediately," Lunitar stated, giving the first to Gideon and the second to a guard. Passing Nicholas to Moventius, he moved toward the door. "Father gave me strict instructions to give them aid, and who to summon for their care. Go with them to the infirmary. I'll meet you there shortly."

Gideon stared at him in surprise. "Father gave you... What? You followed him?"

"In your quarter's huh?" Moventius laughed. "I'm surprised you're here in one piece after pulling a stunt like that. Lunitar.... hehe, your name should be Lunatic!" Laughing heartily, he picked Nicholas up and headed to the infirmary.

Gideon followed him in somber silence.

Lunitar hurried to Reivn's private office, where he summoned one of Reivn's own servants. In minutes, there was a knock at the door.

"Come in!" he answered rather harshly.

The servant poked his head in. "You sent for me, my lord? Uh... Where is his lordship?"

Lunitar frowned. "His lordship on a mission of high importance. However, I have a direct order for you. You are to fetch Lady Reyna and escort her to the infirmary immediately. We have three guests in desperate need of her healing. I will meet you there. Go quickly."

The servant bowed and scurried from the room.

Lunitar took a deep breath and sat back for a second, closing his eyes. "Father..." he whispered to the silence.

Down in the infirmary, chaos ensued as Gideon and Moventius arrived with their charges, the guards behind them. They settled the men down onto beds and tried to make them comfortable.

Gideon looked around. "Moventius, we're going to need sustenance for them to help them regenerate. You see to that while I get clothing for them that isn't shredded or matted in blood.

Moventius nodded and left to retrieve what they would need from his own stores.

Gideon took stock of the three wounded men and roughly gauged their sizes. Then he sat back to watch over them while he waited for Lunitar. *How did he manage to leave here without my notice? Father is going to be furious with me for this...*

Lunitar walked in at that moment and looked over at him. "I'm sorry," he stated.

"You could have warned me," Gideon replied. "I was charged with the protection of this Keep while father was absent. I will hear about this."

Lunitar shook his head. "I don't think so. He was rather infuriated with me and I expect he isn't through speaking to me on the matter. We just got interrupted before we could finish."

Further conversation was interrupted as the servant arrived with Reyna. She entered nervously, not daring to look at anyone.

Lunitar's eyes wandered down to her ankles, which were almost completely hidden by the hem of her plain gown, to see if the anklet was still there, but if it was, it was not visible.

Going to Nicholas, Reyna sat down and began to rudimentarily heal his wounds.

Lunitar stared at her in silence, watching as she ministered to her patients.

The servant stood quietly by waiting for her.

Lunitar glanced at him, his curiosity peaked. *Why is he still here? This doesn't make any sense...* He opened his mouth to ask, but then was distracted when Gideon stood to leave.

Gideon headed to the door, and then looked back. "I know you meant well. But remember in the future that you are not the one who endures the brunt of his wrath if you anger him. When it concerns the safety of this fortress, I am the one he will chastise. Good night, little brother."

Staring after him, Lunitar frowned. His annoyance at his brother's words was tempered by the truth they carried. He had put Gideon at risk. Still. he felt it had been necessary. His eyes settled again on the servant. "You can go. I'll escort the lady to her rooms when she finishes."

The servant shook his head. "I am required to wait for her, sir."

"I am dismissing you of that responsibility. She is perfectly safe and I can escort her wherever she wishes to go," Lunitar stated firmly.

The servant shook his head again, looking slightly uncomfortable. "Begging your pardon, sir, but you don't have the authority to dismiss me from my charge. Only his lordship can do that."

Lunitar growled. "I am Lord Reivn's son. Since when do you have the right to refuse an order from one of us?"

"Since Lord Reivn placed the responsibility of her care on me... sir," the servant answered.

His countenance growing dark, Lunitar turned away in annoyance and stared at the woman still tending to the wounded. *What isn't he telling me? Who is she?*

Unaware of his thoughts, Reyna moved from patient to patient, slowly closing their wounds. Her long black hair was loosely tied back, with small strands escaping to fall unnoticed down her back. Her olive skin was flawless, and her hands moved with delicate grace.

Lunitar thought it unusual to have such a creature brought into their world. *Too gentle, too fragile...* He walked over to her. "Excuse me, my lady. May I offer my assistance?"

Reyna glanced up briefly and shook her head. Her dark eyes were filled with...

*Fear?* Lunitar realized as he stared at her.

As quickly as it had appeared, it vanished again. A mask fell over her expression and she looked away. She finished her work in mute silence and then joined the servant to leave.

"Thank you for your aid, my lady," he called after her.

She stopped at the door and turned, bowing her head slightly. Then she was gone, leaving him to stare at the empty doorway.

Troubled, Lunitar went back to the Wolvens' sides. He sat down beside Nicholas and watched over them in silence while they slept. He was lost in thought. Worried about his father and wondering about the mysterious young woman he had now met three times, he waited for word that Reivn had returned, but the fortress remained quiet. Before long, his thoughts were interrupted by Moventius' boisterous voice in the hall and he looked up. His brother entered the infirmary, his arms loaded with food for their Wolven guests.

Moventius grinned. "Such a morose look, Luni. What's wrong?"

Lunitar shook his head. "Nothing father's return won't cure. Is that for our guests?"

"It is indeed," Moventius smiled. "You may not want to stay though. We eat raw meat, not blood as you do." Moventius put down the load he carried and moved to awaken Nicholas. "Brother, come. Wake. Eat."

Lunitar sighed and got up. "If you're going to be here awhile, I'm going to take my leave and head to the library."

Moventius chuckled. "I think I can handle looking after these three. Just remember the library isn't in the portal chamber."

Lunitar glared at him and then left, heading for the Mastric's library deep in the fortress.

## Chapter Forty-Nine
## A Dragon's Heart

*Even in the bravest of hearts, there are moments of desperate fear that grip you in a vice so tight you want to stop the forward momentum that hurls you toward whatever fate awaits at the end of your journey. The truth that lies behind every warrior though, is that courage and bravery are no more than the determination to plunge ahead no matter how much you fear what lies before you. Whether out of loyalty, love, duty or honor, it is the creed that holds the warrior to his code. That code for me is my honor, my loyalty and sense of duty in the oath I took centuries ago. But most of all it lies in the love I bear my family, my sons and daughter... my wife.*

*I leave tonight to follow her on a mission I myself would not have undertaken alone, and yet my fragile flower, in her outrage at the death of a comrade, has chosen to do so. I cannot bury the dread I feel in this venture, yet I admire her courage. Even if born in the naivety that is so much a part of her charm, I cannot help but admire her persistence and determination. It is the very core of what we Draegons hold so dear. Perhaps she learned that trait from me during all those nights I so relentlessly pursued her. From the moment I first laid eyes on her, I knew my life would never be the same and that she would have some major role to play. When Alora returned and ripped her from me for that brief time, the grief that took me was almost my undoing, and it made me very aware of just how powerful a bond I share with my beautiful angel. Now I follow her into one of the darkest and oldest parts of the western world and can only pray I am not too late. Even warriors with the greatest of courage can lose their lives to a greater enemy than themselves. And Cyrus is one such enemy...*

*Lord Reivn Draegon*

\* \* \* \* \*

They were coming for her.

Angelique dropped to her knees and closed her eyes, waiting for death. Her strength was gone, and she could neither fight nor run anymore. She thought of Reivn, whose face she would never see again, and a tear trickled down her cheek. All around the jungle, shouts rose in the darkness as the Principatus closed in, their victory complete. She was trapped.

Then with the force of a hurricane, a deafening roar broke out from deep in the tree line and the forest exploded in flames.

The Renegades near the jungle's edge scattered in every direction, screaming as the fire engulfed the dense undergrowth around them. Total chaos ensued as they scrambled to get away from the roaring inferno.

Angelique opened her eyes, looking around in confusion.

An enormous dragon emerged from the dense undergrowth, its immense red-tipped wings whipping the air around it into a fierce wind. Roaring its fury, it spewed Dragonfire in every direction. Its hide bore the appearance of a Daemon emerged from the pits, in deep shades of crimson, and it was moving in and out among the Renegades at a frightening speed. Explosions of flames rained down as the terrified Renegades tried to dodge death. But the Dragon reared back on its immense hindquarters and surrounded the scattering Immortals with a swirling white-hot inferno, until everything in its path was engulfed in the searing blaze. Then the creature continued its rampage, moving toward Angelique and killing everyone in its way.

Those still halfway up the side of the pyramid turned and ran in terror.

Angelique alone remained, on her knees and helplessly staring across the clearing.

The creature stopped, its gaze coming to rest on her. Then it headed in her direction.

She closed her eyes and began to shake, knowing it would soon be upon her. Too exhausted to get up and run, she let the tears fall…

Swirls of mist filled the air as the Dragon grew closer, and it began to change. It grew smaller, its claws turned to fingers, and its protruding spines to long, black hair. Then finally, its wings disappeared. Reivn gazed down at Angelique's still shaking form and closed eyes, and he reached down and gently took her hand. Then he pulled her into his arms. "I heard you, angel. I am here and there is nothing to forgive. You are hurt. I have come to take you home."

Angelique shook her head and lifted his hand to her forehead, her eyes telling him what she could not bear to voice.

He reached deep into her mind, searching until he found the answer he sought. "You are not alone," he whispered, his voice painfully quiet. "He jumped bodies?"

She could only nod, her injuries and loss of blood beginning to overtake her.

"No..." His voice shook. "I... I cannot remove him. His magic is Daemonic, and that knowledge is forbidden to our kind. I do not know how to counter such a dark spell."

Her knees buckled and she fell against him, blood seeping from her wounds.

"Why? Why did you go? Why did you not heed my advice, angel?" Reivn growled, forcing himself to maintain control. "I told you to return home and to leave Cyrus to me! Your desire to stop him was every bit as honorable as my own, but you were not ready! And now..." Unwilling to let her go, he held her close.

Angelique pulled away and gazed up at him. "You know what you must do," she reminded him quietly. "You have to contain him, no matter what. As I grow weaker, I can feel him trying to take control. I beg of you, don't ever let him escape. For now, my body is his prison, but your hand alone can hold him. Please... don't let my sacrifice be for nothing."

For the first time in almost a thousand years, Reivn felt such incredible grief that he lost all thought of control. "No! I will not let you do this! I will find another way! I will not let you die!"

Angelique touched his cheek, her lily-white hands trembling at the strain. "To live in the hearts of those we leave behind is not dying. I will live on through you, but you have to let me go," she whispered. Her voice trembled as she spoke. "So many have died at his hands. It has to end. This is the only way."

*She is right*, he realized, seeing his worst fear unfold before him. Desperation washed over him as he recognized he was out of choices. He pulled her into his arms and held her close, unwilling to let her go. Then he kissed her, closing his eyes and committing every moment to memory. "You have done the impossible, angel. You pulled me back from the abyss, giving me hope for the future. You brought light into my dark world and taught me to live again... and now you are leaving me. With all the power I wield, I still cannot save you. Forgive me, angel... for everything... for all of it. And know this... even when my own death comes, I will not forgive myself. For me this is not the end. It is only the beginning."

He helped her to stand and then stepped back, his eyes so full of agony that she could not bear to meet his gaze. He stared at her in anguish, begging God, life, anything to stay his hand and free her. Silence hung like a shroud over the clearing and he closed his eyes. Finally willing his magic forth, the air around them began to crackle with energy. His power massed into a swirling vortex of shadows as he cast his darkest spell: living death.

When he finished the invocation, he hesitated, gazing at her, his eyes pleading. "God help me, I cannot do this..."

"Yes, you can, and you must. It is all right. I love you, Reivn Draegon," she whispered and nodded, recognizing his fear as it mirrored her own.

Reivn cringed inwardly, knowing he would never hear her voice again. "And I love you, my beautiful angel..." his voice broke as he replied. He stared at her pale countenance, trying to remember the rose tinged color of her cheeks when she had first met him, her pallor causing him more grief for the pain she had endured. When he could delay no longer, he closed his eyes and touched her cheek, ushering forth the spell.

Angelique instantly collapsed seemingly lifeless, as a pale shadow melded into her face.

Reivn caught her as she fell. A heart-rending cry shattered the silence of the night as he lifted his head and screamed, his agony filling the air. He pulled her still, battered body close to him and buried his face against her, sinking to his knees. There in the clearing where none could see them, he wept, his tears falling freely in the empty night.

He sat there for hours holding her, feeling far more bereft and alone than he had ever been. His tears falling freely, he swept her hair from her face and stared down at her ashen visage. "I do not know how to live without you anymore. You were the better part of me and all that was left that was good in my heart. You were gentle, forgiving, compassionate... innocent. Without you there is naught but the darkness that now threatens to suffocate me." A lump formed in his throat, the ache boiling forth until he leaned back and screamed again, his grief so overwhelming, he could no longer contain it.

When he finally realized the dawn was not far away, he got up, cradling her in his arms, and forced back his tears. Holding his grief at bay, he slowly looked around at the carnage.

Charred and broken bodies littered the ground, most of which were still burning, and turning as they eventually would, to ash. The ring of blackened, scarred earth where once there had been jungle terrain was immense, and the trees along the forest's edge still smoldered where the moisture in the leaves had not fully quelled the remnants of the flames. Even the jungle's creatures had scurried away, driven deeper into the forest by the fighting and fire alike. Now the silence was deafening.

Sorrow unlike any he had ever known filled him, the pain in his chest all too real as he walked away from the temple and its surrounding city to open the portal to Draegonstorm. Then he stepped through the magical gate, silently carrying her home. His lifted his gaze but a moment on the torches lining the dark hall and they flared at his command.

Gideon ran to the portal chamber the moment he felt it open. But he froze when he saw Reivn and who he carried, and his eyes widened in horror. Stepping back, he moved aside for his father to pass, bowing his head in silence.

Lunitar appeared around the corner, having also felt the portal's opening. Then he saw his father. Dropping his gaze, he stared at the pale figure in his arms and his heart sank. Without a word, he joined Gideon and watched as Reivn bore Angelique past them on his way to the private chamber they had once shared.

Reivn barely noticed their presence. When he reached their door, his eyes fell to the ornate inlays around the wrought iron hinges and locks, remembering how she had once admired them. A twinge of fresh pain shot through him. "My angel..." he whispered and looked down again at the woman in his arms.

Angelique's face was pale and battered from the battle with Cyrus.

Reivn walked into the room and kicked the door closed behind him. Then he went to the bed and gently laid her down. He slowly stripped off the remnants of her torn garments and began to wash her, cleaning the dried blood from her body and matted hair. Then he carefully dressed her in a favored gown.

When he was done, he walked over to the old captain's chest near the wall and pulled out her brush. He stood there numbly turning it over in his hand, noting the faded staining on the wood handle and the worn boar bristles that still held remnants of her hair. Overwhelming grief filled his senses as he sat down beside her, and a flood of memories filled him as he brushed her hair.

When he finally finished, he covered her with a sheer black veil. Then he kissed her forehead gently, as tears drifted unheeded down his face. He stared at her, hating the morose finality of the veil that concealed her fragile frame from the light.

Finally, he went over and took white roses from a vase on a small table, intent on laying them with her. But when he turned back to the bed and gazed down at her still form that lay in its center, he dropped to his knees, the roses falling unheeded to the floor. Taking her hand, he held it and wept, his head resting against it for long, uncounted moments.

When he was finally able to pull himself together, he picked up the roses again and gently pulled them apart, saving only two as he scattered the petals across the bed. Then gently folding her hands across her chest, he placed the last two roses in them. "Sleep now. I will not be long." Then he slowly drew the sheer curtains closed that hung around the bed. "Farewell, angel," he whispered and his voice broke.

With a heavy heart, Reivn summoned the spirals. He wove a powerful spell around the bed, locking it with a protective seal and suspending her in time. Then he snuffed out the torches with a word and left the room.

Lunitar stood in the hall not far from the door. He had been waiting in silence for his father to emerge. He felt Reivn's grief and feared for him. But when he saw Reivn exit the room, he moved into the shadows and looked away, letting his father grieve in private.

Reivn called the spirals again at the door and sealed the room so none but him could ever disturb it. Then he awakened the stone gargoyles that stood vigil over his fortress and ordered them to stand watch. When he was done, he turned away with a heavy heart. His sorrow drew him to the balcony where he had once stood with her to await the sunrise. As he stepped into the last of the night air, he stared out at the mountains. Unable to contain his anguish any longer, his shoulders shook as he wept.

Lunitar followed his father and now stood staring at his back in stunned silence, unsure of what to do. He had never seen so much raw emotion in his father before. Finally, he walked over and stood beside his father.

Reivn met his gaze, unable to speak as he fought to contain his emotions.

Lunitar looked down and fought to control his own sorrow. Then he put his hand on his father's shoulder. "You are not alone, father. We are here." He wanted to say something that would ease Reivn's pain, and he felt powerless in the face of such grief. "I'm so sorry. I know there are no words that will suffice, but please... tell me what I can do?"

Reivn stared at his son. "Guard her well. Let no harm befall her while she sleeps."

"How long is she to sleep, father?" Lunitar asked, his voice painfully quiet.

Gripping the edge of the balcony as though he would fall if not for its strength, Reivn's answer was deafening in the silence. "Aeternally..."

Lunitar bowed and turned without another word, stepping back into the Keep's dark interior as tears slowly fell from his eyes. *Forgive me, father...*

Reivn forced back his emotions and tried in vain to focus his attention on his duties. After several fleeting thoughts, he finally sent a telepathy to Lunitar. *Tomorrow I will go before the Council to report the mission...*

*No, father... not tomorrow...* was Lunitar's silent answer.

Reivn gazed out over the balcony's edge to the world beyond. Hues of pink and yellow mingled with uncounted shades of blue and white to paint the sky as the dawn broke across the mountains. Peace reigned the early morning as he watched Angelique's last sunrise. Then the first rays of light crossed the distant horizon and touched the balcony's edge. He allowed the sun's light to hit him, the pain as his flesh began to smolder going unnoticed.

Lunitar suddenly realized Reivn had not still moved, and he stepped beyond the doorway's threshold. With grim determination, he reached out and grabbed his father's hand. Then he pulled the grieving Warlord into the darkness and firmly closed the door behind them. "...and I will always protect you... even from yourself... Come, father. Life is better."

# BLOOD FEUD

## Chapter Fifty
## Blood Feud

*Fate is the cruelest of taskmasters. It shows no mercy and often strikes from the darkest places, where we cannot see what lies before us. Grief walks hand in hand with all that we love, and leaves nothing untouched. There is no true immortality... no eternity. Death finds us all in the end and shows no discrimination in who it claims. There is no power... no spell we can conjure forth that will stop its march across our lives. I am a Warlord and Commander in Chief of all the armies of the Alliance, and I am prostrate and helpless before its hunger. I have sent so many to their deaths, each time with the knowledge they knew the possible fate that awaited them. Yet with each command I have given, it has taken a little more of my soul with it into the darkness. I never imagined the grief I felt then to be but a shadow of the pain I could know.*

*I stand on the edge of the abyss once more, looking down into the chasm beneath our lives, and all I see is death. Those of my friends, my comrades... my love. This infernal war the Ancients wage, what is it they seek to gain? There will be no reconciliation with those who have broken faith, but there needs not be death for them either. Why can we not come to a resolution that ends the bloodshed and brings peace? The numbers of the fallen over the centuries is greater than the measure of time we have thus far lived and still there is no end in sight. How many more must pay for their arrogance and greed?*

*I stand alone on the edge of night, watching as the dawn creeps again onto the horizon, and I wonder at the future we all share. Can we not find some measure of accountability that will finally bring peace? I know nothing more than the darkness that lies before me...*

*Lord Reivn Draegon*

\* \* \* \* \*

Reivn sat in his office, the journal in front of him open so the ink could dry. He stared at its pages, not really seeing them, as faces haunted him from the shadows. His eyes were gaunt from lack of sustenance and his expression wearied. He got up and strode over to put another log in the fireplace. His motions felt raw and mechanical, as he gazed at the flames, letting his memories drift. Painful reminders of their loss filled his heart and he closed his eyes.

"Father?" A voice greeted him from the door.

Reivn turned to look at his son. "Did you file the report?"

Lunitar nodded. "I did, and sent it to Polusporta. I signed your name to it as instructed. They should know within the hour."

Reivn's gaze shifted back to the fire and he sighed heavily. "They will be pleased that Cyrus no longer runs free. The cost will, no doubt, elude them."

"It does not elude us, though, father," Lunitar answered quietly. "I only wish there was some way to undo what has been done..."

Reivn shook his head. "I have found nothing in the tomes since... that night," he finished after a moment.

Lunitar bowed his head. He too had been searching for a way to save Angelique. "I will not stop looking for the answer. I care not of the cost to me."

Reivn did not reply as he stared at the flames, seeing her copper curls and soft eyes gazing back at him. His grief was still too new, and he could not voice what he felt.

Lunitar stood there in silence. He blamed himself. *If I had been more persistent in forcing her to return home with me, she would never have gone...* He closed his eyes, the enormity of her fate weighing heavy on his shoulders. Reivn had said absolutely nothing to him at all about that night or the nights that had led up to it. He had been hauntingly silent.

In truth, Reivn blamed himself for not being there when she needed him most. His grief was uncontainable, and he had said very little to anyone in the nights that had followed his return with her. He spent most of his waking moments digging through the vast collection of tomes on the arcane, desperately seeking a spell that would free her from Cyrus's grasp. He knew her soul battled for survival every moment it shared her body with the Martulian's, and feared she would be lost to him forever.

Lunitar stared at his father's back, unsure of what to say that could possibly pull him from his near madness. The loss of Angelique had shaken the entirety of Draegonstorm, from the family down to the servants, and the halls had fallen to a somber silence. But his father was beyond consoling, and his grief had turned to obsession. "Have you sought anyone to help you feed, father? Perhaps one of the servant girls could..."

Reivn glanced up sharply, his eyes glinting like cold steel. "Do you not suppose I have already tried?"

Lunitar dropped his gaze, so Reivn would not see the worry in his eyes. "You cannot go indefinitely without some form of sustenance. You need to feed. If we cannot free mother from..."

"I will free her!" Reivn snarled in fury. "She will not stay locked in eternal warfare with that monster! I will not allow it!"

Lunitar's concern for Reivn overtook his own sadness, and he frowned. "I agree with you, father. We will not abandon her. But I am concerned that it will not be expedient enough to prevent your loss of strength due to lack of sustenance. Unfortunately, I believe it will be much longer than that."

Reivn growled and turned his back on his son. He stalked to the window and stared out at the night. His silence was deafening. Finally, he turned around and the haunted look in his eyes chilled Lunitar to the core. "I have no chance of gaining sustenance from any other than her. The curse has wrapped itself firmly around us both. I tried... and killed the girl when I lost control..."

Lunitar looked stunned at his revelation. "I see. So, in addition to finding a solution to Angelique's situation, we need to find a cure for the curse as well, and quickly."

"I have spent years looking for a way to lift this curse from me, and as far as I know, the only way to do so is through Angelic or Daemonic magic." Reivn fell silent and sat down in front of the fire, staring into its depths. His exhaustion apparent, he closed his eyes.

Shaking his head, Lunitar walked over and sat down beside him. "But now I can also search. Do not lose hope, father. Now there are two of us searching. We will find the answer."

Reivn shook his head. "You do not understand. We in our darkness do not have the ability to wield pure Angelic magic. Were we able to use such potent magic, this war would long since have been brought to an end. The strength and pathetic magic of the Renegades together is no match for the will of Zion."

"Yes, that is true," Lunitar admitted quietly. "However, we do not know what the future holds. If nothing else, if we find a solution that uses Angelic magic, then perhaps we can figure out how to emulate it through the Spirals or by some other means."

Reivn leaned back wearily. "I see the influence of Mastric's teachings in you. Your determination is admirable, but it will not always afford you the success you hope for. You may think me pessimistic, but I am also realistic. Out of curiosity, how much do you know of our power or this war in truth? What have you learned over your years in the field and in your studies in the libraries?"

Lunitar thought for a moment before answering. "I know what you have taught me, and Mastric before you, and through study have expanded that knowledge extensively. As far as the war... we fight the Principatus in defense of humanity because the Renegades seek to destroy them and us. Why? Is there more to it?"

Reivn stared in silence at the flames, contemplating his words. Then he said, "More to the war? Quite possibly. It has been raging far longer than Polusporta has even been in the Sahara, and if the secrets buried in the sand there are what I suspect they are, the truth is by far more dangerous than you realize." He turned to gaze at his son. "What I am about to tell you could condemn us all, so you must never speak of it to anyone you do not fully trust with your life. Much of what I know, I have discovered during my many missions, or is information that has been passed on to me by those far older than I am. What I have is a giant puzzle. There are pieces missing I have not yet been able to find, and some secrets that are buried so deep, I may never discover the truth behind them." He paused, letting this sink in before he continued. "I have reason to believe the Ancients are not the original creators of our race, nor even the first generation. They have hidden from us the one who spawned our race and attempted to erase all knowledge of him from the history books. I believe his is the body buried deep beneath Polusporta in a vault where none may enter, and none are supposed to know of its existence. What I do not know is who he was or what part he has played in all of this."

Lunitar was quiet for a moment, his mind working through everything Reivn said. "That is a huge accusation, father. Assuming it is true, then would the principles behind this war, or whatever you wish to call it, still be the protection of humanity? The origins of our race are an entirely different topic all together. But I have to ask, did the war happen because of the mystery behind our origins or was it because of what occurred in Mysia centuries ago?"

"That is where the question gets interesting, and the answer even more so," Reivn replied. "I doubt it has ever been solely about defending humanity. You see, the rifting of the tribes had something to do with the man buried beneath Polusporta. I'm sure of it! Defending the mortals was just the banner they raised to lead us forward. However, the hatred they have of the Principatus, and their own brethren in particular, tends to suggest otherwise. It is uncharacteristic of someone who merely seeks to defend mortal kind. Think about it... why would defending the humans usher forth so much unbridled hatred? They kill without mercy, and want every renegade, no matter how young, unschooled or innocent, wiped from existence. Why?"

Lunitar stared at him, deep in thought. "That is a good question, and I'm not entirely sure how to answer that. As far as I can tell, they carry no blood ties to each other the way we do with the bond of blood, so they would essentially have to be abominations. This leads to some very serious questions I have been contemplating during my own research recently, because the few abominations I have seen are very powerful and their abilities usually quite specialized. So, with any magic they have an affinity for, they could outmatch us. They are naturally powerful. I can only guess that if fully trained, they would far exceed what we who have trained in that magic can do. But I digress. So, to answer your question, I honestly think it has something to do with their blood. That is why the Council wants to eradicate them, am I right?"

Reivn shook his head. "That's just it. It is the blood, but not in the way you think," he explained. "The bond we all share... you to me... me to my father... it is their way of controlling what we do. They manipulate our birthrights and only let us use what they want us to use. Did you know there was a time when I could heal as well as Angelique? Yet I could still wield my magic in battle every bit as well as I do now."

Lunitar's eyes widened in surprise, and he stared at his father. "What? How is that possible? Or better yet... if that is true, then why can you no longer do so now?"

"Mastric and the rest of the Council decided to divide us according to our uses in their war." Reivn hesitated before continuing. Then he said, "The caste system... it was designed to create specific roles within our society throughout the nine tribes, and they manipulated our blood to do so. Mastric took away the ability to heal from those of us he designated as warriors and gave it to those he found useless as such. That was when the Clerics were first created. I felt it when he ripped that power from us... from me. Valfort felt it too. It was one of many reasons he argued with Mastric before he was demoted."

Lunitar fell silent, realization slowly crossing his features. Then he shook his head in disbelief. "I have one question to ask you father... No. I want to ask you this as my friend... Reivn. Did Valfort ask you to join him when he deserted? And if so, how sorely tempted were you? Because I think I would have been."

The silence in the room was deafening as Reivn sat in contemplative thought. Finally, he looked at his son, his expression dark. "I believe he tried to that night at Rowton Heath. But I refused to even consider it. My cause for remaining in this war is my own. If we abandon the humans to their fate, regardless of the Ancient's true purpose, then the Renegades can and will destroy humanity to the last. My honor would not allow me to abandon so many innocents to their fate, nor to leave all those still loyal to that cause to die recklessly. Without our leadership in this war, many more would have fallen. That is something I could not and would not allow, regardless of my distaste for the Council's misuse of us. I do not fight this war for Mastric, nor for any of those who sit in Polusporta. I fight because someone needed to step forward and defend the innocent. I fight because it is the right thing to do. And it was my reason for staying."

"I see..." Lunitar replied as he slowly digested that information. "Well, father... I fight for many of the same things as you, but primarily I fight because of you." His shifted his gaze to the fire as he spoke. "Were you to quit the battlefield, I would follow suit. Now, as always, I stand ready to fight at your side. The reasons for this war may differ from the Council to us, but our cause has always been just, and I believe in it."

Reivn realized Lunitar was worried. "Know that our path is not an easy one. When I first discovered the truth, I was angry... furious in fact. I felt betrayed. I had been lied to and manipulated into doing what they wanted of me. But the first time I found a human child caught in the middle of this incessant killing, I realized I could not walk away. They are the true victims here. For as much as we have power and as much as we know of the real world... the world they never see... I also know that the only thing standing between them and the things their nightmares are made of is those of us who are willing to die defending them."

"Did the Council really provide us with a banner to rally behind with the preservation of the species of mankind?" Lunitar asked as he thought over the possibilities. "Or did they take advantage of our protective nature and use what they view as our weakness to control us and keep us in line so they could use us to fight their war?"

Reivn frowned at the question. "Does it really matter? The outcome is still the same. The humans are still as vulnerable either way. I made this choice on my own and I stand by it. Do you remember when you were first created?"

"Very much so," Lunitar replied quietly.

"I remember mine as well," Reivn explained. "After he turned me, Mastric offered to let me die if I so wished. But even then, I told him I wanted to fight... to free my people from the tyranny of the Persians."

Lunitar chuckled and leaned back, closing his eyes. "If only my own goals had been so noble. I wanted to fight and seek revenge. Fortunately, you showed me a different path."

Reivn laughed and got up to put another log on the fire, then he stirred up the embers. "I remember. You were very angry during your first nights as a blood servant... but you were also full of the desire to learn. That was what drew me to you, among other things. You had a fire in you that equaled my own, and you could be taught. When I looked at you, I saw a much younger version of myself in your eyes and I understood. That was why I asked for you when Mastric offered me a reward. I wanted to give you what he never would... honor." He turned to look at his son. "I have never once regretted that decision. I only wish Angelique could have known you as I do." His eyes filled with sadness again at the thought. "She loved you, you know."

Lunitar looked down so Reivn would not see the tears that had begun to form in the corner of his eyes. "I know she did. During the time I spent guarding her in Atlantic City, we got to know each other well enough to become good friends. Then when she came here and worked so tirelessly over you to bring you back from the brink, I knew she was one of us. She was ready to sacrifice herself to save you. I never told her just how much that meant to all of us."

Reivn nodded, his thoughts drifting back to the loss he felt. "She would have done just that had you let her. She was the best of us all, I think."

Lunitar fell silent, not knowing what to say.

"Do you know she was the first Renegade to ever be brought back into the fold? She proved this blood feud could end if the Council were willing to change their policies about some of the young we find." Reivn shook his head. "Their endless desire to kill the young... it makes no sense. We could take them into our care and teach them our ways. They would be spared, and it would strengthen not only our numbers, but our cause as well." He dropped back into his chair. "Instead, we kill them by the thousands. To this day, I do not know why the Council actually let me keep her and her children, but I think Mastric had a big hand in it and that worries me. He does nothing without a reason. I fear he is not done with me yet. The power he gives me is part of some scheme of his... some plan he will eventually reveal."

Lunitar did not answer. He knew Reivn was right about Mastric. He had seen it many times during his own service. He was worried about where those plans could be leading all of them.

Reivn sat back and closed his eyes as his thoughts drifted to the future. Then he sighed. "You realize that if Mastric calls me back to Vienna to serve him, you will be taking charge of Draegonstorm indefinitely.

Lunitar looked up. "I understand that, but we'll cross that bridge when and if we need to. I will put a contingency plan in place to ensure a smooth transition should it become necessary."

"To be honest, I want nothing more than to bury myself in the arcane and forget the world out there even exists." Reivn got up and went to his desk. Then after looking around for a second, he picked up some papers. "I am weary of the fighting and always looking over my shoulder, and I am weary of leaving this legacy behind me." He handed them to Lunitar.

Lunitar glanced down at the papers in his hand. It was the casualty list from Atlantic City. "Will they not let you step down as Warlord and resume the role of Prince here in Australia?"

Reivn shook his head in frustration. "I see you have not yet heard my new title... I am now Warlord Prefect, Commander in Chief of the military, and Prince of the Australian territory."

Lunitar's eyes widened in shock. "Warlord Prefect? Is that a new rank?"

"It is. They created it that night," Reivn explained in disgust . Then he added, "...as my reward for serving them well."

Lunitar closed his eyes for a moment and shook his head. "My condolences, my... Lord Prefect," he said dryly. "But all joking aside, father, how much more can they heap on you before even your strong shoulders buckle from the weight of responsibility?"

"As much as they want to," Reivn replied bitterly, "...with the full expectation that I will do what is demanded of me, and they will continue to demand their pound of flesh until my bones are ground to dust."

"Then know that you are not alone. The whole family and indeed this entire household will do whatever is necessary to assist you in the execution of these new responsibilities," Lunitar promised. He got up and knelt on one knee in front of Reivn. Then he placed his right fist across his chest. "By the honor we hold so dear, we stand ready, my lord."

Reivn walked over and grabbed Lunitar's arm, pulling him to his feet. "When we are here like this... talking as the friends we were long before you became my son... there is no need for such motions. Please... the Council may demand that you grovel, but I ask only that you stand at my side. I have had my fill of pomp these last few weeks. While my wife was hunting a killer, I was waging a lost cause in a defeated city for a collective of selfish antiques who know nothing of the world they supposedly belong to!"

Lunitar got up and looked him in the eye, gazing at him in admiration. "...and there is the fire of the man I have known all these years. I started to lose you there for a little bit. Welcome back. You're not the only strategist and tactician in this house. I was trained by the best."

Reivn growled and let him go. "I find your antics less than humorous. My light died with the woman in that room. My fire, however, is fueled by my fury at their wanton disregard for the lives of their children... the creations they made through the destruction of lives. They owe us more than they can ever give back. I wonder exactly how long this war of theirs would last if it was them who had to wage it against each other instead of sending off the young to be slaughtered in their stead."

"Not long," Lunitar answered honestly. "But that avails us none. We can wish all we want, and yet we are still the ones standing on the front lines for the very reasons you just spoke of." He paused for a moment, and then added, "We are firmly trapped in this war, quite frankly, by a net of our own making. So, as you pointed out, we must deal with the hand we are dealt and make the best of the situation. I have said this before, and I will say it again. I am yours to command, and I am your son. But most importantly, I am your friend. I will always be here when you need me... even when you don't know that you need me." He laid his hand on Reivn's shoulder. "Now... shall we get some of the necessary preparations done?"

Reivn stood there silently, his mind racing in a dozen different directions. When he lifted his eyes and met his son's gaze, the pain in them was obvious. "I need... more time. I know what is expected, but..." he knew it sounded pathetic, but he could not bring himself to voice the truth. His desire to sleep beside Angelique had been at war with his sense of responsibility to the people he had sworn to lead and protect, and it was tearing him apart.

"Then I will begin the planning and you will come when you are ready. I will be sure not to disturb you." Lunitar squeezed his shoulder and let him go.

A knock at the door interrupted their discussion. Reivn immediately turned around, once more masking his emotions. "Come!"

Girard stuck his head in the door. "My lord? An urgent message just arrived from the Council for you."

Reivn growled. "Well, that certainly did not take very long." He took the letter from Girard and tore it open. Then his eyes filled with fury as he read its contents. "They have summoned me to Polusporta to discuss Angelique and Cyrus."

Lunitar frowned. "What? Why? What else was there to tell them?"

"I do not know," Reivn replied angrily. "But I will know soon enough." He glanced at Girard. "You may go."

Girard bowed and left, closing the door quietly behind him.

Reivn walked over to the desk and began writing furiously. "I am giving you a new assignment here at Draegonstorm. I want you to begin restructuring the Dragon Guard."

"To what end?" Lunitar walked over and stood in front of him.

With a sigh, Reivn handed him the necessary letter. "This territory only has a minimum number of soldiers. We have never operated with more than the company presently assigned here because Draegonstorm has always been little more than our ancestral home." He stood and walked over to the fireplace. Then he reached up and brushed his hand across the Coat of arms that hung above it. "That is going to change. We need to increase our strength."

Lunitar raised an eyebrow. "Should I recruit numbers sufficiently to accommodate defenses appropriate for a territory?"

Reivn turned. "By Council ideations, the company already assigned here is sufficient to hold a territory. However, as my new duties have moved us even more to the forefront of the war, I need soldiers I can count on that are accessible at a moment's notice. The present status of bringing soldiers from all over the world to answer the call has too often left us with less than half of what we need to hold a territory while waiting for reinforcements that might never come. The front cannot suffer another defeat such as Atlantic City, or the bottleneck will buckle, and the North will be lost."

Troubled at his father's words, Lunitar bowed. "Then I will get the staff busy recruiting the necessary personnel and requisitioning supplies immediately. I will have a full report of our progress upon your return. By your leave, my lord?"

Reivn shook his head. "There is more. I want you to keep this as quiet as you can. Open the North wing and garrison the newcomers in the barracks there. Select only those with the utmost loyalty to our banners. No one else. This is more important than expediency."

Lunitar bowed again, his curiosity aroused. "I will see it done. Is that all, father?"

Reivn walked over and put his hand on Lunitar's shoulder. "You are my son, my heir, and my most loyal Commander. Now, I need you to be more. We are entering murky waters here, and we must be careful. Should the Council believe my motives to be anything other than preparing to defend the Alliance, they will do everything they can to destroy this family. Kneel."

Lunitar obeyed, bowing his head in silence.

Placing his hand on his son's head, Reivn decreed, "Lord Lunitar Draegon, you are hereby officially inducted into the Order of the Dragon and promoted to Commander of the elite ranks of the Dragon Guard. You answer only to me from now on, and all the officers here report to you. Continue to enforce the laws as they have been established here. There can be no tolerance for any conduct other than that designated in the creed that was written when the Order was first established so long ago. Honor, fealty and wisdom. Remember it and what it stands for. Honor first... in all things. Fealty without exception... to this house and this bloodline. Wisdom in all acts... tempered with compassion when called for and unyielding discipline when necessary. As a knight of the Order, it is your sacred duty to uphold these ideals. Do you accept this charge?"

Stunned at what his father had just bestowed on him, Lunitar looked up and slowly nodded. "I do, my lord, and upon my oath, I will execute it to the best of my ability."

With a satisfied nod, Reivn walked over and picked up his coat. "Your charge begins now. Should I not return from Polusporta, then you are to see to the safety of all within our walls, including those who sleep aeternally. And remember... courage is merely the decision to move forward in the face of fear. Do not let any actions of those who stand against us sway you. Do what is right and defend those who cannot defend themselves." He walked to the door and opened it, and then stopped. "And always remember... first and foremost, you are a Draegon."

## Epilogue

Valfort slowly came out of his trance and began to stretch. Stiff from the lack of movement for more than three months, his body ached. He groaned and glanced at the altar he had been working over, and then smiled in satisfaction. *It won't be long now.*

A beautiful woman with alabaster skin and long raven hair was lying on the altar. Naked save for the sheet lying across her midsection, she was in a state of repose, seemingly asleep.

He drank down a few more vials of the blood he had been using to sustain himself, gulping the fluid greedily, his hunger insatiable. "You will owe me for this one, my sweet," he growled, staring at the woman. "This was an expensive journey."

Silence was the only answer that greeted him as he prepared to go into the final portion of the ritual he had been conducting. Rubbing his hands to remove some of the stiffness, he sighed and shifted positions before settling in again. Then he began to chant, conjuring black fire that danced like a living entity in the palm of his hand. As he spoke, the magic awakened to his touch, writhing in pleasure and feeling its presence summoned into the world. Encouraging it to grow, he fed it, pulling tendrils from the spirals and dangling them above it.

When it had finally grown large enough to satisfy his needs, Valfort began to weave it through the air like thread on a loom until it was splayed above the body in an intricate pattern that mimicked her shape to perfection. Then guiding the ebony flames, he drew runes in the air above her, lowering them one at a time until they completely covered her. Invoking powerful incantations to open the pathway, he called to Tartarus, his voice echoing through the abyss.

The flames rose, their dark essence reaching into the abyss to form a bridge.

Deep in the depths of Tartarus, a shadowed figure slowly rose from the crimson wasteland and floated across. Following the path, it made its way up and out of Tartarus until it reached the body lying in front of him. It convulsed and shivered slightly, every inch trembling as the muscles awakened and reacted to their new owner. Then it was over.

Breathing heavily from the strain of using so much magic, he finally lowered his arms. He watched as the figure return to its state of rest, and then dropped into a chair and closed his eyes for the first sleep he had been able to claim in over three months.

The day passed in tomblike silence and night came once more. Waking from slumber, Valfort looked over at the altar. The woman had not moved. He got up, walked over, and checked her to be sure she was still viable.

The woman's skin was warm, but her pallor was almost gray.

*Time to awaken,* he thought to himself. He went to a small refrigerator in the corner of the room and grabbed the blood bags he had stored. Then taking them back to the altar, he opened her mouth and slowly began to feed the blood down her throat a little at a time until the bags were emptied. When he was finished, he walked over to the bed to check the clothes he had laid out to be sure everything she would need was there. Then he began to pace back and forth. Every few minutes, he stopped to look at the silent figure on the bed. Then he went back to pacing. His impatience was growing with every passing minute.

"How long have I been gone?" A sultry voice behind him asked.

Valfort spun around and smiled as his gaze settled on the altar.

She was sitting up, her ebon hair spilling softly over her shoulder. She stared at him expectantly through black eyes.

His expression grew dark. "Long enough."

"So... months then," she surmised. "That is unfortunate."

He glared at her. "For who. I've been secluded here for more than three months, starving myself and forcing myself awake to cast the necessary spells. Unfortunate is not the word I would choose!"

Ignoring him, she went to the bed to inspect his gifts, her damp, bare skin glistening in the torchlight.

His eyes followed her appreciatively, noting how sensuously she moved. Then remembering who she was, he looked away.

She donned the clothes had laid out for her and brushed her long, black hair. Then she turned around. "From you, I presume?"

"Of course," he replied. "I hope they are to your liking."

She sauntered across the room to the mirror and stared at the unfamiliar face of her new body. "They'll do. The body is nice, but I'll have to work on the face. I prefer my own. So, tell me all the news. There have obviously been some losses."

He nodded, watching her with interest. "There were, but those responsible will pay for it in blood." He stretched and walked over to the closet. Then rummaging through his clothes, he found what he wanted and pulled out a fresh suit, laying it on a chair. "I have not heard anything in the last three months because of my need to be here. But that will be remedied soon enough."

She touched the mirror and a slight ripple moved across it. "Hmmm, it will be a few nights yet before my power is back completely. I will need to feed to complete the transition first."

Valfort grinned. "I have a few I put to sleep for you upstairs."

Turning around, her eyes settled on him and a sultry smile crept across her face. "And if I am hungry for more than that?"

With a growl, he crossed the room and pulled her into his arms. "Those are words I like to hear, beautiful."

In a flash, she had caught his hand and painfully twisted his arm, pushing it off her. "Slow down, cowboy. That was not an invitation... not yet."

He glared at her and backed off. "Then what was it, exactly?"

She laughed and moved closer to him. Then she kissed him full on the lips. "Perhaps it was a test to see if you still desire me."

A low growl forming in his throat, he wrapped his arms around her again. "You are the most intoxicating woman I have ever known. I desire none but you these days."

"Then it is time to satiate both our desires, my pet," she whispered against his ear. Without warning, she sank her teeth into his neck and sucked greedily.

With a groan, he pulled her closer and tilted his head back, reveling in her hunger. When she licked his wound closed, he kissed her deeply, his desire for her almost uncontainable.

In response, she reached down and undid his robe. Then she slid her hands down the front of his naked body. "Then why don't you let me thank you properly."

"I thought you would never ask," he grinned. He unzipped her dress and ran his hand down her bare back. "I was very selective in finding this one for you. I know your tastes."

"Then you know I like it rough," she replied and grabbed his hair. Quickly ridding him of his robe, she shoved him backward on the bed and climbed on top of him. Then she pulled the dress off over her head and straddled him. She purred like a cat stalking her prey and slowly ran her claws down his chest, drawing blood.

He winced at the pain, and then chuckled as she claimed him. "You haven't changed a bit."

"Did you really think I would?" She laughed at the thought. "If anything, I've had a refreshing trip home, reminding me of things I had almost forgotten. We've only just begun having fun."

Valfort growled like a hungry animal. "I waited for months for you. I have a few surprises in store for you as a welcome home."

She laid across his chest, moving with him and reveling in the feeling of his flesh. "Mmm, I can't wait to see the pets you saved for me. I'm going to be very hungry when we're done."

For several hours, they reveled in each other's carnal and twisted desires. Finally, Valfort strolled to the bathroom to wash.

She lounged in the bed, licking the blood from her fingers with low, guttural noises akin to an animal feasting on a carcass in the midday sun. Finally, she sat up and stared at the door to the bathroom, her thoughts moving elsewhere. "So, you haven't told me... How goes the war?"

Valfort exited the bathroom, towel-drying his hair. He looked up at her question and gazed at her from across the room with a grin. "It goes well. Welcome back, Alora."

*About the Author –*

K.R. Fraser spent her childhood in Europe, visited multiple countries and experienced different cultures around the globe. She is fluent in three languages and knowledgeable in four more. She began theatre and dance training at age three and was composing music on the piano at age eleven. She continued these studies into her young adult years.

Ms. Fraser developed an interest in books very young, and by fourteen had written her first collective of poetry, several of which were published worldwide in later years. At age sixteen, she began writing short stories, and writing became a life-long love. Her first short story in the horror genre, "The Cycle" was published in 2006 and presently remains in circulation. She has since published several other works, has been seriously writing for more than twenty years, and has also been an editor for more than ten years. She also completed her first Associate's degree in multimedia in 2009, and then went on to achieve her Bachelor's and Master's in the media industry. Her works include award-winning poetry, short stories and news articles in various subjects of interest.

She began a small independent company in 2001. However, in 2007 a serious injury Ms. Fraser received during an accident caused a major setback for the company and it briefly closed its doors. This did not discourage her, however, and she turned to writing fiction full-time. Then in 2008 she reopened the company and changed its name, and Dragonrock Enterprises was born. Today, the company includes five divisions, and though still small, the company represents a growing list of clients, and produces quality and professional work in an inviting work environment where creative minds are encouraged to dream.

K.R. Fraser's work is ground-breaking imaginative. Her use of imagery and character dialogue keeps you on the edge of your seat from the first page. This amazing series will easily carry your imagination to new heights and leave you begging for more.

*"Writing is a passion that will live until I close my eyes for the last time. I believe an author is a dream weaver who leads you on a guided tour through their magical world. I want those who go on this journey to live incredible moments with these wonderful characters... crying with them, laughing with them, and cheering them ever forward. In sharing them with the world, I am sharing the love I have for the Unicorn behind every tree, every Dragon in the sky, and every fairy that curls into a flower to sleep at sunset. Welcome to the world of Draegonstorm."*

*~ K.R. Fraser ~*

CPSIA information can be obtained
at www.ICGtesting.com
Printed in the USA
LVHW031310191119
637819LV00001B/21/P